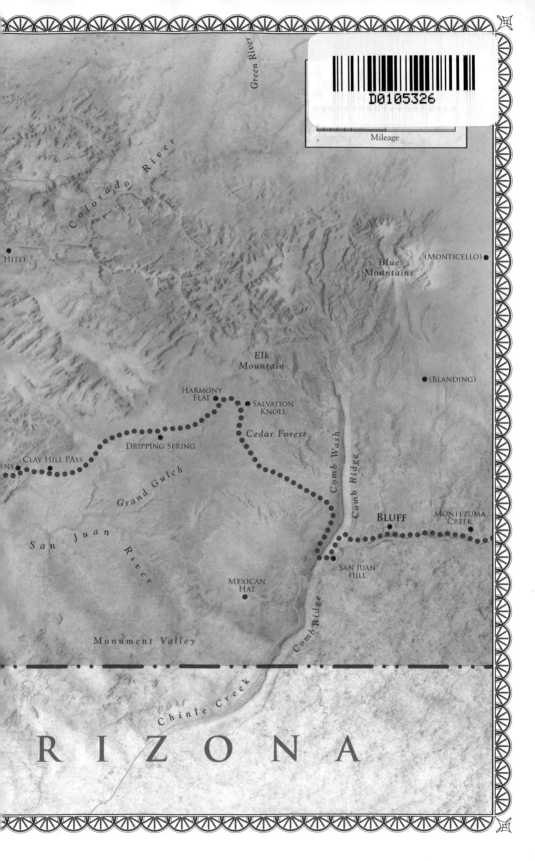

Green River

Colorado River

Mileage

(HITE)

Blue
Mountains

(MONTICELLO)

(BLANDING)

Elk
Mountain

HARMONY
FLAT

SALVATION
KNOLL

Cedar Forest

DRIPPING SPRING

Comb Wash

Comb Ridge

CLAY HILL PASS

NS

Grand Gulch

BLUFF

MONTEZUMA
CREEK

San   Juan

River

SAN JUAN
HILL

MEXICAN
HAT

Comb Ridge

Monument Valley

Chinle Creek

RIZONA

THE
UNDAUNTED

THE
UNDAUNTED

THE MIRACLE OF THE HOLE-IN-THE-ROCK PIONEERS

GERALD N. LUND

DESERET
BOOK

SALT LAKE CITY, UTAH

Maps by Bryan Beach.

Library of Congress Cataloging-in-Publication Data

Lund, Gerald N.
    The undaunted : the miracle of the Hole-in-the-Rock pioneers / Gerald N. Lund.
        p. cm.
    Includes bibliographical references.
    ISBN 978-1-60641-191-9 (hardbound : alk. paper)
    1. Mormon pioneers—Fiction.   2. Utah—Fiction.   3. Frontier and pioneer life—Fiction.   I. Title.
    PS3562.U485U53 2009
    813'.54—dc22   2009022805

Printed in the United States of America
Bang Printing, Brainerd, MN

10   9   8   7   6   5   4   3   2   1

PREFACE

This is a true story. It is the true story of real people who undertook and completed what many called an impossible journey.

It is a story of a group of Mormon pioneers. Unlike earlier pioneers, they were not fleeing persecution or seeking a place where they would have freedom of religion. They were not escaping poverty or trying to join others of their own faith. These pioneers lived in prosperous Mormon communities in comfortable homes. They ran successful businesses or farmed land much more productive and rich than would be available in the place where they were going.

They went because they were called, and because they believed that call was from the Lord.

They went because they believed it was necessary for the safety and good of the overall community.

In short, they went because they believed it was the right thing to do.

The late David Miller, then a professor of history at the University of Utah, wrote this concerning these pioneers:

> In all the annals of the West, replete with examples of courage, tenacity and ingenuity, there is no better example of the indomitable pioneer spirit than that of the Hole-in-the-Rock expedition of the San Juan Mission. No pioneer company ever built a wagon road through wilder, rougher, more inhospitable country, still one of the least-known regions in America. None ever demonstrated more courage, faith, and devotion to a cause than this group . . . who cut a wagon

passage through two hundred miles of this country. . . . Today
their feat seems well-nigh impossible. Yet they proved that virtually nothing was impossible for a zealous band of pioneers.
(Miller, *Hole*, ix)

I was first introduced to these pioneers and their story in the fall of
1996. I was part of a group of Church Educational System administrators
who were invited to travel to southern Utah and cross some of the trail
these pioneers blazed through the wilderness. I was stunned by the country
through which we traveled, and came away completely amazed, deeply
awed, and profoundly moved by the story we were told.

At the completion of that experience, I vowed that someday I would
tell those people's story. It took over ten years to fulfill that vow, but *The
Undaunted* is the result. To be *undaunted* is "to be unwilling to abandon
one's purpose or effort; to be undiminished in courage or valor." I can think
of no better word to describe the men and women of the San Juan Mission.
This book is my tribute to those resolute and indomitable pioneers and
their absolutely astonishing feat.

Although the story told here is true, *The Undaunted* is a novel. It is historical fiction. The two families who take the central role in the story are
entirely fictional. They are the creation of the author, but the story and
setting in which they find themselves are not. The events in which they
participate and the people with whom they interact are real and true. I
have diligently tried to have these fictional creations accurately represent
the real individuals and families who took part in the Hole-in-the-Rock
expedition. I have even taken the unusual step (for a novel) of document-
ing what is history in chapter endnotes so the reader can better determine
where the line between fiction and history is drawn.

During the writing of this book, I was often asked by people what project I was currently working on. When I told them I was writing a novel
about the Hole-in-the-Rock expedition, the most common response was
a blank look. I was amazed at how many people who are members of the
Church and live in Utah know nothing about this remarkable story.
Another frequent comment went something like this: "Oh, yeah, I've

heard about the Hole in the Rock (or seen it while boating on Lake Powell), but I don't know much about it." So one of my goals in writing the novel was to let more people know this incredible story.

But another objective began to form in my mind as the project continued. In many conversations, I noticed a disturbing trend. Among the relatively few who *were* familiar with the Hole-in-the-Rock pioneers— including some descendants—again and again I heard comments about this being a remarkable story but essentially a mistake, a fiasco. Several historians who have written on this subject have drawn similar conclusions. While such individuals are quick to admire the courage and tenacity of those who answered the call, they feel that the very concept was flawed, that it was a serious lapse in judgment to take two hundred and fifty people, including many women and children, into a wilderness as harsh and forbidding as almost any in North America. In their eyes, the decision to take the group over an unexplored route through the torturous red rock country of southern Utah was a serious failure in both Church and expedition leadership. They suggest that well-meaning but overzealous men ignored very real dangers, made decisions based on limited or even erroneous information, and refused to bend in their determination to move the expedition forward. One woman even went so far as to say that, in her opinion, the leaders were despotic in forcing the group forward when they knew it was so dangerous.

By that point I was well into my research, and everything I had learned about those leaders suggested just the opposite. They were human, of course, but they were hardly religious fanatics or stubborn fools. They were wise, experienced men who were widely respected by their peers for their judgment and leadership abilities. So what went wrong? How and why, in this particular case, did these leaders act so differently from the way they had in other similar circumstances? The more I studied and read and contemplated the situation, the more sure I became that this viewpoint was a misperception and did an injustice to the memories of decent, honest, and faithful men.

Then one day, I came across a statement by the very popular and eminent historian David McCullough that gave me a new perspective on the issue. Speaking of historical "facts" and "true history" he said:

> If you think about it, no one ever lived in the past. Washington, Jefferson, John Adams, and their contemporaries didn't walk about saying, "Isn't this fascinating living in the past! Aren't we picturesque in our funny clothes!" They lived in the present. The difference is it was their present, not ours. They were caught up in the living moment exactly as we are, and with no more certainty of how things would turn out than we have. . . .
>
> The truth of history is the objective always. But the truth isn't just the facts. You can have all the facts imaginable and miss the truth, just as you can have facts missing or some wrong, and reach the larger truth. As the incomparable Francis Parkman wrote: "Faithfulness to the truth of history involves far more than a research, however patient and scrupulous, into special facts. Such facts may be detailed with the most minute exactness, and yet the narrative, taken as a whole, may be unmeaning or untrue. The narrator must seek to imbue himself with the life and spirit of the time. He must study events in their bearings near and remote; in the character, habits, and manners of those who took part in them. He must himself be, as it were, a sharer or spectator of the action he describes." (McCullough, "The Course of Human Events," 2003 Jefferson Lecture in the Humanities, http://www.neh.gov/whoweare/mccullough/lecture.html)

We speak of "Monday morning quarterbacks" or "armchair coaches" who are quick to criticize and second-guess what should have happened from the sidelines of the game. We must be careful that we do not make that same mistake here. This turned out to be a very complicated situation with unattractive choices or, in some cases, no other options. Therefore, I have tried to present the "character, habits, and manners" of these men who "lived in the present" and were "caught up in the living moment" of their situation and not just the limited available "facts." In doing so, I hope readers can judge for themselves if this was indeed a failure in leadership or simply men making difficult choices in extremely challenging circumstances.

Let me speak of one last objective I had in writing this novel. President Gordon B. Hinckley once spoke of the importance a study of history has for those of us in the modern world:

> It is good to look to the past to gain appreciation for the present and perspective for the future. It is good to look upon the virtues of those who have gone before, to gain strength for whatever lies ahead. It is good to reflect upon the work of those who labored so hard and gained so little in this world, but out of whose dreams and early plans, so well nurtured, has come a great harvest of which we are the beneficiaries. Their tremendous example can become a compelling motivation for us all. (Hinckley, "Faith of the Pioneers," 3)

The story of these early Saints who labored so hard and did so much has become a powerful example and a compelling motivation for me personally. My hope is that it will become so for others as well.

Acknowledgments

There are many people who have contributed to this book, and though my acknowledgments here are brief, my gratitude for their contribution is enormous.

I would first extend the warmest of thanks to LeGrand and Marcia Black and their family. It was LeGrand and Marcia who led us on that 1996 trek, following the road those pioneers had made. Marcia is a direct descendant of Benjamin Perkins, the Welsh coal miner who was instrumental in blasting a wagon road down through the Hole in the Rock. Though he claims to be a "johnny-come-lately" to the San Juan Area, LeGrand did his master's thesis on the Hole-in-the-Rock trail, and few know it better than he. His and Marcia's love and enthusiasm for this area and the people who made it famous are so thoroughly contagious that all of us were infected within hours. Thankfully, I shall never recover. In the last year, they and their family accompanied us on three additional exploring expeditions. Curtis and his wife, Kristin; Brent, Jill, and Jodi not only provided delightful company but proved to be expert spotters in helping us less experienced ATV drivers negotiate particularly difficult stretches of slick rock. Thank you, Blacks, for our association and friendship. We are truly in your debt.

Second, since I am not a professional historian, I owe a great debt to those historians who have done the research and writing upon which I depended so heavily in writing this book. The bibliography cites their works, but I pay particular tribute to the late David E. Miller and the history he wrote. It is almost universally acknowledged as the definitive work on the Hole-in-the-Rock expedition. The number of citations of his work in the endnotes is indicative of the importance it played in my research.

Others from Blanding joined us in June 2008 for an ATV expedition across the more rugged portions of the east side of the trail. It was arduous and challenging. It was also spectacular and fulfilling beyond our highest expectations. Lynn and Lorraine Laws and David and Ramona Lyman provided guide service and support vehicles, as well as sharing many details about the area and the pioneers who crossed it. Ben and Brett Black, of Blackhawk Transportation in Blanding, not only provided us with ATVs but packed in water, equipment, food, and some of the best Dutch-oven cooking in the state. It is a privilege to call these good people our friends.

Jerry Roundy and his wife provided important information and warm hospitality in Escalante when we did the west side of the trail. Jerry's excellent book on the history of Escalante is included in the bibliography.

The staff at Deseret Book are too numerous to thank by name, for it takes much effort and many hands to bring a manuscript to published book form. But an especial thanks to Cory Maxwell and Jana Erickson. We have now been friends and associates for nearly twenty years and worked on many projects together. My respect and appreciation for them only deepens with the passing years. Emily Watts's editing work is invisible to readers, but it is present on virtually every page throughout the book. Thank you, Emily.

Last of all, a big thank you to my family. They have contributed much in planning and carrying out our three separate expeditions to that area, combining their family vacations to help me with much-needed research. To give some clue as to just what kind of effort that represents, on our last trip, completed in April 2009, we took thirty-nine people (including about fifteen children of elementary-school age or younger). We had a grand time, and it thrills me to see them develop their own love for that area and the story of the Hole-in-the-Rock pioneers.

Last, and most important, my wife, Lynn, has been my never-failing supporter, enduring many hours alone while I have been down working on the computer. She is always my first reader, and her critiques carry great weight with me. She provided numerous suggestions, ranging from minor details to important structural issues. I trust her judgment and always look to her first to see if something is really "working." It has been that way now for nearly fifty years.

The Undaunted Web Site: Undaunted-TheNovel.com

I don't know how many times I have heard myself and others say, after negotiating breathtaking (and hair-raising) portions of the trail, "How in the world did they ever take wagons across this?"

Trying to describe such places verbally in a way that gives the reader a clear visual image is well-nigh impossible. In addition, unlike the Church history sites in the eastern U.S. or the Mormon pioneer trail, which crosses four states, the Hole-in-the-Rock trail is only about two hundred miles long. Thankfully, much of the trail is easily accessible today. Some portions can be traversed only in ATVs or specially equipped high-clearance vehicles, but large portions of it are either paved or on well-maintained gravel roads. Since a large number of readers come from the western states and are within a day's drive of this area, it is my hope that many will desire to see these places for themselves and undertake their own exploring expeditions. Therefore, we have created a web site in connection with the novel. Undaunted-The Novel.com includes the following:

- A large selection of photographs of the area.
- Maps of the trail and its key sites, with links to photographs and related sections of the novel.
- General information and resources for those who wish to visit the area on their own, including recommended routes, GPS coordinates to key places, and suggestions on how to find accommodations.
- Historical information and photographs.
- Links to other valuable web sites, such as one by the Hole-in-the-Rock Foundation.
- An interactive feature where readers or visitors to the site can ask questions.

Be sure to visit us at Undaunted-The Novel.com!

BOOK I

BEGINNINGS

1862–1872

CHAPTER 1

Friday, June 13, 1862

David Dickinson's eyes were wide open. He was staring up at the single window in their one-room tenement flat, willing the light outside to grow brighter. He raised up on one elbow and peered across the darkened room to where a blanket hung from a rope, separating his parents' sleeping room from the main room. Did he dare just rush in and wake them?

He sighed, falling back on the pillow. He had not been allowed to enter their sleeping room when the blanket was drawn since he was three, and—his head came up with a jerk.

"Annie?" It was his father's voice, spoken in a bare whisper.

"I'm awake," his mother whispered back.

There was a rustle of straw and the squeak of rope as someone got out of bed. More rustling, this time of clothing. David lay back and squeezed his eyes shut, heart thumping just a little.

"Is he . . . ?" His mother's voice still sounded sleepy.

"Naw. 'E still be sleepin'. But Ah moost be goin' soon."[1]

"I know."

David cracked an eye open when he heard her bare feet hit the floor, then a whisper of sound as she put on a housecoat. A moment later, the blanket separating their sleeping room from the rest of the flat pulled back, and John Dickinson appeared, pulling up the suspenders on his trousers. David closed his eye again as his father tiptoed across the room and lit a candle.

Softer footsteps moved toward him across the floor. "David?"

He stirred and mumbled something unintelligible.

"Happy birthday, David," his mother said softly, laying a hand gently on his shoulder.

"What?" He stretched, then feigned a huge yawn.

But she knew him too well. "You cahn't fool me, young man." It was her finest London accent. Her hand shot out and found that spot beneath his armpit that she had discovered years before. In an instant he was writhing on the bed, screeching with laughter.

"'Appy bur'day, Laddee," his father said, coming back to stand beside his wife. As David sat up, his father bent down and pulled him close. David felt the scratch of thick stubble and smelled the coal dust and candle smoke on his shirt.

"Tank ya, Dah."

Over his father's shoulder, he saw his mother frown. "Thank you, Dahdee," he corrected himself quickly.

Anne Dickinson was slender and looked pale in the candlelight. The bone structure in her face was fine, almost fragile, and her skin was like the finest of Spode porcelain. She had blue-green eyes and soft, golden brown hair that fell to her shoulders. Her mouth was small and her lips pale, so when she frowned, it was like a shadow drifting across a sunlit meadow. But when she smiled, as she did once again now, it filled her eyes. She was so beautiful, David wanted to reach out and touch her face.

"Ya be most welcum, Son," his father said, ignoring the brief interchange. He gave him another squeeze, then pulled back and stood, smiling down on him. "Noow then, Davee lad. This be yur sixth bur'day. So yur Mum an' me, we 'ave a wee sooprize fur ya."

"What, Dahd?"

"Yur muther be tekin' ya ta Barnslee Town t'day."

David leaped to his knees. "Barnslee? Trulee, Dah?" He turned to his mother, hardly daring to believe. "Ah've never bin ta Barnslee in me 'ole life."

She sighed, wondering if he would ever be able to get past his Yorkshire accent, but decided to let it pass. His excitement was infectious. "You've actually been there two or three times," she said, "but only when you were a wee boy."

Reaching in his pocket, his father withdrew three coins. David peered in disbelief. Each coin was a tuppence, a two-pence piece. That made— he calculated quickly—six pence.

"'Ere be a little sumthin' ta 'elp ya celebrate. Maybe yur Mum be tekin' ya ta the sweet shop." He winked. "Let ya buy sumthin' ta give ya a real bellyache."

"It be joost fur me, Dah?"

"Indeed. Ya can pick oot whate'er ya lek. Whaddya think of that, eh?"

"Oh, Dahdee!" His eyes were round and dancing with excitement. "Thare be nowt bettur in the 'ole wurld than that."

His mother sighed. "Not *nowt*, David. *Nothing.* Say it properly."

"Thare—" He stopped at her look, took a deep breath, and tried again, speaking more slowly now. "*There* be *nothing* better in the 'ole wurld than goin' to Barnslee Town."

She bent down and kissed the top of his head. "Very good."

His father winked at him again. "Yur Mum, she be one fine woman from down near London Town, Davee boy. She teach ya 'ow ta spek joost reet. Use the Queen's English reet proper."

"I hardly speak the Queen's English," she demurred.

He went right on. "She naw murdur the muther tunge lek this old Tyke."*

She started to protest, but he raised a hand, cutting her off. "Thare be no 'ope fur me, Davee boy." Now he was actually exaggerating his accent. "The way Ah spek be burned inta me bones. But ya, Davee, if ya listen well, yur muther she mek ya inta one fine laddee. Reet, Annie?"

Her smile was filled with love as she leaned over and briefly touched his hand. "Reet, John."

She turned again to her son, combing her fingers through the curls of his dark hair. "Ah, David," she said, her voice warm with love, "you're going to be as handsome as your father."

"Aw, gwan!" her husband said.

"No, look at you, John Dickinson, with your brown eyes and dark,

---

* In Yorkshire, a "Tyke" is not a young child; the term is a colloquialism for a Yorkshireman.

wavy hair—and that smile that can charm a pig up into a tree. No won-der this wee lass went weak in the knees that day you first came in the company store."

David was watching this exchange happily. He ran over to the tiny mirror that hung over the kitchen sink and studied himself quickly. "Do you really think I'll look like Dah, Mum?"

She moved beside him. "Look at that jawline—firm and square, just like your father's. And you've got his brown eyes." She smiled at him in the mirror. "I love your eyes, David. When you smile, the laughter ripples up into them as well. Your hair is a little lighter, but thankfully, you got a bit of your father's waviness. Mine be straight as a stick." She bent down and kissed the back of his head. "Aye, you're going to be a handsome one indeed."

"Aw, gwan," he said, blushing, and sounding exactly like his father.

"Ah think ya be taller than me eventually," his father said, moving up beside them.

"Really?" David exclaimed. At five foot seven—just a couple of inches taller than his wife—John Dickinson was one of the shorter men working the Cawthorne Pit, and David worried that he would be like that too.

"I think so too, John," Anne said. "The way he be eating lately, I keep expecting him to sprout ears and turn into a mule." Smiling, she turned away. "Get dressed, David. Your father needs his breakfast. We'll leave right after he does so we can have the whole day together. Maybe there will even be time to trek down to the canal and watch them load the coal into the boats."

His arm shot high in the air. "Yah!"

Eyes warm with affection, Anne rumpled his hair once more. "Go on, now. Get yourself dressed, then out to the loo with you. Be sure you put on some shoes."

She moved to the table but continued to watch him out of the corner of her eye. He gave her an awkward glance, turned his back to her, then slid off his nightshirt. Now she watched him openly, feeling a sadness come upon her all of a sudden.

The baby chubbiness was completely gone. His vertebrae were visible along the center of his back, and when he reached for his trousers, she could also see his ribs. He was still a little boy to her, but once he started in the mines, his body would become as hard and muscular as her husband's. She turned away, not wanting to embarrass him further.

Finished, he gave her a little wave as he went out the door.

She sighed, not wanting to think either about him growing up or about his starting in the mines.

Her husband was gathering his things so he could leave as soon as breakfast was done. Anne moved to a shelf and took down a tin box about six inches square. "Here's your snap, John." She placed it in the pack he would carry over his shoulder into the mine. The packed lunch didn't get its name from the meager fare—two boiled eggs, half a loaf of bread, a chunk of cheese and two small pasties,* but from the way the tin lid snapped when it was closed. "John?"

"Yah, luv." His mind was clearly elsewhere.

"I'm sorry for always trying to correct David. I don't want to make you feel bad. I love the way you speak—" She smiled. "Or spek. 'Tis just that I want David to—"

"Ah know, Annie, luv, Ah know. An' Ah dunna mind at awl."

"And do you mind that I am teaching him to read and write?"

He turned in surprise. "Ah think it be grahnd what yur doin'."

"I don't know that much, but . . ." She let it trail off.

He forced a smile. "Annie, Ah know what ya be tryin' ta do, an' Ah think that it be gud." How did he say what needed to be said? He was of the sixth generation of coal miners in his family. His wife had not been born in Yorkshire and so she found the life and traditions of the mining community difficult to embrace. Thirteen years had softened her to the point where she accepted the hard realities of their lives, but she would never fully embrace them.

John Dickinson loved his wife, totally and without reservation. He never criticized her, not to her face, not behind her back. He knew, as

---

* Pastries, small sweet rolls or buns.

surely as he knew how to bring down a block of coal from the coal face, that she was the best thing that had ever happened to him.

With a start, he realized she was watching him, waiting. "Ah joost wurry a bit," he admitted.

"Go on."

"We be minin' folk, Annie. Naw amoont of fancy talk gunna be changin' that." He rushed on before she could interrupt. "Ah'm not askin' ya ta stop, mind ya. Joost tek care that ya dunna fill 'is mind with dreams that cahrn't be. That's awl Ah be sayin', Annie."

For a moment she wanted to flare out at him, grab his shoulders and shake him until he understood. But he was right. These were grand dreams she was having. Bloomin' madness, some were saying. "Have you listened to him read lately, John?"

"Naw. Naw fur a bit."

"I'm no teacher, John. I barely learned to read myself before—" She shook her head, not wanting to go where that thought would take her. "But he is so quick, John. He's already reading better than me. And he knows his numbers, too."

He was nodding, but she couldn't tell if that was just John, never wanting to hurt her, or if he really agreed. "John, I do not know how long I shall be here with you." One hand came up quickly. "No, John. I hope I'm wrong. But I fear that there were just too many years in the match factory, breathing in that white phosphorus dust."[2]

One hand stole up unnoticed and began to gently massage her jaw, the jaw that now gave her pain every time she ate, though she had not told John that yet. "The doctor says I've got a few years yet, but 'tis not likely I'll be here to see him become a man. And we have to get our heads 'round that. It will be you who is left to raise our son."

"Annie, please . . ."

"I want something more for David, John. We lost our little Annie at birth. Another gift from the match factory, I'm sure. And I couldn't carry any of those other babies for more than two or three months. But David was a fighter. He survived, and he's all we've got. Helping him to learn to speak proper and to read and write—'tis the only way I know how to help him."

He turned and took her in his arms. "Annie?"

"Aye?"

"Ah spek wit Mr. Rhodes, yes'day."

Her eyes widened for a moment, then she quickly pulled away.

"Ah tole 'im that Davee be six t'day, an'—"

She put her fingers to his lips. "Dunna say it," she said softly, perfectly imitating his Yorkshire drawl. "I know it moost be, John, but dunna say it. Naw t'day. Please."

But it had to be said. "Thare be a place for a trapper in Shaft Three. That's me pit, Annie. At least, 'e will be close by so Ah can watch 'im."

She didn't answer. "It be five pence a day," he added softly. "Five p! We need it to buy more med'cine." A long pause, then fervently, "Ah will naw lose ya, Annie. Ah will naw!"

She was close to tears. "How soon?"

"T'day be Freeday. Rhodes wants 'im ta start t'morrow, but I tole 'im Munday."

Her head dropped. It was like there was a great stone in her stomach. Then something fierce flared up inside her. "I know it must be so," she said, "but promise me one thing, John."

His eyes were bleak, but he managed a smile. "Whate'er ya ask of me, luv. Ya know that."

"Promise me that you will get him out of the mines. Not now. But sometime. Promise that you'll take us to America, John."

"Aw, Annie." His voice was filled with pain. "America? Thare be naw way. The passage alone be twenty poonds or more."

"Actually, steerage class is only fifteen pounds. But we need extra for the food. The crossing takes about three months, and the ticket includes only one meal a day." She had been investigating this for some time. "So we need money for that, too." Her eyes were suddenly angry. "Ridiculous! It costs less to go to America than to give us a proper burial here."[3]

He wasn't going to be drawn in with any of that. "We barely be scrapin' by noow, Annie. Thare joost be naw way. It be only a dream."

Her fingers dug into his arm. "No, John! It is our only hope for him. Promise me."

"Aw . . ." He shook his head. "Most trappers be startin' at age five, Annie. Davee awreddy be a year be'ind. Ah started the day after me fifth bur'day."

"And the Colliers Act of Eighteen Forty-Two says that no child under ten shall be employed in the mines," she shot back, eyes blazing.

There was a short, bitter laugh. "Parl'ment be passing laws lek that joost ta mek rich folks feel better aboot 'ow they treat us poor lugs. The mine owners pay the law naw mind, cuz they know Parl'ment pay it naw mind. Naw up 'ere in Yorkshire, they dunna."

She wanted to scream. Not at him, but at life. No, at him, too. Because he was right. He was always so infuriatingly right. Which allowed no room for hope, or dreams, or . . .

He started to turn away, but she grabbed his arm and pulled him back around. "John, I will agree to let David start work on Monday on one condition."

"Annie—"

"Hear me well, John Dickinson." Her eyes were implacable. "Promise me this, or else I'll keep him home. I'll teach him to be a clerk or a teamster or something."

He sighed. When she was like this, there was no moving her. For someone so gentle, so fragile, sometimes she was more rock than cotton. "What it be that ya want me ta do?"

"I will agree to him becoming a trapper, then a hurrier and a spragger or whatever all the jobs are, and even eventually a miner, if you promise me—you must swear it!—that every penny, every shilling he ever makes, will go into the box."

"Wha'?" he cried. "We need that fur yur med'cine, luv."

"No, John. Every shilling, or he stays home."

He looked stricken. Why did she think his family had been miners for six generations? Because there was no way out of the mines. None! But he finally nodded. "Ah mek ya that promise, Annie. Ya 'ave me wurd on it." He blew out his breath. "Ya 'ave me wurd."

She went up on tiptoes and kissed him on the cheek. "Would it surprise you, John, to know that I have already saved about twenty pounds?"

"Naw!"

"I have. I started right after David was born. It's in a shoe box under the floorboards."

He could only stare at her. What kind of dream fired that level of determination?

But it was still just that—a dream. "It tek ten more years ta save e'nuff ta git us awl thare. Davee be sixteen by then."

"And how old will he be in ten years if we don't save our money?" she snapped back at him. "I don't want David to know anything about this. Or anyone else. But you must promise me."

Hearing David's footsteps on the stairs outside, she gave him a quick smile. "Come right home tonight, John. We'll be having Yorkshire pudding and growler[4] for supper."

"We dunna 'ave muney fur growler, Annie."

"'Tis your son's birthday, John," she cried. "And Monday, he goes into the mines. We *will* be having Yorkshire pudding and growler for supper."

Cawthorne was a "pit town."[5] Located about midway between Leeds and Sheffield and three miles west of Barnsley, it was one of dozens of villages that helped sustain the vast coal-mining industry in South Yorkshire. Major seams of coal ran for miles through the area. Sometimes these seams were close enough to the surface to outcrop. Other places they dove hundreds of feet underground. Sheffield, one of the great mill towns in all of England, was just a dozen miles to the south, so Cawthorne was in the heart of one of the richest coalfields in the British Isles.

Cawthorne was home to about a hundred and fifty families, all of them mining families. All the businesses in town—the Cawthorne Dry Goods Store, the greengrocer, a butcher shop, and the Cold Thorne Pub—were owned by Cawthorne Coal Company, as were all of the row houses. Since rent and all transactions in the village used company scrip, the mine

owners kept the prices inflated and the miners in perpetual debt, and
therefore in perpetual servitude.

The row houses ran the full length of the single street in Cawthorne.
They were joined together in one continuous structure, facing each other
like wooden specters having a stare-down. They were dingy, dilapidated,
and long ago blackened by soot and coal dust. Each flat or apartment was
a single room no more than fifteen feet wide and twenty-five deep. A
sleeping area for the parents was partitioned off by a rope and a blanket.
Everything else took place in the main room. There was no inside loo, or
toilet, only a basin for washing dishes. A large bucket for bringing water
from the town pump and a galvanized washtub served as the rest of their
"indoor plumbing." The tub was used both for laundry and for bathing,
though it was barely big enough to hold David's father, and only if he
folded his legs up into an impossible position.

Miners bathed each night to cleanse themselves of the coal dust. The
rest of the family bathed only on Saturday night. David hated that, because
they all used the same water, and he was always last. Not only was the
water mostly cold by then, especially in wintertime, but it was gritty from
the coal dust left by his father. In large families, the water would actually
get so black that you could lose a baby in it. His mother told him that this
was the origin of the old saying, "Don't throw the baby out with the bath-
water."

For the families' other personal needs, the company had built forty
outhouses behind the tenements—twenty on the north, twenty on the
south. Forty outhouses for almost four hundred people. And for all of this,
each family was charged one-third of their monthly earnings as rent. The
soot, the coal dust, the stench, and the raw sewage came at no extra
charge.

"Hurry, Mum." David was out ahead of her, running forward, eager to
be clear of Cawthorne and out into the countryside.

She smiled. How she envied his irrepressible zest for life. "I'm coming,"
she called.

"Hurry. Barnslee be waitin' for us."

Notes

1. For reasons that will become apparent as the novel proceeds, I decided to have the lead characters come from a coal-mining town in Yorkshire, England. This created an immediate dilemma. How to deal with the Yorkshire accent?

The peoples of the British Isles have an astonishing variety of accents, as my wife and I learned during our three-year stay there. Yorkshireans are not only part of that diversity but have an accent quite distinct. One day my wife and I were in the city of York, which is in the northeast of England, to do some family history research. By then, we had become pretty good at attuning our Yankee ears to local speech. But this day, when I asked for some information from one of the clerks (or *clarks*, as the Brits say), the woman gave me a lengthy and detailed response. And neither my wife nor I understood more than a word or two of what she said.

Therein is the dilemma. To have at least some authenticity, I felt I had to reflect the Yorkshire accent to some degree. But if it were *too* authentic, I was afraid readers would find it tedious and difficult to read. Clearly, there had to be a compromise. Here, in brief, are some of the compromises I chose to make:

—The formal *thee, thou,* and *thy* were used in Yorkshire in the 1800s. However, these were pronounced as *thah, thi,* and *tha.* These are used so frequently in conversation that they quickly became a serious distraction, so I went with the more recognizable *ya* and *yur.*

—When a letter is dropped out of a word, it is customary for an apostrophe to be inserted in its place, as in *can't* or *hasn't.* But in Yorkshire, they drop letters everywhere. The initial *h* on most words is silent. *The* becomes just a *t'* and is frequently tacked onto the word it modifies (for example, I'll meet ya at t'pub). *With* becomes *w'* and *of* becomes *o'.* Consonants at the end of words—such as in -ing words—are often dropped. The dialogue became so peppered with apostrophes that it was downright annoying. For example, here is a sentence expressed as a person from Yorkshire might say it: 'E kissed 'is wife g'bye, lef' t'-house w' 'is bes' mate who is o' Barnslee Town, an' walked t' t'mine t'gether."

—Couple those two things with their unique pronunciations, and even the simplest phrase becomes a mystery. For example, "Ge' i' e'en," does not easily translate into "Get it eaten." So I often put in more recognizable spellings to make it easier for the reader.

For these compromises, I apologize in advance to the friends and associates from Yorkshire my wife and I made while in England. I regret my inability to do justice to your rich and delightful way of speaking. My only excuse for even attempting to do so is that my great-grandfather's ancestors came from Heptonstall in West Yorkshire, which is just twenty-five miles west of where this novel begins. So it is possible that I have a genetic bias for the "muther tunge."

2. The East End of London in the latter part of the nineteenth century had several large match factories. Here is an example of the incredibly deplorable working conditions for children and women in eighteenth- and nineteenth-century England. Women and girls

worked six days a week, fourteen hours a day in the match factories and were paid five shillings a week.

Though it had been banned in the United States and Sweden, Parliament refused to outlaw white phosphorus in England because it would be "a restraint of free trade." The white phosphorus vapors caused a yellowing of the skin, hair loss, and a form of bone cancer known as "phossy-jaw." It often led to a horribly painful death (see "Matchgirls Strike," http://web311.pavilion.net/TUmatchgirls.htm).

3. This observation was made by two missionaries from the U.S. about British taxation: "[There are] taxes of *every kind*, . . . for smoke must not go out of the chimney in England without a tax. Light must not come in at the windows without paying duties. . . . There are taxes for living & taxes for dying, insomuch that it is very difficult for the poor to get buried any how, & a man may emigrate to America & find a grave, for less money, than he can get a decent burial for in Old England. We scarce recollect an article without tax except cats, mice & fleas" (in Allen, Esplin, and Whittaker, *Men with a Mission*, 10–12).

4. Yorkshire pudding is even today a staple of the British diet, especially for the Sunday meal. It is not a pudding in the American sense of the word, but an unsweetened, bowl-shaped pastry usually served with brown gravy. Tradition has it that it was first developed in Yorkshire among the very poor because it was an inexpensive way to fill children's stomachs when meat and other staples were beyond a family's means (see *Random House Dictionary*, s.v. "Yorkshire pudding"). At this time in Yorkshire, a "growler" was a small pork pie.

5. Cawthorne and Barnsley are both existing towns in South Yorkshire. Barnsley is a large city, Cawthorne a village of fewer than three hundred people. Specific descriptions of Cawthorne and Pit Number Three are fictional.

CHAPTER 2

Friday, June 13, 1862

By early afternoon, Anne Dickinson was quite exhausted. And yet she felt a deep satisfaction. At least a dozen times that day—the latest just minutes ago—David had paused in his frenetic rush to exclaim, "Oh, Mum. This be the grahndest day of me 'ole life." In fact, it had been such a delight to watch him, she had not corrected his language once all day.

They had walked long and laughed much and he had pelted her with endless questions. Every store became a new adventure. The millinery shop, the haberdashery, an ironmonger,* the tobacconist's and a bookstore. He had to see every one. But it was the sweet shop that absolutely dazzled him. He just stood there, struck dumb, eyes moving slowly across the shelves, counters, and cases. In the end, deciding how to spend his six pence proved to be pure agony.

Anne steadfastly refused to help. "'Tis your money," she kept saying. "You must decide."

He finally settled on a stick of black licorice and six pieces of Turkish delight.†

Now, late in the afternoon, they were finally on their way back to

---

* Monger is an old English word meaning "one who sells" (*Random House Dictionary*, s.v. "monger"). So, for example, a fishmonger is one who sells fish. An ironmonger sells iron products. An ironmonger's shop is what we in America would call a hardware store. Even today, they are much like the old neighborhood hardware stores of the late 1800s and early 1900s in small-town America.

† A candy that seems to have originated in Turkey but is very popular in Britain. It has a soft, jellylike consistency, much like our gumdrops, but it is cut into small cubes and dusted with powdered sugar. It comes in many flavors.

Cawthorne. And for the moment David was quiet. Suddenly he stopped. "What's that, Mum?"

"What, darling?"

"That big building."

"That's the Church of the Holyrood."

"Church of the what?"

"Holyrood. It means the holy cross. It's a Catholic church."

"Can we go see it?"

"No!" The sudden change in her voice brought his head up. "We have to be getting back." But it was still afternoon, and she had said they could stay until evening.

"Please, Mum. It's beautiful. Please."

"It's just a church, David. Like the All Saints Church in Cawthorne."

"So is this our church too?" he asked.

She gave him an odd look. "*Our* church? We don't have a church."

"We have the All Saints Church."

"But it's not *our* church. We don't attend there. All Saints Church is an Anglican church, which means it belongs to the Church of England. That's different from the Catholic church."

"Please can I go see it, Mum? Joost peek in."

"*No*, David! Church be no place for people like us. No church."

⁂

"David?"

He looked up. They were out of Barnsley now, walking leisurely between the hedgerows that lined both sides of Cawthorne Road. She pointed ahead to where a small meadow with scattered oak trees opened up. "Do you mind if we stop and rest a bit?"

He shrugged and turned aside. He hadn't spoken since she had cut him off so abruptly. A heavily loaded coal wagon was approaching, stirring up clouds of dust. "Let's move over under that oak tree," she suggested.

Fifty yards back from the road, the noise and dust receded. David plopped down on the grass, stretched out on his back with his hands beneath his head, and closed his eyes. Anne watched him for a moment, then sat down beside him.

"Are you tired, Mum?"

"A wee bit. But it's been a glorious day together."

"Aye, Mum. It was brilliant."

She cocked her head. "Brilliant? And where did you learn that word?"

The familiar grin reappeared. "Dunno."

She just shook her head, then lay down beside him and closed her eyes. Nearly five minutes passed with neither of them speaking, and she found her eyelids starting to droop.

"Mum?"

"Yes?"

"Tell me aboot when ya were a little girl."

She turned her head, surprised at the request.

"Tell me aboot London."

"I don't know *about* London." She stressed the proper pronunciation. "I did not live in London when I was little, David. I was born in a village called Battersea, about five or six miles to the southwest of London."

"Dahdee says that you lived in a grahnd 'ouse, Mum. Be that true?"

Her eyes closed, warm remembrance and dull pain flooding over her at the same moment. "Aye," she finally answered, "it was a grand house indeed. Guess how many bedrooms."

"There was more than one?"

She smiled. Two bedrooms would seem fantastic to a boy who had only ever known a room partitioned off by a blanket for his parents. "Astle Manor had fifteen bedrooms."

"Whah!" he blurted. "Tha canna be so."

"'Tis true. Lord and Lady Astle were very rich. Lady Astle was related to the royal family."

"Whah!" he said again. "I canna picture such a thing." He sat up, thoroughly fascinated now. "Did you ever get to be inside such a grahnd place, Mum?"

She laughed. "I was actually born inside the house, my darling. We had our quarters in the basement with the other servants."

His eyes were as round as the wheels of a coal trolley. "Dahdee never tole me that," he finally managed. "So were you rich?"

"Oh no, David. My parents—your granddad and your grandmum—were servants at Astle Manor. Papa was a groomsman and took care of the horses and such. Mama was the head chambermaid. That means she took care of all the bedrooms. It was a very important responsibility. Making the beds each morning, emptying the chamber pots, washing the sheets, keeping the fireplaces clean and filled with wood in the winter. When the Astles went to Brighton for the summer—that's down by the seaside—Mama would let me help her, so I got to be in every bedroom at one time or another."

"Was it Grandmum who taught you to read? Or did you go to skoo-ul?"

"In London, they don't say *skoo-ul*, David. It's just school. But no. Neither Mama nor Papa could read. Actually, it was Lady Astle who made it possible. The Astles had a little chapel on the estate, with their own vicar."

"What's a vicar?"

"A minister, a parson, the head of a local church."

"Ah."

"But Reverend Pike served only Astle Manor. He was also a teacher for the Astles' three children. Then Lady A—that's what we all called her, but not to her face, of course—decided it would be useful if a few of her servants could read and write. The adult servants were too busy, so she decided to train up the next generation. She had a few of us attend school with her children.

"We went two hours each morning after the chores were done. Reverend Pike, he taught us some basic reading and writing, and then later our numbers."

"I would give anything to go to school," he ventured wistfully. "Dahd says there ought to be school in Cawthorne, but the mine owners don't like that idea."

"Of course not," she muttered, half to herself, "wouldn't want their little employees getting minds of their own now, would we?"

"What?"

"Never mind. I hope they get a school in Cawthorne someday, but it doesn't matter. I'm going to teach you everything I know, David. You and me, we'll have our own school."

"I am so glad, Mum. I love it." Again they fell silent. Again it was David who broke it.

"So if you lived near London, and Dahd was a miner here in Yorkshire, how did you meet?"

She sat up abruptly, then got to her feet. "It's time to go, David." He looked hurt. She reached out her hand. "Come. We still have to stop at the store and get supper."

He stood and fell into step beside her, confused by her abrupt change of mood. As they reached the road, he tried again. "How come you didn't become a chambermaid, Mum?"

"No more questions, David. You've asked more than enough for one day."

"Oh." His mouth shut and his chin dropped. He moved a step away from her, studying the puffs of dust his shoes made as they hit the roadside.

It was half a mile before the guilt got the better of her. He looked so crestfallen. She touched him on the arm. "I hope it was a happy birthday for you, David," she said.

He brightened immediately. "Aye, Mum, 'twas more grahnd than I could ever imagine."

That pleased her, and in spite of the pall of gloom brought by the thought, she decided it was time to let her son know about the rest of his birthday surprise. "David?"

"Eh?" He was off in his own thoughts again.

"Your father has another surprise for your birthday."

"What?"

"He spoke yesterday with Mr. Rhodes, supervisor of his pit at the mine."

His head jerked up. The excitement in his eyes was like a lance in her side. But she forced a smile. And she told him. Her voice was dull and lifeless, but she told him—about his starting work in the mines three days hence. She didn't tell him about the argument she and his father had had, nor of the deal they had finally struck. His salary would be turned over to his parents anyway. There was no need for him to know where it was going.

By the time she finished, he was literally dancing in excitement. "Ya dunna be teasin' me, Mum, are ya?" he said, lapsing back into the language of his father. "Da ya spek trulee?"

She felt utterly weary. "Yes, I speak truly. On Monday you begin work in the mines."

She looked away. *But, God willing, you will not spend your life there.*

CHAPTER 3

Monday, June 16, 1862

David and his father walked through the first light of dawn toward Cawthorne Pit Number Three. David trotted to keep up with his father's brisk pace. It was five-thirty, and no one else was about. As they approached the entrance to the winding tower, David's eyes kept lifting to the giant winding wheels perched atop the derricklike structure. He had seen the tower many times from outside, but approaching it now, he felt like an ant approaching an oak tree.

"David?"

He looked up to see his father watching him. "Yes, Dahd."

"Do ya un'erstand 'ow important a trapper be in the mines?"

"I think so." Then he shook his head. "I'm not sure."

"Thare be large doors placed throughout a mine. They be fur ven'lation."

"Ven'lation?"

"Yah. That means ta keep the air movin'. That buildin' over thare—" he pointed to a low brick building behind the winding tower—"'olds two big steam engines. One powers the windin' gear, the other pumps fresh air down inta the mine. When the doors throughout the mine are shut, the air be *trapped* an' forced inta the side chutes an' minin' chambers. That's why ya be called trappers. Yur job is ta open the doors when a coal car approaches, then shut 'em agin."

"Oh." David knew that his job was to open and shut doors, but he had not understood why.

"Anuther thing. Op'nin' the doors frum time ta time allows the air ta flow more freely and that stops the gas frum puddlin' up." He peered at him. "Da ya 'member what be fire damp?"[1]

David nodded gravely. "Gasses in the mine that catch fire?"

"Reet. It be cuz of fire damp that they invented the Davy lamp. Best thing ta happen in the mines fur a long time."[2]

"My friend Peter Jones, 'e be a trapper 'til 'e be eight. 'E tole me 'twas naw that 'ard. Ya joost sit 'roond an' wait fur people ta cum wit the coal tubs."

Frowning, his father stopped. "Joost cuz yur Mum be naw 'ere, 'tis naw reason ta change the way ya talk. If ya think it pleases me, ya be mistaken. Do ya un'erstand me, boy?"

He looked up in surprise, a little hurt. "I—"

"Yur Mum wants only what's best fur ya, Davee. Dunna ever furget that."

"I won't, Dahdee."

"Ah warn ya," he said sternly, "sum of the men an' boys be teasin' ya reet fierce aboot 'ow ya spek, but ya pay 'em naw mind, Davee. *Naw* mind! If'n yur Mum be thinkin' ya be doon thare undoin' what she's been teachin' ya, ya naw be stayin' on as a trapper. Do ya 'ear me, Son?"

Shocked a little by his father's intensity, David bobbed his head up and down quickly. "Yes, Dahdee."

"Gud boy." John touched his shoulders. "Awl reet, then, let's git doon thare an' show ya what ya be doin' fur a livin'."

———※———

As they approached the cage that would lower them into the mine, David eyed it warily while his father talked briefly to the winder—the man who ran the winding machinery that lifted or lowered the cage. David was looking at the rope that dropped from the winding wheel high above them and hooked to the top of the cage. It was black with grease, polished to a dull sheen, and looked no thicker than his middle finger. And the cage looked like it was very heavy.

"Are you sure this be safe, Dahdee?" he whispered.

Angus McComber, the winder, roared with laughter. "Aye, laddie. Ya be safe as long as ya be gud to me, lek yur Pap always is. Otherwise, Ah let the lever slip through me 'ands, an' ya be droppin' lek a rock." He cackled gleefully, showing one missing tooth.

John ignored him and stepped across the gap into the cage. "Cum on, Son."

His weight started the cage swinging back and forth, bumping gently against the sides of the shaft. Then David made a mistake. As he stepped across the gap, he looked down. It was straight down for over four hundred feet. Far below he saw tiny pinpricks of light and realized they were lanterns. He gasped and groped blindly for a handhold as a wave of dizziness hit him.

"Dunna look doon, David!" his father barked. "Keep yur eyes straight a'ead. Cum on, in the cage wit ya, boy."

David's face flamed hot. He did not want to shame his father in front of the other man. He took a quick breath, looked straight ahead, and stepped into the cage. His father pulled the door shut and banged twice on the steel framework with the palm of his hand. The sound of the steam engine somewhere off to the left deepened as it took the weight of the cage and began to lower it.

Moving to one corner, his father motioned for David to join him. The walls of the shaft were slipping past them now with increasing speed, and the square of light directly above them was shrinking rapidly. The vertigo rose up again and David closed his eyes.

After a moment, the dizziness passed and he opened his eyes again. The darkness was thick now, but he could still discern their passage through solid rock. He relaxed a little. The cage still rocked back and forth slightly, but it was bearable.

David looked up. The square of light high above them was no more than the size of a thimble now. "Dahd? Has the rope on the cage ever broken before?"

There was a long pause, then his father said, "Ya dunna ask questions lek that, Son."

David's face went hot as he clamped his lips tightly together. Even at six, he knew that miners were very superstitious. They always stood in the same place in the cage when they went down or came up. They liked to eat in the same spot every day. No one ever started a job or moved on a Friday, because it was a bad luck day. And once a man put away his tools at the end of the shift and started for home, he would never, for any reason, return to his chamber. The mine was too close to Satan's domain, and one did not tempt the Evil One.

At the bottom, his father opened the door and they stepped off onto a rough-hewn floor. John shut the door, then banged on the steel frame three times with his hammer. Immediately the lift started up the shaft again. "Twice ta go doon," he explained. "Three times ta go up."

David turned slowly, looking around. To his surprise, the air was cool, enough that he was glad he had brought his light jacket.

"I thought you said it got hot in the mines, Dahd."

"Not 'ere. Only in the work chambers."

The light from the two lamps here was softer, more subdued, and David realized that the air was filled with a fine mist of coal dust. There was also the heavy smell of mule dung coming from a side chamber. No surprise. Once the big cars were loaded from the smaller coal tubs or trolleys, mules would pull them back to the cage for transport to the top.

"Cum," his father said, "our monkey head be this way."

David nodded. You didn't grow up as the son of a miner and not know the language. The main tunnels that brought the cars to the cage and from there up to the surface were called gangways. Going off in both directions from the gangways were the chutes—tunnels big enough to carry full-sized coal cars. Smaller passages, which generally ran parallel to the gangway, connected the chutes into one vast latticework. These were the monkey heads. They connected the chutes with the work chambers where the coal was actually dug.

Lamps were hung at about twenty-five-yard intervals, providing only a dim light, but David found his eyes adjusting quickly. They moved into the gangway, passed three chutes, then turned right, where his father stopped. He stood in front of a tunnel no more than four feet square. This was a monkey head. A set of narrow rails ran into it.

Removing the cloth pack from his shoulder, his father hung it around his neck. He swung the pouch that held his water and ale so that it hung from his belt in front of him. He dropped to his hands and knees and started into the tunnel. "Watch yur 'ead," he grunted, and he disappeared. .

Knowing that a monkey head was a tunnel had not prepared David for actually entering one. He didn't have a pack, only the cloth sack his mother had filled with his snap, two candles, and a water flask. Tying it to his belt, he quickly dropped on all fours and followed after his father. Instantly the darkness closed in around him. He stopped, gripping the rails to fight off a wave of panic. He moved forward again. The floor was rough. "Ow!"

"Try ta keep yur knees on the ties b'tween the rails," came his father's muffled voice, "or ya be bangin' up yur legs real bad."

The ties helped, but in moments, David's knees felt raw and the palms of his hands were burning. David had never been afraid of the dark, but now, with only a faint glimmer ahead from his father's lamp, it felt like the tunnel walls were closing in on him. A suffocating wave of panic swept over him. "Dahd! Are you there?"

"Ah be joost ahead of ya, Son," came the faint reply. "Keep 'old of the rails. 'Nuther 'undred yards an' we be thare."

Sure enough, a minute or two later the glimmer of light around the round shape of his father's rump widened. Another minute and his view to the tunnel was clear. He scrambled the last ten feet and leaped up, hungrily drawing in deep breaths. This chamber was maybe fifty feet square. The roof, rough and undulating, was higher than the chute. It felt wonderful to be in the open again. Four lamps hung from spikes driven into the side walls at twenty-foot intervals. The increased light was as welcome as the open space.

He looked around. The narrow tracks they had followed through the monkey head split and ran off in three directions. Four empty coal tubs sat on the rails. These were not the big cars that carried coal to the cage, but smaller trolleys made of wood, set on iron wheels.

"It is warm here, Dahd."

"When ya be workin' a coal seam, the compressed heat is released. Meks things toasty."

As David turned back to his father, his eyes widened a little. His father's back was to David, but he had already stripped off his pack and pouch and placed them on a narrow shelf that had been cut into the coal face, and now he was removing his clothes. First came the boots and socks, then off came the light jacket followed by his shirt, then the heavy kegs, or trousers.

David looked away. He had never seen his father undressed before. But his curiosity drew him back. His father stood there, bare-legged and bare-chested, with nothing on but a thin pair of grey cotton smalls. He took down a fold of cloth and shook it out, and David saw it was another pair of kegs, but these were made of light cotton, and were as black as if they had been dyed in India ink. John buttoned them at the waist, then pulled the suspenders over his shoulders.

Seeing his son's expression, John smiled. "These be me workin' kegs, Son. As ya can tell, it be too 'ot in 'ere ta work in me regular clothes."

"Do you not even wear a shirt, then? Or shoes? What about in winter?"

A short laugh. "Thare be naw winter in the mines. Or summer or spring, fur that matter."

His father turned back to the shelf, struck a match, lit his Davy lamp, and strapped it on his head. He took down what looked like a folded blanket. Finally, he grabbed one of the several picks leaning up against the wall. "Ah be workin' a monkey 'ole today. It be this way."

"What's a monkey hole, Dahd? Is that the same as a monkey head?"

"No. Cum an' see."

They walked fifty or more feet before his father stopped. At first David saw nothing, only the black roughness of the coal face. But when his father laid down the pick, removed the Davy lamp from his head, and knelt down, David drew in a sharp breath. Where the wall and the floor met, a niche had been cut horizontally into the coal face. It was about six feet long, two feet high, and cut maybe three feet into the face of the wall. It looked like it had been made for a corpse. A shiver ran down David's back.

"This be a monkey 'ole, Davee," his father said, unfolding the blanket. "This be the one thing miners hate above all others."

He spread out the blanket and pushed it into the hole. Then he placed the Davy lamp at one end of the niche so it illuminated the inside. Finally, he lay on his back and scooted himself onto the blanket. One hand came back, groped for a moment, then found his pick.

David was aghast. "You work in there?" His father's nose was just inches from the ceiling.

But even as he spoke, his father's upper body began to move rhythmically. There was the sharp clang of steel on stone. Puffs of black dust immediately filled the space. Chunks of coal were falling now, bouncing off his father's arms and body.

It continued for several seconds, then stopped. His father slid out again, leaving the pick in place but retrieving the lamp. He stood up beside his son.

"When ya undercut the coal face, it makes it easier ta bring the 'ole thing down." Seeing the look on his son's face, he smiled. "It be pure hell, but it do speed up the work."

He waved his hand. "We need ta tek ya ta yur post an' show ya 'ow ta be a trapper, Son."

David fell into step beside his father, trotting to keep up with his long strides. He said nothing more. The awfulness of what he had just seen lay heavy on him. Then came a sudden thought: *That's why Mama hates the mines so.*[3]

Notes

1. *Fire damp* was the name given at this time to a number of flammable gases produced in coal mines, the most common of which was methane. The name probably comes from the German word *dampf,* meaning "vapor," and came into use in England when German miners were brought over to help the British learn deep-mining techniques.

2. Before the invention of the Davy lamp in 1815 (named for its inventor), candles or lanterns were used in the mines for illumination. This often caused the methane and other gasses to ignite and explode. The Davy lamp consisted of a glass cylinder, within which the flame was further encased in wire gauze so as to permit air to enter but prevent the flame escaping to ignite any gasses in the air.

3. The endnotes in chapter 4 will discuss in more detail the conditions in the coal mines and the life of a coal miner as described in the novel.

CHAPTER 4

Monday, June 16, 1862

"As ya can see," his father said, pointing as they walked deeper into the mine, "the coal seam still be runnin' purty mooch level 'long 'ere, though it naw be thick e'nuff ta justify a full chamber." Just ahead of them the area suddenly reduced in width by half and became a tunnel, with the ceiling only about five feet high. His father had to bend at the waist to enter; David only had to duck his head.

"How do the mules come in here, Dahd?"

"They dunna. Naw here. Do ya r'member what a 'urrier is? An' a thruster?"

"Yes, Dahd. Hurriers get their name because they pull the coal tubs through the tunnels and hurry them along. Thrusters help the hurriers by pushing the tubs from behind. And the trapper opens the doors, which are called traps, for the hurriers, the thrusters, and the mule drivers."

"Do it awl mek sense ta ya, Davee boy?"

"It does, Dahd."

"So in monkey heads lek this one, the tunnel be naw large e'nuff fur mules, so the 'urriers become the mules." He turned his head and his lamp shone directly into David's eyes, causing him to squint. "Yur furst station be quite narrow an' confined, cuz the mine bosses, they dunna be trustin' the bigger doors ta a new trapper. But do yur job well, an' they be movin' ya ta one of the chutes in a month or two."

Following close behind his father to take advantage of the light from his lamp, David was peering around him. Just as he saw the outline of a door ahead of him, a terrible stench assaulted his nostrils. "Ew!" he exclaimed. "What is that awful smell, Dahd?"

John ignored that. "This be yur station, Davee. This be whare ya be servin' as trapper."

The door was set in a framework of beams and closed the tunnel off completely. The door itself was made of planks and had a hole about half the size of David's fist on one side. A thick, knotted rope came through it so it could be pulled from either side of the door.

Stepping to one side, his father placed his lamp on a small shelf cut into the wall. The light revealed a mound of old candle wax on the ledge. Turning, David looked around. Immediately he saw the source of the awful smell. Near the hinges of the door, a short, three-legged stool was set in a niche hollowed out of the coal face. Beneath it, in about an inch of coal and rock dust, was a thick, dark paste bearing deep impressions of a child's bare feet. The smell of urine and feces was overpowering. The area was littered with garbage—bits of paper, splinters of bones, wood shavings, a twisted spike from the rails. He jumped as a dark shape moved across his peripheral vision. "Dahd!"

"Joost a rat," his father said. "An' a small one at that. Won't 'urt ya. Joost keep yur snap on the shelf where they can't git at it." He was still looking around, his nose wrinkled. "Rats be good luck, did ya know that? Thare ears be so sensitive, they can 'ear a cave-in b'fur it 'appens."

He walked over to the stool and cursed softly under his breath. "'Ad no idee it be this bad," he muttered. "Stupid nippers. Cahrnt thare mums teach 'em nothin'? May as well put 'em in a pigsty. Goin' ta the loo reet 'ere whare they 'ave ta sit awl day."

Turning back, he said, "Shudda brung a shuvel. Ah be comin' back ta 'ave lunch wit ya aboot midday. Ah'll bring one then."

"Really?" David was instantly embarrassed by the raw eagerness in his voice.

"Joost today. On yur own after that. But we'll cover up that muck wit sum dirt and gravel." He pointed toward the door. "When ya need ta use the loo, Son, thare's a wide spot up the tunnel a way." He half turned. "Gimme one of yur candles."

David untied his sack from his belt and handed it to his father. John retrieved one of the thick, stubby candles and lit it off the Davy lamp. He held the flame to the hardened candle wax on the shelf until it began to soften, then stuck the candle upright into it.

"Each candle be burnin' aboot three, maybe four 'ours. Two candles canna git ya through a 'ole shift. Naw whare close. So once ya git used ta the lay of things, yoo'll want ta blow it oot fur a while. Save it fur when ya canna stand the darkness anymore."

"I'm not afraid of the dark, Dahd."

"Ah know, Son, and that be good. But ya ain't never saw darkness lek this b'fur. Joost wait. It's so thick ya can almost taste it."

"If I blow the candle out, how will I light it again? Do you have a match?"

"Aye, but Ah canna be sparin' it, Son. Each match costs a ha'penny an' we dunna know when we be needin' one at the coal face."

David looked away, feeling the first stirring of panic.

"Yoo'll be awl reet, Son. The 'urriers 'ave candles. Ya can light yurs off'n thares if ya need ta." Sensing David's misgivings, John stepped to the door, grasped the rope, and pulled on it. It creaked and groaned until he had it fully opened. Pointing through the door, he continued, "This be whare the coal be cumin' frum. The crews be workin' a new chamber doon thare."

David saw that the tunnel was descending away from him on a slight angle.

"They be cumin' this direction, widenin' the tunnel, layin' rail, bringin' the first of the coal oot. Once that's done, this tunnel be wide e'nuff fur mules an' cars. No more boys draggin' thare guts oot pullin' the tubs."

Then there was a soft sound of disgust. "Crate-egged* mine owners. They be daft as a dead mule, nowt but spit an' glue.† Easy e'nuff fur 'em ta sit in thare grahnd mansions, smokin' thare pipes an' sippin' champagne, sayin', 'G'wan, ya stupid Tykes. Joost follow Ole Lady Coal whare e'er she leads ya. Pay naw mind ta cuttin' yur way through three 'undred feet of solid rock. Joost cut it on through an' stop yur bellyachin'.'"

---

* *Crate-egg* is a Yorkshire colloquialism for an idiot.

† That is, poorly made, not worth much.

David was smiling in the darkness. His father was not talking to him anymore, and listening to him rant like this was a new experience. He suspected that if he hadn't been here, the soliloquy would have been much more colorful.

Finally, John Dickinson realized what he was doing and gave David a brief smile. He gestured to the door. "Yur turn."

It surprised David how a door not much taller than he was could be so heavy, but he managed to drag it open without it stopping. Then he pushed it shut again, which was easier.

"Gud. The trick be 'earin' the tubs cumin' so ya 'ave the door open in time. The loaded coal tubs be full an' very 'eavy, so it be a real pull fur the 'urriers and the thrusters cumin' this way. If they git ta the door an' it ain't open, they be boxin' yur lugholes reet sharply. Un'erstand?"

"Yes, Dahd. But if the door's shut, how will I know when they are coming?"

"Ya gotta be lis'nin'. Cahrnt be dozin' off or anythin' lek that. But ya be 'earin' 'em whilst they still be maybe 'alf a minute away. That be plenty of time."

Now he turned and pointed toward the way they had come. "When they be bringin' the empty tubs back frum the gangway, yoo'll be seein' thare lights almost b'fur ya 'ear 'em. Each 'urrier 'as 'is own Davy lamp. Since the tubs be empty then, sumtimes the 'urriers stop an' talk. Makes a good brek fur 'em. And fur the trappers, too."

He took a quick breath. "Davee, thare be a couple of very important things. First, if'n yur candle suddenly starts burnin' brighter, in a flickerin' sort of way, git oot of 'ere. Ya cum runnin' fast as ya can scoot an' tell me or one of t'other miners. D'ya un'erstand, Davee? This be very important. D'ya un'erstand what Ah be sayin'?"

"I think so." There was a growing hollow in the pit of David's stomach. *But if my candle isn't lit, how will I know if the fire damp is building up?* He bit his lip and said nothing more.

John laid both hands on David's shoulders. "Yes'day, David, ya be no more than a boy, but t'day ya becum a trapper. T'day ya start bein' a man."

"I understand, Dahd." At the moment, he wasn't feeling much like a man. The elation of his first day on the job had left him about the time he had stepped into the cage.

He felt the hands lift from his shoulders. "Ah must git back. Ah be back at midday."

"Bye, Dahd," David said, forcing a lightness into his voice that he wasn't feeling at the moment. "I be fine."

"I know, Son. I know." He turned, bent down, and disappeared into the tunnel.

In a fit of bravado that he instantly regretted, David snuffed out his candle about quarter of an hour later. He wanted to feel the darkness for himself, see what he was going to have to cope with. He instantly wished he hadn't. It was crushing. Like something primeval pressing in on him, filling his nostrils, pushing down on his eyelids, clamping his arms against his body. At first he thought that once his eyes adjusted, it would be better. He was wrong. After waiting five minutes, he put his hand an inch in front of his nose and waved it back and forth. He could discern no movement whatsoever.

Next he bent down, groping for the track. He decided he wouldn't wait for his father to return with a shovel. He began scooping up handfuls of dirt and gravel and tossing it in the direction of the stool, hoping his father would be proud that he hadn't waited for him to solve the problem. But it was arduous work, and since he couldn't see if he was even throwing it in the right direction, he gave up and groped his way back to the stool.

With the absolute darkness came absolute stillness. Or so he thought. As his ears adjusted to the silence, he began to hear things he hadn't noticed before—the drip, drip, drip of water from the ceiling. The rustle of his clothing when he moved. The creak of the stool when he shifted his weight. Something scurrying past him in the darkness. That one made him stiffen.

He got off the stool and moved to the center of the tracks, feeling around with his hands. He found three or four apple-sized chunks of rock or coal and placed them beside the stool. The next time he heard the whisper of something racing across the floor, he hurled a rock in the direction of the sound. "Git outta here," he yelled. He held his feet off the floor for a time but finally couldn't stand it any longer.

He forced himself to concentrate on the dripping sound. It was steady, always plopping at the same interval. About every two seconds, he decided. After five more minutes, he began to wonder how many times it dripped during a full shift. Wishing he had a paper, he forced himself to do the arithmetic in his mind. One drip every two seconds. Thirty drips per minute. Um. One hundred eighty drips per hour. No. Eighteen *hundred* drips per hour. However, when he tried to calculate how many there would be in a full shift, the math defeated him and he gave up.

⁂

The first cart came about an hour later. He heard the low rumble of steel on steel before he saw the light. It grew larger quickly and, because it was coming from his right, he understood that the hurrier was pulling an empty tub. He quickly swung the door open, then stood far enough back from the track to be out of the way. The light from the Davy lamp bobbed up and down with the movement of the person's head as he bent over and pulled the cart.

"Ain't ya got no candle?" a boy's voice grunted as the cart rumbled past.

Momentarily startled, David blurted, "Yep. Just savin' it." Then, as an afterthought, "I be the new trapper."

But the cart passed him and went through the door. In the diminishing light of the lantern, David saw another boy following behind, hanging onto the tub to hold it back on the slight decline. This was the thruster. He lifted one hand and waved at David as he passed. "Hiya."

"Hullo," David responded, happy even for that single word. Then they were gone, and David was alone again with the suffocating darkness.

⁂

Anticipating that it would take maybe half an hour for them to return with a loaded tub, David waited for what he guessed was a little less than that, then went to the door and opened it a crack. Ten minutes later, he felt the cart coming even before he heard it. The solid floor beneath his feet began to tremble almost imperceptibly.

Eager to follow his father's counsel, he pulled the door full open, even though he could not yet see the hurrier's light. Surprised at how eager he was to see them—anyone!—again, he moved down the track about fifty feet to wait for them.

In a moment, the small point of light appeared; then the sound of the loaded tub came echoing up the tunnel. As the lamp grew brighter and closer, he could see the dim figure of the hurrier, leaning forward into his harness, hunched over so that he was almost on his hands and knees. When the cart trundled slowly past David, there was a momentary jerk of the boy's head as he suddenly realized he was not alone in the tunnel.

"Door's open," David called, knowing they couldn't see that far ahead yet.

But there was no answer, just the grunts and the sound of labored breathing. He fell in behind the thruster, who, to his great surprise, was pushing not only with both hands but also with his head. The upward grade here was taking its toll on both of them.

"Push!" It was the hurrier and it was sharp, angry. "'Arder, Robbie!"

David leaped forward and threw his weight against the tub as well. There was a startled look, then a flash of white teeth. "Thanks, mate."

The cart started to move a little faster, and in a moment they passed through the door. Here the grade leveled a little, so David jumped aside, letting the cart roll on without him. He stared after them well after the light had disappeared and the sound of the tub had died. Finally he groped his way to the door, pulled it shut, and sank down again on his stool.

When they returned about twenty minutes later, David walked forward to meet them. "Beggin' your pardon," he said to the lead boy as he fell into step beside him, "but could I get a light off your candle, please?"

There was a nod and a grunt, nothing more. But as the tub approached the door, the hurrier called over his shoulder, "We be pullin' up, Robbie."

The wheels creaked and groaned as the coal tub rolled to a stop. With one deft movement, the lead boy, the hurrier, removed a short length of stick, called a sprag, from his belt and jammed it under one of the wheels so it could no longer turn.

As Robbie came around from behind, the other boy, clearly the older of the two, undid the belt around his waist and stepped out of it. This was the "gurl belt," a leather girdle about two inches wide to which two chains were attached, one on each side of the buckle. These passed down and between the boy's legs, then joined together at a swivel behind him into one chain that was hooked to the coal tub.

Still not speaking, the hurrier took down his lamp from the strap around his head and handed it to David. David quickly opened the latch on the glass cover, lit his candle from the flame, then handed it back. "Thank you."

In the brighter light, David saw that both boys wore light cotton pants and shirts and flat caps with narrow bills, like his. They wore shoes, but those looked pretty tattered. He was not surprised to see that both of their faces were black with coal dust, smeared here and there where they had wiped away the sweat with the back of their hands. Their eyes gleamed like half-crown coins from out of the darkened features.

"Hullo again. My name is David Dickinson."

The leader nodded. "This be yur furst day as trapper?" When David nodded, he said, "Thot so. Ah be Jimmie Parker. This be me brother, Robbie."

"I am very pleased to make your acquaintance," David said, sounding stiff and formal.

"'Ow cum ya talk funny?" Robbie demanded.

Remembering his father's admonition, he didn't flinch. "Because me mum, she be from down near London, an' she be teachin' me to talk right proper like."

That seemed to impress them, and nothing more was made of it. David turned back to Jimmie. "How long have you been a hurrier?"

"Aboot six months noow."

"My dahd says I can become a thruster, like Robbie here, in a few months, then I can be a hurrier when I'm eight."

"'Ow old ya be noow?" Robbie demanded.

"I just turned six on Saturday."

Jimmie shook his head. "'Ave ta be at least nine ta be a 'urrier. An' ya 'ave ta be a thruster fur at least a year too. Cump'ny rules. It be 'ard work. B'sides, yur too scrawny."

"Am not!" David retorted.

"Robbie," Jimmie said to his brother, "show 'im yur 'ead."

The boy swept off his cap and bowed his head in David's direction. There was a bald spot about three inches in diameter on the crown of his head. David's eyes widened. It was not a natural baldness. It was from pushing the cart.

"Look!" Jimmie said.

David turned, then drew in a quick breath. Jimmie had unbuttoned his trousers and dropped them. He was standing there in his smalls. Then he raised his shirt as well. "Cum on," he said. "Cum see what it means ta be a 'urrier."

As David moved in, he felt his stomach turn over slightly. Jimmie was pointing to a long patch of rough skin that looked like the sole of someone's foot. It nearly circled his waist.

"These be calluses whare the belt rubs," he explained. He lifted one leg, turning toward the light. Several deep maroon circular scars were visible on the inside of his leg, just below the crotch. "The gurl chains rub 'ere. The first day ya git blisters big as soap bubbles. The next day, when ya put on the chains again, the blisters burst lek an egg dropped on a rock. Then the blisters git blisters."

He clearly enjoyed seeing David's eyes growing wider. "When the blisters pop, yur trousers stick ta 'em an' ya be 'ollerin' lek a pig bein' butchered when ya tek 'em off. Teks aboot six weeks ta whare it dunna hurt anymore."

He dropped his shirt and pulled up his trousers. "Sure ya still wanna be a 'urrier, mate?" It was an open sneer.

Feeling a flush of anger, David lifted his head. "I be paid five p a day. What are you paid?"

That caught the boy back a little. "Thrusters get one shillin' fur pushin' the tubs. 'Urriers get one an' sixpence fur pullin' 'em."*

"A day?"

---

* In the British monetary system at that time, there were twenty shillings to a pound, and twelve pence to a shilling. In that era, a pound was worth about four U.S. dollars.

"Yah."

David deliberately lapsed into his best Yorkshirean drawl. "Well noow then, me mum, she worked in a match factory doon in London Town when she were but a wee lass. Me Dahd says thare be e'nuff poison in one box of matches ta kill a man, sure as a dagger in the 'eart. Even after awl these years, she still be sick. Sumtimes bad sick." He took a quick breath. "One an' sixpence a day buy a lot of med'cine, maybe even 'elp git 'er a real doctor."

David looked Jimmie Parker square in the eyes. "Ah dunna care aboot the blisters. Ah dunna care aboot cump'ny rules. Ah will be a thruster in six months, an' Ah'll be pullin' a coal tub b'fur Ah be eight. An' that be awl thare be ta that."

Jimmie retrieved the belt and chains and hooked himself up to the tub. He removed the sprag from the wheel, then motioned for Robbie to take his place behind the cart.

David sprang forward and pulled the door open.

Finally, Jimmie looked directly into David's eyes. "Ah un'erstand," he said. "Gud on ya, mate." He leaned into the chains, and the coal cart rumbled forward and through the door.[1]

Note

1. A word about coal mining and the life of coal miners as found in this and following chapters may be helpful. Yorkshire was a major coal-mining center from the 1700s into the twentieth century, and the Barnsley area was a major center for mining. However, not all of the information used herein is drawn strictly from the Yorkshire area or that specific time period. Some details come from descriptions of other British coalfields, or from mines in Pennsylvania and West Virginia. I have drawn details from various times and places in order to give an idea of what life was like for the miners and their families, especially for children in the mines. Specific conditions described in the novel may not have existed in Yorkshire or may not have still existed at the time described here.

The two most helpful sources were Fiona Lake and Rosemary Preece, *Voices from the Dark: Women and Children in Yorkshire Coal Mines*, and Susan Campbell Bartoletti, *Growing Up in Coal Country*. Their descriptions are superb and the illustrations and photographs included in both books are not only fascinating but heart wrenching. For some of the details of the mining industry in England, Geoffrey Hayes, *Coal Mining*, was also helpful.

A search on Google or Yahoo under "coal mining history" is productive. A *Pictorial*

Walk Through the 20th Century: Little Miners, U.S. Department of Labor, Mine Safety and Health Administration (http:www.msha.gov/CENTURY/LITTLE/PAGE1.asp); and *Children in Coal Mines* (http://www.ancestryaid.co.uk/boards/genealogy-coffee-room/2195-children-coal-mines.html) were especially helpful. (http://en.wikipedia.org/wiki/Hurrying).

As grim as the descriptions included in the novel make it sound, I chose not to dwell too long on some aspects because they were unbelievably awful. For example, no mention is made of "breaker boys," who typically were four to six years old. These boys sorted out the slate, rock, and other refuse that came out with the coal. The coal was dumped into giant crushers and breakers, then sent down long iron chutes. There the boys sat hunched over on planks that straddled the chutes, picking out the unwanted materials as the coal passed beneath them:

As the coal streamed down the chutes toward the boys, it spewed black clouds of coal dust, steam, and smoke, which settled over the boys like a blanket and turned the faces and clothing coal-black. To keep from inhaling the dust, the boys wore handkerchiefs over their mouths. Behind the handkerchiefs, their jaws worked on wads of tobacco that they chewed to keep their mouths moist. "Smoking was not allowed," said James Sullivan. "Chewing tobacco was supposed to prevent the breaker dust from going down your throat" (in Bartoletti, *Growing Up in Coal Country*, 15).

Here are some actual statements collected by the Children's Employment Commission formed by Parliament in 1842 to investigate conditions in England's coal mines:

I have had to hurry [pull the coal tubs] up to the calves of my legs in water. . . . My feet were skinned, and just as if they were scalded, for the water was bad: . . . Had a headache and bleeding (Fanny Drake, age 15).

I'm a trapper in the Gawber pit. It does not tire me, but I have to trap without a light and I'm scared. I go at four and sometimes half past three in the morning, and come out at five and half past. I never go to sleep. Sometimes I sing when I've a light, but not in the dark; I dare not sing then. I don't like being in the pit (Sarah Gooder, age 8).

I stop [after] 12 hours in the pit (John Saville, age 7).

I was five years old when I first went into the pit, and no older (John Hobson, age 13½).

In some parts of these mines the passages do not exceed eighteen inches in height. . . . Not only is the employment of very young children absolutely indispensable, . . . but even the younger children must necessarily work to a bent position of the body (Children's Employment Commission).

Chained, belted, harnessed like dogs to a go cart,—black, saturated with wet, and more than half naked,—crawling upon their hands and feet, and dragging their heavy loads behind them,— they present an appearance indescribably disgusting and unnatural (Children's Employment Commission).

I have to go up to the headings [the coal face] with the men; they are all naked there; I am got well used to that, and don't care now much about it (Mary Barrett, age 14).

All of the above reports are taken from Lake and Preece, *Voices from the Dark*, 8–20.

I have included one of the pen-and-ink drawings from the report of the Children's Employment Commission to give the reader a visual image of what is described in these chapters. This is also taken from *Voices from the Dark*.

CHAPTER 5

Monday, June 16, 1862

Neither father nor son spoke until they had cleared the gate of the pit yard and were on their way home. Then John cleared his throat. "'Ow be yur first day as a trapper, Son?"

David had expected the question and had been thinking about how to answer. He wanted to talk about how slowly the time had passed, and maybe about how he had felt when his second candle had sputtered out, but he sensed that either would be a disappointment to his father.

"It be fine," he said. "I fed a rat today, Dahd."

"What?"

"I was eating the rest of my snap later this afternoon, after you left. Had my candle lit again by then. And I saw this big rat—"

"'Ow big?"

David held up his hands and measured off about eight inches. "That be with his tail, too."

"Oh. That be nuthin'. Sum of me mates claim they've seen sum as large as a cat."

David's mouth fell open.

"Yah. They git real big sumtimes."

"He came out as soon as I opened my snap to eat the pasty I saved. I threw a rock at him, but he came right back. Finally went up on his hind legs and begged, just like a squirrel."

"Shure 'nuff. Seen 'em do that meself. Take yur 'ole lunch if ya let 'em. Seen one wrap 'is tail aroond the handle of a mate's snap and drag it away. Never saw it agin."

A trio of miners walked by them, empty durfeys and darkened Davy lamps swinging from their belts. "Ev'nin', John. This be yur boy? 'Eard we 'ad a new trapper t'day."

John waved back. "Yep. This be Davee. First day on the job."

"Gud on ya, mate," another one called.

David pulled his shoulders back. There was a special bond of brotherhood among the miners, and now he was part of that. And that reminded him of something else. "Dahd?"

"Eh?"

"When we were coming home Saturday, Mum told be about when she were a girl."

"Yes?"

"When I asked her how you two met, all of a sudden she wouldn't talk about it anymore."

"Aw."

"She acted like she were mad at me."

"No, Son. Warn't that. It's joost that . . . sum things aboot 'er early life be kinda painful." He was silent for what seemed like a full minute, then motioned to a spot off the road. They were nearly to the outskirts of the village and, if they continued, would be home in three or four minutes. He found a flat place and sat down, motioning for David to join him.

"'Ow mooch did she tell ya?"

So David told him all that he could remember.

"Well, the vicar an' the skoo-ul, that be key ta un'erstandin' the 'ole story," John started. "B'cuz Lady Astle wanted a few servants who could read an' write, she let yur mum attend the skoo-ul. Ta ev'ryone's surprise, yur mum turned oot to be the brightest of the 'ole bunch. Ya don't git ta see it mooch, Davee, but yur mum, she be real bright, quick as a buggy whip. The vicar, well, 'e saw that, an' started takin' a special interest in 'er. Ta 'er, readin' an' writin' were like bangers an' mash, or bubbles an' squeak.*

---

* These are two popular dishes in England. "Bangers and mash" are sausages (of various varieties) served with mashed potatoes. "Bubbles and squeak" are cold meat fried with cabbage and potatoes.

She could naw git e'nuff learnin'. Soon she was a'ead of awl the rest, even the Astle kids."

His brows knitted, and his mouth pulled down. "Then it awl cum crashin' doon."

"What? What 'appened?"

"When she be 'bout thirteen or fourteen, a snooty cousin of the Astles cum ta stay at the manor house fur the summer. 'E was 'andsome an' charmin', a real dandy, Ah reckon. Fancied 'imself ta be quite the man wit the ladies. So one day, whilst the family were in London, this dandy snuck inta the bedroom whare yur mother were fixin' the beds. 'E cum up be'ind her and put 'is arms roond 'er. Asked 'er fur a kiss. Started tryin' to sweet-talk 'er an' all that."

David's eyes were wide.

"My Annie, she tole 'im to git oot. When 'e wudn't, she gave 'im such a bang on the side of the 'ead with a chamber pot, at first she thot she'd killed 'im."

David clapped his hands in delight. "Did she really, Dahd?"

"She did." He too was relishing the image. "'E 'ad such a black eye that 'e daren't cum doon ta dinner fur two days. Passed it off by sayin' 'e fell off a horse."

"Gud fur Mum!"

"But—" John was suddenly grave. "A week later, a purse full of muney, which Lady Astle kept 'idden in 'er wardrobe, went missin'. Yur gran'mum, she were the only one besides Lady Astle allowed inta that room, so of course they called 'er in. She was 'orrified. Denied everythin'. Then this dandy—" he almost spat out the word—"cums forth an' tells the fam'ly that 'e saw yur gran'mum cumin' oot of the bedroom wit a purse in 'er 'and."

"No!"

"Yes, Davee. Lord Astle went straight to yur gran'mum's room an' found the empty purse in a basket of laundry." John had to stop. When Annie had first told him this, she had wept profusely. It still gave him pain to relive it in his own mind.

"What, Dahd? What 'appened? Was the cousin telling a lie?"

"Indeed," his father said darkly. "An' it be pretty clear why. Yur mum naw only gave 'im a black eye an' a bloomin' 'eadache, but 'is pride was 'urt more than either of those. So 'e got back at yur mum in this way. Evidently, it was 'im who stole the muney an' 'id the purse. But bein' 'e was fam'ly, and yur gran'mum was a servant, they believed 'im, of course."

His sigh was deep and filled with anguish. "If that naw be bad e'nuff, it gits worse. Yur mum went to the vicar. She tole 'im what had 'appened, tole 'im ev'rythin'."

"Did *he* believe her?"

"'E did. Ev'ry word."

"So did the fam'ly believe him?"

"That's joost it, Davee. 'E never tole 'em. Dinna dare. Said Lady Astle was awreddy un'appy that the vicar was showin' too mooch favoritism ta yur mum."

"'E never tole 'em?" David was shocked to the core.

"Said if'n 'e did, Lady Astle wud throw 'im oot too. Said 'e cudn't interfere."

"That's terrible, Dahd."

"Yes, it is." His father stood up. "Cum. Yur mum will start worryin' soon."

"But what happened, Dahd?"

He sat down again. "Aw, Son, that be a real tragedy, joost lek in that Shakespear fella. B'fur the night were throo, yur gran'mum an' gran'dah were oot on the street wit thare two girls. They never saw Astle Manor agin. The fine lady and gentleman—" this was said with bitter sarcasm— "also made sure that they cud never work as servants agin. And times in London then were real bad. They near starved b'fur they finally settled in the East End of London whare naw one knew 'em. Poor Gran'mum. It be like sumthin' joost snapped in 'er mind, that's 'ow yur muther describes it. She were never the same agin. Gran'dah Draper finally got a job sweepin' out stables fur the army. Yur mum—my sweet Annie—'ad ta go ta work in a match fact'ry."

David's eyes were wide. "And that be how she got sick?"

There was a brief nod. "B'tween yur mum an' yur gran'dah, the two of 'em earned barely e'nuff fur a tiny flat. They dinna 'ave e'nuff ta eat. Cudn't afford coal ta 'eat the flat. Yur Aunt Jane, who be three years younger than yur mum, she stayed 'ome an' cared fur yur gran'mum. But it dinna mek any difference. She died seven months after they left Astle Manor. By then, 'er mind was gone an' she no longer recognized anyone.

"A few months after that, my Annie, one mornin' whilst she be gittin' ready fur work, noticed big gobs of 'air cumin' oot of 'er 'ead."

"From the fos—fosfur . . ." He was close to crying and gave up on finding the word.

"Phosphorus. Yes. That's what the doctor said. But Gran'dah Draper, God rest 'is soul, the minute 'e saw that 'is Annie were showin' the first symptoms of phossy-jaw, 'e up an' quit 'is job, packed thare belongin's inta an ole bag, an' started walkin' north."

"So that's how Mum came to Yorkshire," David exclaimed, pleased that the few pieces he did know were finally starting to fit together.

His father nodded. "That were eighteen forty-eight, an' yur mum were naw yet sixteen years ole. By then, the laws said naw women cud work in the mines, so, b'cuz she cud read an' write, she got a job as a clark at the cump'ny store 'ere in Cawthorne."

David nearly jumped up and down. "And that's how you met Mum?"

"It is," John chuckled. "But that be a story fur anuther day." He slapped David on the back. "Run on, noow. Yur muther, she be anxious ta 'ear aboot yur first day at work."

"David?"

His head raised. She was barefoot and he hadn't heard her come. "Yes, Mum?"

"You're not asleep?"

"Not yet."

She sat on the edge of his straw mattress. "You should be. You must be very tired."

"I am, but I'm not sleepy."

She nudged him to move over, then lay down beside him. Behind the curtain where his parents slept, David could hear the deep breathing of his father.

"Do you mind if we talk for a little bit?"

"Ah wud—I would like that."

"You talked at supper some about your first day at work, but I'd like to ask some questions."

"Of course, Mum."

She reached out and found his hand. "Were you frightened, David?"

"Naw," he said quickly.

When she gave him a dubious look, he relented. "Well, maybe just a little. When we were crawling through the first tunnel, it got real dark. I was a little scared then, but just for a minute."

"You crawled through the tunnels? Why on earth would you do that?"

Now he was the expert explaining to the novice. He told her about monkey heads—tunnels too low to stand up in—which connected the main chambers. He explained about hurriers and thrusters and how they used the tunnels to draw smaller coal tubs to the main chutes or the gangway. "Hurriers get their names from havin' to keep the coal hurrying along, and thrusters—"

She squeezed his hand. "I know what they do, David. Your father told me that you were very brave and didn't burn your candles out right away. Is that true?" When he nodded, she said, "What did you like the least about being down there?"

She felt him shrug beside her. "Dunno. The dark, I guess. But you get used to it after a while. And the rats, but they don't bother you."

She suppressed a shudder. "They honestly didn't frighten you?"

He opened his mouth to tell her the truth, but, knowing how she felt about mice in the house, he decided it was better to let it pass. "Oh, that's the other thing," he said. "Time goes really slow. Sometimes it's half an hour or more between the carts." And then he told her in soft whispers what he had done to help the time pass, adding one thing that he had not shared with his father. "When no one was coming, I practiced speaking properly."

"You did?" she exclaimed, clearly pleased.

"Yes. Dahd told me you wouldn't let me keep working there if I stopped talking properly."

"Really? He said that?" She felt her eyes start to burn. Dear, sweet John. "He's right," she went on gruffly. "And there's another thing. Do you know what miners say are the first three things they learned when they were boys in the mines?"

"What?"

"Swearing, smoking, and chewing. Know what's going to happen to you if those are the first three things you learn?"

"I'll get my lugholes boxed?"

She laughed. "Every single night, do you hear me?"

"I won't, Mum," he said.

"Actually, I want to talk to you about how you spend your time down there." A quick breath. "David, you know that your father and I don't keep secrets from each other."

"Yes."

"But I have a secret that will be just between you and me. All right?"

"Okay." She took his hand and pressed something into it. He turned his head. "A candle?"

"*Another* candle. Your father says you can have only two candles per shift because they cost too much. But that's not enough for the whole time, is it?"

"No. They only burn three or four hours."

"I know. So I want you to take another one." And then he felt something bigger, this time placed on his chest. He reached up with his other hand. "A book?"

She leaned close. "In Barnsley there is a town library, a circulating library, it's called."

"Circu- what?"

"Circulating. Several years ago, Parliament passed a law that gave money to larger towns and cities so they could have libraries for the people—all the people—where you can take books out for a time, then bring them back. That's what circulating means."

"You went to Barnsley?"

"Yes. Don't tell your father. He worries about me so, but it was a nice day, and walking does me good." She went on quickly. "I want you to take this with you tomorrow. And the candle. And when there are no carts, you read."

"But Mum—"

"There will be a lot of words you don't know. Just sound them out and then we'll talk about them each night. No, listen to me, David," when he tried to interrupt again. "Now that you are working, I can't teach you in the day anymore. You can't lose what you've learned."

Actually, he was thrilled to think that he could have another three hours of light, aside from the opportunity to read. "What book is it?"

"Oh, no. I'm not going to ruin it for you. It will be a little challenging for you to start."

He turned on his side and put his arm around her. "Thank you, Mum."

"You are most welcome." She kissed him on the forehead. "Go to sleep, David."

"Mum?"

"Yes?"

"Do you believe in God?"

She reared back. "Whoa, mule! Where did that come from?"

"I've been thinking about what you said aboot the Holyrood Church. If we don't have a church, do we have a God?"

"Of course. That's very different, David. You don't have to go to church to believe in God."

"Oh." To her surprise, he sounded more disappointed than pleased. She waited, wondering what was going on in his mind.

"My friend Peter says God watches everything we do, and if we're bad He punishes us. But if we're really good, and pray really hard, then God will bless us and make us happy."

"That's nonsense," she snapped. Then, instantly regretting her tone, more softly she added, "I think that God is out there, but I don't think He sits around in heaven, looking down on us, trying to decide what we need. He has more important things to do than that."

"Hmm," he said. He put his hands beneath his head and stared up at the ceiling.

She watched him for a moment, then very tenderly asked, "What is it, my darling? Tell me what is going on in that quick little mind of yours."

"Nothing." He yawned. "I'm just getting tired."

"And that's all you have to say about what I just said?"

"Yes."

She turned fully to face him again. "Why did you ask about God, David?"

"I . . . I guess I was thinking about Him today."

There was a long pause. "Were you thinking about praying to Him today?" Sensing his hesitation, she continued, "I see. David, all I was trying to say is that He doesn't answer prayers for me. And I don't believe that if something bad happens to us, it is God's punishment. If God is really like that, then I don't want to let Him decide how I live."

"Yes, Mum." He sounded very subdued.

"Ask your father about these things. It's important that you hear what he has to say too."

"Why? Does he believe God hears our prayers?"

She sighed. "I'll let him answer that, Son. But you should know something. Your father has never been to school. He doesn't know how to read or write, but that doesn't mean he is not smart." When he didn't respond, she went on more earnestly. "Listen to me, David. Your father is very intelligent. He always thinks things through very carefully. Did you know, for example, that the other men often come to him when they have a problem that needs solving?"

He turned his head so he could look at her. "Really?"

"Yes. He's very clever. And very wise. So it's important that you ask him your questions too. He does believe that God watches out for us and that He answers prayers."

"Yes, Mum."

She gave his hand one last squeeze, then sat up. "You go to sleep now, David."

"Mum?"

"Yes?"

"There was one time . . ." He drew in a deep breath and let it out again. "My last candle had gone out and I knew it would be a long time before Dahd came for me."

She waited for more, but he fell silent again. "So did you pray?" she asked.

"No. But . . ." He sat up and pulled his knees up beneath his chin. "But I wanted to."

"Did you cry?"

His head dropped. One part of him was ashamed, because he had felt so much like a little boy again today, but he wanted her to know. She understood him in a way that his father didn't. "Once," he finally whispered.

When she spoke it was soft and gentle. "Thank you for telling me that, Son. I understand, and you don't have to be ashamed." She started to turn away, then stopped. "Once, when I was much younger, I cried for three days. And I prayed too. But . . ." She shook her head. "I've said enough. You talk to your father, hear what he has to say."

"But I want to know what *you* think, Mum."

She took a long time before she spoke, and when she did it was like she was far away from him. "All right. I think that when we cry, God does not hear us. I think that when we pray, God does not answer us. And . . ." She shook her head. "And if that is true, then we have to conclude that *God does not care*."

Saturday, June 28, 1862

In Cawthorne Village, the second and fourth Saturdays of each month were considered almost the same as holidays. The workday ended a couple of hours earlier. People put on their finest and gathered as families, then spent the rest of the night mingling in a near-carnival atmosphere. The second and fourth Saturdays were paydays at the Cawthorne Mine.

John Dickinson's family now had two members on the payroll, and tonight David would be getting his first salary. He was fairly dancing as they entered the pit yard with the slow-moving crowd and started for the company office. When he was handed his first pay voucher at the end of the shift it showed he was owed five shillings. Remembering how it had felt when his father had given him six pence for his birthday, five shillings—or sixty pence—almost made him dizzy.

"How much money will you be getting today, Dahd?"

That startled John, and he looked quickly at his wife. Anne smiled and leaned over to her son. "Usually, we don't talk about that, David." Her voice dropped to a whisper. "But your father earns five shillings a day. That be thirty shillings per week, or sixty shillings in all. Since there be twenty shillings to the pound, he's owed three pounds."

That staggered him.

"It be what Ah'm *owed*," his father growled, "but it be naw what Ah am *paid*."

"Why?" David cried in dismay.

"Because we be in debt ta the cump'ny store, an' we be owin' rent on the cump'ny flat, an' we be in debt ta the cump'ny infirmary fur yur mum's med'cine. So the paymaster keeps back 'alf of me pay each payday. It be joost the way life be."

"That's not life, John," David's mother said bitterly, "that is robbery, pure and simple. Nothing more, nothing less."

"That's what Ah said," he agreed with a wry smile. "That be life fur a miner."

CHAPTER 6

Wednesday, December 17, 1862

By the end of David's sixth month as a trapper, he had come to dread the boredom more than the dark or the rats. His father was right. After two months in the narrow monkey head, he had been moved to one of the larger chutes, or side tunnels. Here things were not quite so stifling. The chute was wide and high enough for a man to stand up and for mules to pull the coal cars along the tracks. This also meant lamps were hung along the walls at about hundred-foot intervals. It was hardly light enough to see between those intervals, but it beat the utter blackness, and since they always put a lamp near the door, he no longer needed his own candles. There was more traffic in the chute and therefore less boredom. However, the monotony never quite went away.

The outside world didn't help with that much. It was midwinter now, which meant that when he came to work with his father, dawn was still nearly two hours away. When they finished, it had been dark for another three hours. Sundays didn't change that much. Low-hanging clouds and a grey, dismal drizzle were typical. Occasionally snow would blanket the ground and bring a temporary change of scenery.

He was running out of ideas to help pass the time. He had quit practicing his "London accent" weeks ago. He hadn't told his mother, but she never asked anymore, probably because he found himself speaking that way without thinking about it now. He still read three or four hours a day, and his mother was increasing the difficulty of the books she checked out. But in the dim light and thick air, he found himself getting a headache if he read too long. And what was three hours in a twelve- to fourteen-hour shift?

David heard the sound of rock crunching on rock. A moment later, a dark shape momentarily blotted out the light from the next lamp down the tunnel.

"Davee!"

"I'm here. That be you, Bertie?"

There was an eerie moan. "Noooo. Ah be the ghost of John McCleery lookin' fur me 'ead."

Even as he laughed at this silliness, David felt a little chill dance up his spine. According to legend, John McCleery had been decapitated by a runaway coal car some twenty years before when the car jumped the tracks, hit one of the pillars, and caused a major cave-in. They found McCleery's head, but not his body. Along with other superstitions, miners believed a man who was lost in the mines haunted the chambers and tunnels looking for his body until it was found.

Albert Beames strolled up, cap perched jauntily on his head, both hands thrust into the pockets of his filthy coveralls. "'Owdy."

"Hullo, Bertie." Albert's post, the next one down from David's, was three or four hundred paces away. They had become friends shortly after David had received this new post.

"Ah be bored. Wanna play sumthin'?"

"But . . . what if a car comes?"

"They awl be tekkin' lunch aboot noow. Cum on. Won't be nuthin' cumin' fur near an hour."

For a trapper to leave his post anytime during the day, even during lunch break, was strictly forbidden by the fire bosses and the mine foreman. But that made little difference. In a big mine like this, you might not see the foreman for several days, and the miners themselves winked at the practice. They had been trappers. They well understood the tedium. And, boys were boys.

"Did you leave your door open?"

"Be ya daft?" Bertie said, giving him a scornful look. "Ah be fired fur that. But if'n we play 'alfway b'tween yur door an' mine, we both be able ta 'ear if thare be anythin' cumin' frum either way, even wit the doors shut."

David considered that, focusing on the stillness. Bertie was right. And besides, you could always feel the cars coming, even before you heard them. He looked around, checking again to see if anyone was around. It surely was tempting.

"Yur cars be cumin' uphill, an' movin' slower. My cars will be loaded, but we can feel and hear 'em farther away. We be awl reet."

David still hesitated. He liked Albert Beames, or Bertie, as most of the trappers called him. He was a bit odd looking, with freckles hidden beneath the layers of coal dust, and teeth that were prominent enough that some of the older boys called him Beaver Beames. Bertie was a year older than David and about a stone heavier.* He was totally devoid of ambition and was baffled by David's continual talk of becoming a hurrier. "It be nuthin' but 'ard grunt work," he said dismissively when David told him of his ambitions. But he was affable and had a way of making David laugh even when he tried hard not to. And he was bored.

"Okay," David said. "But we can't be too noisy, or we won't hear them. So, let's play the cowboys and Indians. I get to be the Indian."

Ten minutes later, they changed roles and David became a lanky cowboy with a piece of twisted stick for his six-shooter. He gave Bertie thirty seconds to hide, then began stalking him in a crouch. David was inching his way along the tracks, searching the near darkness, when suddenly his blood froze. In the dim light, he saw little puffs of dust exploding from the gravel in front of his eyes and he realized the ground was trembling beneath him.

He leaped to his feet. "Bertie! Bertie!" he screamed. "A train's coming!"

---

* A "stone" is a measure of body mass equal to 14 pounds or 6.4 kilograms. The term is still in common use today in the British Isles and in some of the Commonwealth countries.

Bertie jumped out from behind one of the supporting pillars. "What!" His head was turning wildly, but his feet seemed frozen in place.

"The door! Open your door, Bertie!" Then, knowing what would happen if he didn't do the same, he turned and raced back toward his own post. "Go, Bertie! Go!" he shouted.

Halfway back to his post, David slid to a halt and spun around. He was too far away now to make out much, but he thought he could see Bertie's shadow pumping down the tunnel. What had started as an almost imperceptible tremor was now a low rumble, and, even this far up, the ground was vibrating. It was a heavily loaded train—three to five cars, most likely.

He couldn't tell how close Bertie was to his door, but when the door was open, David would be able to see the pinpoints of light from the line of lamps farther down the chute. None of those were visible yet. He cupped his hands to his mouth. "Open the door!" he screamed.

His answer was a blast of sound louder than anything he had heard in his life. In the faint light, he saw a dark shape hurtle backwards, impelled by roiling clouds of dust. Another crash was followed by the screech of steel grinding on steel. The blasts came like rifle shots now as one car telescoped into another, leaping the tracks and smashing into solid rock. Then it was no longer individual sounds, but one thunderous roar.

For a second, he could not move, could not believe what he had just seen. Then he turned and ran, ran as he had never done before. The concussion caught him a second or two later and blew him off his feet. He screamed with pain as he hit rough gravel and slid forward.[1]

It took two full hours to clear the tunnel enough to let men crawl through the rubble. David sat on his stool, his head in his hands. *Please, God. If You are there. Please. Don't let Bertie be dead.* He said it over and over, trying not to think about his mother's words.

The first man through the wreckage broke into a run toward David. "Davee! Davee!"

David slowly got to his feet. "I'm here, Dahd," he called. "I'm all right."

His father swept him up with a great sob and gripped him so tightly that it crushed the breath out of him. When he heard David cry out in pain, he set him down and stepped back.

David held out his hands, raw and starting to scab. "The explosion threw me down," he said.

His father took David's hands in his own and examined them in the candlelight. Then his head dropped onto his chest. "Thank God," he whispered. "We thot ya be dead too."

David took a breath, then made the choice that he had been considering with increasing anguish for the last two hours. "What happened, Dahd?"

John just stared at him.

"I heard the explosion. Was there a cave-in?"

"No. We 'ad a train of six loaded cars rollin' doon the chute." He wiped a hand across his eyes. "At the last minute, the spraggers* saw the door warn't open. They tried ta stop the train, but it was too late. It hit the door at near full speed."

"What about Bertie?" David whispered.

"Who?"

"Bertie Beames. He's the trapper there. He's my friend. Did he . . . ?" He couldn't finish.

"I'm sorry, Son. He must have been right behind the door when it hit. One of the spraggers was killed too." John shook him a little. "But ya be awl reet, Son? Yur hands will heal. Are ya awl reet other than that?"

David closed his eyes and lied again. "Yes, Dahdee. Ah be awl reet."

⁂

Mother and father stood in the dark, looking to where their son lay on the straw mattress, curled up in a ball. They couldn't tell if he was asleep or not, but Anne Dickinson doubted it.

"Did he cry when you told him about Bertie?" she whispered.

---

* A sprag was a short but stout length of wood used to block the wheels of a coal car and bring it to a stop. Spraggers were the boys who ran alongside and placed the sprags.

"No."

"What about when he saw the bodies?"

"Naw then, either. In fact, 'e wudn't even look at 'em." His jaw tightened. "It be a terrible thing. Mr. Rhodes wud naw let us tek the boys oot until we 'ad the chute open agin. They were joost lyin' there beside one of the shattered cars."

"He needs to talk about it, John. He's only six years old."

"Ah know, Ah know, but ya canna force him, Annie. That be worse."

She turned away, hugging herself tightly, fighting back the burning in her eyes. *Oh, God!* It was a cry of rage. Of hate. Of bitterness. *If You be right about there being damnation, then damn them! Damn them all in the deepest bowels of hell!*

Note

1. This incident is based on an actual case that happened in West Virginia in 1903, though in that case the young trapper fell asleep (see Bartoletti, *Growing Up in Coal Country*, 31).

CHAPTER 7

Saturday, June 13, 1868

When David entered their flat after going out to the loo, to his surprise, his mother was just inside the door waiting for him. He was instantly contrite. "Oh, Mum. Did I waken you?"

She smiled brightly, but it looked strained. He could see the tiredness in her eyes, and the hollows in her cheeks were pronounced. "That's all right. It's time." She came forward and kissed him on the cheek. "Happy birthday, Son."

"Thank you, Mum."

"Did you know that when you were born twelve years ago today it was a Friday? Friday the thirteenth?"

Then he understood. "No, Mum, I didn't know that."

His father came out from their sleeping room into the main room. "'Appy bur'day, Son."

"Thank you, Dahd."

"Do ya know why yur mum be talkin' aboot Freeday the thirteenth?"

"Because all miners think Friday is an unlucky day. And the number thirteen is an unlucky number. So Friday the thirteenth is an especially bad day."

"Which just goes to show how wrong miners can be," his mother said, stepping back to slip an arm through her husband's. "Friday the thirteenth was the second-best day of my life."

"What was the first?" her husband asked solemnly.

She reached up and kissed him. "You know the answer to that. But look what Friday the thirteenth brought me. The handsomest boy in all of Yorkshire."

"Aw, Mum. I thought I was the handsomest boy in all of England."

She laughed merrily. "You were once upon a time, but now . . ." She peered at him and frowned. "If this keeps up, we may have to send you to the ugly house."

He tried to look offended, but instead ended up laughing with the both of them.

"So," his mother said, "what are we going to do to make your twelfth birthday a special one? I wish it weren't a workday and we would go to Barnsley."

"That would be grahnd, Mum. Maybe another time." He forced a cheerful smile and tried not to look at his father. They both knew that what she really meant was, "I wish I were feeling strong enough to go to Barnsley."

In the last year, his mother had weakened noticeably. Her trips to Barnsley for books had stopped a year ago. Her complexion, once as clear as fine porcelain, had a touch of dullness to it, and from time to time David caught her wincing as she chewed her food—evidence of the advancing seriousness of her phossy-jaw. The doctor at the company infirmary agreed that it was the lingering effects of the white phosphorous in her body, but said she was doing remarkably well considering she had worked in that match factory for almost three years. When David's father had pushed the doctor to explain exactly what he meant by "remarkably well," he finally admitted that he thought she had maybe three or four years left. That had been eighteen months ago.

A stricken John Dickinson had finally shared that information with David so he could help discourage Anne from overdoing, but neither of them had said anything to her about this prognosis. David guessed that they didn't have to. She didn't need a doctor to tell her what was happening.

She was watching him over her husband's shoulder, seeing the pain on his face. She stepped clear and motioned for him. "Come over here, David Dickinson."

He walked toward her, but immediately she turned her back to him, then backed up against him. "Look at this, John. He's taller than me now."

"Aye," his father said. "Ah think 'e be taller than me as well noow." He took her place.

Sure enough, as they stood back to back, David was about an inch taller than his father. That made him grin. "And still growing, Dahd," he said. "No more wrestlin' me to the ground, or Ah be throwin' ya doon and pinnin' yur ears back fur ya."

His father just hooted. "Anytime ya thinkin' ya be up ta that, ya joost let me know, and Ah'll knock a couple of inches off that cocky 'ead of yurs."

It was all blather, but he loved it. David had been in the mines for six years now. His boast about being a hurrier by the time he was eight years old had proven to be just that, an empty boast. But after that setback, he had started exercising every day at his post as trapper when no one was coming, and he had proven himself strong enough to become a hurrier six months before he turned nine, which was the normal age. Now, with three and a half years of putting on the gurl belt, straining every muscle to its limit, pouring sweat, often falling to his hands and knees to keep the tubs rolling, his body was as lean as the rails he walked between and hard as the steel they were made of. He could pretty well hold his own now with all but the biggest boys.

Anne Dickinson moved in and put her arms around these two men she loved more than anything else in life. "So, David, what would you like for your birthday today?"

Hesitating only a moment, he said. "I don't want you to be angry with me, Mum, but I already know what I want."

"And why would I be angry with you?"

"Because I'm tryin' out for spragger today."

"No, David!"

David was watching his father, knowing the victory would be won only with his support. His father cocked his head to one side, giving him a quizzical look. "Ya be only twelve, Son, and barely that. Thare be no spraggers yunger than thirteen. Ya know that, dun't ya?"

"Ah know," he said with a cocky grin. "So Ah be the first."

Anne stepped between them. "John, it is too dangerous."

But his father was eyeing David up and down. "'E be real quick," he mused. "An' stronger than boys twice 'is age." He punched David playfully on the shoulder. "An' bein' ugly, that be one of the requirements fur bein' a spragger."

David felt a warm glow inside him. His father was for it. In fact, he was proud that David wanted it. Then, strangely, David suddenly thought of Bertie Beames. He looked away quickly so his parents wouldn't see the shadow that passed across his eyes. The week after that terrible day, his father had insisted that the foreman move David's station to a completely different area of the mine. He had gone back to the site of the disaster only once. A week following Bertie's funeral, he had slipped out of the house and purchased a small cluster of wildflowers from the greengrocer. The next morning, he had gone early enough to place them near the shattered door. He had stood there for a long time, cap off, head bowed. "I'm so sorry, Bertie," he had finally whispered. From that time forward, he had never spoken of Bertie again, not even when his mother kept trying to encourage him to talk about what had happened.

He turned to his mother and took her hands. "Mum, I've been practicing. I'm real good."

"I don't care. Look at Richard Doyle. He lost his hand. And Margaret Wynche's boy. He got dragged under a tub, now he's hobbling about on one leg. And the Jones boy—"

"Annie," David's father cut in quickly, "thare be naw need fur awl that." It was not the miners' way to talk about mine accidents or the dangers associated with their work.

"Mum," David said quietly, "I get one and sixpence as a hurrier. Spraggers are paid three and two." He squeezed her hands, cutting off her protest. "And besides, I'm getting too big to be a hurrier. I've got sores on my back from scraping the top of the tunnels."

"Davee, I—"

"'E's reet aboot bein' too big, Annie."

She turned away, lips pressed into a tight line, knowing she had lost. Again. And yet, strangely, she felt a little thrill of pride, too. This was her son. He had her will, her determination, her fierceness in grabbing life and shaking it until it conformed to one's will.

David swung around. "Mum? What if we take the extra money and put it into your box?"

She was stunned. "What box?"

"The box for America."

She whirled around to look at her husband, but he was as shocked as she was. "You know about that?" she exclaimed.

A curt nod. "I do. Think about it, Mum. Six shillings a week. Even when I take out my expenses. Every week, six more shillings. Think what that will do for us."

She wanted to slap him and hug him at the same time. How had he known about the box she kept hidden under the floor? And how could a twelve-year-old know that the one thing that kept her going, kept her alive, was the thought of leaving the mines and going to America?

With a cry that was half laugh, half sob, she threw her arms around him. "All right."

Now his father came to him. "Ta even try oot fur spragger, ya need permission from Mr. Rhodes. An' he gonna be sayin', Naw way ya gonna be a spragger at age twelve."

"I was going to stop and see him this morning. There be an opening coming up next week."

"Ah, know, but . . ." John stopped, his eyes lifting to stare at the ceiling. David looked at his mother, and she smiled. They both knew this meant that his mind was working, chewing on the problem, considering it from every angle. Finally, he gave a brief nod. "Here's what ya be sayin' when ya talk to 'im."

Mr. Jonathan A. Rhodes, supervisor of Pit Three, was a short man with a giant ego. Like some small men, he was vicious and mean. He always had a cigar clamped between his teeth, as if that somehow made him more formidable. He had a temper like a bulldog with boils and a tongue like a mule skinner's whip. David hated him with a deep and silent intensity that still smoldered after nearly six years. It was Rhodes who had left Bertie and the spragger lying there, all battered and broken, while the miners cleared the tunnel. There had been no expression of sorrow, only a stream of profanity over the fact that the mine had shut down.

Later David had learned that Bertie's family had had to pay half a pound to have the body brought up top. One more evidence that the most serious offense a miner could commit was to have an accident that stopped work. If a mule died in the mines, the company paid to have the carcass removed. If a man or boy died in the mines, the family had to shoulder the costs, and typically the body was left in place until the end of the shift. But none of this showed on David's face when he knocked firmly on the office door of Mr. Jonathan A. Rhodes.

"Yah!" It was a low bark with not the tiniest shred of patience in it.

He pushed the door open, sweeping off his cap. "Mr. Rhodes, sir? Ah be Davee Dick'nson." There was no way he would be talking fancy London talk here.

He swung around. "Who cares? Why ahrn't ya in the cage? Shift starts in five minutes."

"Beggin' yur pardon, sir, but Ah hurd ya wur lookin' fur a new spragger. Ah'm yur man."

He leaned back. "John Dick'nson's boy?"

"Yes, sir." He held his breath. His father was widely respected among the miners.

"Too late. Awreddy 'ave me a boy picked oot. Sean Williams." Then his eyes narrowed. "'Ow old ya be, boy?"

"T'day be me twelfth bur'day, sir."

There was a rasp of disgust. "Git outta 'ere. Spraggers need be thirteen. See me next year."

"Beggin' yur pardon, sir, but Ah be better than Sean Williams."

For a moment, David thought the man was going to explode, but then a deep chuckle rumbled within him. "Well, ya be cheeky e'nuff." He thought a moment, then shook his head. "Sorry. Awreddy tole Sean 'e cud 'ave it. Noow git."

But David stood his ground. "'Ow aboot a contest, sir?"

~~~~~~~~~~

The place Rhodes chose for the "shoot-out," as he called it, was in Chute Number Four. It was a long chute. The tunnel's roof was five to seven feet high, and the walls about thirty feet apart. That was wide enough and high enough to run a double track and use mule teams. The engineers had made it so the chute had a slight decline. It wasn't dramatic—about a two-percent grade—but it was enough to keep a train of seven or eight cars rolling. Rhodes had chosen Chute Four precisely because of the slope in the floor. Seeing how a boy did on a level stretch was no contest at all. Six loaded cars sat on the rails, three in one train, three in another.

These full-sized coal carts were four feet wide and eight feet long and could hold the contents of six of the small coal tubs. That was about four tons of coal each. The carts had wheels and axles formed from a single piece of steel. This meant the two wheels did not turn independently, nor did they have an independent braking system. This was where the spraggers came in. If a car got rolling too fast down a grade, it would jump the tracks and smash into the wall.

A sprag was a stick of oak or other hardwood about two feet long, which had been milled down until it was round like a shovel handle, only about half again as thick. These were the "brakes" for the cars. The spraggers would run alongside the car, and, if it got rolling too fast, or simply when the car had to be stopped, they would jam sprags up behind the wheels. The sprags would be jerked upward and jam in so tightly that the wheels locked. It was a cheap and effective braking system. Cheap, if you didn't count the danger to the spraggers.

Since the bed of the car extended almost a foot over the wheels on all four sides, placing the sprags exactly right when a car was rolling took speed, agility, and a quick eye. His mother was right. It *was* dangerous work. If you didn't put the sprag in far enough, when the wheel grabbed the wood it could pop the stick right back out at you, cracking your jaw or maybe putting out an eye. If you put the sprag in too far, it could yank you in with it. That was how fingers were crushed or severed. Sometimes hands and arms as well.[1]

So what? David thought. Every job in the mine was dangerous to one degree or another. Bertie Beames was the ultimate proof of that. What being a spragger offered in addition to the higher pay were some very attractive compensations. First of all, spraggers roamed freely through the tunnels. No more sitting in mind-numbing darkness hour after hour, listening to the rats and counting the drips of water from the ceiling. No more crawling along dark passageways, pulling your guts out trying to keep the tubs moving.

And precisely because it was so dangerous and required such quickness and skill, the work was exciting. You never heard spraggers talking about how bored they were. And with that came the extra pay. And prestige. Even the miners viewed the spraggers with respect. If a load was spilled, it was the miner who got his wages docked, so miners curried the favor of the spraggers. Some even brought tobacco or food for them.

David was startled out of his thoughts when someone gave him a hard shove from behind. He turned. Sean Williams was standing right behind him, breathing heavily, his face a stormy cloud. "Ya be the wazak* tryin' ta tek me job away frum me?"

David took a step back, surprised by the hatred in his eyes. Sean was nearly fourteen, a little older than most starting spraggers. He was lean and hard. He too had spent his life in the mines. He was half a head taller than David, which would give him an advantage when it came to placing the sprags. But David hoped he was just enough faster than Sean to make up for it.

David's jaw set. "No, I be the wazak who *be* takin' yur job away frum ya this mornin'."

Sean's face went the color of a plum. The men roared with laughter. David turned, grinning. That was a mistake. Sean lunged. His clenched fist caught David high on the right side of his cheek. Lights flashed and he stumbled backward. His foot caught on a rail and he slipped and went

---

* Yorkshire colloquialism for a fool; a very derisive term.

down hard. Searing pain shot through his right hand as he threw it out to catch himself.

"Fight! Fight!" The shout echoed in the tunnel and instantly the men and boys closed in around them. Sean stepped forward, breathing hard, glaring down at him. "Ya 'ave a big mooth, lit'le boy, but ya canna be a spragger if ya canna even see sumthin' comin' at ya."

More laughter. David remained where he was, still a little dazed. Then he saw Rhodes push into the circle, his head moving back and forth as he took in what was happening. David knew he wasn't there to intervene. That was not the way of the miner. His eyes flashed when he saw David on the ground, but he just jammed the cigar in his mouth and waited.

For a moment, David was tempted to turn his head, search out his father. But he couldn't. Wouldn't. If he didn't do something right now, the contest was over before it started.

Sean spat to one side and turned away. "Cum back in a year or two, wazak."

With a shake of his head to clear the lights dancing before his eyes, David got slowly to his knees, then to his feet. Every eye was on him now. He started toward the retreating back. The shouting and yelling instantly died away. Hearing that, Sean stopped and turned around. When he saw David coming, his fists came up again. "Reddy fur sum more, lit'le boy?"

"Yep," David said. His head was down, and his arms were at his side. "Only this time, let's see if ya can do it when me back's naw turned."

Sean threw another punch, this one aimed straight at David's jaw. David ducked to one side and grabbed Sean's wrist in a pincer grip. Then he smashed his left fist into Sean's nose. Blood spurted. He hit him again. Then again. And this time it was Sean who went down flat.

There was stunned silence. It had happened so fast. David moved to stand over him, chest rising and falling as he stared at him. "I'm back *now*, big boy," he said, his voice hoarse.

"E'nuff!" Rhodes roared. "We ain't gunna settle this wit fists. Git yur sprags. The 'ole mine's shut doon 'ere, so let's git it over wit."

"Awl reet," Rhodes bellowed, raising his hand for silence. "Thare be only one rule. We cahrn't be 'avin' these cars jumpin' the tracks joost cuz we got two nippers who think they be a couple of barnyard roosters. So, we have Dick Canning 'ere, an' Johnnie Brown. They be two of our best spraggers. If'n sumthin' goes wrong, they'll jump in." He swung on David and Sean. "If'n they tell ya ta git outta the way, ya better git outta the way."

He waited for their acknowledgment, then chomped down hard on his cigar. "Ev'rybuddy else stays oot of it. Naw callin' oot advice. If'n that 'appens, the contest be over. Un'erstood?"

Everyone nodded.

"Awl reet," he said, glowering at David. "Dick'nson be tekking the first three cars. Williams gits the second train."

Three cars meant six sets of wheels. David selected six stout sprags, then, as a second thought, took two more. His father had said you always needed extra sprags. He tucked all but one under his left arm, took the last one in his right hand, and walked to the first three cars. Half a dozen men, including his father, stood behind the last car, ready to start the train rolling.

"Ya be ready?" Rhodes called. David's head bobbed once. "Then let 'em roll."

For a moment, there was not a sound except for grunts of exertion as the men leaned into the back of the last car. Then there was a creak, followed by a groan of steel, and the wheels began to turn slowly. David bent down, watching the lead wheel intently. All thoughts of Sean Williams were gone. Now it was just him and these six wheels.

"She be yurs," someone behind him hollered.

He was right. Gravity was taking over and the cars gradually began increasing in speed. David walked along, ignoring the creaking and groaning, which were becoming more pronounced. He had earlier walked this stretch of track twice and had a good feel for what was coming. The slight decline ran all the way to the gangway, which meant that if the train were left alone, it would hit the last curve too fast. From here, the chute was straight for a good three hundred feet. Then the tunnel curved slightly, opened up in another straightaway of a hundred feet, then bent into the final turn before the gangway that led to the cage.

The trick was to keep the train from going so fast that it jumped the track, yet not stop it too soon. If he did that, mules would have to be brought up to take it on into the gangway and the cage. David had watched spraggers work before and had been amazed to see them bring a train to a halt just ten or fifteen yards from the cage.

David broke into a trot as the cars continued picking up speed, rocking back and forth. His eyes darted back and forth from the wheels to the track ahead. He ducked. Just ahead the roof lowered enough that the top of the coal in the cart just barely cleared it. Hit that with your head and the contest would be over, or worse.

He broke into an easy run. The cars were moving at five or six miles an hour now, but they had covered only half the distance to the first curve. *Not yet. Not yet!*

Ten seconds before it reached the curve, the train was running at close to eight miles an hour and he was sprinting hard. It was time. That, or lose control. He leaned in and shoved the first sprag behind the lead wheel. Instantly, there was a spray of sparks and the horrible screech of steel.

David swore softly. He had been so worried about getting his hand caught that he hadn't put the sprag in as far as it should have been. The wheel caught the end of it, and the tremendous pressure on the stick twisted it upward and outward at a crazy angle. No time to worry about that now. He dropped back to the next wheel, snatching another sprag from beneath his arm. This time he really leaned into it, and this time his placement was perfect. The wheel jerked the sprag out of his hand, burning his fingers with the speed of it. He was vaguely conscious of shouts and someone running hard right behind him.

With two sets of wheels locked and shooting sparks, the train was no longer increasing its speed, but neither had it slowed appreciably. His eyes snapped forward. The curve was just ahead. He dropped back to sprag the second car when someone slugged him on the shoulder. It was Johnnie Brown, running alongside him now. "Watch yur front sprag!"

His head jerked forward and instantly he knew he was in trouble. That first sprag was wobbling wildly. There was no way it was going to hold. Even as he darted forward, there was a sharp crack. The end of the sprag sheared off, and the rest of it rocketed back at him like a missile. He ducked to one side, feeling a brush of air as the stick shot past his head.

With the release of that set of wheels, the train shot forward again. It was leaning into the curve now, with the next one just seconds away. Sprinting hard, he grabbed yet another sprag.

"Block 'em awl. Block 'em awl!" Johnnie was screaming.

David barely heard. He knew what had to happen, and how fast it had to happen. Feeling like his lungs were on fire, he bent down, running at full speed. He reached the front wheel, leaned in, and shoved hard. This time there was no mistake. The wheels shrieked in protest as sparks shot out from beneath them. He didn't wait to see if it would hold. Back again to the lead wheel of the second car. *Don't rush it. There!* His hand darted in and out and the wheels locked. Grab another sprag. Drop back. Shove it in. See the sparks and know it's all right.

With the speed of a striking cobra, in went another, and another. And that did it. As the train hit the last curve, its speed dropped dramatically. He slowed, matching the train's pace, head jerking back and forth as he checked each of the six sprags. They were all in solid as a rock.

It was over. The lunging monster swung into the gangway and ground to a halt about fifty or sixty feet later. It was another hundred feet to the cage, but David didn't care. It was stopped. He bent over, hands on his legs, gulping in deep breaths of air. Someone ran up beside him. "Gud work, man," Johnnie said. "Ah thot it was a goner thare fur a bit. Gud job."

"Thanks," he said, not looking up. He couldn't. He felt sick. He had lost, and he didn't need to wait for Sean Williams to prove that to him.

As he was buckling the gurl belt around his waist, readying himself to haul an empty tub through the monkey head to the next chamber, he saw his father approaching. He kept his head down, pretending he hadn't seen him. *Don't tell me how great I did, Dahd. Please.*

When John reached him, there was a brief nod. "Sean did well. Every sprag put straight in."

"I heard." *Do we really have to talk about it?*

A hand rested on his shoulder. "Davee?"

"Yes, Dahd."

"Mr. Rhodes pulled me over b'fur 'e went back up top."

David's head lifted slowly.

"'E said thare be anuther openin' fur a spragger in a few weeks." He socked David playfully on his arm. "Rhodes sez ya got spunk an' ta cum see 'im agin in a month."

Note

1. Much of the information on spraggers comes from Bartoletti, *Growing Up in Coal Country*, 32–34.

CHAPTER 8

Saturday, February 20, 1869

When David returned from the paymaster's office, he slipped quietly into their flat. A candle was burning, but, as he suspected, there was no sign of his mother. He removed his hat and coat and hung them up, careful to avoid any creaky spots in the floor. He moved to the sink and the bucket of water there. Ladling two scoops into the tin washbasin, he bent down and washed his face. As he took the towel and dried off, he eyed himself in the mirror. One hand came up and rubbed along his jawline. Though his mother teased him, saying there was nothing there but boyish hope, he was sure he could feel the first beginnings of stubble.

"David? Is that you?"

He turned, tossed the towel down, and went quickly to his parents' sleeping room. He pulled the blanket back. "Yes, Mum. I'm back."

She looked confused. Then she focused on him and offered a fleeting smile. "Already?"

"It's past nine."

Now she was remembering. "And your father? Did he go to the pub?" She was clearly disappointed with that.

"No, Mr. Rhodes was at the paymaster's office. After Dahd was paid, he called him inside." She looked alarmed, so he added quickly, "He wasn't angry. He was smiling as Dahd went in."

A bare nod told him she had heard. David took the black purse from his jacket and shook it, jangling the coins noisily. "Ten shillings this payday, all of it going into the box."

A wan smile, then her eyes closed again.

That was disturbing. Most times, if he could get her talking about going to America, it enlivened her, cheered her up, lifted her spirits.

As if she sensed what he was thinking, her eyes opened again. "That's wonderful, David. I counted it last night. We have more than sixty pounds now. We need at least eighty. Ninety would be better. Fifteen each for—"

"I know," he cut in, sparing her the effort. "Fifteen each for three tickets. Then thirty-five to forty more for expenses." He could see the thinness of her body, even beneath the blankets. Thankfully, there was not enough light in here to see the yellowish cast that her skin had taken these last few months, or the growing dullness in her eyes. Though she was trying to hide it from him by keeping her hair up in a bun, he knew she was starting to lose that too. That made him want to cry. Her beautiful, golden brown hair was now thin, with no sheen to it.

A nod and a warmer smile. "Do you think I'm crazy, Son? It's such an impossible dream."

He went to her and sat down beside her. "Mother," he said, taking her hands. "You have taken the impossible and made it into reality. Even Dahd believes it is going to happen now."

She squeezed his hands, and the weakness of her grip was frightening. "I know. My dear, patient, beloved John. That's the one thing I can thank Reverend Pike for. I would never have come to Yorkshire and met your father if Reverend Pike had defended my mother." She closed her eyes. "Oh, my darling Davee, I still can't believe it could really happen."

She saw him wince and laughed. "I know, I know. You're twelve now, almost thirteen. Too old and too big for me to be calling you darling anymore."

He changed the subject. "I'll be thirteen in less than four months, and I'm planning to make mule driver before then."

"Oh, David, David. Is this what I've done to you? Look at you. Hurrier before you were nine. A spragger at twelve. Now you want to be a mule driver before you're thirteen. Next thing you know, you'll be owning the mine before you turn twenty."

"Aw, gwan, Mum. Mule drivers start at three shillings per day, and when I can handle six mules at a time, then I get a miner's wages. Five per day. Think of what that will mean, Mum. Almost two pounds per week. I'll put it all into the box."

There was the sound behind them of someone clearing his throat. They turned to see David's father standing in the doorway, flakes of snow in his hair and on his shoulders. He came forward, bent down, and kissed Anne gently on the lips. David watched as the flakes quickly dissolved into water droplets.

She was suddenly anxious. "What did Mr. Rhodes want?"

He shrugged out of his jacket and tossed it on a chair. When he turned back, he was beaming. "'E wanted ta give me four more shillin's per day."

"What?" they exclaimed together.

"Startin' tomorrow, me dear Missus Dick'nson, Ah be the new fire boss in Tunnel Five, an' that means four more shillin's per day."

"Really, Dahd!" The position of fire boss not only paid more, it was a position of great importance. A tunnel fire boss was always the first one into the mine, moving from chamber to chamber, checking for fire damp or other dangerous vapors. No one went in until he said.

Then the implications of that hit David. "Four more shillings per day?" he cried. He jumped up and darted into the main room. He grabbed the slate and a piece of chalk and began scribbling. His mind was racing. At four more shillings per day, that was a full pound every five days, or two pounds eight shillings more per payday. When he made mule driver . . .

He was so excited he had to rub the figures out and start over. When he was finished, he stared at the board. They could save four more pounds each payday! He jumped up and ran back to his mother's bed. "We can do it before the end of the year, Mum! Look."

He sat down and led her through the figures. Her arithmetic was much better than his. John Dickinson watched the two of them in admiration. Arithmetic was a complete mystery to him, and he was amazed and proud at the same time.

"We need thirty more for ninety pounds. At four more pounds per pay day, that's only . . ."

She beat him there. "Eight paydays, or four months." She fell back, eyes gleaming with excitement. "Four months! Oh, David! There's only one more week in February, so don't count that. So March, April, May, June—" She ticked them off her fingers one at a time. Now she was positively glowing. "We could have enough to leave by July."

John Dickinson coughed awkwardly. "Yur furgittin' two things. First, Davee's not a mule driver yet."

"Oh, John, let us have some fun here."

"Second," he went on, stubborn now. "We owe at least thirty poonds ta the minin' cump'ny."

He may as well have poured ice water down their necks. David *had* forgotten. Totally. It was not his worry, and he just never thought about the debt they owed to the company.

"*No, John!*" His mother spoke with such ferocity that it shocked them both.

"No?"

"No! The mine owners are thieves and robbers. They're worse than the highwaymen who prowl the moors. At least *those* men wear a mask and carry pistols. These people are weasels. Rats! Vermin! They charge outrageous prices because we have no choice but to pay them. They dock your pay for the tiniest infraction. And if you don't watch them like a hawk, they'll cheat you at the pay window."

She had to stop. Her chest was rising and falling. "You've given them seventy-five or eighty hours of your life every single week since you were five years old. *You—don't—owe—them—one—farthing!*" Each word came out like a small cannon shot.

Still too shocked to believe what he was hearing, John just stared at his wife.

She was up on one elbow, pleading now. "I mean it, John. No one knows anything about this. We're going to just slip away. Like ghosts in the night. They'll never hear from us again."

A tiny smile suddenly played around her mouth. "When we get to America, we'll write and apologize. Tell them how sorry we are that we *forgot* to pay the bill before we left."

She fell back, the look on her face one of sweet satisfaction. "I'm tired,

John. I'd like to sleep now." She turned over, cutting off any further comment from either father or son.

Friday, May 14, 1869

David had only one thing on his mind as he watched Freddie Robertson lead his three mules down the gangway toward the third side chute. Five empty coal cars rolled along behind Freddie and his "sweethearts."

Just watching Freddie got his blood boiling. David should be the one guiding those mules now. Yet, for all his careful plans, all his boasting, there had not been a single position as mule driver come open. So five paydays had passed without the extra money he had counted on that night with his mother. That was almost ten pounds. That meant they would have to postpone their departure until . . .

"Let's ride 'em back."

David looked up in surprise to see Sean Williams staring at him, a silly grin pasted on his face. They were walking alongside the cars now, for the tunnel inclined upward here. The mules were doing all the work, and there was no need for the spraggers.

David and Sean Williams had become friends of a sort after their contest for spragger last year. But it was not a particularly close friendship. The memories of the fight still stood between them. Often they were paired together on the longer trains, like today, but when they had a choice, they both selected other junior spraggers to work with.

David straightened slowly and looked around. What Sean was suggesting was that when they reached the chute, they would have a downhill run. Freddie would unhook the mules, and they would let the train roll. That was when the two of them were supposed to run alongside and sprag the train if it got rolling too fast. But the grade in that particular chute was not that steep, so if no one was around, the boys could jump on the bumpers and ride the train all the way except for the last little stretch into the work chamber.

"Cum on," Sean jeered. "Ain't nobody aroond. Whaddya say?"

David was tempted. Riding the cars down a chute was exhilarating, but the bosses absolutely forbade it. Nearly half of the fatalities among spraggers came when the boys were struck by a low-hanging outcropping of rock or lost their balance and fell off the cars and were run over.

And there was something else to consider. If they were caught, they wouldn't be fired. Good spraggers were far too valuable, and he and Sean were the best. But they would be fined, at least half a day's pay, maybe a full one if Rhodes was in his usual foul mood. And it would be just like him to pass over David for the next mule driver's position. But . . . the chances of them being caught were practically nil. He grinned. "Why not?"

Freddie had the mules pull the train off into the chute until all five cars were on the decline. David jammed a sprag beneath the lead wheel on his side, and Sean did the same on the other side to hold the train until the mules were unhitched. On the end of each car was the bumper, a small extension of the car's base, which was just wide enough for a man to stand on while driving the teams. Sean pointed. "Ya care which side ya git?"

"No. Let's go."

Sean nodded, leaned down, and knocked the sprag out from behind the wheel. As the wheels groaned and slowly began to turn, the two boys jumped onto the bumper. "See ya at the bottom, Freddie," Sean called. Then he grasped the sides of the car and leaned forward, looking every bit like some mythical figure on the prow of a ship. As the cars gradually picked up speed, David also leaned forward into the wind. When they rolled past the first lamp, he turned and looked at Sean. Their eyes met and they both laughed.

There wasn't much danger of the cars jumping the track in this stretch. But you never knew. Sometimes a large chunk of coal would roll off a car and dent the track. Five cars—even empty ones—carried a lot of momentum.

David crouched down slightly, darting his head back and forth, searching out ahead of them for any bad spots. For now, the tunnel was plenty wide, and the roof was a good six feet high, providing ample clearance. But coming quickly now, the entire tunnel constricted. Another hundred feet and the roof would be just inches above their heads. And jumping off when the clearance on either side was just two or three feet was extremely dangerous.

The line of cars approached the first curve; now they were moving at five or six miles an hour, enough that a man would have to run to keep up. David tensed as they approached the narrowing of the tunnel. He remembered very clearly that just beyond the curve there was a real bad spot. A spot of granite had been found in the coal seam and left where it was. It was like a small, upside-down pyramid. Why no one had bothered to knock it off, he wasn't sure, but it had given more than one miner a raging headache. And it was on his side of the tunnel.

"Whee'yah!"

David turned his head. Sean had one hand raised, letting his fingers brush along the ceiling. His cap was pulled low over his eyes and his chin jutted forward.

Giving a whoop of his own, David let go with one hand and leaned even farther forward, bending his knees to lower his head a few inches. They were between lanterns now and it was hard to make out any contour of the ceiling whipping by just above their heads. That spot should be coming any—*there!* He jerked his head to the left and down. Too late. The blow slammed his head backwards, almost flipping his face up into the coal face. He felt a searing pain, and lights flashed before his eyes. He dropped to a crouch, clinging desperately to stop from falling.

"Ya awl reet?"

He didn't answer. Tears were streaming from his eyes, pushed horizontally back across his cheeks by the wind. Reaching up with his other hand, he discovered that his cap was gone. Then he felt the warm stickiness even as pain shot through his skull. He was bleeding.

"Ahre ya okay?" It was Sean again.

He waved a hand. His jaw was clenched against the pain and he couldn't speak.

And then the roof started to rise again and the floor began to level. They were moving at close to ten miles an hour now, rocking back and forth, but this would be the maximum. The train was already starting to slow. Another hundred and fifty yards and they would roll to a stop at the entrance to the chamber.

That thought brought his head up with a jerk. His hat. If they saw him without his hat, the miners would know instantly what he and Sean had been doing. Most wouldn't care, but if there was a foreman there . . . He looked down, judging the speed, waiting for a wide space. Then he jumped and hit the ground running. He lumbered to a stop, then whirled and ran back up the chute, scanning the ground ahead of him as he went. Bringing one hand up, he gingerly probed his scalp, grunting in pain. It was bleeding, but so far it was all matting in his hair. He felt his face and found nothing. Good. Blood streaks down his cheeks would end it.

His father wasn't working this tunnel anymore, but if David came walking in with a bleeding head, his father would know about it before the afternoon was over. He had to find that cap. He moved slowly now, eyes moving back and forth. There. Up against the wall. He picked it up, carefully placed it on his head, then started back, wincing with each step.

Ahead, the train was down to a slow roll. He saw Sean jump off and sprag the wheels. It screeched to a halt. Behind him, he could hear Freddie coming with the mules.

"It's all right," he called. "Had to get my cap."

"Yur cap?" Sean said incredulously as he reached David. "You jumped fur yur cap?"

"Yeah," David snapped. "First person to see my scalp ripped open and we'd be in trouble."

"Oh! Yah, reet. Ah dinna think of that."

"Well, not a word to anyone. My head's cut, but it'll be all right."

Sean put an arm around David's shoulder, causing him to inhale sharply. "Man, Ah thot fur a minute thare, that outcrop dun tek yur 'ead off."

"It did," David said, forcing a grin. "Luckily, it was still inside me cap."

<hr>

They waited for Freddie and the mules to catch up with them, hitched the animals to the train, then fell in behind the five cars as the mules pulled them into the work chamber.

"Oh-oh," Sean muttered.

David was keeping his head down in an attempt to lessen the pain. His wound throbbed horribly and he felt a little light-headed. When he looked up, his stomach lurched. Tom Cutler, constable for Cawthorne Village and the Cawthorne Mines, stood in the midst of a half circle of miners.

Sean shot him a look. *How could they know already?*

David shook his head, instantly regretting it. "Don't say anything. I'll do the talking."

"David Dick'nson?"

"That's me." He had seen the constable around town a few times, but rarely did he come into the mines. And surely not for some spraggers riding a train just for fun.

"Do ya kno whare yur pa be reet noow, Son?"

They were going to tell his father? "He's a fire boss," he said slowly. "Could be anywhere."

One of the other miners spoke up. "Saw John earlier this mornin'. Said he wuz gunna do sum work in Tunnel Five."

The constable turned and nodded. "Gud. Can sumone tek me thare?"

The same man stepped forward. "Ah can."

David was confused. His head was pounding. The pain was excruciating. But it seemed that this was not about him or Sean. Then a sudden prickling sensation started up the back of his neck. "Is something wrong? Has something happened to my Dahd?"

The constable had started after the other man. He half turned. "Naw, not yur pa." He went to say more, thought better of it, and started off again. David leaped forward and grabbed his arm. "Then who? What's happened?"

The man's eyes were grave and filled with hesitation. He took a breath, then another.

"Tell me!" David cried, tightening his grip. "What's wrong?"

"It be yur mum," came the soft answer. "She were walkin' ta the store, an' joost collapsed." At the shock on David's face, he hurried on. "She be awl reet. They took 'er ta the infirm'ry. She be resting noow. Ya stay 'ere,

Son. Soon as we find yur pa, Ah'll tek 'im up. We'll send word back doon ta ya."

But David was already running toward the chute and the main gangway.

"David!" It was Sean. "Cum back. Ya cahrn't leave yur shift wit oot permission."

David only increased his speed, reaching up with one hand to hold his head as he ran.

CHAPTER 9

Friday, May 14, 1869

"No!"

At the sight of her son rushing into the small infirmary ward, Anne Dickinson pulled herself up on one elbow. "Oh, David! No!" She fell back, face as grey as the sheets that covered her.

"Mum. Are you all right?"

She shook her head, but not in response to his question. "Did you get permission to leave?" she demanded weakly.

He dropped into the chair beside her bed, anger flaring. "I didn't ask."

"David, they'll—" But when she saw the set of his face, she decided to try another tack. "David, I took out the box this morning and counted things very carefully. We have seventy-two pounds. It's not enough. We can't afford a fine right now. We'll never get to America."

David was flabbergasted. She had collapsed on the street. She was in the infirmary too weak to sit up, and she was worried about him losing money?

"Mother . . ." A movement out of the corner of his eye caught David's attention. He turned. The company-owned infirmary served both the mine and the village. There were eight beds, and all but two had patients in them. A doctor and a nurse were working with a man just two beds down from David's mother. The doctor was staring at them. It had been him jerking around that had caught David's eye. When he saw that David was watching him, he quickly turned away.

"Shh, Mum," he whispered. "There are people who can hear you."

It was if he hadn't spoken. "You could lose your job. You know how Rhodes is."

"They're not gonna fire me," he soothed. "And you're sick, Mum. They said you fainted in the street. I wasn't gonna wait until the end of the shift to find out how you were."

She waved that away. "I didn't faint. It was a momentary wave of dizziness."

He just shook his head. This woman was incredible. And maddening. He swept off his hat and kissed her on the cheek.

"David!"

He reared back quickly. "What?"

"What happened to your head?"

He swore inwardly. In the rush, he had completely forgotten about the throbbing wound in his scalp. He put his cap back on quickly. "Uh . . . it's nothing, Mum. I was bringing in a string of cars and bumped my head on the ceiling. Fortunately, I had my cap on."

"Call the doctor over here right now," she said.

"Mum! Will you forget about me? Tell me how you are feeling."

"I'm fine. Just need a little rest." She reached out for him, taking his hand. She could barely hold on to it. A wave of sorrow washed over him. "Go back now, and it will be all right."

"Mother!" Again that won him a piercing look from the doctor, and he quickly lowered his voice. "I am *not* leaving. You are very sick. Stop worrying about me." He took a quick breath, then smiled down at her. "And you wonder why *I'm* so stubborn."

Her eyes filled with love. "You got it all from your father."

He laughed aloud. He couldn't help it. She was hopeless, cheering him up even as she could barely lift her head from the pillow. "The constable went looking for Dahd. He should be here any minute. When he comes, we'll talk to the doctor, see what he says. Then I'll go back."

Thankfully, just then he heard a door open and close. His father, still wearing his lantern and tool belt, rushed in. David stood, leaving the chair for his father.

John dropped down and took both of his wife's hands in his, oblivious to the fact that his own hands were grimy with coal dust. "Annie, do ya be awl reet?"

There were sudden tears in her eyes. "Yes, luv. I knew you would come."

"What happened?"

"She says she was only dizzy." David shot him a look that told him how likely that was.

"I was feeling good this morning," she said, "and it was such a beautiful day."

His voice became very gentle. "Ya promised me, luv. No walkin' wit oot me or Davee."

The door at the other end of the ward slammed open and Jonathan Rhodes stormed in. His cigar was trailing smoke and his eyes were spitting fire. Seeing the two men beside the bed, he started straight for them, boots clumping loudly on the tile floor. Then he saw the doctor and did a sharp right turn. The doctor visibly jumped to attention and said something to the nurse, who fled.

Father, mother, and son all watched this nervously. Rhodes's back was turned to them, but his raspy voice boomed through the hall. "Tell me aboot the Dick'nson woman!" he demanded.

The doctor's reply was inaudible. "'Ow bad?" Rhodes shot back. More murmurings. "Ya shure?" The doctor nodded, his face almost twitching in fright.

Rhodes spun around and started toward them again.

"Mr. Rhodes! Please! The cigar," the doctor cautioned.

Rhodes stopped long enough to glare at him, whip the cigar out of his mouth, and stomp it out on the floor. Then he came on, bearing down on them.

He pulled up in front of David, thrusting his jaw forward. "Who in the—" He glanced down at David's mother, checked himself, and started again. "Who in the grahnd kingdom of Hades gave ya leave ta cum oot of the mines in the middle of the day?"

His father came between them in a flash. Rhodes was at least two stone lighter and a good inch shorter than David's father, and he had been boss too long. For a lean man, he had a sizable beer gut, and his nose glowed from too many nights in the pub. One flight of stairs winded him. Yet to Rhodes's credit, he didn't back down so much as half a step.

"The constable cum fur me," David's father said. "Tole me my Annie 'ad collapsed an'—"

"Dunna tell me what Ah I awreddy know," he snapped. "Who do ya think sent the constable lookin' fur ya?" He went up on his toes and looked at David over his father's shoulder. "But who said *you* cud leave yur shift?"

David stepped forward, wanting to smash this man's face, but his father's hand shot back and grabbed his arm. "Me son wuz wurried aboot 'is mum," he said, the words tight and clipped.

"She naw be that sick," Rhodes sneered.

"How would you know?" David cried. "You don't know about people. You don't care how sick she is. All you care about is meeting the quota. Filling the tubs."

His father swung on him. "David! Shut yur trap. This be b'tween me an' Mr. Rhodes."

But Rhodes pushed him aside, thrusting his face into David's. "'Ow do Ah know? Ah'll tell ya 'ow Ah know." The bulldog face turned. "Doc! Git over 'ere. Reet noow!"

Again David's father inserted himself between the two. When he spoke, his voice was low, filled with menace. "Rhodes, ya naw be spekkin' ta me son. Ya be spekkin' ta me an' me alone."

The doctor hurried up, head jerking back and forth as he took stock of what was happening.

"Tell 'em what ya joost tole me, Doc," Rhodes growled. "'Ow be Missus Dick'nson?"

The doctor licked his lips. "She is very weak. Tired. She needs lots of rest."

Rhodes cuffed him on the arm. "The rest, ya lunkhead. Tell 'em. Is she dyin'?"

David's father shot a quick look at his wife and saw her alarm. "That's e'nuff, Rhodes."

"Is she?" He grabbed the doctor's shoulder and shook him. "Is she dyin'?"

"Uh . . . no. Not in my opinion. With some rest she should—"

Rhodes shoved him aside and he almost sprinted away. "Thare," he said to David's father. "Whad Ah tell ya?" Then to David, "Ya 'ave five minutes ta be oot of 'ere, or ya can furgit ever workin' fur me agin. Ya got that?"

"I ain't going," David answered, suddenly calm. "Not 'til I'm sure she's all right."

"No, David," his mother cried.

"Four minutes," Rhodes snarled.

What happened next was so astonishing, so stunning that it would live forever in David's memory. John Dickinson was thirty-six years old. He had started in the mines at age five. Blessed at birth with a gentle and stoic nature, he had accepted what life had dealt him without resentment or bitterness. He had none of his wife's fierceness nor her dreams of a better life. He simply endured—the cold, the misery, the backbreaking work, the vast injustices of the system and indeed of life itself. But now, something snapped. The dam broke and it all came pouring out.

John lunged forward, grabbed Rhodes by the lapels of his jacket, and slammed him up against the wall, screaming into his face. David could scarcely believe what came out. Mixing in a generous stream of profanity, his father called Rhodes a stupid ox, a pig-headed mule, something not fit for the dung heap, a man with coal dust for brains, and a lazy pile of lard.

Rhodes's face went a chalky grey. His eyes were bare slits. David couldn't tell what the man was feeling more: terror at the fury in his father, or shock at the insults being hurled at him.

David glanced at his mother, whose face was utterly white. That galvanized him. He leaped forward. "Dahd! Don't!" He grabbed him by the shoulders and pulled him back.

The torrent of invective stopped, but John wasn't finished. He dug his fingers into the supervisor's lapels and lifted the mine boss clear off his feet. He shoved his nose within half an inch of Rhodes's face. "My son sez 'e's naw goin' back," he shouted. "'Is mum be sick. Can ya git that throo yur thick skull?" He gave him a hard shove and stepped back, chest heaving. "An' if'n ya ever spek lek that in front of me wife agin, Ah'll brek yur skinny neck. Do ya 'ear me?"

For a moment, Rhodes was frozen in place, eyes bugged out, staring at this raging fury before him. John took a menacing step forward. "Noow git outta 'ere an' leave us alone."

Rhodes stumbled away, gasping for breath. Suddenly David became aware that the entire infirmary was dead quiet. The doctor had his back to the wall and looked like he might throw up. Some of the patients were sitting up, gaping at them. Others were up on one elbow, trying to see what was happening.

Rhodes never lifted his head as he stalked away. It was to his credit that he didn't break and run. As he neared the end of the ward, his head finally came up, and he went out the door with it held high. He slammed the door so hard that the whole room reverberated with the noise. That broke the doctor's trance and he ran out after Rhodes, slamming the door a second time.

Still half dazed, David looked down at his mother. If she had worried about him losing a day's pay, what had this done to her? Evidently, the same thought hit his father. Ignoring the approbation around him, he went slowly back to the chair and sank down into it. "I'm sorry, Annie. I dunna know what got—"

Tears were streaming down her face now. She reached out her arms, and he bent to her embrace. "I love you, John Dickinson," she whispered, clinging to him with a fierceness that matched what they had just witnessed. "Thank you, my dear, sweet luv."

⁂

By five o'clock that afternoon, David knew that his mother was dying. And he was sure that she knew it too. After things in the infirmary had finally calmed down, she had fallen into an exhausted but fitful sleep. David held one hand, his father the other. About half past seven, his father stood and went looking for the doctor.

As soon as he was gone, David looked around. The other patients were either asleep or staring up at the ceiling. He lowered his head and began to speak in a bare murmur.

"Dear God. I don't know if You know me. Or if You can even hear me. But. . . ." He wasn't sure even what to say. He closed his eyes now, searching for the words. "My mother is . . . she's very sick. I don't want her to die, God. She is so good. She wants to go to America."

He cracked open one eye to see if anyone was watching, then continued. "By the way, my mum's name is Anne Dickinson, but my dahd calls her Annie. I just call her Mum. Please, God. If You have to take her to heaven, could You wait until we get to America? She would rather die there than stay here in Cawthorne. By the way, Cawthorne is close to Barnsley. I know you know where Barnsley is, because I saw your house there one day."

He felt a slight movement of the bed as his mother stirred. He clenched his eyes even more tightly shut and hurriedly finished. "Please, God. If you're there, don't let her die. Please!"

When he raised his head, her eyes were open and she was watching him steadily. Her lower lip was trembling, but her eyes were soft and filled with love. "Were you praying, David?"

He looked away, embarrassed. She took his hand. "It's all right. Were you praying for me?"

"Yes, Mum."

"Thank you."

"I don't want you to die, Mum. Please don't die."

She reached up and tousled his hair, then jerked back when he winced and drew away. "Oh, David, I'm sorry. I forgot about your head." Her hand moved down and caressed his cheek. "I don't want to die either, Son. Especially now, when we're so close. And oh, how I would like to be around and see you grow into a man."

She stopped, her hand falling back to the bed. Her breathing now was short, labored.

"Mother, don't try to talk. You need to rest."

She waved that away. "Listen to me, David," she whispered, an urgency on her now. "Don't think I don't believe in God. I do, Son.

Everything in the world tells me that there is a God out there." A fleeting smile came and went. "Well, maybe not coal mines." Her smile broadened. "And certainly not Mr. Rhodes. I'm not sure just who is responsible for him."

"But—"

She pressed a finger to his lips. "No, David. I want to say this before your father returns. I know God is there. But I also know He doesn't have time for people like you and me." She had to stop again. He almost told her that she didn't have to say anything, but he sensed this was important to her.

"I prayed to Him that night the Astles threw us out. I prayed to Him when my mum was dying. I begged, and pleaded, and shed a thousand tears." Her eyes closed. "But I learned that He can't possibly answer everybody's prayers. Think how many more important things He needs to do. How many more important people there are besides you and me."

"There's nothing more important in the whole world than you, Mum." He was fighting tears again, and not successfully. "Maybe if *you* prayed."

Anger welled up inside her. "I did pray, Davee. I prayed until my knees were raw. I cried and pled and promised God to be a good girl. I prayed that He would spare my mother and curse the man responsible for her death. Then finally, I realized that God was off somewhere doing other things. That's when I knew it doesn't matter if you cry. It doesn't matter if you pray. He doesn't hear us, or if He does, He doesn't care."

"Please don't die, Mum," he sobbed. "Dahd and I need you."

"I do believe in heaven," she whispered. "So I won't leave you, Son. I'll be watching you."

Voices sounded, and they both turned to look. David's father and the doctor had just entered. They walked to Anne's bed, and the doctor gave her a cursory examination—lifted an eyelid, peered into her throat, took her pulse. He turned away. "There's nothing more I can do," he whispered to David's father, but loudly enough that both David and his mother overheard. "I'm sorry."

"Then go," his mother snapped, surprising them all. "Just go and leave us alone."

As the doctor hurried away, David's father turned back and knelt beside her. "Annie, I—"

She shook her head, her way of telling him it was all right. "John?"

"Yes, luv."

"Take me home."

"David?"

Instantly he was off his chair and on his knees beside her. She clasped both of his hands in hers. "Yes, Mum?"

Behind him, his father moved in closer as well. "Joost rest, Annie."

She shook her head. "Son, we have about seventy-two pounds."

"Mum, no! Don't worry about that now. Please!"

Her fingernails dug into his hands with surprising strength. "Don't argue. Just listen!"

"Yes, Mum." He felt the tears reappear and start to trickle down his cheeks.

She reached up and brushed them away with her fingertips, her own eyes now shining. "You only need two tickets now. That's just—"

"No, Mum! Don't say it."

She laid her hand against his cheek, smiling up at him. "It's all right, Son. I'm going to a better place." She motioned for her husband to come closer, then reached and took his hand, too. "All you need now are two tickets. That's thirty pounds. That leaves forty-two pounds extra to get you to America. Do you understand what that means, John?"

A sob was torn from his throat. "Ah canna leave ya, Annie. Ah canna."

She went right on. "It means you can go anytime now, John. You don't have to wait 'til August. You can go now!"

David reared back. He was so stricken with grief that he hadn't thought about America, about what her dying meant for their fund. But she had worked it all out in her mind. Even as she was slipping away.

"John, it's likely you'll be fired. And David too."

He shook his head. "He won't dare. Me mates will strike."

David turned in surprise at that. Throughout the evening a stream of miners had stopped at the door to their flat to give their condolences, caps in hand, heads bowed. There were brief whispered conversations with his father, then they would leave again. David could only imagine how fast the word of what had happened in the infirmary must have flashed through the mining community. It would become the stuff of legend. Rhodes was hated with universal passion. His father was right. Rhodes wouldn't dare try to fire John Dickinson.

"Ah'll naw be fire boss any longer," his father went on, "an' Davee 'ere will naw be a mule driver, naw fur a long time, but—"

"It doesn't matter. Not now. Can't you see? You don't have to wait."

To his dismay, his father nodded, not wanting to fight her any longer. David wanted to grab him by the shoulders and shake him. He couldn't just let her go.

"But you have to be careful," his mother went on, more slowly now, laboring with the effort. "They can't suspect you're leaving, or they'll make you pay off all the debts."

"Please, Mother," David begged. "We're going to wait for you."

She completely ignored him. "Will you do it, John? Wait maybe a week or two. When things settle down, then go."

"Yes, Annie."

A sob was torn from deep within her. "And you'll take care of my Davee? Take him to America? Promise me, John."

"Ya 'ave me wurd on it, Annie, me luv."

David's head came up. The bells of the All Saints Church of Cawthorne had just finished chiming out the eleventh hour. He had not been asleep, but his eyes were heavy. Something had changed. He tensed, peering down at his mother in the candlelight, and saw the gentle rise and fall of her chest. He released his breath. She was still with them.

He half turned to see if his father was still asleep in his chair. He was not. He too was intently watching his wife. He stood and came over to stand beside David, putting a hand on his shoulder. For a long time they didn't move, just looked down at her.

Finally, his father reached down and laid his hand on her forehead, as if checking for a fever. Taking it away, he just shook his head. "Try ta sleep a little, Davee. Ah'll sit with 'er noow."

He shook his head. "I'm all right, Dahd."

There was no fight left in his father. He nodded, face bleak, and returned to his seat.

It was about ten minutes later that David's head came up a second time. For a moment, David wondered if it had been only his imagination, but his father had heard it too. He was up in an instant and standing by David's side. Then it came again. Her breathing had been shallow and slightly raspy for the last hour, but now, she inhaled deeply. She held it for three or four seconds, then exhaled in a long, drawn-out sigh of relief. Several more seconds passed before she inhaled again. Again she held it. Again the deep sigh, as if something down deep inside her was being released. David found himself holding his own breath, willing her to take another.

Then, even as they watched, her body almost imperceptibly relaxed. It settled more deeply into the straw mattress. There was one more breath. One last, long sigh, and she was gone.

"No, Mum," he whispered, grasping her hand, tears streaming down his face.

His father gave a stifled sob and fell to his knees beside the bed. His head dropped to rest on her shoulder, and he wept openly. "At last ya be free, Annie," he whispered. "God speed, luv."

CHAPTER 10

Monday, May 17, 1869

A messenger was waiting for John and David Dickinson when they entered the shaft house and approached the cage on Monday morning. It was Bart Wiggins. Wiggins was what was known by the miners as a "candyman." Candymen were little more than thugs and hooligans, down-and-outs brought in by the mine owners to deal with "employee concerns" through raw intimidation. They settled grievances with fists or clubs, evicted families from their homes if they were troublemakers, and helped striking miners gain a "broader perspective" of the issues. The name suggested that they were willing to sell their souls for a little "candy" from the mine owners. The label was an indication of the absolute contempt the miners had for them.[1]

Bart was one of the worst. Huge, ugly, and totally loyal to Jonathan Rhodes, he struck fear into the hearts of even the hardiest miner. At the sight of him, David felt his stomach turn and his step falter. But his father didn't flinch. "Mornin', Bart," he said evenly.

Then David saw something that warmed his soul. Standing around the cage, half in the shadows, there were at least a dozen other miners. Their shift didn't start for half an hour yet, but he immediately understood. They had come to stand alongside their mate.

"Beggin' yur pardon, John," Bart said, sweeping off his hat, polite as a vicar welcoming his parishioners to church, "but Mr. Rhodes wud lek ta see ya an' yur son in 'is office."

There was an angry murmur as several of the miners took a step forward.

Bart whirled on them. "Back off! Ain't nuthin' gonna 'appen. He joost wants ta talk ta 'em."

His father raised a hand to the others. "It be awl reet. We be fine."

But the men fell in behind them anyway, thrusting their way past Bart, not intimidated at all.

"At least 'e waited 'til the funeral was over," John muttered.

The hatred was like bile in David's throat. "Only b'cuz yesterday was Sunday." Rhodes had not shown up at the church—his mother's first time there, as far as David knew—or for the burial.

His father stopped and looked at him. "'E dinna cum b'cuz 'e was afraid."

David snorted. "Ah don't blame 'im, Dahd. You were like a madman in the infirmary."

John ignored that, lowering his voice. Bart was about ten steps behind them, and the men behind him. "Listen ta me, David, an' listen well." His voice may have dropped in volume, but it had noticeably increased in hardness. "Rhodes stayed away, not b'cuz 'e be afraid of me. 'E be afraid of the miners. Thare be a lot of anger aboot what 'appened wit yur mum. Ya dunna know awl that is goin' on noow, so ya keep yur trap shut in thare, d'ya 'ear me?"

David looked up, stung by the sharpness of his words.

"Ah mean it, Son. Ah shamed Rhodes in front of people, an' noow the 'ole village knows it. He cahrn't let that go, or 'e be finished as supervisor. Ah know 'ow ya feel aboot yur muther, an' ya know Ah I feel the same. But ya dunna be lettin' yur temper git away frum ya.'Ear me?"

"Yes, Dahd." But he wasn't quite ready to shut up just yet. "Just don't apologize to him."

His father's look was like the edge of his pick. David vowed not to open his mouth again. But ten steps later, he couldn't help it. "Will he fire us?"

John shook his head quickly. "Dunna think so, but cahrn't be sure. 'E know thare be big trouble if 'e cumes doon too 'ard on us, but 'e cahrn't let it joost pass."

The ache for his mother was more terrible than David had dreamed possible, and his anger at what had happened with Rhodes in the infirmary—which David was absolutely positive had hastened her death—was like a fire in his belly. He wanted to strike out, hit back, make this terrible man rue the day he had chosen to treat Anne Dickinson with such contempt.

And then David remembered something else. A mine was a fertile place for rumors. Accidents were common in the mine—some of them fatal—and on more than one occasion they had "conveniently" happened to those deemed by the management to be troublemakers.

He let out his breath. "I'll not say a word, Dahd."

"Gud."

Rhodes was in his chair, his back to them, and did not turn when Bart shut the door behind them and posted himself outside to stand watch. Through the window, David saw the miners clustered in small groups, glancing from time to time at the office and the candyman.

John swept off his cap and motioned for David to do the same. David hesitated. Last night, after his father had gone to sleep, he had gotten a bucket of water and carefully washed out the dried, matted blood in his hair. The last thing they needed right now was to have Rhodes see it and start asking questions. He removed his hat but kept his head high.

When Rhodes turned around, his eyes were dark, smoldering. His mouth was pinched into a tight line. He was clearly fighting for control. When he found it, he leaned forward. "Ah be reet sorry aboot yur wife, John. Ah dinna know it be as serious as that."

David stirred, but his father's hand brushed against him, warning him off. "Tank ya."

"Ya 'eard what the doc said. 'E tole me she be fine."

"Well, 'e was wrong."

Rhodes replied with a curt nod. "Anyway, Ah be sorry fur what 'appened." He stood up and began to pace. "Ah'll git reet to it, John. Naw waste yur time or mine."

John just waited.

"Yur boy 'ere left 'is shift wit'out permission. That be agin the rules."

"Ah be the fire boss," his father said without expression. "If'n Ah say a man go up top, 'e go up top."

David had to force himself to keep his eyes forward. Had his father just lied for him? No. They had not seen each other on Friday until they met in the infirmary, but his father hadn't said he specifically told David to leave, only that, as fire boss, he had the right to.

The look in Rhodes's eye told them both that he knew better, but he let it pass. "Ya got a bit of a benny on* in the infirm'ry, John. Ya said sum real ugly things."

"Ah did," John agreed.

"Ah cahrn't joost let it go, John. Ya un'nerstand that, dun't ya?"

"Ah do."

The supervisor faced John, feet planted now. "Thot aboot firin' ya. Ah cud, ya know."

"Ya cud."

"Or, Ah cud pull ya off frum bein' fire boss."

"Ya cud."

Rhodes was watching him closely now, trying to read what was behind those inscrutable eyes. "Ah be a fair-minded man, John. An' thare be a lot of strain, what wit yur Annie an' all."

"Don't call her Annie!" David blurted before he even realized what he had done.

He might as well have not been there. In one sense, he was irrelevant in all this.

"So Ah be givin' it a lot of thot, John. If'n Ah joost overlook what 'appened, the men will be thinkin' ole Rhodes be goin' soft on 'em. Cahrn't have that, eh? But knowin' yur grief an' awl, Ah dunna wanna mek things wurse fur ya."

He stopped. Still David's father just waited, watching and weighing what was being said.

"So, Ah think Ah 'ave a way that we can sidestep the problem. Keep things under control." A long pause. "If'n ya be agreeable."

---

* To get upset, to lose one's temper.

David risked a glance up at his father. His face was still expressionless, but his eyes were dark with suspicion. "Ah be listenin'."

"A rider cum in frum Tilburn Castle late yes'day. Lady Tilburn, she sez they be low on coal fur the kitchens an' water 'eaters. Got a bunch of uppity-uppities cumin' north frum London fur the summer. Cahrn't wait fur next week's normal deliv'ry."

His mouth twisted in what David assumed was meant to be a smile, but was actually a horrible grimace. "Cahrn't be 'avin' the lords an' ladies inconvenienced noow, can we?" Still no answer from John. "Way Ah figur, if'n Ah were ta send ya an' yur boy with a wagonload of coal doon thare—no pay fur either of ya, of course—maybe that be penalty e'nuff, consid'rin'."

"What else?"

Rhodes nodded, glad that they were at last communicating. "Ah leave ya in as fire boss, but fur a week ya drop back ta regular miner's wages."

"What aboot David, 'ere?"

The piggish eyes narrowed. "Ah'll leave 'im as spragger, but 'e loses Freeday's wages."

"'E be only gone fur 'alf a day."

Rhodes chewed on his lip for a moment. "Awl reet. 'Alf a day's pay. It goes wit'oot sayin', thare be naw pay fur Sat'day fur either of ya, since ya stayed 'ome ta mek arrangements."

His father nodded. That was a given. "What aboot 'im being a mule driver?"

There was a flash of genuine anger, but it was pushed back. "When be ya thurteen, boy?"

"In a month," David said.

"Ah'll consider it then," he said, looking back to his father. "Naw b'fur."

"An' that be it?" his father asked.

Rhodes hesitated, then finally nodded. "Then it be square b'tween us."

His father nodded too. "Agreed."

David was soaring. His father had stood nose to nose with Jonathan A. Rhodes, terror of the Cawthorne Mine, and come away with no more than his fingers rapped. If only his mother had been here to see this day.

The supervisor returned to his chair, scribbled a note, and handed it to David's father. "Tek this ta the loadin' yard. Ya bin ta Tilburn House b'fur?"

"Naw."

"Be aboot sixteen, maybe seventeen mile sooth of 'ere." Which meant not only a day's work without pay, but a very long day at that. "The loadin' boss give ya directions."

His father took the note and took David by the arm, and they left without another word.

It was a glorious early summer day. The sky was a brilliant blue, and puffy clouds lazily scudded across it from west to east, shadows gliding along at two or three times the pace the heavily loaded wagon was making. They went west to Penistone, which was on the eastern edge of what was called the Peak District. As they turned south and passed through Stocksbridge they were skirting its eastern boundaries. Here the sprawl of city and industry thinned and then gave way altogether as the land began to rise to meet the Pennines, known as the "backbone of England." Vast moors and highlands stretched away as far as the eye could see. It was so totally different from anything David had ever seen before, he couldn't take his eyes away from it.

They passed through little farm villages with delightful names like Springvale, Oxspring, and Wigtwizzle.[2] For a boy who had spent his life in the grey and dreary confines of a mining village, these were a wonder indeed, and he could only gawk as they drove through them. No mountains of culm, or coal waste. No belching black smoke from the boilers driving the steam engines. No thick layers of coal dust covering everything.

The countryside was even more wondrous. The narrow roads were defined by hedgerows thick enough to stop a runaway coal car. The grass along the verge was as high as the mules' bellies. Wildflowers splashed across the hillsides. From time to time they passed fields of rape seed,[3] so brilliantly yellow in the sunshine as to make David lift his hand and shade his eyes.

But all of this wonder and amazement was mixed with a piercing grief. It was his mother who should be here beside his father. This was what she had longed for. How she loved the sunshine. How she treasured fresh air and wildflowers. Knowing it was her death that had brought about this trip only made his grief all the more keen, all the more unbearable.

"'Ow's yur 'ead t'day?"

David turned in surprise. They had barely spoken in the last two hours, each lost in their own thoughts, their own sorrows. "My head?"

There was a soft chuckle. "Didya think Ah wud naw notice it in the infirm'ry when Ah stood over ya?"

"Oh."

"Ridin' the cars?"

That took him even more aback. Finally, he nodded. "Who told you?"

"Just a guess." He reached up and pulled down his collar to reveal a two-inch white scar on the side of his neck. David had noticed this before and had asked him one day what it was, but his father had brushed his question away.

"From riding the cars?" he exclaimed.

"Yep. Mine was a steel spike driven inta one of the supportin' pillars. Jumped off the car an' thot I'd missed it. Lucky Ah didn't tear me throat open."

"Did your Pa ever know?"

An even deeper chuckle. "Yep. Then 'e showed me a scar on 'is leg."

David sat back, warmed by this moment even more than he was by the sun. Then, catching him completely by surprise, his eyes were suddenly burning again. "I miss her so much, Dahd."

"Aye," John sighed. "Ah miss 'er lek Ah dinna think was possible."

About four hours later, as they came up and over a stone bridge that spanned Tilburn River, David's jaw dropped. Tilburn Castle[4] was situated at the base of a forested hillside about a quarter of a mile from where they were. Ahead was a gently rolling dale through which ran the river, a stream about eight feet wide and a foot or two deep. The ground dropped away slightly from where they were, so they had a clear view of the house.

It was huge, bigger than any building David had ever seen in his life. Bigger than the breaker building in the pit yard. Bigger than the Holyrood Church in Barnsley. The house was three stories high, with a central block fronted by massive pillars. Matching wings were attached to both sides, balancing the heavier block in a delicate blend of lines.

"Blimey!" David said, completely awestruck. "I never knew there were a house so big."

"An' this joost be one of their summer 'omes," his father muttered.

David gaped at him. Had he heard that right? But his father wasn't looking at him anymore. He lifted the reins. "Gee on wit ya, mules," he clucked.

As they approached a small lake that had been formed by damming the river, they heard a burst of children's laughter. A moment later three figures darted out of a stand of willows next to the lake and ran across the road directly in front of them. They were shouting and chasing one another, playing some kind of game. They pulled up short at the sight of the wagon.

It was three girls. The oldest was probably David's age. Her long hair shimmered gold, and her eyes were a luminous blue. As she surveyed first his father, then him, her mouth curled disdainfully. Next to her was a girl of maybe ten—clearly a sister—with slightly darker hair that bobbed in tiny ringlets. Though surprise registered on her face as well, she smiled up at them. The third girl was maybe five or six and looked like neither of the other two. They all wore long dresses with full skirts and petticoats, with hair ribbons that matched the color of their dresses. Black patent-leather shoes covered their surprisingly tiny feet.

Suddenly, the oldest one pulled a face. "Ew!" she said, then shouted to the others and darted away. Off they raced, disappearing into the trees on the other side of the road.

David recoiled. The revulsion and disgust in the girl's eyes had been as real as a slap across the face. It was like she had accidentally overturned a rock only to find something very repulsive there.

"Pay 'em naw mind, David," his father said softly.

He didn't answer. The haughtiness, the sheer arrogance, the complete and utter disdain had shaken him. What he had seen in those eyes was pure contempt for a life form lesser than her own.

His father could sense that he was troubled. As they moved forward, he began speaking. "The royalty an' nobility be convinced that they be God's elect. They trulee b'lieve they be chosen fur such a life as this b'cuz they be naturally an' infinitely superior ta the rest of us poor lugs. This—" he waved a hand to include all that lay before them—"in thare minds be thare divine reward for bein' the chosen ones. They accept awl the land, the muney, the titles an' 'ouses an' jewelry and servants ta be the reward fur their natural superiority."

He blew out his breath in an expression of deep disgust. "The 'ole system be like a pile of rottin' carcasses. In my mind, they be more corrupt and evil than even Rhodes an' awl of 'is wickedness. The fact that it be blokes like us, muckin' out the coal and silver and lead and tin that keep 'em in their fancy palaces and their golden carriages, means nothin' ta 'em."

David was staring. It was a rare thing to see his father this exercised about something.

John looked at him, sensing his astonishment. "Sumday," he muttered, "Ah think God be smitin' 'em doon an' consignin' 'em ta the fires of 'ell so that justice may be done."

As they finished shoveling the last of the coal into the chute behind the great house, David happened to glance up. On the second story, framed in one of the great arched windows, he saw the older sister again. She was standing behind a filmy curtain, staring down at them. He saw her visibly jerk back when she realized he had seen her. Smiling broadly, he swept off his cap and gave her a sweeping bow. It gave him great satisfaction that once again she recoiled in horror and disgust and immediately disappeared.

Notes

1. Taken from The North East England History Page, "Owners and Candymen," http://www.northeastengland.talktalk.net/page72.htm. It is not clear where the title *candyman* originated. The supposition given in the novel is speculation.

2. These villages still exist in South Yorkshire. One of the delights of driving through the British countryside is to pass through small English villages with names that bring a smile to your heart. Here are just a few that exist in the U.K. today: Anthill Commons, Barton-on-the-Beans, Biggleswade, Birdwhistle; Blubberhouse; Bokiddick, Buttsbear Cross, Diddlebury, Diggle, Duddlewick, Giggleswick, Goonhilly Downs, Little Snoring, Maggieknockater, Mold, Nasty, Oswaldtwistle, Mousehole, Penpillick, Pothole, Pucklechurch, Ramsbottom, Rows of Trees, Scarcewater, Tiddlywink, Tintwhistle, Ucksford, Ughill, Upton Snodsbury, and Wormbite.

3. The rape seed is in full bloom in May in the British Isles. To come over a hill and see a thousand acres or more of these brilliant yellow blossoms is truly breathtaking. Rape seed gets its name from the Latin *rapum,* or turnip. In North America it is more commonly called canola.

4. There is no such place as Tilburn Castle or Tilburn River, nor were there actual people known as Lord and Lady Tilburn.

CHAPTER 11

Monday, May 17, 1869

With an empty wagon, they made much better time back to Cawthorne, but it was still past ten o'clock by the time they reached the pit yard. The yard was dark, but the loading foreman had waited for them. By the time they helped him unhitch the mules, feed them, and wipe them down, it was close to eleven when they finally approached the door to their flat. "Don't suppose Rhodes would let us sleep late for a couple of hours in the morning," David said.

A low grunt was his only answer to that.

His father unlocked the door, pushed it open, and stepped back so David could enter first. The cloud cover had moved over them and the night was very dark. Inside their flat it was even darker.

David stepped inside and stopped. He breathed deeply. He swore he could smell the presence of his mother—the smell of baking on her clothes, the soap on her hands, and the sweetness of her hair. He closed his eyes, her loss hitting him yet again like a physical blow.

The door closed and his father pushed past him. There was a loud crash and something heavy skittered across the floor. "Ow!" Something crunched loudly as his father fumbled his way toward the table. "What's goin' on 'ere?" David heard him mutter.

There was the scratch of a match on wood, then a flare of light. His father held a match up above his head and turned slowly. It wasn't much light, but it was enough. The room was a shambles. Two chairs were on their sides. Crumpled papers littered the floor; broken pottery glittered in the light of the match. Clothing was strewn everywhere. His father moved to the cupboard as the match went out. There was fumbling for a moment, then the scratch of another match. This time he lit the two candles in the candle holder. In the greater light it was clear that the damage was total. A can of sugar had been dumped on the counter. Flour was sprayed across the floor and looked like snow. Knives, forks, spoons, the teakettle, pots, pans, tin cups, and mugs were tossed about. The straw mattress where David slept had been slashed open and straw scattered everywhere.

That sight spun him around. He walked swiftly to his parents' sleeping room, ignoring the crunch of things beneath his feet. He pulled the blanket back and felt a surge of red-hot anger as he saw the shredded mattress cover where his mother had breathed her last breath just two days ago now. The nightdress that David had folded so carefully before they dressed her for the coffin was heaped in one corner. Someone had walked on it. He picked it up, closing his eyes.

A cry spun him around. His father was on his knees beside the overturned kitchen table. He was bending over a black hole in the floor, rocking back and forth, holding his head.

"Not the box!" David shouted. In three great leaps he was beside his father and down on his knees. The hole beneath the floor that his father had so carefully crafted many years before had been chopped open with an ax. Inside, David saw that the cavity was empty.

He howled in anguish. They had not only desecrated his mother's bed. They had not just soiled her clothing. They had smashed her dreams. They had stolen the one thing that had kept her filled with hope and prolonged her life. The anger in him nearly blinded him.

David saw that his father's face was white. "But 'ow? Naw one even knew we 'ad it."

David groaned and put his face in his hands. "The doctor knew," he said hoarsely.

"What?"

He felt like he was going to vomit. "Mum spoke to me about the box when she was in the infirmary. I think the doctor overheard her."

"Did she say where it was?" He looked around, then answered his own question. "Of course she didn't. Otherwise, why tear everythin' apart?

"She did say how mooch we had saved."

"Aw, David." John got to his feet, moving slowly, as if he had been struck a severe blow. He reached down, picked up one of the chairs, set it up straight, then dropped into it like a sack of coal, shoulders slumping. He looked around, eyes vacant.

After several moments, his eyes came back into focus and he sat straight up. "Blow out the candles, Son. Ah need time ta think, an' Ah dunna want anyone knowin' we're back."

Five minutes later, his father abruptly stood up. "Git a flour sack frum the bottom drawer."

David leaped up. "Yes, sir."

"Yoo'll need ta light a candle ta see, but keep it covered so it be naw seen frum the street." He ignored David's quizzical look. "We'll need clothes, includin' jackets—sumthin' warm. Git whate'er food ya can salvage. Get yur best boots. Mine, too. Yur pocketknife an' the butcher knife if ya can find it. All the matches an' candles ya can find. Any extra stockin's." He thought for a moment. "Ah want me six-poond hammer."

David had seen that over by his bed. He made his way there, dropped to a crouch, and found it immediately. "Here. Where are we going, Dahd?"

John's answer was calm, measured, as if he were reading from a list. "Listen carefully, Son. Ah'm goin' ta the pit yard. As soon as ya 'ave everythin'—an' joost get what ya can—meet me be'ind the pit yard by the stables."

"What about Mum's things?" His voice was quavering.

A sound of pain escaped John. "See if they tuk the little necklace Ah gave yur mum fur 'er bur'day last year. She kept it b'neath our bed in a snuff tin. Other than that, leave everythin'." His grip on David's shoulder tightened. "We 'ave very little time, Son. Be at the stable in ten minutes. No more. Wait thare ootside the fence fur me. Dunna let anyone see ya." Before David could say anything, John spun on his heel and slipped out the door.

One characteristic of a mining village was that, except on Saturday nights, by 10:00 P.M. the entire town became a cemetery. David saw no one as he left the flat and slipped into the street, then made his way through one of the alleyways toward the row of outhouses. Holding the bulky flour sack under his arm to muffle any rattles, and stopping every few moments to make sure no old men with bladder problems were using the outhouses, he made his way to the mine.

The pit yard was black and silent when he reached it. He crept along the back fence until he saw the dark shape of the stables and smelled the mule dung. He set the bag down carefully, making sure it didn't clunk, then peered through the fence into the darkness. "Dahd?"

No answer. No sound of any kind. He was sure he had not taken more than his allotted ten minutes, so he sat down in the dead grass to wait.

Three or four minutes later, he heard the crackle of gravel, and a dark shaped appeared on the other side of the fence. "David?"

"Here."

His father moved to where he was and quickly scaled the fence. He dropped to the ground and touched David's shoulder. "We be goin' in joost a minute."

"Where?"

He pointed to a small brick building that sat back about a hundred feet from where they were. David squinted, then inhaled sharply. "Mr. Rhodes's house?"

John nodded, then put his finger to his lips. "Did ya naw see Bart Wiggins standin' guard ootside the front of the hoose when we passed it earlier t'night?"

David shook his head. He hadn't even looked in that direction.

"There's a weasel in the woodpile, David. Sumthin's up, an' we gotta find oot what." He turned back to the pit yard.

As they waited, David's mind started to race. Of course it was Rhodes. It had to be. The doctor would have gone straight to him and told him what he had overheard. All that blathering this morning about the two of them going to Tilburn Castle as "fair punishment" was nothing but a ruse to get the Dickinsons out of the way. Once night came, he had only to send in one of his goons—probably Bart himself—to do the rest.

But why was Wiggins standing guard outside Rhodes's house? And then it hit him. The box! The box with their money was inside Rhodes's house right now. A thrill of elation shot through him. Suddenly, he sniffed the air. "Dahd, I smell smoke."

John lifted his head. "Aye," he said easily.

David got to his knees, peering through the fence. A slight breeze out of the east was blowing the smoke right to them. He saw an orange glow behind the blacksmith's shop. David knew there was a large pile of refuse there—scraps of lumber, rumpled wastepaper, discarded rags and clothing—which the blacksmith's apprentice used to start the fires each morning.

Even as he watched, the glow flared into flickering flames. At that moment, his father leaped to his feet and started banging on the steel fence post with his hammer, causing David to nearly jump out of his shoes. It made a terrible racket in the still night air.

"Fire! Fire!" His father ran to the next post, closer to the gate. He banged it as well. "Fire in the pit yard!"

"Awl reet," he said, racing back. He grabbed David's arm. "Grab the sack. Let's go."

They heard the first distant shouts as they sprinted out and around one of the great mounds of culm, or coal waste, and approached Rhodes's house from the rear. As they reached it and dropped behind some bushes, his father grunted in satisfaction. "Gud. The windows be open."

It would have been a surprise if they were not. The nights were warm now, and virtually every family in the village slept with their windows open and would until fall. They hunkered down, listening and watching the effects that John had created. People began appearing from everywhere, some in their nightclothes, some pulling on shirts even as they ran, shouting and yelling. They could hear Bart Wiggins banging on the front door and yelling for Rhodes to "cum quick."

The house filled with lamplight, and three minutes later Rhodes and his wife appeared in front of the house with Wiggins in the lead, running for the pit yard.

It took them less than three minutes inside the house to find what they were looking for. Perhaps Rhodes had planned to take his booty to the bank tomorrow, but he had only gotten it a few hours before. As David realized that, again he marveled at how carefully his father had thought things through. In the bedroom wardrobe, beneath a file box of papers and some folded blankets, they found a stout wooden chest with two locks on it.

John told David to douse the bedroom lamps. Then, by the light of the lamps in the main part of the house, he hauled the chest out. With three or four well-placed blows with the hammer, the locks were sprung and removed. And there it was, his mother's shoe box, just as she had left it when she had last counted its contents a few days before.

"Din't even bother ta git rid of our box," he said in disgust. "Shows 'ow frightened 'e be."

David counted swiftly. He sat back, tremendous relief sweeping over him. "It's all here."

"Gud." His father started to close the lid again.

"Wait." David leaned forward, looking inside the chest. There was a cry of triumph as he lifted both hands. One carried a large leather pouch bulging with coins, the other a pocket watch with a thick gold chain. "Ah ha!"

"No, David!"

"*What?*"

"We take only what b'longs to us."

"Dahd, think of all the ways Rhodes has cheated us and—"

His father snatched both bag and watch from David's hands and placed them back in the chest, then shut the lid with an emphatic clunk. "Dunna shame me. We be naw thieves an' robbers."

David stared helplessly as his father replaced the two locks, twisting them so that at first glance they still looked as they had before. He replaced the chest, then the box and blankets on top of it. "Knowin' Rhodes," he said, "furst thing 'e'll do when 'e cums back be ta check the chest. If'n it looks exactly lek it did b'fur, and if'n we be lucky—" He winked at David. "If'n we be real lucky, that wicked old fool won't even think ta look inta the strongbox 'til t'morrow."

"And by then," David cried in fierce exultation, "we'll be on our way to America."

"If we be lucky," his father repeated.

CHAPTER 12

Tuesday, May 18, 1869

They headed east, which was David's first surprise. If they were going to America, they had to get to Liverpool, the major port in England for going to the New World. Liverpool was almost straight west from Cawthorne.

But that became their pattern. It took David about three days to understand it, but then his admiration for his father's wisdom and cunning soared. They would feint one way, then slip off in another. They would leave a clear trail that led nowhere. They deliberately spoke to a constable as they passed through Barnsley about one o'clock in the morning and asked for the way to the canal docks—the docks where canal boats were loaded with coal for Liverpool. As soon as they were out of sight, they turned north, skirting around the canals by at least a mile. The next morning, they bought train tickets for London, then slipped out of the station, shredded the tickets, and headed north. And so it went.

They constantly moved north, never west. It was less than a month away from summer solstice, so daylight came early and lingered well past eleven. It didn't matter. His father seemed in no hurry at all. They moved only after dark, avoided villages, and always slipped off the roads when someone approached. Not until they were north of York did that change.

York was the last large city in their path, and once past that they started moving in the daytime. But even then, his father was ever cautious. When they approached a village, they would separate and pass through it well apart from each other. If they were offered a ride by a passing farmer or merchant, they turned it down. When they needed food, only one would stop at the market. They never took commercial lodging. They slept out in rain, wind, or starry night.

After two weeks, they reached the North York Moors, that vast and empty windswept country where only the hardiest shepherds or settlers chose to live. Only then did they turn west. And through it all, on one thing his father was absolutely insistent. They took nothing without paying for it. They never sought refuge in someone's barn or shed or stable. Not only was it not right, his father kept reminding him, but they didn't need anyone else hunting for them.

One other pattern emerged that David recognized only after they had been on the move for a fortnight. At first, he wasn't sure, but as he searched his memory, he became absolutely certain of it. Since his mother had died, his father had not once called him Davee or Davee boy.

Wednesday, June 9, 1869

David lay on his side, head resting in the crook of his elbow, and watched his father sleep. They had pressed on until after dark, then dropped into an exhausted sleep. David had awakened first. The early light of morning was behind his father, so his face was in shadow, and David could not discern much other than the heavy brows and the beard, now a full inch long.

For all of his growing-up years, David had been much closer to his mother than his father. He loved his father and had the greatest respect for him, but John was gone every day except Sunday for all but a few waking hours. As David had matured and begun working in the mines, their relationship had deepened, but even then, as compared to his mother, David had viewed his father as . . . what? Not weak. He had never thought that. Coal miners had no respect for a weak man, and David had come to realize that his father was greatly respected among his fellow colliers. What, then? Submissive? Maybe. No, a better word was *accepting*. He was accepting of life as it was. He didn't feel a need to be forever trying to change things into what he thought they should be. Life was life, and you just accepted it.

His mother, on the other hand, had a stubborn tenacity in confronting life that was astounding. Life had come at her with the relentless force of an avalanche, and she had simply planted her feet, tipped her head back, and dared it to sweep her away. David was old enough now to realize that he was mostly a product of her strength, her courage, her passion, her intensity. And he would ever thank her for that. So how much had he gotten from his father? Not his patience, that was for sure. Nor very much of his wisdom and sound judgment. David tended to be more spontaneous and impetuous—even rash.

He reached up and rubbed softly across the scar forming on the top of his head. Ask Sean Williams if that wasn't true. Or Bertie Beames. He sighed. A little more of patience from his father might be good.

He returned to his previous train of thought. In these last three weeks, his respect and love for his father had grown much. Every day brought some new revelation of his father's strength, his wisdom, even his cunning. For example, it was not until they were clearly out of danger that David realized something. Setting that fire had not only been an inspired way to get back their funds and cover their escape, but his father had set it against the back of the blacksmith's shop—the *brick* blacksmith's shop. It attracted the attention of the whole village, but the only real damage it would have done was to scorch the bricks black. No one was ever in danger, and no damage was done that would put the miners out of work, not even for a day.

David still thought of his mother every day and greatly grieved for her, but the pain was lessening a little all the time. Their flight had left him with a hollow feeling in one way. Never would he be able to sit beside her simple slate headstone. Never would he be able to lay some spring flowers on her grave. But . . . it had brought David and his father together. And maybe that was some kind of justice of its own.

Thursday, June 10, 1869

As they entered the outskirts of Liverpool, David was completely overwhelmed. On that first trip to Barnsley with his mother, he had thought they had entered the largest city in the world. Now he saw that Barnsley was but a country village compared to Liverpool.

The sidewalks were packed with people, pushing and shoving past each other, stopping to shop at the markets, all of which had sidewalk displays. Some of the streets were completely blocked off to wagons and other vehicles, and vendors had set up their wares right in the middle of the road. Most of the people they were passing were of the working classes, like themselves. But here and there he would catch sight of a couple of dandies in their long coats and tails and ruffles at their throats, or women twirling their brightly colored parasols while they held handkerchiefs to their dainty little noses.

The streets were littered with dung from cattle, sheep, goats, mules, and horses. The stench was powerful even to David, who had long ago grown used to it in the confines of the mine. And with the stink came the flies. Swarms of them. The flies were so bad, in fact, that David saw one street vendor with what looked like a platter of rice cakes filled with raisins. But when a woman stopped to look, the man made a pass with his hand and all the "raisins" flew away.

If the sidewalks were bedlam, the streets were a nightmare. Shepherds tried to keep small flocks of sheep and goats together until they could reach the butcher shops. Children darted in and out among every possible kind of conveyance—wagons, carts, coaches, gigs, grand carriages, drays, phaetons. Merchants trudged along pulling heavily laden donkeys. Several of the upper classes rode on perfectly groomed thoroughbreds. There were also hundreds of bicycles with their huge front wheels and tiny back ones. How they stayed erect as they wove in and out of the rush was astounding to David.

The cry of teamsters rent the air. They swore, they cursed, sometimes even cracking their long black buggy whips over the heads of another team. One driver of a wagon filled with huge bales of cotton savagely whipped his team forward to cut off an oncoming coach. He succeeded in locking his wheels with theirs, bringing both vehicles to a crunching halt. The drivers went at each other with their fists while the people in the coach leaned out and cheered their man on.

David's father paid all of this little mind. He stopped three different people—all from the working classes like themselves—and asked them how to find their way to the docks. They all said the same. Keep on this street for about two miles and they would reach the River Mersey. The docks were to the right once they reached the river.

David suddenly lost interest in the bedlam around him. In one instant, he was tired of it all. It had been almost one full month since they had last slept in a bed, had a hot bath, eaten a warm meal at a table. "Can we find lodging and sleep indoors tonight, Dahd?" he asked plaintively.

"Aye. But sumthin' a little closer ta the docks. Per'aps a wee room wit access ta a bath."

"Promise?"

John laughed softly. "It's been a long journey, eh, David? But it almost be over. Ah be thinkin'," his father continued, half musing. "The less time we be 'ere, the better. So what if t'morrow we split up. What if'n Ah stay back, do the laundry, maybe start lookin' at what we need ta buy fur our passage. An' ya cud go doon along the docks an' see what ya can learn aboot bookin' passage—when the next ship sails, 'ow mooch the tickets be, an' sooch. Whaddya think?"

"We could, but wouldn't it be better if we worked together?"

There was a long silence, then, "Are ya naw furgittin' sumthin', Son? Ah cahrn't read."

"Oh." David felt awful that he had forgotten that little essential.

"But Ah be real gud at doin' laundry. Ah used ta 'elp yur mum, r'member?"

"That's a good idea, Dahd."

"Except thare be one problem."

"What's that?"

"Ah don't think Ah ever be gittin' the body smell oot of yur shirts. Ya be as rank as a skunk in a bath hoose."

"Hey!" David exclaimed, hardly believing that his father had just made a joke. "You should talk. Remember that last village we went through. When you went in, the dogs started barking and coming out after you, like they always do. But one whiff, and they turned tail and ran."

"Spekin' of dogs, ya cheeky little pup," his father growled, "Ah be showin' ya a thing or two if ya dun't put a sock in it."

"Yah, yah!" David jeered. Then he leaped aside to escape being cuffed alongside the head.

Friday, June 11, 1869

The tiny boarding room they secured was just four blocks from the dock. As David prepared to leave the next morning, his father stepped in front of the door. "Do ya r'member that Sunday be yur thirteenth bur'day, David?"

"Actually, no. I hadn't thought about it."

"What wud ya like fur yur bur'day, other than a ticket to America, which we be gittin'?"

"Breakfast in bed."

"Ah be findin' a market later. 'Ow aboot a new name instead?"

David blinked.

"Ah be guessin' that ev'ry shippin' cump'ny be required by law ta keep a list of all passengers. Ah think by noow ole man Rhodes be givin' up any 'ope of findin' us. But 'e be a stubborn ole goat. Wudn't put it past 'im ta keep checkin' fur a year or more."

"But if we be in America? He can't do anything there, can he?"

"Dunno. Prob'ly not, but Ah'd rether naw be wurryin' aboot it. Far as Ah'm concerned, it be time fur David and John Dickn'son ta disappear, go away, vanish."

David pulled at his lip as he considered that. The very idea felt strange, but why not? "Do you have something in mind?"

John seemed pleased that David wasn't going to fight him on it. "'Ow aboot David Moore?"

"Hmm. Why that?"

He shrugged. "It joost cum ta mind. Ya got sumthin' better?"

"I don't care," David went on. "Moore is fine, I guess. What about our first names?"

"Thot aboot that too," John said. "But our first names be pretty common. Ah think we be okay thare. Well, then, Moore it is."

And then came a sudden thought. "No," David blurted. "How many people in Cawthorne knew Mum's maiden name?"

"Draper?" John rubbed his beard. "Not shure. Nobody, far as Ah know."

"Good." Then more softly, "I would like to take her name."

His father gave a slow, thoughtful nod. "David and John Draper. Aye. That be mooch better." Then, to David's surprise, his father's eyes were gleaming. "That be a gud way ta never forget yur mum," he said huskily. "Thank ya, David Draper."

David returned about half an hour before suppertime and found their room filled with shirts. trousers, smalls, and stockings hung up in every available space in their little flat. He sniffed the air. "What's that smell?"

His father laughed. "It be called soap, ya lug'ead."

"Oh." He came over, and plopped down on a corner of a chair that held his shirt, and looked around. "Beats a creek and a rock, doesn't it?"

"They were gittin' purty grey after a month." John transferred a pair of trousers from another chair, then brought it over to sit before his son. "So, what did ya find oot?"

With a flourish, David withdrew a small pad of paper. He had paid Mrs. O'Keefe, their new landlady, a penny for it and a stubby pencil this morning before he left.

"A lot. In fact, it was a wonderful day."

"So the news be gud?"

"Really good."

His father sat back, folding his arms. "Ah'm listenin'."

Moving slowly so as to increase the anticipation, David unfolded the paper, smoothed it out on his leg, and began. "Here's what we know so far. Number one. You don't deal with ship captains or any of the sailing crew personally. Most shipping companies use agents. Number two. Almost all of the shipping agents have offices along the docks or in adjoining streets. I went to six or seven."

"Bless yur mum fur teachin' ya ta read."

"Number three. There has been some terrible sickness in New Orleans—that's a port in America—so now almost all companies go into New York, Boston, or Philadelphia."

"That be awl reet?"

"I think so. Number four. Some of the shipping lines are American. They have shipping offices here, too. In fact, I talked to two 'Yanks,' as they call themselves. You think Yorkshire Tykes talk funny? You should hear them. Anyway, fares seem to be pretty much the same, American or British."

"Still fifteen poonds?"

"Ah, now, that be the good news, Dahd." He consulted his notes. "In the last few years there's been a major change in shipping across the Atlantic. I guess the people Mum talked to in Barnsley a few years back made no mention of this. But, anyway, a few years ago, someone invented what they call a propeller screw—don't ask me what that is. Different than a paddle wheel is all I know. But with the propeller screw, steamships are replacing sailing ships for passage across the Atlantic." He was trying to contain his excitement, doling out the good news one piece at a time, hoping to build some enthusiasm in his father.

He didn't seem that impressed. "So?"

David's grin was huge. "So instead of two to three months to cross the ocean, it now takes only about a week."

That got John's attention. "Only seven days?"

"And that's not all. The docks are all abuzz with news that has just arrived from America. The Americans have just completed what they call a transcontinental railroad."[1]

"Transconta- what?"

"Transcontinental. It means it goes clear across North America."

"An' that be gud fur us?"

"The railroad goes from New York City to California. That's coast to coast. That means we can go clear across America by train if we choose."

"How fur that be?"

That caught David off guard. He hadn't thought to ask. He just knew the people seemed very impressed with the news. "I dunno. A hundred miles or more." He couldn't sit still any longer. He was up, walking back and forth, consulting the paper from time to time. "Do you understand what that means for us, Dahd? The farther west we go, the less chance there be that Rhodes will ever find us. Now, with the steamships and the railroad, guess how long to go all the way to California? That's in the far west."

His father had no way to even venture a guess. He just shrugged.

"Before, it would have taken us about six or seven months, and that's just traveling time." David drew in a breath, letting the suspense build. "Now, they told me we can go from Liverpool to San Francisco—that's in California—in just three weeks!"

His father gaped at him.

David's grin felt like it was going to split his face. "So guess what all of this has done to the cost of traveling to America?"

John's face fell. "Made it much higher?"

"No, Dahd. Think about it. A shipping company had to pay the crew of a sailing ship five or six months' wages to go to the New World and back. Now they only have to pay them for two weeks to make the same trip. Think of how much savings that be for them. They save on food and other costs too."

"Are ya sayin' that the fares be less?"

"Aye, Dahd." He waved the paper in his face. "The fare is now only ten pounds. What do you think of that?"

John jerked forward. "Ten?"

"Yes! So instead of thirty pounds for the both of us, we only need twenty. I just earned us ten pounds today."

To his surprise, his father suddenly looked sad.

"What?"

"If'n we'd known that, we cud 'ave left earlier, b'fur yur mum died. Maybe . . ." He couldn't finish it.

That hit David hard. For a long time he looked at his father, then he finally shook it off. "She could never have made it this far, Dahd, let alone to America."

"Ah know, Ah know."

"Oh, Dahd, I wish she were here too. It would be such a grahnd day for her."

"Aye." John sighed and forced a smile. "It be a grahnd day fur us, Son. And she wud be reet prood if she cud see us."

"Maybe she can, Dahd. Maybe she can." David began folding the paper up again, then something caught his eye. "Oh, one more thing."

"What?"

"If this is true—and it may not be—a man told me there is another shipping company that has tickets for *less than* ten pounds. And—" He held up one finger to cut off his father's exclamation. "And, he said that they include *all* food in the passage, unlike most of the lines, who pay for only about half of what we need."

Again his father started to react, and again David held up his finger. "*And* they will help us do all the paperwork we need to leave England as part of the fare."

"Cud that be true, ya think?" his father asked, clearly skeptical.

David shook his head. "Dunno. By then the shipping offices were all closing. I'll—no, *we'll*—go first thing in the morning and find out for ourselves."

"What be the name of this supposed wonder cump'ny?"

David glanced at his notes. "He called it the Mormons. Don't know if I spelled it right, but that's what the man said. And he even told me how to find their office."

Note

1. The rails of the Union Pacific and Southern Pacific were joined at Promontory Point in Utah Territory on May 10, 1869.

CHAPTER 13

Saturday, June 12, 1869

A bell above the door tinkled as David pushed it open and stepped inside. His father followed right behind him. As they had approached the office a few minutes earlier, his father had insisted that David take the lead once they got inside. He felt awkward dealing with something he knew so little about. More than that, there would surely be things to read, and calculations to be done, and there David was clearly the one to handle things.

The office was spacious enough, but hardly luxurious. It was well organized. There was a large desk with stacks of papers on one corner, an inkwell and blank paper on the other. Two hard-back chairs were set in front of the desk. A worktable in one corner, with a high stool beside it, held more stacks of paper. A bookshelf bore a few books and a large grey ledger. An open door revealed a short hallway where David could see daylight coming from a back room.

On the wall behind the desk hung a framed certificate of some kind. David took a step closer: *The Church of Jesus Christ of Latter-day Saints.*

He gave his father a questioning look. There was nothing else in the office to indicate what their business was, and the letters on the glass door said only, "LDS Emigration Company."

A chair scraped somewhere, then there were footsteps. A moment later, a man appeared in the hallway. He was an older man, in his late forties or early fifties, a bit overweight but with a pleasant countenance. "Good morning," he said with a broad smile. "May I help you?"

An American, was David's first thought. *Good.* "Yes. My name is David

Dick—" He caught himself. "David Draper. This is my father, John Draper."

The man stepped forward and shook their hands with vigorous enthusiasm. "Pleased to meet you. I'm Brother Daniel Miller."

David shot his father a quick look. *Brother* Miller? Was he a Quaker, by chance?

"Come in, come in." He motioned toward the two chairs. "How may I help you?"

"We are interested in finding passage to America. We were told you are in that business."

"Indeed we are. Please, sit down." He went around the desk as they did so. Once they were all seated, he pulled the inkwell closer to him and took a blank piece of paper. "All right, just let me make a few notes, then I'll try to answer your questions." He dipped the quill in the ink. "Names again were David and John Draper, right?" When they nodded, he wrote quickly in large, bold strokes. "Related to William Draper? That's a prominent name in Utah for sure."

Again father and son exchanged puzzled looks, then shrugged. "Not that we know of," David finally said. In the other offices, David had asked his questions, received the answers from clerks, then moved on to the next place. No one had so much as asked his name once they realized he was not ready to make a purchase.

"Where are you from?"

"Uh . . ." They had also determined that there would be no mention of Yorkshire, but again, no one before had asked.

"We be from Surrey," David's father said, "southeast of London."

"Good. And the town?"

"Battersea," David replied. They had taken his mother's name, why not her home, too?

"And when would you be interested in sailing?"

"As soon as possible," David said without hesitation.

The man looked up, a bit surprised. "Oh. All right." He wrote that down. He was suddenly awkward, almost embarrassed. "Uh . . . I don't know if you had heard this or not, but just this year, President Young has asked that all fares be paid in advance. In cash. That includes the train tickets and all other expenses. Would that be a problem?"

"President Young?" David asked, trying to keep up. "Is he president of the shipping company?" This was definitely not going like any of the other interviews.

Brother Miller gave them a long, strange look. "President *Brigham* Young."

"Oh," David said, trying to cover his bewilderment. "Of course, Brigham Young. Sorry."

"We 'ave cash," his father broke in.

A look of greater surprise, then a pleased smile. "Wonderful."

"'Ow mooch will it be?" Again from his father.

"Well, that depends a little on which sailing you choose." He pulled out a drawer and extracted a printed sheet and slid it toward them. David leaned forward. In large letters, the masthead read, *GUION LINE,* and in smaller letters, *"Steamers to New York—Royal and United States Mail."* There was an ink drawing of a flag as part of the masthead, and one of a large steamship just above the main body of text.

"We use the Guion Line exclusively now," the clerk explained, pronouncing it Gee-on. "They have some of the fastest steamers and they are very reliable." He too leaned forward, tapping the sheet with his index finger. "Look at this."

David read aloud to his father: "Fastest Passages. S.S. *Alaska*—six days, eighteen hours, thirty-seven minutes. S.S. *Arizona*—seven days, three hours, thirty-eight minutes."[1]

David was greatly pleased. "So it's true," he said. "It only takes a week to cross?"

"Yes." He pulled a face. "When my neighbors back in the States emigrated to America in eighteen forty-one, it took them eighty-seven days from Liverpool to Boston."

"You're not British, are you?" David asked.

"No, I was born in America, but my grandfather comes from Preston, up in Lancashire. He was thirteen when he came."

"David be thirteen t'morrow," his father said proudly. "What ya be doin' in England noow?"

"I'm here as a missionary."

David started at that, but then something else on the sheet caught his eye and he jerked forward, his heart dropping. "It says here that tickets are ten to twenty-five pounds. But—"

"Aw, pay no mind to that. This is just an advert printed by the news-paper for the shipping company. Those higher fares include a stateroom with private bath and full access to the ship's lounge. We take steerage class, down below decks. The berths are clean and healthy, but we don't pay for all that other stuff."

"So," his father asked again, "'ow much will it be?"

"Well," Miller said, still reluctant to answer the question before they had all the relevant information, "you have to understand something else. Unlike other companies, we have negotiated with Guion to provide suffi-cient food on the passage so you do not have to bring your own on board to supplement it."

Father and son exchanged glances. So that much was true. "And we heard it also includes help with getting the papers we need," David said.

"Yes, it does. Not only here, but to enter the United States as well. We've had a lot of experience in that and we make sure there are no com-plications."

"Fur the same price?" his father asked.

"Yes. And, remember, in our case, the fare also includes the entire trip to Salt Lake City—ship *and* train tickets, lodging in New York while you clear customs and immigration, all food and other expenses. And the cost for that is—"

He snapped his fingers. "Say, do you happen to be craftsmen of any kind? President Young has sent out a call for different kinds of craftsmen. If you are one of those on the list, the Perpetual Emigration Fund will pay for everything except the ship ticket. Once you're settled in Utah, then you pay back that part to the fund as you can."

David shot his father a warning look, but his father ignored it. "I'm a coal miner."

"Wonderful. That qualifies. We recently opened a coal mine east of Salt Lake City about forty miles. In a place called Coalville, appropriately enough."

"Salt Lake City?" David said. "Where is that? And what is Utah?"

That took Miller aback. "Utah Territory."

"Which is where from New York City?"

"You've never heard of Utah?" He was clearly shocked.

"No." David's father was also shaking his head.

Confused, Miller's eyes were now flicking back and forth between them. "It's out West. Not quite as far as California, but close."

"Okay, so 'ow much?" His father was clearly losing patience.

"Well, as I said, actual fare depends on which ship, but let's say you joined the group leaving a week from today. That would be the *S.S. Wisconsin*. Total cost from Liverpool to Salt Lake would be eleven pounds each, or about fifty to fifty-five American dollars."

"Eleven pounds!" David cried. "We were told you were less than the other companies."

"Remember, this is not just for the ocean passage. That includes everything from here to Salt Lake City, including the train ticket. Also remember, the eleven pounds is for you. For your father, it would be just five pounds for the ship ticket."

He mistook their astonishment for dismay and rushed on. "That's a real bargain. Especially knowing how many there are out there who will cheat you blind—make promises they can't fulfill, only pay for half of what you need on the crossing. Many of these unscrupulous agents will leave you high and dry in New York City. We do not do that. We take care of our own."[2]

David was torn. Something was amiss here, but he couldn't decide if this Mr. Miller was playing them for fools, or if he himself was missing something. He took a breath and leaned forward. "Just to make sure I understand: You're saying we can get passage from here all the way to this Utah for both me and my father, including all food and paperwork, for sixteen pounds?"

"That is correct. With the railroad clear across the United States completed now, we project that the total travel time will be about three to four weeks. One week for the crossing; one to two weeks to clear immigration, customs, and health inspections; and five to seven days on the railroad. All of that for sixteen pounds for the two of you. Once your father starts to work, he would then begin paying back the other portion of his ship fare."

David turned to his father. He wanted to jump up and down and shout, but he only said, "What do you think, Dahd?"

John's head bobbed quickly. "We wud lek two tickets. It be better than anythin' else we've found."

"Thank you, Brother Draper. That's exactly what I've been trying to say." He turned to David. "When you said you wanted to go as soon as possible, are you interested in booking on the *Wisconsin*, sailing on June twenty-first, then? We still have several berths available."

"Yes, definitely." David found himself getting a little irritated by all of this good cheer and self-promotion and Brother this and Brother that. And what about that certificate on the wall? How was a church involved in all of this? "What if we're not interested in Utah? Would it be just five pounds then to New York, with some extra for the other services?"

The man visibly blanched. "You're not interested in going to Utah?" And then he shot forward. "Are you Mormons?"

"Are we what?"

"Mormons. Members of The Church of Jesus Christ of Latter-day Saints."

Father and son looked at each other, completely baffled now.

Miller was incredulous. "So you haven't been baptized?"

When they slowly shook their heads, he rose to his feet. "I am so sorry, Mr. Draper. We are not a commercial shipping agent. We provide emigration services for members of our church. When you came in, I just assumed that . . . I am terribly embarrassed."

For a long moment, David's father said nothing. Then he got slowly to his feet. "It be awl reet, Mr. Miller. It be our mistake. But we still be interested in going." He shot David a hard look. "And that be all the way to Utah, too."

One hand came up to rub at his face. "I . . ." He blew out his breath. "I'm sorry, but we provide this service *only* to members of our faith."

"Oh."

The disappointment was like a kick in the stomach. David also stood, but very slowly. "Let's go, Dahd." A total of sixteen pounds to get them all the way out to the western part of America. That *was* remarkable. He had already started calculating what they could do with the rest of their money.

"Wait," Miller said, coming around the desk. "I mentioned that I'm a missionary for our Church. I work here in the office during the day, but I preach the gospel of Jesus Christ in the evenings. In fact we're having a meeting tonight at—"

"No!" David cut in sharply. "We have no interest in that."

Miller swallowed once, then let his eyes slip over to David's father. His head was down, and it was clear he was thinking about what Miller had said.

"It wouldn't be just to get passage, of course. We wouldn't want that. But the message we bring is wonderful. We have had tens of thousands of converts here in the British Isles, including my own family. If you just came and listened, then—"

"*No!*"

His father looked up. "Ya 'ave bin moost kind an' 'elpful. Thank ya, Mr. Miller."

"*Brother* Miller," the man broke in. "We call ourselves brother and sister because we believe that God is literally our Heavenly Father and . . ." He let it trail off. "Well, I apologize for the misunderstanding. I should have asked about that sooner."

He turned, took another piece of paper, and quickly scribbled an address on it. He blew on it, then handed it to David's father. "In case you change your mind. This is where we preach. Sunday services are tomorrow at ten. Tomorrow evening, I'll also be preaching a sermon on the plan of salvation as taught by Jesus Christ."

He handed it to John, then looked at David, who was glaring at him. "I'd recommend the Guion or the Black Ball Lines. They've both been crossing the Atlantic for decades now. Their fare is ten pounds, but they do include all food and provide some help with your papers. Go back to the docks, turn left, then take the first street on your left. They're both in there."

"Thank you." The mistake had been honest enough. "We appreciate that. Good day, Mr. Miller."

***

"Naw, David!" Now his father was getting angry. "Nuthin' ya can say will be changin' me mind. The answer is no."

"But Dahd! Think about it. Sixteen pounds to go all the way across America. That would leave us over fifty pounds. We could even buy some land for that."

"Aw," his father shot back, voice heavy with sarcasm, "so noow ya be awl excited aboot goin' ta Utah, eh?"

"I don't care where we go," David said, throwing up his hands. "If Utah is farther west, so much the better. Ole Man Rhodes would never reach us out there."

"An' ya wud become a Mormon fur that?"

David made a growling sound in his throat. "In name only. It doesn't hurt them. He was ready to give us our tickets. So we go to Utah. Say thank ya very much, and go our own way. What's the harm?"

"*No!* Ah naw be lyin' ta God just ta get cheaper tickets."

"Lying to God? Come on, Dahd." He spun away. "Who cares? It's just another religion."

"Yur muther wud be ashamed of ya, David Dickinson."

"Draper," he shot back. "And no she would not. You know how badly she wanted to go. And you know how long it took us to save seventy pounds. She would be the first to say do it."

"E'nuff!" he roared, making David jump. "Ya will naw be smearin' yur muther's name in that way. Joost b'cuz she didna go ta church doesn't mean she would mek a mockery of them."

"But Dahd."

"I mean it, David. Yur muther 'ad naw use fur organized religion. Thot they awl be a bunch of crooks, looking doon thare noses on people lek us.

She wud never, not in a 'undred years, join a church joost ta save a few poonds. She wud naw do it."

He raised a hand in warning, cutting off David's objections. "Ah'll naw be 'earin' anuther word, David. Naw anuther word."

⁂

They had been back in their room about half an hour, moving about in a strained silence. His father had wanted to go immediately to the Black Ball line and buy their tickets, but David refused. He said he was too tired. They would go back later this afternoon. His father knew exactly what David was doing, but he said nothing. Once they bought their tickets with Black Ball, it would be settled. There would be no changing his father's mind.

A sharp rap on the door sounded, startling them both. David turned, gave his father a questioning look, then called, "Who is it?"

"It's Mrs. O'Keefe, Mr. Draper," came the reply. "Beggin' yur pardon, sir, but Ah 'ave somethin' 'ere fur ya."

"Maybe some food left over from lunch," David whispered hopefully.

His father stood and went to the door. "What is it?" he started to say as he opened the door, but it was cut short in a gasp of astonishment.

Mrs. O'Keefe was already disappearing down the stairs. Standing at the door was Tom Cutler, constable from Cawthorne. He swept off his hat, grinning wickedly. "Well, well. Wud ya look at that. It be John Dickinson an' son. What a pleasant surprise."

⁂

Tom Cutler sat in a chair across from father and son. His legs were crossed and he twirled his cap in his hand. He was trying to appear relaxed and affable, but his upper body was tense, his eyes wary. He had opened his jacket so that the pistol in his belt was prominently displayed. "Ah be a reasonable man, John," he began.

"'Ow did ya find us?"

A triumphant smile spread across his face. "Patience. Rhodes sent four of us 'ere ta Liverpool, but the others tired after a couple of weeks, said ya be awreddy gone. But Ah thot better of ya than that, John. Ah figured ya wud tek yur sweet time gittin' 'ere. So Ah found me a cheap room, joost lek ya did, an' been broddlin'* aroond ever since."

"So ya saw us this mornin' an' followed us back."

"Ya got it, John. Figured ya'd be cumin' ta one of the shippin' lines sooner or later. Warn't naw problem ta follow ya 'ome." He was clearly quite pleased with himself.

"We're not going back," David said hotly.

"Go back?" He looked hurt. "Who sez yur goin' back?"

As father and son looked at each other, Cutler put his cap back on and sat up. The down-home country boy demeanor had vanished. "Okay, noow, let's see," he mused. "'Elp me r'member 'ow much thare wuz in the strongbox that night? Seventy poonds of yurs, an' a 'undred and sixty-five poonds of Rhodes's. That be a lot of muney, John. A lot of muney."

David rocked back. "What? We didn't—"

His father's hand shot out and clamped down hard on his knee, cutting off his words. His eyes never left Cutler's. "So that be Rhodes's game, eh? Moost be 'opin' the mine owners will cover 'is loss. Easy way ta double yur muney."

Cutler's eyes narrowed. "What ya be sayin'?"

"We never took a farthin' frum Rhodes's bag. Took only our own back."

The constable sat back, weighing that. "Be just lek 'im," he finally allowed. "'E be a reet rascal, shure 'nuff."

"Lek ya said, Tom," David's father said, his voice cold now. "Ain't no sense wastin' time. Ya be 'ere fur the purpose of extortion, so git ta it."

"Noow, John. No one, includin' me, be sayin' that what Rhodes did ta ya an' yur missus be awl reet. An' it was wrong fur 'im ta tek yur muney. But Ah can't change any of that. Ah've only got a couple of choices 'ere, way Ah see it. If Ah cum back *wit* the two of ya, Rhodes will naw only pay me the extra bonus 'e promised, 'e'll also pay me costs 'ere as well. On the

---

* To broddle means to poke around, dig out information.

other 'and, if Ah come back *wit'out* the two of ya, Ah ain't gonna git nothin'. Maybe even lose me job."

David's father said not a word, just watched the other man calmly.

Cutler was all business now. "'Ow mooch of that seventy-two poonds is left?"

"Only sixty," David said.

"More like sixty-five," his father answered. "'Ad to eat. An' then thare be the train tickets we 'ad ta pay."

There was a raucous laugh. "Ya done good on that one, John." He turned to David. "Yur pa 'ad us lookin' awl over London Town fur the two of ya. 'E be a real shrewd Tyke." Then back to his father. "So, if Ah were to tek, let's say, uh . . . awl but five poonds of that muney, Ah be willin' ta go back an' swear Ah cud naw find ya. That way, even if Ah dunna git paid, Ah wud cum oot awl reet, if'n ya know what Ah mean."

"Five pounds!" David shouted. "Are you daft?"

"Noow, dun't be gittin' radgy* on me, Davee boy. This be b'tween me an' yur pa."

John was sitting calmly, watching Tom as he spoke. Without looking at David, he asked, "Awl but five poonds, eh? Tell me, David, what wud that mek Tom's salary, considerin' 'e be oot 'ere fur nigh onto a month noow?"

David figured quickly. "Sixty pounds for four weeks would be fifteen pounds per week."

"An' ya mek 'ow mooch a week as constable, Tom? Five shillin's? Eight shillin's?" He didn't wait for an answer. "Them's purty rich wages, Tom."

"If'n Ah tek ya back, ya both be facin' leg irons. Ya know that shure as thare be black lung in the coal mines."

"And 'ow mooch of that wud ya 'ave to pay Bart Wiggins an' the other fellas?"

"Whaddya mean? Why pay 'em anythin'?"

John Draper got slowly to his feet. "'Cuz that be what it tek ta bring us back." He still spoke easily, almost lazily, as if he were contemplating

---

* Bad-tempered.

things very carefully. But the threat in his demeanor was unmistakable. "Thare be two of us, Tom, an' as ya can see, me boy 'ere, 'e be gittin' ta be a reet strappin' lad. Taller than me noow. 'Ow far da ya think ya'd get, tekin' us over thare by yurself?"

Tom got up quickly, his hand resting on the pistol butt. His eyes were nervous, darting back and forth between them. "It be only three days back ta Cawthorne."

"Can ya go three days wit'out sleep, Tom?"

"Ya be bluffin', John," he said, licking his lips. "Ya naw be that kind of a man."

"Ah ain't never bin pushed so hard inta a corner b'fur."

For a long time they both stood there, eyes locked. Then John spoke again. "Maybe thare be anuther option, Tom."

"What?"

"As long as Davee an' me be in England, we be in danger frum Rhodes. We be checkin' fares fur passage. That's what we be doin' this mornin'. Best we found so far be wit the Black Ball Line. But the fare be ten poonds each. Ya tek awl but five poonds, we be stuck 'ere. An' 'ow do we know ya dunna be tellin' Rhodes ya found us, soon as ya git back, so maybe 'e pay ya after awl, eh?"

He let Tom digest that a minute. "We gotta 'ave twenty poonds fur passage, Tom. And five poonds for expenses."

"Ten pounds," David blurted, seeing now where his father was going with this.

"Just twenty-five poonds, Tom." He flicked a glance in David's direction. "'Ow mooch that be leavin' 'im, David?"

David gritted his teeth. "Forty pounds."

"That still be the best wages ya ever made in yur life, Tom."

The constable licked his lips once more, then nodded. "Take oot twenty poonds, but nothin' more. Ya can work fur yur expense muney. An' Ah give ya me word that Ah'll naw be sayin' a word ta Rhodes aboot ya."

"No, Dahd," David cried. "We can't. It's not enough."

His father walked to the bed, lifted the mattress, and extracted a small leather purse. He tossed it to David. "Count out twenty poonds, Son. No more. No less. An' then Tom will be on 'is way."

⁂

David followed the constable down to the river. He turned east there, and David followed him for another mile. When he returned, his father had their belongings back in the sack and his cap on. As soon as David entered the room, he pointed to the window that led onto the roof. An hour later, they found a deserted warehouse by the wharf and had a place for the night.

They ate a simple meal in silence, still contemplating what had befallen them. After much internal debate, David cleared his throat. "You know what we have to do now, Dahd, don't you."

John's head was in his hands and he was staring at the floor.

"There's no choice. We can't spend all our money on tickets and leave ourselves with no expense money. And if we wait here until we earn more, Rhodes could be back."

"Ah dunna think Tom will tell 'im." It was spoken to the floor. His voice was devoid of life.

"This is stupid, Dahd. This time, you are wrong. This is what Mum lived for. This is what kept her alive for the last seven years. Who cares if we become Mormons or not. Certainly not Mum."

He moved about the large room, kicking at the debris as he passed. Finally, he sat down in one corner, putting his back against the wall. He lowered his head and began to massage his temples with his fingertips.

Almost ten minutes passed; then his father slowly got up. David raised his head to watch. But his father didn't look his way at all. He went to the bag and began rummaging around in it.

"What are you looking for, Dahd?" he said wearily. "There's no more food."

John shook his head, looking more forlorn than he had even on the night they had discovered the break-in and the missing box.

"What do you need?" David asked again.

"Do you have the directions to the meetin' Mr. Miller told us aboot?"

David leaped up, reaching in his shirt pocket. "I have them right here."

He felt light-headed. Dizzy with elation. His mind was racing. "We'll have to be careful, Dahd. We've got to convince them that we aren't just doing this to get passage. We're gonna have to act really sincere. Can you do that?"

"Can ya?" he shot right back.

"I can." He grinned. "In fact, I feel religion coming on right now."

His father whirled on him. "What did ya say?" His eyes were twin points of fire.

"I . . . sorry, Dahd. I know that this is difficult for you."

For a long, long time his father's eyes searched his. Then he shook his head. When he finally spoke, his voice was low and filled with sadness. "Wud ya know what be the most difficult thing fur me in awl this?"

"What?"

"That me own son be naw the slightest bit bothered by the terrible thing we be aboot ta do."

That hit him like a physical blow. "But Dahd, I . . ."

"Yur mum an' me dinna raise ya ta 'ave calluses on yur soul." He started to turn away, then swung back. Now his eyes were full of shame. "May God 'ave mercy on our souls fur this."

Notes

1. The Guion Shipping Line became the line of choice for the Latter-day Saint emigration efforts from Europe. Its ships transported more members of the Church to America than any other line. The figures on crossing times and fares come from an actual advertisement printed about 1886 (see Bloxham, Moss, and Porter, *Truth Will Prevail*, 187).

2. Conditions among dishonest and irresponsible shipping agents became so bad in the latter half of the nineteenth century that Parliament initiated investigations. Since the LDS Church—also known as the Mormons—was a major shipping agency, they too were investigated. An article in a Scottish newspaper summarized the committee's findings:

"It is the conclusion of the House Committee that no ships under the provisions of the 'Passengers Act' can be depended upon for comfort and security to the same degree as those under the administration of the Mormons. . . . The Mormon ship is a family under strong and accepted discipline, with every provision for comfort, decorum, and internal peace."

Thereafter, the British press reported that members of that House Committee expressed the opinion that Christian ship owners could learn much from the Latter-day Saints about "how to send poor people decently, cheaply, and healthfully across the Atlantic" (*ibid.*, 178).

CHAPTER 14

Thursday, July 22, 1869

Brother Daniel Miller's estimate of how long it would take the Drapers to travel to Utah was off by one week, but that was not his fault in any way. The S.S. *Wisconsin* left Liverpool on Monday, June twenty-first, and arrived in Boston six days, twenty-two hours, and sixteen minutes later. Another Mormon shipping agent met them as they disembarked. He had all of the necessary paperwork and marched them through U.S. Immigration Services in one day. Since each of the Drapers carried only one small case of personal belongings, almost all of which was clothing, the Customs Office cleared them in two days and sent them on for health inspections.

It was there that they hit the snag—or, more accurately, stepped off a cliff. When the officials learned that both John and David had worked in the coal mines, they were slapped into quarantine for black lung disease. When his father argued long and loud that the doctors in Yorkshire said that the disease was not contagious, the answer to that was a condescending, "Of course, that's what everyone says." When local doctors agreed that it was not, the officials quickly adjusted: The weakening of the lungs from the coal dust made one more susceptible to diphtheria, which *was* highly contagious and a deadly killer. Therefore, the Drapers had to stay in quarantine.

And so for the next two weeks they underwent tests, endured examinations, filled out a hundred forms, answered ten thousand questions—many of them the same ones over and over, and most of them totally unrelated to anything to do with the Drapers. And they waited.

To David's astonishment, the Mormon shipping agent in Boston didn't abandon them. Ten days following their arrival, all their fellow passengers on the ship were gone, on their way to Utah, but someone from the Church came two or three times a week. Even though these agents were not allowed into the quarantine center, they always left notes, reading material, and small baskets of fruit, breads, cheeses, and sweetmeats.

Finally, on July sixteenth, John and David were given their clearance papers and released. Two days later, the agent had them on the train headed west.

Thus it was that six days later, the evening of July twenty-second, 1869, two months and five days after fleeing Cawthorne, John Dickinson Draper and David Dickinson Draper stepped off the train at Union Station, Ogden City, Utah Territory. Black with smoke and soot, stiff and sore from sitting and sleeping on hard wooden benches, stomachs aching with hunger, and tired beyond imagination, they stood on the platform, heads turning right and left to take in their surroundings. Then father looked at son, weary grins split their grimy faces, and they fell on each other's shoulders and began pounding each other on the back.

"Excuse me."

They turned, embarrassed to have been caught in their exuberance. A young man in cowboy boots, denim pants, and with his cowboy hat in his hand was standing just behind them on the platform. "Are you Brother Draper and his boy?"

"Yah. We be them," John said, straightening and removing his cap.

"I'm Brother Walter Griffeths, Jr.—but everyone calls me Walt. Me and my father and some others have been sent up by Brigham Young to bring emigrants down to Salt Lake City. We got a telegram earlier today saying you two would be coming in on the late train, and that we should take you with us as well. If it's all right with you, we have a place for you to stay tonight. Then we'll leave in the morning."

His father turned to David, trying to suppress a smile, but then he chortled aloud. "What d'ya think, Son? Wud that be awl reet wit us?"

David grinned at Walter Griffeths, Jr. "I think it would."

Friday, July 23, 1869

Next morning, when they arrived at the train station, their designated gathering place, it was 5:00 A.M. The sun was not yet above what looked like a great black wall to the east of them. Outside the station, there were four covered wagons and three long carriages parked side by side. Each was pulled by three span of mules. The men with the wagons had already loaded all but a few pieces of the personal belongings of the emigrants when David and his father arrived. Walt was not there, but they met his father, Walter Griffeths, Sr. He was a large, jovial man with thick, mutton-chop whiskers and a flat Bostonian accent.

There were twelve or fourteen others already there—families, mostly—and others kept streaming in until there were nearly three dozen in all. There were too many for the carriages, so those with families were assigned there, and those without children, like the Drapers, were assigned to ride with the wagons.

The senior Griffeths waved for everyone to gather around him. "All right, folks. We know you're anxious to get this journey over with, so let's get you loaded up and on your way. It's about thirty-five miles to Salt Lake City, and, barring any breakdowns, we hope to be there by sundown. On your arrival, there will be a committee to meet you. All of you will be staying with families in Salt Lake for the next few days, while the Church gets things arranged for you. Most of you, as you know, will not be staying in Salt Lake, but will be going out to the settlements. Normally, you should be on your way by about next Tuesday or Wednesday."

There was a murmur of excitement at that news. John looked at David. "Ah dinna think we be able ta be settled quite that fast. That be wonderful."

"We welcome you to Utah," Griffeths continued. "We know that many of you have come a great distance, even across the ocean in some cases, to join with the Saints. Actually, you have arrived at a very special time. Today is July twenty-third." Murmurs of acknowledgment and even a few exclamations were heard from among the group. David and his father exchanged looks, not sure what they had just missed. There was still so much they had to learn.

"That means that you will be in Salt Lake City tomorrow for what we call Pioneer Day. It was twenty-two years ago tomorrow that Brigham Young looked out over the Salt Lake Valley and declared, 'This is the right place. Drive on.' That was the beginning of finally finding our home in the Valley. It's a big celebration—a parade, speeches, potluck dinners, fireworks—and you'll be privileged to be part of it. Very few get that opportunity on their first day in the Valley."

"How many are there in the Valley now?" a man called out.

"Twelve thousand in Salt Lake City alone, probably another couple of thousand scattered around the Salt Lake Valley. But about seventy thousand of us have come to Zion in those twenty-two years. And there are about twenty thousand more still back in their home states or countries, many waiting to come to the west just as you have."

That stunned David. Ninety thousand! He had been picturing the Church as a little sect with a few thousand members at best. David raised a hand. "So how many settlements are there, and are they all right around Salt Lake City?"

That brought a rich chuckle from Griffeths and the other drivers. "Not quite, my boy," came the answer. "There are about three hundred settlements now, branching out in all directions, some as far away as four hundred miles. Anywhere there's water and good farm or grazing land, you'll find a settlement of Mormons."

Now there was much excitement in the group. It appeared that most, like David and his father, knew they wouldn't be staying in Salt Lake—but four hundred miles? This was a shock.

"Well, that's enough for now. Let's have a prayer and get under way. Once again, brothers and sisters, welcome to Utah. We hope that very soon you will feel like this is home."

When the brief prayer was concluded, John and David turned, not sure where they should go. Then they heard a voice call out, "Mornin'."

They turned. Walt, Jr., was coming toward them. "You're riding with me, if that's all right."

"Tup of the mornin' ta ya, Tommy me boy," John said, adding a touch of Irish to his already broad Yorkshire accent. "We'd be reet capped ta be goin' on doon the road wit ya."

Walt just looked at him, a bewildered expression on his face. David laughed. "My father says we would be delighted to ride with you."

It was the mountains that were the most astonishing thing to the Drapers. For three days they had traveled across the Great Plains—so flat that, as one of the train's conductors had quipped, you could see a rabbit coming three days in advance. Yesterday, they had come across from Laramie, Wyoming. Except for some mountains in the distance, the land on both sides of the tracks was flat, barren, and desolate, stretching off in every direction for as far as the eye could see. About the time when they had finally reached the mountains yesterday evening, it had been dark and they had seen nothing but looming shapes rushing by.

Now, in the full sunshine of a hot summer morning, both David and his father were astounded. To their left, stretching north and south as far as they could see, was a wall of mountains. They seemed almost to leap from the valley floor. Skirted around the bottom by golden-brown foothills, those quickly gave way to steep, green-clad slopes and towering peaks. Against the backdrop of a crystal clear, brilliantly blue sky, it was a majestic sight.

Young Walt clearly enjoyed their reaction. "We call 'em the Wasatch Mountains. Name comes from a Ute Indian word meaning 'mountain pass.' They stretch about a hundred and fifty miles from north to south, and some of them top twelve thousand feet in elevation."

David just shook his head. Unbelievable. But then, North America was unbelievable. For example, they had traveled two thousand miles without ever seeing the ocean. Yesterday, they had traveled for hours without seeing a single human settlement. It was quite the land. Here, the valley floor along which they were traveling was over four thousand feet high, according to Walt, who was very much enjoying the role of tour guide. When David remembered that the highest point in all of England was a peak just over three thousand feet in elevation, it boggled his mind.

His father stirred beside him. "Ah be reet speechless, young Walt. Ah heard thare be mountains like this in the wurld, but Ah never dreamed Ah'd ever git ta see 'em."

Friday, July 30, 1869

As it turned out, David and his father not only got to see this magnificent range of mountains, they got to live right in the heart of them.

It took them about twelve hours to get to Salt Lake that first day, and then began a whirlwind of activities. They were housed with a family from South Wales who had been in the Valley for ten years now. The next day, Pioneer Day, turned out to be everything Walt Griffeths had promised and more—a parade that made David feel like a little boy again, fireworks, picnics.

The next day was the Sabbath, and they gathered into a building that just about left David speechless. They called it the Tabernacle, and it was something to behold. The roof was an elongated dome, somewhat resembling half an eggshell, and inside the building's cavernous interior there were benches enough to sit six thousand people. Because of the unique design of the roof, not a single pillar blocked anyone's view.[1] And Brigham Young himself came and spoke to the new arrivals, warmly welcoming them to Zion. That was a term they were hearing with increasing frequency, but it seemed to be used as though it meant they were finally Home—with a capital H.

To his considerable surprise, David liked President Young. He was somewhat portly, shorter than David had imagined him to be, and was now approaching seventy years of age, but he was funny and friendly. He gave an especially warm welcome to those from the British Isles and briefly talked about his years there with the other Apostles—another new vocabulary word—in 1840 and '41. Afterward, he stood at the door and shook hands with the immigrants. When he heard John's accent, his eyes began to twinkle. Then he lapsed into a perfect imitation of an East London cockney accent, which delighted everyone around him.

Monday began their orientation. David wasn't comfortable with how religion kept creeping into almost every conversation, but the people were nice enough. There was no question about them being helpful and trying to get the Drapers on their way. By the time they went to bed that next Wednesday evening—their last night in the Valley—David had decided he and his father had also come to the right place. Their journey was over at last. Jonathan Rhodes and the Cawthorne Pit were somewhere far away in both time and distance. David and John Dickinson were no more. The Drapers had come to America in fulfillment of his mother's dream. It filled him with a deep sadness whenever he thought how she would have loved to have been part of this, but her years of planning and saving and fighting back the disease within her had finally come to fruition.

⚜

And so they had come to Coalville. They traveled to Ogden by carriage, stayed overnight there in a boardinghouse, then caught the east-bound train into Weber (pronounced Wee-bur, everyone told them) Canyon. Disembarking at Henefer, at the mouth of yet another canyon, they transferred by stagecoach and made the final hour-long, jolting, dusty ride to Coalville.

It was even more beautiful than Weber Canyon. Nestled between verdant mountains on either sides, hay fields and lush meadows surrounded the settlement. This was more like England—green, pleasantly cool, with high, puffy clouds constantly appearing from behind the western mountains. The Weber River ran along the west side of the valley, sparkling in the sunshine. Their coach driver regaled them with tales of fishing for trout in the river and streams, and hunting for deer, elk, and an occasional antelope to provide meat for their table.

As the coach pulled away, David's father turned slowly, taking it all in. Then he sighed contentedly. "Ah, David," he finally said, "Ah ne'er thought Ah'd be findin' a place as purty as Yorkshur, but Ah think Ah be content ta call this our new 'ome."

Before David could answer that, they saw a couple hurrying toward them. The man and woman were both dressed in Sunday best, even though it was a weekday. "Are you the Drapers?" the man called even before he reached them.

"That be reet," his father answered.

"I'm Bishop Wright, bishop here in Coalville. Welcome. If you would like to come with us, Sister Wright has some lunch for you, and then we'll take you to the mine and sign you up." As they turned for their luggage, the bishop waved them off. "My son's on his way with a small cart. He'll take your things to your home, then join us for lunch."

"We have a home?" David blurted.

Sister Wright laughed. It was a pleasant, welcoming sound. "Of course. It's not much. Just three rooms. No indoor plumbing yet, but there's a well just out back."

"We 'ave our own well?" his father said, awestruck.

"You do indeed," the bishop laughed. "That's one thing about Coalville. The winters take some getting used to, but there is water aplenty." He turned to David. "And you're David, right? How old are you?"

"Thirteen."

"Did you work in the mines over in England as well as your father?"

"Yes, as a trapper, hurrier, and spragger."

None of those terms seemed to mean anything to the man. "So, are you looking for work in our mines too?"

"Yes," David replied.

"NO!" his father burst out at the same moment.

As David stared at him, his father quickly explained. "He didn't actually work as a collier, usin' pick an' shovel ta git oot the coal. Only as a helper." He turned to Sister Wright. "Do ya 'ave a skoo-ul 'ere in Coalville? David ain't ne'er been ta skoo-ul."

"Dad!" David cried, "I don't want to go to school. I can already read and write. We need to earn money." He looked at the bishop. "Yes, I am hoping to work in the mines."

His father stepped between them, looking earnestly into the bishop's face. "Ah made a promise ta 'is mum, who passed away in May of this year, that Ah wud naw be lettin' me boy ever wurk in the mines agin. Ah canna go back on me wurd."

"I understand," the bishop said, slowly nodding.

"We do have a school here," his wife broke in, looking at David with new interest. "If you didn't ever go to school, how did you learn to read and write?"

"Me Mum taught me," he said. "I really don't need more school."

"We have a wonderful teacher. I think you'll find she has much to teach you."

"Then it's settled," his father cut in before David could protest. "David will be goin' ta the skoo-ul, and Ah be workin' in the mines." He glowered at David, daring him to contradict him. "An' that be that."

David stood his ground. "I'll do what you say, Dahd. But only until I turn sixteen. Then I'm going to find me a real job and earn some money."

His father looked at him for a long time, a sadness in his eyes. "Ya got a real 'unger in ya, don't ya, Son." Then he made up his mind. "Awl reet. If ya stay until ya be sixteen, Ah'll naw be tryin' ta stop ya after that."

Thursday, June 13, 1872

David awoke early on the morning of his sixteenth birthday. His father had gone to work an hour before, and with school over for the summer, he lay in bed, indulging himself with a brief spell of sheer laziness. As he lay there, his mind went back ten years. He remembered very clearly waking up that morning on his sixth birthday and what a special day that had been. That was the day he and his mother had gone to Barnsley and spent the day, and coming home he had learned that he would start working in the mines the following Monday. How thrilled he had been with that news. How far away that time and that life seemed now.

While he had chafed somewhat these last three years with his confinement in Coalville, David had to admit that they had been good years. His father's experience quickly moved him up to foreman in the mines, and he was able to pay back his debt to the Church. And though David was the second-oldest student in the school, and sometimes felt awkward with the younger children, he had thrived on it. Mrs. MacArthur, a newly married convert from Scotland whose husband worked in the mines with David's father, was a wonderful teacher. In some ways she reminded David of his mother. She had the same deep love of learning, but she especially enjoyed challenging the thinking of her students by throwing questions or problems at them, then critically analyzing their responses. Just as his mother had become the favorite of Reverend Pike when she was a girl, so David had become Mrs. MacArthur's favorite student. She had rekindled his curiosity about life and his insatiable love of learning.

Pleased that he wasn't fighting him about school, his father arranged for David to work in the pit yard after school and on Saturdays. During the summers he became a shoveler, riding the coal wagons down to various settlements not served by the railroad, where he helped unload the wagons. Not only had this provided a good supplement to their income, but David loved being on the road and seeing new places. By the time he was fifteen, he was a teamster, driving the teams himself, with a shoveler of his own to help him.

Gradually, David found himself assimilating into the religious and social life of Coalville. He went to church every Sunday with his father. He found himself terribly bored in some meetings, and faintly interested in others. He quickly learned to suppress his troublesome questions about God and prayer because they always brought deep creases to the foreheads of his teachers or a counseling session with the kind and wise Bishop Wright. He became adept at putting forth a pleasant and conforming facade.

And that was all right. If he was not converted by all of it, at least he was comfortable. On the other hand, his father was totally involved, accepting calls to serve, always volunteering for this need or that, and making some deep and lasting friendships. David couldn't help but wonder how much of John's "conversion" was driven by his guilt for joining the Church under false pretenses, but David never said anything to him. His father was happy. And, if he were to be completely honest with himself, so was David.

But it was time. He was sixteen. Coalville, lovely and charming as it was, was too confining. It was time to spread his wings and fly on his own.

✳

In the three years since they had come, the railroad had run a spur up from Henefer to service the mines in Park City, a few miles to the southwest. David and his father stood near the stagecoach stop, now serving as the train station as well.

"Thare be nothin' Ah cud say that be changin' yur mind?"

David shook his head slowly. "No, Dad. And this has nothing to do with you. You were right. It was a good thing that I stayed in school. And I have loved being with you these three years. But there's better money out there." He waved his hand in the general direction of the west. "I don't know yet what I want to do with my life, but I know this. It will take money, and I've got none of my own. I'm a man now. It's time I stopped living off my father."

His father said nothing.

"They're laying railroad lines everywhere, and telegraph lines into Southern Utah. And they're paying good money for horse wranglers and teamsters in Wyoming Territory."

John's face fell. "An' when will Ah ever see ya?"

"I promise I'll come up at least twice a year. Since you're going to conference in Salt Lake now, what if I meet you there each April and October?"

That had not been expected and it pleased his father. "Ya promise?"

"I do, Dad. You know how much I love you. I'm hardly gonna be forgetting you."

His father drew in a deep breath and let it out slowly. Then he stepped back and eyed David up and down. "Ya be reet, David. Ya be a man now, an' a strappin' one at that. Ah guess thare be naw way Ah be wrestlin' ya ta the groond an' holdin' ya 'ere, eh?"

David laughed, stepped forward, and put his arms around his father. "I love you, Dad. I'll write as soon as I light somewhere." He put his cheek against John's, feeling the roughness of his whiskers.

"Ya tek care of yurself noow," came the gruff reply. "Ya 'ear?"

Note

1. The Salt Lake Tabernacle was constructed between 1864 and 1867. The first conference was held in it in 1867. At the time represented in this chapter, the balcony, which is part of the Tabernacle today, had not yet been added. That came in 1870 and increased the capacity of the building to 7,000-plus.

BOOK II

SETTING

1873–1874

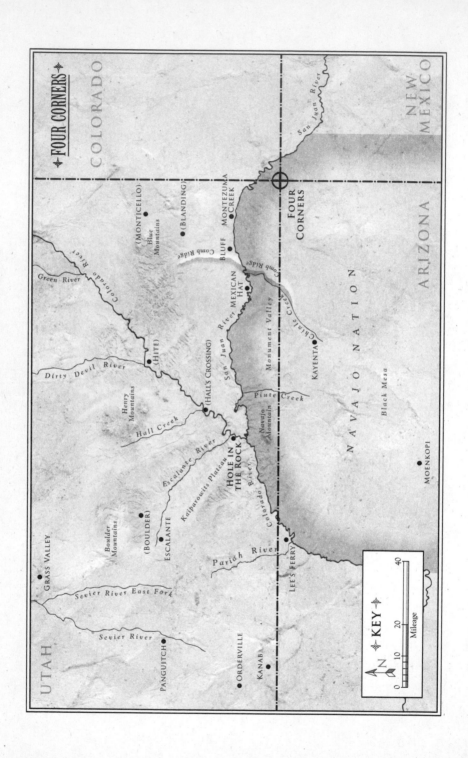

CHAPTER 15

December, 1873

In man's feeble efforts to draw borders and put his own stamp on the landscape of the world, natural features are often ignored and lines are drawn based on the invisible markers called latitude and longitude. Such man-made borders were laid down in an area of North America that is one of the most desolate, forbidding, and unrelentingly harsh places on the continent. As Congress carved up the West, defining various states and territories, a unique thing happened. The state of Colorado and the territories of Utah, Arizona, and New Mexico came together at a single point on the map. It is the only place in North America where four entities share a common point. Not surprisingly, it came to be known as the "Four Corners" area.

For centuries the Four Corners area had been a staging ground for war. Three major groups of Native Americans—the Utes, the Paiutes, and the Navajos—had raided each other's herds and flocks for longer than even the wisest sage could remember.

When the white man, including a flood of Mormons, came into the Great Basin, the Indians acquired a new competitor and a new enemy. And a rich one. The largest of the tribes was the Navajos, or the *Diné—the people*—as they called themselves. For centuries, the Navajos had crossed the Colorado and San Juan Rivers to raid the Utes and Paiutes. Now they had a more lucrative temptation.

Finally, in 1863, the U.S. government had had enough. Six thousand Navajos were rounded up and marched 250 miles east to Fort Sumner on the Pecos River. When the Navajos returned from their "Long Walk," they were so destitute that they began raiding across the rivers again, hitting Mormon settlements especially hard. In one year alone, over 1,200 head of cattle were driven south across the rivers. Even the Mormons, whose policy was to befriend the Indians, decided they could not tolerate this. The resulting conflict came to be known as the Navajo War, and, as 1870 began, it raged along the borders of Utah and Arizona. Finally, thanks to the astonishing influence of two key individuals—the nationally famous explorer Major John Wesley Powell and a Mormon missionary from southern Utah by the name of Jacob Hamblin—a treaty of peace was negotiated. By the end of 1872 and the beginning of 1873, southern Utah was entering a time of unprecedented peace and prosperity for both Indians and whites.[1]

On a day late in December of 1873, four young Navajo braves were caught in a full winter blizzard in Grass Valley along the Sevier River. These four young men were from the Kacheenay-begay clan, who lived deep within the heart of the Navajo Reservation. Two were sons of Kacheenay himself, the clan chief. They had come north almost a month before to trade with the Mormons and the Utes along the Sevier River Valley. They were anxious to return to the reservation and report on their great success. In addition to the extra horses, they were bringing back buffalo robes, saddles, bridles, several bows and quivers of arrows, and a rifle. Because they had not planned to stay so long, what they were not carrying was extra food. They were down to a few pieces of jerky and a small pouch of corn.

Holing up in a deserted line cabin used by cowboys in the summer grazing season, they waited out the storm. To their amazement, a day or two later, several cows and a young heifer wandered up to their door. Seeing this as a gift from the Holy People, their sacred ancestors, and desperate for food, they killed the heifer. Knowing they were in the country of the "Mormons," whose policy was to feed the Indians rather than fight them, they believed that the owner of the cow would not mind, especially if he knew of their circumstances and if they paid him for it, which they were prepared to do. Unfortunately, the line cabin they found and the heifer they killed did not belong to the Mormons at all.

✦

Frank McCartey, like several other ranchers who had come to this area because of the rich grazing, was not a Mormon. In fact, he took great pride in making it clear to anyone who would listen that he was not one of those—then would follow a stream of profanity—Indian-hugging, pulpit-pounding Mormons. McCartey ran cattle in Grass Valley. He and his cowhands had an unsavory reputation among their few neighbors. There were rumors of their willingness to solve problems through violent means, and even of an occasional foray out of the valley as cattle rustlers and highwaymen.

Ugly of temper, quick to take offense, and meaner than a wolverine, there could not have been a worse man to receive the news that a bunch of "them filthy Indians" was butchering McCartey cattle up at the cow cabin in Grass Valley.

✦

The following morning, the Navajos were packing up. They each had a week's worth of smoked meat in their packs now. What they hadn't stripped from the hind quarter, they had taken outside and hung with the rest of the animal. It was time to saddle the horses and start for home.

"Hey! You there in the house."

Four heads snapped up. They didn't understand the words, but they understood the tone. The voice was harsh, flat, angry. The Navajos' leader went to the shutters and pushed them open enough to look out. There were five riders, heavily bundled against the cold. He could see the path their horses had made through the deep snow, and where they had crossed the creek on the ice. They were only about fifty yards away. He also saw that all five had rifles out and laid across their saddles. "The *belagana* are here," he said. "Five of them."

His brother snatched up the rifle and brought it to him. He hesitated, then shook his head. He fingered the leather pouch tied to his belt, making the coins inside jingle softly. "It is all right," he said nervously. "I shall speak to them. Offer them money." The other three, all with bows and arrows notched in the strings, were clearly frightened. They weren't so sure that was the best thing right now. "It is all right," he said again. He opened the door, took a deep breath, then stepped out, keeping his hands in plain sight.

The first bullet caught him high in the shoulder, jerking him violently around. The second hit him squarely in the back as he started to fall. He was dead before he plowed into the snow.

His brother screamed and leaped for the door.

"No!" one of the cousins shouted, diving to intercept him. Too late. The young boy was through the door and on his knees beside his brother. Another shot. The bullet hit him in the chest and flung him backwards into the snow. His legs jerked spasmodically for a moment or two; then he was still.

"Get down! Get down!" the cousin screamed at his companion, who had fallen back and was standing by the fireplace, bow drawn, looking around wildly. He grabbed the rifle, frantically trying to lever a shell into the chamber. There was a sharp crack, and a bullet splintered the thin wood of the shutters. Instinctively, he dropped to the floor. Then he heard a moan. He turned and saw his cousin on the floor, face white, back against the stones of the fireplace, a red stain spreading high up on his shoulder.

The older Navajo grabbed a piece of woolen cloth from one of the packs, scrambled across the floor, and stuffed the cloth up under the buckskin hunting shirt of his cousin. He pointed to the window opposite from where they were. "I will draw the *belagana* off. Go out the window. Don't let them see you."

"No!"

"Run!" He gave him a hard shove, ignoring the scream of pain. "Go!"

As his companion opened the shutters and heaved himself out the window, the Navajo grabbed the rifle and flung himself out the door. Firing blindly in the direction of the riders, he crouched low and ran like the wind. He dove left and felt a bullet whip past his face. He heard the crack of the gunshot an instant later. He scrambled behind a cottonwood tree and stood up, drawing in huge gulps of air. He risked a peek. The men were shouting now as they fired. Bullets whined past or thudded into the thick bark. As the *belagana* spurred their horses forward, he held the rifle out with one hand, fired off another round, then took off, running hard, dodging back and forth between the trees.

To his left, the trees ended and the ground started to rise toward a low ridge about forty yards away. If he could draw them over that, the cabin wouldn't be visible to them. He sprinted away, slipping and sliding in the snow. He didn't turn. He didn't need to. He could hear the thunder of hooves behind him. Twice they fired at him, but there was no way they could hit him while they were riding and he was running.

He crested the hill and dropped down the other side. He had made it. But what stretched out before him now was a quarter of a mile of nothing but open country. Zigzagging wildly, taking great leaps to push his way through the deep snow, his lungs on fire, he ran as he had never run before, all the time praying that the Holy Ones would give him enough strength to draw the *belagana* after him.

A searing pain in his back knocked him rolling. He bounced once, then slid for eight or ten feet, facedown in the snow. His mind commanded him to get up, to run. Another voice told him to play dead. Then he remembered his cousin. With a gasp, he pushed himself up with his hands. It was no use. His body refused to obey what his mind told him to do, and he fell again.

He heard the horses come pounding up behind him, heard the triumphant shout from one of the men. For a moment, he thought they might run over him, trample him. But they stopped. The horses were snorting and blowing, just feet away now. One of the men grunted something that he didn't understand. This was followed by the sound of a shell being levered into the chamber of a rifle. He closed his eyes, calling on the Holy People to protect his cousin.[2]

Notes

1. The brief summary of the history of this time period and the ensuing Navajo War is drawn from several sources (Miller, *Hole*, 8–9; Hamblin, *Journals and Letters*, 45–91; Lyman, "Fort, Parts I and II," 688–89, 719–20).

2. Hamblin, Lyman, and Corbett all give accounts of the tragedy in Grass Valley (Hamblin, *Journals and Letters*, 99–114; Lyman, "Fort"; Corbett, *Jacob Hamblin*, 343–44). Other sources recount it as well (see Brooks, "Jacob Hamblin," 254; Kumen Jones, "Navajo Peace," 214–15). We know what the Navajos had with them from a letter later written to McCartey by Jacob Hamblin demanding that he return those goods to the families of the Navajos or make appropriate payment to satisfy them (in Corbett, *Jacob Hamblin*, 343, 367–68). Kumen Jones mentions "McCartey brothers," but all other sources refer to only one McCartey. No first name is given, so "Frank" is my addition.

CHAPTER 16

Saturday, January 17, 1874

Jacob Hamblin was in the barn, pitching hay into the mangers for his three milk cows and two horses. It was going to be a beautiful winter day in Utah's Dixie. The sun was not quite up yet, but the sky was a brilliant blue, the air was pleasantly warm, and when he finished here, he planned to spend the rest of the day preparing his garden for spring planting.

His head came up as he heard the clatter of hooves on the dirt track that rose from the wagon road down below. He pitched one last forkful into the manger, stuck the pitchfork in the hay, then climbed down and walked outside. Two horsemen swept into view, coming at a full gallop, kicking up dust behind them. He squinted, then started in surprise. John D. Lee?

He removed his hat, wiped at his forehead with the sleeve of his shirt, then replaced the hat as the horsemen swept into the yard, pulled up short, and dismounted.

"John?" Jacob said, going to meet them. "This is a surprise."

John tied the reins to the hitching post and came forward, extending his hand. "Hello, Jacob." He turned and pointed to his companion, a younger version of himself. "Have you met my son, Benjamin?"

They too shook hands, then Jacob turned back to his friend. "What in the world brings you to Kanab?" Lee's Ferry, on the Colorado River, was fifty miles to the southeast.

The horseman shook his head, a shadow darkening his eyes. "We rode all night. There's trouble, Jacob. Big trouble."

Jacob sat on the ground, his back against a cedar tree, slowly massaging his temples to ease the throbbing. He looked up to where father and son were drinking deeply from gourds that hung over the well. "We had heard that three Indians were killed up in Grass Valley by a white man by the name of McCartey," he said. "But he's not a Mormon. It was supposedly over a stolen cow." He blew out his breath in a long sound of discouragement. "I just assumed they were Utes. That's Ute country that far north. Now you're telling me they were Navajos?"

"Yes. And it gets worse. All of them were of the Kacheenay-begay clan."

Jacob visibly winced. "Ah, John. This is not good."

"Two of them were his sons."

There was an audible groan. "I stayed in the hogan of Kacheenay some years ago. I probably met them."

"I'm not finished, Jacob," Lee said gravely.

He grimaced. "There's more?"

Lee nodded and continued, "There weren't three Navajos in Grass Valley. There were four."

"What?"

"The fourth one was wounded but got away. Don't ask me how, but he managed to stanch his wound and make his way back in the dead of winter over more than a hundred miles of wild country. Took him almost two weeks. He arrived at Kacheenay's camp a few days ago. And here's the story he's telling his clan brothers. According to him, the four of them were caught in a blizzard and holed up in a cow cabin in the valley. They were out of food, so they caught a calf and butchered it."

"Oh dear Lord," Jacob breathed. "One of McCartey's cows."

Again there was a curt nod. "They thought it was a Mormon cow. They believed the Mormons would understand their need. The boy said they had money and planned to pay for it."

"So they think it was us who did it?" His head dropped back in his hands.

"The boy said they weren't given a chance to explain. The chief's oldest son was shot down like a dog when he stepped outside with his hands in the air." He waited for a response, but Jacob was in too much pain to say anything.

"The Kacheenay clan are out for blood and crying for revenge. The chief has sent runners out across the reservation calling for war. One of those who was called is friendly to me and my family. He figured the ferry was the closest Mormon settlement and I needed to be warned. He thinks we are in grave danger. And not just at the ferry. All the settlements."

That galvanized Jacob at last. He got up, pushing back the weariness. "All of our work, two years of peace, shattered in one instant by wicked, terrible men. We'll have to warn the settlements. I'll send a wire to President Young right away."

"That's fine," Lee said, "but Jacob, you have to come as soon as you can. You're the only one who can reason with the Indians. There are two miners at the ferry. They said they'd stay with my family until Benjamin and I can return. They said they'll go with you."

He acknowledged that with a nod. "I'm going to the telegraph office. I'll also send some of the Paiutes here in town as runners to spread the word." He stopped for a moment, a scowl darkening his face. "And I'd better send someone to Grass Valley. We have to know if Mormons were involved." He blew out his breath. This was a bitter blow. "Come, we'll get you some food. Then you get back to your family, John. I'll get there as soon as I can."

As the two men started toward the house, Jacob spoke very quietly. "I will be blamed for it. I was the one who promised them the Mormons would live in peace with them. I was the one who told them that peace was the best way."

Tuesday, January 27, 1874

In spite of the urgency, it was ten days before Jacob Hamblin reached Lee's Ferry. Much of that time was spent waiting for two things— confirmation that Mormons had not been involved, and further instructions

from President Brigham Young. Those instructions came in the form of a
telegram:

> JACOB STOP CRITICAL YOU VISIT NAVAJOS STOP ONLY
> ONE THEY TRUST STOP GO AS SOON AS PRACTICAL
> STOP TELL THEM MORMONS NOT INVOLVED AT GRASS
> VALLEY STOP THE LORD BE WITH YOU STOP BRIGHAM
> YOUNG.[1]

Jacob left the following morning.

Friday, January 30, 1874

Hamblin stopped at the ferry only long enough to take some refresh-
ment. The two miners, brothers by the name of Smith—neither of them
Mormons—were still there, as promised. And in spite of Jacob's warnings
about endangering themselves, they insisted on accompanying him. They
had a fresh horse for him and put a pistol, holster, and belt in his saddlebags. Jacob objected to that as well—he had never worn a gun among the
Indians—but once again they insisted, and, once again, he agreed.

As they traveled east into the land of the Navajos, they found growing evidence of possible war. The Hopis, or Moquis, as the Navajos called
them, who were a peaceful people, fled eastward to escape being caught
up in it. Fifteen miles east of Moenkopi,* they saw a lone rider approaching. He turned out to be a Paiute, sent by the Navajo chiefs to meet
Hamblin.

The Smith brothers were shocked that the clan already knew that
Hamblin was on their land and coming to them. Jacob was not surprised
at all. "How far?" was all he asked.

It was close to a full day's ride, and it was nearly dark when they arrived at a "village" on Black Mesa. There were only two hogans, but quite

---

* Near present-day Tuba City, Arizona.

a few cattle, horses, and sheep were gathered in corrals nearby. The dogs started barking while the men were still half a mile away and went into a frenzy when they arrived—barking, howling, darting in to nip at the horses' legs.

About a dozen Indians milled around. At the sight of Hamblin, an outcry went up. They jeered at the three white men in open contempt. But then grey-heads came out of the bigger hogan, and Jacob felt great relief. These had to be some of the chiefs. That was good. He had been afraid he would have to deal strictly with a group of young, hot-blooded warriors.

Their Paiute guide whispered that this was the hogan of Kacheenay himself and that the other was the hogan of Po-ee-kon, Kacheenay's son. However, neither of them were here at present. They had gone to fetch more braves for the council.

Jacob only nodded, but he felt the chill go into his bones. They were in the very place from which the murdered young braves had left on their trading mission.

As the three swung stiffly out of the saddle and began to stomp their feet to get the circulation going again, Jacob spoke in low tones to his companions. "Remember, don't speak to a Navajo unless he speaks to you first. And keep your hands well away from your guns."

Saturday, January 31, 1874

As it turned out, not much happened that night. The three whites were treated courteously by the chiefs. They were fed and led to comfortable, warm beds of sheepskin. This did nothing to relieve Jacob's anxiety; he knew they were simply waiting for more braves to come.

The additional Indians finally arrived about midday. The dogs gave the first warning, and a distant rumble of horses confirmed it. When they appeared, Jacob counted twelve of them. And that was probably just the first group. His hopes sank.

Jacob and the two miners were wandering around outside, trying to pass the time. When he saw how many were coming, he turned to his two companions. "I think it's time to begin," he muttered. "I'm sorry you boys are in on this."

The older Smith managed a sickly grin. "I'm a little sorry myself."

"I'll ask the chiefs to let you go. They won't bother you. It's me they've got their eye on."

"Hell and daisies," came the reply, "we'll not leave you alone now." The man looked around quickly. The Indians around them were focused on the incoming riders. He spoke in a low voice. "Jacob, I think it's time you took that pistol out of your saddlebags and put it on."

There was a moment's hesitation, then he nodded. This was different from any situation he had ever been in. Turning his back to the surrounding Navajos, he took out the gun and strapped it on, Just then, the three chiefs suddenly appeared at the door of the hogan and motioned their "guests" to come inside. Through the translator, the oldest of the three asked Jacob and the Smiths to remove their pistols. They did so, but hung them on pegs just behind where they were going to sit.

When the warriors threw back the blanket and strode inside, their painted faces were twisted with anger and hate. Several carried long knives or tomahawks at their belts. Worse, Jacob immediately recognized one of them. The lead brave was Po-ee-kon, the fiery son of Chief Kacheenay, and therefore brother to the two Navajos who had been slain. Jacob had met him before, and knew that he was renowned for his courage and his utter contempt for the white man. Jacob had been told that he had taken more than one scalp of his enemies. The only glimmer of hope was that Chief Kacheenay was not among them too. To have a brother to deal with was serious enough. To have the father as well could well prove disastrous.

They waited for another hour—the three whites in silence, the Navajos talking among themselves in low, angry voices, all the time smoking cigarettes. Po-ee-kon dominated much of the conversation, shooting dark looks at the three men in the corner. Then, once again, the dogs began their wild barking outside, and in a few minutes they heard the sound of more horses.

A moment later, eight more Navajos entered—seven young braves, also wearing war paint, and another chief, older than the seven, but not as old as the three chiefs who were already there. The newcomers barely glanced at the three white men as they sat down around the fire and joined the others in lighting more cigarettes and venting their anger to each other.

Another ten minutes passed while they all smoked; then finally the newly arrived chief arose. Instantly all went quiet. He walked to a place in front of the door where he was facing the three white men directly and could see all of the others as well. The Paiute interpreter moved quickly to stand beside him. Suddenly the chief's face twisted with rage. Words tumbled out in a torrent—hot, bitter, livid. When he finally stopped to let the translator speak, he had to wipe flecks of spittle from the corners of his mouth.

"Jacob Hamblin has come to our lodge," the Paiute said, clearly nervous to be translating for someone that angry. "Jacob Hamblin has come to tell us that the Mormons did not kill our young men. He comes to tell us that the Mormons are not to blame."

He started again, and now the Paiute tried to keep up with him. "I say Jacob Hamblin has forked tongue. He lies. It was Jacob Hamblin who convinced us to cross the river and trade with the *belagana,* the white men. Jacob Hamblin promised there would be peace. Now three of our sons lie dead, murdered by the Mormon *belagana,* their bodies eaten by the wolves."

A growing chorus of angry imprecations rose with every sentence. The young braves shook their clenched fists at Jacob. Several gave war whoops. A couple drew their knives and shook them in the air.

As the interpreter raised his voice to be heard over the tumult, Jacob sat quietly, arms folded and face impassive. The host chief let the anger run for almost a minute, then raised a hand. The shouts died away, but the low mutters and angry gestures continued.

"Jacob Hamblin must not think that he will be going home," the new chief said. "The other *belagana,* who have done no wrong, may go if they wish, but Jacob Hamblin will not be going home. Jacob Hamblin shall be tortured. Jacob Hamblin must pay for this terrible thing he has done to our people."

The chief stopped again, letting the translator interpret. The noise crescendoed while he stared coldly at Jacob. Then he raised his fist and stabbed the air above him. "Jacob Hamblin must die."

The room exploded. Jacob, who had barely blinked through this rampage, slowly held up one hand, motioning to the more elderly chiefs that he wished to speak. When they signaled their permission, he half turned to face the two prospectors. The Smiths, of course, had not understood anything because the translation was coming in Paiute. Speaking in a low, calm voice, barely audible over the uproar around them, Jacob told them of the chief's offer. "There is a good chance that I shall be killed," he said, "but the way is open for you to leave. But you must do so now."

There was not a moment's hesitation on the part of either of the brothers. "We'll not be going until you do," the older Smith said.

"Thank you." Jacob shook his head to the interpreter, who then spoke to the chief. There was a quick nod, and a new respect showed in the eyes of all the chiefs. One of the things Navajos most despised was fear. The calm courage of these two companions had made an impression.

While this was going on, Jacob deliberately straightened his body enough that his head bumped against the holster of the pistol he had hung there earlier. He looked up, feigning surprise, then said to the interpreter, "These are in the way. What shall I do with them?"

As the interpreter translated that for the Navajos, Jacob didn't wait. Careful not to touch the pistols themselves, which might have looked like he was making a threatening move, he handed two of the guns back to the miners. "Keep them close at hand," he whispered, "but make no move of any kind unless we are obliged to do so." As casually as if they were putting away a piece of clothing, they took their weapons and slid them out of sight behind their legs. The young bucks were now in a heated discussion with the four chiefs, and if any of them noticed the action, they did not react to it. Jacob let out his breath in a long, slow sigh.

The discussion raged on for some time, the interpreter standing back and translating nothing for the white men. The Navajo way was that only the grey-haired chiefs formed the actual council, but all present were allowed to speak. And the young bucks had much to say.

After half an hour of heated discussion, the eldest chief finally cut it off, gesturing to Jacob Hamblin. The interpreter said, "You speak."

Jacob unfolded his legs, then got stiffly to his feet. For a long moment, he let his eyes move from man to man, resting just a little longer on each of the chiefs. It was important for them to see that his eyes held no fear, no guilt.

"My brothers of the Navajo nation. I thank you for letting me speak to this council." He took a deep breath while that was translated. "I have long been acquainted with your people. I have a great love for your people and the Navajo culture. It is well known that I have labored many days to bring peace between us."

Again he waited. The murmuring among the braves was rising again.

"I know of your anger. I know of your sorrow. A great and terrible wrong has been done to your sons. My heart understands and weeps for them. My heart understands why you seek revenge and say that someone must die to make this right."

He laid his hand over his heart. "But I also weep many tears inside my heart to think that my Navajo brothers, who know I do not speak with forked tongue, have decided that I must die. It was *belagana* who did this terrible deed," Jacob said softly, letting his voice drop to little more than a whisper. It quieted them more effectively than if he had shouted at them. "But those *belagana* were not Mormons. My people had nothing to do with this terrible act. I give you my word of honor that this is true." He sat down again.

Po-ee-kon leaped to his feet and said something to the senior chief. The chief thought for a moment, then nodded.

Po-ee-kon was heavily muscled and fierce of face. Sweat glistened on his forehead, and the war paint had started to run a little in the heat. He didn't look at Jacob or his two companions, or even at his own companions. He spoke directly to the four chiefs. They were the ones who would decide what happened this day.

The interpreter moved quietly over to stand beside Jacob. His eyes were wary and filled with anxiety. And rightly so. As Po-ee-kon poured out a torrent of angry words, the others who had accompanied him cried out in support, or turned and gave Jacob dark looks. Most alarming, in response to what he was saying, the new chief kept drawing his hand across his throat.

The interpreter listened for a full two or three minutes without saying a word. Finally, he leaned over and spoke very softly. "The young men are afraid that the council will not allow justice to be done. Po-ee-kon says that the blood of his three brothers cries from the ground for vengeance. There is only one thing that can bring them and their families justice."

Jacob guessed. "And that is the blood of Jacob Hamblin." It wasn't a question. It was the Indian way, blood for blood, suffering for suffering, life for life.

Suddenly Po-ee-kon strode to the door, pulled back the blanket, and barked something. Then he stepped back and let another person enter. It was a young brave, maybe sixteen or seventeen.

"Oh-oh," Jacob murmured. "That must be the boy who was wounded." This was not good.

Po-ee-kon motioned with his hand. The boy dropped to one knee facing the others. In one swift motion, Po-ee-kon pulled the buckskin shirt up and over the boy's head and flung it aside.

Jacob heard the gasps of his two companions, but they were quickly drowned out by the shouts of the Navajos. High on the youth's left shoulder was a bright scar the size of a half-dollar. This was where the bullet had entered. The skin was pinched together by its initial healing, but it was still an ugly, angry crimson.

The warrior touched the boy's bare shoulder and turned him around. The exit wound was even more shocking—two to three inches in diameter and jagged and torn.

Jacob grabbed the Paiute's arm. "I want to hear every word. Understand?"

The interpreter nodded, looking as if he might be sick. If the mood had been bitter before, the sight of this young boy had turned it downright ugly. The boy began to speak, slowly at first, then with more animation as he continued.

And it all came out. Their success in trading with the Mormons, the snowstorm, how the Holy People had brought them food. He stopped now and looked directly at Jacob. His face was impassive, but Jacob could see his jawline tighten and his skin stretch more tightly across his high cheekbones. The silence in the hogan was utterly complete. No one moved. Some hardly seemed to breathe.

As the youth started again, the interpreter just looked at him in horror. Jacob grabbed his arm. "Translate!" he commanded.

In an animated voice, the boy told how the riders had come, how Kacheenay's older son had refused to take the rifle, how he had stepped outside with arms outstretched to show he was not armed. At that point, Po-ee-kon cut in with a question. Jacob heard the word "Mohr-mohn" and knew what had just been asked. Were these men Mormons?

The boy's head bobbed emphatically. "*Ouu'!*" Several of the young bucks shot to their feet, yelling and shouting. Above the rest Po-ee-kon screamed something at the four chiefs.

"Po-ee-kon say Hamblin lies," the interpreter said, his voice so tight now it was hard to understand him. "He say Hamblin took life of his brothers. Only Hamblin's death will pay."

Jacob wanted to close his eyes and be sick too, but he could not. He had to show nothing. Behind him, one of the Smith brothers moved. His hand was stealing toward the butt of his pistol. "No," Jacob hissed, "do not make the first move."

And then an impression came to him, clear and pure and sweet. "If we do nothing, they will not be able to agree on what to do. They will make no move against us."

The two miners stared at him in astonishment. "But—"

Jacob gave a quick shake of his head and turned to the interpreter. "I wish to speak."

The man had backed into a corner and was staring at the bedlam around him. His eyes were wide with terror and he was visibly trembling. It was not unknown for the Navajos to kill an interpreter if they didn't like what they were hearing. "Tell them!" Jacob barked. But the man just shook his head and dropped his gaze to the floor.

Jacob turned to the chiefs and lifted both hands in an imploring gesture. The young braves sensed that something was up and ceased their shouting. The eldest chief said something, and one of the young men stood up and led the interpreter out. A minute or two later, he returned with another Paiute. This man looked almost as frightened as the first, but the chief spoke some soothing words to him and he finally nodded. Then the oldest chief gestured for Jacob to speak.

It took every ounce of his willpower, but Jacob got slowly to his feet, as calm and unruffled as if he were getting up from the table after supper. He stood fully erect, his shoulders thrown back, his hands hanging loosely at his sides. Not a muscle in his face twitched. His eyes were fixed on the four chiefs and never flickered away, not even for an instant. The chiefs had been swayed by the testimony of the young boy. They were being swayed by the passion of the young bucks. Now they must hear another voice.

"I would remind my Navajo brothers," he said quietly, "that you have known Jacob Hamblin for many winters. He has worked without tiring for peace between his people and your people."

He stopped and let the translator get that all out. The braves were still muttering and whispering among themselves, but the four chieftains had given him their full attention.

He went on. "I ask that Po-ee-kon bring one person forward who can say that I have cheated them. I ask that he bring one person forward who can prove I speak with a forked tongue."

Again he waited. He felt a quick thrill of elation shoot through him as he saw the eldest of the chiefs bob his head in a tiny movement. Jacob strode forward boldly into the circle and dropped to one knee. He started drawing in the dirt as he spoke. "Here are the great rivers that form the northern boundaries of your homeland." He pressed his finger into the dust to make a small circle. "We are here, at Black Mesa." He made another circle. "Here is the crossing of John Lee, who is also a friend to your people." Now his finger moved far to the left before it pressed down again. "And here is the hogan of Jacob Hamblin. It is four days' ride."

He waited for them to grasp that. Most were craning their necks. Those who were farthest from him stood up and came closer. He moved his hand more than a foot higher and made a fifth circle. It was as far above his house as his house was from Black Mesa. He tapped the spot slowly. "And here is where your young braves were murdered."

He looked up. He had their full attention now. "Grass Valley is over a hundred of our miles from my hogan. It takes me three suns to get there. I have no cattle there. I do not live there."

He straightened, coming up so his face was just inches from Po-ee-kon's. "Why then does Po-ee-kon say that Jacob Hamblin killed his brothers? He says it in anger, but reason tells you that it cannot be so."

When Po-ee-kon heard that, he leaned forward until their noses were almost touching. Jacob neither flinched nor blinked. One of the chiefs barked sharply. Po-ee-kon glared at Jacob for another moment, but finally stepped back. Jacob returned to his seat as the four chiefs moved closer together and began to talk.

It was almost an hour before the chiefs agreed. The oldest one waved the interpreter forward and spoke quickly, with the others speaking up as well from time to time. The interpreter listened intently, and Jacob thought he could see a touch of relief on his face. When he came over, he spoke loudly so the Navajos would not think he was favoring the white men.

"The chiefs have decided. They believe the words of Jacob Hamblin. They believe that he did not shed the blood of their sons. But they do not believe that Mormons had nothing to do with this."

Jacob sighed, but the man went on quickly. "So, instead of blood revenge on you or your people, you will pay the Navajo people one hundred head of cattle for each of the three boys. And fifty more for the boy who was wounded. This will also pay for the things that were stolen from them. You must give the chiefs a writing that you agree."

There was a deep intake of breath, then Jacob slowly exhaled. They had passed the crisis. Here was a way out. He could sign the writing, and they could walk away. But . . .

His head lifted. To sign would be an admission of guilt, to say nothing of obligating the Church to pay out three hundred and fifty head of cattle. That was a minor fortune.

He stood again and shook his head. "I thank the great chiefs for believing the words of Jacob Hamblin. It gave me great sorrow that they thought I would kill my Navajo brothers. But I cannot sign the writing. That would say that my people are murderers, and *this is not true!* I will not do it."

Before the translator had finished putting that into Navajo, Po-ee-kon was in his face again, screaming invectives. He pointed to the fire in the center of the hogan and screamed something else. The Paiute blanched.

"What did he say?" Jacob asked. "It's all right. I must know."

"He said . . ." The man took a quick breath. "He said if they stretch Jacob Hamblin over this bed of fire, he will sign the writing."

Jacob stood calmly, knowing every eye in the hogan was on him. "You tell Po-ee-kon that Jacob Hamblin does not lie. The Mormons did not kill those braves, those sons, and it is not right that they should pay for what the other *belagana* did. Let the family of Kacheenay go to the ranchers in Grass Valley. He will learn that they are not Mormons. They are evil, cruel men. Let them pay. I will not sign the writing, fire or no fire."

"*Imme-cotch-navaggi!*" Po-ee-kon shouted into his face.

The interpreter audibly gulped. "Are you not afraid?" he translated.

Jacob turned away and looked around the circle, again letting his gaze stop at the chiefs. "Why should I be afraid of my friends?" He seemed perplexed. "If I were, why would I come and put my life into your hands? What is there to frighten me?" he concluded.

"The *Diné*," Po-ee-kon spluttered, half in disbelief.

Jacob understood that word. "I am not afraid of my friends," he answered softly.

Now the Paiute blanched. He turned and spoke to Jacob in great interest. "Jacob Hamblin. You do not have a single friend in the Navajo nation. Navajo blood has been spilled on Mormon land. You have caused a whole nation to mourn. Are you not the least afraid?"

Jacob peered deeply into his eyes. "No. My heart never has known fear." He gestured toward the chiefs. "Tell them what you just said. And tell them my answer."

The negotiations went on all through the rest of the day and into the night, but by midnight an agreement had been made. Jacob would return to Lee's Ferry in twenty-five days to meet a delegation of Navajo chieftains. He would then escort them to Grass Valley, where they could learn for themselves who had killed their sons. A few other particulars were worked out; then suddenly the old chief clapped his hands three times.

Immediately women appeared with a roasted sheep on a large clay plate. As they set it down near the fire, the chief motioned with his hand and spoke.

The interpreter smiled broadly. "The chief says Jacob Hamblin is to have the first rib."

Jacob started to bow, but suddenly the smell of the meat, the effects of sitting cross-legged for nearly twelve hours, and the tension they had endured was too much. "I am sick," he blurted.

He made it to the door in three strides, pulling the blanket back. He didn't want to offend the Navajos. Not now, for sure. So he didn't go out. He just stood there, half in and half out, gulping in huge breaths of the cold night air, fighting down the bitter taste in his throat.

Finally, he straightened and returned to join the circle. The chiefs were watching him closely, but it was the younger Smith brother who spoke. "Are you all right?"

"I am now."[2]

Notes

1. In his brief account, Hamblin does not say how President Brigham Young was informed, only that "when President Young heard of it, he requested me to visit the Navahos [sic] and satisfy them that our people were not concerned in it" (Hamblin, *Journals and Letters*, 99). A runner was sent from Kanab to Grass Valley to learn more details of the murders. Once the runner returned, confirming that Mormons were not involved, and Jacob received word from Brigham Young, he says that he "left at once" (*ibid.*).

2. We have two firsthand accounts of this dramatic Navajo council meeting that was to have such significant consequences for the Mormons. One is Hamblin's own report (see *ibid.*, 99–106). The other is the firsthand account of "J.E.S.," one of the two Smith brothers present through it all (we have only his initials, no first name). He wrote a report for a local newspaper just a few days after the council had occurred. Jacob included that article in the narrative account of his life (see *ibid.*, 107–13). Corbett (348–57) has done the best work on Hamblin's life and particularly this event. He conducted many interviews with Jacob's family and other settlers, and so provides details not found in either of the eyewitness accounts. Even so, there are still a few discrepancies between the accounts.

It should be noted that later, two other Mormons, Ira Hatch and John L. Blythe, were also taken by the Navajos and underwent a similar harrowing experience. They also demonstrated great courage, as Hamblin and the Smiths did, and were also eventually freed (see Kumen Jones, "Navajo Peace," 215). Ignoring their experience in this narrative is not meant to diminish their efforts in any way.

It took many more months for the situation to eventually resolve itself, but finally Chief Hastele, considered the great chief of the Navajos, went with Hamblin to Grass Valley. There they met with Mormon leaders and Hastele was convinced that the Mormons were not involved. He returned to his people and spread the word that Jacob Hamblin and the Mormons spoke the truth. Finally, on August 21, 1874, an agreement was signed by the Navajos formally declaring that they had been satisfied, and war was averted.

BOOK III

THE CALL

1878

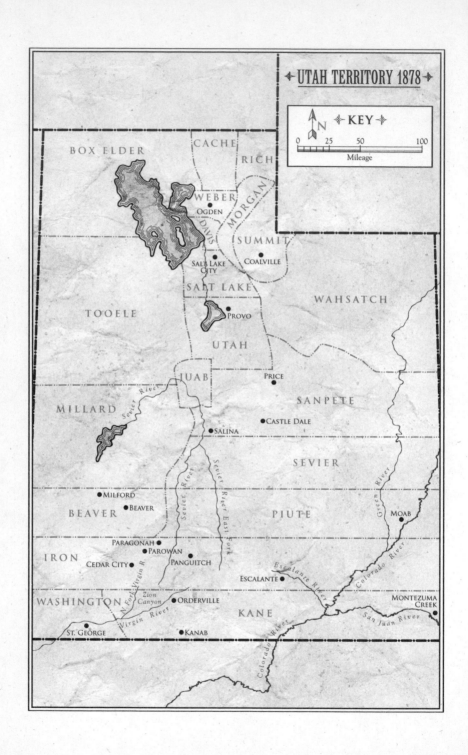

★ UTAH TERRITORY 1878 ★

KEY

N

0   25   50   100
Mileage

BOX ELDER

CACHE

RICH

WEBER
OGDEN

MORGAN

DAVIS

SUMMIT

SALT LAKE
CITY

COALVILLE

SALT LAKE

WAHSATCH

TOOELE

PROVO

UTAH

JUAB

PRICE

SANPETE

MILLARD

Sevier River

CASTLE DALE

SALINA

SEVIER

Green River

Sevier River

Sevier River East Fork

MILFORD

BEAVER
BEAVER

PIUTE

MOAB

IRON

PARAGONAH

PAROWAN

CEDAR CITY

PANGUITCH

ESCALANTE

Escalante River

Colorado River

WASHINGTON

N. Fork Virgin R.

Zion
Canyon

ORDERVILLE

Virgin River

KANE

Colorado River

San Juan River

MONTEZUMA
CREEK

ST. GEORGE

KANAB

CHAPTER 17

Tuesday, August 13, 1878

David Draper reined his horse to a stop, then stood up in the stirrups and stretched. He yawned mightily, glancing up at the sun. It was low in the sky. Dropping back in the saddle, he guessed it was about half past six, which meant he had been on the road for over fourteen hours. No wonder he was numb from the waist down.

He snapped the reins. "All right, Tillie. That's Coalville. We're almost there. And guess what, girl. Coalville has gotten a little more respectable since I was last here." He reached down and patted the mare's neck. "Of course, it has been six years."

⁂

"Excuse me," David said. He was leading Tillie now, moving slowly up the street, marveling at how much the town had grown. Just ahead, a young girl, maybe sixteen or seventeen, was approaching. He saw that she was watching him from beneath lowered lashes. He doffed his hat. "Excuse me, miss. I'm looking for the home of Mister—Brother—John Draper. It used to be right here, but . . ." The house he was looking for had been converted to a shoemaker's shop. He pulled a face. "This place has really changed since I was here last."

She flashed him a quick look, blushed, and lowered her eyes again. "Brother Draper has moved." She turned and pointed. "It's the small cabin at the end of the next street over."

He bowed slightly. "Thank you, miss. That's a right pretty dress you have on today."

Momentarily startled, she beamed, then did a quick curtsy. "Thank you, Brother Draper."

He jerked forward. "You know me?"

Her cheeks were touched with pink now. "I remember you from school."

He peered at her more closely. "Tell me your name."

"Gwendolyn Watson, but everybody calls me Gwen."

He snapped his fingers. "You sat in the front corner, next to Henry McGuire."

"*Yes!*" Her joy was instantaneous. "I didn't think you would remember me."

"Hey," he said, "how could I not? No boy, especially one who sat in the back corner, could ever forget a girl who got one hundred percent on every test Mrs. MacArthur ever gave."

She ducked her chin. He climbed back up on Tillie, then raised a hand in farewell. "It has been a pleasure to meet you again, Gwen Watson. Not only are you pretty as a meadow full of flowers, but when you blush, you're absolutely enchanting."

Laughing as she flamed a bright scarlet, David nudged Tillie forward. If he were to come back to Coalville in another six years, he would bet that Gwendolyn Watson would still remember David Draper.

As he rode up to the small cabin at the end of the street, he was surprised to see a patch of grass in the front and a flowerpot on the porch. It was filled with geraniums and petunias and some other things he didn't recognize. Flowers? His father was planting flowers?

He dismounted and wrapped Tillie's reins around the hitching rail. But even as he did so, the door flew open and John Draper burst out. "David!"

"Hullo, Dad."

"Wud ya look at ya! Ya cud knock me over wit a feather."

David laughed as they embraced tightly for several seconds, neither speaking.

"It's good to see you, Dad," David said when they stepped back. "How are you?"

"Gud. Great, actually. Me 'ealth be better than Ah deserve, an' the older Ah git, the wiser Ah becum."

"An' the more 'andsome too." It felt so good to hear that accent again. "Ya still spek lek a Yorkshur Tyke, that be fur sure."

"Aye, laddie. As they say, ya can tek a Tyke oot of Yorkshur, but ya canna ever be changin' the pure an' delightful way that a Yorkshur Tyke speks."

David put an arm around him as they started into the house. "We've been nine years in America. Hasn't being around all these Yanks taught you anything?"

"What Yanks?" his father shot back. "Ah'm foreman of me shift noow, an' Ah 'ave only two Americans. Thare be three Germans, five Irish, half a dozen Welshmen, and one Italian, who speks very little English. 'Ow am Ah supposed ta be learnin' ta spek bettur in that kind of cump'ny?"

"Question withdrawn," David said with a chuckle.

His father gave him a searching look. "But ya, David, ya sound lek a bloomin' Yank yurself. Yur mum dinna teach ya ta spek like that. Ya naw be furgittin' yur Yorkshur roots, surely."

David just shook his head. There was not much his father missed. "I think it was all that coaching Mum gave me when I was little. It gave me a quick ear, and I guess I just naturally start speking—speaking—like those around me."

His father led the way into a small sitting room and motioned toward a chair. "Sit doon, Son." David did so, but his father stayed standing, looking down at him. "It be so gud ta see ya, David. But why dinna ya write an' tell me ya be cumin'?"

"Didn't have time. I've been offered a job as a mail rider down in the southern part of the territory. I'm on my way there now. Because it's this late, I probably won't make it back up for conference in October, so I decided to swing up here on my way."

"Did ya git me letter fur yur bur'day?"

"I did, Dad. Thank you. You never forget."

"Yur mum would cum back and haunt me if Ah did. Yur bur'day be the most important day of the year ta 'er. Wasn't sure whare ta send it, so

Ah joost sent it ta the Salt Lake postmaster. Figured 'e wud be knowin' whare ya be."

"He did. I got it two days before my birthday. Thanks for remembering."

He shook his head. "Twenty-two years old. Cahrn't b'lieve it. It be six years noow since ya left Coalville. Whare the time be gone?" Then, realizing he was talking to himself, he asked, "So whare will ya be livin'?"

"Cedar City. My circuit includes half a dozen outlying settlements to the east. I don't even know which ones yet."

"So ya be changin' yur employment yet agin." It was not a question, nor did it carry any hint of criticism. "How many jobs that be since ya turned sixteen?" Not waiting for David to answer, he started ticking them off on his fingers. "After layin' telegraph wire in the south, ya worked fur a time layin' rails up in Idaho. That's two. Then ya ran freight across Wyoming."

"Yep, between Laramie and Denver. That's three."

"Then ya becum a mail rider between Salt Lake and Ely, Nevada. That's four."

"No, that was number five. You missed ranching."

"Aw, that's reet. Ya becum a cowboy up in . . . whare were it agin?"

"North of Laramie. I was there almost two years." He turned and pointed out the window. "In fact, it was in Laramie that I got Tillie there. We rounded up a bunch of wild horses from up on the high plains. When we started breaking them, there was this one mare that turned out to be a real fighter. Ornery as a badger with ingrown toenails. Nobody could stick on her back. The foreman finally offered to give her to anyone who could tame her." David grinned. "You know me and a challenge, Dad. Best horse I've ever had."

His father went to the window. "Tillie, eh? That dunna sound lek a very fierce name ta me."

David chortled at that. "Do you remember that place where we delivered coal the Monday after Mother died?"

"Of course. Down by Sheffield. Castle sumthin' or other."

"Tilburn Castle."

"Yaw, that be it."

"Do you remember the three girls we saw by the lake that day?" When John nodded, David went on, "Especially the oldest one, who was so disgusted at the sight of us coal-blackened Tykes?"

"Ah r'membur it well. Ya dinna lek her attitude one bit, did ya."

"No," he said shortly. The memory was still so clear in his mind that he felt his anger rise each time he thought of it. But then a smile stole in around the corners of his mouth. "I actually named the horse *Lady Tilburn*, but I just call her Tillie."

His father slapped his hand against his leg. "Ya named yur 'orse after that gurl?"

David's grin only broadened. "I did. I've been strongly tempted to write her a letter and tell her. Think she'd be honored?"

His father, still chuckling, shook his head. "Aw, Davee, me boy, ya be a real rascal sometimes. Tank ya fur cumin' ta see this ole man of yurs."

They fell silent, both enjoying the moment, then David continued. "So anyway, from there I went to the mail job, and now I'm just transferring routes down south, so you can't really count this as a new job."

"But ya be movin' 'roond a lot, Son."

"Yes, and coming up here today, I realized something. Know what all of those jobs have in common? They're all outdoors. No tunnels. No monkey heads. No coal tubs. I guess I got enough of that to last me for the rest of my life. I love the wide open spaces."

"Aw," John said, understanding now. "That be gud. Yur mum wud be reet prood."

"What about you, Dad?"

"Ah be a miner, Son. Dunna know anythin' else. Dunna even think aboot it anymore."

"Why don't you quit and come south with me? I'm tired of these winters up north here, freezing my smalls off every time I'm out on the road."

His father's face softened. "Aw, Ah 'aven't 'eard underwear called 'smalls' in a long time. It be gud ta know ya 'aven't completely stopped talkin' like an Englishman."

"Now, Dad," he chided, "I talk just fine."

"See what Ah mean. It naw even be Dahd anymore. Just Dad. Ya soond more lek a Yank than the Yanks themselves." But he was smiling, and there was no sting to his words.

"Ya cum sooth wit me, Dahd, an' Ah be spekin' lek a Tyke at least once a week, joost ta mek ya feel at 'ome."

"Aw, David," he sighed, neatly sidestepping the request once again. "Duz it naw seem ta ya like England be another life?"

"It does." He turned. "And speaking of another life, what's with the flowers out front?"

To his amazement, his father actually blushed. "They be nuthin'."

"Come on, Dad. You're planting flowers now? I mean, I think they're lovely and all that, but it certainly is not what I expected."

David was just teasing him, but to his further surprise, his father was suddenly defensive. "It be 'er idee, naw mine."

One eyebrow came up. "Oh? And who is her?"

"One of the ladies at church. She be determined Ah need sum color in me new digs."

David sat back, holding in a smile. "Well, well, well."

"Gwan!" his father snapped. "Ain't nuthin' lek that. She be nice e'nuff, but she canna tek naw fur an answer."

"And what are you going to do if she wants to marry you and won't take no for an answer, eh? Tell me that."

His father lumbered to his feet, glowering at him. "Ya want sum supper, or wud ya prefur ta sleep in the shed an' eat wit yur 'orse?"

David got up too, thoroughly enjoying his father's discomfort. "I've got to unsaddle Tillie, but supper sounds good, Dad."

"Tell ya what. Thare be beans an' bread in the cupboard. Ya start supper an' Ah'll tek yur horse oot back an' put 'er away." He gave him a droll look. "Be an 'onor ta associate wit a real lady agin."

Wednesday, August 14, 1878

They sat together on the porch in the last of the evening twilight. Being on the east end of town, the cabin was high enough that it overlooked the Weber River and the mountains beyond. Now, however, the only thing they could see in the valley were the lights of the town and a few scattered points of light beyond it.

It was a pleasant evening, and much of that was the pleasure David took in being here with his father again. He was glad he had decided to make this hundred-mile detour before heading south. It had been too long since they had spent time together.

"It really is a beautiful place," he said, half to himself.

"Winter be kinda ruff," came the answer, "but the summers be a joy."

"I remember someone once telling me there wasn't any winter in a coal mine."

"Aye. That be true."

"Dad?"

"Yes, Son?"

"Are you still okay?"

"Meanin', do Ah 'ave the black lung?"

"Exactly. You've been in the mines a long time."

"Last time Ah be down in the Valley, 'ad a doctor check me oot. Sez 'e be 'earin' a little rattle in me lungs, but naw ta worry aboot it. Ah be fine."

"I was serious about you coming south with me, Dad. I've been thinking about maybe finding a little spread somewhere, getting some cows, maybe a few horses, and doing some ranching. You could retire and come down with me. Old as you're getting, we could get you a rocking chair, and you could just sit on the porch and watch the sunset. Just like now."

"Retire?" He feigned a deep wound. "Ah be only forty-seven. B'sides, what Ah be doin' thare? Ya want me ta trade in me pick and shovel fur spurs an' a lariat? Gwan."

David had to laugh. He had to admit that such an image was a bit of a stretch. "You could be the cook." He nudged him. "Maybe plant us some flowers along the walk."

"Ya want yur lugholes boxed, Sonny," he growled. "Ya ain't gonna tempt me by bein' cheeky." Then he went on the offensive. "Are ya tellin' me ya be reddy to settle doon, David Draper?"

"Well . . . uh . . . yeah, I guess that is what I'm saying. Sooner or later."

"That's what Ah thought. Naw, tank ya." Then he grew more serious. "Actually, Ah be learnin' ta be a blaster noow. Means anuther ten dollars a month."

That took David by surprise. "You're using black powder down there?"

"Yaw. Got those Welshmen ta teach me 'ow it be done. Ah tell ya, David, it be mooch easier than crawlin' inta them monkey 'oles an' cutting away at the coal face wit a pick."

"I know that, Dad, but that's dangerous stuff. You be careful."

"Ah be real gud noow," he replied. "Dun't ya be worryin' aboot yur pa."

"Well," David said, "I'm glad things are good here, but I still think it would be good for you to get out of the mine. I'd love to be together, even if it's not for another year or two."

"When ya write an' tell me ya've foond sum sweet lassie an' be settlin' doon an' givin' me sum gran'kids, Ah be cumin' the next day."

"Sounds to me like I may not be the first one in this family to marry," he quipped.

So fast that he didn't have time to react, his father smacked him a good one on the shoulder.

"Ouch!"

"Ain't got no plans fur marryin'," his father growled.

David looked more closely at him. "Why not, Dad? You're still young and in good health. Mum wouldn't mind. In fact, I think she would encourage you to—"

He was shaking his head.

"Why not?"

"Yur mum is the only woman Ah ever luved, an' ever will." He gave David a sidelong look. "Ah be sealed ta 'er now, ya know."

"Sealed? What's that supposed to mean?"

"Never mind. Joost git it outta yur 'ead that Ah be marryin' sumone else." Then, before David could protest further, he decided to change the subject. "Do ya still go ta church?"

"I . . ." He blew out his breath. "Not that much since I left. As a mail rider, I'm not very often in town on Sundays."

"An' that's awl yur gonna say?"

Not sure what had brought this on, he decided to joke his way out of it. "Well, I do attend every social and dance they have. Does that count for anything?"

There was a grunt, and his father looked away, which only caused David's irritation to flare. "I'm a *good* Mormon, Dad. I don't smoke or drink or chew or chase women." He flashed a quick grin. "Mum actually gets the credit for most of that. Said she'd pull me out of the mine if I started any of that." He was getting really peeved now. Why was it they had to have this conversation every time they were together? "Look, Dad, I know that you've gotten into this whole Mormon thing, and if that makes you feel better about what we did in Liverpool, good for you. But I'm—"

The hardness that swept across his father's face stopped him short. "I . . . I didn't mean it that way, Dad, I was just—"

"Yaw, ya did." He took a breath, clearly fuming. "It be one thing ta be cheeky when we be funnin' 'roond, David, but dunna be mekin' fun of things that ya dunna un'erstand."

David finally nodded and sat back. "Sorry."

"Ya dunna feel any obligation, do ya?"

"To what?"

"Dunna be obtuse, boy. It does naw becum ya."

"All right." As usual, his father couldn't leave it alone. "Do I feel obligated to attend church because we took passage on a Church ship under false pretenses? No, I don't. They knew we came to that meeting in Liverpool because we wanted to go to America. They were so eager to get us baptized, they didn't care what we believed."

"An' that's yur way of mekin' yurself feel gud aboot bein' deceitful?"

"How often do you go to church, Dad?"

"Ev'ry Sunday."

"Good for you. And has nine years of church attendance been enough to erase your guilt?"

His father stiffened, and David instantly regretted his words. He put up his hands. "Let's talk about something else."

"Naw, let's talk aboot this."

"Come on, Dad. All we do is fight."

"Thare be sumthin' that ya still dunna un'erstand, Son, an' Ah guess that be me own fault." His eyes were challenging now. "If'n ya dunna want ta 'ear this, then joost git up an' walk away. But it be sumthin' ya need ta know."

"Dad, come on. You know I was just popping off."

John went on as if he hadn't spoken. "Ya be reet aboot one thing, Son. Ah was deeply ashamed that night. What we were doin' was wrong. It *was* deceitful." He gave him a long, searching look. "Do ya even r'member what Brother Miller talked aboot that night?"

David shook his head. "All I was thinking about was that we were going to America." He looked away. "And about how terrible I felt that Mum wouldn't be going with us."

"Ah was thinkin' a lot aboot yur muther too. Brother Miller spoke on what 'e called the plan of salvation. 'E spoke of the Savior an' the resurrection. Said 'ow Jesus makes it possible fur us ta be reunited wit our luved ones agin." He was lost now in the remembrance. "'E said that we be part of our 'Eavenly Father's family, an' that 'Eavenly Father meks it possible fur us ta be wit our fam'lies agin after we die. That our relationship does naw end wit this life."

David was staring at him. "He said all that?" That didn't sound even vaguely familiar.

His father looked at David squarely. "Ah was stunned. What yur muther an' me 'ad was the most important thing in me life, David. An' ta 'er too. Ah always b'lieved she wud be goin' ta 'eaven an' awl that. She be an angel, if ever thare were one. But ta be t'gether as 'usband and wife? Ta 'ave that luv continue? Ah never dreamed sumthin' lek that be possible."

There was a deep sigh. "Ah guess Ah shud 'ave tole ya this b'fur, David, but when we first went in ta that meetin', Ah was reddy ta tell Brother Miller that we wud naw be goin' ta America wit 'em after awl. It dinna matter 'ow mooch we needed ta go. What we were doin' was dead wrong. But when 'e began ta spek . . . Ah dunno. Ah joost never felt anythin' lek that b'fur."

"So you're saying . . ." David took a quick breath. He had been deeply touched by his father's emotion, and didn't want in any way to make him feel like he was rejecting it, but . . . "So you're saying that you were converted that night?"

"Naw," came the quick reply. "Naw at awl. Ah joost . . . it was joost e'nuff ta mek me wanna 'ear more." And now there was shame in his eyes. "An' it was joost e'nuff ta mek me decide per'aps it wud naw be so terrible if we became Mormons an' came wit 'em ta America."

David didn't know what to say. After almost a full minute, he stood up. "I'm real tired, Dad, and I've got to leave early in the morning. Thank you for telling me that. I truly did not know."

"Ah be sayin' one more thing, David, then Ah be leavin' ya alone."

David audibly sighed, but didn't move.

"At furst, Ah went ta church b'cuz Ah was feelin' guilty. And then . . ." He stopped, searching for words. "Aw, David, Ah 'ad naw idee, naw idee at awl."

"No idea about what?"

"Aboot what this awl meant."

"The Mormon Church, you mean?"

"Naw. The gospel. Aboot 'ow mooch thare be ta learn. Aboot 'ow mooch our 'Eavenly Father wants us ta be 'appy. 'Ow many blessin's 'E 'as ta give us."

Embarrassed, he looked away. "That be awl Ah 'ave ta say ta ya, Son. Thank ya fur naw laughin' at yur ole Dahd. Ah guess as Ah git older, Ah be gittin' too sen'imen'al."

David went to him and put his arms around him. "I luv ya, Dahd," he said. "I'm sorry that I have to go again so soon."

John said nothing in reply, just held him tightly for a long time.

CHAPTER 18

Saturday, August 24, 1878

When David approached the outskirts of Cedar City ten days later, he was ready for a bath. It was hot—in the high nineties, at least—and the air was perfectly still. The steady plop-plop of Tillie's hooves left little puffs of dust hanging in the air, adding in their own small way to the thick summer haze. To the east, a range of hills shimmered in the heat.

When he had come south to work the telegraph line a few years before, it had been October. The air had been clear and crisp then, with the promise of snow. He still remembered how the sight of those hills had impressed him: the brilliant red soil sprinkled generously with the deep, rich green of the junipers—or cedar trees, as most people called them—and the snowcapped mountains behind them. Today, however, those same hills seemed lifeless and dull. He heard a far-off "caw, caw." Looking up, he saw two crows circling lazily high above him.

Though he had passed through numerous settlements on his way south, he had chosen to sleep in the open except for one time when he had taken refuge in a barn to escape an evening thundershower. The cost of hotels and boardinghouses came out of his pocket, and therefore took money out of his "ranch fund." Tonight, he would make an exception to that rule. Starting Monday, board and room would be included in his salary, but tonight, ranch fund or not, he was going to get himself a hot bath, a good meal, and a soft bed, in that order. But first, he had to find the postmaster and let him know he had arrived.

Cedar City was one of the anchor points on the "Mormon Corridor" established by Brigham Young shortly after bringing his people to the Great

Basin. He had created a series of settlements between Salt Lake City and San Bernardino, California—including Las Vegas in Nevada Territory—to provide an alternate route to California that avoided the High Sierras and Donner Pass. Cedar City, like Coalville, had grown significantly since David had last been here. Looking out across the town now, he estimated its population to be somewhere in the vicinity of a thousand. But he expected he would find the post office on Main Street.

The post office *was* on Main Street, but to David's surprise, it was housed in one end of the McKenna House (subtitled "Hotel and Dining Room"). The hotel was impressive. It had a two-story central block, with smaller wings on both ends. Made of brick laid on a stone foundation, it had a spacious veranda across the front of it, with two large glass doors leading into the main lobby. The south wing had a separate entrance, and the words *Post Office* were posted over the door. A large covered carriage was pulled up at the front of the hotel, disgorging ten or twelve passengers into the building. The driver and his helper were up on top, tossing down suitcases, carpetbags, and valises to a teenaged boy waiting below.

David pulled Tillie up to the rail in front of the post office. He swung down, tied her to the rail, then patted her on the shoulder. "Be back in a second, old girl. Then we'll get you a manger full of hay and a bucket of oats and you can rest for a while." As he stepped up onto the veranda, he removed his hat, combed his fingers through his damp hair, then slapped the worst of the trail dust off his shirt and pants. Replacing his hat, he opened the door and stepped inside.

He stopped, letting his eyes adjust for a moment to the dimmer light. The room was divided off from the main hotel lobby by a partition and occupied the full width of the building. Three chest-high writing tables stood along the wall to his left. The far wall was filled with a full-length counter. Behind it were rows of shelves and one section with crosshatched pigeonholes. Many of those contained letters or newspapers. On the door of a workroom, a neatly painted sign showed various rates for letters and parcels based on distance.

Just then, a woman stepped out. "Good afternoon," she said. "May I help you?"

David swept off his hat without thinking. She was young—probably seventeen or eighteen. She was dressed in a long, full skirt, beige in color, and wore a pale blue blouse with long sleeves puffed at the shoulder but tight at the wrist. It emphasized the slenderness of her waist and made her look taller than she was. Probably five foot two or three, he guessed. But it was her hair that arrested his gaze. It was honey-blonde and cascaded down her back in long, soft curls. In the dimmer light he couldn't see the color of her eyes but guessed they were a light blue. She was, without question, one of the most comely women he had met in a very long time.

Her head cocked to one side. She gave him a quizzical look. "May I help you, sir?"

He moved forward, wanting a better look. "Well now," he said, flashing his most boyish grin, "aren't you about the prettiest thing a man ever laid eyes on."

In quick flashes her face registered surprise, then pleasure, then cool mockery. "Well now," she mimicked, "aren't you one for kissing the Blarney stone?"*

He laughed aloud. "What? Ahre ya Ireesh noow, mee gurl?" he said, grandly rolling his *r*'s.

That did it. The smile came stealing back. "My father was born in the Emerald Isle, near Limerick Town. He's warned me about handsome young men who are full of the blarney."

He looked up at the ceiling, speaking to an unseen audience, still in a rich Irish brogue. "Didya 'ear that, laddies? The bonnie wee lass called me an 'andsome young man."

She grimaced. "Are there really girls empty-headed enough to find that line irresistible?"

He couldn't turn away from her eyes. They were neither green nor

---

* The Blarney stone is a block of blue stone built into the battlements of Blarney Castle, which is about five miles outside of Cork, Ireland. According to legend, kissing the Blarney stone endows the kisser with "the gift of gab." The word blarney has thus come to mean "clever, flattering, or coaxing talk" (see Wikipedia, s.v. "blarney").

blue but grey, pale as an overcast sky, but flecked with tiny spots of light brown around the iris. Finally, her question registered. "What would you say if I told you that you were the first girl I've ever said that to?"

She gave a short hoot of derision. "Sir, I would say you have either a very poor memory or a habit of playing somewhat loosely with the truth."

He was greatly enjoying the repartee. "I confess that, while my memory may fail me on rare occasions, I can say with the utmost sincerity that never in all my life have those words been uttered more honestly, or with more heartfelt feeling. You are indeed the prettiest girl I have seen in a long, long time."

That took her completely aback, and her cheeks instantly colored. Before she could recover, he stuck out his hand. "Hi. I'm David Draper. I'm your new mail rider."

"Oh!" That flustered her even more. "Really?"

He reached out, took her hand, shook it quickly, then let it drop again. "The proper response to that is, 'Hello, David Draper. I'm pleased to meet you. My name is . . .'"

"Molly Jean McKenna," she said, finally smiling again. "And I am very pleased to meet you, Mr. Draper."

"Molly?" he exclaimed. "Why, of course it's Molly. It couldn't have been anything else." He stepped back, still smiling at her. "So, father or uncle?"

"I beg your pardon?"

"We're in the McKenna House. Father or uncle?"

"Oh. That's my father."

"I see. And where might I find the postmaster to let him know that I'm here?"

She was recovering quickly. "He's not here now. Won't be back until four." She smiled, looking secretly amused about something.

He nodded. "Well, Miss Molly McKenna, I shall go and arrange lodging for myself at the board and room I passed a street or two back. There I shall take a bath, and—" he rubbed at the stubble on his chin—"shave so you can see how truly handsome I am."

She laughed merrily. "You are shameless, Mr. Draper," she said, shaking her head.

"Guilty as charged," he said with a jaunty grin, pleased to note that beneath the cool and calm demeanor, she was enjoying this interchange as much as he was. "Would you be so kind as to let the postmaster know I shall be here at four o'clock?"

"I shall," she said, merriment literally dancing in her eyes now. "He keeps an office just off the hotel lobby. Inquire there when you return."

He replaced his hat, bowed deeply, and started for the door. "Until later then, Miss Molly."

He decided Tillie's needs came first. He asked a man outside the post office how to find the livery stable and was directed one block west. It was a large red barn set back from the street, with sheds and a spacious corral in back. The corral held several horses. David saw a large sign painted in white letters just below the barn's hayloft: *McKenna & Son, Livery.* He studied it for a moment. So Molly McKenna was the daughter of one of Cedar City's more prominent citizens. Did that make a difference to him? Probably not, but it was something to keep in mind.

He rode Tillie through the large doors and into the coolness of the barn. He pulled up and looked around. "Hello!" he called. Nothing. He got down and, leading Tillie by the reins, went deeper into the dark interior. "Anyone here?"

Then he saw a paper tacked to one of the wooden posts supporting the loft. A pencil hung on a string beside it. He walked over and read the block letters: *BACK IN HALF AN HOUR. HELP YOURSELF TO WHATEVER YOU NEED. LEAVE YOUR NAME AND WE'LL SETTLE UP LATER. A. M.*

There were several empty stalls. He led Tillie to the nearest one and unsaddled her. Finding a currycomb and brushes, he brushed her down, then got her a bucket of oats. By then, a quarter of an hour had passed, and there was still no sign of A.M. He went to the paper, took the pencil, and scribbled: *This is my horse. Staying at the boardinghouse. Back after five. Thanks. David D.*

As he gave the mare one last pat and started for the door, he heard the sound of voices coming from behind the barn. He turned on his heel and headed in that direction. The back double doors were open about two feet and he slipped through them, blinking in the sunlight.

What he saw was not the livery man, but three boys over behind the tack shed. Disappointed, he started to turn back, but something about the scene arrested him. One boy was backed up against the wall of the shed. He was the shortest of the three, a towhead with short-cropped hair and deep brown eyes. He wore a pullover striped shirt, faded jeans, and scuffed shoes. He stood stiffly, and something about his stance told David that he was frightened. The other two boys were clearly older, the biggest of them a full head taller than the towhead. They stood in front of him, blocking any escape he might seek.

Curious now, David moved slowly toward them, keeping the corral fence between him and them and placing his feet carefully so as not to make any noise. He stopped behind the corner post, just ten or fifteen feet to one side. None of the three saw him or heard him.

From this position, he could see a large circle in the dirt with several marbles on the ground. He also saw that the small boy held a leather sack bulging with more marbles. His eyes were darting nervously between the two boys. Yet he was standing his ground.

"Give us the rest of our marbles, Pajamas." It came from the taller of the two boys. He held his hand out, motioning with his fingers for the smaller boy to hand over the pouch.

Pajamas? David had heard a lot of insults kids hurled at each other, but this was a new one.

"They're not your marbles," the smaller boy said. He stepped forward and bent down to pick up the remaining marbles from the ground. The taller boy moved quickly, sticking out his foot. He stepped on a marble and the younger boy's fingers at the same time.

"Ow!" The towhead pulled free and straightened, backing away a step, holding his hand.

"What's the matter, P.J.?" the taller boy jeered. "Don'tcha want this marble? Thank you very much." He picked it up and put it in his pocket. He quickly scooped up the others as well, then held out his hand. "Now gimme the rest of them." The other boy moved up beside him.

The marble owner jutted out his chin, frightened but determined. "Give me back my marbles, Sammy."

David had to smile. He liked the feisty look on this kid's face. He wasn't backing down, even though he was outnumbered two to one and outweighed by double or more.

"Give me my marbles back, Sammy," Sammy mimicked in a singsong voice. He turned to his friend. "How would you like a name like P.J.?" he sneered. Then in the same singsong voice, "Patrick Joseph, what a name. Call him P.J., it's the same. Pajamas. Pajamas. Pajamas."

Understanding the nickname now, David realized this little chant hadn't been made up on the spot, nor was it the first time this little scrapper had heard it.

They started again. "Patrick Joseph, what a name." Then, quick as a snake, Sammy's hand shot out and snatched the sack of marbles from Patrick's hand.

"They're mine," Patrick exclaimed in a quavering voice, but he didn't try to take them back.

Sammy the bully held them just out of his reach. "Then come and get 'em!"

Patrick was fast, but Sammy was faster. He jerked the bag away just as Patrick's fingers touched it. Then Sammy leaned in and gave Patrick a hard shove with his free hand. "Come on, little boy. Come and get it." He gave him another shove. The second boy moved in and shoved him in the other direction.

"Hey!" David yelled, stepping out. All three boys were startled, and Sammy and his companion started backing away. David cut them off. "No, you don't. Stay right there."

He herded them back over to the circle. The relief on Patrick's face was dramatic. He also looked like he was near tears. "What's going on here?" David asked.

"They took my marbles," Patrick said.

"Did not!" Sammy cried. "They're ours. We left them here earlier. He stole 'em from us."

David turned. "That true, son?"

He shook his head. "He's lying."

The other boy took a step forward, raising his fists. "You calling me a liar?"

"Liar!" Patrick said hotly, his chin jutting out.

David was trying not to laugh. Banty roosters, just like him and Sean Williams. He turned to the two bigger boys. "Ain't right, two of you picking on him, seein' how you're both bigger." David turned to Patrick. "Are the marbles really yours, son?"

"Yes."

"Then why don't you take 'em back?"

That startled him, and David saw Sammy stiffen too. Patrick's eyes were large, fearful.

"I'll keep the other one out of it," David went on softly, "so it'll be just you and Sammy."

"I . . ." Patrick fell back a step, dismay twisting his face.

"Scaredy-cat," Sammy taunted.

David went down on one knee in front of Patrick. "Listen to me, son. I can make them give you your marbles back. And I'll do that if you want me to. But that won't end it. They'll catch you another day, when no one's around. And they'll take 'em back. You want that?"

He shook his head, his jaw setting.

Out of the corner of one eye, David saw that the two boys were starting to edge away. He shot them a hard look and they stopped instantly. "So, do you want your marbles or not?"

"*Patrick Joseph!*" The cry from behind spun all of them around. A young, dark-haired woman wearing a short-sleeved dress of simple cotton was bearing down on them. Her hair was pulled back in a ponytail and her face was brown from the sun. Fire was dancing in her eyes, which were so dark brown they looked almost black. "What is going on here?" She started towards them, walking swiftly.

"Stay out of this, ma'am," David called. "They're just settling a couple of issues here."

She shot him a frosty look, then rushed forward. David stepped in front of her, blocking her way. When she went to step around him, he matched her step for step. "Leave it be," he said.

"Get out of my way!" she hissed.

"They've gotta settle this on their own," he said. "Stay out of it."

"He's my brother," she shouted. "You get out of my way."

That took him aback, and she used that moment to dart around him. She dropped to her knees and put her hands on Patrick's shoulders. "Are you all right, Patrick Joseph?"

David moved closer, seeing Patrick's eyes watching him over his sister's shoulder. "How old are you, son?" he asked gently.

"He's six."

"I wasn't asking you," David snapped. "Patrick, how old are you?"

"I'm six."

"Big sister has to come and save Pajamas," Sammy said, half giggling to his buddy.

With that, Patrick couldn't hold it back and the tears started.

His sister whirled on the two boys. "Go home, Sammy, or I'm going to tell your mother."

David used that moment to slip between brother and sister again. Ignoring the girl, he bent down to face Patrick. "Tears won't make this go away, Patrick. If you cry, nobody except your sister's gonna hear you. And these guys, they're just gonna call you a baby. So let me say it again. You can run away today, but sometime you're gonna have to face it. And if that is true, then why not right now and right here?"

The sister spun on him, eyes blazing. "How dare you? Who are you, anyway?"

David ignored her. "End it now, son. I'll keep the other one out of it."

"Get away from my brother." She was so livid she could barely speak. Sammy and his buddy started to edge away. Seeing an opening, they turned and ran.

Patrick launched himself like a rock from a flipper. He shot forward past his sister, who gave a low cry of dismay. It was her cry that spun Sammy back around just in time to be butted in the stomach. He howled, as much in surprise as in pain, and went flying. Instantly he was up again, fists flailing. But Patrick waded into him, connecting one to his head, then one to his face.

Sammy clubbed back at this ball of fury, trying to get him off of him. It worked. Patrick fell back, blood trickling from his nose. They stood there, two young stallions, each sizing the other up.

"*Patrick Joseph!*" His sister shouted his name and leaped forward.

David lunged and caught her around the waist, dragging her to a halt. "Let 'em play it out."

But it was already over. Sammy's nose was bleeding too, and he was crying. He jerked the leather pouch from his pocket, threw it at Patrick's feet, then turned and ran, his shocked companion stumbling after him.

David let go of the girl and stepped back as she went to her brother. "Are you okay?" she cried, taking him in her arms.

He pulled away and reached down for his marbles. "I'm okay, Abby," he said. He touched his finger to his upper lip and seemed surprised to see the blood. He wiped across his nose with the sleeve of his shirt, smearing blood across his cheek. Then he looked over at David. His eyes were filled with wonder. And pride.

"You done good," David said soberly. "Go over to the trough there and wash your face."

The sister came at him then, fists up, eyes blazing. "You get out of here."

David raised both hands to ward her off. "I'm going. But don't you be babying him. Don't you take away what he just did."

"Git!" she shouted.

David started to back away. Patrick stared at the two of them with wide eyes.

"Does your family really call you Patrick Joseph?" David called to him.

As the boy nodded, to David's surprise, the girl turned and ran to the tack shed. David ignored her. "No wonder they call you a sissy. P.J. doesn't help much either, does it?"

He shook his head slowly.

The girl reappeared, and, to David's utter astonishment, she held a buggy whip curled in her hand. "You leave now, or I'll take this to you. I swear."

He turned his back on her. "Tell you what," he said to Patrick. "The way you butted ole Sammy there, it was just like a billy goat. I'm gonna call you Billy Joe from now on. Now, there's a real name for a boy."

The whip cracked viciously about five feet above his head. "I am not kidding, Mister. You git, and you git now. And if that's your horse in the barn, take it with you."

David turned, smiling lazily. "Ah couldn't do that, ma'am," he drawled. "I am confident that a nice lady such as yourself wouldn't punish a man's horse just to git even with him."

He waved to the boy and started backing away. "Big sisters sometimes just don't understand man stuff," he said in a conspiratorial tone. "Think you'll be safe with her? She looks pretty mad to me."

Billy Joe shot a look at his sister, and a mischievous grin stole out across his face. "Yeah, if I let her hug me a couple of times."

"*Patrick Joseph!*" Then she turned on David again. He jumped to one side as the whip cracked, this time two feet closer than before.

"See ya, Billy Joe," he called, and started moving toward the barn. He deliberately didn't hurry, but neither did he mosey along. He felt like he had pushed the sister to her limits. He entered the barn; grabbed his saddlebags, rifle, and bedroll; then went out and turned up the street.

CHAPTER 19

Saturday, August 24, 1878

By the time he had bathed, shaved, and eaten some lunch, David was in high spirits. His mind kept swinging back and forth between his experience in the post office and his experience behind the barn. Interesting first day. Maybe Cedar City was going to be more than just another place to briefly hang his hat.

As he entered the lobby of the hotel shortly before four P.M., he stopped dead. Helping an elderly couple at the front desk was the girl from the livery stable. The plain cotton dress had been traded for a dressy black skirt and maroon blouse. Her dark hair, which before had been tied back in a ponytail, was now combed out fully and gleamed a rich ebony in the sunlight coming through the windows. He was dumbfounded. Why would a girl who worked in the stables be clerking behind a hotel desk just an hour later? But there was no mistaking it. It was her.

Then his eyes fell on a wooden nameplate sitting on the counter beside her. *Abigail McKenna.* He gaped at it, mind racing, then he groaned inwardly. "A. M." Abigail McKenna. It *was* her. She was working here because her father owned both the hotel and the livery stable.

Almost instantly, he groaned again as another realization hit him. This was Molly's sister, or possibly a cousin. She didn't look like Molly. But as he looked more closely at her, he changed his mind about that. Her eyes were a dark brown, almost black from this distance, but they were wide set and filled with intelligence. Her nose was shorter, perhaps not as graceful, but her mouth was definitely Molly's. As she smiled at something the couple was saying, he saw the resemblance clearly. Abigail didn't have

Molly's remarkable beauty, but she was, now that she wasn't coming at him with a buggy whip, quite pretty in her own right.

And with that came another terrible thought. He could picture two sisters, heads huddled together, sharing their individual experiences with the new mail rider in town, alternating between hysterical laughter and rather unflattering names.

At that moment, Abby's eyes lifted and she caught sight of him. She visibly stiffened, then quickly turned back to the couple.

His only escape was his appointment with the postmaster and he swung around, searching for his office. There were several doors, but he couldn't—he froze as he heard sharp footsteps coming up behind him. "May I help you, Mr. Draper?"

He turned. The couple was moving away and she was coming toward him, eyes cool and distant. He took a quick breath. "I'm here to see the postmaster. I was told that—"

"My father's office is just across the hall," she said, pointing. "He has someone in with him at the moment."

"Your father?" he managed to croak. "He's the postmaster?"

There was the tiniest smile of triumph. "Yes. He asked me to tell you that he will be with you shortly. And yes, Molly is my sister. You remember Molly, surely?" she added sweetly. "The prettiest girl you've ever seen? Right?"

Now her voice turned sticky sweet. "Isn't that nice?" And with a flounce of her hair, she spun around and stalked away.

Then, as he moved toward the door she had indicated, the last piece of the family puzzle fell into place. He was close enough to read the nameplate on the door. He stopped, his jaw dropping. *Patrick J. McKenna, Postmaster.* His eyes slowly studied the first part of the name. *Patrick J. McKenna. P. J. McKenna.* He smacked himself alongside the head and groaned yet a third time. In the course of less than three hours, he had managed to shamelessly flatter one daughter of his new boss, totally alienate another daughter, and goad his son . . . he suddenly remembered the sign on the barn. *McKenna and Son.* So he had goaded what was probably this man's only son into a fight that sent him home with a bloody nose.

Idiot! And as that thought came, the door to the office opened and two men appeared. They were shaking hands. As the first man left, the other turned to face David. "Ah, Mr. Draper, I presume. Come in."

Patrick J. McKenna was not what David had expected. First of all, he was younger, not yet fifty, David guessed. He had expected someone older because of his accomplishments—a hotel with accompanying dining room, his own livery stable, postmaster of a post office in a substantial town. The first signs of grey were showing around his temples, but other than that his hair was the same dark brown as Abby's and full and thick. In fact, as they shook hands and introduced themselves, David saw that Abby took after her father. She had his wide-set, dark eyes; the higher, more defined cheek-bones; and the more serious demeanor.

Secondly, David had dealt with successful, well-to-do people from time to time since coming to America, and in almost every case they had treated him with an air of condescension, like the girl at the lake near Tilburn Castle. But McKenna greeted him warmly. His handshake was firm, and he held David's hand for just a moment longer while he looked him square in the eye. As he did so, David studied him. And he liked what he saw. It was an open, honest, confident face.

"Tell me about yourself, David," he said after they were seated.

David, never one to sidestep a problem, decided there was no sense postponing the inevitable. He leaned forward. "Shall I do that before or after you fire me?"

He blinked. "Fire you?"

"Surely your daughter has told you by now what happened at the livery stable."

He laughed and sat back again. "Ah, yes. I did hear a pretty impassioned account. "

"I'll bet."

"Actually, it took me about ten minutes to get her calmed down enough that I dared send her out to deal with our guests." His chuckle was deep and resonant. "But—and you'd have to know Abby to appreciate this—she's scrupulously honest, even with herself. Or maybe I should say, *especially* with herself. So when I asked her how Patrick was doing after all of this, she grudgingly admitted that he hasn't stopped beaming all afternoon."

"Well," David said, feeling a flood of relief. "I shouldn't have interfered, but—"

He waved that away. "If you thought I would terminate you for that, you've misjudged me. I'll forgive that this one time." He was teasing him now. "Just don't let it happen again."

"Yes, sir."

His eyes had a twinkle in them now. "And there's no need to mention your first meeting with Molly, either." When David rolled his eyes, McKenna said, "I got that report from Abby as well. Molly only told me that our mail rider had showed up. Abby gave me all the interesting details."

He laughed at David's rueful expression. "You've got quite a talent, young man. You've made rather a strong impression on my family. I can't wait to see how my wife reacts to all of this."

David blew out his breath. "Could we consider postponing that meeting for a year or two?"

"Or three, maybe," McKenna mused. Then he chuckled, and the look on his face at that moment was pure Molly. Suddenly David realized why she had looked so amused earlier. She had been thinking about David's little surprise when he learned who the postmaster was.

"So now, will you tell me about yourself?"

David sat back, relaxing a little. "What would you like to know?"

"For starters, how old are you?"

"I turned twenty-two in June."

"I've had a full report on your service as mail rider from the postmaster in Salt Lake City. Very positive. So no need to bother with that. You fill in the rest."

"Well, I was born in England, down near . . ." He hesitated. He had almost said London, but it was nearly a full decade since he and his father had fled Cawthorne, and this man reminded David of his father. Except for that time with Bertie Beames, David had never lied to his father. He decided right then that he didn't want to lie to Patrick McKenna either. "I come from Yorkshire," he went on, "which is in the northeast of England."

"You don't sound much like an Englishman," McKenna said. "I was born in Ireland myself, near a wee lit'le village near Limerick." He pulled a face. "Unfortunately, I came to America when I was only two and never picked up the Irish lilt. Much to my mother's dismay."

David thought about his interchange with Molly about being Irish, but he wasn't about to comment on that. "When we—my father and I—first arrived here, I got tired of the bullies in school telling me I talked funny. So I punched the biggest one in the mouth, then learned how to talk like a Yank."

"Where was that?"

"Coalville."

"Did you work in the mines there?"

There was an emphatic shake of his head. "No, sir. Had enough of that in Yorkshire. Started when I was six. Left when I was thirteen. Besides, my father promised my mother before she died that he'd keep me out of the mines."

Feeling more comfortable with every minute, David quickly summarized what he had been doing the last six years—teamster, work hand, wrangler, cowboy, mail rider.

"So you were a cowboy?" McKenna said when he was finished.

"Yep. For almost two years. I really enjoyed it, actually."

"Why'd you leave?"

"Mostly got tired of the winters."

"The letter I received from Salt Lake said that you have spent some time down in this area."

"Yes. Constructing a telegraph line. We strung wire from here in Cedar down to St. George. When we finished that, we took it on over to Fredonia and eventually up to Kanab."

"So you know this country pretty well."

"Suppose so. Sure covered enough of it on a horse."

"And you've spent a lot of time out in the open."

"Sometimes it's easier than sleeping in town with all them prickly pears."

"Prickly pears?"

"People."

It was McKenna's turn to laugh. "I see. Yes, good description. In fact, I've got a few of those on my payroll."

David rubbed his chin. "I know. I met one of them this afternoon down at the livery stable."

McKenna hooted. "Abby can be a mite prickly, I'll agree. Especially if she thinks someone's messing with her little brother. Those two have a special bond."

"Where'd she learn to use a buggy whip like that?"

McKenna's mouth fell open. "She used a buggy whip on you?"

"Well, close enough to get my attention."

He shook his head, but his eyes were actually filled with pride. "Both of my girls can handle horses well, but give Abby her way and she would only work at the stables. She likes that much better than working here or in the post office."

He fell silent, and David sat back, waiting for him to continue. Finally, he seemed to make up his mind. "I'm sorry to be so inquisitive, David. And by the way, do you prefer David, Dave, or Davy?"

"David."

"Good. My name's Patrick, and I'd like you to call me that, soon as you're comfortable with it." He gave him a sharp look. "If you are looking to get yourself fired, call me *Paddy* or *Pat*."

David laughed. "I'll try to remember that." He was liking his employer more and more the longer this conversation continued.

Then McKenna got serious again. "I know this all seems a little strange, being that we've just barely met, but something's come up since we sent the offer to you. Something additional I'd like you to do, if you're interested."

"What is that?"

"In a minute. First, let me ask one more question. The answer to this won't change things either way, but I'm curious. Are you a member of the Church?"

David had certainly not expected that. "A Mormon?"

"Sorry," McKenna chuckled. "It's so easy in Utah to say 'the Church' and assume everyone knows you're talking about the Mormon Church."

"Well, I . . . yes." He could feel McKenna's eyes on him as he fumbled a little, so he stopped. He remembered his determination to be honest. "My father and I were baptized in Liverpool, just a few days before we boarded the emigrant ship."

"Me and my parents came through Liverpool too, though I can barely remember it."

"Look, Mr. McKenna, I'll be straight with you. I am a Mormon. But I'm not much of one. Oh, I observe the basic commandments. Most kids my age learned to smoke and chew in the mines, but my mother threatened to skin me alive if I did. Same with drinking. Never been one to chase after women. Another stern lecture from my mother."

He thought for a minute how to say it. "But, as for being involved in the Church, most of my years since becoming a member I've been out away from things, where there are no meetinghouses, no congregations. So I'm not a big churchgoer." He flashed a quick grin. "In fact, to be right honest, sometimes I've been known to linger a little longer out in the country on a Saturday afternoon rather than ride into town so as to be there on Sunday, if you know what I mean. Wouldn't want you to think otherwise, if that makes a difference to you."

The silence stretched out for several moments, and David wondered if honesty had been the best tactic after all. Then McKenna seemed to make up his mind. He abruptly sat up and leaned forward. "I like you, David. I like the cut of you. I like your honesty."

"Thank you, sir."

McKenna frowned. "*Sir* is right up there with *Paddy* and *Pat*, David."

"Yes, sir," David said with a straight face.

McKenna laughed again and then got to it. "Here's what I'm thinking, David. You leave on your first circuit Monday morning, right?" When David nodded, he went on, "I'll have a map and the list of all the settlements for you then. You'll be going full circle from here over to Panguitch, then down to Kanab, continuing on to St. George, and back to Cedar. That's about three hundred miles, or roughly two weeks with rest stops. Since St. George is fifty miles to the south of us, it will take you about twelve days to get there."

David was calculating in his own mind. "First time around, a circuit always takes a little longer. Let's say thirteen or fourteen days to St. George to be safe."

McKenna stood and walked to a wall calendar behind him. He tapped Saturday, August twenty-fourth, with his finger. "Here's today." He moved his finger to Monday. "If you leave on the twenty-sixth—" He started counting quietly to himself, then lifted the page to September. "Fourteen days would put you in St. George about Monday the ninth. Right?"

"That's how I figure it."

"I have some business in St. George. I'll be bringing my family with me. My wife has a sister down there, so we'll be staying with them."

"Do you want me to meet you there?" David asked, a little puzzled by this turn in the conversation. His first circuit, and his boss didn't want him to complete it as quickly as possible?

"Eventually, but we won't get there until the thirteenth or fourteenth. However, there are some things I need you to do before we arrive. We'll meet up that following Saturday or Sunday." He was tapping Saturday the fourteenth.

"And what is it you need me to do?"

He returned to his chair. "September nineteenth is Abby's twenty-first birthday. I want to do something really special for her, as a surprise."

"Okay," David said slowly, not sure what her birthday had to do with him.

"Do you know of a place northeast of St. George called Zion Canyon?"

"Yes. On the Virgin River, near Springdale. Beautiful country."

"One of my employees, a man by the name of Carl Bradford, will be going with us. Good man. I lean on him heavily. In fact, you'll meet him tomorrow at church." He winked. "That is, if you'll be in town."

David had made that decision before he had ever reached Cedar City.

If this was going to become home to him, which he now hoped more than ever, then he had to attend church. In Mormon communities, you weren't ostracized if you weren't a member, but you surely stood out from the crowd. "I'll be there."

"Good. Anyway, back to what I was saying. Carl is . . . well, he's more like me. I've spent some nights out on the trail, but at heart I'm a city person. So is Carl. He's arranged for a guide from Springdale to accompany us on this trip, but as I've thought about it, we could really use another person, someone who can handle horses and teams, someone who can help set up camp, maybe even cook up some beans and bacon."

"Ah," David said, understanding now. "That would be me. As long as you don't set too high a standard on the quality of the food."

McKenna chuckled. "Would something like that interest you?"

"How many in the party?"

"Just me, Carl, and my two daughters. And the local guide. So six of us, including you." He wrinkled his brow. "My wife doesn't do well on trips like this, and besides, she wants to have time with her sister there in St. George. So she and young Patrick—" He stopped, and a sardonic smile played around his eyes. "Or Billy Joe, as he is sometimes known—will stay in St. George."

"You're paying my salary, Mr. McKenna—Patrick. I'm happy to do whatever you ask of me."

"Actually, this is quite important to me, so there'll be a bonus in it for you." He sat back again. "And if this works out like I hope, I might have other things for you to do from time to time. Supplement your mail rider's salary."

"Which means I'd better get this one right, eh?"

"Something like that," McKenna laughed. Then he was immediately serious again. "We'll plan to leave for the canyon the Monday after we arrive. That will give you almost a full week in St. George to get things ready. Do whatever you think is necessary to prepare for the trip. I'll arrange a line of credit for you at the bank there. I've already wired the livery stable and told them we'll need horses and a couple of wagons. I'll—"

"How much luxury can you afford?"

"I beg your pardon?"

For a moment David was afraid he'd gone too far. "It would be helpful to know what level of comfort you want for your daughters. We can take two or three wagons and have things pretty nice, or we can rough it somewhat. Probably can't take wagons too far into the canyon, though."

"I see." He pursed his lips. "They're city girls too, but I'd say they're both pretty adventuresome. What do you recommend? And by the way, not a hint of this to either of the girls. I want to surprise them with it."

No challenge there. He had no plans to talk with either sister anytime in the next decade. "We'll definitely need one wagon to get all of our stuff to Springdale," he said. "Then I'd suggest we pack in with horses and mules. We'll definitely want tents: one for the girls, one for us. This late in the summer we could easily see rain—snow in the higher elevations, if our luck's bad. So we'll also need warm clothes and some good Navajo blankets. But I wouldn't take even straw mattresses. No pillows—you use clothes for that, or a saddle. A simple plate for each person. A fork or a spoon to eat with, but not both. Plain grub. Nothing fancy. That sort of thing."

"Perfect. I trust your judgment." A bit of a devilish smile crept around McKenna's mouth. "I'd like to make it . . . how shall I put it? An *experience* for my girls. Fair enough?"

David nodded. "That's exactly what I needed to know." He paused, then added, "I'll make a list and have it for you tomorrow."

McKenna stood and extended his hand. "Thank you, David. You have put my mind at ease. Services tomorrow begin at ten A.M. Did you see the meetinghouse as you came in?"

"I did."

"Then we'll see you tomorrow. Why don't you plan to sit with our family?"

David rubbed at his chin. "Well, I'm not sure."

That deep resonant chuckle sounded again. "It's okay. We always make the members check their buggy whips at the door."

"That's good. What about their mothers? Any protection there?"

He laughed. "Oh, I think you're in for a surprise there."

CHAPTER 20

Sunday, August 25, 1878

"Brother Draper?"

David turned in surprise. A tall, slender man with a neatly trimmed beard was approaching him, hand outstretched. "Yes?"

"Carl Bradford."

David took his hand, trying not to look too perplexed. This guy was too young to be a bishop. David had come early and moved into the very back pew so he wouldn't have to greet a lot of people. But this guy had taken one look at him and come straight over.

The man had sandy hair a shade lighter than his beard, and clear blue eyes. He was smiling, enjoying David's obvious confusion, and David saw that he had a slight dimple in his right cheek. He was about three inches taller than David and dressed in a dark, pin-striped Sunday suit with a knee-length coat and a black bow tie at his throat.

"Patrick told me you might be here. I'm the assistant manager of the hotel. Carl Bradford."

Then it clicked. This was McKenna's employee. The city boy. "Oh, yes. You're going to Zion Canyon with us. Or," he quickly corrected himself, "I should say, *I'm* going with *you*." He had already offended every person associated with the McKennas so far, and he was determined to keep a tight rein on his tongue today. "Sounds like quite a trip. Tell me about the guide you've lined up for us."

"Patrick said you've been to Springdale before, so you probably know the Behunins. They were the first settlers up there."

"I do. Stayed overnight at their house, in fact."

"Did you happen to meet Ben Mangleson? Young guy, about your age, I would guess. One of their hired hands out there."

David ignored the comment about his age, not sure if it was meant to be a deliberate put-down or not. "I did, as a matter of fact. He helped us bring the cows down to St. George. Good man."

"Ben claims to know the area even better than the Indians. Goes exploring on his days off."

David was nodding. "You've made a good choice. I totally approve."

That pleased Carl, and it showed. Carl seemed just a bit stuffy—or maybe *formal* or *proper* were better descriptions—but he was pleasant enough. More to the point, what little David now knew of Patrick McKenna as an employer told him that Carl Bradford would prove to be highly competent in whatever he set out to do.

"Hi!" The sharp cry of a young boy's voice turned them both around.

Along with a couple of other families, the McKennas were just entering the church. Billy Joe was holding his father's hand, but when he spied David, he jerked free, nearly knocked an older woman down, ignored the cry of dismay from his mother, and shot over to where David was standing. "Hullo," he said happily.

"Good morning, son." He looked closer and suppressed a laugh. Billy Joe had one heck of a shiner around his left eye.

"Hey, Patrick Joseph," Carl said, peering down at him. "What happened to your eye?"

"Call me Billy Joe," he said proudly.

"Billy Joe?" Carl echoed, looking puzzled.

"Don't ask," Abby said from behind them. She had moved ahead of her parents and joined them. She gave David a quick, cool glance. "Good morning."

"Mornin', Miss McKenna."

"I prefer *Sister McKenna*," she said coolly.

"Mornin', Sister McKenna," he repeated in the same polite tone.

"Hello, Brother Draper," Molly said as she joined them. Her smile was most appealing, a good sign, since her sister had surely been attacking his character, motives, and ancestry.

"I prefer David," he said, straight-faced and not altering his tone of voice.

Molly laughed merrily at Abby's glowering look of response. Then she turned to Carl. "Morning, Brother Bradford," she said sweetly.

"Morning, Molly." Then Carl turned back to Abby. "And how are you?"

"Good." She went up on tiptoe and kissed him on the cheek, giving him a warm smile. Then she slipped her hand through his arm and moved in close beside him.

So, Carl is not just an employee, David thought. *Well, well.* Being as proper as he was, he probably even got along with her.

Patrick McKenna came up to join them then, holding his wife's hand and bringing her forward. "Good morning, Carl. Good morning, David. David, I'd like you to meet Sister McKenna. Sarah, this is the young man I told you about. Meet David Draper."

He bobbed his head as he took her hand. "I am very pleased to meet you, Sister McKenna."

"And I you," she said, smiling warmly. It reminded him of Molly's smile.

He couldn't resist. "You wouldn't straight-out lie to me, would you now, Sister McKenna?"

She was startled for a moment, but behind her, Molly hooted. Her husband was smiling. Then she laughed as well. "All right. Yesterday, if I could have laid my hands on you . . ." She didn't finish, but reached out and pulled Billy Joe to her, her eyes softening with love. "But this morning . . ." She tilted his chin up. "Tell Brother Draper what happened just now."

Embarrassed, he did what any six-year-old would do. He played dumb. "What?"

"You know. Outside, as we came in. Tell him about Sammy."

That was all he needed. His eyes started to dance. "'Member how Sammy took those marbles that were on the ground and put 'em in his pocket?" When David nodded, he rushed on. "Well, he found them when he got home, and he gave them back to me this morning. And he said he was sorry, too."

"My goodness," David said solemnly. "That *is* progress. Did his mother make him do it?"

The boy wrinkled his nose quizzically. "Dunno. I don't think so." Then he lowered his voice. "I think he was just skeered that I would remember he still had 'em."

"I think so too," David whispered. Still smiling, he turned to Mrs. McKenna. "That's one fine boy you have there. I really am sorry about yesterday. I just . . ."

He saw that Abby was watching him closely, dark eyes flashing as she waited for him to finish that sentence. "It was none of my business," he finished lamely.

Molly's mother cocked her head, deciding if he really meant it, and David was struck at that moment with how much Molly looked like her. Abby favored her father, but Molly was her mother. Were it not for the age difference, they could have passed as sisters. She was lovely and gracious, and David found himself instantly liking her.

"Apology accepted," she finally said, her eyes teasing him now. "Patrick Joseph was very grateful that you interfered. He told me this morning that you are his best friend now."

He turned to see the boy's sudden apprehensiveness, lest David should disagree. "Thank you, Billy Joe," he said. "I consider that a great honor."

Abby winced. "The family prefers that you call him Patrick, or Patrick Joseph."

He eyed her steadily for a moment, then looked down at the boy. "What do you prefer?"

"Billy Joe," he said without hesitation.

David turned to Abby and shrugged. "Sorry. A man's got a right to choose what people call him, I'd say."

But she had already turned away and was pulling Carl with her toward the front of the chapel. As Billy Joe and his parents started to follow, Molly fell in beside David just behind them. "You know, David," she said in a low voice, "you and Abby might actually become friends if you'd stop needling her like that."

He gave her an incredulous look. "Are you talking about the Abigail McKenna I know?"

Monday, August 26, 1878

David had told his new employer that he wanted an early start on Monday morning, so when he arrived at the post office a little before seven, he was not surprised to see lamps burning inside. As he swung down from the saddle, the door flew open and a small figure shot out. "Hi, Brother Draper," Billy Joe cried, a huge grin splitting his face.

"Mornin', Patrick Joseph."

That pulled him up short, and his face fell in disappointment. David took the reins and began wrapping them around the hitching post. "You call me Brother Draper," he growled with mock severity, "and I'm gonna call you Patrick Joseph, or P. J. Deal?"

"Okay, David." He jumped down beside him. "What's your horse's name?"

"Lady Tilburn, but I call her Tillie."

He started patting her nose. "Hi, Tillie." Then in an instant he was back at David's side. "Is this your gun?" he asked, touching the revolver at David's hip. "Neat!"

"Yep."

"It's a Colt forty-five, isn't it?"

David was surprised. "It is. Actually, most people call it the Peacemaker. I prefer its other name—the Equalizer."

Billy Joe peered up at the saddle, squinting against the morning light. "And that's a Winchester Henry rifle, isn't it? That yours too?" He reached up and caressed the stock, rushing on without giving David a chance to answer. "That's called the gun that won the West, right? Shoots a forty-four caliber bullet."

Laughing softly, David took the rifle out of its scabbard and handed it to him. "You're right. This one happens to be the Centennial model. Know what that means?"

Billy Joe looked disgusted by the question. "Put out two years ago to celebrate America's one hundredth birthday. Can I hold it?"

David made sure the hammer was locked and handed it to him. "How come you know so much about guns?"

"Because he spends an hour or two every day down at the dry goods store."

David turned to see Molly and her father standing on the veranda. "Fortunately," her father said, "Brother Williams, who owns the store, finds Patrick quite entertaining. He lets him look at the gun catalogs in exchange for sweeping out the store. This six-year-old knows more about guns than a lot of adults." It was said with great affection, and he reached out and tousled his son's hair. "Don't you, young Patrick?"

Molly was looking at David. She hesitated, then gave him a brilliant smile, those wide grey eyes mesmerizing him. "Good morning, David."

"Mornin', Molly." He managed to pull his gaze away to look at her father. "Mornin', Patrick."

"This is so neat," Billy Joe was saying. He lifted the weapon and sighted down the barrel, barely able to hold it steady.

"Son," his father said gently, "what have we said about pointing guns?"

He lowered the muzzle immediately. "Sorry, Daddy."

"David has to be on his way, Patrick. Let him come inside."

As David replaced the rifle in its scabbard, he reached down and touched Billy Joe's shoulder. "Maybe when I get back, we can go out and shoot some tin cans together."

His eyes widened and his mouth fell open. "*Really?*" He spun around to his father. "Could we, Dad? Could we?"

He smiled. "We'll see. Now let David come inside."

Once inside, Molly pulled her brother off to one side while her father and David discussed the mail route. McKenna had a map laid out on the counter and a paper with the list of the settlements David would visit. When they finished tracing the route on the map, McKenna folded it up and handed it to David, then went behind the counter and brought out a heavily laden mailbag.

"This is fuller than usual," he said. "We missed one circuit when our last rider left us. They'll be anxious to see you."

"Always nice to be welcomed," David said.

"Had word last week of some Paiute trouble south of Panguitch," McKenna was saying.

Billy Joe's eyes grew big. "Indians?" But Molly shushed him.

David shouldered the bag. "How bad?"

"Not real serious. Four Paiutes stopped a couple of drovers, said they wanted to trade for some food. While they were talking, two more tried to steal a couple of the horses. Don't think it's anything to be concerned about, but keep your eyes open."

"I always do that. Anything else?" When McKenna shook his head, he tipped his hat to Molly, then cocked his thumb and finger and "shot" Billy Joe dead in the heart. "You start collecting some cans, all right?"

"I will!" he exclaimed, puffing out his chest.

David moved to the door and opened it. "See you in a couple of weeks in St. George." He waved one last time, exited, and shut the door behind him. A moment later he was mounted and on his way, heading north toward Parowan.

Molly and Billy Joe both moved to the window and watched him until he disappeared.

"All right, young man," his father said. "I told your mother I'd get you breakfast if she let you come down here this early. So off you go. They're expecting you in the dining room."

For a moment he looked like he would protest, but then the idea of food changed his mind and he was gone.

"Father!"

McKenna turned in surprise. Abby was just coming in from the hotel lobby. "What is this about you seeing David in St. George?"

"Well," Molly said, "aren't you the early bird?"

"I am always the early bird. The miracle is that *you're* up and dressed before breakfast." Then she turned to her father again. "Well?"

"That's right. He's going to meet us there."

"You can't do that."

"Oh?" he said, raising one eyebrow. "And why is that?"

She shot him one of her pitying looks, then bent down and kissed Billy Joe on the cheek as he started past her. He immediately rubbed it off, then hurried away before she could do it again. "Because he is insufferable," she finally said.

"I think he's sooo handsome," Molly said, coming over to join them.

The look Abby gave her sister was withering. "You think every mail rider is *sooo handsome*. But that's all right. I'm sure Mr. Draper totally agrees with you."

"Well," Molly said airily, "if he does, he would be right."

Abby whirled back to face her father. "Why, Daddy? What's so important that you need him in St. George? Of all the people, why him? Especially for our family trip. You barely know him. But he's arrogant, conceited, and insufferable."

"And cute," Molly said, thoroughly enjoying this, and secretly delighted with the news. "Now that he's shaved, I think he's adorable." She deliberately let her voice go soft and dreamy. "Those big brown eyes, the dark hair with just that touch of curl at the back of his neck, the cleft in his chin."

"Oh, stop it," Abby snapped, knowing her sister was just baiting her.

Their father held up a hand. "Okay, you two. Abby's question is a fair one. Before I answer it, you need to understand something. I was going to keep this a surprise, but the more I've thought about it, the more I think there may be as much value in the anticipation of the gift as in the gift itself. So—" He looked at Abby. "I've been planning a surprise for your birthday."

"My birthday?"

"Yes. Several weeks ago, I asked you what you wanted, remember? I said that since this would be your twenty-first birthday, we should do something really special."

"Yes, and I told you I didn't know what that would be."

"But the next day Carl let me know that you told him something that you didn't tell me. Something that you really, really wanted to do some-time in your life."

Her head came up with a snap. "Zion Canyon?" she exclaimed.

He nodded, pleased with her reaction.

"We're going to Zion Canyon, Daddy?"

"Yes. This last trip Carl made to St. George included a detour out to Springdale. He's found us a guide who will take us in. We'll spend about a week there."

Abby threw her arms around him. "Oh, Daddy, I can't believe it."

He wagged his finger at the two of them. "From what this guide told Carl, this isn't going to be a picnic in the park. This is rough country, a lot of it still unexplored.[1] But from what little Carl saw around Springdale, he says it is spectacular. Enough to take your breath away."

"Yes!" Abby cried. "That's what I want for my birthday. To have my breath taken away."

Molly was laughing excitedly. "Can I go too, Daddy? Please?"

"We're all going. Well, not your mother or young Patrick, of course, but the rest of us. Carl, me, and the two of you." He paused, then added, "And David Draper."

Abby's face instantly went from joy to dismay. "Why, Daddy? Oh, don't spoil it."

"Because this isn't a trip where we stay in cabins or hotels. We'll be camping out every night. It will be bedrolls and campfires, hardtack, jerky, and johnnycake. Hardly what the two of you are used to. Or me and Carl either, for that matter. David has spent much of his life on the trail. He's exactly what we need."

"What about the guide?" Abby asked. "Couldn't he do that?"

He shook his head. "He's our guide, not our cook and wrangler. And besides, with six of us, one man isn't enough. So your personal differences are going to have to be set aside."

"Please," she begged. "Anyone but him."

He was suddenly impatient. "If you feel that strongly about it, then we'll just forget it and come straight home from St. George."

"No, Daddy," Molly cried in alarm. Then to her sister, "Abby, you have to go. Zion Canyon! Think of it. Everyone says it's like being taken into heaven."

For a long moment, Abby's head turned back and forth between the two of them. Then she stamped her foot. "*Ohhhh!*" she cried in complete disgust, and stormed out of the room.

_____

Note

1. Today, Zion Canyon, which was made a national park in 1919, is visited by over two million visitors each year. However, considering how many important European or American exploring parties passed through this area, it is surprising that it didn't become better known until the early years of the twentieth century. In 1858, a Southern Paiute guide led a young Mormon missionary and interpreter into Zion Canyon. His favorable report about its agricultural potential brought settlers into the area, eventually forming the towns of Virgin, Springdale, and Rockville.

Isaac Behunin settled in the canyon in 1863, farming near the present site of Zion's Lodge. He grew cotton, tobacco, and fruit trees during the summer, then wintered in Springdale a few miles to the south. According to tradition, it was Behunin who gave the canyon the biblical name of *Zion*, meaning a place of transcendent beauty, peace, and rest.

CHAPTER 21

Saturday, September 14, 1878

David had pushed himself hard. In spite of Tillie's throwing a shoe, which required him to walk her the last six miles into Kanab, he finished the mail circuit in two days less than he had allowed himself. He had arrived in St. George late Saturday evening a week ago. And it was a good thing he had, because it turned out that he had needed every day since then to get ready.

After attending church on Sunday—in case Patrick asked—David got a horse from the livery stable and started for Springdale. He left Tillie at the stable to get a much-needed rest.

He arrived at Springdale midmorning on Monday and met with Ben Mangleson, the guide Carl Bradford had secured. That afternoon, Ben took David into the canyon and they spent the rest of that day and Tuesday morning picking out possible campsites along the river. Returning to Springdale on Tuesday, they spent the rest of the day making a long list of supplies and equipment they would need. David then returned to St. George on Wednesday. On his arrival, shortly after dark, he went straight to the telegraph office and sent a telegram to Patrick.

CLOTHING FOR GIRLS A PROBLEM STOP CANYON TOO
RUGGED FOR WAGONS STOP RIDING SIDESADDLE NOT
IDEAL STOP BEN PLANS DIFFICULT HIKES STOP
FULL SKIRTS A PROBLEM STOP RECOMMEND YOU
DISCUSS WITH MRS M STOP DAVID

Now it was Saturday night and all was finally in readiness. The wagon was in a shed, loaded with equipment and food. As he dragged himself back to the boardinghouse shortly after eight o'clock, David went over everything again in his mind, making sure he hadn't overlooked anything.

He opened the door and went inside and there found Mrs. Cosgrove waiting for him, as usual. "There you are, David," she said. "Did you get everything finished?"

He nodded. "Finally." She was a grandmother of seven who had been a widow for nearly fifteen years and who, as near as he could tell, was not a member of the Church. She had taken David in that first day he arrived and mothered him like he was her own.

"Are you hungry? I have some supper still warm in the oven."

He shook his head. "No, thanks, Mrs. Cosgrove. I ate just three days ago."

She laughed. "You are such a tease, David. How about a hot bath instead? I can have the water ready in ten minutes."

"Now, *that* would be wonderful. Thank you."

"Your Mr. McKenna came in a couple of hours ago. Left a note. I put it on your dresser."

He waved his thanks and trudged up the stairs. Tossing his saddlebags in one corner, he sat down and pulled off his boots. Then he went to the dresser and found the folded paper.

David—Was delayed in Cedar. Just arrived this afternoon. Carl reports you have been hard at work. Anxious to hear your report. Church is tomorrow at ten. Love to have you join us. Will stop by for you at 9:30. Might be interesting. Rumors abound about a possible mission to Four Corners area. Could provide some business opportunities.

Sarah's sister insists you join us for Sunday dinner after church. Fried chicken with all the trimmings. That will give us time to hear your report. She won't take no for an answer. Patrick

P.S. Young Patrick, otherwise known as Billy Joe McKenna, is very anxious to see you again. Says he collected 26 tin cans before we left Cedar. Plans to hold you to your promise.

P.P.S. Warmest wishes from Molly. Somewhat less enthusiastic greetings from Abby. However, both are greatly anticipating this coming week.

P.P.P.S. Sarah says thank you for your concern about the girls' attire. Has worked out what she says will be an acceptable solution. Grateful that you and I don't need to worry about it.

Sunday, September 15, 1878

Rachel Reynolds, Sarah's sister, and her husband, Robert, lived in a pleasant two-story house just two blocks from the St. George Temple. With both families, there were fourteen people present for dinner, and tables were set up in both the kitchen and the parlor. The meal was excellent. After almost three solid weeks on the trail, eating cold beans and hardtack, David greatly relished it. During the dinner, however, he was mostly quiet, speaking only when directly addressed, satisfied to sit back and listen.

Patrick had stated right up front that there would be no discussion about the Zion Canyon expedition until afterwards, so most of the time the conversation focused on the speculations about a Four Corners mission, and David had nothing to contribute there. Billy Joe might have given him someone to talk to, but he was in the parlor with the younger children.

Molly, seated directly across from him, would draw him in from time to time, but she was seated by a cousin of her same age who was telling her about the social activities in St. George. That gave David a chance to study her. Once again he was struck with her loveliness. The lines of her face were so graceful. Her eyes sparkled with her sheer exuberance for life. Her laugh was like the ripple of a breeze on a warm day. It warmed him just to be in her presence.

Gratefully, Abby and Carl were at the end of the table on the same side as David, so he didn't have to make polite conversation with her. Other than a curt nod at church, she had studiously avoided him. Which was fine. He was too jaded to get into another spitting contest with her.

Now, as they finished the dessert, an excellent green-apple pie, Billy Joe came in and stood beside David's chair. Expecting a discussion on tin cans and shooting practice, David turned and gave him a smile. But, in true Billy Joe fashion, his first question took David by surprise.

"Did you get attacked by them Indians?"

For a moment, David didn't understand. Then he remembered that morning at the post office and the report from McKenna about the Paiutes. He shook his head. "Nope. Saw some Navajos trading in Kanab, and some Paiutes further north, but they were friendly. Never even took my pistol out of the holster."

"Oh." He looked terribly disappointed. "Did you already deliver all the mail?"

"I did. Picked up a bunch more and brought it back with me, too. Why?"

Billy Joe's shoulders lifted and fell. "Puffy died." It was said in a matter-of-fact tone.

"Puffy?"

"Our cat," Molly supplied. "He was quite old."

"Oh." Then to Billy Joe, "That's too bad."

"We gave him a funeral." Again, it was a statement of fact without emotion.

"I see. And did you cry?"

The boy's head reared back and he looked disgusted. "No."

"But you were sad, right?" Abby asked. She had leaned out to see the two of them.

He nodded, but his eyes never left David's. "Do you think Puffy's in heaven?"

Now it was David who reared back. He hadn't seen that one coming. There were chuckles from up and down the table. "Yes," Billy Joe's father said. "That's a good question, David. Do cats go to heaven?"

"I . . ." He was fumbling. "Well, I suppose they could. Don't know why not."

"But you're not sure?" That was from Billy Joe, who still had him pinned with his eyes.

He laughed. This kid was so single-minded. "No, I'm not sure."

"Do you have God's address?"

David nearly knocked over his glass. "I'm sorry. Say that again?"

"Do you have God's address?" He was clearly put out that he wasn't being taken seriously.

"Ah . . . well, not actually. Why do you need His address?"

"I wanna write Him a letter and ask Him if Puffy's in heaven."

"Patrick Joseph," his mother said. "When we have questions for Heavenly Father, we ask Him in our prayers."

His head moved back and forth in quick movements. "I did, but He didn't answer." He turned his focus back to David. "You're a mail rider. Why can't you take a letter to God?"

Abby's eyes were soft. She was looking at her brother, but she spoke to David. "That seems like a fair question." She was obviously enjoying his discomfort. "I think we'd all like to know God's address. That is, if you have it."

"Well," David began, ignoring her and looking only at Billy Joe. "I guess I'd have to say—"

He stopped. Billy Joe had reached in his back pocket and extracted a crumpled envelope. He held it out to David. David looked down and read "To God" in large, carefully printed block letters. "Will you take it to Him on your next trip?" the boy asked.

"Uh . . ." David was speechless. And then he remembered how he had petitioned heaven while his mother lay dying in the infirmary. He reached out, nodding. "I'll do my very best, Billy Joe," he said softly.

"Good." And that was it. Billy Joe pocketed the letter and rejoined the other children without another word.

The table was quiet for a moment, then Patrick slid his chair back. "Let's get the dishes done. Then we need to hear what David has to say about tomorrow."

Everyone stood now. As David started gathering up his plate and silverware, he saw that Sister McKenna was looking at him. He gave her a crooked smile and shrugged helplessly.

"Thank you," she mouthed, her eyes moist.

To his greater surprise, when David started into the kitchen, Abby, who was just ahead of him, stepped back to let him pass. She didn't speak, but her earlier cool disdain was gone. She nodded politely as he passed.

When the dishes were cleared, washed, dried, and put away, and the tables were removed, all of the children except for Molly and Abby went outside and the adults gathered in the living room. David suddenly felt like an outsider again. The McKennas sat on a divan, holding hands. Aunt Rachel and Uncle Robert were together on the couch. Abby and Carl Bradford sat on the floor with their backs against the wall, also holding hands. Molly took a chair next to her father, leaving David the chair in the corner. He was determined to give a quick report and excuse himself. He needed at least half a day to rest up and get himself ready.

"We have a birthday in four days," Patrick McKenna began, "and we're off to celebrate it in a most unusual way. Since David says we need to leave by five o'clock in the morning, we need to keep this short." He turned to David. "You have the floor. Tell us what we need to do."

And so he did. In short, clipped sentences, he told them of his trip to Springdale, meeting with Ben Mangleson, and the arrangements they had made together. He laid out the schedule as well as he could, going day by day, concluding with their return to St. George ten to twelve days later. He described the tents and their sleeping arrangements. He warned them about the simple nature of the meals, about the possibility of rain, rattlesnakes, and scorpions. "And," he concluded, "even though I know you all ride horses quite a bit, be prepared for very stiff legs and a numb bottom, because we'll be spending about six to eight hours in the saddle on average every day."

"Stop!" Molly laughed. "Are you trying to change our minds?"

He grinned. "No, I just don't want you to have any illusions."

"Do you really think we're that naive?" Abby said. Any points he had made earlier were clearly forgotten. "It is fifty miles from Cedar to St. George, and we managed to survive that."

To David's surprise, her comment embarrassed Carl a little. "But, Abby," he said, "that was riding in a carriage. After going by horse forty miles out to Springdale to meet Ben Mangleson last month, I could barely walk when I got down. David's right to be concerned."

David raised a hand. "Yes, but after being inside the canyon, I can promise you a fantastic experience." He looked directly at Abby. "I didn't mean to suggest that any of you weren't up to it."

She nodded, somewhat contrite.

Looking at Patrick, David went on. "Our ride out to Springdale will be good preparation. Even though we have a wagon, I would suggest you ride the horses as much as possible on the way. When you start getting sore, then ride in the wagon awhile. Once we go on from Springdale, it will be horses all the way."

"Good recommendation," Patrick said. "What else?"

Sister McKenna spoke up. "I want to thank you, David. I have been quite worried about this since Patrick first told me what he was planning. But you have put my mind at rest." She looked wistful. "You almost tempt me to go with you. However, Rachel and I shall just have to console ourselves by shopping the whole time you are gone."

As they laughed at that, a voice behind them suddenly cut in. "Can I go, Daddy?" They turned. Billy Joe was standing in the doorway. His face was forlorn, his eyes imploring as he spoke to his father. "Please, Papa. Please. Please. Please."

"No, Patrick Joseph," his mother said firmly. Then, as his face fell, her expression softened. "This is not a place for a six-year-old."

But this six-year-old was wise enough to know that no hope lay with his mother. He ran to his father and dropped down in front of him. Abby cut in. "No, Patrick." She came to him and put an arm around him. "It's going to be a very difficult trip."

His eyes filled with tears. "You don't want me there for your birthday?"

She melted and took him in her arms. "Oh, Patrick. We'll have a party when we get back."

Seeing no support from his sister, Billy Joe turned once again to his father. This time he said nothing, just stood there with those large, beseeching eyes.

David had been watching Billy Joe's father through all of this. To his surprise, the senior Patrick seemed to be considering it. Finally, he looked at David. "Any comment, David?"

"No, Patrick," his wife cried.

But he held up one hand and nodded at David. "What do you think?"

"Daddy," Abby said, sensing what was about to happen. "You heard what David just said about how *very hard*—" the last two words were said with heavy irony—"this trip is going to be."

Patrick's jaw set a little. "I know that, Abby, but I'd still like to hear what David has to say."

David took a quick breath, knowing he was about to get himself in trouble again. "Well, as far as the practical goes, that's not a problem. I bought a couple of extra bedrolls, in case one of them gets wet. And we have plenty of food."

Molly, who seemed not at all upset with the idea, laughed aloud. "Are you sure? Remember, this boy eats more than any one of you three men."

"Do not!" Billy Joe said hotly. He looked at David anxiously, afraid this might do him in.

"I think your sister's right, Billy Joe. I saw you putting away that pie at dinner. But," he went on quickly before he could protest further, "we have enough to keep you from starving."

Billy Joe's face lit up as he realized that David wasn't going to vote against him. David, however, was watching his mother. Now it was her eyes that were pleading with him. He sighed. "Sister McKenna, it is not my decision whether Billy Joe goes or not. That's up to you and your husband. But I cannot agree that a trip like this is no place for a six-year-old. I've talked to men who walked across the plains when they were four and five."

"That's not a fair comparison," Abby said tightly.

"Abby," her father warned. "Let David finish."

David took in a breath, trying to hold his temper. He had no desire to offend Billy Joe's mother, but his sister needed taking down a peg or two. And there was something that needed saying here. So he took another breath and plunged.

"I started as a trapper in the Yorkshire coal mines three days after my sixth birthday," he said quietly. "A trapper is a boy who opens and shuts the doors in the coal tunnels to help control ventilation. I worked twelve hours a day, six days a week. Most of that was in total darkness. The thing I hated the most was hearing the sound of the rats scurrying past my feet and not being able to see them, or know if they were eating the lunch I brought each day."

He ignored the shudder that ran through Molly's body and the look of horror on Sister McKenna's face. "By the time I was eight, I was hauling coal tubs through the monkey heads—tunnels no higher than this." He held a hand at waist height. "We strapped on leather girdles with chains attached. We hooked them to the carts, then pulled our guts out, crawling on our hands and knees so we didn't hit our heads on the tunnel roof."

He stopped, realizing that his chest was rising and falling a little. Seeing their shocked, wide-eyed, open-mouthed expressions, he forced a wan smile, then said, "Sister McKenna, if you don't want Billy Joe to go with us, that's fine. But don't decide that just because he's six. Even at six, a boy can start becoming a man."

"I'm sorry to hear that you had a deprived childhood, Mr. Draper," Abby said in a tight voice, "but this is our family and you have no say in what happens."

"Abby!" her father said sharply. "That's enough."

David swung on her. "You're right, Miss Abigail. You shouldn't care what I think. But you should care about Billy Joe."

"His name is not Billy Joe," she snapped. "And for your information, I love my brother."

"Maybe too much," he murmured.

Abby went livid. "How dare you!"

He whirled on her. "Then stop calling him Patrick Joseph. That's an honorable name, and maybe when he's twenty, he'll like it. But he's a kid now. That's not a kid's name." He turned to the parents. "Do you know what started the fight the other day at the livery stable? The other kids were making fun of his name. They call him P. J. or *Pajamas*."

There was a sharp intake of breath from Sister McKenna. "Is that true, young Patrick?"

He hung his head. "Yes, Mama."

"So I gave him a nickname," David said calmly, "a nickname that he earned, by the way." He turned to Patrick senior. "Abby's right, Patrick. I am not part of your family. And it's not my decision. But I know about boys. And I know that sometimes they can be protected too much. Sometimes they just need to do something exciting and manly."

"Yeah!" Billy Joe cried.

David ignored that, though it was hard not to smile. "So since you asked, yes, I would be happy to have Billy Joe join us. In fact, I think it is one of the best things you could possibly do for him right now."

He stood and went to the door, feeling every eye upon him. "If you want to find someone else for tomorrow, I'll understand. Just leave word at the boardinghouse and I'll head on back to Cedar City. But either way, I'll have the wagon here at five o'clock."

Monday, September 16, 1878

When the door opened, David fully expected that Brother McKenna would be the only one to come out. But he was wrong. Abby came first, dressed in riding clothes. She walked past him with a curt nod, but said nothing. Her father was next, followed by Molly, dressed in the same manner. She didn't speak, but gave David a little wave and a bright smile.

Then Carl came around from the back of the house, leading four horses. "Good morning, David," he said, as if nothing unusual had happened here the previous afternoon.

"Mornin', Carl."

Well, at least I still have a job. He was relieved. He had hoped it would go this way, but the more he had replayed the conversation in his mind yesterday, the less certain he had become.

Then his head came around slowly. Sarah McKenna was framed in the light of the doorway. Her sister was standing next to her, and Billy Joe stood between them. He wore a wide-brimmed hat, a leather jacket, and cowboy boots. At the sight of David, he gave his mother a quick hug and a kiss, then came on a dead run.

"Well, hello there, Billy Joe," David said. "What are the chances I could get you to ride up here with me and help drive this team? They're a little ornery this morning."

"Yahoo!" he shouted and clambered up beside him.

Sister McKenna came down the walk, smiled briefly up at David, then went on and gathered her two girls in her arms. "You have a wonderful birthday, Abby."

"I will, Mama. I'm so excited."

Sarah and her husband then embraced. "Be careful, Patrick."

"I will." He took the reins of his horse from Carl. "We'll be back in about ten days."

She finally turned to David.

He swept off his hat. "Sister McKenna, I . . . I'm sorry for what I said yesterday."

She was quite grave, but a smile teased the corners of her mouth. She looked up at her son, who already had the reins in his hands. "Watching my son this morning, I'd say no apology is necessary." Suddenly her eyes were shining. "Will you take care of him for me, David?"

"I will."

She laughed to cover the huskiness in her voice. "Well, my daughters too. And Patrick, of course. He'll be your biggest challenge." Then she had to stop, pressing her lips together to keep them from trembling. "Promise me," she said in a fierce whisper.

David looked her directly in the eye. "You didn't have to ask. You have my word on it."

CHAPTER 22

Thursday, September 19, 1878

"Good morning, Sister Abby," David said, looking up from the fire. "Happy birthday."

"Thank you." She moved over to stand across the fire from him, warming her hands. "How can it be so warm in the day and so cold at night?"

"That's the desert for you."

She bent over and sniffed the air. "Umm, flapjacks."

He reached down to where he had several already done and sitting on a plate. He picked one up and tore it in half. "Here, try it. But no honey and butter until breakfast."

She took it, pulling off small pieces and eating it a little bit at a time. "This is so good."

"Nothing like being hungry to improve the taste of food." He flipped over two flapjacks, watching her as she turned to look at the sun, which was just peeping over the eastern cliffs. She wore a sheepskin jacket over her blouse and long skirt. Beneath the hem, he could see sturdy hiking boots. She also had a cowboy hat pulled down almost to her ears, but tufts of her dark hair stuck out all around it. With the new sun on her face, her eyes were almost golden. As she stood there, her breath showed like little puffs of silver.

"By the way," she said. "Out here, just plain Abby is fine."

"But I could never think of you as just plain Abby," he quipped. "You actually look quite fetching this morning. This desert air must be good for you."

"*Oh, please!*"

He looked up in surprise.

"Why do you do that, David?"

"Do what?"

"That thing you do with girls, that—" her voice dropped into a low growl—"Why-hello-there-little-darlin'. My-ain't-you-the-pretty-little-thing-now?"

He blinked. "I said all that?"

"I used to think it was because you viewed all unmarried females over the age of ten as scatterbrained, flighty creatures who need your adoration to keep them all fluttery inside."

"Whoa! What'd you do, sleep on a rock last night?"

"See what I mean? I can't even have a serious discussion with you. But I'm on to you, David Draper." She was actually almost smiling as she said it. "These last few days I've come to see beneath that game you play to charm the girls, keep them all atwitter so they can't get to know the real you."

He stood slowly. "Is this what you're like when you're all atwitter?"

She kicked dirt at him. "Stop it. It's not funny."

"I wasn't trying to be funny," he snapped, irked now. "Look, Abby, you want honesty. All right, I'll be honest. You scare the heck out of me."

"Go on!" she burst out incredulously.

"I mean it. When you got that buggy whip out, I decided right then and there that here was a woman I was going to take very seriously. I was afraid that if I misbehaved again, you'd strap on a gun and come looking for me."

She tried to glare at him, but she couldn't hold it. The laughter bubbled up and burst out of her. "Well," she said, "you really did make me angry that day."

"Who, me?" he asked innocently.

"You have this ability to irritate people," she went on, "and I can't decide if it's a natural gift or if you've been working on it all your life."

"It's natural. But you've helped me greatly enhance it."

She laughed again. "You're hopeless."

But he wasn't done. "Do you feel like I treat you with respect?"

Startled, she considered that, then finally nodded. "Yes. Not at first, but now, yes."

"So you're not just another pretty face?" he asked softly.

"*Ohhh, you!*" She threw her hands in the air. "There you go again. Why do you do that? It's not you, David. It's a game. And you're not a little boy anymore."

He didn't flinch. "That was not a little boy's question."

That stopped her. "What is that supposed to mean?"

"So, you think I was playing when I said you looked fetching this morning?"

"I . . . of course. That's just you."

"You don't consider yourself pretty, do you? Not compared to Molly."

Her face flamed instantly red. "I feel no obligation to answer that."

"Sorry. You just did." He returned to his cooking, turning the bacon and checking to see if the flapjacks were done. Then, as he watched her face, his voice softened. "Sit down, Abby. I shouldn't have said that."

"Then why did you?"

"Because you *are* a pretty face," he shot back at her. "You too are a lovely woman. You don't have to look like Molly to be pretty, or be like Molly to be an attractive, interesting person. And if you think that's just me trying to sweet-talk you into going all fluttery, well, so be it."

"I . . ." She looked away, clearly uncomfortable with what had just happened. "Where are Carl and Daddy?"

"Down at the river with Billy Joe, washing up."

She gave him a fleeting, halfhearted smile, pulled her jacket around her more tightly, and started away. David lifted the frying pan and waved it at her. "If you're going down there, tell them breakfast will be ready in ten minutes."

She waved, but several steps later stopped and turned back, shoving her hands deep into her pockets. "I will say one thing. You were right about Billy Joe coming with us. I was wrong. And I apologize for that comment about your childhood. That was totally uncalled for."

That took him by surprise. Then he remembered what her father had said about her scrupulous honesty, especially with herself. He grinned slowly. "Well, maybe not totally. And I'm sorry for saying you love Billy Joe too much. He thinks the world of you, Abby. It's fun to watch the two of you."

She smiled awkwardly. Finally she lifted a hand and turned to go again. But once again she remembered something else and turned back. "One more thing."

He tried not to smile. She was really unloading the saddlebags this morning.

"Thank you for thinking about what kind of clothes Molly and I would need up here." She was suddenly flustered. "Riding sidesaddle all this time would have been. . . . Well, let's just say we could have done it, but this is much better." She pulled out the front of her skirt to show that beneath its fullness it was actually tailored so as to be separated into what looked like men's trouser legs.

"Well, I'll be. So that's how you did it?" He chose his words carefully. "I just thought you and Molly were tucking all that material up beneath you on the saddle when you rode."

She laughed. "You can do that, but—" she pulled a face. "But it ain't very comfortable." Then she reached in her pocket and brought out what looked like two men's garters. Her face colored even more. "I know Ben is worried about hiking today, but watch this." She bent down, gathered half of her skirts around one ankle, then slipped the garter over her foot to hold them in place. She did the same with the other side. When she straightened, she looked like she was wearing a pair of very baggy men's trousers. "It's not very flattering." There was an amused smile. "Molly is still adjusting to the idea. But it will work."

"Women are a marvel," he said, really meaning it.

"Well, again I thank you. We wouldn't have come prepared if you hadn't said something."

"It was just one of those flashes of insight. Surely it wasn't me. Maybe it was me Mum, telling me from heaven to treat you two properly."

She pursed her lips. "If that's true, that would answer my question."

"What question?"

"How in the world David Draper ever thought of such a feminine thing." And with a jaunty wave, she turned and walked swiftly away.

David watched her for a moment, glad that the contentiousness between them seemed to be softening a little. This trip had been good in that regard. It had been an amazing experience so far. The scenery was spectacular! Every bend brought another jaw-dropping sight. Sheer rock cliffs jutted straight up out of the valley floor fifteen hundred to two thousand feet high. The variety of colors in the stone was astonishing—deep vermilion to pale pink, dark chocolate to light tan, soft yellow to brilliant white. Billy Joe perfectly described one mountain as a cake piled high with mounds of white frosting. The whole experience was having an effect on all of them, drawing them closer together in the sharing of it.

There had been other insights as well. David's admiration for Patrick McKenna grew with every passing day. He was also finding an unexpected depth to Molly beneath that dazzling, bubbly exterior. Carl Bradford, stuffiness and all, was all right too. He was steady, always pleasant, quick to contribute in discussions or to give a hand when there was a task to be done. David liked him, and he hadn't expected that. Carl would be a good match for Abby, if he ever got a little more romance into the relationship. Sometimes David wanted to sneak over behind him and whisper, "She's cold, put your arm around her. When she's talking, don't just nod. Watch her eyes. That's how you can tell what she's thinking." But he said none of that, of course. Abby seemed content with how things were, and it certainly wasn't his place to interfere.

As for Abby and her sister, David found that relationship even more intriguing. They were so different in temperament and physical appearance that it was surprising they weren't more competitive with each other. Where Molly was impetuous, Abby was steady, almost contemplative. Where Molly was gregarious and talkative, Abby was quiet, more reserved. They were both very articulate, but expressed themselves in different ways. Abby was more reasoned, more precise, where Molly let it all come tumbling out.

A crunch of footsteps on leaves brought him up. Molly was just coming out of their tent, pulling on her jacket and yawning mightily at the

same time. She was definitely not the early riser in the family. "Mornin',
Molly."

"Good morning, David. Oh, it smells good." She looked around.
"Where is everybody?"

"Your family and Carl are down by the river. Ben's saddling the horses
and hobbling the mules. We're leaving camp here and will be coming back
tonight."

She came to the fire and looked down at the stack of flapjacks he had
cooked. Suddenly, her eyes lit up. "Do you have any more of that stuff,
David?"

"For the flapjacks, you mean? Yes, some."

"Make me a real big one, can you?" Not waiting for an answer, she ran
back into the tent.

Five minutes later, when the family returned, David and Molly were
standing in front of the fire. Molly held something behind her. As Abby
reached her, she brought it around to the front. It was a plate with a very
large flapjack on it. In the flapjack were two birthday candles. "Happy
birthday, Abby."

Then, handing the plate to David, she rushed to Abby and threw her
arms around her.

They rode upstream for about three miles, following the river in single
file, Ben in the lead, David bringing up the rear. They rode for over an
hour, mostly silent as each new bend in the river brought another astonishing view. The air was so clear, the colors so brilliant, that Abby kept
blinking to make herself believe it was all real and that she was really there
seeing it for herself. She stood up in the stirrups and twisted her body so
she could see the full length and breadth of the canyon.

David, just behind her, looked up. "It really is something, isn't it?"

"Unbelievable," she breathed.

She reined her horse in a little, letting David come up beside her. "I
have another confession to make," she said.

He gave her a questioning look. "You didn't like my flapjacks?"

She laughed lightly. "No, they were wonderful. Molly and I are going to make them for supper some night when we get home. She's going to ask Mother if you can come and join us, see what they taste like when they're done properly."

"Ouch!"

"Just teasing. They really were delicious."

"So that's your confession?"

Her head dropped. "Actually, I wanted to apologize for something else."

"About you not wanting me to accompany you on this trip?" he guessed.

She gave him a sharp look. "Did Daddy say something?"

"No." He grimaced. "It was a little obvious, you know. So . . . apology accepted."

Just then, Ben Mangleson, who was about a hundred yards ahead of them, shouted and waved them forward. "Here we are. Come take a look at this."

"This" was stunning. About a quarter of a mile away was a single monolithic tower of deep red sandstone jutting straight up out of the canyon floor. Skirted by a base of red soil, huge blocks of fallen rock, and green juniper trees, it rose majestically—nothing but sheer cliffs for a good thousand feet or more.

Ben was like a little boy showing them his new horse. "There it is. Angel's Landing. Happy birthday, Abby. What do you think?"

"Incredible. Breathtaking."

Her father laughed in delight. "You said you wanted to have your breath taken away."

"So," Ben said, still grinning broadly, "how would you like to go up top?"

As they dismounted at the base of the tower, Molly removed her hat and tipped her head way back. "We can't possibly climb that, Ben."

"We go around and up the other side. Come on, we'll hobble the horses and leave them down by the river."

Billy Joe suddenly stopped. "Be careful," he said, raising a warning hand. "In the desert you have to watch out for snakes and lobsters."

There was a momentary startled silence, then an explosion of laughter. Billy Joe blushed deeply.

"Did you mean scorpions?" Abby asked after a moment. "They do look like little lobsters."

"Oh, yeah." The irrepressible grin was back and he was laughing at himself. "Snakes and scorpions." And he was off, hoping to see the very things he had just warned them about.

As they unbridled the horses and turned them loose to graze, Patrick turned and looked up at the massif that towered over them. "Have you been up there?" he asked.

"Yes," Ben said. "I've climbed it twice since Carl was out here a month ago."

"How bad is it?" David asked.

"Well, we've named it Angel's Landing," Ben laughed, "because only an angel could ever get up there." Then, seeing their looks, he went on quickly, "Just kidding. I'm certainly no angel."

Billy Joe's head whipped around. "Angels? Are there angels up there?"

They all laughed at that. "No, Patrick," his father said. "They just call it Angel's Landing."

"Oh." His face fell and he looked at the ground.

Probably because it was her birthday, Ben decided it was Abby he had to convince. "I'm telling you, Abby, from the top, you'd swear you *were* an angel in heaven. It's like nothing you've experienced in your whole life."

"How bad is the climb?" David asked again.

"The first two-thirds of it has some pretty steep places, and we'll be feeling it in our legs and lungs, but I think even Billy could handle that. The last third . . ." He grinned. "Well, that's the breathtaking part. This main tower here, what we call the Landing itself, is connected to the rest of the mountains by a narrow spine of rock. It's kind of like a huge stone bridge that connects the tower to the line of cliffs, but it's solid rock all the way down." He grinned again. "When I say all the way, that's about eight hundred feet of vertical drop on both sides. In a couple of places, the spine is no more than fifteen or twenty feet wide. It really is amazing."

Eight hundred feet! Abby felt her stomach flutter.

"Just to be safe, I strung ropes across a couple of spots. Gives you something to hang on to, steady yourself." He turned to Patrick. "Brother McKenna, there's a nice overlook just above where the spine starts. I'd recommend we all go that far; then anyone who isn't comfortable going on can wait there for the rest of us. Even if you go no farther, the view from up there is absolutely spectacular."

Abby cut in before he could answer. Billy Joe was off stalking a lizard, and she inclined her head in his direction. "I don't think Billy Joe should go up at all, Father." She turned to David, daring him with her eyes to disagree. "I mean it, Daddy," she hurried on. "You know how he is. He sees something and he darts off without thinking. Mama would never allow it."

David nodded. "I agree with Abby, Patrick. That is no place for a boy. I'll stay with him while the rest of you go up."

Abby released her breath, thanking him with her eyes.

"Thank you, David," Patrick said, "but I'd rather have you up top helping Ben. I'll stay." He looked at his two daughters, then back to David and Carl. "I'm trusting you two to be wise up there. If it looks too bad from the overlook, don't go."

David looked at Carl, then they both nodded.

Just then Billy Joe came on the run, waving a letter in his hand. "Can I go, Dad?"

His father shook his head. "No, Son. This one is just for grown-ups."

David decided the boy had overheard their conversation, because he didn't fight that. Instead, he turned to David. "Then will you take this up for me?"

"What is it?" David asked, already knowing the answer.

"This is my letter to God," he said. His head tipped back to look at the great tower looming over them. "Maybe the angels will know where He lives."

CHAPTER 23

Thursday, September 19, 1878

Two hours later, the five of them stood looking down on what Ben had called the "spine" or the "bridge" that linked towering Angel's Landing to the mountain ridge behind it. No one spoke. There weren't words to express what they were seeing.

It really was a remarkable geological formation. Angel's Landing was at least a mile in circumference at the base, but the rocky crown was no more than four or five hundred yards around. The massif stood completely apart from the cliffs that formed the western wall of Zion Canyon except for this narrow, solid-rock umbilical cord anchoring it to its "mother."

Ben's warning that the crossing had some "rough places" was an understatement. Much of it was typical mountain terrain—rocks, gravel beds, scattered juniper trees—that could be crossed without much difficulty. But right at its narrowest stretch, thick sandstone blocks had broken off and lay in great chunks, partially blocking the way across the spine. One boulder looked to be as much as six feet higher than the base of the ridge and would have to be climbed over. That stretch would have been daunting enough if the drop-off on either side had been fifteen or twenty feet high. But this narrow crossing was like a single strand of spiderweb spanning two great chasms.

On the right side, the cliff dropped into a slot canyon so narrow that they could not see the bottom. What they could see was six or seven hundred feet of vertical drop into nothingness. The left side was worse. Here there was no other wall. Far below them, the Virgin River Valley spread out between the walls of Zion Canyon. The river itself looked like the silvery track a snail leaves behind as it crosses a sidewalk. The valley floor was at least a thousand feet down, and about eight hundred of that was a sheer cliff face of what looked like seamless stone.[1]

Ben spoke. "Well, there it is. Who's game for going across? Abby? It's your birthday."

She pressed a trembling hand against her skirts, now fastened into trousers by the garters. Her face was pale. "I'm not sure yet."

"Molly?"

She didn't answer. She was staring down. Her tongue flicked in and out, licking at her lips.

"What about you, David?" Carl asked.

"I'd like to." He smiled wryly. "May be my only chance to see what heaven's like, but this isn't my trip. I'm here to do whatever Molly and Abby want."

Abby turned to Molly, her eyes questioning.

"I am scared absolutely to death," Molly whispered, "but I want to do it. What about you?"

Abby shuddered in spite of herself. "I don't know if I can. You, Carl?"

"I'll stay with you if you decide not to."

"But you want to do it?"

He hesitated, then his head bobbed. "Yes."

"Then go," she said, with a touch of snappishness. "I don't need a baby-sitter."

Carl looked confused and a little bit hurt. "I . . . ."

"I have a suggestion," David came in smoothly. "Suppose we let Carl go first, with Ben taking him across. That way you and Molly can see how difficult it is. Then you can decide."

"Good idea," Ben said. "There's a small landing right where the spine begins. Let's go that far. Whoever decides not to go can wait there for the rest of us."

Abby, Molly, and David watched the two men as they moved across the spine. At first, Ben went ahead, barely looking back, not wanting to make Carl feel like he was being mothered. But when they reached the part where the first rope was secured between some juniper trees, Carl lost his confidence. Ben came back to help him negotiate the rockfall and the large block they had seen. When Abby saw him pulling himself up over that big rock, grasping the rope like it was life itself, she had to close her eyes and look away.

Five minutes later, they were past the rough stretch. Carl turned back and waved. "It's a bit hairy," he called. "But it's all right. You can do it."

"Carl, you go on," Ben said. "I'll go back for Molly."

Abby cupped her hands to her mouth. "No, Ben. Stay with Carl. Please!"

"It's all right, Abby," Carl called. "It's easier from here on."

"Please, Ben!"

He waved and turned back to rejoin Carl.

David pulled on his leather gloves, eyeing the two sisters. "Well?"

Abby swallowed hard, then looked at Molly. Molly's hands were clenching and unclenching, but she answered firmly. "I wouldn't miss this for anything in the world."

"Do you want her to go first?" he asked Abby. When she gave him a quick nod, he turned back to Molly. "Okay, let's go." He gave her an encouraging smile. "I won't tell you not to look down. You have to do that to see where you're putting your feet. But look *only* at your feet. It's looking down into those depths that brings on the vertigo."

"Okay." Her voice was quavering noticeably.

Abby watched them go, amazed once again at her sister. She knew Molly was as frightened as she was. Cute, flirtatious Molly. There was some steel down inside that fluffy exterior.

Moving forward, David was also impressed. He could hear Molly's breath coming in panicky gulps, and he could see her hands trembling, but she didn't stop. She watched his every move, then did exactly the same thing. She followed his instructions to the letter. Once, when her boot slipped on a loose rock and she threw her arms around him to catch herself, she blushed deeply. Then, with eyes twinkling, she looked up at him and said, "I've wanted to do that for quite some time." Which made him laugh aloud.

When they reached the place where the spine widened out and became a full ridge again, she turned. Her face was radiant and her eyes danced with excitement. "Thank you, David. Thank you for believing in me." Then, to his surprise, she went up on tiptoe and kissed him on the cheek. "You go back for Abby now," she said. "I'll be fine."

Abby was seated on a shelf of rock, watching him with narrowed eyes as he made his way back to her. When he reached her, she spoke. "That was tender."

"What?" Turning, he saw that where he and Molly had parted was in plain sight of where he and Abby were now. He flashed a grin. "There's nothing like walking across a tightwire to increase one's feeling of gratitude."

She laughed in spite of herself. "And to have one as pretty as Molly express that gratitude with such sincerity is a burden one just has to bear, right?"

"You do what you have to do," he grunted. He changed the subject. "By the way, we got interrupted down there. You were about to apologize for something. I'd really like to hear that."

"Oh, no, you don't," she said quickly. "This isn't the place for that. I think we need to stay focused on the question at hand, which is, am I crazy enough to go across that?"

"And what have you decided?"

Before she could answer, they heard a shout. Ben was coming back down the hill from the top of Angel's Landing. "Carl's up top," he shouted. "Be right there."

Abby's hand shot out and gripped David's arm. "No. If I go, I'd rather it be with you."

David shot her a quizzical look, but stood and waved him off. "We're all right," he called. "You stay with Carl and Molly up top. We'll meet you there."

Even from this distance, they could see his disappointment. "Poor guy,"

David said. "Two beautiful damsels in distress and he doesn't get to help either one."

"Am I a damsel in distress?" She was completely serious again now and answered her own question before he could. "Of course I am. I don't know if I can do it, David. Just looking at it from here makes my head spin."

"Abby, listen to me. There's nothing you have to prove here. Not to me. Not to Carl. Not to yourself." And then, as an afterthought, "And certainly not to Molly."

"I know, but . . ." Her eyes were staring across to the Landing. "I really want to do it."

"Then I'm here to help you. You can change your mind at any point."

For a long moment her eyes probed his. "All right."

At first, the rocks were almost like steps, or actually more like small landings. The layers of sandstone had split into blocks, forming a rough, natural stairway. It was easy going, and she raised her eyes to see how far that would continue. That was a mistake. She had to stop and clutch David's arm as a wave of dizziness swept over her.

"Remember," he said easily, "don't look out at all that empty space. Focus only on the little square of ground where you're putting your feet."

"Right," she said through clenched teeth.

When they left the "steps," they started down a forty-degree incline. Fortunately, the path was at the base of a slanting rock wall on their right side. It tilted away from them at just enough angle that she could lean against it. More important, for the moment, it blocked any view of the chasms below.

But the wall lasted only about three rods before it rounded away from them. And there before her lay the worst of Ben's "rough spots." With a sinking heart, she saw that it was much worse than it had looked from above. She felt sweat pop out on her forehead, and her neck beneath the collar of her blouse was suddenly sticky.

"Just stay focused on your boots," David said, speaking as though he were directing her how to braid a rope or tie a bowknot.

"Oh," she murmured through tight lips, "does that mean I have to keep my eyes open?"

He laughed softly. "You're doing fine. Just watch how I maneuver over this big rock."

They were standing on another level platform of rock, but blocking the path directly ahead was the sandstone block. It was easily the size of a small carriage. When it had split off centuries before, it had come to rest right in the center of the spine at its narrowest spot. The block was chest high and oval in shape, somewhat resembling a squashed egg. It was its roundness that caused her breath to catch. It actually overhung the platform where she was standing, leaving a two-foot gap between them. This meant that there was nothing beneath that overhang to place her boots on, no foothold for her to use. She was going to have to grasp the rope and, with legs dangling, pull herself up and onto the rock by the sheer strength of her arms. And when she did, those hellish drop-offs would be right there in front of her eyes, with just two or three feet of rock on either side of her.

She watched David closely. He grasped the rope, then, exactly as she had feared, hauled himself up while his feet dangled free. But he was soon up and off the block. He turned. "Okay."

"I don't think I can do it," she whispered.

He stretched out one hand toward her. "I'm right here, Abby." But there was no way he could reach her until she got up on top of the block. If he came back, there would be no room for her. She would be on her own for several seconds. She closed her eyes, knees trembling.

"Abby?"

She opened them again. He had come a step closer. "If you look on the left side of the rock, you'll see where Ben carved a toehold for you." His voice was quiet, calm, confident. "Put your left foot there first, then grab the rope and pull yourself up."

Her mouth was filled with cotton, her heart was pounding, and she could feel the veins in her neck throbbing. "I can't."

"This is the worst place," he said in that same level voice. "After this, it gets easier."

"Liar!" she hissed.

He laughed again. "Guilty as charged, but not today. This *is* the worst. You can do it. Think of this as kind of a leap of faith."

"*Don't use the word 'leap'!*" She nearly screamed it at him. Then her eyes started to burn. "I can't, David," she whispered. "I just can't."

He came back then, lowering himself down to stand beside her. "It's all right, Abby. Let's go back."

"No!" It came out fierce and hard. "I'll not have you miss it because of me. You go. I can make it back from here."

For a long time he looked at her, gauging her words. Finally, he gave a quick nod. "We shouldn't be too long. But don't try going back down the mountain by yourself. Wait for us."

She turned away, the bitterness rising. "I will. Just go."

When he reached the top, Molly, Ben and Carl were standing quietly on the eastern edge of Angel's Landing. After explaining that Abby had decided not to come across, he moved up to join them. And then he understood why Ben, or the Behunins, or whoever had named this place, had called it Angel's Landing. It was unbelievable. They were higher than most of the mountains around them and could see for fifty miles in every direction. It was a stunning and magnificent vista. But straight down, far, far below, was the bottom. He searched the trees along the river, but decided that Patrick and Billy Joe were farther around, closer to the mountain, and couldn't be seen.

Strangely enough, the sight turned his thoughts to his mother. Maybe it was the talk of angels and heaven. But suddenly her memory was as sharp and real and painful as it had been the day of her funeral. He finally had to back away.

Then, remembering something else, he removed the envelope from his shirt pocket, found a large rock near the edge, and placed the letter beneath it. He looked up and saw Molly watching him, her eyes glistening. "For Billy Joe," he said.

"Thank you."

A few minutes later, when they started talking about going back so that Abby wouldn't have to wait any longer for them, he shook his head. "You do that, and she'll feel even more awful."

Molly's eyes were sorrowful. "Will she be all right?"

"Abby? Of course." He let his voice drop into his cowboy drawl. "Ain't nothin' wrong with being smitten by a good old dose of common sense every now and then. I'll go back across and wait with her." He flashed her a jaunty grin. "She'll think it serves me right for being so cheeky with her."

Without waiting for Molly's response, he turned and trotted back the way he had come.

As he approached the east end of the spine and started to descend, a figure stepped out from behind a juniper tree. He gave a low cry and visibly jumped. Then he recognized who it was. "You came across alone?" he said in astonishment.

Abby just looked at him, unable to hide her elation. "I did."

"What happened?" he asked.

"I met someone back there on the trail."

His eyes widened. "Who?"

She looked him straight in the eye. "I met me, and I didn't much like what I saw."

He shook his head. "Amazing." After a moment, he turned and looked back up the way he had come. "Do you want to go up top? It's an incredible view. And it's no problem from here."

"Not really." Her lips puckered into a disgusted expression. "Actually, my knees are still shaking so badly, I'd never make it."

"Understood." He teased her now. "How about going back across on your own, being the expert that you are now?"

She slugged him hard on the arm. "What? Are you insane?"

Back on the west side, they found a spot in the shade of a juniper tree and sat down to wait for the others. Neither spoke for a long time. Then, when the three figures appeared across from them, just starting down from the landing, she began speaking in a low voice.

"When I was eight years old, one day Molly and I were playing in a tree fort at our friend's house. This was in a big old cottonwood tree, and the fort seemed like it was a hundred feet off the ground." She smiled briefly. "Later I measured it. It was only ten feet."

He turned to face her fully, surprised by this turn in the conversation.

"The only way up and down was on a rope ladder with loops in it. One day, just as I started down, I lost my footing. Fortunately, my foot was hooked in the loop. I fell headfirst, but it caught me, leaving me dangling there about eight feet up."

Her eyes dropped. She barely whispered now. "Ever since then, I've been terrified of heights."

He gaped at her, deeply shocked. "And yet you . . ." He could only shake his head. "Miss Abby, you are a wonder."

She managed a shaky laugh. "Or insane. Like you."

Note

1. Angel's Landing is considered one of the premier hiking trails in all of North America. From the top, the view is considered to be the most magnificent in all of Zion National Park. One would expect that its narrow rock fin and dizzying drop-offs on both sides would discourage all but the most courageous of hikers, but it is widely popular and is frequently climbed by people of both genders and all ages. Chains have been anchored into the rock along several stretches of the narrowest or steepest places.

As for its name, a minister who passed through the park in 1916 is commonly credited with calling it Angel's Landing. But the Mormons had been in the area by that time for more than forty years. It seems more likely that they would have given Angel's Landing its name, as they gave religious or scriptural names to many other features in the area.

CHAPTER 24

Wednesday, December 25, 1878

"Dad. Before you open your present, I want you to answer a question for me."

John Draper raised his head. "What?"

"I thought for a long time about what I could get you for Christmas." David pulled a face. "You're not an easy man to buy for."

"'Cuz Ah awreddy 'ave ev'rythin' Ah need. Ya cumin' up 'ere ta spend the holiday wit me is the best gift Ah cud 'ave received."

"And for me too, Dad." He coughed awkwardly, suddenly finding a lump in his throat. "I don't know why, but ever since going to Cedar City, I've been thinking a lot about us. About being so far apart. Mum wouldn't like that."

"Ya got ta go whare the work is, Son."

"I know, but . . . well, anyway, here's my question. And I want you to really think about it." He drew in a breath. "If you could have anything in the world—and I'm not just talking material things—what would it be?"

"Ta be closer ta ya."

"No," David chided. "We're already working on that one. If you're serious about quitting the mines, like we talked about last night, I'll have you down in Cedar City two days later."

"Ah be real serious about it, David. Lek ya say, fur sum reason, Ah be thinkin' a lot aboot being t'gether, too. Maybe me sweet Annie is workin' on the both of us. Be joost lek 'er, wudn't it?" He was suddenly lost in his own thoughts.

"Come this summer," David said softly, "it will be ten years since she left us. And ten years in the mines here. That's enough."

There was a gruff nod. "Aye. Since the Church sold the mine ta the coal cump'ny, it not be the same anymore. Ah be reddy, cum summer."

"Wonderful. So, if you could have anything, any wish, what would it be?"

He looked at David for a long time, then finally shook his head. "Ah dunna know."

"Yes, you do. Think about it. Would you like to go back to England, visit Yorkshire again?"

"No." It came out fast and hard.

David grinned. "Me neither." Then he sobered. "Except to see Mum's grave. But other than that, there's nothing there for us."

"Nothin' but trouble."

"So, is there anything you'd like to do with your life?"

John sat very still for a few more moments. Then he began to nod. "Ah always wished Ah cud 'ave gone ta skoo-ul. Learned ta read an' write, like ya an' yur muther."

"Aye," David said, elated with that answer. "Ah was hopin' that be what ya might say, ya old Tyke." He got up, went over, and laid the brightly wrapped package on his father's lap. He bent down and kissed him on the head. "Merry Christmas, Dad."

His father hefted it, then looked up in surprise. "A book?"

"Open it."

He did so, almost reverently. Tossing the paper aside, he looked at the book. It had a leather cover, but with no printing on it. He opened it, looked surprised, then began riffling through the pages. "Thare be nuthin' in it." He looked up. "Ahre ya playin' a cruel joke on me?"

David laughed, took the book from him, and opened it to the first page, which was half covered in handwriting. "Would you like me to read you what it says?"

"Aye."

"*Dearest Dad. When I was six and became a trapper, Mum secretly gave me an extra candle each day, and brought me books from the circulating library in Barnsley.*"

"Ha!" his father harrumphed. "She joost thought it was a secret."

David nearly choked. "You knew?"

"Frum the first day."

"Aye," David whispered. "I should have guessed." He took a breath, let it out, then went on. "*It is time to share that gift with you. This empty journal awaits the time when you come to live with me. When you do, I shall teach you to read and write, just as Mum taught me.*"

His father's head came up. He was blinking rapidly and his eyes were glistening. "Do ya really mean that, Son?"

David nodded, not trusting himself to answer. He swallowed hard and continued, "*Since I am often gone on the mail circuit, I have obtained the services of one Miss Elizabeth Morris, the local schoolteacher, who will tutor you three days a week. This book will give you a place to practice your writing lessons. My only request is that when it is full, the book comes back to me, as your gift, to be passed on to your grandchildren.*" He took a deep breath, then finished, "*With all my love, your son, David Draper.*"

Thursday, December 26, 1878

Father and son embraced fiercely as the train whistle pierced the air. Their breath hung in the early morning air for several seconds before dissipating. Beyond the canopy of the train station, it had started to snow again.

"Sorry I can't stay longer," David said, finally pulling away. "Patrick's telegram said he really wants me there for the stake conference this weekend. There's something big brewing."

"If Brother McKenna be gittin' ya ta go ta church fur any reason, Ah be naw complainin'."

David ignored that. "I'll write."

"You should 'ave left yes'day," his father said. "Ahre ya sure ya can mek it back in time? Wudn't want ya doin' anythin' ta displease Brother McKenna."

That surprised David. "Why not?"

"Ya be 'appier now than . . ." He shrugged. "Dunna want ya losin' it."

"I . . ." David paused, then nodded. "Yes, I am. Cedar City is actually starting to feel like home."

"Cudn't 'ave anythin' ta do wit that little filly named Molly, cud it?"

David laughed aloud. "Filly? Now you're sounding like an American." He laughed again. "However, I wouldn't call Molly a filly to her face, if I were you."

John nudged him with his elbow. "Joost answer the question."

"Yes, I can make it back in time. I'll be in Salt Lake before noon, and with that big silver mine opened down south now, the railroad runs all the way to Milford. Be there late tonight. Then it's about fifty miles on horseback to Cedar City. I'll be home tomorrow night."

"That be naw the question Ah meant."

David gave him another quick hug. "I know," he smiled. "But here comes the conductor. Got to go, Dad. Love you."

Friday, December 27, 1878

David figured it to be about half eight in the evening* when he tied his horse in front of the McKenna House and dragged himself up onto the veranda. It was snowing lightly, and the night was cold enough that the snow squeaked beneath his boots. The lights of the hotel glowed a warm welcome, but he was disappointed to see that Patrick McKenna's office window was dark. Not surprised, just disappointed. There was hardly anyone out on the streets now.

He stepped inside, expecting to see the night clerk or perhaps Carl Bradford, who often worked late as the assistant manager. Carl was there, but so was Abby. They were shoulder to shoulder behind the front desk going over a large ledger book.

"There you are," Carl said, straightening. He put the pen down and

---

* "Half eight" is the British way of saying eight-thirty, or half past eight.

immediately came around to shake David's hand. "Welcome back. Good trip?"

"It was. Good evening, Abby."

"Hello, David."

"I know you must be tired," Carl said, "but Patrick was really hoping that he could see you tonight, if it wasn't too late. Do you mind waiting while I go find him?"

David very much wanted to ask if it couldn't wait until morning, but he just nodded.

Carl stepped to a row of pegs and retrieved his coat. "Patrick and Sarah are out visiting some people. It might take me a few minutes to find them. You're welcome to wait in the office." He waved and hurried out the door.

As he left, Abby came out to join David. "You do look tired," she said. "Come sit down while you wait."

They crossed the lobby, and Abby led the way into her father's office. She rummaged in a drawer, found some matches, and lit the kerosene lamp. David dropped into a chair, extending his legs to their full length. They were still stiff after two days on a train and in the saddle.

"I'm sorry," she said, "but he really is anxious to talk to you. The main sessions of the stake conference aren't until Sunday, but he and Carl have to be there tomorrow for leadership meetings. They're leaving early in the morning on horseback. Dad's hoping you could drive the rest of us up a little later in the carriage."

He shrugged. "That's not a problem. My next mail run isn't until Wednesday or Thursday."

She started toward the door.

"Sit down, Abby," he said. "Talk to me so I don't fall asleep."

"I . . . I should finish the books."

"I don't hear them calling for you. With the door open, you can see if anyone comes in."

She sighed. "I have been on my feet a lot today." She walked around her father's desk and took his chair. From there she could see out into the lobby as well as talk directly to David.

"Tell me about this stake conference," he said. "Why in Parowan? I would think you had more members here in Cedar City than up there."

"*We* have more members, David," she teased. "Remember, you're part of this stake too."

"Oh, yeah," he said sheepishly. "Keep reminding me."

"Parowan was the first settlement here, and they have two wards, where we only have one."

That made sense. "Your father's telegram said there might be something going on."

"Remember when we were in St. George? There was a lot of talk about sending a mission to the Four Corners area?"

He leaned forward, interested now. "I do remember. You think that's what this is about?"

"Daddy thinks so. Elder Erastus Snow, one of the Twelve Apostles, will be there. He lives in St. George but has responsibility for all of the settlements in southern Utah. The speculation is running wild. We do know that Elder Snow wrote a letter last summer to President Taylor." She stopped. "That's John Taylor, president of the Church."

He gave her a reproving look. "I may not be much of a Mormon, Abby, but I do read the newspapers. I know who the president of the Church is."

She flushed a little. "Sorry. Anyway, Elder Snow recommended that a colony be sent to the area around the San Juan River.[1] Rumors are flying that he is here to make that official."

"Hmm. When would they go?"

"Don't know. Nothing's official yet. May still be nothing but rumors."

He saw the dejection on her face. "You don't think it will affect your family, do you?"

Her eyes raised to meet his. They were nearly black in the lamplight, but they were clearly troubled. "I don't think so. Father hardly qualifies as a frontiersman, Mother even less so. He was raised in Boston. Started as a hotel janitor at age twelve. Worked his way up to manager by the time he was twenty, and owned the hotel when he was twenty-seven. So he's a gifted businessman, but I don't think there'll be much need for a hotel in San Juan country for a long time."

"Dunno," he observed. "All them rustlers have got to stay somewhere."

There was a soft snicker. "I can just see the sign now: *McKenna House—Rooms half price for outlaws and reprobates.*"

"*Steel bars at no extra charge.*" His humor was partially to hide his huge relief. Having the McKennas leave would be a real blow. He liked working for Patrick. And with the extra jobs he kept pushing David's way, David had added another hundred dollars to his ranch fund. There was also Billy Joe. He would miss the boy's crooked grin and unabashed exuberance for life almost as much as he would miss Molly. He laughed softly to himself. And, of course, there was Molly. *That* would be a real loss.

He saw that Abby was watching him steadily. A wisp of dark hair had escaped down across her forehead. *Fetching*, he thought. It was a good word.

The Angel's Landing experience had significantly altered their relationship. To David's surprise, Abby did not tell the others that she had gone across the spine. She just smiled as Molly told her how wonderful it was and how sad she was that Abby hadn't made it across. That had puzzled David at first, but then he understood. This was *her* victory, *her* personal conquest, and she didn't need to share it. As far as David could tell, he was still the only one who knew what she had done.

"Did you have a good Christmas?" Abby had been watching his face, wondering what was going on behind those pensive eyes.

"We did," he said. "Dad and I had a really good visit. I was delighted when he agreed to retire from the mines this summer and come down here to live."

"Really? Wonderful. I'm anxious to meet him. I plan to be really impressed by him."

"That's an odd thing to say."

She was a little embarrassed. "I've watched your face when you talk about him. I have decided he must be a remarkable man."

"He is remarkable. Simple. Plain-talking. Uneducated. But very wise." He paused for a moment, then decided to tell her about his gift to his father. "He actually cried," he said when he was finished. "The only other time I've ever seen him cry was when my mother died, then again at her funeral."

She was touched. "So he never went to school at all?"

He shook his head. "He started in the mines when he was five."

"*Five?*"

"Yes."

She closed her eyes. "I cannot begin to fathom how horrible that would be. When I was five and six, all I had to do was play with dolls and make my own bed in the morning."

His eyes had a faraway look in them now. "It was the only thing I ever remember me Mum and Dad fighting over. All the boys started at five. Families were anxious for them to do so because they needed the money so desperately."

"You almost sound like you were disappointed that your mother made you wait."

"I was then. Terribly so. All my friends were working and getting paid. It was a pittance, of course. Only a few pence per week, but still. . . . Instead, Mum kept me home and taught me to read and write." There was a scornful laugh. "You can bet that won me a few black eyes. They called me a sissy. Little Davee-Do-Good. Couldn't get my hands dirty."

She was nodding slowly. "So that's why you wouldn't let Billy Joe just walk away from Sammy that day." It was not a question, but an expression of her sudden insight.

"Yes. I knew what would happen. Sammy's kind always come back until you show them you're not a weakling."

Silence filled the room as both were lost in their thoughts. Finally, he gave her a wry look. "Thank you for calling him Billy Joe. It really was pretty cheeky of me to jump in like that, with a boy I didn't even know."

She laughed. "We all call him that now. Even Mother."

"I know. But you were the first."

"The first time I caught myself doing it, I was mad at you all over again because it came out so natural for me. You were right. *Patrick* suddenly didn't seem to fit. And it made me angry that you saw that before I did."

"If you get mad every time I'm right," he said lazily, "you're always going to be angry."

To his surprise, she laughed, openly and with delight. "You are something else, David Draper."

"Which reminds me," he said. "You owe me an apology."

"What for?"

"Dunno. Remember in Zion Canyon you started to apologize, then we got interrupted."

"Oh." She looked embarrassed. "I . . ." She shook her head. "Doesn't matter now."

"Are you kidding? You think I'd let an apology from Abby McKenna go to waste?"

There was a slow smile. "They come so seldom because I am so seldom wrong, just like someone else I know." Then she grew serious. "I . . . I just wanted to say that some of the things I said that morning at the campfire—about you always trying to get girls . . ."

"All *atwitter* was the word you used, as I remember."

She nodded. "That was unkind. You do have a gift for getting under my skin, but all of that was uncalled for."

"Apology accepted, and I shall try to be more circumspect when I am around you."

She openly hooted at that. "That will be the day." Then, very uncomfortable now, she quickly changed the subject. "Billy Joe wanted to wait here until you came. Molly too, but where Dad and Mother—" she gave him a quick smile—"he and Mum were out visiting, Molly had to stay with Billy Joe. They were both grumping about the house when I left." Now her eyes met his. "He really thinks the world of you, David."

"He's great," he laughed. "He tickles me. Reminds me of myself when I was a kid."

"Was it awful?" she asked softly. "When I try to picture Billy Joe in those tunnels—" A shiver ran down her spine.

"Back then I didn't think of it as being awful," he said. "It was just life."

"Will you tell me about it?"

He gave her a sharp look. "Pretty boring stuff."

"Please."

And so he did. He started from the beginning, talking about being a trapper, about the terrible darkness, the loneliness, the tedium, the rats. He told her about his mother giving him the extra candle and getting him books. He described life as a hurrier, bent over double pulling the coal tubs through the monkey heads, and about his contest with Sean Williams for the position of spragger. And then, he did something totally unexpected. He told her about Bertie Beames and his part in his death. He suddenly wanted to unburden himself of it.

"That was really the only thing about the mines that was truly awful," he finished, his voice a bare whisper, his eyes dark and hooded. "Even now, sixteen years later, I can picture his body lying there beside that shattered coal car, nobody even bothering to put a blanket over him. They didn't care. Not the mine boss. Not the mine owners. Just keep the money coming so they can live in their castles and palaces and look down their haughty little noses at the dirty, unwashed, black-faced coal miners and their kids."

"Have you ever heard of Elizabeth Barrett Browning?"

"I don't think so."

"Her father made a fortune in sugar in the West Indies, and bought a large estate in Herefordshire." She pronounced it HUR-furd-shire. "Is that how you say it?"

"More like HARE-ah-furd-shur."

She nodded. "As a girl, Elizabeth had everything. But she was very sensitive to the evils of the world around her. She became one of England's most famous poetesses."

"Sorry. Never heard of her."

"Somehow, she learned of the appalling conditions in the mines, especially for children. She once described a mine as a dark and ruthless place where a child sacrificed not only his innocence but also his claim to childhood."

"Amen," he murmured.

"She wrote a poem called 'The Cry of the Children.' When I was sixteen, our teacher made us choose a more lengthy poem to memorize. I chose that one."

He studied her face. Though her eyes showed no tears, he could tell she was having a hard time with her emotions. "Will you tell it to me?"

"That day at Aunt Rachel's house, when you were so angry, and you told us about working in the mines, I was horrified. As soon as we got back home, I went to the library and found it, and memorized it all over again. It's very long. I'll only do a few portions of it." She closed her eyes.

> Do ye hear the children weeping, O my brothers, ere the sorrow
>   comes with years?
> They are leaning their young heads against their mothers—and
>   that cannot stop their tears.
> The young, young children, O my brothers, they are weeping
>   bitterly!—
> They are weeping in the playtime of the others in the country of
>   the free.
> But the young, young children, O my brothers, do you ask them
>   why they stand
> Weeping sore before the bosoms of their mothers, in our happy
>   Fatherland?
> "For oh," say the children, "we are weary, and we cannot run
>   or leap—
> If we cared for any meadows, it were merely to drop down in
>   them and sleep.
> For, all day, we drag our burden tiring, through the coal-dark,
>   underground—
> Now, tell the poor young children—

David's head came up as Abby stopped. The tears had finally come and she was trying vainly to blink them away.

> Now, tell the poor young children, O my brothers, to look up to
>   Him and pray—

> *So the blessed One, who blesseth all the others, will bless them*
>   *another day.*
> *They answer, "Who is God that He should hear us, while the*
>   *rushing of the iron wheels is stirred?*
> *Is it likely God, with angels singing round Him, hears our weep-*
>   *ing any more?*

"Wait," David blurted. "Say that last again."

"I don't know if I can."

"Please. Where it talks about God."

She finally nodded, and started again.

> *Is it likely God, with angels singing round Him, hears our weep-*
>   *ing any more?*

His eyes were stricken. "Those could be the very words of my own mother." He dropped his head in his hands. "Go on."

> *"But no!" say the children, weeping faster, "He is speechless as a*
>   *stone;*
> *Do not mock us; grief has made us unbelieving—We look up for*
>   *God, but tears have made us blind."*
> *And well may the children weep before you; they are weary ere*
>   *they run;*
> *They have never seen the sunshine, nor the glory which is*
>   *brighter than the sun:*
> *"How long," they say, "how long, O cruel nation, will you stand,*
>   *to move the world, on a child's heart,*
> *Our blood splashes upward, O you tyrants, and your purple*
>   *shows your path;*
> *But the child's sob curseth deeper in the silence than the strong*
>   *man in his wrath!"[2]*

Neither spoke. Nor did they until Abby's father returned with Carl ten minutes later.

Notes

1. Erastus Snow sent a letter to President John Taylor discussing the situation in the Four Corners area. It was dated June 11, 1878 (see Miller, *Hole*, 6).

2. A full copy of Browning's poem can be found on www.bartleby.com/246/260.html.

CHAPTER 25

Sunday, December 29, 1878

The first session of the conference at the Parowan meetinghouse was scheduled to start at ten o'clock Sunday morning, but by nine-fifteen, when David arrived with the McKennas, the fields around the Old Rock Church were already filling with carriages, wagons, buggies, and a few carts. Patrick had been right to suggest they go early. In spite of the bitter cold, people had come in from the surrounding towns and settlements that constituted the Parowan Stake.

Since the hotel in Parowan was just a block or two from the church, the McKennas had walked. As they came up to join the throngs moving toward the doors, Sarah exclaimed, "Oh! There are the Nielsons." She waved and called a greeting.

David looked over and saw a family group walking toward the chapel. They looked familiar. The man leading the small group was older, quite tall, and walked with a rather severe limp. "Who's that?" he asked. "I've seen him around town, I think."

"That's Jens Nielson and his family," Sarah explained.

Molly got a dreamy look in her eyes again. "See the young couple in the back? That's his daughter, Mary. She and her husband, Kumen Jones, were married in the St. George Temple just a week ago. He's a rancher out west of town. Oh, doesn't she look just radiant?"

"She just looks cold to me," David observed.

Billy Joe sniggered, but Molly kicked David in the shins. "Oh, you!"

"What happened to Brother Nielson's foot?"

"It got frozen," Billy Joe blurted.

"Not so loud," his father shushed. Then he looked at David. "The Nielsons came across the plains with the Willie Handcart Company. His feet were badly frostbitten one night."

Molly moved in and lowered her voice. "Sister Nielson—everyone calls her Aunt Elsie—she's the little tiny woman beside Brother Nielson." She sighed. "Aren't they cute together? She probably only weighs half of what he does. Anyway, when Brother Nielson couldn't go any farther, Aunt Elsie put him in the handcart and pulled him the rest of the way to Salt Lake City."

"Not to Salt Lake," Abby corrected her. "Just to the camp where the rescue wagons were waiting for them."

"Whatever. It was still a long ways, and tiny as she is, she wouldn't let him die. She made him get in the cart. That is so romantic."

"I think *courageous* is the better word." Abby was clearly peeved with the starry-eyed fluff.

"Oh," Sarah cut in, "there's Brother Francis Webster from our ward. He's another handcart pioneer. He and his wife were in the Martin Company that lost so many people."[1]

"Bishop Nielson and Aunt Elsie are two of my favorite people," Molly continued, refusing to be deflected from her story. "And—"

"Bishop?" David asked. "I thought Bishop Arthur was the bishop in Cedar City."

"Brother Nielson's not the bishop *now*, but he was over in Panguitch." She was losing patience with all the interruptions.

Her father broke in. "And I think we'd better keep moving or we aren't going to get a seat."

The Parowan meetinghouse was packed to the rafters. One could almost taste the excitement as they sang the opening hymn and had an opening prayer. With that done, the stake president, Henry Lunt, finally stood and came to the pulpit. Instantly the hall went quiet.

"Brothers and sisters, we are so pleased to have Elder Erastus Snow with us again this morning in our conference. We so appreciate his

willingness to come up from St. George and—" he paused for effect—
"brave a *real* winter."

There was a ripple of laughter at that. It became a roar when Elder
Snow, clearly visible on the stand, hugged himself and feigned a shiver. The
"upper settlements," the ones north of the Black Ridge and therefore of
considerably higher elevation than St. George and its surrounding settlements, enjoyed poking a little fun at their brothers and sisters to the south.
They called them hothouse plants whose leaves got nipped with the first
sign of frost. The lowland St. Georgians answered that by saying jealousy
always makes the tongue a sharp critic.

"We shall be pleased," the stake president continued, "to hear a dis-
course from Elder Snow later in the program, but he has an item of business to conduct before that. Since this is a rather unusual item of business,
Elder Snow should like to offer a brief explanation before it is presented to
you for your consideration. Elder Snow."

A buzz filled the hall. Mothers started shushing their children. It was
hardly normal to have anyone—let alone an Apostle—explain an item of
business before it was presented.

The president stepped back, and Elder Snow rose and came to the pulpit. "Thank you, President Lunt." He paused and let the buzz die down.
Then a slow smile stole across his face. "I have to say that there is some
validity to President Lunt's comment. Just the other day, I had an elderly
sister come up to me. 'Elder Snow,' she said, 'can you tell me if they named
that fluffy white stuff I remember seeing as a little girl after you?'"

The laughter exploded in waves now. He had them totally with him.

While they had waited for the meeting to begin, Patrick had briefly
filled David in on Elder Erastus Snow. He was ordained an Apostle just
two years after the Saints had come to Utah and was one of the pioneers to
the southern part of the territory. He was much beloved and respected by
the Saints, according to McKenna.

Elder Snow waited a moment, growing more serious as he adjusted his
spectacles, letting the people settle down again. Then he began. "As many
of you know, at the request of Brigham Young, which was reaffirmed by
President Taylor, I have made a specific recommendation to the Church

for establishing a colony in the Four Corners area, somewhere along the San Juan River."

David leaned forward and glanced at Abby, who was sitting to his left on the other side of Molly. She was looking at him, her eyes mocking. "That's John Taylor," she whispered. "He's the president of the Church now."

Molly turned and gave him a strange look. "You don't know who John Taylor is?"

"I don't know who your sister is," he growled.

"We have need of other settlements as well," Elder Snow was saying. "On the Little Colorado and the Salt Rivers in Arizona, for example. The time has now come to move those plans forward. Therefore, I have asked the stake clerk to read a list of names of those being called in this conference to serve as missionaries and help establish these new settlements."

That did it. That was the confirmation they had all been waiting for. The room virtually exploded with conversation. Again Elder Snow stopped, waiting until it died away. "After the stake clerk is finished, I shall ask for a sustaining vote on the proposal."

Elder Snow moved back to his chair and sat down as a man with grey hair and spectacles came forward. He officiously removed a folded paper from his jacket, smoothed it out on the pulpit, then peered up over his glasses to see if everyone was paying attention. That made David smile. You couldn't have found a person over age five in the room whose eyes weren't glued on the man. He cleared his throat and began to read.

"The following names are put forward to you to serve as missionaries to be called to Arizona, or as otherwise directed." He paused, letting the anticipation build. "Silas S. Smith."

There were gasps and exclamations of approval all around them. Patrick McKenna, who sat on the other side of David, leaned over. "He's from Paragonah, just north of here. Highly respected. Member of the legislative council. The fact that his name was read first probably means he'll be captain."

"Shhh!" someone behind them said.

Fortunately, the clerk had anticipated just such a reaction and had paused for it. Now he went on, pronouncing each name slowly and distinctly. "S. H. Rogers. Davis Rogers. H. H. Harriman. George Hobbs. H. Harrap."

With each name there were exclamations of surprise or approval. From somewhere directly behind them, David heard a woman's voice cry out as a name was read, "Oh, no!" David turned to see who it was and saw a woman's head drop. She began to cry softly.[2]

"Solomon Wardell. Carl Decker." As the clerk read each name, ripples of surprise, shock, happiness, dismay, and bewilderment continued to spread through the congregation.

"Hans Joseph Nielson. Francis Webster, Jr."

Sarah leaned over to her husband. "Did he say Jens Nielson?"

"No," he said, shaking his head. "*Hans* Nielson. Or Joe." Then to David, "He goes by Joe. He's Bishop Nielson's oldest son."

"John Lister. Jacob Gould. Simon Topham. P. J. McKenna."

Out of the corner of his eye, David saw Patrick and Sarah stiffen as if hit by the same blow. Molly gasped. Abby's hand shot out and grasped Carl's arm so hard that her knuckles showed white. David could see Patrick out of the corner of his eye. His face was stiff, his mouth pinched. But then he began to nod. He seemed relieved to finally know.

"David Hunter," the clerk was droning on. "George Urie. Samuel Rowley."

Solemn as a judge, he folded the paper and nodded to Elder Snow. "Elder Snow, that completes the reading of the names as given." He returned to his seat.

Elder Snow came back to the pulpit. "Brothers and sisters, I would now propose that we sustain the proposal as read. All in favor, please show it by the uplifted hand."

Hands shot up all around David, including the McKennas'. As he looked around, as near as he could tell every hand was up.

He suddenly realized Molly was giving him a sharp look. "Raise your hand," she mouthed.

He was startled. "I'm not . . ." But he was. He was a member of this stake, in name, at least. And more and more, with the help of the

McKennas, he was in reality as well. Feeling a bit foolish, he slowly raised his right hand along with all the others.

"Those opposed may likewise signify."

Again David turned to look. Not a single hand was visible.

Elder Snow smiled. "The voting has been unanimous, brothers and sisters. Thank you for your sustaining faith."[3]

President Lunt returned to the pulpit and announced the rest of the program. There were several speakers, including himself, but none of them made more than brief reference to what had just transpired. Then the congregation stood and sang a hymn. Again President Lunt stood. "It will now be our pleasure to turn the remainder of our meeting over to Elder Erastus Snow of the Quorum of the Twelve Apostles. Elder Snow."

The Apostle got to his feet, murmured something to the stake president as he touched his arm, then came to the pulpit. He stood there for a moment, letting his eyes take in the congregation in both the lower hall and the balcony. Patrick had said Elder Snow was in his early sixties, but David thought he looked younger than that. Unlike most of the other Church leaders, he was clean shaven, which perhaps gave him a more youthful look. He had a high, receding hairline, quick, perceptive eyes, and a pleasant demeanor. It was obvious that he felt like he was among friends, for he seemed completely comfortable.

When the noise stopped, when all of the crying babies had been shushed or taken out, and all the fidgeting little boys quieted by a hand on the shoulder from their fathers, he began.

"Brothers and sisters, as many of you know, this matter of establishing a settlement in the area of the San Juan River was much on the mind of our beloved President Brigham Young before his death. And it has been of similar concern to President Taylor.[4] Now, the decision has been made to move forward. Nor is it done. There will be other calls extended, and we ask any who have an interest in this matter to volunteer themselves as well.

"We fully understand the impact this decision will have on you, on your families, and on our communities, so we believe it important for you to understand why the decision was made."

He looked around, searching faces, then held up one finger. "The issues are these: First, our missionaries continue to have success around the world, and more and more Latter-day Saints are answering the call to come to Zion. We have not only filled up the valleys and fertile farmlands of Utah Territory, but we have extended settlements to the surrounding states and territories. But the influx of people is not over. More are coming. We need more settlements."

He held up another finger. "Second. A few years back, we experienced a long, drawn-out war with the Navajos, a war that wrought havoc among us and caused a loss of life on both sides. A treaty was eventually signed," he continued, "and we made peace. But that peace was nearly destroyed just four years ago when some young Navajo braves were brutally murdered by wicked men. Only the courageous and tireless efforts of men like Jacob Hamblin, Thales Haskill, and others prevented full-scale violence from erupting."

The mood in the hall had gone quite somber now. Elder Snow himself was very grave. He raised three fingers. "Third. For the past decade, cattlemen from Colorado have been bringing large herds into our territory to strip off our grasslands. Many of the cowhands they hire are ruffians and hooligans, crude men who drink hard and are quick with a gun. Recent discoveries of gold, silver, and other precious metals have also brought vast numbers of people into the mountains of southwest Colorado. Some of these so called 'boom towns,' with all their attendant vices and social ills, are no more than a hundred miles from the Four Corners area. Others gravitate to that area naturally because there is no law there, no civilization to curb their violent ways.

"Who lives in that area now? A few decent people, but mostly it is populated with bank robbers, horse thieves, cattle rustlers, train robbers, jail breakers, tramps, and ne'er-do-wells looking for trouble. In short, every kind of desperado and general criminal imaginable are moving into that country over there. And that is not all. Because there is no nearby military presence, the Indian tribes, who have a long tradition of raiding the herds and flocks of their neighbors, now sweep down from Colorado or raid across the San Juan with impunity."

There was not a sound in the hall. This was not what the people had been expecting.

"'Oh yes, Brother Snow,' you may say, 'that is a terrible picture that you paint. But what has that to do with the Parowan Stake, or with the Cedar City Ward? There are two hundred miles of impassable badlands between us and them. We are at peace with the Navajos, with the Utes, and with the Paiutes. Let the outlaws and the ruffians fight it out amongst themselves. It cannot touch us in St. George. We are safe in Kanarraville. Parowan and Paragonah are secure.'"

He slammed a fist down. "But I tell you in all soberness, my brothers and sisters, *Parowan is not secure.* Cedar City and St. George are *not* safe. We are all at risk."

The shocked silence stretched on for what seemed like a full minute. David and Patrick exchanged glances. Sarah was giving her husband anxious glances. Abby was sitting forward, her eyes fixed on the man at the pulpit.

"So what is the answer to this terrible dilemma? How do we prevent another Grass Valley? How do we make sure that another non-Latter-day Saint doesn't grab a rifle and shoot more Navajos down in cold blood?" One hand came up to his face, and he rubbed pensively at his eyes. "I tell you, this weighs heavily on my mind both in the waking hours of the day and in nightmares that trouble my sleep.

"I know what I ask of you, my brothers and sisters," he went on, his voice dropping dramatically, causing everyone to lean forward a little. "This will be unlike any settlement we have thus far established. You will be far from the nearest towns. You will be going into a harsh and cruel climate. Your neighbors will be thieves and robbers, violent and wicked men, sometimes hostile Indians. There will be no sheriff to call on, no nearby military garrison to flee to. There are not even established wagon roads as yet by which help can be sent to you.

"I do not wish to alarm you, but you need to understand what we are asking of you as you go to your homes today and discuss what you shall do.

Why do we ask such a difficult thing? Because we have no choice. There is only one real solution to our problem. We need a settlement that will become the buffer between our established settlements and the growing problem with the Indians and the outlaws."

He gave a short, humorless laugh. "*Buffer*," he mused. "That's not a comforting term, is it? Other analogies come to mind as well. What we need over there is a rod that will draw the lightning away from the other settlements down upon itself. You shall be like the shock absorbers on a carriage, taking the jolts to yourself so they do not upset the balance for the rest of us." He shook his head slowly. "None of those are very comforting images, are they?"

Then his voice deepened, and he spoke the next with great emphasis. "*But that is exactly what we need*, my good brothers and sisters. We need someone to act as a buffer, someone to absorb the shocks, someone to diffuse the lightning bolts of war.

"I know what some of you are thinking. 'Yes, Elder Snow, we understand the need there, but surely you are not talking of sending women and children? A fort, perhaps. Maybe several companies of militia to establish order. Surely not a settlement of families in a place as dangerous as you describe?' Well, I have pondered much, prayed much, about that very question. And here are my conclusions. A settlement is the *only* thing that will bring a permanent solution to the problem there."

As murmurs started again, he thundered, "*Yes!* I say again: A settlement is the only permanent solution to our problem. Think about it. You cannot have a permanent influence for good without families. You cannot have law and order without lawful and orderly people. We need people who will come to stay, who will till the land and build schools and erect churches. We need people who will work with the Indians instead of killing them. We need citizens who will drive out the criminal element with the very presence of their goodness."

There was a long pause. David Draper was reeling. It was a stunning concept. Daring. Bold. Lasting. A real solution. Not a mustard plaster stuck on a festering sore. Even he had been swept up by the passion of this man.

Elder Snow stood there for another long moment, pensive and deep in thought. When his head finally lifted, his voice was vibrant with conviction. "Shall I tell you what we need there, my dear brothers and sisters? If we are ever going to find a permanent solution, what we need is, very simply, a people of uncommon valor."[5]

Notes

1. Francis Webster, one of the 1857 handcart pioneers, was living in Cedar City at this time. One day in Sunday School, the teacher was being critical of the decision of Church leaders to send the handcart people forward so late in the season that year.

On that occasion he said: "I ask you stop this criticism. You are discussing a matter you know nothing about. Cold historic facts mean nothing here, for they give no proper interpretation of the questions involved. . . . I was in that company and my wife was in it. . . . We suffered beyond anything that you can imagine. . . . I have pulled my handcart when I was so weak and weary from illness and lack of food that I could hardly put one foot ahead of the other. I have looked ahead and seen a patch of sand or a hill slope and I have said, I can go only that far, and there I must give up, for I cannot pull the load through it. I have gone on to that sand and when I reached it, the cart began pushing me. I have looked back many times to see who was pushing my cart, but my eyes saw no one. And I knew then that the angels of God were there. Was I sorry that I chose to come by handcart? No. Neither then nor any minute of my life since. The price we paid to become acquainted with God was a privilege to pay, and I am thankful that I was privileged to come in the Martin Handcart Company" (cited in McKay, "Pioneer Women," 8).

2. It was customary at this time to issue mission calls in public meetings, with no prior warning, no previous personal interviews, or other preparatory actions. There is also evidence that some spouses or other family members reacted to their calls with open dismay (see Miller, *Hole*, 10).

3. With the exception of the McKennas, all of the names come from the minutes of the conference (Parowan Stake Historical Record, in LDS Church Archives, No. 22125, 174; as cited by Miller, *ibid.*, 16). Not all of the names read that day are included here. The official minutes show that *John* Joseph Nielson was called, but the Jens Nielson family say that it was *Hans* Joseph Nielson, oldest son of Jens Nielson (see Carpenter, *Jens Nielson*, 35).

4. Several sources agree that before his death Brigham Young contemplated what eventually became known as either the Hole in the Rock Expedition or the San Juan Mission. However, his death in 1877 postponed any action for a time (e.g., see Andrew Jenson, "Pioneers and Pioneering", 710–11; Miller, *Hole*, 4–9).

5. Kumen Jones, who was an important member of the Hole in the Rock expedition, wrote the following: "At the suggestion of Apostle Erastus Snow, himself a pioneer,

statesman, colonizer, and patriot, whose prophetic visions pierced the future, the decision was reached to plant a colony somewhere in the neighborhood of the 'Four Corners' where the territories of Utah, Arizona, New Mexico, and the state of Colorado cornered together. This was at a stake or district conference held at St. George in the latter part of the year 1878. And at a stake conference held at Parowan, Iron County, Utah about the 27 day of December 1878 a number of young men were called to explore this part of the country" (Kumen Jones, "Writings," 2).

While the minutes of the Parowan stake conference confirm that Elder Erastus Snow was present, no details are given about his address. Elder Snow's remarks in this chapter are therefore my creation. Nevertheless, the concepts he shares are an accurate reflection of the circumstances and conditions that led Church leaders to determine to create a presence in the southwest corner of Utah Territory (see, e.g., Albert R. Lyman, "Fort, Part IV," 44–45; and "Fort, Part IX," 506; Burton, "Back Door to San Juan," in Miller, Hole, 8–9).

It has been surprising to see how many historians and even members of the Church believe that, although the San Juan Mission was an incredible example of faith and courage, in concept it was seriously flawed, and that the mission itself was a mistake. Therefore, having Elder Snow reflect the compelling reasons behind the decision may help correct such misperceptions.

The phrase "uncommon valor" comes from Blankenagel, Portrait, 15.

BOOK IV

REACTION

1879

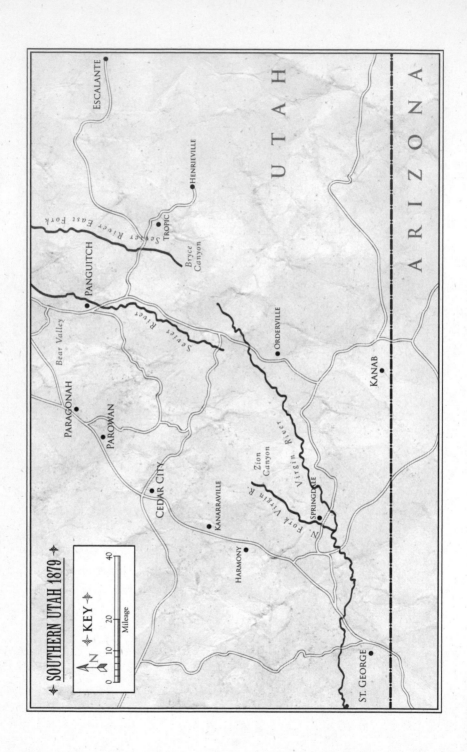

CHAPTER 26

Sunday, December 29, 1878

The McKenna family were among the last to leave the Old Rock Church following stake conference. They had sat there for several minutes after the meeting ended, stunned by what had just happened and the enormity of its implications for them. When they finally stood up to go, President Lunt, who lived in Cedar City, called several other brethren from Cedar City to gather with him and Elder Snow. Patrick was one of those summoned. There was a huddled conversation that lasted two or three minutes; then Patrick returned to the family.

"There is a special priesthood meeting at seven-thirty this Thursday for all of those called from Cedar City and nearby towns. He will give us more specifics and answer questions."

Sister McKenna, who seemed to be the hardest hit from the morning's announcement, managed a wan smile. "I would think there might be one or two of those."

"I've got a couple of hundred myself," her husband said. Then he turned to David and Carl. "There is much to do in Cedar City before the meeting. So I would like to leave at first light. I'll ask the dining room to have an early breakfast for us." He turned. "David, when are you scheduled to leave on your next mail circuit?"

"Wednesday. I already postponed it a week because of being gone up north for Christmas."

"Yes, I know that, but I would really like to have you at the meeting."

David wasn't the only one surprised at that. Everyone was looking at Patrick quizzically.

"But Daddy," Molly said, "David wasn't called."

"The meeting is not just for those called, dear."

"You're the postmaster," David said easily. "Whatever you say. I'll leave Friday morning."

Then Patrick took Sarah by the elbow. "I'd like our family to have some time together now," he said, still talking to David and Carl. "We have much to discuss, but we should like the two of you to join us for supper in the dining room at six."

When David had accompanied the McKenna family to Parowan on Saturday afternoon, they had checked into the Parowan Hotel on Main Street. Patrick had reserved three rooms for them—he and Sister McKenna were with Billy Joe in one, Molly and Abby took another, and Carl and David shared the third.

It was after four now. David was on the bed, pretending to sleep. Carl sat at a small writing table working on something. They had said little since returning to the room. By unspoken mutual agreement, they chose not to talk about what had happened this morning, even though the implications for both of them could be enormous too.

He let out his breath and sat up. Carl turned and looked at him, but David just shook his head. He got up and went to the window. Friday's light snowstorm was gone now, leaving the town glistening under a brilliant blue sky. But it was still cold. He could see the breath of the few people who were out and about.

He started, then drew the curtain back. Directly below him, Molly stepped out of the hotel. She was bundled up in her coat and woolen bonnet and mittens. She stopped for a moment, looking this way and that, then turned and walked slowly up the street, her head down.

"I'm going for a walk," David said. He grabbed his coat and was out the door.

Molly heard his footsteps on the walk and turned. Instantly she smiled and stopped, wiping at her cheeks with the back of her hand.

"Mind if I walk with you?" he said, pretending he hadn't seen the tears.

"I was hoping I might see you," she murmured.

David took her elbow and they moved on again. He was tempted to make light conversation, to see if he could cheer her up a little, but decided to let her lead out when she was ready. She kept her head down as she walked. From time to time, he would feel her digging her fingers into his arm. He was pretty sure she was not even aware she was doing so.

Just ahead was the Old Rock Church. "It's cold, Molly. Want to go inside and talk there?"

She looked up, almost as if she was startled to see the building, then quickly shook her head. So they walked on by, still not speaking.

Finally, as they reached the northern outskirts of the town, she slowed her step and stopped. She turned to look at him. In the gathering darkness of the winter evening, her grey eyes were almost a slate color, and red from crying. "Are you all right?" he asked gently.

She stared at him; then her face crumpled. Her head dropped, and she covered her face with her hands. "Oh, David," she whispered, "what am I going to do?"

Caught by surprise by this outburst, he touched her arm. "Am I to take it from that, that your father is considering accepting the call to go?"

She gave him an incredulous look. "Considering it? David, there's never been a question in his mind. If the call came, we would go. That's it. End of discussion."

That rocked him. "No question at all? But . . ."

She sniffed back the tears, her mouth tightening into a thin line. "He considers this call a reflection of the Lord's will, and when it's the Lord's will, you answer. It's that simple."

He fumbled for something to say. "Elder Snow talked like this was more of an invitation than a commandment."

"Of course he did," she sniffed. "That's the way of the Church. They issue the call, and leave it up to each individual to decide if this is the Lord's will for them."

What if the Lord doesn't care? But he wasn't fool enough to say that aloud. Feeling a sinking feeling in his stomach, he couldn't resist asking, "And you're all right with that?"

"*All right?* What do you think?" She reached inside her coat pocket and withdrew a white handkerchief to cope with a new wave of tears. "I can't believe this is happening. Not to us. It's always been somebody else."

She dabbed at the tears, then blew her nose. Then, once again, she caught him completely by surprise. "I feel so awful, David. So guilty."

"Guilty? Why guilty? That seems like a pretty normal reaction to me."

"Because I should have the same attitude as Daddy. I should want what the Lord wants for us. But I don't want to go. Not in any way. I don't want to leave Cedar City. I love it there. I love working in the post office and meeting people." She looked away, suddenly sheepish. "I love our nice home. I love it that Abby and I each have our own separate bedrooms."

"Is that so wrong?" he asked.

She didn't seem to hear his question. "Why am I so worldly? Why can't I be more like Daddy? Or Abby?"

"Because you're not them," he replied tartly. "What about your mother? How does she feel about it?"

"Awful. Like me. She looks like she's going to be sick."

"You both need to talk to your father. Tell him your feelings, that you don't want to go."

"He knows how we feel."

"So, just like that, you're going to give in?" He felt the anger rising. "Surely your father wouldn't make your mother go if she doesn't want to. Or you."

Her head came up slowly. "You don't know my mother very well, do you?"

"I know her well enough to know she's not one who simply salutes because her husband speaks. And I know your father well enough that I can't believe he would say, 'This is how it's going to be,' and not even listen to your concerns."

"You're right," she said in a low voice, "but you still don't understand. Mama won't go simply because he says so. She will go because she believes this is the thing to do. Because she believes this is a question of faith, and her faith is every bit as strong as Daddy's."

"What about common sense? What about this agency you're always talking about in the Church?" He looked away. "Aw, Molly, don't say it. Don't tell me you're going. Not now."

He had withdrawn his hand in his agitation. Now she reached out and took it. "Why not now?" she asked in a bare whisper.

That took him aback.

"Why not now?" she asked again.

He had thought about this moment all the way back from Coalville, and he certainly hadn't pictured it like this. He had planned to use the two weeks he would be gone on the mail circuit to rehearse his every word, determine the best time and place, see if he really had the nerve to do what he was considering doing.

He drew in a deep breath, looking into those deep grey eyes that made him melt inside. "Molly, I . . . look, Molly, I've been thinking a lot about things, and . . . well, what I'm trying to say is . . ." He looked down at his hands, feeling like a dolt.

When he lifted his head again, she was still waiting, her eyes filled with a touch of hope now. Then, on impulse, he told her about "the box" and how for years it had sustained his mother with its promise of getting them to America, and how during that time, he had put every farthing of his earnings into it. He stopped, giving her a chance to reply, but she never moved, never let her eyes leave his face. So he plowed on. "I guess saving every penny was such a habit by then that I just continued on. By the time I left Coalville when I was sixteen, I had saved a hundred dollars. By the time I was twenty, it was five hundred."

"And how much do you have now?" she asked, the amazement showing in her eyes.

"Thanks to the extra work your father keeps giving me, just over eight hundred dollars."

She gave a low whistle. "My goodness."

"No one knows any of this except for me and my father."

"And now me," she said softly.

"Yes, and now you."

"Why are you telling me this now?"

He drew in a deep breath, then plunged. "Because I don't call it 'the box' anymore. Now I call it my 'ranch fund.' Since coming to Cedar City four months ago, I've realized I'm tired of living on the road. When I was in Laramie, I came to realize that I loved ranching."

She was hanging on his every word. "And you want to have a ranch of your own?"

"Yes."

She leaned forward, eyes literally dancing with happiness now, which knocked David completely off balance. Her next words came like a smack to the side of his head. "Are you thinking of getting serious with me, David Draper?"

He rocked back, nearly choking.

She hooted in delight. "Sorry. Mama always tells me to stop and think before I speak."

"No, I . . ." He could feel the heat spreading across his face.

"No? What *are* you saying then?"

"Molly, I . . . doggone it, girl, you've gone and got me all taffled."

She laughed all the merrier. "Taffled?"

"Yeah, all tangled up, all flustered."

"Hooray for me! That's the first time I've ever seen you at a loss for words." Then she became instantly serious again. "I'm sorry, David. That was terribly presumptuous of me."

He spoke slowly now, trying to choose the right words. "Molly, it's too early to even hope that you and I might . . . well, that we could someday . . ."

"Get serious?" she cried happily.

"Well, yes."

"But you have been thinking about it?"

He sighed. "All the time, but . . ." The knot in his stomach had tightened even more. "Ah, Molly. This is crazy. What am I doing? Look at us. There you sit, all beautiful and gracious, dressed to the nines, daughter of one of Cedar City's most influential and well-to-do citizens. And look at me."

"I am looking at you," she said, her voice soft and warm now.

"I'm a cowpuncher, Molly, a mail rider, a teamster, a construction gang grunt, an old has-been Yorkshire coal miner."

"You don't seem that old to me," she teased.

He rushed on before she could say more. "Molly, I own a horse, a saddle, a bedroll, and a rifle." He threw up his hands. "I don't even own a decent Sunday suit."

"You have eight hundred dollars in cash. How many young men of your age can say that?"

"Yeah, but . . . this is crazy. Why would you even consider . . . ? Your dad will likely toss me out on my backside."

"For what?" she asked, still pressing him.

"When I ask him for permission to come courting his daughter."

"Ah," she breathed, "I was wondering how long it would take you to finally say it. But shouldn't you ask me first? Make sure I won't toss you out on—"

He took her by the shoulders, leaned forward, and kissed her gently, cutting off any further words. And for all that she had been hoping that this very thing would happen, the suddenness of it took her breath away.

When he let go, she was breathing rapidly. "Now who's all taffled?" she whispered.

He laughed and kissed her again. This time it was even softer, but it lingered long enough for her to reach up and put her arms around him and kiss him back.

When they stepped back from each other, there was a quiet joy in her eyes. "I was afraid that I'd be gone and you'd still be trying to find nerve enough to ask Daddy." Now she was teasing him. "Wanna go ask him now?"

He jumped as though she had stuck him with a hatpin. "No!" He shook his head, then said more softly, "Especially not now."

"Then when?"

"I worry about it being too soon, Molly. Yes, I've been here four months now, but in that time I've made five mail circuits and a trip to Coalville. I'm gone more than I'm here. And when I am here, it's not like we spend a lot of time together."

"Not nearly enough," she said, reaching out and stroking his hand.

He was suddenly forlorn. "And now this. I'm not sure what to do."

Tears welled up again. "Don't you know, David? That's what upsets me the most. Knowing that now, when things are finally starting to happen between us, then . . ." She took in a deep breath. "I agree that we need more time, so what do we do?"

"I don't know. But does this mean I have your permission to ask your father if I can start courting you, Molly McKenna?"

She looked up at him. "I don't know." Her eyes closed as she leaned in closer. "Ask me again."

And he did.

When Molly slipped back into the hotel room, Abby was sitting on the bed reading. She watched as her sister removed her bonnet and unbuttoned her coat. "Where have you been?"

"For a walk." She turned her back on her, but not before Abby saw her cheeks flush a little. Abby laid the book down.

"With David?"

"Yes."

There was a pained sigh. "Did you go to his room?"

Molly's chin lifted with a flash of defiance. "No. I went out by myself. He saw me and came out to join me. Why are you making such a big thing of this? It was just a walk."

Abby studied her for a long moment. "You don't act like it was just a walk. What happened?"

Molly didn't seem at all surprised at the question. "Abby, David's gone."

"Gone? Gone where?"

"Back to Cedar City."

"What?"

"He said that he has so much to do before he has to leave again."

"But Daddy told him . . ." She blew out her breath. "Okay, what happened?"

Molly dropped down on the bed beside her sister. "Abby, if I tell you something, will you promise not to say anything to Mama and Daddy?"

"Not if it's something they need to hear."

"Oh, it's nothing bad," Molly snapped. "Promise?"

Abby inserted a bookmark and set the book on the lamp table. "All right, I promise."

Molly's face lit up. She scooted across the bed to sit beside Abby. "Okay. Please don't interrupt until I'm finished."

Abby didn't. She had to bite her tongue when Molly told her how she had blurted out the hint about marriage, but calmed down somewhat as she described David's response. When she finished and sat back, Abby wasn't sure whether to laugh, give her sister a lecture, or hug her. "Did he kiss you?"

"None of your business." But she instantly laughed. "Yes. Three times."

"And is that your first time?"

"Well, the first time since Jimmy Roberts kissed me behind the barn when I was six."

"Molly, Molly, Molly," Abby said with a sigh.

"Don't, Abby. Don't ruin this for me."

Abby turned to face her fully. "Actually, I was just feeling a bit envious."

"About David?" she asked in surprise.

"No, about Jimmy Roberts. He took me behind the barn too, but only to play mumblety-peg." She grew thoughtful. "I beat him, too. Maybe that was why he never kissed me."

Molly laughed, greatly relieved. "Oh, Abby. I've been hoping and hoping he might be interested in me. What do you think Daddy will say? David is really worried that Daddy and Mama will think he's not good enough for me."

Abby didn't respond to that.

Molly instantly bristled. "You think Daddy cares about him not being rich enough?"

"No, not in any way."

"Then what, Abby? Why that look?"

"I am very happy for you, Molly. If this had happened a few weeks ago, I'd . . ." She decided she didn't want to say that. "Back then I considered David Draper to be a shameless flirt whose impudence was surpassed only by his high opinion of himself. But now—well, he still has a natural gift for scraping his fingernails along my chalkboard, but he's a good man."

"So you approve?"

"Of him courting you? Yes, I do."

"But not of me marrying him?"

"Molly, it is way too early for that, and I'm happy that David was wise enough to see that. All he is asking for now is to court you."

"Don't play games with me, Abby. Something is bothering you. What is it?"

Abby paused before answering. "Daddy will say yes to David when he asks. It would not be like Daddy to try to cut it off at this point, even if he does have serious concerns about it."

Molly was up in an instant, tossing her head angrily. "Serious concerns? No, Abby! I don't want to hear this. You *are* ruining it for me."

"Fine. You were the one who asked."

"You always do this," Molly cried. With a flounce, she stomped to the door, jerked it open, and stormed out. But it wasn't five seconds later that she was back. She marched to the foot of the bed and glared down at Abby. "All right. Tell me."

Abby got up, went to the settee, and sat down. She patted the cushion beside her. Molly stood there for several moments, then finally came over and sat beside her. "I don't want you trying to argue with me," Abby began. "I'll just say it, then you decide what you do from there."

Molly folded her arms and sat back as if she were waiting for the verdict in a courtroom.

Abby gave her a sidelong glance and smiled a little. "Can I get a stick or something for you to bite down on while I say this?"

"I already know I'm not going to like what you're going to say. So just say it."

"Okay." Abby looked at her sister, trying to decide how delicately to put it. Finally, she decided delicate was not what was needed here. "I don't think you and David share the same convictions about religion and God."

She jerked her head around. "What?"

"You heard me."

"Why do you say that? He's a member of the Church."

Abby shot her a scornful look. "And you think that makes everyone perfect? You know as well as I do that there are Mormons who are members in name only."

"And you think David's like that?" Molly said hotly.

"I . . . no, I'm not sure I'd credit him with that much of a commitment."

"Well, you're wrong, Abby. He goes to church with us every time he's in town."

Suddenly Abby knew this was futile. Molly was so high in the clouds that she couldn't even guess where solid earth was. "I'm just saying that you need to see if there are differences," Abby concluded.

"Fine, I'll do that."

Abby sighed and stood up. "You asked, and I told you. Now it's up to you."

"What would I ever do without my big sister to keep me out of danger?"

Abby bit back a sarcastic retort. She started back toward the bed, then whirled around again. "If you didn't really want to know, why didn't you say so, and save us both the time?"

"That's it. I'm done." Molly shot to her feet. "You just can't let me be happy, can you? Thank you very much for your wise and sage advice, Abigail McKenna. I don't know what I would do without you."

She went out the door, slamming it behind her, leaving Abby to stare morosely at the wall. Then a slow smile softened the corners of Abby's mouth, and she whispered, "I wonder how long it will take you to remember that you are sleeping in this room with me."

CHAPTER 27

Thursday, January 2, 1879

David arrived at the Cedar City Social Hall a little after seven that evening, fully expecting that this would be another packed meeting. But he was wrong. There were a few horses tied up at the hitching posts, and a couple of carriages, but that was all. As he stood on the sidewalk waiting for the McKennas, a few older men and others who looked like their sons walked past him, nodding and smiling.

At the door, President Henry Lunt, president of the Parowan Stake, and C. J. Arthur, bishop of the Cedar City Ward, greeted the incoming brethren with warm handshakes and hearty words of welcome. David had hung back, not wanting to run that gauntlet without Patrick and Carl.

He had not deliberately avoided Molly and the rest of the family since they had returned home Monday night, but he had kept himself busy, still trying to decide when the best time would be to talk to Patrick.

Yesterday, Abby had come into the livery stable while he was settling Tillie, and she had completely caught him by surprise by her brief comments. She had thanked him, and when he asked her for what, she said, "For going slow with Molly. It's totally contrary to Molly's impetuous nature and it's driving her crazy, but it's the wise thing to do." When he just nodded, a tiny smile played around her mouth. "To be honest, I expected less of you. Thank you for surprising me once again." He took that as an encouraging sign.

Someone called his name, and he saw Patrick and Carl Bradford coming from the direction of the hotel and post office. He waved and moved forward to greet them. "Hello."

They shook hands, then went inside, pausing to shake hands with President Lunt and Bishop Arthur. Patrick introduced David to President Lunt, stating only that he was one of Patrick's employees and that Patrick wanted him to know what was happening with the calls. The president shook his hand firmly and welcomed him there.

Inside, as they waited for others to come, David looked around. There were still a lot of men that he didn't recognize, probably because this meeting included some from outlying settlements, but he did see several he knew. One of those was a few rows ahead of them, an older, bearded man sitting between two younger men. It was the Danish gentleman with the twisted feet that Molly had pointed out to him up in Parowan. David remembered that his son had been one of those called. He nudged Patrick and pointed. "Brother Nielson, right?"

"That's right. Bishop Jens Nielson. That's his son, Hans Joseph— everyone calls him Joe—sitting on his left. He's nineteen and single. I'll bet his call gave the Nielsons pause."

"Why's that?" David wondered.

"The Nielsons lost their only child—a little boy about Billy Joe's age— on the handcart trek, the same night when Jens's feet were so badly frozen. They also lost a young girl they were bringing to America for another family. Joe was their first child born after that. So, in a way, he's their first-born. He and his father are very close."

David was studying the two of them. They looked much alike—tall with broad shoulders, broad faced and square jawed, though Joe was clean shaven.

Patrick went on. "The man on Brother Nielson's right is Kumen Jones, a son-in-law."

"Oh, yeah," David said, recognizing him too. "The one who married the Nielsons' daughter."

"Right."

"I don't remember Brother Nielson being called, right?" David said. "Probably a good thing, him being older and with his handicap and all."

"Yes," Patrick answered. "But Joe and Kumen are both good men. Kumen is one of the best men with a team of horses I know of. He'll be invaluable on the trek." He looked around. "Actually, there are several who were in the Willie or Martin handcart companies. Those two men down front, the white-haired man just to the left of the pulpit and his son. That's Francis Webster and Francis Jr. Young Francis was also called to go with us. They're from England too. Came across in fifty-six in the Martin company. Francis Sr. endured terrible suffering as well. And there's George Rowley. He came with the Willie Company. He was fourteen at the time."

David found himself smiling. This was one of the things he loved about a small town. Everybody knew everybody, and everybody knew everybody else's business. "And now they're being asked to leave again," David murmured. "Seems like if they survived that experience, they'd be left alone now."

Both Patrick and Carl gave him a strange look, and David realized that he was letting his thoughts run out of his mouth without any censorship. But the look passed as Patrick saw someone else. He pointed to a short, burly man with a neatly trimmed mustache and goatee, just coming into the hall with some other men. "That's Ben Perkins and his brother, Hyrum. They're coal miners too, from Wales. Like you, he started in the mines at age six, carrying water for the miners. We'll have to get you two together sometime, let you compare notes."[1]

After a prayer, Bishop Arthur, who was conducting the meeting, stood. "Brethren, I should like to briefly state our purpose here this evening, then turn some time to President Lunt for any remarks he may have. After that, we shall invite responses from those present."

He let his eyes sweep across the assembled group. "The primary object in calling this meeting is to ascertain if those whose names were read and sustained in conference last Sunday are willing to go, and if their parents . . ." He stopped. "You may have noticed that many of the names read out on Sunday are of young men who are not yet married. The reason for that should be obvious to all. But we are anxious to ascertain if the parents of these young men are willing to have their sons go and to assist them in doing so.

"We also wish you to understand clearly that there is no compulsion in this matter. Whether you choose to answer the call issued is a matter of personal agency, as only you can decide what is best for you and your family."

David glanced at Patrick to see how he reacted to that comment. Would it change his mind? But his face was expressionless, and he was actually nodding as Bishop Arthur spoke.

"However, for those who choose to go forward, may we ask that you do so with cheerful hearts and a glad countenance." He waited while a few heads bobbed in agreement. No one spoke, so he went on. "Also, I remind you that Elder Snow invited others who were not called to volunteer themselves if they have a mind to."

David felt a nudge and turned to see Patrick smiling at him. "Why don't you do that?" he whispered. "If you volunteered, I wouldn't have to pay you."

"Pay me?" David whispered back. Was he joking? Then he understood. David would stay on as a mail rider after the family left. If he went with them, his salary would end.

"And you, Carl," Patrick added. "There you go. You don't have to wait for a call."

Carl seemed pleased, and nodded his assent. No surprise there. If Abby was going, Carl would be interested in going too.

Now the bishop thumped the pulpit for emphasis. "Brethren, we know that this call brings with it much upheaval to your lives. We know that it affects far more than just you who are here tonight. Your wives and children will become as much a part of this as you will. I hope you will sit down with them and discuss the reasons behind this call, as Elder Snow so carefully explained them to us. Help them to understand that this decision was not made lightly or without consideration for your feelings and the feelings of your family. I commend you for your faith. I commend you for your willingness to brave the unknown so that others throughout the territory may have peace and may live in safety and security."[2]

He drew in a deep breath as he once again let his eyes go from face to face. "We shall now hear from President Lunt." He stepped back. "President."

"Thank you, Bishop Arthur. And thank you, brethren, for making time to be with us tonight. I say amen to what your good bishop has said, and I too look forward to hearing your expressions concerning these calls. I strongly advise you to put your full trust in God, and all will go well with you."

David's head lifted slowly. *Thank you, President, but if it's all the same to you, I would suggest putting your trust in wise planning, careful preparation, the best teams and wagons.*

"Let me add two or three things of a more practical nature. First, we know that at this point the exact location of your settlement has not been determined. We know you are anxious to know that, but it will have to wait for now. I shall say more of that in a moment.

"Second, we know that many are asking how soon you will be expected to depart. That is easier to answer, though not completely settled. Elder Snow told us as a presidency that he hoped the expedition could be ready to leave by around the first part of April."

A low murmur broke out. Obviously most had not heard that.

"So we have that as a target," he continued. "But, as you know, there are no roads into the area. There are no other settlements there, only isolated homesteads and Indian villages. We cannot simply strike out into the wilderness blindly with two or three hundred people, including women and children. So what we have under consideration right now is a proposal to send out an exploratory party in advance of the main company."

Again he had to stop and let the reaction run its course. "We not only need to know where we are going, but which route is the best to get us there. The exploring party will seek out a southern route so that we cannot be locked in by the snow over the high mountain passes. How long will this exploration take? We cannot say for sure. But for those who will stay behind, I think we can say with some confidence that it is not likely that we will have word back from the exploring party in much less than six months. So those of us going with the main company will have until late summer or possibly even early fall to get ready."

David wanted to stand up and whoop. Six months. That gave him and Molly plenty of time to work things out. He looked at Patrick, who also looked greatly relieved. That would allow time for him to dispose of his businesses.

President Lunt acknowledged the reaction with a smile. "Now, to my third point. As Bishop Arthur has already noted, many of you here tonight, and those being called from other areas, are young single brethren. We strongly recommend that, as part of your preparation, you find a young woman to court, and that you do so with some dispatch so that you can marry before we leave."

This brought much laughter and backslapping, to the embarrassment of the young men.

"We assume that the young men will not find this assignment too burdensome," President Lunt added with a droll smile.

As the congregation roared at that, David kept his eyes forward. He didn't dare look at Patrick. What was going through *his* head right now? There sat Carl, already semi-courting Abby. And here he was, clearly interested in Patrick's other daughter. Theoretically, at least, it was possible that Patrick might end up with both of his daughters going as married women. He shook his head. That was a little much to digest right now.

He looked up, realizing the president was through and had turned the time back to the bishop.

"All right, brethren. We don't wish to prolong the meeting, but we would now invite you—including you fathers—to express your feelings." He immediately returned and sat down again. For a long moment, there was not a sound, then an older man got to his feet slowly.

"That's Jim Nealson," Patrick whispered.

"Thank you, Bishop. Thank you, President, for your stirring words. I would like to say that I hereby signify my willingness to do all in my power to assist my son so that he can go and fulfill this mission." He sat down again as others around him smiled their approval.

"Francis Webster," Patrick whispered as the white-haired man Patrick had earlier pointed out to him stood. He laid a hand on the shoulder of the young man sitting beside him. The younger Webster was looking up at his father, and David could see the strong resemblance between them.

"President Lunt. Bishop Arthur. I hereby pledge to do all in my power to assist my son, Francis Jr., to fulfill his duty." And he sat down again.

Next came George Urie. He was brief, blunt, and quite different from the others. David found it quite refreshing. "President Lunt," he began, "I am sorry, but I am not prepared at this time to say whether I will be going or not. However, I do promise that it shall have my most careful consideration." And he sat down.

One after another they rose and gave brief expression to their feelings. One said that he felt like he could live about anywhere anyone else did, so he thought he'd be on hand when it was time to go. One of the Welshmen stood and, in halting English, said he would be ready to go and hoped all could go together.

Then a man stood who was close to thirty, maybe a little older. He didn't have anyone with him. Patrick's soft commentary continued. "James Davis. Owns a prosperous store here in town. Married. Four children. Wife expecting another."

David jerked around. *He's taking a pregnant wife?*

"Due in July or August, I believe," Patrick said. "Here's another one of those soft, pampered businessmen who shouldn't be going, right?" he whispered.

"Those are your words, not mine," David countered. Then he turned to watch the man.

Davis didn't look at those in the congregation, only at his two leaders. "I just wanted to say this. The other night I was warned in a dream that I would be required to go and live in the Arizona country."

David instantly noted his British accent—southern England, he guessed. Maybe around London. He sounded quite a bit like David's mother when he spoke.

Brother Davis started to sit down, then changed his mind and straightened again. "As many of you know, my wife is with child, expecting sometime in July. Sister Davis has also been in poor health for some time." He stopped, Adam's apple bobbing as he fought to control his feelings. "So when we heard my name read out on Sunday, we were much surprised." He shook his head. "Much surprised. We feel bad about having to leave our store and our home, and considerable other property we own. We expect we shall sell it at a loss. We are particularly worried about my wife's health, but as we talked about it, we decided that we had been called by servants of the Lord, and so we determined we would try to magnify our call."

David was shaking his head in disbelief. Dreams? A pregnant *and* sick wife. What was going on here? Seeing that Patrick was watching him, David kept his face impassive.

James Davis stood there for several long seconds, trying to gain his composure. Then his chin came up and he held his head high. "So I say to you, I shall do all in my power to be ready with my family when the company prepares to depart."[3]

And what about your wife? Does she know you're down here tonight committing her to go with four children and another on the way? David wanted to stand up and shout that at him. But of course, he didn't. He just sat there fuming.

It was no surprise to David at all when Patrick stood next. Every eye turned to him, and David could see the respect they had for him. He glanced quickly down at Carl, then looked at David, his eyes holding him for a moment longer before he turned back to the two leaders. "When my wife and I were baptized into this Church, we made a covenant with the Lord that we would take His name upon us so that we could be called His people. We made a covenant that we would bear one another's burdens, that we would mourn with those who mourn, and stand as witnesses of God in all things, at all times, and in all places." There was a quick smile. "And I assume that includes San Juan country. So, with the full blessing of my wife, and with the full agreement of my children, I pledge to you this day that the McKennas have every intention of living first by covenant and then, and only then, by comfort and convenience."

Notes

1. All of the people mentioned here are either listed in the minutes or were likely there because we know that they, or a family member, were among those called. The personal information about individuals shared here is accurate (see Jenson, *LDS Biographical*

Encyclopedia, 3:441; Miller, *Hole*, 186; Carpenter, *Jens Nielson*, 35, 38; Jessie M. Sherwood, *Life Sketch of Mary Jane Wilson* [daughter of Benjamin Perkins], 2, 5).

2. The first of Bishop Arthur's remarks reflect the summary made by the clerk who kept the minutes of the meeting. The second part of his address was summarized by the clerk in this brief sentence: "The Bp. gave timely and fatherly instructions" (Cedar Ward minutes, 332).

3. The expressions of actual individuals given here come from the minutes of the Cedar City Ward or Miller's summary of that meeting (see Miller, *Hole*, 12–13). As it turned out, James Davis and his family did not end up going on the main Hole-in-the-Rock expedition. They joined the exploring party, which left Cedar City on April 13, then stayed on the San Juan River to await the arrival of the main company. More will be said of them in future chapters.

CHAPTER 28

Monday, January 13, 1879

David Draper banked the campfire and stood there for a moment, looking down into the glowing coals. Then he walked over to where Tillie had found a patch of grass and made sure her hobbles were secure. He stroked her neck for a moment as she nuzzled his arm, then came back to the fire. Earlier he had cut a dozen or so cedar branches to make a thick base for his bed on top of the snow. He untied his bedroll from his saddle, peeled off the half of a buffalo robe he had purchased some years before, and laid it out across the branches. He put it so the hide side was down and the hair side up. That would provide him a waterproof base in case any melting snow came through the branches.

Finally, he unrolled his blankets. He wasn't worried about sleeping warm tonight. A gentle south wind had started about midday, and the temperatures had softened. It probably meant a storm was coming tomorrow, but by then he'd be farther south and at lower elevations. Rain he could live with.

He removed his boots, took off his revolver and gun belt, and laid them beside his "pillow"—the mailbag covered by his folded slicker. He next took off his belt with its heavy buckle, coiled it up, and shoved it inside his hat so that the hat couldn't blow away in the night. Finally he stretched out on his bed. He lay back, hands behind his head.

Above him the sky was clear, and the myriad of stars seemed closer than usual. He could clearly see the long band of soft, filmy light stretching from horizon to horizon that gave the Milky Way its name. Half of a waning moon was up about a third of the way on its journey across the sky. It glistened off the snow in silvery softness. Somewhere in the distance he heard the yipping of a coyote, and the answering hoot of an owl. Together, it all made for good company, and David felt himself relaxing.

For a change, he wasn't thinking about Molly. He was thinking about land and cattle. He had been on the road now for twelve days, four days longer than it would normally have taken him to get this far. He had taken a day and a half in the Panguitch area, riding up and down the valley looking for possible ranch sites or land for sale. What he had found was not encouraging. The valley was filling up, and land prices were already rising. So he took two more days and rode over the virtually treeless and bitter cold Paunsaugunt Plateau past Bryce Canyon, then dropped down into Tropic and Henrieville. The temperature difference between the top of the plateau and the valley below was dramatic enough that the first settlers in the valley had felt like they had entered the tropics, and named their town accordingly.

Here the land situation looked much more promising. These were newer settlements, and the valley was less populated. Eager to bring more people into the area, when the settlers learned of his interest, they welcomed him warmly. They showed him large areas of good, still-unclaimed grassland. If he were to settle there, some of it would be given to him for free. The rest he could buy for fifty cents an acre. They also told him that the surrounding mountains provided good summer grazing. It was a beautiful little valley—in many ways, exactly what he was looking for.

But could he really bring a woman like Molly to such an isolated and primitive place? He sighed in frustration. The road he had followed was barely a track. Some of the settlers still lived in dugouts cut into one of the side hills. No one had anything larger than a one-room cabin or a simple adobe hut. Then there was the problem of isolation. Even pushing it, it was a four-day trip to get back to Cedar City. He audibly groaned. Cedar City? What was he thinking? Molly's family wasn't going to be in Cedar City. They were going to be in San Juan. There were no roads between Tropic and San Juan. It would take weeks to go around. Knowing how close she was to her family, could he really ask that of her?

As he lay there, growing more frustrated with every minute, he suddenly jerked up. He rose up on one elbow, peering at Tillie. She was a frozen statue, head high, ears cocked sharply forward. She snuffled her breath, peering directly down the hillside below them.

David was instantly out of his bedroll and groping for his boots. He moved quickly but silently. A bear? A wolf? His ears were straining to hear as he pulled his boots on. Then he went cold. In Panguitch, and again in Hillsdale and Hatch, the locals had warned him to be on the lookout for a small band of renegade Utes or Paiutes who were raiding the homesteads up and down Long Valley. Indians out looking for an occasional loose horse or stray cow were not unusual, but it was reported that this band was led by a white man who rewarded the Indians with generous amounts of liquor in exchange for whatever stock they could steal. One settler down in Orderville had been seriously wounded trying to stop them from emptying his corral.

Boots on, he retrieved his pistol and strapped it around his waist. Then, moving carefully on hands and knees, he started toward his saddle, where his rifle was still in its scabbard.

"Leave it!" a deep voice yelled at him from the trees to his right.

David forgot the rifle. He dropped and rolled, yanking at his pistol, scrambling for cover behind his saddle. There was a bright flash and the blast of a rifle. He heard the snap of the bullet as it passed just above his head. Suddenly a man burst out of the trees, and in the pale moonlight David saw he held a rifle. He leaped up, raising both hands high in the air and waving them frantically back and forth. "All right! All right!"

"Drop the pistol!" the man barked.

David did so, keeping his hands plainly in sight.

"That's better," the same voice said. He shouted something that David didn't understand, and instantly David heard the crunch of footsteps behind him. Out of the corner of his eye, he saw a dark shape bend down and pick up his pistol. He gave a low cry as it was jammed hard against his back. Speaking almost in his ear, the second man hissed something unintelligible. David had interacted enough with Indians to recognize that this was not another white man, like the man with the rifle. His heart sank. This was not good. This was big trouble.

Then behind him, just out of his line of sight, David heard the crunch of more footsteps. He turned his head enough to see two more men—also Indians, judging from the floppy hats and the bows strung over their shoulders. His mind was racing. How many more? And where were they? The reports had said a "small band" of Indians and a white man. Did three Indians constitute a small band? Or were there others? Probably. At least one, staying back with their horses. His mind was working furiously.

The man with the rifle came forward. He was tall and heavily built. A thick beard covered the lower part of his face. He grunted something in the same Indian tongue, and the man holding the pistol in David's back stepped away from him.

"Unbuckle your gun belt and toss it back to him," the big man growled.

David awkwardly complied, using only one hand, keeping the other high so they wouldn't think he was going to try something. When it was loose, he tossed it lightly to the Indian.

"Now step back."

David did so, and the Indian moved around to where he could cover him with the pistol.

There was another burst of Ute or Paiute, and the Indian darted over to David's saddle and retrieved his rifle. He also picked up the mailbag. He walked them over to the leader and held them out.

Never letting the muzzle of the rifle waver from David's chest, the big man set the rifle and the bag down. He grunted something again, holding out his hand. The Indian turned sullen, but finally holstered David's pistol and tossed that on the pile as well. With a jerk of his head, the big man gestured toward Tillie.

David turned to look. The two Indians were moving slowly toward her, talking softly in their native tongue. Tillie didn't like it, and she was backing up slowly, tossing her head. The one who had shoved the pistol in David's back trotted over to join them.

"You only got the one horse?" the man barked at David.

"That's right."

He called that information to them, then came forward warily. When he was close enough he jammed the end of the rifle hard against David's chest, causing him to wince. "You the mail rider?"

David nodded, still breathing hard from both shock and his burst of exertion.

"How much money's in the bag?"

"Mail riders don't carry money," David said, keeping his voice even.

"People send money through the mail to their families."

David was quickly regaining control. "Well, I certainly don't go through the mail to find out who." Then he added, "You know that stealing United States mail is a federal offense. You'll have the Pinkertons after you."

There was a bark of derision. "Oooh," the man exclaimed. "The big bad Pinkertons." He jabbed David again. "Open it. I know you have the key." He backed off a couple of steps.

Just then, Tillie snorted, then whinnied sharply. They both turned to see what was happening. The three Indians had spread out in front of Tillie and were moving in slowly toward her, hands out, talking softly. Tillie snorted again, backing up in little hopping steps because of the hobbles. Then the closest Indian lunged forward, grabbing her by the halter. Triumphantly, he shouted to his companions.

The first Indian came running back to David and his captor. He grabbed the bridle, which was draped over David's saddle, then trotted back. As he approached his companions, holding it out for them to see, the one holding Tillie's halter snubbed her head down and held it tightly. The third man grabbed one ear and twisted it hard, pulling Tillie's head with his full strength. Tillie whinnied in pain, but her head dropped, and the one with the bridle darted in. In a moment, they had the bridle in her mouth and slipped it up and over her ears.

When they released her head, Tillie laid her ears back and snapped viciously at the closest man. They laughed, yelling warnings to each other. Tillie snapped again, and they jumped back. And in that instant, David had the first flash of hope. He glanced at his captor, who still held the rifle steadily on him, now about ten feet away from him. But the big man was watching the battle between horse and man, grinning at the sight.

David turned back. One of the Indians reached down between Tillie's front legs. There was a dull flash of moonlight on metal, then the leather hobbles fell free. Tillie didn't like that, either. She tried to rear up, but was jerked down again sharply. Her ears lay back again, but again, the one holding her head didn't give her enough slack to be dangerous.

"I think they like your horse," the man chortled. He reached down and picked up the mailbag. "Give me the key," he demanded.

David pretended not to hear, pretended to still be engrossed in what was happening over with Tillie. "If they plan to ride her," David warned, "they better get the saddle. She hates bareback."

The big man roared. "You think I'm gonna tell an Indian how to ride a horse?"

David's mind was racing. If there was someone staying back with their horses, it was probably just one man. And the horses were probably a good hundred yards or more away, or David would have heard them. He tensed.

He drew in a silent breath, then poised himself, hoping against hope that they would try to mount his horse. They did. As the first Indian held Tillie's head tightly, the second one grasped her mane and threw himself up on her back. At that same instant, David gave a shrill whistle. Tillie's head jerked up so fast and so hard that it sent the first Indian flying. The next instant, she erupted into an explosion of bucking, twisting, pounding fury. The second brave had barely straightened himself on her back. The spine-cracking jolt sent him flying as well.

David didn't wait to see what the third Indian was going to do. He leaped forward, bringing both hands together to form a club. The big man had turned to gape at the battle going on to his left. He heard David and swung around with a cry. The rifle blast nearly deafened David, but he was already past the muzzle and knocked it aside, then swung at the big man's head with a fury of his own. The man saw the blow coming and tried to duck away, but he was too late. David's interlocked fists connected with the side of his face, snapping his head back sharply. He dropped to his knees, one hand coming up to ward off another blow.

Ignoring the pain shooting through his hands and arms, David grabbed the rifle by the barrel and snatched it out of the big man's grasp. In one smooth movement, he whirled, swinging the rifle like a club. The man's hands were up to shield his face, leaving his body unprotected. The swinging butt of the rifle caught him squarely on the left side of his chest. There was a soft snap as a rib or two broke, followed by a scream of agony. He fell, writhing and screaming, to the ground. David leaped in, kicked his rifle and pistol clear, then levered another shell into the chamber and whirled to face the Indians.

The one was still down, rolling in the snow and howling with pain, holding one arm. The other two were staring at David. Then one of them started clawing for the bow over his shoulder. Dropping to one knee, David fired. A plume of snow exploded about ten feet to the right of the nearest Indian. He jacked another shell in and fired again. This time it was five feet away. They jumped back, yelping in surprise. He pumped another round into the chamber. "Get outta here!" he shouted. "Go!" He fired a third time, this time into the air.

That did it. They grabbed their companion and dragged him to his feet. He screamed, holding his arm like it was broken. Off they went, slipping and sliding as they raced away down the gentle slope toward a grove of junipers about sixty or seventy yards away. He fired again just to let them know he was still there.

He swung around, rifle coming up, but his former captor was no longer a threat. He was curled in a ball, arms hugging his chest, moaning in pain. In three steps, David reached his own rifle and pistol. He picked them up and tossed them clear. Then he grabbed his saddle and ran back to where he had a good view down the moonlit hillside. He dropped it and flopped down behind it. It wasn't much, but it was all the cover he had.

Not ten seconds later, four horsemen came bursting out of the trees. David jacked another shell into the chamber, but then lowered the rifle. They weren't coming up the hill. Stretched out low over their horses' necks, the four braves raced away, shouting and whipping their horses into a hard lope. Feeling a tremendous rush of relief, he stood, lifted the rifle, and fired one more shot into the air just for good measure. Then, trembling violently, he slowly sank down to the snow, leaning back against his saddle.

Wednesday, January 22, 1879

It was the last of lingering twilight when David entered the outskirts of Cedar City. A light snow was falling, the large flakes swirling slowly downward in the still air. Tillie plodded along, head down, hooves muffled in the snow. And, anxious as David was to get her to the stable and himself into a hot bath, he didn't push her. She had earned the right to plod.

They had left here twenty days before. With the two side trips he had made, and with having to backtrack to Orderville to turn over his prisoner, David guessed she had carried him for close to four hundred miles. She was near the edge of her limit as much as he was.

Like Tillie's, David's head was down as he slumped in the saddle. He was physically spent, mentally exhausted, cold clear down to his bones, and so ready to be out of the saddle that he could barely stand it.

He was suddenly aware that Tillie had stopped. David lifted his head. Just ahead of them, standing squarely in the middle of the road, was a dark figure.

"Hello, Tillie," Molly McKenna said softly. She came forward and began to stroke Tillie's face. "So you finally brought him home to me."

David stared at her. There was a dusting of white on her shoulders and bonnet. "What are you doing out here?"

Molly laid her head against Tillie's. "How's that for a greeting, Lady Tilburn? Not so much as a 'Hello, Molly.'"

"Hello, Molly," David said, swinging down out of the saddle, wincing as every muscle in his body protested. "What are you doing out here?"

She came to him, taking his hands in hers. "Hello, David." And then, surprising him and herself, she kissed him quickly and lightly on the lips. "Welcome home." She reached up and rubbed at his chin. "My goodness. Do you never shave when you're on circuit?"

"Right. I should have asked one of those fancy hotels for a razor."

She stepped back, giving him the once-over in the fading light. "You need a haircut, too."

"Well, I planned on taking care of all that in the morning. I didn't plan on meeting this beautiful woman in the middle of the street. How long have you been waiting?"

"An hour. The post office in St. George sent a wire, telling us when you left, so I figured it would be sometime this evening when you arrived." Her eyes lowered. "Are you vexed?"

"No, of course not. I'm delighted to see you. It's just—"

She cut it off, slipping an arm through his. "I'm just teasing you." She rubbed Tillie's nose again. "You look exhausted. Both of you. Come on. You ride, I'll walk alongside."

"You want me to get back in that saddle? What are you, a sadist?"

That was more like it, and she laughed happily. "Are you too tired to walk, Mr. Hero, sir?"

He groaned. "No. Don't tell me."

"Yep. It's all over town. We knew within a couple of hours of when you turned your prisoner in at Orderville. Went out over the telegraph. Made all the papers the next morning." She lifted her hands and formed a head-line in the air with her fingers. "'Mail Rider Captures Outlaw Gang. Singlehandedly Fights Off Three Hundred Indians.'"

He started, then realized she was teasing him.

"I saved a copy of the paper for you so you can show it to your grand-children." She jumped aside to avoid his swiping hand. "I also sent a copy to your father."

"You didn't."

"I did. Didn't know the address, so I just put it to Mr. Draper, care of Coalville Post Office. I was pretty sure he would never hear it from you."

He walked for a moment in silence, then reached up and patted Tillie's neck. "This one is the hero. Or heroine, I guess you'd say. Weren't for her . . ." He let it go.

"Did you think you were going to die?" she asked gravely.

He nearly brushed that aside, then decided to be honest. "I wondered there for a bit, but rough as the leader was, I don't think he planned any-thing violent, long as I cooperated."

"Did you pray, David?"

"Pray?" he snorted. "Things were happening a little too fast for that."

"Not even a thought about asking God to help you?"

He tried not to show his irritation. "Molly, look. He had a rifle pointed at my chest and another man had a pistol at my back. I wasn't thinking about God at that moment."

"Hmm," she murmured, speaking half to herself. "At a time like that, God is the first thing I would have thought of." She looked up at him. "I was praying for you," she said softly.

"What?"

"I've been praying every day since you left. I asked God to protect you from danger."

"Thank you," he said, touched, even as he felt his temper rise a little. He opened his mouth to say more, then clamped it shut again. He was tired and irritable and it was better to let it go. "So," he asked, "anything new happening on the call to San Juan?"

"They officially announced that Silas Smith will be the captain of the company."

"That's good, right? If I remember, your father said he's a good man."

"Yes, Daddy's very pleased. Which reminds me, Daddy would like to meet with you in the morning at nine o'clock."

"I guess he hasn't changed his mind about going?"

There was a soft explosion of frustration. "We're going. That's settled."

No real surprise there. He said nothing.

She stepped closer and pressed her shoulder against his. "I am so happy you're back, David. I've missed you. A lot."

"And I missed you." She looked up, clearly anticipating more. "A lot," he added solemnly.

Her smile turned impish. "Oh, I should tell you about the parade."

"Parade? What parade?"

"The one on Saturday they're giving in your honor."

He stopped dead. She pretended not to notice and walked on slowly. "You'll be the grand marshal, of course. They've asked the governor of the territory if he can attend, and . . ."

He quickly caught up with her and grabbed her elbow. "You'd better be kidding, Molly McKenna, or I'm going to show you exactly what I did to that guy up there on the mountain."

She raised the back of her hand to her forehead. "Oh, dear me. I do believe I'm going to faint."

Molly watched as David unsaddled Tillie, filled her manger with hay, and gave her a bucket of oats. Finished, he took Molly's arm. "You'd better get home. Your parents will wonder what's happened to you."

"Mother knew what I was doing."

He gave her a sharp look, but decided to let it pass. "I'll walk you home."

"No you won't," she said firmly. "I will walk you to the boardinghouse and tell Mrs. Halliday to put you to bed."

"I won't fight you on that one."

As they left the barn and started up the street, she became pensive. He hoped she wouldn't start on what he guessed was going through her mind, but she did anyway.

"Have you thought any more about asking my father if you can court me?"

"Only all the time," he muttered.

"And?"

"Aw, Molly. I don't know what to think anymore."

Her step faltered momentarily, and her chin dropped. "Oh."

"It's not what you think, Molly." He stopped and faced her. "I thought about you every waking moment. I close my eyes and all I see are those wonderful eyes of yours."

"Mmmm," she murmured. "That's better."

But instantly the frustration was back. "I went to Tropic, Molly."

She looked blank. So he told her about his search for land in Panguitch, and then about making the side trip over the mountain to Tropic and Henrieville.

"And?" she asked again.

"There's plenty of land. Good land. But . . ." He took her arm and started walking again, feeling the hopelessness rising again.

"What, David?"

"Molly, I met a lot of the families there. Good people. But I also found women living in caves dug into the hillsides. I ate supper in a house with a sod roof. When it rains, bugs and mud and an occasional mouse drop out of the ceiling onto the table. I met women who haven't seen their families for over a year."

It was like his words had frozen her.

His voice softened. "I talked to a man who takes his cattle up in the mountains all summer and doesn't see his wife until he comes down again. Is that what you want?"

Her eyes went cold. "Poor little coddled Molly. What kind of rancher's wife will she make?"

He grabbed her shoulders. "Molly, those men that attacked me had been raiding the ranches up and down the Sevier Valley, hitting isolated homesteads like the ones I just described. They shot one settler when he tried to stop them. All I have been able to think about since that night is, what if that had been you, out there in Tropic, with me gone up in the mountains for a month or more? As beautiful as you are, it gives me the chills to think what would happen."

His horror washed the anger out of her. "You really were thinking about me in that way?"

He threw up his hands. "Of course I was. I told you that before I left."

She moved closer. "David, I think I'm falling in love with you."

That startled him. Then he gave her a wry smile. "What took you so long?" he growled. "I fell in love with you that morning when you accused me of kissing the blarney stone."

Her eyes widened, and she laughed merrily. "Really?"

He looked around quickly to be sure that they were alone, then took her in his arms and kissed her firmly. Then he sobered again. "But that doesn't just magically make everything right."

"It doesn't?" She laid her head against his chest. "It sure feels like that to me."

He wanted to push her back, grab her and shake her, try to make her understand. But instead he put his arms around her and began gently stroking her hair. "You're leaving, Molly. What are we going to do about that?"

"I'm praying about that, too," she said.

He took her by the shoulders and held her at arm's length. "Molly, Molly, Molly," he sighed. "I wish it were that simple."

"I'm not asking *you* to pray," she shot right back at him. Then she went up on tiptoes and kissed him softly. "Just hearing you say you love me is enough."

He started to shake his head, but she pressed her fingers to his lips. "Not now, David. You're exhausted. I'm sorry I brought it up now. Let's get you home. We can talk tomorrow."

Before his frown could deepen, she raised up and kissed him again, only this time a little longer than before. He closed his eyes and encircled her in his arms and let the kiss linger, savoring the sweetness of her.

CHAPTER 29

Thursday, January 23, 1879

Molly was not around when David entered the hotel shortly before nine the next morning, but Abby was behind the front desk.

"Well," she said when she looked up and saw him. She immediately reached for a piece of paper and grabbed the pen from its inkwell. "Do you give autographs?"

"Not you too," he said, making a face.

"Oh, yes," she said, her eyes filled with mischief. "In Cedar City, we take our heroes seriously. Five to one odds. That's impressive."

"Stop it," he growled.

Her smile faded. "Really, are you all right?"

"I'm fine." He raised a hand to wave away any further comments. "It just happened, Abby, and fortunately it turned out well. People are making way too much of it."

"Well, we're grateful it turned out as it did. But if you think Billy Joe thought you were great before, just wait until you see him now." The mischievous twinkle stole into her eyes again. "In fact, we're thinking of putting your name forward for sheriff in the next election."

His look of disgust made her laugh right out loud. She pointed to the door across from them. "Daddy's waiting for you. He said to go right in."

Just then the door to her father's office opened and Patrick McKenna stepped out. "Ah, David," he called. "There you are."

"Good morning, Patrick."

"Come in." To Abby, he said, "Will you make sure we're not disturbed?"

As he turned back and went inside, David shot her a quizzical look, but she just shrugged and shook her head. He followed Patrick in and shut the door behind him.

"How are you, David?" Patrick began. "Molly said you looked exhausted last night."

So he knew she had been out to meet him. "I was, but twelve hours of sleep helps."

"Good. This was quite the trip you had."

"Sorry I took so long."

"Well, I don't think anyone over around Orderville is complaining. In fact, they're hailing you as the conquering hero."

"Please," he moaned. "If anyone gets the honors, it's Tillie."

He nodded absently. "Did you get some time to look at ranch property?"

So Molly had told him more than just that she had met him last night. "Some," he said. "Tropic looks the most promising." He shrugged. "Buying a ranch isn't in my immediate future. I was just looking, trying to get some ideas."

"Well," Patrick said, making a steeple with his fingertips, "maybe I can help in that regard." At David's startled look, he continued, "But more of that in a moment. When are you scheduled to leave again?"

David frowned. The very thought of it sounded awful. "I'm supposed to leave Monday, but I was going to ask permission to postpone that a couple of days. Let my horse rest up a little."

"And you too, I'm sure. Permission granted." His employer sat back, his face thoughtful. "Do you mind it?" he asked.

"What?"

"The circuit. Being out on your own. Sleeping under the stars. Cooking over a campfire all the time." He grinned. "Having to corral the local bad boys and haul them off to jail."

Surprised by the question, David hesitated. Then he shook his head. "Normally, no. This one seemed especially long. I guess because it was."

"What if you got a better offer?"

David's eyebrows lifted at that. After quick consideration, he said,

"Well, I guess if it were truly a better offer, that makes for a simple decision."

There was an answering chuckle. "Well said."

Again he sat back, watching David, but he seemed far away in his thoughts. Feeling somewhat bold, David decided to risk a question. "In that last meeting, Bishop Arthur said that these calls were a matter of agency, that those called should not feel any compulsion to go."

Patrick came back to him. "Yes, and that if we go, we should go with cheerful hearts."

"That, too." He took a quick breath. "If I might speak frankly, Patrick, why do you suppose they called you and Sister McKenna?"

He snickered softly. "Because we're such strong pioneer types, you mean?"

David flushed. "I didn't mean it that way." He hesitated, then said, "Well, maybe I did. But it's more than that. You are a successful and astute businessman. I can see where that would be of value to a new settlement eventually, but why in the initial stages? Seems like while they're getting things started, there's more of a need for road builders, teamsters, hunters, and farmers—those who make their living out of doors, and with their hands—than for a businessman."

Sobering, Patrick responded, "I know, I know, David. Believe me, we have asked ourselves the same question. Why us, of all people?" He grew even more serious. "I don't know, David. I just know that we are going to answer the call. That's what we do."

"Will Abby go?" David asked. He had almost said Molly, but thought better of it.

His employer looked surprised. "If we go, Abby will go." He thought for a moment. "She'd probably go if we didn't go. She's actually quite excited about it. A new adventure and all."

David's head came up slowly. He wondered how much the Zion Canyon experience had influenced her.

Patrick sighed. "It will be hardest on Molly. Her mother, too, of course. But Molly especially. But no. No one will be staying. We're all going."

"What if Molly decided she didn't want to go?" David asked, as if the thought had just come to him.

Patrick's brows furrowed. "I suppose she's old enough to make up her own mind, but . . ." He shook off the thought. "No, she'll go. What else would she do?"

Before David could answer that—if he had chosen to answer it—Patrick leaned forward, looking at David in earnest now. "What about you?"

"Me? I wasn't called."

"So? You heard Bishop Arthur. Volunteers are welcome. Let's see now, of the list of qualifications you mentioned, you qualify as an outdoorsman, a road builder, a teamster, and a hunter. Also, after your latest episode, it sounds like you would be a good man to have around if there was any Indian trouble."

"But, I'm not—" he almost said, "a Mormon," but quickly caught himself.

"You're not what?"

"I'm not looking for somewhere to go. I've got employment here. I hope to get my father to move down and live with me before the summer's over."

"I remember you saying that." Patrick grew thoughtful. "So bring him, too. Didn't you tell me that he's a blaster in the mines? Building roads to where we're going will require explosives."

"*What?* I'm having a hard enough time convincing him to come here. Besides, I have a job here and can't just up and leave it."

"Which brings me to what I would like to say." He pursed his lips. "I have a proposal for you, David. Please hear me out first, before you answer."

"All right."

"I've been thinking on this for some time, but your little incident over near Orderville was like putting the final stone in the wall for me." He took a quick breath. "I'm really not suggesting that you volunteer to go, David. Nor is what I am talking about a call from the Church. It is an offer of employment."

David's mouth opened, then shut again.

Patrick smiled. "That's right. As you so diplomatically noted a minute ago, the McKennas are hardly model pioneers. What we need is someone who is. Someone who's good with horses and teams and wagons and camping out and coping with the wilderness and fighting off nasty outlaws and renegade Indians and . . ." He laughed softly. "I suppose that's enough. I am offering you eighty dollars a month to help get us ready, then one hundred dollars a month to take us across the trail."

David was flabbergasted.

"If your father comes, I will hire him, too, as my contribution to the road-building efforts."

They talked for another half an hour—David, still half dazed, firing questions at him, Patrick answering them, his excitement growing because it was clear David was considering it.

David finally sat back, his questions exhausted, his mind whirling. "A hundred dollars a month?" He shook his head and gave a low whistle. "That's incredibly generous, Patrick."

"Not if you're as desperate as we are to get some competent help." He sat back and watched David thoughtfully. "So while I'm at it, let me see if I can sweeten the pot a little. I don't know if you knew this or not, but Brigham Young's policy has always been to give new emigrants land at little or no cost to them. John Taylor is continuing that policy."

David leaned forward, eyes suddenly intent. "Say that again."

"You heard me right. And while you think about that, remember that Elder Snow said a major concern over there is cattlemen running their herds into Utah. What does that tell you?"

It clicked instantly. "That there must be some pretty good rangeland over there."

"Exactly. The Church is eager to get legal owners on that land to counteract that influence. I know you're putting your money into the bank. What if you didn't have to spend it to buy land? What if you could use it to buy your own herd, build a house and barns and stables?"

David sat back, his mind reeling. And not with just thoughts of land and cattle. Molly wouldn't be leaving him in a few months. If they did ever marry, she would still be close to her family. It was just one stunning possibility after another.

Patrick leaned in, pressing his point. "I'm not making that a condition, David. We hope you would stay, but that's up to you." He took a quick breath. "I want to say all of this now, before you have to leave again. I want you to think about it while you make your next circuit. When you return, you can give me your answer, and if—"

"I accept," David said quietly.

Patrick's eyes widened. "Just like that?"

David chuckled. "This sounds like a better offer to me. I'd have to be three ways from stupid not to accept."

Patrick stood up and extended his hand. "Then consider yourself hired." As David took his hand, the grip was powerful and held him fast. "Sarah will be ecstatic."

David didn't get up, and after a moment Patrick, looking puzzled, sat down again. "Yes?"

"I have something to ask you, and it may make a difference in your feelings."

"Go on."

"As you know, I . . . well, Molly and I have . . . uh . . ." He was fumbling badly. "What I'm trying to say is . . ."

"You would like my permission to start courting her?"

David breathed a sigh of relief. "Yes, sir, I would."

"Granted." He laughed at David's expression. "Why do I get the feeling that was harder for you than facing that band of renegades?"

"Only because it was." He grimaced. "Maybe five times more. But thank you, Patrick. I will treat her with the utmost respect."

Patrick leaned forward, elbows on the desk, resting his chin in his hands. "This won't change my answer, but I'm curious about something. May I get personal with you?"

"Of course."

"Do you believe in God, David?"

David felt the breath go out of him. But he knew that he had to be honest, especially if this man was going to end up as his father-in-law. "To be right straight with you, Patrick, I do. I believe in a Supreme Being, the Great Creator, Divine Providence, or whatever else people call Him. But you shouldn't read more into that than is there. I would have to say that my feelings about God are very likely quite different from yours . . . or Molly's."

"In what way?"

"I don't believe in a God who watches over us all the time and inter- venes in our behalf when we get in trouble. For example, Molly asked me if I thought I was going to die when that man had his rifle in my chest. Then she asked if I'd thought of God in that moment of crisis. If I'd prayed for help."

"And how did you answer her?"

"I had to say no. I don't think the idea of asking Him for help even crossed my mind, whereas Molly said it would have been the first thing to come to her mind."

"I see," Patrick said thoughtfully.

"My mother experienced great tragedy in her life. When she turned to God for help, nothing ever happened. Eventually, her own mother died be- cause of it." David looked away, and his voice went soft. "I watched my mother die too. I was thirteen at the time."

"And you prayed and nothing happened there either?" Patrick guessed.

He nodded. "Mum always said that God had better things to do than watch over poor people like us. We had to learn to make our own way in the world. She said when we cried, He wouldn't hear us, basically because He didn't care."

Patrick said nothing, so David went on. "I know how important your faith is to you, Patrick. And to be honest, it makes me a little envious that you view Him as such a personal being. But I don't feel that way. Not sure that I ever can or will."

Patrick leaned forward, quite earnest now. "Does Molly know any of this?"

David chewed on his lower lip for a moment, then shook his head. "I think she may suspect, but no, we haven't talked in these kinds of specifics."

"Abby told me a little about your mother. She also told me about sharing Elizabeth Barrett Browning's poem with you. That's why I asked my question."

So, David thought, he already knew. He felt a rush of gratitude that he had been forthright in his answer. "If that makes a difference in how you feel about Molly and me, then—"

Patrick waved that away. "I told you that your answer wouldn't change mine, and I meant it. My only question is this." Then he gave a quick shake of his head. "No, it's not a question, more like a suggestion. When the time is right, you need to tell Molly that. Don't hold back on her, David. This is too important. She needs to know, so she can deal with it."

"I will." Now it was David who stood. "And thank you again for your confidence in me, Patrick. You really took me by surprise." Then another thought came. "Does Molly know you've offered me this job?"

"No. Nor Abby nor Billy Joe. Only Sarah." A slow smile stole around the corners of his mouth. "Actually, this was partially her idea. As for the others, maybe it's best if we don't say anything quite yet. I'd still like you to have a chance to think on it. When you come back we can make it official."

"Fair enough."

Cedar City, Utah Territory, January 23, 1879

Dear Dad,

I am sending this letter via the postmaster in Coalville and have asked him to find someone to read it to you when it is delivered. There is much to tell you.

I returned to Cedar City after Christmas to find things in turmoil. I told you about the stake conference in Parowan which Bro. McKenna asked me to attend with his family. It proved to be momentous. The Church has called dozens of people to open new settlements in the southeast corner of the territory and in northern Arizona. The

McKennas were among those called. Big shock for them. And for me. I wasn't sure what this all would mean for my employment and my situation down here.

Turns out it has great implications for me. And for you! Brother McKenna will definitely answer the call and take all his family with him. That is amazing in a way, because he is a businessman, a city person, and this will be a challenging task. BUT!!! Just today, he asked me if I would accompany them as his employee. I will be his "wagon boss," as it were, which means simply that my job will be to prepare them for the journey and get them through safely. The salary is most generous and will add significantly to the "ranch fund."

Therefore, I leave on my last mail circuit next week, and on my return (about February 12th or 13th) will begin my work with him. Dad, Bro. M. knows that you have agreed to quit the mine and come live with me. He wants to hire you as well and have you GO WITH US!!! We will need people with road building experience, especially blasting knowledge. I know this comes as a shock, but please think about it. PLEASE! Pray about it. (I know that sounds odd coming from me, but you believe in prayer and maybe it will help convince you.) This feels right, Dad. I am certain it is.

It is important that you decide quickly and clear your affairs to get here as soon as possible. There is much to do, and we may be leaving as early as April. So don't think about it too much. Just do it. Hope to have a letter from you saying you'll come when I return.

Love, David

CHAPTER 30

Wednesday, February 12, 1879

When David reached Cedar City after completing his final mail circuit, the sun was about an hour from setting. Not wanting to see any McKennas until after he'd had a chance to wash off two weeks of trail grime, he avoided Main Street and went right to the livery stable. He was relieved when a boy he didn't recognize came out to help him.

Soon David was soaking in a hot tub in the boardinghouse, thinking about Molly. Today was going to be a surprise—more likely a genuine shock—to her, and he was anticipating that very much. He thought back to that morning two weeks ago when he had come to the post office to pick up the mailbag before starting on his last circuit. She had been waiting at the post office with her father. He could tell from her circumspect behavior that her father had not said anything about David requesting permission to court her. He was glad for that. It would be best coming at the same time as Patrick's announcement about their new "wagon boss."

***

Half an hour later, as he came down the stairs of the boardinghouse, he stopped in surprise. Molly and Billy Joe were there waiting for him near the front door. Billy Joe's grin was half a mile wide, and he started waving wildly the instant he saw David. Molly's smile was warm and welcoming, with just a touch of shyness. "Hi, stranger," she said, moving over to meet him.

"Hello, Molly. Hi, Billy Joe. How did you two know I was back?"

"Daddy left word at the stable that they were to let him know the minute you returned."

"Oh. Does he want to see me?"

"Actually," she said, "Billy Joe and I are here to escort you home. Your company is requested at our supper table tonight. Mama said to tell you there were to be no excuses. She's made your favorite, roast beef and mashed potatoes. And—" she paused for dramatic effect—"English trifle."

"You're kidding."

"Nope. Sister Rowley up in Parowan taught Mother how to make it. She and her husband are from Worcestershire." She said the last word *Wor-chester-shire*.

"Us natives," he drawled, "pronounce that *Wooster-shur*."

She blushed. "I know, but us foreigners can never remember that." Then came that wonderful smile again, and the warmth in it made him tingle. "We are to go straightaway."

He looked at them both more closely. Billy Joe had on knickers and thick woolen socks. He wore a light blue, long-sleeved shirt beneath his jacket. His hair had been wetted and slicked down—except for the ever-present rooster tail—and he looked like he was headed for church. Even his shoes were polished. Astonishing!

Molly was also dressed more nicely than her everyday dress. Her skirt, full and to the ankles, was a dark blue, and beneath her winter coat she wore a white blouse with ruffles around the collar. Her hair was brushed back from her ears and tied loosely with a ribbon that matched the color of her skirt. This allowed it to cascade across her shoulders and down her back.

"What's the occasion?" he said, nodding his approval. "You're not sneaking me off to some church meeting, are you?"

"No," she laughed. "Just supper. But Daddy insisted we dress up for it. He's actually more excited about it than Mama, which is unusual."

So he plans to make the announcement tonight. Good. As far as David was concerned, the sooner the better. He and Molly had much to talk about. He smiled at her. "So," he said, "a little mystery with our roast beef? Sounds interesting. Lead on."

As they reached the walk and started up the street for the McKenna home, David reached out and squeezed Billy's shoulder. "How have you been?"

"I taught Paint a new trick," he said proudly.

"Paint? Who is Paint?"

The boy's face lit up. "That's right. You weren't here. I got a new horse for my birthday."

"Really? When was your birthday?"

"A week ago. On the sixth."

"Is your horse a pinto?"

Billy Joe put his hands on his hips, tipping his head to one side. "How did you know that?"

"Just a guess," David chuckled. "Whoo-ee! A new horse. Maybe there'll be time after dinner to show me. So what trick did you teach him?"

"I taught him to say thank you after I give him an apple or a carrot."

"You don't say," David said. He glanced at Molly for confirmation.

"Don't ask me how he did it," she nodded, "but he did. That crazy horse actually nods his head after Billy Joe gives him something to eat."

The boy was beaming. "Won't do it for anyone but me."

"Smart horse," David said. "Do you want to teach him to come when you whistle?"

"Yeah! That would be neat."

"Okay. You've got school tomorrow and the next day, so how about Saturday? Maybe we could go riding." He winked. "Maybe even have a race. Think Paint can beat Tillie?"

Billy Joe's face fell. "I don't think we should race."

"Oh? Why not?"

A grin began at the corners of his mouth and spread all the way up to his eyes. "Cuz we'll beat you so bad, you won't want to be my friend anymore." Then, convulsed with laughter, he broke into a run. "I'll tell Mama you're coming."

Patrick was waiting for them at the front door. He grasped David's hand and pulled him into the vestibule. "Welcome back, David."

"Thank you. It's always good to be back."

"Last time. How does that make you feel?"

Molly whirled. "Last time for what?"

She had started to remove her coat but stopped with one sleeve half off. Her father stepped forward quickly and helped her. "Your mother wants you to take out the biscuits, dear," he said.

"Last time for what?" she asked again, this time looking to David for help.

Her father gave her a little push. "Mama said they need to come out *now*. Off you go."

She went, but not without casting a curious look over her shoulder.

Once she was gone, David turned to Patrick. "So, you plan to tell them tonight?"

"You haven't changed your mind about going with us, have you?"

"No way. In fact, I even started making a list of things that need to be done."

"Wonderful. I'm absolutely delighted, David. This will be such a relief to Sarah and me. I'll make the announcement right after dessert."

"And . . . ?" David gave him a searching look.

He tried to look puzzled, but couldn't hold it in. "Yes, I'll announce that too."

David wrinkled his nose. "Not sure how Abby will take it."

"What? The news about you coming with us, or the news about you and Molly?"

"Both," he said glumly. "I'm not sure she will approve in either case."

"Oh, I think you may be surprised. It might interest you to know that several times in these last two weeks, when we've been talking about what all this means—" He gave a short laugh. "Actually, we talk about little else anymore. But several times, Abby's said, 'Maybe we ought to ask David what he thinks about that.'"

"Really?"

"Yes. A legacy from our Zion Canyon outing, I think."

"So has there been a departure date set? Did they decide to send out an exploring party?"

"Yes, that's official. Silas Smith will lead that. He hopes to leave the first week of April. And they're still talking like that expedition may take as long as six months."

"How many will be going?"

"Silas is still working that out. He's thinking a party of twenty-five, or thereabouts." His brow furrowed. "Right now, it looks like a couple of families will be going with them."

David reared back. "Families? On an exploring expedition?"

"I know. I had the same question. But, according to Silas, they're anxious to go. They want to be the first to answer the call, as it were. You kind of know one of them. Do you remember the man who got up and spoke in the meeting we had with President Lunt? He said his wife was with child. His name was James Davis."

"I do." Then the implication of that hit him. "But I thought you said her baby wasn't due until July or August."

"That's right. But they are determined to go now. Also the Harrimans. Don't know if you know them or not. They're from Parowan. Good family. They also have four children."

David couldn't help it. His look was openly skeptical. "Eight children and a woman with child on an exploring expedition? Seems a little . . ." He shrugged. It wasn't his call, nor his concern. "So that means that the main company will have eight or nine months to get ready, rather than two or three. That's good."

"I had exactly the same thought," Patrick agreed.

They fell silent for a few moments, and David wondered why they were still out here in the vestibule and not going in. Then Patrick grunted. "Ah, here he comes."

David turned. Coming up the walk was Carl Bradford, Patrick's number-one assistant. "He had to wait for the night clerk to cover for him at the hotel," Patrick explained.

"Has he decided what he's doing?" David wondered.

"Not yet. Maybe when he hears our announcement tonight, he'll declare himself."

"I thought you were thinking of having him stay here and manage the hotel for you."

"I am, but I won't say anything about that until he decides about going."

"Got you," David said. "I'll be careful about what I say."

Patrick chortled. "Why do I find that a little hard to believe?" Then he stepped forward and opened the door. "Evening, Carl. You're just in time."

✦

"So," Sarah McKenna said, watching David finish the last of his dessert. "How was the English trifle?"

He frowned deeply. "It was just awful, but . . ."

Her eyes widened, and both Molly and Abby looked shocked.

"But I can't be absolutely sure of that," David said, looking perplexed, "so I think I'd better have another bowl to make absolutely certain."

That redeemed him. Laughing, Sarah leaned forward, took his bowl, and refilled it. "It's a good thing you finished that sentence, young man."

He took the bowl and ate another large spoonful. "It is delicious, Sister McKenna. I mean really wonderful."

"How does it compare to what you had back in England?"

A frown creased his forehead. "Actually, I can't answer that. I don't remember ever having trifle before."

Her mouth opened slightly. "You're from England, and you've never had . . ." Then she laughed. "You're joking, right?"

He lifted another bite, wishing he had said nothing. But he decided he couldn't just let it go now. "Actually, I'm not. I don't remember ever having afters, or desserts, as you call them, following a meal. In fact, for a long time, I thought dessert was an American thing."

No one said anything to that, but their dismay was evident.

David went on. "Part of it was being poor, I suppose. That's the life of a coal miner's family. But since I've grown older now, I've wondered if much of it may have been because my mother was saving every penny and shilling she could scrape together so we could come to America."

Abby leaned forward enough to look past Carl at David. "And it worked."

"Aye," he said softly. "It worked. She was frail as a ghost physically, but pure steel in every other way." He cleared his throat and picked up his spoon again. It was time to change the mood. "Anyway, Sister McKenna. Though it is my first experience with English trifle, I do have to say that this is the best I've ever eaten."

She laughed again. "You must have been a handful for your mother when you were a boy."

"Hear! Hear!" Abby murmured.

Patrick chose that moment to stand up. He nodded to his wife. "Thank you, Sarah, for a wonderful dinner." There was a round of echoing sentiment to that.

"And thanks to the girls for their help."

"I peeled the potatoes," Billy Joe reminded.

"And to Billy Joe for the potatoes." He let the family quiet down, then became serious. "I have three announcements to make tonight. That's partly why the special occasion. The first will come as a surprise to everyone but myself. The second and third will come as a surprise to everyone but David, Sister McKenna, and me."

David looked at him more sharply. Something even he didn't know about? He glanced at Molly.

She shook her head, as puzzled as he was. "Like you said," she whispered with a little giggle, "a little mystery served with our roast beef."

Patrick reached in his pocket and brought out a folded paper. "I received a telegram this afternoon from Salt Lake City."

"Not another call," Molly groaned, feigning deep pain. Everyone laughed, but it was noticeably strained and quickly died out as they realized that might be exactly what it was.

Patrick unfolded it, then put on his reading glasses. "Actually, it originated in Coalville."

David had been toying with the rest of his trifle, but his hand stopped in midair.

Now Patrick was looking directly at him. "It was addressed to me, and I think you'll see why in a few moments. He took a quick sip of water, then began to read: "'To Patrick McKenna. Cedar City, Utah. Regards: David Draper. Please inform my son am in receipt his letter. Have considered request to come south immediately. Find the idea much to my liking.'"

David's cry of joy caused Patrick to pause for a moment, then he went on. "'Find the idea much to my liking. Hope he is serious. Will arrive Cedar City March 15.'"

"March fifteenth!" David exclaimed. "He's coming? He's really coming?"

"I'd say that's a yes," Patrick said dryly, greatly enjoying this moment. He lifted the paper again and finished. "'Look forward with great anticipation to meeting your family. David says nothing but good. Hope you can put up with an old Tyke.' And it's signed John Draper."

He handed the telegram to David. "It worked, David. He's coming. Congratulations."

David read it through again quickly, scarcely believing it. Then he folded it and put it in his pocket. "Thank you, Patrick. Thank you for making it possible."

"What wonderful news, David," Sister McKenna exclaimed.

"That's marvelous," Molly cried. "After all you've said, we can hardly wait to meet him."

"What's a tyke?" Billy Joe asked.

David chuckled. "Well, over here a tyke is a young boy, but where I grew up, a Tyke was a Yorkshire man. Often it was used specifically to refer to coal miners."

"What's Yorkshire?"

"Oh, well, that's a pudding."

Everyone laughed again as Billy looked all the more puzzled.

"I'll explain it all later, dear," Sister McKenna told her son.

"That is wonderful, David," Abby said quietly. "Is he going to be as hard to live with as his son?" It was said soberly, but her eyes were twinkling.

"Aw, Abby me gurl," he said, "ya 'ave naw idee, naw idee." He dropped the accent as he went on. "As my mother once said, my father can charm a pig into a tree. He's a real corker. I'm afraid after you meet him, you'll find his son to be quite boring."

Patrick cleared his throat. "Before you all rush over here to congratulate David, let me make the second announcement. That will explain why David thanked me for making this possible."

He picked up his glass of water and lifted it high. "I should like to propose a toast."

They all reached for their glasses, smiling in expectation. "I would like to propose a toast to David Draper. This is a big day for him. He has just learned that his father is coming to live with him. And . . ." He let that hang for a moment. "And on this very night, David has agreed to leave his service as a mail rider and accept new employment."

Molly nearly dropped her glass, her face draining of color. "You have?" she blurted.

Her father answered that for her. "Starting tomorrow morning, David will begin work as the foreman for the McKenna family wagon train to San Juan."

Jaws went slack. There were loud gasps. Molly gave a soft "Oh!" Billy Joe looked bewildered. Abby and Carl turned and looked at each other in astonishment. Only Sarah, who already knew, was smiling. Seeing that his attempt at a toast had been completely forgotten, Patrick set his glass aside. He rapped on the table for their attention. "That's right. After the call came, your mother and I spent a lot of time discussing what this meant and how we were going to accomplish it." He rubbed his chin ruefully. "Or cope with it, is probably a better way to say it. I think we all recognize that we are hardly what you would call a pioneering family, so your mother and I decided we needed a little help."

Molly was staring. "Does that mean you'll be going with us, or just helping us prepare?"

"I'm coming with you," David said. "And Dad too. We'll also stay with you until you are safely settled and established."

"But no longer?" Abby said.

"Maybe. I hope someday to become a rancher. If there proved to be an opportunity there, I would stay. If not . . ." He shrugged again. "Cattlemen have to go where the grass is."

Billy Joe was tugging at David's arm. "You're coming with us?" His eyes were dancing.

"That's right, Billy Joe. All the way."

"Promise?"

David nodded, then turned and looked at Molly, whose face was a study in wonder, amazement, and joy. "I promise."

Billy was out of his chair and doing a little Indian dance. "Yippee!" he shouted.

"Starting tomorrow, you said?" Molly asked her father. "So no more mail circuits?"

"No. I've already found his replacement."

She sat back slowly, shaking her head. And in that instant, David knew exactly what she was thinking. She had just gotten an answer to her prayers.

Sister McKenna stood and came over to David. "I cannot tell you what a tremendous relief it is to know that you accepted, David. I am now at peace about going." She bent down and laid her cheek against his for a moment. "Thank you."

David started to make some flippant remark, but his voice suddenly caught. "It is a tremendous honor for me," he whispered, looking up at her. "Thank you for your trust."

"Well, well, well," Abby murmured. "You do know how to drop a surprise on us, Daddy."

"I'll say," Molly responded.

"Wait, wait!" her father cried. "There's one more thing." He looked at his wife. "Why don't you make the final announcement, Sarah."

She was still standing by David. She nodded and laid one hand on his shoulder. "David has asked your father for permission to court his daughter." She turned to Molly, her eyes suddenly shining. "And your father said yes."

Molly's hands flew to her mouth. She looked first to her father, who smiled and nodded, then to David, who smiled and nodded. Then, in a perfect imitation of Billy Joe, she lifted her hands and began to do a little dance in her chair. "Yippee!" she said softly.

For the next five or six minutes, everyone swarmed around David to congratulate him. Patrick let it play out, then said, "While it is tempting to ask David many questions now, we must remember that he's been on the road all day and it's getting late. I'm sure he's very tired."

At that moment, a yawn hit him and David stifled it without thinking. Only when he saw them all grinning at him did he realize what he had done.

"I rest my case," Patrick said.

Carl raised his hand. "I have a little announcement of my own, if that's all right."

They all turned. He hadn't said much all evening.

"I spoke with President Lunt earlier today," he said. "I have submitted my name as a volunteer, and it was accepted. I too will be going to San Juan."

"Bravo!" Patrick said, clapping his hands. "Would you consent to travel with us as well, Carl? We would be honored."

"And we do need another man," Molly said. She gave Abby a pointed look, which caused her to do something David rarely saw. Abby blushed. "To drive one of our wagons, of course," Molly added, with a devilish little smile.

Once again, Patrick lost control of the "meeting" as everyone congratulated Carl. Finally, he got them settled down again. "I am delighted that you will be with us, Carl. You have much to contribute as we make our preparations and then depart."

"Thank you, Patrick. Like David, I consider it an honor to be with you."

Patrick turned back to David. "I think before you start meeting with the family to give us instructions, it would be helpful if you and I and Carl rode up to Paragonah to meet with Silas Smith. I'd like to do that tomorrow and come back Friday night. Then we can have our first family meeting on Saturday morning. How about seven o'clock?"

Molly groaned. "Seven o'clock? On a Saturday?"

He ignored that. "We start our shifts at the hotel and the post office at eight. That would give us an hour. Is that enough, David?"

"More than enough for the first meeting. We'll have others as we go along."

"Then seven it is. Let's meet here. Wouldn't want to have Molly seen in public that early."

Abby turned to her sister. "You could just put on your robe and a hair net over your curlers. Come as you are, like you always do for breakfast." She gave a little devilish smile of her own. "I think we need to start preparing David for what he's in for."

CHAPTER 31

Saturday, February 15, 1879

It was no surprise to David when he entered the dining room of the McKenna home at ten minutes to seven on Saturday morning that Molly was already there. Her hair was brushed until it gleamed; her skin was soft, almost translucent, in the lamplight. She was dressed like she was ready for church, with not a wrinkle in her blouse. She had a leather-bound book that looked like a journal on her lap, and a pencil between her fingers. "Good morning, Brother Draper," she said primly.

He laughed. "Hello, Molly. You look lovely this morning."

"Thank you." She turned to her father, voice all sticky sweet. "Would you like me to go up and tell the others we're ready to start?"

He shook his head, chuckling as well. "I'll do it." And with that he ran lightly up the stairs, calling out to his wife, Abby, and Billy Joe to hurry.

David took a chair across from her. "You really do look beautiful this morning, Molly."

Her lashes dropped to screen her eyes. "Why thank you, Brother Draper."

"So," he said, lowering his voice, "can we talk today?"

She nodded. "I have the afternoon shift at the livery stable. I'll be there all afternoon."

"Good. I told Billy Joe I'd help him teach Paint to respond to a whistle, so I'll be there too."

"He's really worried about that, you know," she said, smiling fondly. "He can't whistle. Been practicing all yesterday. It's really quite amusing to watch how serious he is about it."

Just then there was a knock at the door. Molly got up and came back a moment later with Carl Bradford in tow. He and David shook hands, and he took the chair beside David. A moment later, they heard Patrick's footsteps in the hall above. As he started down the stairs, David caught Molly's eye. "I'll be there around two," he said softly.

She nodded and sat back, hands folded neatly in her lap.

Patrick had Billy Joe give a short prayer to open the meeting. After saying the usual kinds of things, he cracked one eye open to see if his mother was watching, then in rapid-fire order asked for a blessing on Paint that he would be smart, and on himself that he might learn how to whistle. As he said amen and sat down again, his mother was shaking her head, and both of his sisters looked like they wanted to hug him.

"All right," Patrick said. "We're in your hands, David. Tell them how things went with Silas Smith, then take us wherever you think we need to go."

David nodded and stood up. He looked around, pleased with what he saw. Billy Joe sat by his mother, eyes alert, expression attentive. He was the only one who didn't have something to write with. Abby and Sister McKenna both had pencils and journals similar to Molly's. Patrick had a lap board and sheets of paper. Carl had what looked like a ledger book from the hotel.

"To be honest, this is a little intimidating. I've never 'taught school' before."

"You'll have quite the challenge with this class," Abby quipped. "So be kind."

"And patient," Sarah McKenna added with a smile. "Be very patient."

"All right, ladies," Patrick broke in. "Don't make this any more difficult for him than it is."

Actually, their light banter helped to relax David, and it hit him just how comfortable he had become around this family, and how happy he was to know that the relationship wasn't ending.

He took a quick breath and began. "Although Abby was teasing—" He pulled a wry face. "I hope you were teasing—her point is well taken. We do have a challenge before us. I don't wish to add to your anxiety, but we also have to be realistic. Our visit with Brother Smith has only confirmed that this expedition is going to be very difficult. And, by the way, I think Patrick and Carl will agree, Silas Smith is an impressive leader. They've chosen the right man for the job."

He went on. "Anyway, we will be crossing harsh terrain where there are no roads, and few if any settlements. There'll be no stopping at the nearest ZCMI[1] to replenish supplies. We hope that the Indians, knowing that we are Mormons, will be at least tolerant—if not friendly and helpful—as we pass through their lands, but we must be prepared for possible hostilities."

"Did you have to say that?" Molly sighed. She was half jesting, but only half.

"Unfortunately, those are realities. Another reality is that we shall have to carry not only everything we need for the trip but sufficient supplies to live on until we can get a settlement established. With me and Carl, there will be seven of us. Silas hopes that once the exploring party blazes a road, we can make the trip in about six weeks. But to be safe, we have to plan for as much as six months, counting the time until we become self-sufficient. Carrying enough food to last us six months will be a tremendous challenge of its own."

"I don't think you should give us only the good news, David," Sister McKenna said, her eyes twinkling. "Isn't there any bad news we ought to be aware of?"

"Sorry," David said with a chuckle. "I didn't mean to sound overly grim. I just—"

"No," Patrick said. "We don't need it sugarcoated."

"Can't we supply some of our food along the way through hunting?" Carl asked.

"We can if we're willing to eat lizards and scorpions." He looked at Billy Joe and smiled. "Although I have heard one can sometimes find lobsters out there."

Billy Joe ducked his head and giggled softly. "I meant scorpions," he told his mother.

"But in the desert there won't be much—if any—larger game. Maybe we can find a few sage hens, but I think we have to assume we will eat mostly what we carry. Therefore, we will need four wagons. On the other hand," David went on, "there are some encouraging things as well."

"Oh, goody," Molly said, lifting her pencil for the first time. "I'm ready for some of that."

"First, the group we are traveling with is going to be highly qualified for the task ahead. The Church has been wise in calling people from down here. You know the country and you are adapted to the climate. Silas says we'll have a whole range of skills in the group—stockmen, teamsters, blacksmiths, carpenters, masons, farmers, and road builders such as Ben Perkins."

"And John Draper," Patrick added.

David nodded, still getting used to that idea.

"What about experienced hotel owners and postal clerks?" Abby asked. "Any of those?"

He laughed. "Only one family that I know of. But don't be too down on yourselves. The McKennas are not the only ones who don't fit the classic pioneer mold."

"Yeah," Carl said glumly. "You've also got me."

David turned to look at Abby and Molly. "I never said anything about your family to Brother Smith, but do you know what he said to me as I was leaving? He said, 'Patrick McKenna and his good wife were chosen not so much for what they can do but for what they *are*, and what they can contribute to the settlement.' Coming from a man like Silas Smith, I would say that is a real compliment."

"If it's all right, David," Abby said, her voice soft as she looked at her father, "could we travel with them? Maybe some of it will rub off on Molly and me."

"What else?" Patrick said, uncomfortable with this turn in the conversation.

"You have another advantage," David went on. "Thankfully, your father has been successful in business. That means he has the resources to fully outfit the family. You will be about as well stocked and well equipped as any family going. That will a real asset, not just to you but to the whole company."

"Thank you, David," Sarah said. "Thank you for reminding us of that."

He nodded. "A third important positive is that we have time. Silas did confirm to us that an exploring party will be leaving Paragonah—or Paragoonah, as you all say it—around the tenth of April. When they return, we'll know exactly where we're going. And they will also be building roads as they go, which will greatly simplify things for those who follow.

"So, in summary," he said, "I am really much encouraged, to tell you the truth."

"If you're encouraged," Abby said, "then we are greatly so."

Billy Joe raised his hand, and David nodded at him. "Can I take Paint?"

As the others smiled, his father answered that one. "Of course, Son. In fact, that's why we bought him for your birthday. We'll be taking most of the horses and mules we own from the livery stable, and it's time you had a horse of your own."

Sarah reached out and touched his cheek. "Oh, Billy. I think you're going to be the one who loves this experience the very most."

"Other questions?" David asked.

Abby's hand came up. "What about our own personal preparation? I'm guessing there are some skills we need to learn."

"Excellent point. I would recommend three things. First, we need to toughen up physically. The trail will do that automatically once we start, but it's much less painful to get started on that in advance. Walking as much as possible will be important, not just around town, but longer walks. Ten to fifteen miles in one day on the trail won't be unusual, and you'll find out very quickly that riding in a wagon is not like riding in a carriage. A wagon going across open country can be a pretty bruising experience.

"Second, how many of you have ever cooked over an open fire? Other than helping me in Zion Canyon?" When all three of the women shook their heads, he said, "Well, this will sound silly, but as soon as the weather warms up a little, we need to start doing that. We'll build a campfire, maybe out behind the livery stable, and let you practice. You'll find it very different from cooking on a stove or baking in an oven. We'll purchase some Dutch ovens so you can practice baking, too."

"Actually, that sounds fun," Molly said. All of this was weighing her down, and she was happy to find something that had any lightness to it.

"It will be fun here," he said. "Out there it will be critical."

He saw momentary hurt pass across her face and realized that his answer had come out sounding blunt. He smiled at her. "And it can be fun, too."

She smiled back.

"Next, we need to make sure all of you, including the three women, know how to handle both a pistol and a rifle. If you already know how, we'll seek to improve your marksmanship."

"Why?" Abby said. "With the three of you—" She saw Billy's head come up. "With the four of you men, do you really think that's necessary?"

"Good question," David said. "Did you know that of the tens of thousands of people who crossed the Oregon trail, more died from gun accidents than from trouble with Indians?"

"No," Abby said. "You're just saying that."

"Sorry, but it's true. Here's what happens. Someone who hasn't handled guns very much lays his rifle in the back of the wagon. Soon people are piling clothes and other things on top of it. Then he sees an antelope or an Indian. He grabs his gun by the barrel and yanks it out. The trigger catches on something, and . . ." He shrugged. "His wife is left a widow."

Abby was contrite. "Sorry."

"I hate guns," Molly said suddenly. "Can't the others do it for me?"

"Unless you happen to be alone when a sage hen . . ." He paused, debating about finishing, then decided it needed to be said. " . . . or a rattlesnake comes along."

Her body involuntarily shuddered.

Patrick stirred, his face somber. "David's not saying everything that needs to be said. We all heard what Elder Snow said in conference. One of the major reasons for us going over to San Juan country is because peace with the Navajos is very fragile. Suppose there is another tragic incident like the one in Grass Valley. If a group of hostiles were to come when us men weren't there, you'd have to be able to defend yourselves."

There wasn't a sound. The faces of the three women had paled. Molly looked like she might be sick. Abby was staring at the floor.

David went on, more gently now. "That is not likely. Frankly, I don't expect any trouble, but if it does come, it will be too late then for shooting lessons."

"Sign me up," Molly said in a low voice. "I'm sorry I asked."

"I won't be afraid," Billy Joe said.

No one laughed. It hadn't come out as a little boy's boasting, but as the calm assurance of a would-be little man.

"I know you won't," David said. "You're already becoming an excellent shot. In fact, maybe I could get you to help me when I teach your sisters." He looked at Patrick. "This boy knows more about guns than I do."

Billy Joe's chest puffed out and his chin came up. "I can help, if that's what you need."

It sounded so grown-up that the mood in the room instantly brightened. David glanced at the clock over the mantel. "We have plenty of time to sort all this out. That's the good news. So, Patrick, unless you have something to add, I think everything else can wait."

Patrick nodded and got to his feet. David sat down beside Carl. He expected Patrick to thank him for what he was doing and give the family a little pep talk, a let's-go-do-it kind of thing. But he didn't. He stood there for almost a full minute. David saw his Adam's apple bob up and down several times as he tried to get control of his voice. When he did, it was low and husky. "I love my family," he began. "More than anything else in the world."

He stopped. Sister McKenna, eyes shining, was watching him intently. So were Abby and Molly. Even Billy Joe sat perfectly still.

"I've always been proud of you," he went on. "Each of you." Then he was suddenly fierce with emotion. "But I want you to know, I have never been more proud of you than I am at this moment. Thank you for standing with your mother and me in this. Thank you for what you are and for what you are willing to do."

Note

1. ZCMI, or Zion's Cooperative Mercantile Institution, was a cooperative retail enterprise started by Brigham Young in 1868 to "bring goods here and sell them as low as they can possibly be sold and let the profits be divided with the people at large" (see Ludlow, *Encyclopedia of Mormonism*, 2:621). The cooperatives quickly spread to many settlements in the territory, and for over a century, ZCMI was the largest retailer in Utah.

CHAPTER 32

Saturday, February 15, 1879

When David arrived at the stable that afternoon, he saw through the door that Molly was carrying a bale of straw toward the nearest stall. "Hey," he called, "let me do that."

Molly set the bale down and turned to smile. As he entered the barn, someone else greeted him. Billy Joe was in the hayloft above. "Hi, David."

"Hiya, Billy Joe," he said. "How you doing?"

"All right," he grumbled.

Molly was directly below her brother and out of his sight. She gave David a helpless shrug.

David moved over to the straw and picked it up. He carried the bale into the stall, pulled out his pocketknife and cut the twine, then began to spread the straw out. Molly came in to help. "Sorry," she whispered. "I didn't know he was coming. Mama says he has to work here for an hour."

They worked together for nearly half an hour, cleaning out the stalls and putting in fresh straw while Billy Joe forked down hay for them from the loft. The work kept their conversation to a minimum, and Billy Joe prevented it from getting too serious. Finally, Billy Joe came down the ladder. He was covered with hay dust and sweating heavily. "Has it been an hour yet?"

It hadn't, but Molly wasn't about to quibble. "It has. Thank you, Billy Joe."

David brushed the worst of the dust out of Billy Joe's thick brown hair. "You really worked up a sweat there, Billy Joe." Though it was only in the forties outside, inside it was quite pleasant. David took out his bandanna and handed it to the boy. "Here, use this."

Billy wiped the sweat away from his forehead, his eyes, and the back of his neck. He handed the bandanna back, then began rubbing at his hair vigorously with his fingertips. "It itches."

"Yeah, sweating does that when your hair is longer, like now. Maybe your mom will give you a butch cut now instead of waiting for summer."

"How come God just doesn't make our hair so we can take it off when we get hot?"

David hooted aloud. "Billy Joe, you are one creative thinker."

Molly came over to join them, and rubbed his hair for him. "That's my Billy boy."

David was still chuckling. "You expect a lot from God, don't you? Which reminds me," David said, "did God ever answer your letter about Puffy?"

"Yep." Billy Joe gave his hair one last swipe, then started away. "I'll be out with Paint."

David grabbed his arm and pulled him back. "Whoa there, boy. You got an answer?"

"Yep."

"*Billy Joe!*" Molly exclaimed. "You never told me that."

He shrugged, starting to squirm under the attention.

"So," David asked, "is your cat in heaven?"

"Yep."

"Are you telling me you got a letter back?" David asked, intrigued now.

"Nope. Didn't need one. I saw Puffy in a dream."

Molly knelt down in front of him. "You did? What happened? I mean in the dream."

His shoulders lifted and fell.

"Are you sure it was her?" David wondered.

At his look of disgust, Molly murmured, "Puffy was a boy cat."

"Sorry. So how did you know *he* was in heaven?"

Billy Joe was looking at his feet. "I just did." Then, before any more questions came, "Can I go?"

Molly touched his cheek briefly. "Of course."

They watched him trot out the back doors to the paddock where his horse was pastured.

"Well, that was a surprise," Molly said.

David was still looking at the empty doorway, considering the sweet simplicity of Billy's words. "To say the least," he finally said.

"Do you believe him?" she asked.

He turned, caught off guard by the question. "Why wouldn't I?"

"I mean, do you believe that his dream was from God?"

He sighed. He knew what this was about. After that night when her father had announced they were courting, David had sat her down and quietly shared his feelings about God. He said nothing about it being a re-quest from her father, because he had planned to do it anyway. She took it quite stoically, but he guessed she had given it much thought since then. This wasn't a question about Billy Joe. This was about David. So he chose his words carefully. "I think God has special feelings for young children. Especially one as delightful as Billy Joe."

She gave him a chiding look. "Well, that was a safe enough answer. Do you think his dream was from God or not?"

"Does it matter? I mean, Billy was really concerned about Puffy. Now he has his answer. It would be a natural thing for him to dream about the cat. If that convinced him that Puffy's in heaven, what does it matter where it came from? The result was the same, either way."

He was tempted to say more, to say that it troubled him how so many people in the Church tried to make a miracle out of every little thing that happened. But he didn't, of course.

Something in his expression must have warned her they had just moved into sensitive territory, because she decided to change the subject. "I thought when you started working for Daddy on this new job, I'd see more of you." She formed her lips into an exaggerated pout. "It's only been three days and you've been off to Paragonah to see Silas Smith. Now you and Carl and Daddy are going to Salt Lake for a month to buy wagons."

"Five to seven days is hardly a month."

"But it will feel like a month," she said.

"I'm here now."

"Yes, you are," she said softly. She motioned to the large bin where they kept the oats. "And I have some things I want to say."

They moved over and sat down, arms touching. He nudged her. "Go ahead."

"All right. First, did you know about Daddy's job offer before you left on this last circuit?"

"I did, but he asked me not to say anything until I returned."

"And what about asking Daddy if we could court? Earlier, you said it was too soon."

"When he offered me the job that day, suddenly it seemed like the right time."

She pretended to be offended. "So I'm the last to know."

"Not really. I didn't tell Tillie until after your mother made the announcement."

She slugged him.

"Well," he said, "she's the one I always confide in."

She moved closer and slipped her arm through his, then laid her head against his shoulder. He sensed that her mood had just changed. "What's the matter?"

Her eyes searched his, then her face crumpled. "Oh, David! I don't know if I can do it."

"What? The mission, you mean?"

She nodded. "It sounds completely awful to me, and I feel terrible about that. Abby's actually excited. Can you believe that?" Her lips pulled down. "That's what's worrying me. That it *will* be a whole new experience."

"I shouldn't have spent so much time talking about the challenges this morning."

"No," she exclaimed. "It's not that. We need to know what to expect. But . . . it's me, David. I'm not a good cook, even in a nice kitchen. Going without a bath or washing my hair for more than two days makes me very grumpy. I love my soft bed. And I hate guns. I close my eyes and plug my ears before anyone pulls the trigger." She pulled a wry face. "Is it possible to do that while trying to keep a bunch of Indians at bay?"

"That does present a challenge," he said with a laugh. "Molly, you're worrying too much. It won't be easy, but you're tough."

"Ha!" she snorted. "Where have you been?" But then she shook it off before he could answer. "What kind of wife does that make for a rancher?"

He considered that. "Well, maybe we could put up a sign telling the Indians about your cooking, and that would do it."

She slugged him again. "I'm serious, David. Am I really cut out to be a rancher's wife, living in a dugout with gunnysacks for curtains, a thousand miles from the nearest nowhere?"

"And am I really the man you want to marry?" he fired right back. "A doubting skeptic who goes to church only because you do?"

She didn't answer, which told him that she had asked herself that very question.

"Look, Molly," he said, "I didn't ask your father for permission to marry you. Only permission to begin courting you. Isn't that what courtship is for? To get a chance to really know each other and see if this is what we should do?"

She straightened. "You're right. Of course, you're right. Why must I always be so impatient? I don't want to see *if* it's going to work out, David. I want it to work out right now. I agree with President Lunt. You need to just hurry up and marry me before we have to leave."

"Is that what you really want?" he asked softly.

"If I said yes, would you do it?"

There was a trap if ever he saw one, but even as he thought about it, she shook her head. "Sorry. This *is* just a courtship. You're right. Just tell me to be quiet and let things take their proper course." She let out a long, pained sigh. "I'm sorry I'm not strong, David."

"You are strong! You're going, aren't you?"

"I don't want to look like a sissy in front of you. I want to be more like Abby—Abby, who does everything; Abby, who rides and shoots and walks for miles and bakes pies that float off the table, they're so light."

"She shoots?"

"Yes. Carl took us out yesterday. I wouldn't say she loves it, but she did quite well." Her nose wrinkled into that mischievous look that was so her. "Me? Well, let's just say that with my eyes closed, I was lucky to hit the mountain on my third shot."

"There is one thing I know for sure, Molly McKenna. I love you. I've never said that to any other girl. But part of loving a person is making them happy. And right now, I can't honestly say that I know marrying me will make you happy."

"Oh, David, it would. More than you know," she breathed.

He sat back, trying not to show his frustration.

She touched his arm. "I know, David. I know what you're saying. And you're right. We're not engaged. We're not even promised."

Those large grey eyes searched his for a long moment, then looked away. "Do you know what I worry about the very most?"

"If I can ever change?"

Her eyes widened momentarily at that. Then she shook her head. "No. I think you are changing. You just don't know it yet. No, what really frightens me is that, if I did turn out to be unhappy as a rancher's wife, you would give it up for me. And when I try to picture you like Carl Bradford, living in town, working behind a desk, clerking in a bank, selling sugar and flour and thimbles in a dry-goods store, it makes me want to weep. I can't do that to you, David."

Deeply touched as well as astonished by her openness, he could only nod. "So," he finally said, "let's give it time. The Lord has answered your prayers. At least we're going to be together to work this out."

She reared back, her eyes mocking. "What? Did I just hear David Draper say we might have gotten an answer to our prayers?"

He smiled sardonically. "No, I said *you* might have gotten an answer to *your* prayers. But think about it. Two or three months on the road, crossing trackless deserts, living out of a wagon—I can't think of a much better place to find out if this is going to work or not."

"You're right. So we just let it happen, right? And see what comes of it?"

He felt a tremendous relief. "I couldn't have said it better myself."

She cocked her head and looked at him. "Then I have only one more question."

"What?"

She tipped her head back and closed her eyes, letting her dark lashes lie softly against her cheek. "Do you want to kiss me right now?"

"Have to think about that." He took her by the shoulders and gave her a long, lingering kiss.

"Umm," she murmured. "Think about it some more."

He did. Then both of them jerked apart as Billy Joe's voice rang out just behind them, "Molly's kissing David. Molly's kissing David."

Molly turned a deep scarlet as David jumped up and strode toward him. Billy Joe gave a yelp and ducked into one of the stalls, slamming the door behind him, cackling with delight. When he peeked through the slats that formed the manger, he started singing again. "Molly's kissing David. Molly's kissing—"

"Do you want me to teach you how to whistle?"

The chant stopped instantly. "Yes!"

David bent down. "Do you know what you have to do, if I do that?"

He tried to wink, but it was more of a grimace. "I can't tell anyone?"

"That's right. Do you know what'll happen if you ever *do* tell anyone I was kissing Molly?"

"Yep. You'll give me a fat lip, right?"

David fought hard not to smile. "Fat enough that you'll never whistle again."

Billy Joe came out and ran to Molly. He gave her a quick hug around her legs, then pulled her face down to his. "I'm glad you kissed him, Molly," he said in a loud whisper. "I really like David."

Laughing, she caught him up and planted a kiss on his forehead. "And I like him too."

He howled and squirmed free. "Don't kiss *me!* Ugh!"

She bent over and looked him squarely in the eye. "If you tell Mama or Abby about this, I'm going to kiss you every day for at least a year."

That did it. Away he went. But as he went up the ladder to the loft again, that irrepressible giggle erupted once more. This was one grand and delightful secret. "Molly's kissing David," he sang softly, laughing happily to himself.

Wednesday, February 26, 1879

David pulled the buckboard to a halt in front of the McKenna residence. "Well, we did it," he said as Patrick climbed stiffly down. "To Salt Lake and back in seven days."

"Yes, we did," Patrick said. "A very productive trip. We now have ourselves four wagons."

Carl Bradford stood and jumped down as well. "I'm just a block over, David. I can walk from here. You just head for the livery stable. It's been a long day." He grabbed his valise and walked swiftly away.

"Let's get together in the morning, Carl," David called after him. "We're going to have decide what to do for teams before we go up to Milford and take delivery on those wagons."

He got a wave in response.

"Go take a hot bath," Patrick said to David, "and forget about all this for at least tonight."

"Sounds good to me." But just then, the front door of the house burst open and Molly came running "David! David! Come quick."

Startled, he jumped down. "What is it, Molly?"

"Hurry!" She was urgently beckoning to him.

He glanced at Patrick. Gone for a week and not even a hello? And why just David? If something was wrong with the family . . . he started toward her, Patrick following.

As they reached the porch, Molly did something even more strange. She blocked her father's way. "No, Daddy, let David go first." She stepped back and opened the door wide for him.

He went through the vestibule in three strides and burst into the living room. Then he stopped dead, his jaw going slack. David's father stood in the center of the living room. He was dressed in a white shirt with a string tie and Sunday suit. His hair, even more grey than when David had last seen him, was short cropped, in the fashion of coal miners, and he was sporting a short beard that ran from ear to ear and covered his chin. That was an addition since Christmas, which, surprisingly, made him seem younger rather than older. Pasted on his face was a grin so big he looked like a kid who had just won a sackful of all-day suckers.

"Well, wud ya lookee thare," he drawled. "Ah do b'lieve that boy might be related ta me."

They sat at the table, sipping the cocoa that Sister McKenna had prepared. David was beside his father. Patrick sat holding hands with his wife. Billy Joe sat between Molly and Abby. None of them spoke. This was a time for father and son, and they didn't want to take away from that in any way. David kept turning his head to stare at his father.

"Your telegram said you wouldn't be arriving until the fifteenth of next month," David said. "Patrick and I were just in Salt Lake. If we had known, we could have come back together."

"Naw," John said. "Ah be 'ere two days noow. If'n Ah'd waited fur ya, Ah wud naw 'ave got ta know these lovely ladies 'ere. An' this strappin' laddee name of Billy Joe."

"But your telegram said . . ."

He waved that away. "When Ah got yur letter, Ah put in me notice. Reet noow, they've got plenty of 'elp, so they let me go early."

"And we're so glad he did, David. We think he is the cutest thing we've ever seen," Molly said, smiling brightly at him.

"He is a delight," Abby agreed. "He keeps us all in stitches."

"See what Ah mean, Davee boy. 'Tis e'nuff ta warm the cockles of me 'eart."

David rolled his eyes as everyone laughed. He looked at Molly. "You once accused me of having kissed the Blarney stone. Well, now you know where I got it. He's a rascal," David said with great affection. "But I'm stuck with him now."

"If he hadn't come early," Molly said, "we would never have learned all those very interesting things about you, David."

David groaned. "Aw, Dad, you didn't."

John looked hurt. "A father's got a reet ta brag aboot 'is son, no? But dunna worry. I dinna tell 'em any of the real gud stuff. Dunna want 'em thinkin' any the less of ya."

Molly turned to Abby. "Don't you just love the way he talks?"

"Don't, Molly," David said. "Dunna be spoilin' this ole Tyke, or ya be mekin' 'im nigh on impossible ta live wit."

Molly clapped her hands in delight. "You should talk like that all the time, David."

"That's not worthy of an answer," he growled.

Patrick stepped forward, extending his hand. "It is a great pleasure to meet you, Brother Draper, and we—"

One hand shot up, cutting him off. "Beggin' yur pardon, Bruther McKenna, but who be this Bruther Draper fella ya keep referrin' ta? Dunna know any Drapers 'ere but a man named John an' 'is cheeky son, David."

Patrick nodded. "Fair enough, John. But only if I'm Patrick to you."

"Aye, an' begorrah," he said in a near-perfect Irish brogue, "thare be a fair Irish name if'n ever Ah hurd one."

"Cheeky," Abby was saying to her mother. "Now, there's a word to describe David for you."

Billy Joe had been watching this interchange with great interest. Now he turned to David's father. "You talk funny," he said.

"What ya be sayin', Billy boy? A Yorkshur Tyke dunna talk funny. Only ya bloomin' Yanks. Ah can 'ardly unnerstand a wurd, what with yur flat 'A's' and yur mushy consonants. 'Tis the queen's English Ah be spekin', son. Nuthin' but."

"Don't you believe it, Billy Joe," David said. "If Queen Victoria were here today, she would no more understand him than you do."

"Ha!" John said, speaking to the girls. "What did Ah tell ya? Cheeky as a pup." Then he looked at Billy and in a near-perfect American accent said, "Tell you what, Billy Joe. I can teach you how to speak real proper like, if you want."

"Would you?" Billy Joe cried. "That would be neat."

David watched in amazement. His father was charming the socks off them, and evidently had been doing so for two days now. He reached out and laid a hand on his father's knee.

"What is it, Davee boy? Be ya tryin' ta say Ah be runnin' off at the mooth too mooch?"

David shook his head. "No. It is so good to hear your voice." His voice cracked a little. "Welcome to Cedar City, Dad."

CHAPTER 33

Thursday, March 20, 1879

The next month proved to be the happiest time of David's life. It also proved to be the busiest and most stressful.

The first item of business was to move his father out of the hotel where the McKennas had put him up into a room next to David's at the boarding-house. Since everything he had owned in Coalville had been either sold with the cabin or packed into one steamer trunk, that didn't take long. But it proved to be a wonderful choice. Every morning and night, father and son took their meals together. And in the evening, they would spend the rest of the night just talking.

Patrick immediately put John on the payroll and put him to work. However, John refused David's offer to have him work directly with him. He wasn't going to "stand 'roond lookin' stupid whilst David did awl the work." Instead, he offered to help Patrick prepare to either sell or leave his properties. He did minor repairs on the house and in the hotel. He painted the entire barn with Billy Joe's help—all the while teaching him how to speak with a Yorkshire accent that was even more atrocious than John's. Though the McKennas would be limited in what they could take with them, one advantage for these "pioneers" was that once they arrived at their destination, they could eventually send wagons back and bring more of their belongings. So a major part of John's work was helping Sarah and the girls prepare things for storage.

In spite of the fact that preparations for an exploring party were well under way, David had this nagging worry that Silas Smith might ask the McKennas to accompany the group. With four grown men and no small children, they could be a boon to the other two families. Patrick kept assuring him that this wasn't going to happen, but David felt compelled to do as much preparing as possible just in case.

For David, first priority was procuring the wagons and teams with the required harnessing and hardware. Since Patrick and Carl were too busy to accompany them, David and his father, with two hired teamsters, took a string of rented mules north to Milford and brought back the four Conestogas they had purchased in Salt Lake.

One afternoon was spent at the tinsmith's shop with Sarah, Abby, and Molly. Just walking through the door almost instantly doubled the number of things on their "essential" list. Though Sarah already had many items, Patrick insisted she leave those and take everything new. When they finished, they had boxes filled with hurricane lanterns, candleholders, candle-making molds, milk pails, cake and pie pans, cookie cutters, pewter mugs and plates, and flat pans with sliding covers to protect their food from mice, cockroaches, and other pests.

At the cooper's shop, David and Carl purchased about thirty barrels of various sizes. There were large, watertight ones that could hold more than thirty gallons of water each. The medium-sized ones were for assorted dry goods—beans, dried peas, rice, and the like. Specially lined barrels would carry molasses, honey, pickled cod, salted ham, slabs of smoked beef, sides of bacon. Some were specifically designed for wagon grease, an absolute necessity in the desert landscape and climate. Smaller barrels would hold a wide variety of "necessaries," such as powdered soap, liniment for the animals, and ointments and other medicines.

And so it went. They spent two different half days at the dry-goods store purchasing tools, blankets, cooking pots, Dutch ovens, frying pans, soup kettles, extra rifles, boxes of ammunition, and a dozen other things they would need. In addition, they put in an order for bags of flour, sugar, salt, potatoes, carrots, turnips, dried fruit, and other staples. If they left in April, they would have the order filled. If they left in September, it would be on consignment until then.

David stoutly resisted Sister McKenna's repeated invitation to him to accompany the women to the dress, millinery, and notions shops. It took him until the third invitation to realize that she—ever with a completely straight face—was simply pulling his leg.

He abruptly changed tactics, much to their dismay, and accompanied them shopping to the local ZCMI. When he innocently made as if to follow them into the "foundations" area of the store, he was ushered out by three very red-faced women. And that ended that.

At David's insistence, their personal preparation went forward apace with all the rest. When the weather was acceptable—and it was proving to be an early spring—they "ate out." David's father built a fire pit out back of the livery stable, and two or three times a week they cooked their meals over the fire and ate sitting on the ground around it. Twice, when it began to rain, David wouldn't let them go into the barn. They sat out there, wet, bedraggled, and miserable, silently smoldering at this man who was proving to be a draconian tyrant.

David and Carl set up a shooting range just outside of town, using the mountain as a backdrop. That proved to be wise. Many were the wild shots that kicked up puffs of dust on the hillsides high above their targets. Patrick and Carl quickly proved themselves adequate marksmen and no longer joined them. Surprisingly, Billy Joe was nearly as good as his father, but with his love of guns, he insisted on being to every practice and regaling the others with facts on muzzle velocity, caliber of bullets, and the makes and models of rifles, pistols, and shotguns.

Sarah turned out to be another surprise. She had a good eye and a steady hand. Molly was able to get over closing her eyes with every shot, but seemed content when she was able to hit the side of the mountain. Abby proved to be confident and comfortable with the weapons, though not as accurate as either her mother or Billy Joe—a fact that peeved her enormously.

They took long walks when the weather was good. When a late, slushy snowstorm hit, David gathered everyone up and made them walk for nearly four miles through it. They also took the horses out regularly and started toughening up their backsides by riding for hours at a time.

It was hard. It was intense. It was exhausting. But out of that experience, an interesting thing began to happen. The McKennas were already a

close family, but the bonding taking place between them now was gratify-
ing to watch. They laughed together, they moaned and groaned to each
other, they proudly displayed every new blister. And they all did a little
Scottish jig when Molly actually put a bullet within ten feet of one of the
targets.

As David watched all of this, he decided that this unforeseen conse-
quence of their efforts might prove to be the single most important thing
they were doing. His only regret was that Patrick and Carl were missing
out on much of it. As the days passed, more and more the two of them
were consumed with getting Patrick's affairs in order. From a comment or
two that David overheard between them, it was clear that Patrick had
other business interests that he hadn't known about. He was a minority
partner in the local bank. He owned some property out west of town. Also,
he had decided to keep the hotel. This, in a way, created more complica-
tions for him than if he had simply sold it.

To balance that out, however, was Molly. There were no more long,
painful talks about his faith or her inadequacies. In terms of their preparation, she did it all and never complained. She was almost always cheerful
and enthusiastic. When she failed, she would frown, mutter a few words
to herself, then dig in and try again. When they started cooking in the
Dutch ovens, her biscuits burned black. Her "lumpy dick"* was lumpy
enough to eat with their fingers. She had stared at it balefully, then
shrugged. "I thought we were making wallpaper paste."

But she had her strengths, too, and David was quick to point these out
to her. Her ability to organize things was prodigious, and she kept David's
lists of purchases updated and current. She worked with Carl to keep the
books on all expenditures. She calculated what it would take to feed eight
people for a day, then multiplied that by two months, three months, and
six months. Her father was so impressed that he put her in charge of purchasing all the food.

Gregarious by nature, she began talking with any and all who had any

---

* A simple meal made by pouring flour into boiling water, then adding a dash of sugar or
molasses to it.

kind of pioneering experience. From them she gleaned dozens of practical ideas that would be useful in their own experience: recipes, tips for starting a fire with wet wood, suggestions for doing laundry in a stream or river, ideas for coping with dirt when there was no stream or river. She had David buy her a compass and learned how to read it. She ordered a star map from a mail-order catalog and quickly taught the others how to use various constellations to find their way.

The intensity of their preparations threw David and Molly together almost every day, and gradually the romantic awkwardness of their relationship softened. They were rarely together alone, so they had little opportunity for physical affection, and this helped. They became more friends than sweethearts, more partners than suitors.

And what a wonderful thing having his father there turned out to be. David had never seen John like this. In those early years in Coalville, it had been just the two of them. They had had little time to play, and even less to laugh. Or at least, that was how David remembered it. But in this last month John Draper had absolutely blossomed. David had hired the schoolteacher to tutor him. He was amazingly quick and could now read most of the newspapers and quite a bit in the Bible. The McKennas adored him and had him and David for supper two or three times a week. People of all ages called out to him and stopped to talk anytime he was out on the streets. And lately, several widows went out of their way to talk to him at church and community activities. And he was thriving on all of it.

All of this was on David's mind as he walked slowly back toward the boardinghouse. He was bone-deep tired and ready for a break from the mental as well as the physical exhaustion. He actually welcomed the thought of putting it all aside and going with the family to Parowan for stake conference. They were leaving a day early—tomorrow—which would give them all a chance to lay aside the pressures they had undergone these last weeks.

As David started up the walk to the boardinghouse, he checked his watch. It was not quite eight o'clock, so he had missed supper. He wondered if his father had eaten without him.

As he went inside, Tamera Halliday, daughter of the owners, was at the desk. She was thirteen. "Hi, David," she called cheerily.

"Hi, Tamie. Is Dad home?"

"Yes. Came in over an hour ago."

"Did he have dinner?"

"Yes, but Mum left some in the oven for you."

He turned, making a detour for the kitchen. "Bless that woman," he said.

"There's milk in the icebox," she called as he disappeared.

It was almost nine when David went upstairs. As he reached his room, he stopped and checked the door next to his. There was a light under it, so he moved over and knocked softly. It was not unlike his father to lie on the bed to practice his reading until he fell asleep.

"Come. It's open."

He pushed the door open but stepped in only partially. His father was at the small desk studying a newspaper. He looked up. "Ah wondered if'n ya were ever gonna mek it home."

"I stopped and had supper." He moved inside and shut the door, then went over to stand behind his father. He grunted when he saw what John was reading. The large, bold headline read: **Mail Rider Stops Cattle Thieves Near Orderville**. This was the newspaper Molly had sent to his father right after that incident had happened. "What are you doing, Dad?"

"Joost lookin' at it. Tryin' ta r'member all that it says. Ah can mek oot quite a few of the words noow, but naw awl."

"It may be good reading practice, but you surely could find better content than that." He moved over and sat down on the other chair. "Would you like me to read it to you?"

"Naw. Molly tole me ya were mooch peeved when she sent it ta me."

"They made a big deal out of nothing, that was all." He sobered as he remembered that night. "Could have gone either way, actually," he finished, somewhat lamely.

"But it dinna go the other way. Sumone was watchin' o'er ya that night."

David laid a hand on John's shoulder. "Just wanted to say good night. Haven't seen you all day."

"Ah be glad ya did. Thare be sumthin' Ah've been meanin' ta talk ta ya aboot."

"What's that?"

He folded the newspaper and pushed it aside, then fiddled with it, making sure it was straight. David looked at him more closely. He was suddenly nervous, and he wasn't sure why.

"What is it, Dad?"

John finally looked up. "Never mind. Ya look tired. Ah'll tell ya in the mornin'."

"I'm not that tired. What?"

He turned around in his chair, then got up to face David. David studied him, noting that his father was starting to age somewhat. Not a lot yet, but there were wrinkles around his eyes and lines across his forehead.

"Thare be sumthin' ya need ta know, so ya naw be thinkin' Ah be sneakin' b'hind yur back."

That came as a surprise. "Sneaking behind my back? You haven't been flirting with one of the widowed sisters in the ward, have you?"

There was not even a flicker of a smile. David apologized. "Sorry. Go on."

"Ah naw be feelin' reet aboot goin' on a mission witout bein' called."

David just gaped. "Say that again?"

"Ya 'eard me," he growled. "So Ah sent me name in to Silas Smith as a volunteer. Patrick says thare be an invitation ta do that. Ah ask 'im if it be possible ta get an official call at stake conf'rence this weekend."

David threw up his hands. "Aw, come on, Dad. What difference does it make if you're called or not? You'll be doing exactly the same thing either way."

"It mek a diff'rence ta me." His jaw was set. His eyes dared David to disagree. "An' if'n thare be no diff'rence in yur eyes, then why wud ya care either way?"

David started for the door. "You know what? You're right. It doesn't mean anything one way or the other to me. Good night."

"Thare be one more thin' ya need ta know."

David stopped, not turning.

"If'n it does turn oot to be a mission call, Ah dunna feel reet aboot tekin' a salary fur doin' what the Lord 'as called me ta do."

David stood there, feeling his temper rise. That did make a difference. His father had just put half of his first month's salary into their ranch fund. Then he just sighed. It was his money, and his life. "Still trying to get over the guilt, are you, Dad?"

David had turned his head as he spoke and saw his father flinch as though David had struck him. Then John's eyes went cold. "If'n Ah be an embarrassment ta ya, boy, ya joost let me know an' Ah'll be 'eadin' back up ta Coalville ta see if I can get me ole job back."

David blew out his breath, highly frustrated. "You were right, Dad. I am tired. Let's talk about this at breakfast."

"Ya sure ya won't be too embarrassed ta be seen in pooblic wit me?"

"Good night, Dad," he said, fighting to hold his temper. "I'll see you tomorrow."

The door was almost shut when suddenly his father was there and yanked it open again. "Yur muther went through a terrible tragedy, David, an' it soured 'er on religion, an' even on God. But she 'ad gud cause, an' ya dunna. Ya 'ave a gud life. The Lord 'as blessed ya and watched over ya agin and agin. So dunna be blamin' yur muther fur bein' so sour about other people's beliefs."

"Good night, Dad." He tried to pull the door shut, but now his father's eyes were spitting fire. His hand shot out and gripped David's arm, the fingers dug into the flesh. "Ah be yur fahther, David. Ya 'ave no cause ta be turnin' yur back on me."

That shot went home. He turned back slowly. "You're right, Dad. I'm sorry. Say what you have to say."

For a long moment John stood there, looking up at his son. In that moment, the anger drained away, to be replaced by a deep weariness. "David, ya refuse ta see what is obvious ta ev'ryone else. Ya refuse ta see that the Lord be tekin' a 'and in yur life, tryin' ta touch yur 'eart."

"Right," he said, no fight left in him.

"But since ya refuse ta listen, then the Lord gonna be knockin' ya alongside the 'ead until 'E gits yur attention. Life be gonna start comin' at ya likc rocks frum a catapult, until ya learn ta bend the knee an' bow the 'ead. It gives me great sorrow ta say it, becuz it be a 'ard way ta learn, Son, a very 'ard way." His eyes bored into David's now. "But Ah know, as sure as Ah know Ah luved yur mother, that it be cumin'."

"And how is that, Dad?" he flared. "Are you reading the future now?"

The sadness in John's eyes made David fall back a step.

"Becuz I pray fur it ev'ry night an' mornin', Son. *Ev'ry* night an' *ev'ry* mornin'. That's 'ow Ah know it be cumin'."

CHAPTER 34

Sunday, March 23, 1879

As usual when they went to stake conference in Parowan, the McKennas took rooms in the Parowan Hotel—Patrick, Sarah, and Billy Joe took one; Abby and Molly took another; David and his father were in a third; and Carl Bradford was alone in a fourth.

By unspoken mutual agreement, David and his father had not reopened their conversation from that night. It really wasn't any of David's business if that was what his father wanted. And when John had told Patrick of his decision the next morning, Patrick had insisted on continuing to pay him until they actually left Cedar City. When David's father protested, to David's surprise, Patrick dug in his heels. "If you were working in the coal mines and got a call," he pointed out, "you would continue to work there until you left." And that settled that.

David kept telling himself that none of this really mattered, but it still grated on him, and that had put a strain on their relationship. The thing that irked David the most was the nagging guilt. It was never said, but it was there, just underneath the surface: *Why don't you volunteer? Why not make it a mission call for David Draper as well as John Draper?* He gave a soft snort of derision. Wouldn't that please Molly? It might even convince her he was softening up a little.

A soft knock on the door brought his head up. "I'll get it, Dad."

His father stuck his head out of the small washroom. He had lathered up and was trimming his beard with a straight razor. He nodded and disappeared again.

To his surprise, Silas Smith was standing at the door when David opened it.

"Good morning, Brother Draper. Sorry to disturb you. I know you're getting ready for conference, but I wondered if I could have a word with you."

"Sure. Let me get my boots."

When David returned, Silas steered him to a corner of the hotel lobby where there was a cluster of chairs. There were a few people about, but this gave them at least some privacy. They sat down across from each other, and David, quite curious, turned to face the mission leader.

"David, let me get right to it. I was hoping to get a chance to visit with you yesterday, but—" He shrugged. "Too many meetings, I guess."

"It must be a busy time for you, what with you leaving in just a week or two now."

"Extremely," he said with a smile. "It seems like every day brings some new crisis."

"Only one?" David was still trying to figure out what this was about.

Silas laughed. "Did I say every day? I meant to say every hour."

At about fifty years of age, Silas Sanford Smith was probably one of the oldest men to have received a call to the San Juan. His very demeanor and bearing bespoke wisdom, experience, and good judgment. He was not particularly tall, only an inch or two taller than David's five-foot-nine, but he was lean and fit, and strong as a blacksmith. His full, neatly cared for beard and mustache were just starting to gray. He had a high, broad forehead with a sharply receding hairline. Heavy brows shaded piercing, dark eyes that were quick to smile.

Silas was from Paragonah, just six miles north of Parowan. That little village was very proud that one of their own had been chosen as president of the mission. At a dance held on Friday night, the Paragonians had been eager to tell everyone what they knew about him. And it was impressive.

He had come to the Salt Lake Valley in 1847 at age seventeen. He wasn't in the first company led by Brigham Young, but his family was in one of those that followed shortly thereafter. His roots in the Church went back much further than that. His family had joined and had come to

Kirtland, Ohio, while the Church was in its infancy. They fled to Missouri when the persecutions in Ohio boiled over. There they were caught up in the conflagration caused by the infamous Mormon extermination order issued by Missouri's governor. They fled as exiles to Nauvoo, Illinois, then had to leave again in 1846 when they were driven out for a third time by government militias. Silas and his wife had been among the first settlers in Parowan and then later moved to Paragonah. He had fought as a major in the militia in the Walker Indian War, been called to serve a mission in the Sandwich Islands at the age of twenty-four, and returned to become a bishop in Paragonah. He had also been a member of the Utah Territorial Legislature for nearly twenty years, a deputy U.S. marshal, a probate judge, and a prosecuting attorney. He was widely known, deeply respected, and greatly loved by the people of southern Utah.[1] All of that only added to the positive impressions David had received about Silas when he and Patrick and Carl had met with him a few weeks before.

He cleared his throat. "Brother Draper, I should like—"

"Just David," he said quickly. "Please."

There was a fleeting smile. "Okay. David, I should like to put a proposition to you. Before doing so, however, you should know that I have discussed this with President Lunt and Elder Erastus Snow and have their full concurrence in the matter."

"All right," David said slowly, feeling a sudden uneasiness.

"I should like to put your name forward in conference this morning to be officially called as a missionary to the San Juan." He held up one hand quickly as David jerked forward. "The specific intent in doing so would be to ask you to accompany the exploring party."

David's heart dropped. He felt like he had just been hit with a brick.

"I know this is rather sudden," Silas went on when he didn't respond, "and that it gives you very little notice, but we need a man with your experience, David. In fact, there are few who are better qualified than you for the task we have before us."

"I . . ." He blew out his breath. "I'm not sure what to say, Brother Smith."

He laughed softly. "Silas is fine for me, too."

"Silas, I . . . whew! You really know how to sandbag a man, don't you?"

There was a soft chuckle. "Sandbag. Waylay. Ambush. They probably all describe what I'm doing to you right now, actually." He leaned forward in much earnest. "Look, I know what you're doing for the McKennas, and that is a tremendous thing. I also took the liberty yesterday of discussing this with Patrick. He turned a little grey around the gills when I told him what we were thinking. But," he rushed on as David made as though to speak, "he was also quick to give his permission. In fact, he said you have done so much already that he thinks they can continue on in your absence. And your experience with us would be of great value to them."

David's mind was whirling. "Is it true that you're thinking it will take six months?"

He nodded gravely. "Roughly. Two months to get there. Two to three months to get the two families who are going with us well established, then a month to six weeks to return."

"Silas, I am greatly honored . . ." He rubbed his eyes. "It's not just helping the McKennas. There are some personal matters that make leaving for six months very difficult right now."

"Patrick told me about you and Molly. Is that part of it?"

That surprised him a little. "Yes. And also my father. As you may know, my father just came down here to live with me a few weeks ago. And that was only because I pressured him to do so. We've not been together for over six years. To turn around and leave him for six months, would . . ." He sighed deeply. "It would not be good."

"I understand."

David felt awful. "I would be truly honored to serve with you, Silas. I have the greatest respect for you, but this simply is not a good time. In fact, it is really a very bad time."

"I understand. I'll ask the clerk to strike your name from the call list." He stood, and David rose as well. Silas stuck out his hand. "Will you let me know if you change your mind?"

David nodded, shook hands, and headed back to his own room. When he got there, his father was waiting for him. "Who was that?"

"Silas Smith."

One eyebrow came up. "An' what did 'e want?"

David just shook his head. "Nothing. He just had a couple of questions."

The same clerk who had read the names at the December stake conference came forward, this time without any introduction from Elder Snow or the stake president.

"Brothers and sisters," he began, looking out on the congregation over his spectacles, "we would propose that the following names be added to those previously called to fill missions to Arizona and the San Juan areas, specific sites yet to be determined."

He peered sternly at them for a moment as the soft noises of anticipation spread across the room. Then he raised his spectacles, lowered his head, and began to read. "Jesse N. Smith. Silas S. Smith, Jr."

Patrick leaned over to David and whispered, "Silas's son. Married, with two children."

The clerk continued, pronouncing each name slowly and distinctly. "Joseph Fish, Smith D. Rogers, Amos Rogers, John R. Hulet, John H. Rollins, Cornelius Decker."

Once again, as the names were read, reactions rippled through the crowd.

"Lehi West, Sister West, John A. West, Zechariah B. Decker, Jr., John Dickinson Draper."

On the other side of Patrick, David saw Sarah's head come up in surprise. Abby, who sat between Carl and David's father, reached out and touched his arm, smiling broadly. Molly was sitting beside David and was likewise surprised. She looked up at him, but he pretended not to see her. And he deliberately did not look at his father.

The clerk was droning on. "N. P. Warden, Lars Christiansen, Jens Nielson—"

At that, there was an audible ripple of surprise. David turned to Patrick. "*Our* Jens Nielson?" he whispered. "The one who's crippled?"

Patrick nodded. "Only one I know of."

"Samuel Cox, Jane Perkins, Sarah J. Perkins, David Dickinson Draper."

As his head snapped up, Molly's hand shot out and grabbed his arm. "Really, David? You've been called?"

David just stared at her. Down the row he saw that Abby was stunned. His father's jaw was slack. Sarah leaned forward, smiling at him in astonishment. Only Patrick seemed not surprised.

David spun around, looking for Silas Smith. When he spotted him about three rows back, Silas looked baffled. He shrugged his shoulders and mouthed, "I'm sorry."

✻

Silas came up to David the moment the meeting ended. "I am so sorry, David," he said. "I sent word forward to the clerk to strike your name, but he must not have gotten it."

Molly, who had almost been floating for the last hour, spun around.

"I truly apologize for any embarrassment this may cause you," Silas said again, and then he turned and was gone.

"You withdrew your name?" Molly faltered.

The others had heard it too, and David felt like a little boy in school who had just been caught putting a bug in the teacher's water glass. "It was a mistake," he said. "My name wasn't supposed to be on there."

"A mistake?" Abby exclaimed. "You mean they didn't intend to call you?"

David ignored that, still focusing on Molly. "They wanted me to go with the exploring party," he said quietly, hoping the others wouldn't hear. "I would be gone for six months."

Her mouth opened in a big O, and she fell back a step. Then David turned and walked away.

✻

At dinner in the hotel dining room, the family studiously avoided speaking of David's "call" or lack of it. There were a lot of congratulations for David's father, which didn't help David's mood much, and several dis-cussions about names of those who had been called.

Abby looked at her father. "Was Bishop Nielson's call a surprise, Dad?"

"It was to me," Sarah said.

Patrick shook his head. "I had heard that he had put his name forward, just as John did. Not a surprise, really. As you know, their oldest son, Joe, is going. So is their daughter, Mary, and her husband, Kumen Jones. Joe and his father are very close. I think Jens wants to go with his family and help them get established."

"How old is he?" David suddenly asked, the first he had spoken dur-ing the meal.

"Just over sixty," Patrick said.

"And crippled," David muttered under his breath.

He evidently had said it louder than he intended, because every head at the table turned to look at him. "What was that you said, David?" Sarah asked.

"How can he go?" he said, "when it is so difficult for him to walk?"

"He gets around just fine," Abby said tartly.

"Getting around Cedar City is one thing," he said, wishing he hadn't started this, but angry enough to finish it. "A two-hundred-mile trek across very difficult terrain is quite another."

"But isn't that his choice?" Abby shot right back.

"It is," David snapped. "But that doesn't make it right. It does affect others, too."

"David," his father said, "Ah think that be e'nuff. It be naw yur deci-sion."

"Look," David said earnestly. "I'm not criticizing Brother Nielson. From what you say, he is a man of great faith. It's admirable that a man of his age and with his handicap would be willing to accept such a call. But that doesn't mean it's the wise thing to do. This trip will be more chal-lenging than any of us can imagine. I'm just saying that I think it is a mis-take for the Church leaders to ask him to do something like this."

Patrick had been watching David carefully. Now his head lifted. "Silas plans to ask Bishop Nielson to be the wagon captain for the Cedar City/Parowan/Paragonah contingent."

David snorted in soft derision. "Figures," he said.

"Brother Nielson is as strong as an ox," Carl ventured. "And he gets around pretty well."

David raised his hand, warding off any further comments. "I'm sorry. Dad's right. It is none of my affair. It's just that . . ." He let it hang there in the awkward silence. "Never mind."

"Do you know *why* he's making this 'mistake'?" The last word was said with heavy sarcasm. David turned. Abby was across the table from him. She was clearly ready for battle.

"It doesn't matter. It's not my decision. I'm sorry I dared to express an opinion."

That only made her anger flare higher. "As you know, the Nielsons came with the Willie handcart company in eighteen fifty-six."

"I know," he said, tired of it all. "I know they suffered tremendously. And I have nothing but the greatest admiration for them."

"You didn't answer my question," she said coldly. "*Why?* Why would a sixty-year-old man with twisted, frostbitten feet volunteer to go on yet an-other difficult trek?"

"Because of his family."

"No, not good enough. He could let them go, then visit them later. Or he could keep them home. Tell them to refuse the call as well."

"You tell me, then, Abby. Why would he?"

Everyone around the table was frozen into silence, and several other tables of people kept glancing over at them, sensing the tension.

Abby's head was up and her voice trembled a little. "On the day they had to pull their handcarts up and over Rocky Ridge in order to reach the rescue wagons, Jens and Aunt Elsie, as we all call her, lost their only son, who was just Billy Joe's age. He froze to death. They also lost a young girl named Bodil Mortensen, whom they were bringing with them for another family. She went out to gather firewood. They found her frozen by a clump of sagebrush. Brother Nielson's feet were also badly frostbitten at that time. They never healed properly."

She faltered a moment. "That night, when they tried to put up their tent, Brother Nielson was the only man left in the tent group. The other four had all died. It was bitter cold and snowing hard. The canvas was stiff and unmanageable. The ground was frozen so hard that they couldn't drive the tent pegs into it. They were exhausted, freezing, and emotionally shattered.

"Brother Nielson was struggling to get that tent erected—and remember, these were twenty-man tents. They were large and heavy, difficult to set up even in the best of circumstances. But as he struggled, he couldn't do it. He asked some of the largest and strongest women to help him, but they couldn't do it either."

She had to look away, and David saw her swallow quickly a couple of times. When she turned back, her eyes were glistening. "I shall try to quote him as best I remember him saying it. 'When it looked like we all should die, I offered a prayer to my Heavenly Father. I remember my prayers as distinctly today as I did then. I said that if the Lord would let me live to reach Salt Lake City, then all the rest of my days should be spent trying to be of use to Him under the direction of the priesthood.'"[2]

She sniffed once, then went on, her voice very low. "Going to San Juan will be Jens and Elsie Nielson's sixth move since coming to Utah, David. Now, if that bothers you somehow, perhaps you should take it up with Bishop Nielson directly and tell him you think it's a mistake for him to fulfill a promise he made to the Lord over twenty years ago."

David returned to the hotel about half past seven to find his father in the room practicing writing his words. David had excused himself from dinner and gone for a long walk out of town, where he could avoid seeing anyone. He had deliberately stayed away this long so that he wasn't back for supper with the family. Now he slipped into the room without a word.

When his father looked up and saw him, he gave a soft grunt of acknowledgment but said nothing more. That was fine with David. He washed his face, got a drink of water, then sat down on the bed with a pad of paper and a pencil and went to work outlining what had to happen this coming week.

About ten minutes later, he looked up and said, "When we get back to Cedar City, I'll be going south to Springdale to get those mules. I'll be gone a week to ten days."

His father turned slowly. "Do ya need me ta go wit ya an' 'elp?"

David shook his head. "No. I'll be fine."

For a long, searching moment, his father just looked at him. Then his head bobbed up and down one time. "Awl reet," he said, and turned back to his reading.

Notes

1. Most of this information on Silas S. Smith comes from Jenson, *LDS Biographical Encyclopedia,* 1:801–2. Kumen Jones, who served under his leadership on both the exploring party and the main expedition, also described his character and qualities as a leader ("Notes on the San Juan Mission," 7–8).

2. The account of Jens Nielson's prayer that night near Rock Creek, Wyoming, comes from his own history (see Lyman, *Bishop Jens Nielson,* 4). After their arrival in Utah, the Nielsons helped settle Parowan, then subsequently lived in Panguitch, Circleville, back in Parowan, and finally in Cedar City. Thus the move to the San Juan was their sixth move in just over twenty years (see Carpenter, *Jens Nielson,* 21–30).

CHAPTER 35

Tuesday, April 8, 1879

David was back from Springdale nine days later with twelve mules in tow. He had so much dreaded returning to face the family after the fiasco in Parowan that he had almost driven the mules home by way of Denver. It turned out to be not as bad as he had feared, but nowhere near as good as he had hoped. He first went to Patrick and Sarah and made apologies for having been so obnoxious at dinner. He used as his excuse the fact that he had been deeply shaken by Silas's invitation that morning. They were both understanding and said not to worry about it. However, he could sense Patrick's disappointment that he had so quickly dismissed Silas's invitation.

Sarah, on the other hand, seemed happy that he wasn't going to leave them for six months, but was more bothered by what had happened at dinner. She was cordial, but occasionally he sensed a little distance. David suspected that in time that would pass.

The strain between David and his father was still there, but neither of them brought up what had happened that Sunday, and gradually things settled back to some kind of normalcy there as well.

When David apologized to Abby, she coolly brushed him off, saying that he was under no obligation to account to her about accepting a call or not. As for Jens Nielson, she had felt compelled to confront him on that because David was not only absolutely wrong but totally out of line in saying it. Thereafter, both were happy to stay pretty well clear of each other.

Surprisingly, Molly took it the best. Like her mother, she seemed to feel an enormous relief that David wasn't going to leave them for six months. As for the other issue, she seemed as anxious to avoid further discussions on their spiritual compatibility as David was. Whenever they were together alone, which wasn't that frequently, she kept the conversation on neutral ground.

Billy Joe was the only bright spot. The supper-table experience seemed to have passed right over his head. He always came on the run when he saw David, and he was quick to share the latest triumph in his training of Paint. When he wasn't in school, he often became David's partner in whatever project was under way. That was encouraging in a way, because it meant that at least Sarah and Patrick did not yet see David as a negative influence on their son.

He went to church with the family on the Sunday after his return. To his dismay, as they came outside after the meeting, they ran headlong into Jens Nielson and his family. David was formally introduced all around, managing to avoid meeting Abby's eye during the whole process.

He was saved from further awkwardness when he learned that Joe Nielson and Kumen Jones were both signed up for the exploring party expedition. Kumen was going to be a scout; Joe, one of the teamsters. He took the opportunity to ask questions about their departure and avoided any further conversation with Bishop Nielson.

Other than that, the last week had been what David thought of as "hunkering down" time—quiet, uneventful, and conflict free. Today would be the same. He was taking some of the horses and mules to spring pasture up Cedar Canyon.

As he stepped off the porch of the boardinghouse into a light rain, he was momentarily tempted to go to the post office and say hello to Molly. Then he remembered that Molly was working the hotel desk this morning and the post office in the afternoon. That increased his chances of bumping into Abby, so he turned instead toward the livery stable.

⁂

It was late afternoon when he stabled Tillie again and walked out of the livery stable. The rain had stopped and the air was sweet and fresh and crystal clear. He pulled out his pocket watch. It was five minutes to five. He immediately changed directions and headed for the post office. If he was lucky, he would get there just as Molly was closing, and perhaps they would have a chance to be alone. Maybe even go for a walk.

When he walked in, Molly was working with one of the elderly sisters, helping her address an envelope in the proper manner. He moved over into the corner and pretended to read one of the notices posted on the wall. A moment later, the woman left, thanking Molly as she went. Molly followed her to the door, locked it, then pulled down the shade. "There," she said.

David noticed that she didn't pull the shade on the door that led directly into the hotel lobby, but she did turn over the small card that said "Open" on one side and "Closed" on the other. Finally she turned to him. "This is a pleasant surprise."

"Hello, Molly." He came over and took both of her hands. "How are you?"

"Better now, thank you."

"Because of me," he teased, "or because the post office is closed?"

"Definitely, the post office." She squeezed his hands. "But you're a close second."

Then she snapped her fingers as she remembered something. "Where's your father today?"

"He's not back? I took some stock up Cedar Canyon for pasture. He took the rest out west of town. I assumed he would beat me back."

She walked over to the pigeonholes and withdrew a letter. "I sent Billy Joe over to the boardinghouse just a few minutes ago, but neither of you were there." She handed the envelope to David. "This letter came for your father today. Can you take it to him?"

"Sure." He took it and looked at the return address. *Box B, Salt Lake City, Utah Territory.* "Hmm," he said, slipping it into his inside coat pocket. "Didn't know Dad knew anyone in Salt Lake." As he turned back to her, she was looking at him very strangely. "What?" he asked.

"Do you know what Box B is?"

He shook his head. "No, do you?"

She hesitated, then shook her head. "Not for sure. Never mind."

"So, are you up for a walk?"

Her face fell. "Mama's helping the Relief Society with a quilt, and I promised I'd start supper. Want to come help?"

He shook his head, and she laughed aloud. "Scaredy-cat." Then she looked out into the lobby. "But I don't have to leave for a few minutes. We can talk here if you'd like."

"Good. I just wanted to see you, see how your day was."

"It was good. And yours?"

"Quite enjoyable. With the rain everything's so fresh, and Cedar Canyon is almost as green as England. It's beautiful."

"Maybe we could go for a walk up there on Sunday if the weather is good."

They were leaning toward each other across the counter, and David's hand stole across and took hers. She looked up and smiled, then put her other hand over his. She began to trace little patterns on the back of his hand and up onto his wrist. "David?" she finally said. "Do you mind if we talk about us for a minute or two if I promise not to get all weepy?"

"Not at all. Are you feeling weepy?"

"Not really. But it always seems to come when we try to get too serious." She pulled her hands back and straightened so as to be looking at him more directly. "Do you ever pray about us, David?"

He was thinking he should have been surprised by that, but he wasn't. Not really. "In my own way, I suppose," he answered after a moment.

"What does that mean?"

"I haven't knelt down by my bed and actually spoken aloud, if that's what you're looking for. But I think about it all the time. I wonder, and ponder, and hope. Don't the scriptures somewhere talk about the 'prayer of the heart'?"

"Yes, they do."

"Well, I guess that's how I pray. In my heart."

"But you don't specifically speak to Heavenly Father?"

He shook his head.

Her expression was one of mixed hope and sadness. "I pray for us all the time."

"I know."

"I plead with Heavenly Father that He will help us to know if this is right, if we are meant to be together forever."

He made a shrewd guess. "Especially after days like that Sunday up in Parowan."

She couldn't meet his eyes. "Yes."

"Molly, I was being just plain stupid that day. I'm still not sure what got into me."

"Will you pray with me now?"

David swallowed quickly, realizing that she had been thinking about this for some time, just waiting for the right moment. "You mean right here?"

She glanced quickly out into the hotel foyer again. "Why not?"

"All right," he said after a long pause. Up in Cedar Canyon, ironically, he had decided it was time to either move the relationship forward or . . . "As long as you're voice."

She was motionless, her eyes wide and questioning, not quite daring to believe. "Really?"

"Do we have to kneel? That feels kind of funny, knowing people can see in here."

She took his hands again. "No, right here is fine."

Two hours later, David was lying on his bed staring up at the ceiling, thinking on the experience he had gone through with Molly. He was a little taken aback by his reaction to it all. It had turned out to be a sweet experience for him as well as for her. Her prayer had been quite simple. In a soft but clear and steady voice, she had thanked the Lord for bringing her and him together, and for bringing David to Cedar City so he could help their family answer their call to serve. Then a tremor crept into her voice as she began to plead with Him. It reminded David of a child explaining something to a parent, even though the child knew the parent already knew it. She prayed for guidance in their relationship. She asked that they might know if they were meant to be husband and wife, and if not, to give them both the courage to accept that. But if they were—now she was weeping softly—would He please work things out between them.

The prayer was pure and sweet and filled with longing. David was surprised how much it had touched him. The single kiss that followed was much like the prayer—pure, sweet and filled with longing. As they pulled back from each other, he realized with a keen and surprising intensity just how truly wonderful a woman Molly was, and how much he wanted to do whatever it would take to make her happy.

He sat up eagerly as a knock sounded on the door. "That you, Dad? Come on in."

His father came in, removing his coat. "Hi."

"You're just back?"

"Yeah. Took longer than I thought. The one pasture was pretty well flooded so I had to take them out a little farther west."

"Good."

"You eaten dinner already?"

"No, but I'm not hungry. You go ahead."

John looked at him more closely. "You sure?"

David nodded and lay back. As his father started to back out of the door again, David remembered. "Oh, by the way. Molly gave me a letter for you. It's there on the lamp table."

He came in and shut the door. "A letter? For me?" He picked it up, looked at the envelope, then turned to David. "Salt Lake City?" His question was hesitant, unsure.

"Yeah. Who do you know in Salt Lake City?"

"Ah know *aboot* a lot of people thare, but none of them know me." His father sat down, took out a pocketknife, and slit the envelope open. He looked at it, then looked up. "It be written in some pretty fancy cursive. Ya ahre goin' ta 'ave ta read it ta me."

David swung his legs off the bed and stood up. He went over and took the letter from his father, curious now too. When he saw the letterhead, he did a double take.

Office of the Quorum of the Twelve Apostles
The Church of Jesus Christ of Latter-day Saints

He sat down slowly and began to read: "It's addressed to you, Dad. *'Dear Brother Draper. After careful consideration, you have been recommended . . .'*"

He stopped, his eyes almost popping out. His father was leaning forward, intent on every word. "What, David? What is it?"

He rubbed at his eyes, then started again. "'*You have been recommended as a full-time missionary for The Church of Jesus Christ of Latter-day Saints. If you can accept your call, please report to Salt Lake City as soon as possible, where you will be set apart as—*'"

"No!" He dropped the letter as if it were suddenly hot.

His father shot to his feet. "*What?* Tell me."

David just stared, not even seeing his father. It was like he had been hit in the stomach.

Greatly exasperated, his father shot to his feet, reached out, grabbed David's shoulders, and shook him lightly. "Tell me what it says, David."

David slowly picked it up again. "'. . . *where you will be set apart as a missionary in the British Mission with headquarters in Liverpool, England.*'"

John sat down heavily on the bed. "England?" he said in a hoarse whisper. "They want ya ta go to England?"

David slowly shook his head. "Not me, Dad. *You.* This is your letter, not mine." He lifted it again. "'*You are to make your way from Salt Lake City by rail to either New York City or Boston, and there take passage for Liverpool. On your arrival, you will report to President William Budge, mission president, at the address which is furnished you below. Your term of service . . .*'" David's eyes skipped quickly across the line. Then he looked up, the shock giving him a gaunt, haunted look. "Your term of service is for three years."

David couldn't go on. He started over again, reading the last paragraph again to himself.

"Don't stop," his father cried. "Read it oot lood, please."

David tipped his head back, then rolled it around, trying to loosen the sudden stiffness in his neck. The first feelings of betrayal were starting to rise within him. And anger. He let his eyes drop to the signature line, then let the letter drop in his lap. "It's signed by President John Taylor, President of the Quorum of the Twelve."[1]

He slowly folded the letter and handed it back to his father. "A mis-sion'ry?" John said, his voice filled with awe. "Hoow can that be? Ah can 'ardly read and write."

David swung around on him. "*That's* what you're worried about?"

"David! Hoow can Ah possibly teach the gospel if I canna read or write?"

David was astonished. "You're thinking of going?"

He blinked. "Why wouldn't I?"

David was incredulous. "Because you're almost fifty years old. Because you just moved down to live with me. Because you have Mr. Jonathan Rhodes and who knows how many candymen waiting to get their hands on you in England." He had to stop to catch his breath. "And . . . and . . . because you already have a call to go on a mission."

That last came out with great relief. "That's right, Dad. You already have a mission call. Salt Lake just doesn't know that yet." He smiled. "You can write and tell them that."

John scoffed aloud. "That call was naw frum the Quorum of the Twelve Apostles, David. Thare be a great diff'rence."

David was up in an instant, facing off against his father. "Dad. This is insane. You are not going on a mission to England."

The coffee-brown eyes turned on him and went very dark, almost beetle black. "What's that ya be sayin'?" he asked. "Ya be talkin' like this be yur d'cision and naw mine. The letter dinna cum to ya. It cum ta me, r'member?"

"Don't even think about it," David said hotly. "This is crazy." Then he was pleading. "Dad, you just got here. After almost seven years, we're fi-nally together."

His father dropped his head into his hands. "Ya think Ah dunna think aboot that? Ya think me 'eart isn't achin', joost thinkin' aboot leavin' ya?"

"Then don't." It came out blunt and hard.

There was a stubborn set to John's jaw now. "If'n President Taylor be sayin' the Lord 'as called me ta England, then Ah be goin' to England. This ain't joost aboot you and me, David."

"You're not going, and that's final. I won't let you."

John stood slowly, putting the envelope in his inside jacket pocket very carefully. When he turned back to David, his face was resolute, and David knew he had lost.

David sat down on the bed and leaned forward, head in his hands. "You can't go on a mission, Dad. Not now. You just can't."

"Maybe naw, David," he said with great finality, "but Ah am. That be awl thare be ta it."

Notes

1. President Ezra Taft Benson made "Box B" famous when he told the story of his father getting a mission call from the First Presidency showing that it came from Box B in Salt Lake City (see Benson, *Come unto Christ*, 87). Box B, the postal address for Church Headquarters, was in use at this time (see *Conference Report*, April 1880, 160).

President John Taylor became president of the Church on the death of Brigham Young in 1877. However, the First Presidency was not reorganized until three years later, so in 1879 he presided over the Church as president of the Quorum of the Twelve.

CHAPTER 36

When David stopped by the post office the next morning, his mood hovered somewhere between gloom and rage. He had barely slept after battling with his father for another two hours, which had only left them both more deeply entrenched than ever in their opposite opinions. The only concession David won was that his father would talk to the Twelve when he got to Salt Lake and explain to them about his call to the San Juan Mission. But David knew nothing would come of that. After a fitful night, David had knocked on his father's door on his way down to breakfast, but John had either already gone or was refusing to undergo any more of David's attacks.

As he entered the post office, he was disappointed to see that it was Abby behind the counter sorting the mail and not Molly. She looked up and nodded soberly. "Good morning, David. Molly's in Daddy's office, doing the books."

"Oh? Thank you."

As he started toward the hotel lobby, she said, "I hear congratulations are in order for your father."

He turned in surprise. It was barely eight o'clock. Seeing his look, she explained, "He came by the house early this morning to tell Daddy he won't be going with us. That made us all sad."

"Yeah, tell me about it," he grumbled.

"He said that you were very angry." There was a moment's hesitation. "David, I—"

"Don't!" he snapped. He was in no mood to start another round.

Her head came up. "I was only going to say that I'm sorry."

"I don't want to talk about it. Is Molly alone?"

"She is," Abby said after a moment. And with that, she went back to sorting the mail.

He knocked softly on the door to her father's office, then opened it. She was sitting behind the desk with a large ledger book before her. But it was closed, and the pen was in the inkwell. She had been crying. "Is it true?" she asked, sniffing back tears.

"Is what true?"

"That you told your father not to accept his mission call?"

He rolled his eyes. "No, it's not true. I told him not to accept *another* mission call." When she tossed her head dismissively at that, he said, "He already has a call from the Lord, Molly. Remember? That's what you all told him. 'Oh, John, this is from the Lord. You're doing the Lord's will.' What do you have to say about that?"

When she looked away, he leaned forward, wanting to take her hands. But her hands were in her lap now. "Look. I don't want to fight with you about this. He's going. There's no way I can change his mind."

She looked down at her hands. After a moment, her shoulders began to tremble. He was instantly contrite. "Molly, please. Can't we talk about something else? I have to ride out to New Harmony this morning. Would you like to come? We can take the buggy."

She didn't look up. When she finally spoke, her voice was choked, barely a whisper. "And what happens if we marry, David?" Finally her head came up, and the tears were coursing down her cheeks. "What will you say to our sons when they get *their* mission calls?"

He sat back, the breath going out of him. He wanted to yell at her, shake her, strike back, walk out and slam the door.

"David, I think it is better if we don't court each other anymore."

For a long moment, he just stared at her. She refused to meet his eyes. "Don't do this," he said quietly. "Not now. Not today."

"I am so sorry, David. But I think we have our answer." She wiped at the tears with both hands, went to say something else, then shook her head. "I'm sorry, David."

He slowly got to his feet, looking down on her, feeling a great hollow in the pit of his stomach. And then suddenly, with perfect clarity, he knew what he had to do. "Fine," he said. He turned on his heel and went to the door. "Good-bye, Molly."

He went straight to the post office. Abby looked up, startled to see him. Then she grew alarmed at the look on his face. "David?"

"Where's your father?"

"He's with Carl down at the livery stable. They have a potential buyer."

"Thank you." He started for the door.

"David, is everything all right?"

"It is now," he said.

When David walked into the livery stable, Patrick and Carl Bradford were standing near the stalls with a man whom David didn't recognize. Patrick looked up in surprise, then lifted a hand in greeting. "Be right with you," he said.

David shook his head. "I'm sorry, but could I see you for a moment now, Patrick?"

Patrick hesitated, clearly taken aback.

"It's urgent."

He cocked his head, his eyes questioning, but then he nodded. "Excuse me for a moment." He came over, his face concerned. "What is it, David?"

"I thought you should know. After thinking about it, I have determined to accept Silas's invitation to go with the exploring party."

Patrick's eyes widened in shock. "But . . ."

"I'll be leaving this afternoon."

He was stunned. "This afternoon?"

"They're supposed to be leaving anytime now, if they haven't already."

Then understanding dawned. "Is this because of your father?"

"This has nothing to do with my father," David said, his voice clipped. "I don't expect to be paid while I'm gone. And on my return, I still plan to go with you, if you still want me."

"Of course we still want you. But, David—"

David stuck out his hand. "Thank you, Patrick. I hope this will allow me to be of greater value to you and the family."

"David, I . . ." But he was left to stare after him as David walked away, not looking back.

Dear Dad,

I am so sorry for the things I said last night. You are absolutely right. No son has the right to tell his father what he can or cannot do. Please forgive me. And please forgive me for taking this solution. It's not because of you. It is just best all around if I leave right now.

It is not likely that we shall be where we can get any mail or send it, but please write to the McKennas and I shall catch up on everything when I return.

I am so proud of you. You will make a great missionary. It's not what you can read or write that matters, but what is in your heart, and you have the greatest heart of anyone I know.

I have put my extra things in the two boxes that are in my room. Could you please put them in one of the storage sheds for me? I will pay my bill here at the boardinghouse as I leave.

I love you with all my heart. This last month has been the happiest of my life. Thank you for that. Three years seems like a long time, but maybe by then, when you return, it will be to "our ranch," wherever that may be. May God go with us both.

David

Dear Abby,

I wish there had been time to say good-bye. You have become a trusted and wise—and honest!!!—friend.

I hope that you can help Molly understand why I left so suddenly. It is for the best. She will blame herself, but you will know what to say. It truly is for the best. (I hope you are nodding in agreement right now.)

You once told me I was denying reality because I refused to see the connection between Molly's prayer one day and your father offering me a job the very next morning. Well, tell me what you see when you look at this. Yesterday, for the first time in a very long time, I said a prayer. Well, Molly actually said it, but I stood with her. And my heart was with her. She prayed that the Lord would bless our relationship so that we could be brought closer together, so we could resolve our differences. And here I am, less than twenty-four hours later, with my father leaving for three years and my relationship with Molly ended. I will be anxious to hear your explanation of that when I return.

My love to your mother. She reminds me in so many ways of my mother, and I could not pay her a higher compliment. Please tell Patrick Joseph (also known as Billy Joe) I'm sorry for not saying good-bye. I will miss him fiercely. Tell him he's got the loudest whistle of anyone I know.

I shall return in about six months. To what I cannot say.

David

My dearest Molly,

I am sorry that I am saying good-bye in this way. I know it shall make you cry (yet again). Once the tears are gone, you will see that this is best. I could not bear the thoughts of seeing you every day and only nodding politely to you or smiling like amiable strangers passing on a sidewalk. Perhaps, in six months' time, I will be able to be around you without being swept away in the depths of those beautiful eyes, or in the joy of your laughter. I shall miss you more fiercely than I can express. Maybe by then, I can bear the thought of being "just friends."

Please try not to relive our last conversation, for I know you well enough to know that you shall take all the blame upon yourself, and leave me, who caused it all, innocent in your mind. (Is it any wonder that I love you so?) What hurts most is that you see me more clearly than I see myself, that you know me more honestly than I know myself.

I read in the New Testament where John the Baptist went out into

*the desert and found holiness there. Perhaps six months in our barren
red rock country will do me good as well.*

*There is so much more I would like to say, but words and time fail
me. I love you. I'm sorry for making you cry so often.*

David

Monday, April 14, 1879

As David came out of the dining room of the Parowan Hotel, he
stopped dead. Carl Bradford was in the lobby, speaking to the desk clerk.

"Carl?"

Carl spun around, then said to the clerk, "Oh, there he is right now.
Thank you."

They came together in the center of the lobby and shook hands. "This
is a shock," David said. "What brings you up here to Parowan?"

"I hear you're leaving tomorrow."

"Yes. In fact, you're lucky you caught me. I'm going up to Paragonah
later this morning. That's where the company is forming up. We leave at
first light." Then, as he watched Carl's face, he raised one hand as though
to push him away. "I hope you've not come to try to change my mind,
Carl."

He shook his head, then reached in his pocket and extracted an envelope. "Nope. Just delivering your mail." David took it, preparing to refuse it, but when he saw the name in the top lefthand corner, his mouth
dropped open. It was not from Molly. "From Abby?"

Carl nodded. "She was very anxious that you get this before you left."

He was dumbfounded. "You rode twenty miles just to bring me a letter?"

Carl grinned. "It seemed to be very important to her." Then he stuck
out his hand. "Good luck, David. See you in six months."

He stared at the man's hand for a moment, then slowly shook it.
"Thank you, Carl."

Back in his room, David sat on the bed and took out his pocketknife. He slit the envelope open, not sure he was ready to be chastised for how shabbily he had treated Molly. But finally curiosity got the better of him and he extracted the folded sheets of paper. He counted them. Three pages. He took a deep breath, returned the knife to his pocket and began to read.

Dear David,

    I wish to tell you a story.

He laughed in spite of himself. How perfectly Abby. No preamble. No mention of what had happened. Just raise the gun, pick your target, and fire.

    Supposedly, this is a true story. In a way I'm glad that you are not here to interrupt me as I tell it, for I know this will greatly irritate you, especially in your present mood. But our friendship compels me to share it with you.

He chuckled again, knowing that she had him pegged exactly.

    In India there is a religious sect that has great reverence for life. They don't eat meat of any kind. They never harm fish, birds, animals, or insects. They feel so strongly about it that they even watch where they step so they don't accidentally step on an ant or a bug. One day some Christian missionaries came to that area and began to preach about Jesus. When the people found out that Christians did not share their reverence for living things, they refused to listen to them anymore. One frustrated missionary tried to convince them that their beliefs were extreme, that this was more than was expected by God. When he failed to do so, he decided to confront them with the inconsistency of their own position.

    He offered the leader of the sect a glass of water. After he had drank it, the missionary took an eyedropper and put a drop of that same water on a glass slide and put it under a microscope. "Look," he told

the man. When the man looked into the microscope, he saw swarms of
bacteria, amoebae, and other microscopic creatures. "Those are all
living things," the missionary said triumphantly, "and you just drank
them all. See? It isn't possible for you to live consistently with your be-
liefs." What do you suppose the man did next?

He stopped. What an odd story. Carl had ridden forty miles round-trip
to share this? And then he frowned. "Oh, please!" he muttered. "Don't tell
me that the man converted to Christianity and lived happily ever after."
But her next line took him totally aback.

> *He broke the microscope!*
> *Before I say more, I want to make something very clear. This is not*
> *about Jens Nielson. This is not about your father. And believe it or not,*
> *it's not about you and Molly. This is about you. And it needs to be said.*

His lips pressed into a line. He could almost hear her voice, daring him
to disagree.

> *The reason you are in such pain is that you are a microscope*
> *breaker, but down deep you are much too honest with yourself to be*
> *comfortable with that. Let me explain. That day after conference, when*
> *we were at the dinner table, we were all shocked by the vehemence of*
> *your feelings about Jens Nielson. As you talked, I kept asking myself,*
> *"Why did Jens Nielson's call make David so angry?" You said yourself*
> *that it was none of your business, especially since he asked to go. Then*
> *I decided it was really driven by what happened with Silas Smith earlier.*
> *You were angry with him for putting you in such an awkward position.*
> *A Church leader had extended a call without knowing all of the indi-*
> *vidual circumstances. And then to have it not cancelled.*
> *I can just hear you now, David. "It wasn't a call, it was an invita-*
> *tion." BAM! Don't like the idea of it being a call? Well, then, just smash*
> *the microscope and say it was only an invitation.*
> *Then comes the real blow. Just when you're getting things back to*
> *normal, along comes a letter from Box B. Talk about the ultimate*

"mistake"! How dare they call your father? He just came to Cedar City. He already has a mission call. And then, to add insult to injury, while you're still seething about that, Molly announces that it's over for her.

Oh, David, what irony. When you finally agree to pray with Molly about your situation, the whole mountain caves in on you. So much for a Heavenly Father who blesses His children and answers their prayers, right?

Please don't think I am making light of this. I weep for your pain even as I write this. (Well, that's metaphorically speaking. As you know, the Lord shorted Abigail McKenna on tear ducts when she was born. I think he gave them all to Molly.)

You are especially not going to like this next part, so please take a deep breath before you continue. Or you may want to bang your head against the wall a couple of times.

"Oh, Abby," he laughed. "And you think I have a gift of getting under your skin?"

Here is a question for you. Did you ever consider that Molly is right, that what has now happened was your answer? Not HER answer, YOUR answer. I'm not talking about you and Molly now. I don't wish to speak about that. Think about it. Silas Smith calls you to go with him on the exploring party. You tell him no, flatly refusing to even consider it. But what if the Lord wants you to go? What if He needs you there? Or, more likely, what if YOU need to be there? But you kick back. You won't even give it a second thought. So the Lord says, "Does he think he can simply ignore Me?" Oh, David, for a man who believes that God is off somewhere in the universe doing other things, it must be terribly difficult for you when it appears not only that He is there, but that He has chosen not to bless you but to thwart you, to block you at every turn. That has got to be particularly unsettling.

Jesus once said of some people that "seeing, they see not, and hearing, they hear not." In another place in the scriptures, the Lord said, "wo unto the blind who will not see." Am I being too harsh on you,

David? Perhaps. Particularly at this time when you are in so much pain. But I use the following examples to make my point:

Example 1. You are completely alone out in the wilds when four men attack you—five, if you count the one watching the horses. They catch you totally by surprise, disarm you, hold you under the barrel of a rifle, and what happens? By this quite remarkable and marvelous coincidence, Tillie reacts violently when one of the Indians tries to mount her. That distracts the others and—my, how fortunate for David Draper.

Example 2. When the McKennas are called to leave, David Draper is sick at heart because that means he and Molly are going to be separated right when things are finally going well. Molly announces to David that she has started to pray about it. Then, by this quite remarkable and marvelous coincidence, the very next morning Molly's father offers David a job that will not only keep them from being separated but will actually draw them together like never before.

"Right," he muttered darkly. "And now look what He's done to us."

Final example. You and your father are living in Yorkshire, England, where you have never so much as even heard of a people called the Mormons or a place called Utah. But through a tragic series of events, you have to flee your home. You make your way to Liverpool, and by this remarkable and marvelous coincidence, someone just happens to mention to you that there is another shipping agent called the Mormons. You and your father go there and learn that the only possible way for you to get the cheaper passage is to—

"No!" he said angrily, dropping the letter on his lap. "If God wanted us to come to America, why not just let my mother live? Why allow Rhodes to steal our money? Now who's not facing reality?" But after a moment, he picked the letter up again and continued to read.

—the only possible way for you to get the cheaper passage is to convert to Mormonism. Thus you come to Utah, end up in Cedar City,

where you meet this incredibly difficult person named Abigail McKenna who keeps insisting that you take another look through the microscope.

So I say only this, David, and then I'll close. Did it never occur to you that when you have to use the words "remarkable and marvelous coincidence" again and again to describe what has happened, perhaps "coincidence" is no longer the right word?

I know that you discount our feelings of faith and belief as being the product of our own emotional makeup, or perhaps because we were born and raised (some would say indoctrinated) in Mormonism, but I would say this. After Molly told me what happened between you and her, and then we learned that you were gone, I had the strongest feeling that you were finally where the Lord wanted you to be. That you were finally doing what the Lord wanted you to do.

Sorry, but I do feel that way. If that is too completely uncomfortable for you, then just grab a hammer and swing away. You shall be in all of our prayers.

> *Your friend always (I hope),*
> *Abby*

BOOK V

EXPLORATION

1879

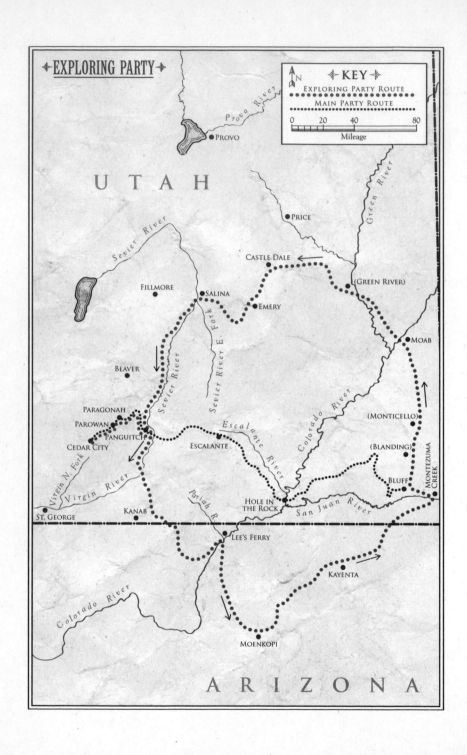

CHAPTER 37

David had never participated in a full wagon train before, but he had seen a few over the years, and they were a sight to behold. With the coming of the transcontinental railroad, the great wagon trains that had gone west across the Oregon/Mormon Trail had become a thing of the past. But David had read of one that had over two hundred wagons strung out along the trail for nearly five miles. As he looked on their little company, here to the north of Paragonah in the first light of morning, it seemed somewhat of an understatement compared with that. There were only a dozen wagons, a couple of hundred head of stock, about twenty-five men, and two families. Each of the families had four children aged thirteen and younger.

Though the scale of their trek was smaller, there was still much confusion. Cows bawled, horses snorted, mules brayed, dogs barked. Men shouted back and forth to each other as the two mothers tried to keep their children out of the way. The children, of course, thought it all a grand adventure, and they darted in and out, screeching and yelling.

David sat back in the saddle, enjoying it all. For the moment, he had nothing to do. Eventually, Silas planned to use him as a scout, but for the first few days, they would be on established roads, and the greater need was to keep their stock from bolting back home.

He stood up in the stirrups and looked over the herd milling around him. All the action on the road was starting to make the animals restless. He turned to Nielson—or Niels—Dalley, head wrangler for the company, who sat astride his horse on the far side of the herd. Niels, like David and most of the other men, was about David's age and not married yet. "They're getting anxious to be on the move," David called.

"Yeah," Niels called back. "I'm with them. What's the holdup?"

"Silas is getting the wagons into line now," David said. "Hopefully then we can move."

David hooked one leg up and over his saddle horn and turned again to watch the company. All twelve wagons were here, and Silas Smith and his two lead scouts, Kumen Jones and George Hobbs, were riding up and down trying to get them lined up in some kind of order.

This was not as simple as it seemed. The recommendation given in the letter of call from Salt Lake City had been that each wagon be drawn by four horses or mules. That was wise, considering the country they were going to be crossing, but handling four animals was always more challenging than handling two. And this was the first day. The teams had not had a chance yet to settle into the routine of the trail.

The wagon directly east of David was trying to pull into its place between two other wagons, but the driver was having trouble. David saw at once that he was not experienced. He was hauling back on the reins at the same time he was calling out to the horses to move. "Ease up a little," David murmured. "Give 'em some room."

He nudged Tillie forward, watching more closely now. The animals were confused and started to balk, tossing their heads and snorting. The lead span began backing up even as the rear two were pushing forward. "Whoa there!"

David jerked forward. It was a woman's voice. He dug his heels into Tillie's flanks, and she leaped forward. There was the sharp crack and rattle of chains as one of the horses kicked back against the whiffletrees. In another minute they were going to get tangled in the traces, and that meant serious trouble.

"Pull 'em out of the line," he shouted, waving his hand. "Come around and make another try."

If the driver heard, she gave no sign. From the rapid, spasmodic movements of her hands, he could tell she was near panic. "Whoa! Whoa!" she screamed. This only spooked the horses all the more. Out of the corner of his eye, David saw Silas or one of the other horsemen wheel around and start for her too, but he was too far away.

David swung down from the saddle and hit the ground running. "Move over, ma'am," he shouted as he reached the wagon and vaulted up into the seat. "I'll take 'em."

She shoved the reins at him, and as he took them, he caught a glimpse of a very white and frightened face. The off-horse in the front team half reared, neighing wildly. Now, all around, men were racing in to help.

David pulled the left set of reins hard to the left, snapped all the reins hard across the horses' backs, and yelled, "Hee yaw! Gee-up, boys! Gee-up!"

Startled by the sudden authority in both hands and voice, the four horses lunged forward, hitting the tugs, turning sharply to the left as they did so. David saw the wagon ahead of them rock a little as the nearest horse pushed against it, barely clearing it. Then they were free. David pulled them out into the road, well clear of the other wagons.

He heard the woman make some sound beside him, but he couldn't tell what she said and didn't have time to find out. "Easy, boys," he soothed. "Easy, now."

Pulling together at last, the four animals quickly settled into their normal rhythm, and the potential crisis was past. David made a wide circle in the adjoining field, brought them back onto the road, and pulled them into their place in line without incident. "Whoa!" he called. As they came to a stop, he reached down and set the wheel brakes. Only then did he turn to look at the woman. "There you go," he said, giving her a warm smile.

"Thank you," she said, her voice trembling.

David lifted a finger to the brim of his hat. "No problem, ma'am. They're just a little skittish this morning. Once they get on the road, they'll settle down."

She nodded, her eyes filled with gratitude. She was older than David, perhaps in her mid-thirties. She had dark brown hair, light blue eyes, a thin face with pale skin. There was a scattering of freckles on her cheekbones, but these were nearly obscured by the dark shadows around her eyes. She looked as if she had not slept for some time. Her accent was pure British, and . . .

David heard a whimpering sound behind him. He turned to look back into the wagon. Four children were sitting on a quilt, eyes wide and frightened. Two older boys, maybe ten and twelve or thirteen, sat behind a girl about Billy Joe's age. She had a little boy sitting in her lap. She was holding onto him around the neck as if he were about to fall off a cliff. He was the one whimpering; David wasn't sure if he had been frightened by the horses or if he was on the verge of being strangled by his sister.

"Are we gonna die, mister?" the girl cried.

David gravely shook his head. "No, sweetheart," he said in the same soothing tone he had used with the animals. "We just turned the horses around to get back in line."

"Promise?"

He shifted the reins to one hand and quickly drew his finger across his chest. "Cross my heart and hope to die, poke a stick in my eye, if I ever tell a lie," he said solemnly.

The woman beside him laughed softly. "It's all right, Emmy. No one's going to die. So let go of John's neck before he turns blue."

Only then did the girl realize what she had been doing. Embarrassed, she let her little brother go and laughed nervously. The boy scrambled away, ducking behind one of his older brothers for safety.

David turned back around to face the woman and handed the reins across to her. "Be sure you release the brake when you're ready to move," he said.

"Thank you so much," the woman said. "My husband has been teaching me to drive a team, but . . ." Her head dropped. "But I guess we didn't get to backing up yet."

He let it pass, knowing that talking about it would only embarrass her more. "You're from England. Down around London town, I would guess."

Her eyes lifted in surprise. "Middlesex, actually. How did you know that?"

"Cuz Ah be born in South Yorkshire meself, o'er near Barnsley, if'n the truth be known."

She cocked her head. "So which is the real you? Yorkshire drawl or southern Utah twang?"

He laughed, finding himself liking her immediately. "Combination of both, I guess."

She stuck out her hand. "My name is Mary Elizabeth Davis." When he didn't respond to that, she added, "James Davis is my husband." That still didn't register with him. "We're one of the two families who are going with you and staying there once we find out where 'there' is."

"Oh," he said. And then it clicked, and he fought back a startled look. James Davis was the man who had stood up in the priesthood meeting held in Cedar City after the stake conference. He was the one who said that he had been shown in a dream that they were to answer their mission call in spite of the fact that his wife's health was not good and she was carrying a child. Without thinking, his eyes dropped to where the roundness of her stomach showed beneath her dress. "You're the one who's—" He caught himself just in time.

She was blushing, but held his eye. "Yes, I'm the one having a baby."

Now it was David who felt his face go hot, for he was remembering the irritation he had felt that a husband would put the Church over the needs of his wife. And now here he was sitting beside her. He didn't know what to say.

"And you're Brother Draper." It wasn't a question.

"You know me?"

"I know of you. I've seen you in Church with the McKennas." Another smile, only this one teasing him a little. "And who in Cedar City doesn't know about you and Molly?"

A voice behind him blurted out, "You're the one who captured those outlaws?"

David turned. It was the oldest boy, a lean and gangly kid in his early teens with hair that hadn't seen a comb in a while. He was leaning forward, his expression one of awe.

"Eddie," Sister Davis said, "don't be impertinent." Turning to David, she said, "Let me introduce my family to you. Our oldest son, the one with his mouth open and his eyes bugged out, is Edward. He just turned thirteen ten days ago. Next to him is James Henry—we call him Young James, or Jimmie—he'll be nine in October. And this is our only daughter, Emily Ellen. We all call her Emmy. She'll be six in June. And our baby is John Orson, who will soon be three."

David swept off his hat and nodded. "It is a pleasure to meet you." Then to her, he said, "That's one passel of mighty fine-looking children." He winked at Emmy and leaned in closer. She had long, carrot-colored hair that fell down her back in soft curls. Her eyes were a bright green and looked out over a pug nose and a mouth that, at the moment, was pulled down as she gazed at him. A generous dose of her mother's freckles added to the effect and made her absolutely adorable.

"Where did you get those beautiful eyes? From your mother?"

She snorted in disgust. "No, silly. Mama's eyes are blue. Mine are green."

He reared back, pretending shock, and turned to her mother. "Well, would you look at that. I think you are right, Miss Emily."

"I got my eyes from Heavenly Father," she said, quite indignant now.

"Ah. And what about those freckles? I didn't think Heavenly Father gave those away."

"Those are angel kisses," she shot right back at him. "That's what Mama says."

He straightened, completely charmed by this little pixie. "I see. There must have been a lot of angels come to say good-bye when you left heaven."

She giggled, then looked at her mother. "He's nice, Mama," she whispered.

"So *are* you the one who captured that outlaw and ran off all them Indians?" Eddie persisted.

"Eddie!" his mother exclaimed.

David ignored her. "*All* them Indians happened to be only four," he said confidentially, "but don't tell the others. It makes a much better story your way."

Sister Davis suddenly jerked up. "Oh, good. Here comes James."

David turned to see a man coming at a full run toward them. "Mary, are you all right?" he called even before he reached her.

"Yes, dear. We're fine. Thanks to Brother Draper's quick thinking."

"I'm so sorry," he said, reaching up and taking her hand. "I was back with our extra horses. Someone just told me you were having problems."

"Everything's all right, James. Really."

David stood and jumped down beside her husband. "She did good," he told him. "She didn't panic or do anything foolish."

Emily poked her head over the side of the wagon. "Brother Draper saved our lives, Daddy."

James laughed and extended his hand. "If you saved Emmy's life, then I am much obliged."

David took it, liking the firmness of the grip. James had much the same accent as his wife, only with a little deeper rounding of the vowel sounds. "Glad I was nearby," David said. He looked up at Emily. "After all, it's not every day you get to save a beautiful damsel in distress."

She put her hands on her hips, and her lower lip jutted out. "I'm not a damsel."

David bowed low. "Beggin' your pardon, m'lady." Then to her father, "It's not every day you get to save the life of a beautiful *princess* in distress."

Emily's hand flew to her mouth and she giggled softly.

He turned back to Brother Davis. "The horses are feeling all the excitement. They'll settle down once we hit the road." He looked around. "Speaking of which, it looks like it's about time to do so. I'd better get mounted."

James Davis turned and walked with him back to Tillie. "I really do appreciate it, Brother Draper, I—"

"Please," David inserted quickly. "We're going to be together for the next six months. How about just David?" He was trying to feel a little peeved at this man who was dragging a pregnant wife and four young children into the wilderness, but he was having a hard time doing it. James was as pleasant and likeable as his wife.

"And I'm Jim to everyone but my wife. She still insists on calling me James. But thank you again." He lowered his voice, glancing back over his shoulder. "I feel terrible making her drive a wagon, especially in her condition, but when you have two wagons there's no choice. I'm teaching Eddie how to drive," he went on, "but he still needs a little more experience."

David picked up Tillie's reins. He put a foot in the stirrup and swung up into the saddle. "You have a fine family, Jim. That little Emmy is a charmer."

His eyes softened. "I think so too." He started away, then turned back. "We'd be right pleased to have you join us for supper tonight, wherever that happens to be."

"The first few nights with the cattle will be a challenge and I'll be riding night herd, but once we get them settled into a routine, I would be honored to join you. Thank you."

Sunday, April 20, 1879

In his early life, David had never given much thought to Sunday other than it being the best day of the week because the mines were closed. It had become the Sabbath only when at age thirteen he had arrived in Coalville with his father. Every Sunday, in spite of numerous and vigorous protests from his son, John Draper had taken David to church, and Sunday had become not only a day of rest but a day of worship. (Though, David thought wryly, to be truly honest, it was a day of worship for his father, and more like a day of endurance for David.)

That pattern had basically ended when he turned sixteen and left home to go out on his own. When he was visiting his father on a Sunday, he went to church with him. Occasionally he would visit a local ward if he happened to be in town, but mostly Sunday became his day again—to rest, to get things done, to do something for himself.

All of that had ended about eight months ago when he had come to Cedar City to accept a job as mail rider and had bumped headlong into the McKennas. Since then, worship services had become a part of his life. Although he didn't find them all that objectionable, if it had been totally up to him, he probably would not have gone every Sunday.

David was thinking about all of this because he had just come from their first Sunday worship service on the trail. It had been simple. The people were seated on the ground around Silas Smith's wagon. They sang a hymn and opened with prayer. The sacrament was passed—small chunks of bread baked in Dutch ovens, and two tin cups of water passed from person to person. Silas Smith took about half an hour and spoke of their mission and the importance of keeping faith. They sang another hymn, had a closing prayer, and that was it.

There was never any question about participating in religious activities. Mormon wagon trains traveled on Sunday only if they were in critical circumstances, such as having to press on to reach water or to avoid danger. There was always a worship service on Sunday—and usually on Thursday evenings as well. In addition, each day the trumpet would blow at 4:30 or 5:00 A.M. to wake everyone up, and then at six it blew again to call everyone together for morning prayers. At 9:00 P.M., the trumpet signaled time for lights out, and they would gather for evening prayers before retiring. Religion and religious worship seemed to permeate everything in the Mormon way of life, and although that left David feeling somewhat uncomfortable, he grudgingly admitted that at least they weren't Sunday-only Christians.

Most of the company stayed around Silas's wagon to visit, but David slipped away, preferring to be alone with his thoughts. Now he sat under a cedar tree, his back up against the rough bark, and contemplated things. They had been on the trail for six days, and he pretty well knew everyone now—some better, some less. There was a good spirit among the group, and David was quickly growing comfortable with them.

Then, before he could catch himself, his thoughts turned to his father. Had he left Cedar City by now? He certainly had been anxious enough to leave. How long would he stay in Salt Lake City? David had left Cedar City eleven days ago. Theoretically, his father could have gone to Salt Lake, gotten whatever it was he was supposed to get there, and boarded a train for New York or Boston by now. He might even have booked passage on a steamship.

When he had passed through Panguitch yesterday afternoon, he had thought about writing a letter and sending it to his father. In another few days, there would be no more settlements and no more post offices, so if he was going to do it, it had to be pretty soon. But he had finally rejected the idea. He had no idea of the address of the mission headquarters in Liverpool.

But he had no excuse not to write to the McKennas, especially Molly. David's replacement as mail rider would be through before long and could take his letter back to Cedar City. But he didn't write. He also thought of answering Abby's charge that he was a microscope breaker, but quicky nixed that as well. He could hardly write Abby and not Molly. So, in the end, he did nothing.

He turned his head at the sound of footsteps. It was Jimmie and Emmy Davis, the two middle children of Jim and Mary Davis. He stood up and brushed the dirt and juniper needles from his backside. "Hey, you two," he called as they approached. "Where are you off to?"

They were both still dressed in their Sunday clothes. Jimmie's hair had been plastered down with water earlier, but now sprung loose again in all directions. His white shirt was unbuttoned at the neck and both wrists. He was a boy who looked greatly relieved to be done with church.

Emmy looked more like she was going to church, not coming from it. Her red hair was brushed out and looked like the embers of a campfire. She was in a blue gingham dress and white bonnet, but wore her walking shoes—heavy brown clunkers. And yet, as he watched her coming, arms swinging, eyes sparkling, he decided even the shoes fit. This was Emily, a spunky leprechaun in a blue dress and brown clunkers.

"We came to get you," Jimmie said as they reached him. "Mama sent us to find you."

Emily nodded vigorously. "Daddy said you promised to eat dinner with us."

"Oh, yes." David had made excuses several times now, but the herd had settled down, and starting tomorrow, David would begin scouting duties with Kumen Jones, Joe Nielson, and George Hobbs. "Okay. How soon?"

"Mama says to come right now," Emily blurted.

"Are you sure?"

"Yes!" She was very emphatic.

"Eddie wants to show you something, too," Jimmie said. The two of them looked at each other, some secret passing between them, then hid a wave of giggles behind cupped hands.

"Emmy!" Jimmie shushed fiercely. "Don't give it away."

She darted up to him and grabbed his hand. "Come on, David. Let's go."

Dinner, and the time afterwards, turned out not to be as awkward as David had feared. In fact, it proved to be quite delightful. The children were excited to have a guest for dinner, especially one who had driven off a whole tribe of Indians, arrested all of the cattle thieves in Utah Territory, and who, just a few days before, had raced to their rescue and saved Emily from certain death. Mary, a little embarrassed by their unabashed hero worship, kept trying to tone them down, but David waved her away. This was fun, and it was good for him right now.

Finally, their parents sent them off to the river to wash the cooking pots and the dishes. Jimmie and Emmy mightily protested, begging their mother to let Eddie show David the big surprise first, but both father and mother were adamant, and finally the three adults were alone.

"I am so sorry, David," Mary said. "I shan't let them bother you too much if I can help it."

"No apologies are either necessary or accepted," David said. "Your children are wonderful, and I enjoyed every minute of it. I never had brothers or sisters, so this is really great for me."

"Well," Jim said, sitting down beside his wife on a blanket, "thank you for being so patient with them. They can be pretty nonsensical at times."

David chuckled. "'Shan't.' 'Nonsensical.' Do you know how good it is to listen to you two? Your accents remind me so much of my mother." He turned to Mary. He shook his head, his tone suddenly wistful. "It really is quite remarkable."

"Mary told me you're from Yorkshire," Jim said. "I would never have guessed that."

"Thanks to my mother. She worked very hard to teach me to speak more proper. She said I had a good ear for language."

"Was she from London, then?" Mary asked.

"Near there. She was born and raised in Battersea, southwest of London."

"Know exactly where it is," Jim said. "It's just a few miles from where we grew up."

From then on, David had no problem talking with them. He asked them questions and listened to their responses. Jim answered a few of them, but seemed content to let his wife do most of the talking. And while David had thought of Mary Davis as being somewhat reserved by nature, she opened up and talked freely about herself and her family, and seemed pleased—almost eager—to do so.

They had both been born in Middlesex County, which included London in its boundaries. Both were raised in working-class homes. Both had been converted to the Church there and emigrated to America together. After arriving in Salt Lake, they were sent to Cedar City.

"That was right after we were married for eternity in the Endowment House in Salt Lake City," Jim said. He turned and smiled at his wife. "April twenty-third, eighteen sixty-four. Fifteen years ago this next Wednesday, actually."

She was momentarily startled. "Oh dear. This Wednesday? It is, isn't it."

He laughed. "Aye, and for our anniversary, I thought we might ask David to watch the children for the day so we could take a sailboat ride down the River Thames." Of course, he pronounced it *Tems*, not *Thaymes*, as Americans tended to do.

Her eyes softened. "Ah," she sighed, "now you're making me homesick, James."

"Molly told me that when you first came to Cedar City, you lived in a dugout."

"True," Mary said.

"For almost three years," Jim added.

"Our first two children were born there," Mary went on. "Mary and Edward."

"Mary?" David asked. "Do you have a daughter I haven't met?"

A shadow passed over her face. "Mary was our firstborn. She died when just a baby."

"I'm sorry," David said, feeling stupid for asking the question.

"That seems to be our lot in life," James said quietly.

Close to tears, Mary kept her head down and stared at her hands. "We've actually had four girls and four boys," she whispered. "We lost Mary at two months. One son died at fourteen months, and two other girls passed away, at six months and five and a half months."[1]

David was shocked. Four children! And all at a tender age. He could barely fathom what that would cost a mother and father. And suddenly his mother was in his thoughts again. Here was another woman who had faced terrible loss and tragedy. Why hadn't Mary Davis turned bitter, like his mother? Why wasn't she cursing God? Four out of eight children? If God was so good to them, like Jim seemed to think, why hadn't He blessed them in this aspect of their lives? These were good people. They were trying to be faithful.

He realized that she was watching him closely, puzzled by the expression that had come over his face. "So you're hoping this one is a girl?" he said quickly.

She managed a smile. "It is."

The conviction with which she spoke surprised him. "It is?"

"Yes." Her smile noticeably warmed. "Emily told Heavenly Father that she already has enough brothers. This one better be a little sister or she's sending it back."

"I see," David said, chuckling softly. "If I was Heavenly Father, I'd probably not cross Emily, either. She's pretty strong-minded for such a little wisp of a thing."

"Who, me?" Emily called.

They turned to see the four children returning, arms laden with dishes. Even little Johnnie, not yet three, carried a small teakettle as he toddled along. They trooped to their mother and let her do a quick inspection. "Very good," she said. "Put them away in the wagon."

"*Then* can I show David my surprise?" Eddie wailed.

"Yes," Emmy cried. "Can we? Can we?"

Mary laughed, "Yes, children. If David is up to it."

David shrugged. "It takes a lot to surprise me, Eddie."

Off they raced to the wagon. There was a clank of dishes and metal; then, a moment later, they all reappeared, Eddie in the lead. He was holding a piece of paper in both hands. Jimmie and Emily were right behind him, whispering instructions to him, eyes dancing with excitement.

When Eddie's father saw what his son had in his hand, he groaned, but his wife poked him sharply. "Don't give it away," she said.

David was a little taken aback to see that the sorrow that had filled her eyes just moments before was completely gone now. She seemed almost as excited about this as the children.

They all gathered around David, the parents leaning in to see, the children crowding into a half circle. Up close now, David saw that what Eddie held was not a sheet of paper but a letter-sized envelope with the flap tucked down inside it.

"We found these yesterday here in camp," Eddie said. He tipped the envelope enough that David could read some crudely scrawled words on the front of it. He looked more closely. *RATTLESNAKE EGGS*. That was scrawled in rough letters across the top. On each corner, written diagonally, were smaller letters: *Handle with care. Keep warm. Do not shake. Danger.*

He looked up at Eddie. "You found rattlesnake eggs?" he asked skeptically. "Come on. You don't expect me to believe that, do you?"

Eddie just nodded, very solemn now. "Wanna see?"

David looked around at the others. "All right. What's the catch?"

"It's no joke," Emmy said gravely. "Really."

"Give it to him, Eddie," Jimmie said. "Let him see for himself."

Eddie extended the envelope toward David. "All right. But be careful. Don't take them out. Just peek inside."

David looked to Mary for some clue as to what was going on. She gave him an enigmatic smile. "Only one way to know for sure," she said.

Still highly suspicious, David took the envelope. Eddie quickly stepped back, as if to make sure he would be clear if something happened.

Laughing, knowing that something was up but not sure what it was, David gently felt the contents through the envelope. There was some kind of a bump in the center, then a flatter, wirelike something surrounding it. He looked at the circle of faces. They had all gone very still now, squirming with anticipation. Carefully, he pulled the flap open with one finger. He couldn't see inside, so he used his finger to spread the envelope open.

BRRRPP! The rattling sound was like a gunshot in the silence. At the same instant, something vibrated hard against the palm of his hand. With a yell, David flung the envelope into the air and fell back. Heart pounding, mouth suddenly dry, he watched in shock as it fell to the earth. The family exploded with a roar of delight. Emily shrieked with laughter. Jimmie was dancing up and down, whooping like an Indian. Eddie was grinning like he had just won the three-legged race at the county fair. Mary and Jim were chuckling.

"What in the world?" David exclaimed. His face went red as they laughed all the harder.

The envelope had landed next to Mary, so she picked it up and handed it to David. "Take a look," she said, barely repressing a giggle, sounding very much like Emmy at that moment.

David took the envelope, somewhat gingerly now, and felt it carefully again. Nothing had changed. Carefully he opened it wider, steeling himself for another surprise. Then he snorted in disgust. "You've got to be kidding!" he cried.

"I told you it was rattlesnake eggs," Eddie chortled.

David reached in and pulled out the contents. What he held was a V-shaped piece of spring steel. A rubber band had been stretched across the two upper ends of the V. In the center of the rubber band a large coat button, about an inch in diameter, had been threaded. Not sure exactly what he was looking at, he held it up, giving them a querying look.

Mary reached out and took it from him. "Watch," she said. She held the bottom of the clip in one hand, then started winding the button with the other. Still puzzled, David watched as the rubber band began to twist and tighten, pulling the two ends of the clip closer together.

And then he got it. "Give me that," he growled.

Holding the button so it couldn't unwind, Mary picked up the envelope, inserted the clip, then carefully tucked the flap in. Only then did she hand it back. "There you go," she said, suppressing a smile. "Rattlesnake eggs."

He took it, shaking his head. As he had done before, he held the envelope up and used one finger to open the top again. *BRRRPP!* Even though he was expecting it this time, it still made him jump. The vibration against his hand, coupled with a sound that was eerily like that of a coiled diamondback, still gave him a jolt.

Once again the children shrieked with laughter. Their little joke had gone off perfectly. Feeling sheepish, David turned to them. "Okay, you three," he said darkly, "you know this means war. You hear me? I will get even. That is a promise."

Note

1. The conversation between James and Mary Elizabeth Davis and David Draper, who is a fictional character, is obviously not based on any known record. The details given about their life, however, come from "History of the Life of James Davis" (see Miller, *Hole*, 155).

CHAPTER 38

Wednesday, April 30, 1879

Lee's Ferry proved to be a turning point for the exploring party expedition. To that point, with the exception of Buckskin Mountain, they had traveled along well-established roads. While crossing the Buckskins, they had taken a wrong turn and ended up having to unload the wagons and lower them over a fifty-foot cliff by ropes. But, other than that, it had been easy going. They had never been more than a day and a half's travel from one of the settlements. They had frequently passed isolated homesteads or ranches where they could replenish their food or get help with needed repairs. And the only Indians they had seen were a few individual Utes or Paiutes going peacefully about their business in the settlements.

Lee's Ferry was named for John D. Lee, who was sent by the Mormon Church in 1872 to provide ferry service at the confluence of the Paria and Colorado Rivers. Paria Canyon provided a natural opening in the otherwise impenetrable Colorado River gorge. Lee was no longer there, having been arrested and eventually executed in 1877 for his yet unclear part in the infamous Mountain Meadows Massacre. That had happened west of Cedar City during the Utah War of 1857, but even now, more than twenty years later, and two years after Lee's death, his guilt or innocence was still being hotly debated all across southern Utah.

His widow, Emma Lee, and some of her children, along with a few others who helped run the ferry, lived nearby at what they called the Lonely Dell Ranch. What they had created in that arid, desolate, red rock canyon country was astonishing. It was a virtual oasis in a vast desert. With unlimited water from two rivers, they cleared about twenty-five acres of land

and put it under cultivation. They had fruit trees, sugar cane, cantaloupe and other melons, several kinds of vegetables, and deep green fields of alfalfa. In addition to beef and milk cows and a few horses, they raised pigs, chickens, and ducks, supplemented their diet with fish from the river, and kept several beehives. Travelers were amazed to find they could purchase honey, milk, butter, cheese, eggs, fish, ham, bacon, and beef—either fresh or dried as jerky. The two rivers also provided abundant firewood in the form of driftwood deposited each year during spring runoff.[1]

It was as if the little exploring company from Paragonah had been wandering in the wilderness for forty years (even though it was only seventeen days) and had somehow stumbled into a land of milk and honey—literally. It was such a rejuvenating experience that several proposed that they lay over for several days to recuperate.

But Silas Smith was unbendable. They arrived just before noon. Once they were settled in camp, their captain called a meeting and announced they would start ferrying across the river first thing in the morning. They had come about 175 miles now, but that wasn't even halfway yet, and by far the worst portion of the journey still lay ahead. In the meantime, they should rest up, do their laundry, purchase what they needed, and otherwise enjoy their brief stay here.

Since leaving the high elevations, 6,600 feet in the Panguitch area, they had dropped about three thousand feet. They had also traveled a hundred and fifty miles farther south. Down this far, it was no longer spring. The daytime temperatures were now consistently in the high eighties or low nineties. Feet and hands that had been tender and soft when they started were thick with calluses. Faces and arms that had been wintry-pale when they left were now a deep brown. The children looked like little Indians, and often the boys went without their shirts.

As David came out of the trading post, he heard the cries of the children and turned to look. Just above the west ferry landing, the riverbank curved gently inward, making a small, shallow area where the water whirled in slow eddies. The Harriman and Davis children were making the most of this "swimming pool," as Emmy called it. David saw that Mary

Davis and Sister Harriman were sitting nearby in the shade of a juniper tree, enjoying the chance to relax.

As he watched the children for a moment, he was once again astonished at their resilience. They seemed to bear up under the rigors of the trail better than the men, women, or even animals. He saw Emmy scoop up a bucket of water, sneak up behind Eddie, and dump it on his head. In seconds he had scooped *her* up and dumped her unceremoniously into the shallow waters.

That gave David an idea. He walked quickly to his campsite and put his purchases into his saddlebags. Then he strode into the forest of juniper trees that lined the banks of the river and began searching along the ground. In two minutes he found what he was looking for—a two-foot length of dead juniper branch that was dark grey and, like most juniper branches, twisted and gnarled. He picked it up, brushed it off, then sighted down it. Perfect! Grinning broadly, he stuck it in his belt at the small of his back and started for the river.

Pausing only long enough to tell Mary to be sure to watch, he strode on down to where the children were playing. Emmy and the younger Harriman children were now sitting in water up to their waists. She saw him and waved. "David, come swim with me."

He waved back, but turned and headed in another direction. About twenty yards away, Jimmie and Eddie and the oldest Harriman boy were digging "canals" to the river with one of their dad's shovels. This was good. He wouldn't be frightening the younger children.

David stopped about ten feet away. "Hey, Eddie."

The thirteen-year-old looked up. The sun was behind David, and Eddie had to squint to see him.

"Remember those rattlesnake eggs?" David called.

Eddie sniggered. "Yep. Wanna see 'em again?"

"No need," David replied. "I think I found the mother." And with that he pulled the juniper branch out from behind his back and gave it a gentle flip toward the boys. Up it went, arching gracefully, rotating in the air as it flew, looking every bit like it was alive.

Jimmie gave a shout and rolled away. The Harriman boy screamed and fell back. Eddie was squatted down over his "canal." He gaped for an instant, then scrambled backwards, howling with fright. The stick hit the sand and gravel right in front of Eddie's jerking feet, bounced once, and slithered to a stop, almost touching the bare flesh. Eddie exploded upwards, tried to run, but tripped and went sprawling.

David ran to the stick and picked it up in one smooth movement. He held it by the "tail" and rolled it back and forth between his fingers, causing it to dance in his hands. "Come on, Eddie," he cried. "She won't hurt you."

And then Eddie saw what it was and started to laugh. He got to his feet, reached out, and took the stick from David. He examined it for a moment as the other two boys edged closer. Then he gave a whoop and slapped his leg. "You got me, David. You got me real good."

"You, my boy," David said solemnly, "have just received what in England is known as your comeuppance." He winked. "I would say that we are now even."

Thursday, May 1, 1879

It was going to be a costly day for the company. Although the Lees were members of the Church, the fact that the exploring company was on an official Church mission made no difference. Income from the ferry was what the Lee family lived on. The fees were set and there would be no exceptions and no discounts. Each wagon with its teams was two dollars. A horse and rider was two dollars, unmounted horses or mules a dollar, and cattle twenty-five cents per head. That added up to a lot of money for a cash-poor company.

They were up at first light and started the wagons down to the ferry landing. The Harrimans crossed first, followed by the Davis family. George Hobbs, one of the four scouts with the party, helped the Harrimans over. George was Sister Harriman's younger brother.

Joe Nielson and Kumen Jones came to help David load the two Davis wagons on, then helped push the ferry out into the current. As they turned to see who was next, David noticed that Silas Smith was standing over near the herd of livestock. That was a little surprising, since the animals would be the last to cross over. Two of Silas's grown sons had accompanied their father on this expedition, and the three of them were conferring now, heads together. Then, as David looked more closely, he saw that Silas had separated out his horses from the rest of the herd. He had about a dozen in addition to the ones pulling his wagon.

Silas looked up, saw David watching him, and motioned him over. "Bring Kumen and Joe," he called. As the three of them started toward the herd, Silas walked toward the river, his sons with him. David, Kumen, and Joe angled so they joined them at the water's edge.

For several seconds, Silas didn't speak. He was looking at the river, his face lined with concern. It was a very intimidating sight that lay before them. They were in the height of the spring runoff. The water was chocolate brown and filled with debris. Branches, driftwood, tumbleweeds, and full-sized juniper logs floated by. David watched one log for a moment, calculating its speed. He estimated that the current was probably moving at five or six miles per hour, faster than a man could comfortably walk.

About half a mile upstream from where they were, the river came out from between high, narrow canyon walls. Another half a mile below them, it entered Marble Canyon, where it again was squeezed into a narrow channel. Even from here they could hear the water roaring in protest. Lee had chosen this site for his ferry because the channel widened out to about a hundred and fifty yards here and the water was relatively smooth. But now, at high water, it was choppy enough to leave tiny whitecaps. And the river was bitter cold.

"We've been talking," Silas said after a moment. "I think we're going to ford the horses."

All three of the other men jerked up at that.

"I know, I know," he said. "But I can't spare that kind of cash, brethren. It'll cost me six dollars for our three wagons. Nothing to be done about that. But at two dollars a head for the three of us, and a dollar more for a dozen horses, that's just more than we can afford."

Kumen Jones had run a cattle spread out west of Cedar City and was one of the most experienced stockmen in the company. "Silas," he said,

choosing his words carefully, "look at that current. And I'll bet ten or fifteen feet out from shore, it's over the horses' heads. They'll have to swim it
most of the way."

"One of those logs hits you or one of the animals," David said, "and
it'll be over. Cost you more than twenty-four dollars if you lose even one."

There was a clipped nod. "Considered all that." He looked at his boys,
all grown and adults now. They nodded in answer to his unasked question.
"But I think we're going to try it."

He turned and looked across the river to where they were unloading
the two Davis wagons. "George Hobbs is already over there. If you three
boys went over with the next load, you'd be there to help us if we get in
trouble." He turned and looked upriver. "We'll take them upstream as far
as possible. That should give us enough angle to cross before we hit the
rapids."

Kumen gave David and Joe a long, searching look. They nodded, and
Joe spoke for all of them. "If you're committed, Silas, we'll be there to pull
you out."

"We're committed," he said in a low voice.

They waited until all twelve wagons were safely on the other side.
Even while they were still unloading Silas's wagon—the last to cross—
David, George Hobbs, Kumen Jones, and Joe Nielson stripped off their pis-
tols and anything else they didn't want to get wet. Each grabbed an extra
lariat; then they called the other men together. The mood was somber, and
David sensed that he was not the only one with a sense of foreboding.

"We're not sure where they'll come out," Kumen began, "so we want
you brethren to space yourself evenly from the ferry landing all the way
down to where the rapids begin."

"They can't get in those rapids," George Hobbs said. "There won't be
any saving them then."

"The four of us will be on horses," Kumen continued. "We'll ride along
with them as we see them coming down, then, when they're close enough,

go out and help them. But, as you know, we can't go out very far or our own horses will be swimming too. That won't do them much good."

No one moved. David turned to James Davis. "Jim, you and Brother Harriman make sure your wives keep the children back. We can't have one of them getting bumped into that current."

"They're clear over there in the trees," Hank Harriman said. "They'll watch them close."

Kumen took a deep breath, then let it out. "Okay. George, give Silas the signal."

⁂

"Here comes the first rider," George Hobbs yelled.

David had already seen him. He squinted, trying to make out who it was. But with the sun glinting off the water and the men laid low over their horses' necks, there was no way to tell. And then, strung out in a jagged line behind the lead rider, David could make out other dark spots coming toward them—horses' heads held high to keep their noses out of the water.

David felt his stomach lurch. They had already covered half of the distance downstream from their starting point but were only about a third of the way across the channel.

"More angle! More angle!" David shouted. He lifted his lariat and started making a loop.

"We're too high," grunted Kumen. "They'll be lucky if they make the ferry landing." He kicked his horse and raced back toward the ferry, which was about a hundred yards away. David followed right behind him. As they pulled up, George raced past them. "I'll have the men below the ferry bunch up closer," he shouted.

Joe Nielson shot past them too. "They're going to need a horse lower down," he called.

David and Kumen were just above the ferry landing. David turned in the saddle, his eyes searching the dark surface of the river. He could make out all three riders now—two in front, leading the way for the horses, and one behind to help any animal that got in trouble.

"It's going to be close," David said. He turned Tillie's head and they plunged into the river. He gasped as the cold water hit his legs. Kumen did the same, going in about twenty yards farther downstream from David.

David urged Tillie into the river until she was chest deep but still on firm footing, his eyes never leaving the dark shapes riding the current. He could make out more detail now. The two lead riders were low over the necks of the horses, one hand twisted in the animals' manes. David could hear them yelling encouragement to their mounts as they fought to keep their horses' heads turned crosswise to the river's flow. The horses' eyes were wild with fright, and their heads bobbed up and down as they lunged against the powerful current.

"Help!" The closest rider had released one hand and was waving wildly. David saw it was Silas Smith. The fear in his voice was evident. Though they were out of the swiftest part of the current, the river was still sweeping them downstream. It looked like they were going to go right past David and Kumen.

David began swinging the lasso. He waited, judging his speed and distance, then threw. He led the horse a little too much, but Silas stood in the stirrups, stretching high, and caught the loop. In one quick movement he had it over his saddle horn and pulled tight. David wheeled Tillie around and urged her out of the water. She grunted as the weight of the other horse hit the line, but she never faltered, and in another thirty seconds, they were both out.

Silas slid off his horse and hit the ground running, shouting at Kumen to throw the rope to his boy. Kumen's throw was better than David's. The loop sailed out, then gracefully settled over the horse's head. Kumen backed his horse up and out of the water, bringing Stephen Smith and his horse with him. Father and son grasped each other's wrists for a brief moment; then again they were off, yelling at Albert, Silas's other son. But Joe was already moving to him, sailing his rope out right into his hands.

They nearly lost the last horse as it was swept into the rapids, but two men there waded out and managed to put a rope around its neck and drag it in.

Five minutes later they were all gathered near the ferry landing. Silas and his boys had blankets around their shoulders, shivering violently. No one was saying much. It had been too close and they all knew it. As the last of the horses were brought up, Silas shrugged off the blanket and walked over to them. He counted swiftly, and then his shoulders sagged with relief. He gave David and Kumen a crooked grin. "Best twenty-four dollars I ever saved," he gasped.[2]

Tuesday, May 6, 1879

It took the company five more days to reach Willow Spring, just forty miles south of Lee's Ferry. In those five days, they learned for themselves the challenges and hazards of desert travel. Hour after hour, they plodded along through the thick, choking dust, bonnets and hats pulled low to shade their eyes from the blinding glare and searing heat. They learned what it means to make a dry camp. It starts with going all day on nothing but an occasional sip of water to ease the pain of cracked and bleeding lips. That night each person gets another sip or two, but none for cooking or washing. The next morning it's up and at it again for another ten to twelve hours.

The dry washes seemed to come every mile or so, the sand soft enough and deep enough that the wagon wheels sank in over the fellowes.* Teams already weakening with thirst exhausted themselves trying to pull the wagons through. In the deeper washes—which proved to be pure hell—several men would have to get behind the wagons and push until they were up and out the other side. Otherwise the teams would just grind to a halt. The animals' necks were often snow-white with lather. As the miles wore on, they moved more and more slowly.

Even though they left the livestock with the drovers at Bitter Spring to wait until a wagon could refill the barrels at Willow Spring and return for them, they still lost twenty head of cattle. As they moved south, they

---

* The inner portion of the wheel rim where the spokes are attached. Usually the fellowes were about two inches thick.

left a trail strewn with carcasses that would soon be stripped by the coyotes and the ravens, the bones left to bleach in the sun.

It was hot, backbreaking, exhausting work, made worse by the ravenous thirst, the deepening sunburns, and the pasty grit that filled every wrinkle in their bodies. To add to the joy, any metal on the wagons or harnessing got hot enough to blister if you accidentally leaned your hand against it.

When they finally pulled into Willow Spring, the company was too exhausted to go on. Even though Moenkopi, the first settlement in over a hundred miles, was just a few miles away, the unanimous decision was to stop and rest for the night.

The Davis family gathered together near the small creek below the springs. They had drunk their fill earlier, but the children lined up, cupping their hands and drinking deeply. Again. That finished, Mary announced it was time for a little personal hygiene. She took out a rag, dipped it in the water, and began to sponge off the grit and grime from Emmy's neck.

"Oooh," the little girl said. "That feels so good, Mama."

"I'm next," Jimmie declared.

His mother looked shocked. "Say that again, young man. Did I just hear Jimmie Davis ask to take a bath?"

"How about taking a real bath?" David said.

Mary whirled. "Don't you be saying that unless you really mean it, young man."

"I do mean it. Tomorrow we will be in civilization again."

"Sivel what?" Emmy asked, looking up at him with those enormous green eyes.

He bent down. "Civilization. That means a big city."

"Moenkopi is a big city?" the elder James asked skeptically.

"Absolutely. Silas thinks there are at least a hundred people there. Maybe even a hundred and one."

"Oh," Eddie said, disappointment clearly written on his face.

"Scoff if you will," David said, waggling his finger back and forth in front of their noses, "but Silas says they have one of the largest bathtubs in the world."

Emmy's eyes grew very large. "A bathtub."

Mary stepped in front of him. "David, I'm warning you. If you're just pulling our leg, you will being calling down the famous Davis wrath upon your head."

"I'm just telling you what Silas told us. It's called the Moenkopi Reservoir. It's no more than a hundred yards wide, but—" He held up a finger as a slow smile stole across his face. "It's nearly three miles long. Just like some great, giant bathtub."

Notes

1. Lee's Ferry and the Lonely Dell Ranch, located about seven miles south of Page, Arizona, are now listed on the National Register of Historic Places. Emma Lee continued to run the ferry for some years after her husband's death. The ferry finally stopped operating in 1928 when Navajo Bridge was built over Marble Canyon a few miles downstream (see Wikipedia, "Lee's Ferry, Utah," and Land Use History of North America: Colorado Plateau, "Lee's Ferry," http://cpluhna.nau.edu/Places/lees_ferry.htm).

2. The exploring company journal for May 1, 1879, records: "Silas S. Smith having a small bunch of horses did not want to pay $1.00 per head for their being ferried over, so drove them into the river to swim them across. The river was one-fourth mile across and the horses struck below the landing and had to swim back nearly losing one over the rapids" (see Miller, Hole, 19).

CHAPTER 39

Wednesday, May 7, 1879

It was early in 1874 that Jacob Hamblin and two non-Mormon prospectors rode into the heart of the Navajo nation to confront a tribe on the verge of war. When they left the next day, Hamblin had been able to convince the chiefs that the Mormons had nothing to do with the murder of three Navajo braves in Grass Valley. That led to an eventual treaty, and war was averted. Once it was evident that the treaty would hold, Brigham Young called numerous people to move into northern Arizona and establish new settlements.

One of the locations chosen was a Hopi village in Moenkopi Wash. The Hopis, or Moquis, as the Navajos derisively called them, were a peace-loving people who received the Mormon missionaries much more warmly than the other tribes. Many had been baptized, including their chief, the greatly beloved Chief Tuba. He and his wife had later been taken to St. George by the missionaries, where they were sealed together in the temple.

Thus, in 1875, a group of families from southern Utah Territory came to Moenkopi Wash and started a settlement there. Not surprisingly, they called it Moenkopi.

✳

When the exploring party came over a slight rise about midday on May seventh, they stopped in wonder. There, about a mile ahead of them, stood a collection of buildings—a square stone fort, some adobe and mud huts, and several Indian hogans. Small patches of green by the houses were clearly vegetable gardens. Larger patches of deeper green marked fields of corn—or maize, as the Indians called it—and alfalfa. But the most stunning sight was David's "bathtub." To see that much water in this vast desolation was absolutely astonishing. For a long moment, the group just gaped, wondering if it was a mirage. Then suddenly someone whooped out a single word: "Water!" A great cheer exploded spontaneously from up and down the line.

It was a time for rejoicing. The desert stretch had been crossed without any serious accidents or loss of human life. No wagons had been lost and no critical supplies had been abandoned. The loss of twenty head of cattle was a serious one, but one of the reasons they had brought such a large herd was to cover just such losses. What Moenkopi meant for the company was rest, fresh vegetables, roast lamb, cornmeal, and, most importantly, water—water enough for cooking, water enough for the stock, water enough to do laundry, and water enough to bathe in.

And there was something more. This was a Mormon settlement. The astonishment of the townspeople when they saw a whole company of fellow Church members coming up the main street of the village was nearly as great as the company's joy when they saw the Moenkopi Reservoir.

That night the two groups gathered together in a joyous celebration of the company's arrival.[1]

Thursday, May 8, 1879

The next morning a meeting was called for the men in the company and the leadership of the Moenkopi settlement. When David and Jim returned to the wagons it was almost noon. Mary was waiting with three-year-old John playing nearby, but the other children were gone, down at the reservoir playing in the water with the Harrimans. "There you are," she said when she saw them. "I about gave you two up."

Jim blew out his breath. "Turns out the settlers here assumed we had come to join them, that our mission was here in Moenkopi. When Silas started asking them about the roads east of here and about perhaps getting a guide to help us cross the Navajo Reservation, they were dumbfounded."

"Oh dear."

"They were not at all happy when we told them we were moving on," David added. "Silas had to remind President Brown three different times before they finally accepted that we are under call to explore a route to the San Juan." He looked around. "Do I smell corn bread?"

She laughed. "Actually, Emily saved you both a great big piece. It's in the Dutch oven there by the fire. I'll get the honey."

Once they had their bread, Mary sat down beside Jim and immediately pressed them for more information. David waved a fork at Jim, signaling him to begin because David's mouth was full.

"Well, there is some good news. The company's going to stay here for about a week."

"Really!" she exclaimed. "A whole week?"

"Well, maybe a little less. We'll just have to see. The teams are exhausted—"

"As are we," David cut in.

"As are we," Jim agreed. "They've got a good blacksmith here. The wagons are in need of some work. Brother Silas wants every horse and mule in the remuda checked to make sure their shoes are good. There'll be harnessing to fix, tools to sharpen—"

Mary broke in. "Clothes to wash, shoes to repair, dresses to mend."

"Exactly."

David picked it up from there so Jim could take a bite. "Four scouts—George Hobbs, Bob Bullock, Kumen Jones, and myself—will leave day after tomorrow to scout out a road, at least for the first fifty or sixty miles. The settlers have sent for a man by the name of Tanner to guide us."

He speared another piece of bread, so Jim picked it up again. "There's also the not-so-good news. We've seen the last of any wagon roads."

David said nothing. When Jim called it not-so-good news, he was softening it for his wife, and David wasn't about to correct him. What he didn't say was that the leaders of the Moenkopi settlement had flat out told them that what they were thinking was impossible. "There is no way we can take wagons beyond here, according to them," Jim said, quoting President Brown. "The only paths east of here are sheep trails and goat tracks. They say you need an experienced guide to even find your way from village to village."

David didn't add what the counselor in the presidency had said next. He had jumped to his feet, almost spluttering in his astonishment. "Water is everything out here, and there is precious little of that. During the winter, natural rock tanks and potholes hold rainwater and snowmelt, but that will be mostly gone now. You can't just take twelve wagons, forty people, and a couple of hundred head of stock across Navajo lands. Listen, these people fight *each other* over water. What few springs there are have been protected and guarded for generations. There is simply no way. You have to stay here with us."

"It took Silas some time to convince them," Jim soothed, "but they finally agreed that we have to fulfill the mission we were given. So they've sent for this Brother Tanner, who they say knows this country better than any white man alive. He'll guide our scouts.[2] In the meantime, we'll stay here and rest up. Oh, another good thing is, they have work for our men."

"Work?"

"Yes, they're building a mill here to help process the wool they purchase from the Navajos and Hopis. It will provide work for the settlers and a market for the Indians. They want our men to help with the construction while we wait for the scouts to return. They'll pay us in cornmeal."

"Wonderful," she exclaimed. "Manna in the wilderness, as it were, eh?"

"Yes," the two men said together. Then they shot a quick look at each other.

She picked up on it immediately. "What?"

Jim hurried and took another bite and waved his fork at David. "You tell her," he mumbled.

Giving him a dark look, David took a quick breath, then turned to face Mary. "The council made another decision. Actually, I think it's a blessing for you. Well, for the family," he hastily amended. "They are recommending that you stay here, even after the rest of the company goes forward." He rushed on as her mouth dropped and her eyes widened. "Not permanently," he said. "Just until we find where we're going. Then we'll come back for you."

Jim decided it was time to rescue David. "They have several concerns," he said. "First, this last five or six days has been very hard on the cattle. You saw it for yourself. The younger heifers, and especially the calves, have sore and bleeding hooves."

A shadow of pain crossed her face. "Yes." She had been horrified to see bloody hoof marks when the animals crossed patches of rock pan. Emily had cried when she saw it.

"Well, those aren't going to heal in a week. So Silas wants to leave all the loose stock here while the company presses forward. It's also probably best not to have the stock trailing us while we're wandering around trying to find the way through."

"Go on," she said slowly.

"So they want us to stay here with the cattle until they can come back for us."

"*Us?*" she cried. "Does that mean you'll stay too?"

He was startled by that. "Of course. I would never leave you and the children."

The relief in her eyes was enormous. David saw her visibly relax. Then immediately her lips pressed together. "This is because of the baby, isn't it?"

Jim winced. "Mary, I . . . we need to . . ." It trailed off as her eyes challenged his.

"You're darn right this is because of the baby," David blurted. "I keep thinking about us out there—limited water, no idea where we are, maybe facing some less than friendly Indians, and with only one other woman in the whole company to help you. It gives me nightmares. And if that's how I feel, I can only imagine what's going through Jim's mind."

To his utter surprise, she burst into a merry laugh. "You really worry about me?"

"I do," David said. "More than you know."

"As do I," Jim said. He went to her and took her hands. "Mary, I've been just sick about it. If you lose another baby, I . . ." He couldn't finish.

"I'm not going to lose this baby," she said firmly. "I'm not." She drew in a deep breath, and looked up at her husband. "But you'll be here with us until they come back for us?"

"Yes."

"Until I come back for you," David affirmed. "If you stay, you have my word that I'll be one of those that comes back to get you."

She smiled at him. "I already knew that," she said softly.

He felt a surge of elation. She was going for it. "Now maybe I can get some sleep again."

"How long will it be before you will return, do you suppose?"

Jim looked away. David sighed. "Well, that's the rub, Mary. As we already noted, we're heading out into a trackless waste. Even with these guides they're getting for us, it's going to take a while to find the way. And once we're in San Juan, we need to get some crops in. Silas is talking about building you and the Harrimans a house before we head back to Cedar City." He paused. "It could be as long as two months."

She nodded thoughtfully. "Staying here does have its attractions," she finally said. Then, as another thought came, "Are the Harrimans staying back with us?"

Jim slowly shook his head. "No, Silas recommended they do, but Henry said they're going to push on. So it will just be us."

To David's surprise, she accepted that without a word. Her gaze moved back and forth between the two of them. "And you really think this is best?"

Jim's head bobbed vigorously. "I do."

"Absolutely," David affirmed.

She abruptly stood, holding the roundness of her stomach with one hand. "Okay. Let's go down and tell the children."[3]

When David finished saying good night to the children and returned to the campfire, Jim and Mary Davis were seated on a half log in front of it, shoulders together and holding hands. He walked up to them and smiled. "You're not having second thoughts, I hope," he teased.

She shook her head emphatically. "Not in any way. In fact, it has lifted a burden off my mind to know we can stay here for a time."

"Good. Mine too." He started to turn away. "Well, I have to pack. We're off at first light."

"Oh, no, you don't," Mary said, pointing to another log. "I've seen what you're carrying. You can pack everything you own in under a minute. So come and sit with us for a while."

"Yes," Jim said, "we won't keep you up too late."

He hesitated. Then, pleased that they would ask, he went around and took the seat opposite them.

As he got settled, Jim asked, "So there are four of you leaving tomorrow?"

"Six if you count Seth Tanner and the young Navajo he's secured to help us. They'll scout out a possible route for the first fifty or sixty miles; then a couple of us scouts will return to bring the rest of the company while the lead scouts press forward."

"We'll miss you, David," Mary said quietly. "Emmy cried when I told her."

"She made me cross my heart and hope to die when I promised I'd be back. Then she hugged me until I nearly lost my breath." His eyes softened. "I'm going to miss all of you. You've come to mean a lot to me, but especially Emmy. She has really won my heart."

"And she knows it," Mary laughs. "You spoil her something awful."

"Sorry, but I'm having a hard time feeling guilty about that."

She nodded and they fell quiet for a time. Then Jim and David began discussing what the future now held—where they would finally settle, how soon the main company would come east to join them, how the children would adapt to a new and isolated home.

About fifteen minutes later, a cry turned their heads in the direction of the wagon. "Mama! Mama!"

Mary started to get up, holding her stomach as she raised herself from the log. "She's having a nightmare."

Jim quickly put a hand on her shoulder and gently pushed her down again. "I'll go."

They watched him climb into the wagon, then heard the whimpering stop as the murmur of his voice soothed his daughter. Mary, who had been anxiously watching the wagon, finally turned back. "He'll tell her a story. She'll be all right."

David nodded, surprised at the sudden envy he felt. Mary, watching him closely, saw the look and guessed what it was. "David," she asked, "why aren't you married?"

The question so startled him that he just stared at her.

She flushed a little. "Sorry. When it comes to impertinence, I'm as bad as Eddie, aren't I?"

"I . . ." He was still completely taken aback. "What made you ask that?"

She was teasing now. "Well, you're devilishly handsome. If I were ten years younger and not madly in love with my husband, I'd go after you myself."

"Gwan!" he scoffed.

Her laughter tinkled softly in the warm night air. "You rescue damsels in distress. You are wonderful with children." She stopped, peering at him. "You're what, twenty-two now?"

"I'll be twenty-three next month."

"And not yet married. That is strange indeed." Then she waved a hand. "You don't have to answer. It's really not mine to ask."

"Tell you what," he said, having a sudden thought. "I'll answer your question if you'll answer one of mine."

She gave him an appraising look. "Is it an impertinent one too?"

"Absolutely," he said.

She didn't hesitate a moment. "Of course. But you have to go first."

And so he began to tell her of his life since coming to America, about how he had left Coalville to go on his own, about the various jobs he'd taken since then. "Aren't many women in a railroad camp or on a cattle ranch," he concluded. "And the few there are, are either married, grandmas, or allergic to men from Yorkshire. But anyway, that's been my life. Not much chance for courting a girl."

"Until Cedar City," she said.

He gave her a sharp look. "Until Cedar City," he agreed. "For all the good that did me."

"David, I . . . we heard about you and Molly breaking up, just before we came up to Paragonah. I'm so sorry."

"Nope," he cut in quickly. "None of that. It's my turn now."

"Your turn for what?" Jim Davis said. They hadn't heard him, but he was out of the wagon and coming back over to join them.

"Is she asleep?" Mary asked.

"Yes. She was barely awake." He sat down by Mary again, looking at David. "So?"

Mary answered for him. "David was just about to ask me an impertinent question." At his raised eyebrows, she smiled. "I asked him why he wasn't married. So now it's his turn."

"Want me to leave?" Jim asked, looking at David.

"No, actually, I've changed my mind. It's none of my business, really."

"Oh, no, you don't," she said. "Your marital status was none of my business, so ask away."

He watched them for a moment, considering. With Jim here, he wasn't sure he wanted to ask it now. But then, in a way it was as much a question for Jim as for her. "All right," he said. "But if I cross a line where you are uncomfortable, you just tell me that this is a spot of bother, as we Brits say, and I'll shut up and go to bed."

"I think we're sufficiently prepared," Jim said easily.

David drew in his breath, trying to decide how to best start. Finally, he turned to Jim. "I was there that day in the meeting when you stood and said you were going to accept your call. I was sitting by Patrick McKenna, and he was kind of giving me a running commentary on who people were. To be honest, when he told me that your wife was with child and in poor health, I . . . ."

"You thought it was just plain stupid? Is that what you're trying to say?" Mary smiled.

David laughed softly. "I was looking for a little softer word than that."

"I thought it was just plain stupid," Jim said.

"And so," Mary said, "your question is, why are we out here?"

"Not actually. Close, but not exactly. Before I ask it, though, it would be helpful if you understood something about me." He managed a quick smile. "You see, I've been hiding the real me from you."

She leaned forward, looking very much like Emily at the moment. "Oooh," she murmured. "A dark side we don't know about. Please, tell us."

So he did. He didn't go into all of it. He said nothing about his mother's experience at Astle Manor, and only briefly talked about her problems caused by working in the match factory. "She just had a very difficult life," he concluded. "I think that turned her sour on religion and made her quite skeptical about God. I'll just give you one quick example, because it will help you better understand my question. On my first day in the mines—remember, that was just three days following my sixth birthday—there was one point where I was so terrified of the darkness that I started to cry. That night, Mum questioned me about my first day. She specifically asked me if I had cried, or if I had wanted to pray to God for help."

He stopped, once again staring into the fire. "When I finally admitted that I had done both, she said, 'David, there's something you need to remember. I think that when we cry, God does not hear us. I think that when we pray, He does not answer. And if that is true, then we have to conclude that God does not care.'"

"Oh, David," Mary whispered.

He brightened. "It's all right. That was a long time ago. But over the years, I came to that same conclusion for myself. Watching the exploitation of children in the mines, I asked myself many times, if there really was a God, why didn't He intervene in our behalf? I saw a young boy, no older than me, killed right before my eyes because he took a few minutes out of his miserable life to play a child's game." His voice caught for a moment. "And when my mother was dying, I begged God to spare her life." He had to stop and look away.

"And that's when you knew your mother was right, wasn't it?" Mary asked.

"Yes." He straightened, speaking quickly now before either of them could respond. "But all of that is just to give context to my question, which is this: Why aren't you two bitter? You've lost four out of eight children, all while they were still babies. So why aren't you shaking your fist at God like my mother did? Why would you continue to believe in Him? And yes, when the call came, and your situation was so precarious, why would you ever say yes?"

Husband and wife looked at each other for a moment. She nodded for him to begin, but he shook his head. "I think that's really your question, Mary."

For a long time she studied the ground, not looking at David. Then finally her head came up. "There is so much I would like to say, David. So many things that might help you to understand, but maybe that will come another time. I would only say this."

He interrupted her. "Mary, if this is too much for you, just forget it."

"No, it's a fair question. Even if we answered the call, why come with the exploring party? Why not wait until the baby was born, make sure everything would be all right?"

"Exactly. Can't good old common sense balance out revelation every now and then?"

She didn't seem to hear him. Jim began speaking very quietly. "When we heard our names read out in conference, we were both stunned," he said. "Mary's health hadn't been good for a long time. And losing one baby after another was . . ." He swallowed quickly. "It had been difficult for us."

Now she picked it up. "As we talked about it on the way back to Cedar City the next day, we were—I was—very emotional. 'How could they ask this of us?' I kept saying. But then we talked about the blessings that have come to us when we have tried to be obedient."

David shot her a skeptical look.

She ignored it. "We were so troubled by the whole thing that James and I decided to go to Bishop Arthur and ask him what he thought we should do. At first, he would only say that this had to be our decision, both *whether* to go and, if we did, *when* to go. He reminded us that President Lunt had said that people shouldn't feel compelled to go, especially if they were facing unusual circumstances." She pulled a face. "Surely, I thought, if ever there were special circumstances, we qualified."

"Ten times over," David murmured.

She barely acknowledged that. "But then Bishop Arthur asked if I wanted a blessing." Her eyes half closed in remembering. "As he spoke, I could feel something in him change. At first he was very tentative; then suddenly he began to speak with more assurance. He told me . . ." She took a quick breath, fighting her emotions. "He told me that if I would go, if I would accompany my husband in answering this call, that my health would be restored, and that—"

A stifled sob rose up, cutting off her words. Her husband put an arm around her and held her for a moment. She wiped quickly at her eyes, then, head high, finished. "He told me that my health would be restored and that I would never again lose another child."[4]

David rocked back. Suddenly he remembered her words from yesterday. "I am not going to lose this child. I am not."

"And you believed him?" David found himself saying. The words had come out unbidden.

"No!" she said fiercely. "As Bishop Arthur spoke those words, I didn't just *believe* him. I *knew* that what he was saying was true. I knew it with all my heart. I can't explain that to you, David, but I felt it so strongly. I just knew."

David said nothing. How could you question something like that? How could you scoff when she sat there right before your eyes, looking healthy and strong and happy? She wasn't the same woman as the one he had climbed up beside that first morning to help with her team.

"Do you understand what I am saying, David? My heart just weeps at the thought of your mother and how she must have suffered. But I am here to tell you that God does hear our cries, He does see our tears, and *He does care.*"

As they watched David walk away five minutes later, James slipped an arm around his wife's waist. "I thought for a minute you were going to tell him about Abby."

She looked up at him. "I thought about it, then decided tonight wasn't the time."

"Tell me again what she said when she came to see you the night before we left."

There was a long sigh. "She told me about what had happened with David and his father, and how Molly broke off their relationship the very next morning. She said he was deeply hurt and angry, especially because it all happened just hours after he had agreed to pray with Molly."

"Oh?"

"Knowing we were going to be with him for the next several months, Abby wanted us to know the situation. She asked, if there ever might be a chance, that we would become his friend and let him know that he's not been abandoned."

"Interesting," Jim mused.

"Yes, isn't it." She was smiling as she watched the dark figure disappear into the darkness. "Before we even left Paragonah, look who ended up sitting beside me in the wagon seat. None other than David Draper himself."

James pulled her closer to him. "Very interesting indeed."

Notes

1. Moenkopi (also spelled in the journals as Moan Coppy or Moyancoppy) is located just a short distance south of Tuba City, Arizona. After two earlier attempts, a group of several families, led there in late 1875 or early 1876 by James S. Brown, finally succeeded in starting a settlement there. By 1879, when the exploring party came through, it was a small but thriving community (see Garrett and Johnson, *Regional Studies*, 141–45).

2. Nielson Dalley's account of the exploring party also mentions Thales Haskell as one of the guides. Since Dalley is the only one who mentions Haskell, Miller assumes that he didn't go all the way to San Juan with them (Miller, *Hole*, 30). Therefore, he was not included in the novel.

3. In his life story, James Davis records the following: "Crossed the Colorado at Lees Ferry, and stopped at a small village called Moencopi. . . . They advised us with families to stay there on account of the dangers ahead of us. And let the young men go and find a suitable country to locate" (in *ibid.*, 156). The other details about the week's layover to rest up and repair and the sore feet of the young cattle are supplied by Miller (*ibid.*, 20).

I remind the readers again that the history of this company is not detailed enough to provide in depth character studies or personal conversations. These details, including the personalities of James and Mary Elizabeth Davis, are of my own creation. However, I have tried to be true to the situation, the circumstances, and the few recorded details about their lives that are available. I hope that the descendants of this wonderful couple will see that the liberties I have taken in depicting them in this story come out of my profound respect and admiration for them both.

4. The account of this blessing from Christopher Arthur, bishop of the Cedar City Ward, comes from the "Life of James Davis" (Miller, *Hole*, 155).

CHAPTER 40

Tuesday, May 13th. *I have determined that henceforth I shall keep a journal of my travels as a member of the exploring party to the San Juan River. Actually this was at the suggestion of Sister Mary Davis, wife of James Davis. They are one of only two families traveling with us. She strongly encouraged me in this endeavor because she believes our little expedition is making history & should be recorded. I find that a bit optimistic, but like the idea anyway. She helped me locate some paper & a small leather pouch to keep it in. Purchased it from one of the settlers here. So I begin. It was one month ago tomorrow that we departed from Paragonah. Wish I had thought to start then, but when I have time, I shall write a summary of the first month.*

After exploring possible routes with three others—Kumen Jones, Robert Bullock, & George Hobbs—George & I returned to Moen Coppy to bring on the rest of the company. Had supper with the Davis family. Delightful time with the children. Hadn't expected to see them again for several more weeks so this was a treat.

Left M. C. abt. 11 am with 9 wagons & a few loose horses. Started from home with 12, but George Hobb's broke an axle & left it at Lee's Ferry for pickup on return trip. Davis family's two wagons remain with them. Cattle will stay in M.C. until we make a road & return for them. Traveled abt. five miles. Road that far already broken through thick stands of greasewood, some as high as Tillie's head. M. C. settlers provided ox teams to help clear the road in return for us bringing bring back wood to the settlement. Trumpet blew at 9 pm. Lights out & bed.

Wednesday, May 14th. Again started at 11 a.m. Three yoke of cattle used to pull a forked tree through heavy greasewood to break open a road. Finally left greasewood for more elevated country—tall mesas on both sides. No wagons have gone through here before. Two men from M.C. helped break through last of the greasewood, but will not continue farther.

Thursday, May 15th. Delayed by lost horses. Company moved on while a few searched for them. Finally brought into camp by Wm. Gardner, an Indian interpreter. By then so late we made camp for the night. When horses were turned loose to graze, Niels Dalley's horse & one of S. Smith's horses took umbrage with each other. In the fight, Dalley's horse broke the hind leg of Smith's. He had to be put down.[1]

Friday, May 16th. First trouble with Indians today. Started at 9:30. Drove 5 miles to ranch of son of Navajo chief, named Po-ee-kon.[2] This is one bad Indian. He openly brags he was the one who shot George A. Smith, an Indian missionary, some years back. According to our guides, he is a brother of the young Navajos killed in Grass Valley. P. is ugly, mean-tempered, & hates whites. Had several men with him. He had one rifle, the rest only bows & arrows.

When captain asked for permission to water our horses, P. refused, saying there wasn't enough for his flock. Some of us young bloods got a little hot under the collar at that. There was plenty enough water & our teams were pretty jaded by then. When we protested, he pulled out a club & savagely struck one of the boys. That was plain stupid. Abt. 20 of us had our guns drawn in an instant. For a moment, it looked like there would be blood. But our wise captain suggested we move away from the pool, & dig wells nearby. We dug several small wells & found water not too deep. After our animals drank & we refilled our barrels, Smith then presented the wells to P. That defused the situation, but he was still plain mean-ugly.

Monday, May 19th. *Been several days since my last entry. Urgency is such that we drove all day yesterday, not stopping for Sabbath. Making good time, but learning that water is our greatest anxiety. The Navajos know this very well & resent our presence. (Haven't told them that we have 200 cows coming later.) Whenever we find a damp place or anywhere there are green plants, we dig down &, as a rule, plenty of water is found. We then turn these wells over to the Indians, who gratefully receive them. This has eased our way a great deal. The news of our success has spread far ahead of us. Usually we are greeted warmly by small bands of Navajos. They even bring mutton to give us, or trade. The meat is much welcomed by all.*

One interesting event associated with water. At one place, we were able to dig a few small wells, but these barely filled our urgent needs. Then one brother went to a sandstone ledge & drove his pick into the stone. To our astonishment, a small stream of water gushed out. This proved to be sufficient for our needs, & a blessing to the Indians after we left.[3] *Our captain says we are not a Moses in the wilderness striking a rock with our staff to get water, but we continually seem to find enough, even if it takes picks & shovels.*

Robert Bullock, one of our scouts, & Seth Tanner, our guide, met us today. They have ridden 75 miles ahead & say the way is open before us. They found a large sandstone tank, or lake, with plenty of water ahead.

Friday, May 23rd. *Making good progress. Been scouting ahead with Bullock & Tanner. Water still a challenge. On Wednesday found a large sandstone tank, but Indians bring thousands of sheep there to water. It was much fouled, abt. the same color as water running out of a corral. Had no choice but to drink. Heat is relentless every day now.*

Once again S. Smith proves himself worthy to lead. Nearly had more trouble with Indians—Paiutes this time—but Silas wisely dealt with it & defused it. The night passed without further incident.

Wednesday, May 28th. *Accompanied scouts—Bullock, Jones, Hobbs—searching out road. Reached the San Juan River this* *afternoon! Much elated, returned to camp to report. Last few days very difficult. Did more work on road yesterday than any day so far. After traveling down a canyon for some miles, came against a solid rock hill, very steep. Had to cut notches in the rock to provide footing for the horses, then put 8 horses per wagon to pull them up. After that traveled on solid rock for some miles. Incredible. Just solid red rock hills & canyons as far as the eye can see. Dramatically different from England's verdant scenes, but has a remarkable beauty of its own. Heat is becoming unbearable. Sometimes we travel at night to escape it.*

Saturday, May 31st. *We have reached our destination!!!! After three very arduous days, with much difficult road building required, & much sand in the lower washes & canyons, full party camped on south bank of San Juan River. Ate fresh fish for dinner last night. To our surprise, when Bob Bullock crossed the river, he found several families farming at what they call McElmo Wash & Montezuma Creek. Peter Shirts is a Mormon. Bullock knows him well. He was much surprised & happy to see us, as were the others. Much rejoicing on our part too. We have come 400 miles in six weeks, the last 150 through trackless country where no wagons have ever gone before. I am proud to have been part of it, in company with as fine of men as I have ever been privileged to know.*

Saturday, May 31, 1879

"Billy Joe? Would you offer a blessing on the food, please?"

Patrick Joseph McKenna looked up at his father and nodded. All five heads bowed.

"Dear Heavenly Father," Billy Joe began, "I thank Thee today for the food. Bless it to our good. We thank Thee for all the blessings You give us. Bless the sick and those in need. Bless Paint so that he will come when I whistle. Bless the exploring party, especially David and Tillie. Keep them safe. In the name of Jesus, Amen."

His mother, father, Abby, and Molly looked at him with great fondness, but he paid them no mind. He grabbed the bowl of mashed potatoes sitting beside him and, even as he scooped out a large spoonful, said, "Pass the gravy."

"Please," his mother reminded him.

"Please," he said. "But hurry. I'm hungry."

The food was passed and dished up, and as they began to eat, Patrick reached in his pocket and withdrew an envelope. He waved it back and forth. "Guess what came today."

Molly actually dropped her fork. It hit the plate with a loud clunk. "From David?" she cried.

His face fell a little. "No, dear, I'm afraid not. It's from Sister Mary Davis, though."

"Really?" Sarah exclaimed. "How is she? Any problems with the baby?"

"Does she say anything about David?" Molly blurted. "Is he all right?" She was leaning toward her father, almost like she might snatch the letter out of his hand.

"Yes, of course she does." He looked to his wife. "And she's fine. Wonderful, in fact, according to her. It's written from a place called Moenkopi, in Arizona Territory. She and James stopped there while the rest of the party went on. They'll come back for them later."

"Can I read it, Daddy?" Molly said eagerly.

He opened the envelope and extracted three folded sheets of paper. "I shall read it for you, and for all of us," he said. "As you can see, it is quite a long letter, all of which I think you will find to be very interesting."

Abby was sitting in the chair beside her bed, reading by lamplight, when she heard the creak of footsteps in the hallway. When they stopped outside her door, she didn't wait for the knock. "Come in, Molly," she called.

Molly slipped through the door. She was in her nightdress and a robe, as was Abby. She moved to the bed and fell heavily upon it. "Oh, Abby, why won't he write? He could have sent a letter from Panguitch, or Hatch, or Orderville."

"I don't think they went through Orderville," Abby noted. "They turned east before then."

"Stop it," she wailed. "Don't rub it in." She was near tears. "But why won't he write?"

Abby got up and went over and lay beside her sister. She laid one hand on her arm. "Molly, you know the answer to that. You tell me."

"Because I told him it was over between us."

"Yes. I'm guessing that's got quite a bit to do with it."

"I know. But I thought he would at least write and tell us he's all right."

"When you basically asked him not to?" she chided. "He's too proud for that."

"I would have written to him if I thought a letter could have caught up with him."

"And what would you have said? That you were wrong? That you are sorry for what you said? That everything is all right between you now? All is forgiven?"

Molly turned over onto her side to look at Abby directly. She studied her for several moments, and then her lips pulled into a pout. "I was hoping for a little sympathy here," she finally said. "I'm not going to find it, am I?"

"I'm sorry, Molly," Abby replied. "I'm not trying to be cruel, I'm just trying to be . . ."

As she searched for a word, Molly finished it for her. "Realistic?"

"Well, yes." She sat up, pulled her knees up, and folded her arms around them. "There's something you need to consider, if you haven't already, Molly. I think it's important in understanding what's going on."

Molly sat up as well and scooted around so she was facing her sister. "What?"

Abby's shoulders lifted and fell. "You sure you want to hear this?"

Molly's look answered that.

"All right. I want you to think about all of this from David's point of view."

"You don't think I have?" she exclaimed. "I know how I hurt him. I know that the timing was awful, coming right after that whole thing with his father as it did, but—"

"*Why* was it awful?"

That took her aback. "Why? Because he was already angry that his father was going away. After all David had done to get him down here, I'm sure he felt betrayed."

"By whom?" Abby asked softly.

Her irritation was rising. "By his father, of course. And then by me. What are you trying to say, Abby?"

Abby got off the bed and went over to her dresser. She pulled out a piece of paper and came back to stand over Molly. "Here's the note David wrote to me just before he left. I want to read you one part of it." She held it up and began, "'*Yesterday, for the first time in a very long time, I said a prayer. Well, Molly actually said it, but I stood with her. And my heart was with her. She prayed that the Lord would bless our relationship so that we could be brought closer together, so we could resolve our differences. And here I am, less than twenty-four hours later, with my father leaving for three years, and my relationship with Molly ended. I will be anxious to hear your explanation of that when I return.*'"

"Why didn't you ever let me read that note before?" Molly asked.

Abby gave her an incredulous look. "I did. Right after you read me his note to you."

"Oh, yeah. I wasn't very coherent at that point, was I?"

"No, you weren't," she said, her voice a mixture of exasperation and love.

Molly took the note and read it again slowly. "Okay, now ask me your question again."

"You said he felt betrayed. I asked you by whom."

Molly lifted it again, reading more slowly now. When she looked up, her eyes were wide and shining with tears. "He feels betrayed by God."

Abby retrieved the note, folded it up, and returned it to its place. "Remember what he said about crying to God when his mother was dying? What happened then?"

"God didn't hear him. Or at least that's how he saw it."

"So, after many years, when he finally cries out to God again, what happens?"

Molly stared at her sister for a long moment, then dropped her face into her hands. "He didn't answer him."

"Oh," Abby said quietly, "I think it was much worse than that. God didn't just ignore David. It's like He jerked the rug out from under him. Hit him when he was down. Rubbed his nose in his own foolishness." She gave Molly a faint smile. "I'm speaking as if I were David now."

"Oh, Abby. No wonder he ran."

"But that's the real question, Molly. Don't you find it strange *where* he ran to?"

"What?"

"After that kind of a betrayal, why not throw up his hands, say to heck with the Church and us Mormons, and head for California or Wyoming or anywhere people wouldn't be trying to get him to be a believer. Of all places he could have gone, why join the exploring party?"

Molly's eyes were wide as she considered the implications of that. "I don't know," she said.

"I don't know either," Abby said after a moment. "But if you can figure that out, maybe you'll know what to do when he comes back here in another four months."

"*If* he comes back," Molly said, suddenly desolate.

"Oh, he'll be back," Abby said with great conviction. "I'm just not sure why."

Notes

1. Nielson Dalley's journal places this on May 15th, but the camp record shows it as happening on May 26th (Miller, *Hole*, 25, 150).

2. The name of the hostile Navajo is variously spelled in the journals and histories as Peokon, Peocorn, Peoquan, and other variations (*ibid.*, 23, 149, 152). I have gone with the earlier spelling used when Po-ee-kon was a principal player in the Jacob Hamblin settlement of the Grass Valley incident.

3. Nielson Dalley is the only one who mentions this incident and places it at the Po-ee-kon ranch—which he spells as Peokon (see *ibid.*, 149–50). Albert R. Lyman's account of this incident, from which we get the most details, states that they dug "several wells" and found water at a shallow depth (in *ibid.*, 22). Though the camp record makes no mention of the sandstone ledge, it does say they "dug out some good springs" that day (*ibid.*, 23).

CHAPTER 41

Tuesday, June 17, 1879

David Draper rapped sharply on the side of the wagon box. "Silas? You in there?"

"I am," came the immediate answer. "That you, David?"

"It is." He walked around to the back of the wagon and pulled the flap back. Silas Smith was sitting cross-legged on a quilt with a flat box on his lap. Using it as a lapboard, he was writing a letter. Beads of perspiration were visible on his forehead beneath his hatband.

"Pretty hot to be sitting inside a wagon, even if it is in the shade," David observed.

Silas wiped at the sweat with the sleeve of his shirt. "You got that right, but I'm almost done."

"Go ahead and finish. I'll be outside here."

"Okay. Give me two minutes. I want to send this off tomorrow."

David moved over to one of the many cottonwood trees, smoothed out a place in the dirt under its sheltering branches, and sat down. True to his word, Silas appeared a short time later and came over to join him.

"Whew!" he said, removing his hat, "that does feel better."

David had to smile. Silas was going bald—or, as he liked to put it, his hairline was creeping over the top of his head looking for his ears. The lower two-thirds of his face was a deep brown, but just above his eyes, where the hat brim came, his skin was white as a sheet of paper. "I can hardly wait until July and August," David noted. "This place must be an oven by then."

"I hope we're on our way back by August," Silas said. "I'm sure the folks back in Cedar and Parowan are most anxious to hear from us."

"Are you thinking of going back the same way we came?" David asked.

He shook his head emphatically. "Water will be in even shorter supply by then. The Navajos won't stand for it."

David was pleased to hear that. He had been worried about that very issue.

Silas sat down and leaned back against the tree, putting his hands behind his head. "No, I'm afraid our trip has been basically for nothing. I can't go back and recommend the route we took to the brethren. There is just no way it will work."

"I wouldn't say for nothing," David said. "At least we know what our destination *is* now. And we've started a dam, built homes for the two families, and gotten a few crops planted."

"And I do take satisfaction in that. However, one major purpose was to find a route and build a road—which we did, but it looks like we'll never use it." He exhaled wearily. "This is not going to be received as good news back home. In fact, the letter I was writing is for Elder Snow. I'm recommending he send out another scouting party to find a central, shorter route."

"How in the world are you ever going to get mail out of here?"

"Now that things are getting established here, my boys are going to take a wagon and go upriver a ways. We'll see what the possibilities are for other settlements; then we'll go on into southern Colorado and purchase some supplies. I'll post the letter there. Hopefully it'll make it back to St. George in about a month."

David nodded. "Wish there was better news, but I completely agree with you." He frowned. "In fact, I'm worried about bringing the cattle we have back at Moenkopi across the route even now. How is Po-ee-kon going to react to two hundred head?"

"That weighs heavy on my mind," Silas said. "It was a good decision to leave them, considering Sister Davis's delicate condition, but the sooner we get them here, the better I'll feel."

"Actually, that's what I wanted to talk about," David said. "Joe tells me that you are sending some men back for the family and the cattle."

"Four, actually. Jim Decker—I've asked him to be in charge—Niels Dalley, Ham Wallace, and Parley Butt."[1]

"How about making it five?"

One eyebrow cocked up. "Meaning you?"

"Yep."

"We're sending out other parties, too. Me and my boys will go east for supplies. I want another group to explore the country up north around the Blue Mountains. I was thinking of sending you out with that one. Knowing your interest in becoming a rancher—"

"I'd really like to go back to Moenkopi."

Silas gave him a searching look. "You got kinda close to those children, didn't you?"

"I did. I also came to have great regard for Jim Davis and his wife. I promised them I'd come back for them."

Silas replaced his hat and tugged it into place. "All right. Knowing Po-ee-kon, it won't hurt to have another gun. And I hate to have a man break his word, especially to one as cute as that little Emily. Get your things together. They plan to cross the river this afternoon. You'll be taking only one pack horse. I want you out of Navajo country as quickly as possible."

Sunday, June 22, 1879

James Davis had his wagon parked behind the home of Brother Brown, president of the Indian Mission in northern Arizona. It was nearly sundown and Jim was building a fire that Mary would use to cook dinner and the family would use to keep warm. For all of the blistering heat of the day, when night came on in the desert, it could rapidly get quite chilly. He wouldn't light the fire until dark, but—

"Look, Pa!"

He turned. Eddie had gone inside the wagon for something. Now he was standing on the wagon seat, pointing to the east.

Mary straightened and hurried over to stand beside her husband. "Indians?" she asked.

"No," Eddie cried. "They're wearing hats. I think it's them."

Jim climbed up beside his son and squinted up the road. Since the riders were coming through the thick stands of greasewood on both sides of the road, it was a little hard to make out how many there were. At least five. Maybe six. Just then a shout went up from the village. Others had seen them too, and were running forward. He looked down at his wife, grinning like a kid. "I think Eddie's right, Mary. I think it is them."

✷

David searched the faces of the group streaming down the road toward them. They were whooping and hollering, waving their hats, running. With the sun at their backs, it was hard to make out individuals, but then suddenly a tiny figure broke free of the rest.

"David! David! David!" She was waving both arms high above her head.

He reined Tillie to a stop and was out of the saddle in one swift leap. The other four pulled in their horses and started to dismount too, but David didn't wait for them. He broke into a run. As he and Emily met, he swooped her up in his arms and swung her around and around. She squealed in delight, then threw her arms around his neck and planted a huge kiss on his cheek.

When he finally lowered her, he bent down. "Hi," he said solemnly.

She looked up at him, her eyes enormous and filled with joy. Then, very gravely, she reached up, took his face in both of her hands, and pulled him closer, peering into his eyes. "I knew you would come," she whispered. And then she kissed him again on the cheek, only this time very gently.

Thursday, June 26, 1879

Though the plan had been to get the herd rounded up, the Davises packed, and the group on the road the next day, things didn't work out quite that way. That night, two horses came up missing. After searching for them for a couple of days, Jim Decker decided they couldn't delay any longer. Mary was now just a few weeks from delivery. If they didn't start soon, she was going to have this baby somewhere out on the Navajo Reservation, and that thought left them all very nervous. Leaving two men to look for the horses, the rest of them, along with the Davises, started east.

It was a tearful farewell for the family. The family had been there for about six weeks now and had quickly been adopted by the community. The children had made several good friends, as had Mary. However, nothing could dampen the euphoria of finally being under way.

With the farewells done, everyone stepped back as James helped his wife up into the wagon seat, then lifted little Johnnie up to her. As he joined them and took the reins, she turned and looked back. David was driving their second wagon and letting Eddie help bring along the cattle. Emily and Jimmie were on the seat beside him. David was showing Jimmie how to hold the reins, while Emily begged him to let her try it too. Just behind them, Eddie sat on Tillie, proud as punch that David was trusting him with his beloved horse.

Mary smiled at her husband. "I think the children are even more excited than I am."

He snapped the reins. "I don't think anyone in the world could be more excited than you, dear."

Saturday, June 28, 1879

By Saturday, Jim Decker was quite worried. There was still no sign of the two men they had left behind, and they were rapidly approaching the area where they had confronted Po-ee-kon earlier. Decker was very reluctant to enter his land without having all of them together, and so he called for a halt. They nooned at one of the rock tanks. The water was almost gone, and by the time the last of the cattle finished drinking, it was little more than a mud hole.

After a quick consultation among the men, it was decided that they would make camp here and wait for the other two to catch up. Decker then took Parley Butt and rode ahead to try to learn if the bad-tempered Navajo was still around. He left David and Eddie in charge of the cattle and Jim Davis and his family gathering enough firewood to last for a couple of days.

To their immense relief, Decker and Butt came riding back into camp a couple of hours later, leading the two missing horses! They had gone only a few miles up the road when they came across two young Navajo braves who just happened to be riding the missing animals. Though it galled him greatly to pay out precious cash for what was rightly theirs, Decker wisely decided it wasn't worth riling up the Indians, especially so close to Po-ee-kon country.

Parley Butt got a fresh mount, then, leading the two horses, started back for Moenkopi to find Niels Dalley and Ham Wallace. The others settled uneasily into camp to wait for their return.

"David?"

He looked up in surprise. He was standing night guard on the herd, seated on a dead cedar stump, thinking of Molly and his father. There was a half-moon, and in its light he saw two figures approaching. The voice was that of Jim Davis. "Over here," he called.

They made their way over, Mary cradling her stomach with one hand and holding onto Jim's arm with the other. "Mind if we join you?" Mary asked.

"Love the company," he said, standing up and brushing off the stump for her. She smiled and gratefully sat down. Jim came up and stood behind her. "Kids asleep?" David asked.

"Except for Eddie. He's talking with Brother Decker about what our new home will be like."

"Hot," David said shortly. "But that probably comes as no surprise."

"No," Mary groaned. "I thought St. George was hot, but this is terrible."

They fell silent for a moment, watching the shifting shapes of the cattle and hearing the low sounds they made as they bedded down. Then Jim spoke. "Mary has a question for you."

"All right."

She gave her husband a quick look, but he nodded his encouragement, and so she began. "Is it true that this Po-ee-kon is the one who killed Apostle George A. Smith a few years back?"

David was not greatly surprised by the question. He had watched Mary's face every time they had spoken of their experience with the Navajo on their way through the first time. He didn't want to add to her anxiety, but he decided she had a right to know.

"Yes and no," he said. "No because, according to Silas, it wasn't the Apostle, it was his son George A. Smith, Jr. He was an Indian missionary down here with Jacob Hamblin and others almost twenty years ago now. But yes, according to the reports, it was Po-ee-kon who actually pulled the trigger. From what we've heard, the little group of missionaries were con-fronted by a rather hostile band of Indians. While Hamblin and the oth-ers were trying to placate them, George A.'s horse wandered off and he made the mistake of going after it alone. Po-ee-kon and a couple of oth-ers followed. When they were alone, Po-ee-kon asked George A. if he could look at his pistol. Not wanting trouble, the boy took it out and handed it to him. Po-ee-kon walked around behind him, then shot him in the back three times."[2]

"How awful!" Mary exclaimed.

David nodded. "According to our guide, it happened within just a few hundred yards from where we were camped that night before we ran into him ourselves. Back then, Po-ee-kon was a young brave and maybe trying to prove his manhood. Now he's kind of a sub-chief under his father, Kacheenay. He has a nasty reputation for hating white men."

"You didn't see him as you came back through, did you?" Jim asked for Mary's benefit.

David shook his head. "We were traveling a lot at night by then to beat the heat, and there were only five of us and a packhorse." He was watching Mary closely. "But you can bet that by now those two Navajos who had our horses have told him exactly where we are, exactly how many cattle we have, and exactly how many of us there are."

She swallowed hard. "So you think there'll be trouble?"

"I hope not anything serious. Po-ee-kon was the only one who had a rifle last time. He's full of bluster and blow, and he may try to pick a fight, but we're all carrying rifles and pistols. He'll think twice about going up against that kind of firepower."

"Well," Jim said, "we'll add two more to that. Both Eddie and James have their own rifles."

"*James!*" Mary cried.

"I'm not talking about them fighting," he said stubbornly, "but if it comes to that, having a couple more rifles in evidence won't hurt."

David reached out and touched her arm. "Jim's right, Mary. The more guns he sees, the more likely it is he'll keep a lid on that temper of his."

"You think a thirteen-year-old and a nine-year-old are going to frighten an Indian chief?"

He shrugged. "You have to remember, by the time Navajo boys are nine, they are taking a herd of sheep out by themselves. They are taught to scare away coyotes, to drive a wolf or mountain lion off. No, if Po-ee-kon sees your boys with rifles, he won't think of them as boys."

"What if they attack at night? You said you had to camp there because of the water."

Her husband answered that. "The settlers at Moenkopi told me that the Navajos have a great reverence for the sun. They believe the sun can see what they do and then tells the Great Spirit. If the sun can't see them do something, then the Great Spirit cannot know about it, so they don't like to fight at night. Is that true?"[3]

"Not sure, but that's essentially what Silas said too."

That seemed to relieve her a little, so he shared something else he had learned. "They also say that the Indians, including the Navajos, are superstitious about hurting or killing Mormons."

"Really?"

"That's what Silas told me. I guess our people have done a lot to help the Indians. And they've seen some of the missionaries give healing blessings. They think we have strong medicine, which makes it bad medicine for them to hurt us. I guess the idea of good and bad medicine is very big in their beliefs."[4]

She squinted up at him. "Are you just saying that to make me feel better?"

He straightened to his full height, then pulled a finger quickly across his chest twice. "Cross my heart and hope to die; stick a finger in my eye; if I ever tell a lie."

She tipped her head back and laughed. "No wonder Emmy adores you. You're a bigger imp than she is." Then she got to her feet. "I know I shouldn't worry," she sighed. "I just can't seem to get this knot in my stomach untied. And I can't tell if the feelings I'm having are from the Lord, or just my natural tendency to worry."

"Sorry," David said, smiling to take away any sting. "I don't know much about feelings from the Lord. I'd have to go with the worry option."

She gave him a quizzical look. "Yes," she mused. "That's what Abby said too."

His head snapped up. "Abby?"

Jim was giving her a warning look, and she quickly tried to change the subject, but David wouldn't let her. "What did Abby say? And when did you talk to her?"

She feigned a great yawn. "Put me to bed, James," she said. "I'm suddenly very tired."

Monday, June 30, 1879

Fully expecting that Parley Butt, Niels Dalley, and Ham Wallace would catch up with them soon, Jim Decker had them break camp about nine o'clock on the morning of the second day and start moving forward at a leisurely pace. His estimate proved to be accurate; the three men caught up with them as they were nooning. It was a great relief to all of them to be back up to full strength. Decker hurried them along, and they were moving east again by half past twelve.

About five hours later, they reached the area where the desert gradually gave way to low ground, which was mostly a swampy marsh with one large, muddy pond. It was surrounded by thick stands of reeds, cattails, and a few clumps of willow. The cattle, having gone all day without water, rushed forward to drink from the pond, and the drovers let them run. They wouldn't leave this place without being driven.

They took the two wagons on past the pond for a short distance, where Decker pronounced they would stop until morning, even though there were still a couple of hours of daylight left. They quickly dug two or three shallow wells and found good water, though they had to let the mud settle out of it first.

While Mary was with the children, David quietly told Jim that this was the very place they had seen Po-ee-kon before, and that he should keep the children together and his rifle close.

It wasn't ten minutes later that they heard a cry. Where the land rose gently to the north of them, five Indians were striding toward them. The lead one was a tall and powerfully built man in faded Levi's but no shirt. He had a rifle in one hand and a belt of ammunition around his waist. The others were similarly dressed but carried only bows and quivers of arrows.

"It's Po-ee-kon," David said quietly.

All of the men of the camp were already gathered in around the two wagons, but they instinctively moved in a protective circle around Mary and the family. Jim Decker immediately began speaking in a low voice. "I want every man to quietly pick up a rifle. Just keep them crooked in your arm, muzzles pointed at the ground. We don't want them thinking we're looking for a fight. Mary, get the two younger children and keep them with you. Eddie and Jimmie, get your rifles and stand behind your father."

He turned. "Parley, you get over there beside the rear wagon where you can watch the cattle. Don't want somebody running 'em off while they keep us occupied. Ham, you and Niels take a position to my left where you can watch the trail. David, you'll be my backup."

As everyone moved into position, he lowered his voice even more. "I'm guessing it's just the five of them, so stay calm. Don't let them see that you're scared." He flashed a quick grin. "Even if you are."

The sun was still at least an hour from setting, but the rays were

coming from low in the sky. In the sunlight, the dark skin of the five
Indians glowed like burnished gold, making them look all the more frightening. As David watched them come, he had to give Po-ee-kon his due.
He was a commanding and intimidating presence. His mouth was pulled
back into an arrogant grimace, and his eyes were like cold pieces of
obsidian.

"He'll try to provoke us," Decker said. "But no matter what happens,
stay calm. The Navajos greatly respect courage in the face of danger. No
one fires the first shot, understand?" Then he turned to face the oncoming men squarely. "*Ya'at'eeh*," he called, raising one hand in greeting.
"*Ya'at'eeh*, Chief Po-ee-kon."

His answer was an angry bark. "Go away, Mormons. This *my* land! You
no stay. No cows. No water. You go."

Decker smiled and nodded as if he agreed with every word. "We come
as friends. We come in peace. We have gifts."

"You go!" Po-ee-kon shouted, his tone ratcheting up from angry to bel-
ligerent. "No want Mormons here. My land. My water."

"We must have water," Decker said, still speaking slowly and with great
calm. He turned and pointed to the piles of dirt where they had dug. "We
dig wells. You have. More water for your sheep. Free to you when we go."

The Navajo raised his rifle and shook it in Decker's face. "You no
stay!" he roared.

As casually as though he were simply getting more comfortable,
Decker shifted his rifle from his left arm to his right. The muzzle was still
pointed at the ground, but, casual or not, the Indian saw the movement
and understood it for exactly what it was. The white men were ready to
fight.

Po-ee-kon turned, muttering and cursing, and stepped back about ten
paces. He motioned for the others to gather in around him, and they began
talking in low, angry tones. Decker half turned. "Mary, we're going to go
on with our supper." Her face looked totally drained of color. "Are you up
to that?" he asked quietly.

She hesitated a moment, then nodded. They were having cold mutton, sliced squash, and corn bread. As she took a carving knife and began

to slice the mutton, David thought he saw her hands trembling a little, but her face was calm. She looked to her children. "Come, help me."

David turned his attention back to the Navajos. They were working themselves into a lather. Po-ee-kon kept shooting the whites threatening looks. David saw him staring at Mary as she moved to Eddie and started to fill a plate. He turned to the others, sneering. His hand moved back and forth in front of his stomach, emulating the shape of her pregnancy. There was a burst of raucous laughter from the others. Fortunately, Mary had her back to him and didn't see it.

"Heap that plate up pretty full," Decker suggested. "Put on lots of corn bread."

When she brought it to him, he set his rifle against the wagon, took it from her, then walked forward a few steps. "Food," he called. "Come. Eat. We be friends."

None of the five Indians moved, so Decker set the plate on a rock and stepped back again. Po-ee-kon stared at it for a moment, then savagely kicked at the ground in front of it. A spray of dirt and sand flew into the air, covering the food.

"Just ignore him," Decker said, backing up slowly. "Keep those plates coming."

"Sit down in a circle," David added. "Let's eat as though they weren't here. And no matter what, don't let them provoke you. Just keep cool."

Eddie brought David the second plate. He stood his rifle against the wagon wheel, where it was within easy reach, and took the plate. The boy's eyes were wide and his hands were trembling too. "Easy, Eddie," David said softly, smiling broadly as he did so.

As Eddie walked back to his mother, David sat down on the wagon tongue. He saw out of the corner of his eye that Po-ee-kon was watching him, so he reached down with one hand and adjusted his gun belt, pulling the holstered pistol a little more to the front. Again, it was not meant to threaten, just to remind them that he was still armed. Then he began to eat with gusto.

Po-ee-kon took three long steps and stood over David, glowering down at him. "You hitch horses," he shouted. "Go now."

David took a bite, not even bothering to look up. Again the Indian gave a savage kick, and again his moccasins sent sand spraying across David's plate. Without so much as a blink, David took another bite, chewed thoughtfully for a moment, then turned his head and spat out a few grains of sand. He turned to Mary. "Very good," he called.

Mary had laid the carving knife on the small wooden folding table she was using to serve the food. Po-ee-kon, seething now, left David and went to the table. Mary drew back, moving closer to her husband. Po-ee-kon snatched up the knife and started hammering it against the table, trying to break off the blade. When that didn't work, he moved to a rock and tried again. Hands stole toward pistol butts. Po-ee-kon stared around the circle for a moment, then flung the knife aside. He pulled a hunting knife with a long steel blade from a scabbard on his side.

He waved it in the air, turning slowly so as to face them each in turn. He stopped, looking directly at Mary. Though he was a good ten or fifteen feet from where she and the children were, David didn't like the way this was going. He set his plate down and picked up his rifle, laying it across his knees, his eyes never leaving the Indian. So far, the other four braves were letting their chief take the lead. That was good. They didn't seem anxious to start something yet.

"Steady, Mary," Decker called. "He's just trying to frighten you."

She gave him a bright smile. "It's working," she said through clenched teeth.

Jim Davis moved over closer to his wife and motioned the children to gather in with him. He handed them plates, then beckoned for them to begin eating. Watching all of this, his face almost a mottled purple now, Po-ee-kon took a step forward. "Hey, squaw!" he shouted. "You take children. Go home. Or you die." He brought the hunting knife up to his throat, then pulled the knife across it, the blade less than an inch from the flesh.

She never even looked up, and David felt a thrill of pride at her courage.

"You hear me, squaw? You go or you die." The knife flashed again.

David jerked forward. Standing just behind his father, young Jimmie

Davis had moved. His face was white and his hands were trembling violently, but the muzzle of his rifle was lifting. His father saw it too, and half turned his head. "No, Jimmie. Don't you be the one to shoot first. Just stand still."

That was enough. David got to his feet. Moving lazily, he walked toward the family, holding his rifle in both hands, the muzzle pointed to one side. He was pleased to see Jim Decker moving too. Then Niels and Ham were coming up behind him. One by one they moved over and stepped between the raging Indian and Mary Davis.

Po-ee-kon didn't move, but David saw a flicker of uncertainty in his eyes now.

"We want no trouble," Decker said easily. "We come in peace, but we fight if we must. You go now. We'll be gone when sun is in the sky again, and the water will be yours."

The Navajo's eyes were tiny slits, but he lowered the knife and stepped back. He looked directly at Mary, who was holding a whimpering Emily. "You go, squaw. Take girl with fire for hair away, or she die." Then he glowered at Decker. "When sun is in the sky, we return."

Decker simply nodded. "We'll be waiting," he said.

Po-ee-kon's chest rose and fell as he looked back and forth from face to face. Then he shoved his knife back in the scabbard and spun away. He stalked back to his friends, yelling directions at them. They immediately turned and broke into a trot, going back the way they had come. Po-ee-kon followed, but as they neared the top of the rise, he stopped and turned. "Po-ee-kon find more braves. We come. We kill *belagana*. You see. You die."

He turned and began to run, joining the others as they disappeared.[5]

Notes

1. These four men are named by both Miller and Nielson Dalley as being the ones who returned to Moenkopi (see Miller, *Hole*, 26, 152). Reay adds Kumen Jones to the list, but doesn't give a reference (5). No other mention is made of Kumen being there, so he was not included here.

2. The full story of the murder of George A. Smith, Jr., son of George A. Smith of the

Quorum of the Twelve Apostles, can be found in the history of Jacob Hamblin, who was there (see Corbett, *Jacob Hamblin*, 183–91).

3. This piece of information about the Navajos not liking to fight at night comes from James Davis's history (see Miller, *Hole*, 156).

4. Several writers mention the superstition various Indians of southern Utah and northern Arizona had about killing or harming the Mormons (see, for example, Hamblin, *Journals and Letters*, 35–36).

5. We have two accounts of this second confrontation with Po-ee-kon, one by Nielson Dalley and one by James Davis. Both accounts are included by Miller (see *Hole*, 27, 156).

CHAPTER 42

Monday, June 30, 1879

The moment the five Indians disappeared over the low rise to the north, Mary Davis fell into her husband's arms, shaking as violently as if she had been seized with a terrible chill.

David walked swiftly to Emily and John. The little boy had started to cry, watching the adults, looking bewildered. Emily's lower lip was trembling. David scooped Johnnie up into one arm, then knelt down in front of Emmy and took her by the shoulder. "You were so brave, Emmy," he said. "I am so proud of you."

With a great sob, she threw her arms around his neck. "I was scared, David."

"So was I," he said. He pulled back to look at her. "Then I saw you and Eddie and Jimmie being so brave, and I decided I had to be brave too."

"Really?" Her eyes were wide with wonder.

Jim and Mary Davis moved over and joined them. John held out his arms to his mother, and David handed him over to her. Jim turned to his two older sons. "You acted like men today," he said in a husky voice. "I am proud of you both."

"If he had tried to hurt Mama—" Jimmie began, but his father cut him off.

"I know, and you weren't going to let them do that, were you? You were a real man today, Jimmie. I am real proud to call you my son."

"Why did that Indian say I have fire in my hair?" Emmy asked, tugging on David's shirt.

He laughed. "Not *in* your hair, Emmy. He was saying that your hair is as beautiful as the flames of a campfire."

She reached up with one hand, preening it back. "Hmm," she said, quite impressed.

And with that they all started talking at once. The relief was so intense that they had to let it out. After several minutes, they gradually calmed down again. Jim and Mary sent the children back to finish their supper, then joined the other men, who were deep in conversation.

"Should we pack up?" Mary asked, looking at Jim Decker.

He shook his head. "The cattle need the water and the rest. And we're better here than out in the open if they decide to come back tonight."

"Do you think they will?" Jim Davis asked.

"I don't think so." He looked to the others, inviting them to offer their opinions.

"Possibly," volunteered Ham Wallace. "But if he had more braves close by, I don't think he would have talked about being back when the sun was in the sky again."

Parley Butt spoke. "Remember, when we came through here before, Seth Tanner told us that Po-ee-kon just uses this area for summer pasture. His village is actually ten or more miles away. If there was help nearby, he would have brought them with him."

"Maybe it's all bluff," Jim Davis said.

"Perhaps," Decker agreed. "That's his way, all right. But he's pretty steamed right now, and we just humiliated him in front of his companions. He's got a lot of face to save."

"Then we leave first thing in the morning?" David asked.

Again Decker shook his head. "If they're coming, and I think they will, we're better off making a stand here. Out in the open they could easily ambush us. We'll post guards tonight, of course, then be ready at dawn for whatever comes." He looked around the circle. "Agreed?"

They all nodded.

"Good. But let's be ready to move quickly. Niels, you and Parley bring the cattle in a little closer. David, you and Jim pull the wagons right up alongside each other." He tipped his hat back, looking at the sun, which was now almost ready to set. Then he turned to Mary. "It's going to be all right, Sister Davis. They know we mean to fight. You and Jim see if you can calm the children enough to get them to sleep. We'll worry about all the rest of this."

Tuesday, July 1, 1879

By seven o'clock the next morning, the sun had been up for two hours. Those had been two long, tense hours. David and the other men were posted around the perimeter of the camp, watching for signs of anyone approaching. But nothing was either seen or heard, and the relief they had felt the night before gradually began to return.

At quarter past seven, Jim Decker called all of the men in. "It looks like our friend couldn't get enough men to form a war party. Or maybe it was all just bluster after all. I would suggest we hitch the team, then build a fire and have some breakfast before we get on our way."

No one objected to that, and they fell to work. David helped Emmy, Jimmie, and Eddie gather firewood, while their mother and father began preparing the food. It was an indication of the resilience of children that by the time they brought the wood back to the wagons, they had made a game out of it and were giggling and laughing.

Dalley and Butt saddled the horses and hitched the teams. Wallace began pushing the cattle together so they would be ready to move at a moment's notice. Decker remained on watch, circling the camp slowly, searching the skyline for any signs of life.

But it was Jim Davis who was the first to see something. David heard him give a low cry. When he turned, Jim was looking south, where the land gradually rose to a low mesa about three miles away. About a quarter of a mile away, a figure was silhouetted in the morning light. It was a single man, an Indian, judging from the brightly colored blanket around his shoulders.

Instantly the camp went on alert again. The men grabbed their rifles and gathered in around the family. Decker walked to his horse and retrieved a pair of field glasses from his saddlebag. He came back, leaned back against the wagon to steady himself, then raised them to his eyes.

"It's an old man," he said. "Seems to be alone. Definitely a Navajo. Not armed in any way that I can see." Pause. "Quite old, actually. Grey hair. Not one of those here yesterday."

He lowered the glasses and handed them to David. "Cover me. I'll go talk to him."

Leaving his rifle behind, Decker strode away. David watched through the glasses as Decker and the Navajo met and started talking. The old Indian was excited about something. He kept turning and waving his arms, pointing to the northwest. David watched his face closely through all of it. "He seems quite worried," he reported, "but not angry."

Then David watched as Decker gave a curt nod, shook hands with the Indian, then spun on his heel and came trotting back. The others gathered in around him.

"All right," he said as he reached them. "Change of plans. We're leaving immediately."

"What?" Parley asked. "What's the matter?"

"This old man claims to be our friend. Speaks passable English. Says that Po-ee-kon has about twenty-five warriors on their way here. He's promising them lots of loot and a rich haul in cattle and horses. He says they're about an hour away."

"Do you believe him?" Niels asked. "Or could this be a trap?"

"We can't dismiss that possibility," Decker said tersely, "but I don't think so. He's very agitated. Says we must leave immediately. He'll go with us, show us a different way to get out of here. But he says we must move now."

He bit his lower lip, looking at the others. "What do you think? Do we trust him?"

Everyone was silent; then David said, "You talked with him. What do you think?"

"I believe him. I feel the Lord's hand may be in this."

"Then let's go," Jim Davis said.

Decker was all business now. "All right. Brother Davis, you and the boys kick out that fire, then you and Eddie get that first wagon rolling.

Stop and pick up the Navajo. He says he wants to ride in the wagon so he can see farther."

As Jim, Eddie, and young Jimmie sprang into action, Decker turned to Mary. "You take the children in the second wagon with David. He'll drive. Ham, you and Niels start those cattle moving. I want to keep them right close behind the wagons. Parley and I will scout out ahead, make sure he's not leading us into a trap." He looked around. "All right, let's go, let's go."

For almost three hours, the old Indian urged them forward. He sat on the wagon seat between Jim and Eddie Davis, directing them. He would stand up on the seat every few minutes and search the countryside around them. Decker had said he was agitated, and that proved to be an understatement. He seemed genuinely frightened and constantly urged them to go faster. Where possible, he kept them moving along the bottom of dry washes. That kept them out of sight, but it also put them in deep sand. The wagons kept bogging down, and from time to time they had to stop and let the teams rest. Each time they did, he got quite annoyed. "Must go! Hurry! Hurry! Must go!" he would shout again and again.

But by eleven, as they pulled up and out of a narrow wash onto a long, gently rising mesa, he finally relaxed. He told Jim and Eddie to pull up, and signaled for David to do the same. He stood on the wagon seat one last time, steadying himself against the bow of the wagon as he turned his head back and forth, scanning the vastness of the country around them. Finally, he grunted and jumped down. "We safe now," he declared. "They not follow. We rest. We eat."

For a time, as they prepared a cold noon meal, the men continued to scan the horizon, looking for any sign of a war party on their trail. The change had been so abrupt that they were still skeptical, but the change in the old Indian's countenance was so dramatic, and his relief so evident, that finally they relaxed. Mary fixed him a heaping plate of cold mutton, bread, and cheese, washed down with canteens of water, and insisted that he sit with them to eat. He did so, but said little while the others talked all around him.

Something about all of this didn't make sense to David, and he decided to put it to rest in his mind. He caught the Navajo's eye. "How did you know where we were?"

"I follow wagons and cows."

Decker flinched at that. They had not seen anyone. "For how long?"

"Four suns."

"Why?" David asked. "Why were you following us?"

He turned and looked directly at James Davis. "You not remember me?"

Jim leaned in, looking the old man up and down. "I don't think so."

"I come your store many times."

Mary's head came up. "In Cedar City?"

His head bobbed. "Yes. Cedar Town. Come many times. You always good to me. Give food. Very kind."

Her face suddenly registered understanding. "That was you?" she cried.

He cackled in delight, showing a mouthful of crooked and yellowing teeth. "Me young then. Very . . . how you say? Handsome?"

"Oh, my word," she breathed. Then she laughed. "I can't believe it. Your name is . . ." She searched in her memory. "Your name is Yaheeno, right?"

He beamed even more broadly. "Yah. Yaheeno."

"Yaheeno Begay?" Jim blurted. "Well, I'll be."

David was having a hard time believing it too. What an incredible coincidence! However, the old man's pleasure was genuine. He was almost laughing, he was so pleased. But David was still trying to understand. "How did you know the Davis family was in our party?"

Yaheeno Begay looked at David and saw that the other men were also listening carefully. They were not yet completely satisfied that he was all that he claimed to be. "One moon ago, I hear family of James Davis travel with Mormon wagons to San Juan. When they come to Black Mesa, I watch. No James Davis. Must be wrong."

"We stayed in Moenkopi while the others went on ahead," Mary broke in.

There was an emphatic nod. "I have cousin. He go Moenkopi, trade sheep. He say family of James Davis in Moenkopi. I go to Moenkopi. But you gone already. Mormons say family of James Davis is from Cedar Town. So I follow."

He gave David and the others a quick glance. "You not see, but I follow four suns." He pointed to his eyes with two fingers. "I watch. I see James Davis. I see family." He turned and looked at Mary. "I see Mother Davis. I see she is with child. I follow close. Make sure no trouble for family of James Davis."

Her eyes filled with tears. "Thank you."

David was finally satisfied, as were the others. All around the old man, the faces were smiling and nodding their approval. "Welcome, Yaheeno Begay," David said. "We thank you for your help. Po-ee-kon is a bad Indian."

There was a disgusted grunt. "Bad man. Bad medicine. Much anger for Mormons. I watch last night. Very bad. Very angry. When he leave, I follow. He go for warriors. Very angry. Plan to kill Mrs. Davis and James Davis. That very bad. I must stop."

He shrugged, as if those last three words summed it all up. Jim Decker stood and went to his saddlebags. When he returned, he had a small bag of tobacco makings brought along for this very purpose, a sack of dried corn, and a handful of coins. He faced the old man. "You are a good friend and brother, Yaheeno. Your medicine is good. We thank you. We wish we had more to give you, but thank you. Thank you for helping us."

That gave David an idea. He got up and went to the back of the wagon where his things were. He found his small valise, rummaged around in it, and came back with a silver and turquoise Navajo bracelet that he had purchased at Lee's Ferry. He had planned to give it to Molly as a peace offering on his return, but this was more important. Holding it where the Indian couldn't see what he had, he went to Mary and stood between her and Yaheeno. "Here," he whispered, handing it to her. "Let this be your gift of thanks to him."

She stared at it. "David, I can't—"

"Yes, you can. Giving a Navajo a piece of Navajo jewelry is a little odd, but I think coming from you, he will treasure it. And it wasn't cheap. I paid two dollars for it." When she still hesitated, he said, "We owe this man a great deal, and we need to show him that we are truly grateful. But I want it to come from you. He did this for you and Jim."

The tears spilled over. She wiped them away quickly, stood, and walked to the old man. Gravely, he got to his feet to face her. She struggled for a moment with her emotions, then began. "You are a true friend to my family, Yaheeno Begay. We thank you for what you have done this day." She held out the bracelet. "Please accept this as a token of our gratitude— our thanks—to you."

The old, wizened eyes stared for a moment at the bracelet, then lifted to meet her gaze. To David's surprise, his eyes were shining. Finally, he reached out and took the bracelet. He bowed his head. "Yaheeno thanks Mrs. Davis. You good woman. Good family." He paused. "Good friend. Yaheeno very happy. Yaheeno very glad Po-ee-kon no find you."

"Are you going to be in trouble with Po-ee-kon?" Niels Dalley asked.

There was a snort of disgust. "He know nothing. He stupid like sheep. Yaheeno like clever goat." He carefully shoved the bracelet and the coins into the pocket of his trousers, then retrieved the sack Jim Decker had given him. In with the tobacco and the cornmeal went the remainder of his mutton and corn bread. All of them watched him without a word.

Finally, he closed the bag and swung it over his shoulder. "Must go now. You safe."

"Thank you so much," Decker said.

Jim Davis stepped forward and clasped his hand. "You are a good friend. We shall never forget you. Thank you."

"Never," Mary said, ready to start crying again.

His eyes dropped to look at her stomach. "Maybe you call baby Little Yaheeno, no?" He threw back his head and cackled again, delighted with his little joke. Then he spun on his heel without another word and walked away, not once looking back.[1]

It was about four in the afternoon and the little party of two wagons, six men, one woman, and four children was rolling slowly eastward, back on the road that had been blazed several weeks before. They had come about fifteen or sixteen miles since they had left Yaheeno. Not only had there been no further sign of Po-ee-kon, but they had not seen another living thing, and they finally knew they were out of danger.

David was still driving the second wagon. In spite of Mary's insistence that she could drive now, especially while the road was pretty flat, David had decided, with Jim's concurrence, that he was going to drive her all the way to the San Juan.

Out of the corner of his eye he saw the wagon flap pull back, and a moment later Mary climbed up to sit beside him. "Are they asleep?" he asked softly.

"Finally. Emily is still so excited about all that happened, I thought she was never going to give up." Then she looked around. "Where's young James?"

He pointed to a rider alongside the lead wagon. "With me driving, Tillie's feeling a little rejected, so I asked Jimmie if he would take care of her for a while."

There was immediate skepticism. "He asked you first, didn't he?"

He drew a finger across his lips. "If you don't ask, I don't have to tell."

"And who's going to spoil my children when you leave to go back to Cedar City?"

"Are you kidding? Living in the lap of luxury over there in San Juan? They'll be so spoiled before year's end, you'll need me to straighten them out again."

Her chuckle was soft and amused. She looked up at the sky. "How long before we stop?"

"Decker wants to push on until dark."

"Good. The farther we go, the better I feel."

They fell silent for a time, letting the sway and bump of the wagon lull them a little. "I was really proud of you last night," David finally said. "Things got a little dodgy there for a time, but you never flinched."

"Oh, yeah? Good thing you couldn't see the inside of my stomach. It was doing flip-flops the whole time that beast was waving his knife around."

"Well, it didn't show on your face, and that's what's important."

"Thank you."

Another five minutes went by. Finally, she drew in a deep breath and turned to look at him. "David, there's something I need to tell you."

"All right."

"The night before we left Cedar City, Abigail McKenna came to see me."

That brought his head around with a jerk. "Abby?"

"Yes." She looked a little sheepish. "We're very good friends. Both she and Molly have watched our children for us from time to time."

"And what did she want?" he asked darkly. "Did she ask you to watch over me, see if you could redeem my soul while we're traveling together through the furnace of affliction?"

She laughed merrily. "Abby was right. You really are defensive about this, aren't you?"

He softened a little. "Sorry. I . . . I just get a little tired of being everyone's project."

"I see," she said thoughtfully. "Do you think that's how Jim and I see you? As our project?"

"No," he replied instantly. "And thank you for that. It's been refreshing to be just David." He hesitated. "So what did she have to say?"

"Not much. She told me what had happened with your father and Molly. She said you were hurt and angry, and probably could use a friend."

He gave her a long look. "Ah, so that whole thing with the skittish team that first morning was nothing but a trap?"

She touched his shoulder briefly, laughing again. "Of course. Couldn't you tell? I thought Emily's 'You saved my life' speech was an especially nice touch."

"All right," he growled. "Point well taken." He looked directly at her now. "And did Abby lay out my whole history for you—tell you of my traumatic childhood and how it has soured me?"

"No, but you did that yourself the other day." Then she pursed her lips slightly. "She did say one thing that I found rather strange. She said that, in her opinion, your problem is that for you, God is an abstract."

He was totally taken aback by that. "An abstract?"

She shrugged. "That's what she said."

"And what is that supposed to mean? That sounds so like Abby."

"I'm not sure. When I asked her, she refused to say any more." She cast him a quick sidelong glance. "I've thought about it a lot, actually."

"And?" he said, a little wary now. His expression made her chuckle again.

"I'm not going to preach at you," she said after a moment, "so you can relax."

He did relax, feeling the defenses immediately lower. He couldn't resent this woman whom he had come to admire so much. "So, did you come to any conclusions?"

"Usually *abstract* refers to something that is unclear or difficult to define."

He was shaking his head. "I don't find the idea of God difficult to understand. And I don't have trouble defining what He is. I think what bothers Abby—and especially Molly—is that my definition happens to be quite different from all of yours. I just don't see Him as hovering over us, interfering in our lives and—"

"That's an interesting choice of words."

"What, *hovering?*"

"Well, that too. But I meant *interfering.* I don't believe God interferes in our lives either. Intervenes? Yes, definitely, but not interferes. I don't believe He ever forces Himself on us."

He brushed that aside. "Interfering, intervening—I don't see a lot of difference. Anyway, I think He's out there. I think He created the world—and us—and now has gone on to other things."

"So you think we are His creatures?" At his puzzled look, she continued, "You said that He created us, so that makes us one of His creatures. Like an elephant or a beetle or a . . ." It trailed off.

Sensing a trap, he nodded slowly. "Yeah, I guess."

"Not His children?" she asked softly.

"Well, in one sense, but—"

"No, not in one sense, David. Do you believe that He is our Heavenly

Father? That we are literally His offspring, just like Johnnie and Emmy are my offspring?"

"No," he said shortly. "I believe He is our Father in the same sense that we say George Washington is the father of this country."

There was a long moment of silence, then a soft sigh. "Now I understand what she meant."

"So enlighten me," he said, suddenly finding himself getting a little irked by it all.

To his surprise, she shook her head. "No, I want to think about it for a time."

"Come on, Mary, I can take it."

But she just shook her head, and for the next quarter of an hour she refused to say another word. When she spoke, her words once again took him by surprise. "Do you remember when we talked about the blessing Bishop Arthur gave to me?"

"Of course."

"I don't think I told you this then, but in the blessing he promised us that if we went, we would be protected from harm."

"No," he said slowly, "you didn't mention that."

"So here's my question to you, David. And I'm just going to say it straight out, okay?"

He laughed. "So you're trying a new approach, eh?"

That made her laugh too. "James says it's my best and worst trait." She took a deep breath. "All right, here it is. We are out here, two hundred or more miles from home, in a forbidding and desolate land where Jim and I have never been before. Suddenly, we are confronted by an enemy who hates us. Unbeknownst to us, he is so angry, he rounds up twenty-five more braves with the intent to come back and massacre us all. Then, at the moment of gravest danger, an old Navajo shows up. This man has just happened to learn that a family by the name of Davis is traveling through the area. And this particular Davis family just happens to be the same one who treated this Navajo kindly many years ago. And so this Navajo just happens to decide to follow us and just happens to be close enough to see the danger we're in and just happens to show up in the nick of time to save us."

She paused, but only for more breath. "Oh, and by the way. During all of this, fervent prayers are being offered by the Davis family for God to intervene and protect their family. In fact, even as a knife is being waved under the nose of the mother of this family, the only thing going through her mind is, 'Please, Father. Help us. Protect my children.'" Have I got that pretty much right, would you say, David?"

She had him, and they both knew it. "Yes."

"You were an eyewitness to this, David. You saw it with your own eyes. So are you just going to pass it off as another—" she made quotation marks in the air with her fingers—"*remarkable coincidence?*"

"Ouch!" he said. "Just how long did you and Abby talk?"

"Long enough." She smiled. "So answer my question. Can you truly, after that experience, still maintain that you do not believe in a God who hears our prayers and cares for His children?"

He was silent for a long moment. She simply watched him and waited.

"No," he finally murmured. "I can no longer say that."

Tears came to her eyes. "Thank you. No further questions. When you return home, I should like you to take a letter back to Abby for me."

"And what are you going to say?"

"I'm going to tell her she's wrong. God is no longer an abstract for you."

Note

1. James Davis provides the account of this old Indian and his pivotal role in the deliverance of the Davis family and those who were bringing them on to the San Juan. Some details, such as the name of the old man, and how he learned that the Davis family was traveling across the reservation, have been added to flesh out the story. But the fundamental facts—his having received kind treatment years before from the family, his tracking them while they traveled, and his urging them on in order to escape Po-ee-kon's wrath—all come from Davis's own words (see Miller, *Hole*, 156).

CHAPTER 43

Saturday, August 2, 1879

David set his shovel against the cottonwood tree and walked over to the barrel of water. He removed his hat, wiped at his perspiring brow, then filled the dipper and poured it over his head. It was cooler than the late afternoon air, but barely. Didn't matter. He took another, then did it a third time. Suddenly, he saw a movement and turned. Eddie Davis was standing a few yards away, hat in hand, looking at him.

David hung the dipper over the side of the barrel and jammed his hat back on. "Is it time?"

Eddie nodded. "Pa thinks it will be any time now."

Forgetting the shovel, David walked swiftly to him. "Let's go then, boy," he said, slapping him on the shoulder. "Let's not be dawdling here."

✤

About an hour later, Elizabeth Harriman, the only other woman who had traveled with them, came to the entrance of the Davis house and pulled back the burlap sacks that served as their front door. Jim Davis shot to his feet, as did David and all four of the children.

Before she could speak, they heard a tiny wail from inside the house.

"You have a new baby, Brother Davis. Congratulations."

"How's Mary?" he said.

"Fine. Tired, of course, but she did real good."

"Is it a girl?" Emmy cried, running up to her.

Sister Harriman laughed. "That's not for me to say, darling. Let's let your Daddy go in first, and then in a minute or two you can go in and see your new baby."

Five minutes later, Jim reappeared at the door. The children gathered in around him, clamoring to know what it was. Jim's relief was such that it looked like he needed to sit for a few moments. But instead, he dropped to one knee and looked Emily in the eye. "Emmy, do you remember how you said that if you didn't get a little sister, you were going to send it back to Heavenly Father?"

She started to nod. Then, as it hit her what he was saying, her face fell. "Is it a boy?"

He laughed and swooped her up in his arms. "Well, we're going to name it Ethel Olive Davis. That's a pretty funny name for a boy."

Emmy stared at him for a moment, then shrieked in delight.

"You have a little sister, Emmy. A precious little sister. "[1]

Tuesday, August 19, 1879

Silas Smith rode up the line of wagons, checking with each driver to make certain they were ready to roll. When he reached the end of the line, he swung down. The Harrimans and the Davises stood together behind the last wagon, looking somewhat forlorn. David stood with the Davis family, holding Tillie's reins.

"So," Jim Davis said to Silas, "you're going back another way."

Silas looked somewhat disappointed. "We are. I think we're all agreed that the route we took coming over just isn't going to work for the main company."

"I think that is a wise decision," Mary Davis said. Holding little Ethel in her arms, she stood beside her husband. "I can only imagine how Po-ee-kon would react to that."

"So," Hank Harriman said, "should we be watching to the north for your return?"

Silas shook his head. "That's the way we're going back, following much of the Old Spanish Trail, but I'm not sure that's the answer either." Then he smiled. "But we will be back, one way or another." He swung back up on his horse. "In the meantime, you'll be in our prayers."

"And you in ours," Sister Harriman said. "Most fervently."

Silas looked down at David. "And we'll see you back in Cedar City."

As he rode away, Jim gave David a sharp look. "What's that supposed to mean?"

"I talked to Silas this morning. Because of my commitment to the McKennas, he's agreed to let me ride on ahead and not wait for the wagons. That will save me at least a week."

"Great idea," Mary said. "I'm sure they are very anxious for your return."

Behind them, they heard Silas shout something. A moment later the first wagons began to roll. With that, the Harrimans shook hands with David, turned, and walked away. David watched them go, then turned solemnly and shook hands with each of the two older Davis boys. "You're all grown up now, Eddie," he said. "You're pulling the weight of a man, and I'm proud of you. And you, Jimmie," David said, holding him in his grip for a moment, "for a moment there, I thought you were going to take on old Po-ee-kon all by yourself."

He flushed a little. "Well, it made me real mad when he started scaring Mama."

His father looked at him, eyes warm with pride. "I've never been more proud of you boys."

"We'll go shooting when I get back," David said. "Maybe go up on the Blue Mountains and hunt some deer. You, me, and Eddie." He dropped to one knee and gathered little Johnnie into his arms. "Tell you what, John. When I come back, I'm going to bring you a whole sack of all-day suckers. Would you like that?"

His head bobbed so vigorously his whole body wiggled.

David turned to Emmy, who immediately threw her arms around him. "And what about you, little princess? What do you want me to bring you?"

"I don't want you to go, David," she wailed.

"I have to, Emmy. I promised Brother McKenna I'd help him bring his family back here."

"Can I go with you, then?"

He shook his head. "Then baby Ethel wouldn't have a big sister to watch over her. We couldn't have that, could we?"

Her shoulders fell. "Promise me you'll hurry."

"You have my word on it," he said. He kissed her on the cheek, held her tightly for a moment, then stood up and faced her father.

"Thank you, David," Jim said. "Thank you for all you've done for my family. We owe you a great debt."

"On the contrary," he replied. "Getting to be part of your family has been one of the best things that's ever happened to me. I'm sorry for ever thinking it was a mistake for you to come."

Jim hooted softly. "And I'm sorry for wondering if it was a mistake for us to come."

Finally, David turned to Mary. She handed the baby to her husband, then reached in the pocket of her apron and withdrew a letter. She held it out, and David saw "To the McKennas" written across the front of it. "Would you deliver this for me?"

He took it, stepped back, and put it in his saddlebags. "So, you're making me a mail rider again," he teased. "Do I get to read it before I deliver it?"

"*No!*" Then her mouth softened. "But it's not what you think it is."

"Which is?"

"It's just not what you think it is." She came to him, put her arms around his shoulders, and hugged him as tightly as Emily had done. "Goodbye, David. Thank you."

He found his throat suddenly tight. "And what can I bring back for you, Sister Mary Davis?"

"You. With Molly by the hand. Maybe a ring on her finger."

Startled, he gave her a long look, then laughed. "I can promise the first. Can't do much about the second."

"Yes, you can," she said fiercely. And then suddenly her expression changed. A look of wonder filled her eyes. "On second thought, I won't hold you to either of those."

Totally taken aback by her words, he said, "You don't want me to bring Molly?"

She laughed merrily. "Of course. And Abby, and the rest of the family too. But not with a ring." She was very serious now. "Not even with the promise of a ring."

That really rocked him. "But why?"

"It's not time for that. Not yet." She paused, as if her thoughts were surprising even her. "You have to find yourself first, David."

And then, as he stared at her, she stepped forward and kissed him on the cheek. "Good-bye, dear David. And may the Lord be with you until you return."[2]

Notes

1. Mary Elizabeth Davis carried her baby to full term. She gave birth to a little girl just a few days after their arrival at the new settlement on the San Juan River, the first white child born in the San Juan Mission. She went on to have two additional girls while living there in Bluff, giving her four girls and three boys (from the Family Group Sheet of James Davis and Mary Elizabeth Fretwell Davis). True to the blessing of her bishop, she never lost another child.

2. Leaving the Harriman and Davis families settled at what eventually became Montezuma Creek, the exploring party started on their return journey sometime in mid-August. They took a northern route up through Moab, Green River, Castle Valley, and back into Paragonah via Bear Valley. Miller gives a good summary of their return journey, then states: "It was mid-September when they again reached Paragonah. . . . They had made a circuit of almost a thousand miles and had built several hundred miles of road through the desolate desert country. Most important of all, they had located a site for the San Juan Mission settlement" (Miller, Hole, 29–30).

BOOK VI

RESPONSE

1879

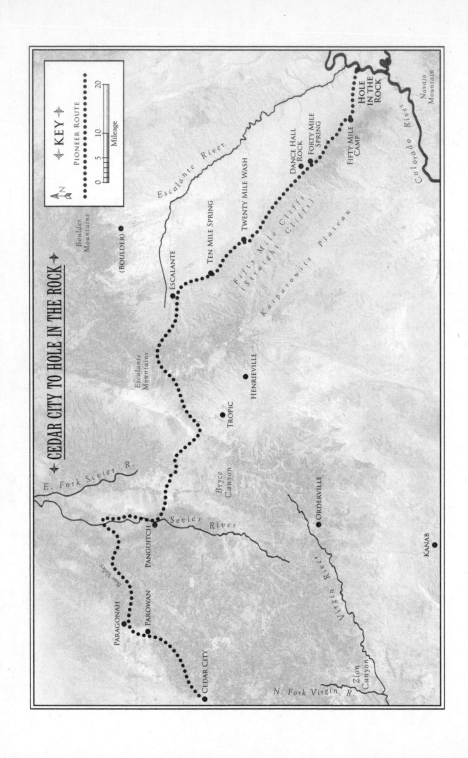

✦ CEDAR CITY TO HOLE IN THE ROCK ✦

KEY ✦
PIONEER ROUTE

Mileage
0 5 10 20

N

Boulder
Mountains

(BOULDER)

Escalante River

ESCALANTE

TEN MILE SPRING

TWENTY MILE WASH

DANCE HALL ROCK

FORTY MILE SPRING

FIFTY MILE CAMP

HOLE IN THE ROCK

Navajo Mountain

Colorado River

Fifty Mile Cliffs (Straight Cliffs)

Kaiparowits Plateau

Escalante Mountains

HENRIEVILLE

TROPIC

Bryce Canyon

E. Fork Sevier R.

Sevier River

PANGUITCH

ORDERVILLE

KANAB

Bear Valley

PARAGONAH

PAROWAN

Virgin River

CEDAR CITY

Zion Canyon

N. Fork Virgin R.

CHAPTER 44

Tuesday, September 2, 1879

"Patrick Joseph McKenna! Breakfast's ready. You get down here right now, or you're going to be late for school."

"Coming, Mama." A moment later, a head appeared through the railing near the top of the stairs. "Mama, I can't find my shoes."

Sarah McKenna shook her head. "If I don't end up with grey hair and ulcers, it won't be any fault of his."

"I'll go help him." Abby got up. "And I'd better get Molly going, too."

"Take a trumpet," her mother said. "Maybe she'll think it's resurrection morning."

Patrick McKenna appeared at the door to his study. "Won't make any difference. Molly will ask if she can't wait until the second resurrection."

Just then there was a resounding thud as something hit the floor directly overhead. Abby and her mother exchanged startled looks and bolted for the stairs. "Billy Joe?" Sarah called.

They heard a window being thrown open, then Billy Joe yelling, "David! David!"

The two women stopped dead, staring at each other. Patrick whirled and strode to the dining-room window that faced the street. "Well, I'll be," he cried. "It is David."

They stared at him. Then, as Billy Joe came shooting out of his room and down the stairs whooping and hollering, Abby said, "This is better than a trumpet. I think I'll wake Molly."

David pushed his chair back. "Sarah, that is the best meal I've eaten in six months."

She laughed, pleased. "Knowing where you've been, that's not much of a compliment."

"Well, it was wonderful."

"*Now* can we ask him questions, Mother?" Molly cried.

"No, Molly," her father answered. "Look at those poor bloodshot eyes. David needs to go to bed. We'll have him back for supper tonight—then we can all ask him all the questions we like."

She gave a soft groan of protest, but nodded.

David watched her, trying not to stare. She looked wonderful. Even having just been awakened, she was still luminous. Her eyes seemed brighter even than he remembered them. She had on a starched white linen blouse with long sleeves buttoned at the wrist, and a dark forest green skirt that went to her ankles. She still wore slippers, and her hair had been hurriedly brushed and tied back with a ribbon, but the sheer loveliness of her made him ache.

"You rode all night," Billy Joe said.

David wiped up the last bite of his pancake with syrup, ate it, then nodded. "I was going to stop in Parowan, then I thought, why not just go on and get this over with. So here I am."

"And we are so glad," Sarah said.

"Which reminds me," David said. "Mary sent you a letter. Billy Joe, it's in my saddlebags."

Billy Joe grabbed an apple from the bowl in the center of the table. "Can I give this to Tillie?"

David laughed. "She'll think she's died and gone to heaven."

Billy Joe raced out and was back quickly with the letter. He handed it to his father, who handed it to his wife. "Let's wait to read it," he suggested. Then to David he said, "We've been holding a room for you in the hotel. Your boxes are there. Tomorrow, we can get you set up again in the boardinghouse."

David stood up. "Thank you. A real bed sounds wonderful right now."

"You look real different," Billy Joe said. "Your beard and hair is so long." Before David could comment on that, he added, "Did you see any Indians?"

"Quite a few," David chuckled. "In one place, about five more than we wanted to."

"Wait," Molly cried. "How come Billy Joe gets to ask questions, and I don't?"

"There'll be time tonight," her father said. "For you too, Billy Joe."

"But," Abby exclaimed, "you can't just drop a comment like that and not explain yourself."

So he told them quickly about their two meetings with Po-ee-kon, not dwelling too much on how he had brandished his knife at Mary and threatened to kill them all. Then he explained how the old Navajo had shown up and helped them get away. When he finished, all of their eyes were wide, but Billy Joe's were like silver dollars. "Neat!" was all he could think of to say.

"I'm sorry, David," Sarah said, "but I have one question too. How is Mary? Did she have the baby all right?"

He smiled, feeling the deep weariness now. "She did wonderful, and Emily now has a new baby sister. I'm sure she'll tell you about it in her letter."

As the women gave soft exclamations of joy and began to talk excitedly with each other, Patrick took David's arm. "Okay, that's all. Billy Joe, you take Tillie to the livery stable and get her unsaddled and put away. David is going straight to bed."

※

David slept for seven hours straight. Still feeling like he had been stuffed through a knothole, he got out a clean change of clothes and, stopping only to make sure Tillie's needs were met, went straight to the barbershop. A hot bath, a shave and a haircut, and a set of clean underwear and clothes did wonders for him. Telling the barber to burn his old clothes, he stopped to look at himself in the mirror, then replaced his hat and stepped outside.

"Well, hello there. Are you new in town?"

He turned in surprise. Molly sat on a wooden bench. She stood and
came to him. One hand came up and touched his cheek momentarily. "My,
you do clean up real good," she said.

"Well," he said, "this is a surprise."

There was a quick flash of the impish Molly he had met that first day
in the post office. "I was hoping you might say, 'Well, this is a *pleasant* surprise.'"

He laughed and moved to her. "It is a pleasant surprise." Then his eyes
narrowed. "How long have you been out here?"

"I'd rather not answer that."

He nudged her. "Come on. How long?"

She blushed a little. "Not that long." Her cheeks colored. "I . . . I
wanted to talk to you alone before we all get together."

He gave her a long look. She had changed clothes since this morning
and was even more lovely than she had been at breakfast. Her eyes were
clear and bright, but they were filled with sadness, where this morning it
had been only joy. It made him want to take her into his arms and hold
her, help wipe away the hurt he knew he had caused her.

He sighed, then nodded slowly. "I'm sorry you had to wait. Shall we
walk?"

"Yes, but not up Main Street. The whole town's already buzzing about
your return."

She was right, of course. Two people had already come into the
barbershop to talk with him while he was being shaved. "You lead the way
and I'll follow."

⁂

Her destination turned out to be just outside of town. It was a grassy
spot in the shade of the cottonwood trees along Coal Creek. The afternoon sun was low in the sky, and a slight breeze flowing off the mountain
just to the east had taken the edge off the heat. The creek level was low
this late in the season, but there was still enough water that it murmured
softly.

She led the way into the shade of the trees, and David realized she had

chosen this spot deliberately. They were still in clear view of the road—
thus maintaining propriety—but most passersby would probably not notice them. She sat on a fallen log and motioned for him to sit on a large
stone so he would be facing her. She had not spoken since leaving the
barbershop. As they settled onto their respective seats, he wasn't sure if he
should speak or wait for her to begin.

After watching her for a few moments, he decided the former was the
wiser course. "Molly, I . . ." She looked up, her eyes anxious. He smiled.
"It is so good to see you again."

She instantly began to cry. "Oh, David. I am so sorry," she whispered.

"Sorry?" he said quickly. "No, Molly. Don't be sorry. What you—"

"Please," she cut in quickly. "Let me speak first."

He nodded and sat back.

Reaching in the pocket of her dress, she pulled out an embroidered
handkerchief. She looked away again as she dabbed at her eyes, sniffing
back the tears. It took her almost a full minute to regain her composure.
Only then did she face him. She took a quick breath, then another. Finally,
she sighed a deep, sorrowful sigh. "I am so sorry for what I said that morning, David. No, more than that. I'm sorry for *how* I said it and *when* I said
it."

"Molly, I'm not looking for an apology."

She waved that away. "I should have seen how deeply you had been
hurt. But I was so wrapped up with my own hurt, my own frustrations, my
own pain. And so I unloaded on you. At the worst possible time for you."

"Molly," he said softly, "you said only what needed to be said."

She was fighting the tears again. "Perhaps. But it didn't have to be
right then. And for that, I am truly sorry. I was thinking only of myself."

He smiled sardonically. "Well, it did feel like I had walked straight out
of one ambush into another." Then he immediately sobered. "But that
doesn't change the fact that you were right."

"Any more, I'm not sure that I was right," she whispered.

"Molly," he said sharply, "don't back down." Then immediately, he saw
that this was getting them nowhere. He thought of that last puzzling conversation he had had with Mary Davis. "Look, Molly, we can hash and

rehash what happened, but it gets us nowhere. The real question is, what now?"

"I would like to know the answer to that very much." Then, before he could answer, she patted the log beside her. "Will you come hold me while we talk? I've missed you so much."

He stood and went to her. But when he sat, he didn't put his arms around her. "Molly, I've had a lot of time to think about us, especially these last two weeks when I've been alone in the saddle for ten or twelve hours a day. And finally, just last night, I made a decision."

"What?"

He turned so he was facing her, trying hard not to be lost in the beauty of her eyes, the loveliness of her face. "Let me start by sharing two things I know to be true. First, we can't just pick up where we left off. Too much has happened. There are still too many questions, too many issues." He drew in a breath. "And yet, I'm back. I have a contractual commitment to your father and to your family to help you make this journey. That means now—starting tonight—we're going to be thrown together virtually every day."

"And that's bad?" She was half teasing, but half serious.

He didn't answer. "The second thing I've learned is that a wagon company is a unique social setting, if I can use that phrase. It's unlike anything else I have ever experienced. Everything kind of boils down to the day-to-day fight for survival. All the extraneous is stripped away and only the core remains. That significantly alters the dynamics of personal relationships."

"I'm not sure I understand what you're saying."

"Because the experience has such a narrow focus, normal things tend to get magnified out of proportion—petty irritations can lead to massive blowups, minor disagreements can become highly divisive, harmless competitions turn into full-out contests. Everyone knows everything about every person in the company. It's ten times more intimate than even a small village. If we are trying to work out some of the kinks in our courtship—and I think we both have to admit that there are several—it will quickly become everyone's business. For example, if we were on the

trail right now having this talk, before we could even get back to the wagons, everyone in the company would be wondering what we were saying."

"My goodness," she said. "I hadn't considered that."

"This is going to be hard enough for us without that kind of intense
scrutiny."

"So are you saying it's over between us?" she asked slowly.

"No, Molly! I love you. Perhaps more now than when I left. But that
doesn't change things. We still have much to work out. And maybe it
won't work out. All I'm saying is that I don't think we can work it out in
this particular setting."

He saw the first glimmer of hope in her eyes. "But after we get there?"
she asked.

"Yes! Then we go at it straightaway, give it our all, see if this is meant
to be." He was leaning forward in his earnestness. He took her hand. "Silas
says he hopes that once we determine which road to take, then—"

Her startled look stopped him. "Yeah," he said glumly, "I'll say more
about that tonight, but the route we took isn't going to work. We're looking for another way." He ignored her questioning look and plowed on.
"Silas says that once we decide which way to go, he hopes we can be there
in no more than six weeks. Even if it's another month before we leave,
that's still only three more months, Molly. Isn't it worth putting things on
hold for three months rather than risk having them fall apart altogether?"

She was searching his face. "So you're not just trying to find a way to
let me down easy, tell me that it's over, that you want nothing more to do
with me."

He was incredulous. "Is that what you think?"

"If you did, I wouldn't blame you." Then she shook her head. "No,
David, I see what you're saying. And though it makes me want to cry, I can
see the wisdom in it."

An immense relief washed over him. It had taken him a long time, but
he had finally decided this was what Mary had been trying to tell him.
Putting a ring on Molly's finger or making promises to each other would
only complicate things and destroy any chance they had. "So you agree?"

She hesitated, then smiled, though it was tentative and filled with sorrow. "I think so. Tell me what that means. We can't just ignore what has already happened between us."

"You're right, but we can set it aside for now, put it on the shelf, as it were."

"Be more specific," she said.

"Okay, tonight we tell your parents that we are no longer officially courting. They'll think it's because of what happened, but that's all right. We become just friends. We don't go off and have long talks like this one. No physical affection, not even holding hands."

Her head dropped. "I was afraid you were going to say that." Then she looked up again. "I don't know if I can do what you say," she whispered.

"You can—*if* you think it is the right thing to do."

"And you do? You're really sure of that?"

He wanted to take her and shake her. *I'm not sure of anything anymore!* But he finally just nodded. "I am. I think it is our only hope."

"All right," she murmured finally. She didn't sound at all convinced.

"Molly, think of it this way. You keep telling me that you believe that God is a loving Father who knows us personally and cares for us as His children. You say you believe that He intervenes in our lives, blessing, protecting, and watching over us. Right?"

"I do."

"Then trust in that."

Her mouth opened, then shut again as the implication of his words hit her. He could see that she understood. "I do trust Him, David. I do with all my heart. But the question is, do you?"

"I'd like to think I do. But it doesn't matter. My lack of faith can't cancel out yours."

That startled her even more.

He was watching her closely now. "Can it?"

"No, I . . ." Her mouth set in a firm line. "No. You're right. It can't. I just have to have faith that He will help us work through this."

"Then we're agreed?"

She sat there for a long time, her hands twisting in her lap, her eyes down, but finally there came a slow nod. "Yes."

He got to his feet. "Are you sure?"

She rose as well and stepped forward to face him. "No, not in any way," she said, but she was nodding as she spoke. Her head tipped back as she looked up at him. There was a deep longing in her gaze. It was too much for him. He took her by the shoulders and drew her closer. She closed her eyes and her lips parted a little.

But as he bent in to kiss her, she jerked back. "No, David. If this is the best thing for us, then we have to start now. No last farewell kisses. No last tearful good-byes."

"I agree." Then he stepped forward, took her by the shoulders again, and drew her to him. He kissed her softly, his hand coming around behind her neck to hold her there. For a moment she was startled; then her arms came up around him and she kissed him back. They clung together for several seconds before he released her and stepped back.

"That wasn't a farewell kiss," he grinned. "That was just saying hello after six months."

She cocked her head to one side, her eyes teasing. "Eh? What did you say?"

And so he said it again.

CHAPTER 45

Wednesday, September 3, 1879

When David entered the lobby of the McKenna House the next morning, there was no one behind the front desk, and he could see that the post office wasn't open yet. He went right to Patrick's office and knocked on the door.

"He's not there yet."

He turned. Abby had come out from somewhere and was now behind the desk. He turned and walked over. "Mornin', Abby."

"Good morning, David." She glanced at the office door. "Daddy and Carl are having an early meeting at the bank to set up things for the hotel after we leave."

"Oh. Did your father decide to sell it, then?"

She shook her head. "He's selling everything else, but he's decided to keep the hotel. Carl is going to return here after we get to San Juan and manage it for us."

"He's coming back? But I thought . . ."

She blushed. "A lot happened while you were gone, David."

"Meaning what?"

Her color deepened even more. "Carl came to Daddy about three months ago and asked for permission to court me."

"Finally," David blurted. Then it was his turn to blush. "I didn't mean it that way, it's just that Carl is so . . ." He stopped, realizing he was only digging the hole deeper.

"I told Daddy that I wasn't interested."

David's head came up with a snap. "You turned him down?"

She was playing with the ledger book, moving it back and forth on the desk.

"No wonder he's coming back here."

Her eyes flared. "Knowing that Carl was just being obedient to President Lunt's counsel for single young men to marry before we leave didn't seem like a good enough reason to me."

"Oh," David said softly, "I think it was much more than that for Carl."

She stared at him for a moment, looking like she was ready to bristle, then smiled quickly to hide her embarrassment. "Besides, I knew that Carl could never be happy living in some isolated, tiny settlement. That's just not Carl."

"Well, well, well," David said. "That must be a relief to your father."

She gave him a strange look. "Which? Having Carl take care of the hotel, or not having Carl as a son-in-law?"

At David's startled expression, she laughed right out loud. Then she decided to change the subject. "Dad told me that he gave you your mail. How are things with your father?"

He leaned his elbows on the counter. "Wonderful, actually. He's been spit on, yelled at, called a Yorkie by the Londoners, and even spent one night in jail. And yet he sounds happier than I've ever heard him in my life. They've now sent him up to what they call the Black Country, near Birmingham. He's working in the villages in South Staffordshire, which is a huge coal mining and steel center." He laughed as he thought of one thing his father had written. "He claims that the Black Country accent is so terrible, even he can't understand it." His eyes went soft. "He's baptized almost a dozen people so far."

"My goodness," she said, with a puckish smile. "It's a good thing no one was able to talk him out of going to England."

He winced. That was Abby. Rapier sharp, and straight for the heart.

"Sorry," she said. "I was just teasing."

"No you weren't," he said lightly. He reached in his jacket and extracted a letter. "You'll be happy to know, however, that I've just written him. I didn't have an address for him before, so I haven't been able to write until now. I've asked him to forgive me."

Her eyes softened. "He had forgiven you before you were halfway to Parowan. He stopped by here shortly before he left for Salt Lake, and we had a long talk."

He sighed. "I'd appreciate it if you didn't tell everyone what a fool I've been."

She scoffed aloud. "Don't have to. They already know that."

"Ah, Abby," he chuckled, "I think I shall appoint you as my humility monitor."

Though she was trying to keep a straight face, he could see the laughter in her eyes. "There's no need for that. Ain't that much to monitor," she drawled.

This time he openly guffawed. "But you're still on the job anyway, aren't you."

Now she was laughing too. "It is good to have you back, David."

He handed her the letter. "The post office isn't open yet. Could I get you to post it for me?"

"Molly's in there," she said. "It's just not quite eight o'clock yet."

"Ah . . . well, I've got to run. Could you just post it for me?"

"I see," she said slowly. "And are you running *to* somewhere or running *from* someone?"

At his look, she just shook her head. "I'll take it to her."

"Thank you. Let me know how much it is and I'll pay you when I come back." He waved and started for the front door.

"David?"

He stopped and turned.

"Thank *you.*"

He almost asked her what for, but he already knew the answer. "So she told you?"

There was a soft laugh. "Of course."

She came around the counter and walked over to join him, still holding his letter. She lowered her voice as she reached him. "It *is* the right thing to do, David. Thank you for being wise enough to see that."

"Did she tell your parents, too?"

"Only that the two of you had decided not to have a formal courtship right now because of the trip. I'm sure they think it's because of what happened when you left."

He grunted.

"I was worried that she would be so afraid of losing you that she would decide she had made a mistake when she told you it was over and . . ."

"And you don't think it was a mistake?"

"No. Do you?"

"Not in any way."

She tapped his arm with the letter. "Good answer. *Now* I'll post your letter for you."

But once again, as he started to leave, she called out to him. "One more thing. Did you know that Mary sent a separate letter to me in that envelope?"

"She said she wanted to write you," he said slowly.

"She said that God is no longer an abstract for you. Would you like to comment on that?"

"Maybe sometime. Not now." He took a breath. "I will say this much. I told you once that the last time I prayed to God was when I was thirteen years old and my mother was dying."

"Yes."

"Well, I can't say that anymore."

Her eyebrows shot up. "Are you saying—"

"See you later, Abby." Then as he started to turn, he stopped. "Please don't say anything to Molly about this. It will only complicate things."

Tuesday, September 16, 1879

The next two weeks were almost a blur for David. From the moment he arose in the morning until his head hit the pillow at night, the day was crammed with things to do and places to go. Six months had gone by, and the departure of the main company was imminent.

His first priority was to learn where things stood with the preparations for their upcoming departure. After meeting with Carl for three hours, he took the rest of that day and half the next going over the books and the

lists of things they had acquired while he was gone. Carl and Molly had
done an outstanding job in David's absence. Their methodical and deliberate approach was perfect for something as complex as this.

His second priority was putting "the plan" concerning him and Molly
into effect. The morning after his return, he moved out of the hotel and
back into the boardinghouse. Sarah objected, saying that if they were leaving in a month, it was silly not to just stay where he was. However, David
insisted, and Patrick, who seemed to understand why it was important,
made only token resistance. Patrick also defended him when David told
Sarah that he was not going to be a permanent fixture at the McKenna
supper table. There was simply too much to do. By then, even she seemed
to sense what he was doing, and accepted it with minimal protest.

Through it all, Molly was surprisingly compliant. Since the hotel was
Patrick's headquarters, David was in and out regularly. He often saw her
behind the front desk or in the post office, but she was always bright and
sunny, treating him no differently from how she treated everyone else.

On Sundays, he went to church with the McKennas, but he sat next
to Molly only if it accidentally turned out that way. He was inundated with
questions from the members, especially those who had been called, but he
demurred. Silas Smith was their leader, and it was not David's place to give
any kind of official report until he returned.

A few days after David's return, Bishop Jens Nielson—who would lead
the Cedar City contingent until they met up with Silas Smith in
Paragonah—received a letter from Elder Erastus Snow. The Apostle had
received the letter sent by Silas from Colorado and knew now that the
southern route was not viable. He also let Bishop Nielson know that clear
last spring, Silas and he had determined to start at least a preliminary exploration of a possible central route. Elder Snow had directed some of the
brethren over in Escalante, the farthest east settlement between Cedar
City and San Juan, to undertake that task. They would come to Parowan
for the next stake conference and report their findings.

On September twelfth, a telegram for Elder Snow arrived in St. George
and was immediately forwarded to Cedar City. Silas Smith and the exploring party had reached Salina and expected to be back in Paragonah in five

to six days. Thereafter, Silas and Bishop Nielson would immediately travel to St. George to confer with Elder Snow.

Wednesday, September 17, 1869

David had gone up Cedar Canyon to make sure that there was enough good grazing to leave the stock up there until the departure or until the weather turned cold. It was nearly dark when he rode up to the McKenna livery stable. The barn still had the McKenna name over the front doors even though it had been sold, but David suspected it would be changed once they left. He unsaddled Tillie, put her in a stall, brushed her down, got her a bucket of oats, and was just starting to leave when Billy Joe McKenna came rocketing through the back doors. He slid to a halt, surprised to see David standing there.

"Hey, there, Billy Joe."

"Hi, David. Somebody said you were back. Can I help you with Tillie?"

"All done. But you can walk me to the boardinghouse."

As they left the barn, David ruffled his hair. "How's school?"

The boy's head dropped, and there was a pained expression on his face. "Not so good. I had to write, 'I will not bring stink bugs into class' fifty times on the blackboard after school yesterday."

"And why would the teacher make you do that?" David asked solemnly.

He shot David a scornful look. "Because I brought five of them in a bottle and they got out."

"But you don't know how they got out?"

His nose crinkled up as he squinted up at David. "Well, I did crack the lid a little."

Just then a figure appeared, coming out of the boardinghouse. David was surprised to see it was Molly.

"Hi," he called.

"Hi, Molly," Billy Joe said.

She hurried up. "David, Dad wants you to come over to the house right away."

"Okay," he said slowly. "Anything I need to bring?"

"No. There are four brethren there. One of them is named Silas Smith." She laughed at his delighted expression. "One is Jim Decker, one is Joe Nielson, and one is Kumen Jones. Abby's gone to get Bishop Nielson. He'll be so excited to have his two boys back."

"Wonderful." This was good news indeed.

"Brother Jones said to tell you that you'd better hurry."

"Why's that?"

"Because when I left, they had Mother and Daddy laughing so hard they were holding their sides. He was telling them something about some rattlesnake eggs."

David groaned. "They weren't."

"They were. And as I left, Brother Decker was saying something about you scaring the pants off the Davis boys by throwing a rattlesnake at them. Would you like to comment on that?"

"No," he growled. "Come on. Let's hurry. Those brethren are notorious exaggerators."

"That's funny," she said. "That's exactly what they said about you."[1]

Note

1. I could find no specific date for the return of the exploring party. George Hobbs said it was the middle of September (see "History of the San Juan Stake," 7). I have some of them in Cedar City on the seventeenth, but their first welcome would have been in Paragonah and Parowan since they were returning by way of Panguitch and Bear Valley.

CHAPTER 46

Saturday, September 27, 1879

In conjunction with the stake conference, a special meeting was called for all of those who had been called as missionaries, including parents of single missionaries. It was set for one o'clock on Saturday afternoon. The McKennas, along with Carl Bradford and David, were there at 12:20 and still ended up two-thirds of the way back in the Rock Church on Main Street. By the time President Henry Lunt, president of the Parowan Stake, stood to open the meeting, every seat was full, and several people were standing in the back.

Following the opening hymn and prayer, President Lunt came to the pulpit. Quickly the chapel quieted. He stood there for a moment, letting his eyes sweep across the assembly; then a slow smile stole over his face. At a time of such high excitement, every eye should have been on him, but many were still craning their necks to see the two strangers seated on the stand behind him between Silas Smith and Elder Erastus Snow.

"Brethren and sisters," he said, trying to gently chide them a little. "If I could have your attention, please, we'll introduce the two brethren at whom you are all gawking."

That won him some good-natured laughter. As it died away again, David glanced quickly at the family. He was on the one end, next to Billy Joe. Abby was next, then her father and mother. Carl sat beside Sister McKenna, and Molly was on the far end, as far removed from David as possible. He smiled inwardly. The same was true of Carl and Abby. This was going to be an interesting trip.

Finally, President Lunt began. "Brethren and sisters, normally the custom in such a meeting as this would be to hear from myself first, and our esteemed leader, Elder Erastus Snow, second."

Someone groaned audibly near the back, and another ripple of laughter filled the hall.

President Lunt turned to look at the Apostle. "I shall take that as an affirmation that we should not proceed according to custom." More laughter, now open and appreciative. Then he sobered. "Considering the unique circumstances of our situation, and in consultation with Elder Snow, who presides at our meeting, the order of the program shall be changed as follows. Elder Snow wishes to say a few words of introduction. Thereafter, he will invite others to speak to us as he sees fit. When that is finished, we shall open the time for questions."

Now the undercurrent of sound turned into a solid murmur of approval. By the time the McKenna group had arrived in Parowan last evening, the whole town was buzzing with the news: Two men from Escalante had arrived in Paragonah, six miles to the north, earlier that day. They were staying with President Silas Smith at his home there. Elder Snow had gone north to meet with them.

The rumors flew wildly on every side. These were the scouts sent by the Church to look for a better route. No, they were only a couple of cattlemen come to do business with Silas Smith. They *had* found a shortcut, which would save the company three or four hundred miles of travel. (David found that one especially amusing, since it would have meant they would have had only about ten miles to go to reach their destination.) They had scouted all across the area but had come to report there was no way through. And on and on it went.

But one thing was for sure now. The two weren't just cattlemen, or they wouldn't be seated on the stand now. That was what was creating all the buzz in the meeting.

"Brethren and sisters," Elder Snow began, "thank you for coming. We were afraid when we called this meeting that hardly anyone might show up."

There was a roar of laughter at that.

He sobered quickly. "We are here today for one purpose and one purpose only, and that is to settle on a route to the San Juan and get you good people on your way as soon as possible."

"Hear, hear," someone murmured.

"I should like to say a few words of introduction, then invite President Silas S. Smith, president of this company and of the San Juan Mission, to say what is on his mind. He may then call on his two associates to speak as well. Following that, I shall make one or two concluding remarks; then, as President Lunt has suggested, we shall entertain questions."

There were many heads bobbing as he paused. "First of all, I should like to formally introduce you to these two brethren who have you all so curious. A few of you may already know them. They are both from Escalante and are here at our request."

He half turned. "Brethren, if you would stand as I introduce you. First, Bishop Andrew P. Schow, bishop of the Escalante Ward of the Panguitch Stake of Zion."

The man closest to Silas Smith got slowly to his feet. David leaned forward. He was shorter than the Apostle by several inches but was thickly built, with broad shoulders. Like Elder Snow's, his hairline receded back quite far on his head. Where he had hair, however, it was thick and black, as was his full beard. Dark, intense eyes peered out from beneath bushy brows. David guessed that he was in his late thirties or early forties.

"Bishop Schow was born in Aalborg, Denmark. He and his family came to Utah in eighteen fifty-four and have helped settle several towns. He and his wife lived in Panguitch for a time, then moved farther east when he was called to lead a party of six men to explore Potato Valley on the east side of the Escalante Mountains. They did so and eventually established a settlement there, which they called Escalante.[1] It was my privilege to call Brother Schow two years later as bishop of the Escalante Ward. Thank you, Bishop."[2]

Schow sat down.

"I should now like to introduce Brother Reuben Collett." As the second man stood up, there were soft exclamations of surprise. When he had entered the hall with Silas Smith and Elder Snow, he had been flanked on both sides and so the people hadn't been able to see him clearly. He was a lean man, and taller by half a head than Schow. He too wore a thick beard, but he had a full head of light brown hair. None of that, however, was what had created the reaction. One of the sleeves of his suit coat was pinned to his shoulder. He was missing one arm!

If Elder Snow noticed the crowd's reaction, he gave no indication. "Brother Collett, who is originally from Cache Valley in northern Utah, was also one of the early settlers of Potato Valley. He is a successful farmer, rancher, and businessman. He grows sorghum there and is involved in the manufacture of molasses. He also serves as the constable for that area."

That brought another soft intake of breath from the crowd. A one-armed constable?

Collett sat down again, not waiting to be invited to do so. Elder Snow smiled out at the audience. "Brother Collett will not appreciate me doing this, but I think it will help you to better understand why we have such confidence in him. As you have seen, Brother Collett is missing one arm. He lost it in a threshing accident while still a young man. In spite of that, while living in Cache Valley, he was made the constable there. Brother Collett's reputation as a lawman was established when he pursued a dangerous criminal and, by himself, subdued the man, then relieved him of both of his guns and brought him back to the county jail for trial."[3]

David glanced at Patrick, who was nodding thoughtfully. If Elder Snow's purpose had been to give these two men some credibility, he had just done that very effectively.

"So," the Apostle concluded, "these two men were asked by President Smith—acting in his capacity as president of the mission—to scout out a possible route from Escalante eastward to the San Juan River Valley. I have tremendous respect for them both, and for their experience. I have listened to their reports very carefully. Like Silas Smith, both of these men are seasoned scouts. Therefore, I commend them both to you."

He stepped back from the pulpit, "President Smith. Take what time you need and share your feelings, and then let's hear from these two brethren."

Silas Smith rose and came to the pulpit as Elder Snow sat down. David watched him closely. When he had come to Cedar City about ten days before, he had looked tired, almost haggard. Now he looked rested. His beard and hair had been carefully trimmed. His eyes had that brightness and clarity of purpose that David had come to know so well.

"Brethren," he began, his voice ringing out with confidence and exuberance, "it is good to be back among you once again. It is also good to look into the faces of those with whom I traveled for the last six months. And it is good to look into the faces of those with whom I shall be traveling again soon. I look forward to that a great deal."

He paused, his eyes moving from face to face. "I should like to give you a brief report of our experience on the exploring expedition, even though I know by now that most of you have heard many of the details. Then I should like to make one or two summary statements before turning the time to these two brethren." He stopped and looked back at Schow and Collett. "Will you both speak, or just one?"

Bishop Schow spoke up first, loud enough for the entire congregation to hear. "Yah, Brodder Smith. I vas yoost saying to Brodder Collett dat my English not so gut, so he shood all the talking do. No?"

Reuben smiled at him. "Your English is just fine, Bishop, but I'll do whatever you say."

Silas turned back. "So after I speak, Brother Collett will address you, and then we will turn the time back to Elder Snow."

Silas took a deep breath and began. In short, concise sentences he quickly summarized the experience of the exploring expedition. It was masterful, and David wondered if he had made notes and memorized them, or if it was all just that clear in his thinking.

When he finished, he let it sink in for a moment, then continued, speaking more slowly now. "Brethren and sisters, it is my studied opinion—which I think I can say is shared by the brethren who accompanied me—that the road we took will not work for us. We absolutely must find another way to the San Juan."

That didn't get much of a reaction. It was common knowledge now that the southern route was being rejected. But what he said next did get their attention. "Please remember, when I say 'the road we took,' I am talking about both the southern *and* the proposed northern route. Let me say that again. We traveled every mile of both routes. That's over a thousand miles. We know that of which we speak, and it is only after much careful thought and deliberation that I say to you again, neither the southern nor the northern route is practical. *We must find another way.*"

Now he had their full attention.

"The southern route is simply not feasible. First, it is a long route, about four hundred wagon miles. Much of it lies through difficult country. Far more serious is the fact that water is very scarce. We lost over twenty head of cattle, or about ten percent of the herd, and that was in springtime when water was the most plentiful. We are now estimating that the main company will have somewhere between two hundred fifty and three hundred people in about eighty wagons, and will be bringing along well over a thousand head of stock. Maybe even fifteen hundred."

There were several low whistles.

"And it will be late in the fall by the time we reach the desert. Hopefully, some winter rains will replenish some of the water supply, but we cannot rely on that.

"A third serious problem is the Indians. Much of the southern route lies across Navajo tribal lands. They were much concerned when they heard of our coming. Fortunately, we had only one near-violent confrontation, but again, that was with twelve wagons, about three dozen people, and a small herd of livestock. It doesn't take much to imagine how the Navajos will react to a company nearly ten times that size. We and any who may follow will likely face vigorous and hostile resistance."

Out of the corner of his eye, David saw Molly's head drop as she clasped her hands tightly together. That was one of her greatest fears, and she had interrogated him more than once about their clash with Po-ee-kon.

Silas reached down to where a pitcher of water and two glasses sat on a small table beside the pulpit. He poured himself a glass of water and drank it as he let the people digest that. He set the glass down with a loud thunk, and everyone instantly quieted.

"So why not take the northern route, Brother Silas? you may ask. And that is a valid question. There is much to commend it, most important of which is that it follows established wagon routes for all but the last hundred miles. South of the new settlement of Moab there were no roads, but we took the time to build the beginnings of one as we returned home. So why not go that way? First, because it is about four hundred and fifty miles from here to Montezuma Creek via the northern route. But from here to there as the crow flies is just over two hundred miles." He flashed a quick grin. "Now, we know that wagons aren't crows, so it will be somewhat longer than that, but think about that difference. With the stops we make for the Sabbath or to rest the cattle or to repair wagons and build roads— all the normal things required on a wagon trek—we average around five to eight miles a day. Four hundred fifty miles will take us three full months, twice as long as it will take to cover two hundred miles. That difference cannot be ignored."

Several men were stirring, and David saw one hand tentatively raise, but Silas went on. "More to the point, it is now the last of September. If we push hard, as the First Presidency has asked us to do, we will be lucky to have the first wagons rolling by mid-October. Should we decide to take the northern route, we will be traveling through the dead of winter. And may I remind you quickly what the northern route includes? The Upper Sevier River Valley, which is seven thousand feet in elevation. Grass Valley and Castle Valley, both right around six thousand feet in elevation. That's to say nothing of several mountain passes of eight to nine thousand feet. In addition, we will be going northward two hundred miles before we turn east again. The climate there is much colder and those areas are prone to deep and prolonged snow.

"Is it a better route? An easier route? Absolutely. *If* it were spring or summer. But it is not. If we decide that is what we need to do, then put your wagons in the barns, brethren, turn your horses out to pasture, go back to work in your stores and businesses, because we won't be leaving until spring."

He paused, looking very grave. "Not unless we want another Willie and Martin handcart experience on our hands."

There was total silence now as the grim reality of that settled in upon them.

"This is why," Silas continued, sounding weary now, "this is why I contacted these two brethren last spring. I had high hopes for the southern route, but I wasn't completely confident that it would be viable. So I asked these two trusted friends to find another way, a better way, a shorter way, a warmer, safer way."[4] His shoulders lifted and fell. "I would now ask that Brother Collett share what they found. Listen well, and then we must decide."

As the lean constable got to his feet and moved to the pulpit, every eye was on the empty sleeve pinned to his shoulder. Like David, the people were trying to picture him bringing in an outlaw singlehandedly—literally singlehandedly.

"Brothers and sisters," he began, "as I give the report President Smith has asked us to make, may I remind you that this is not a decision for Bishop Schow and me. We stand ready to help in any way we can, but we are not going with you. We do not have to live with the consequences of whatever decision you make. I am here only to give you information. The decision is yours."

Again heads were moving up and down all around the chapel. That was an important point.

"I shall summarize what we have learned into several key points for you to consider. First, I would remind you that if you choose to come to Escalante, that gives you about eighty-five miles of established wagon roads. That's almost half the total distance you have to cover. Second, Escalante is the farthest settlement east of where we are now. Although we are a small settlement, we are thriving. That means before you have to jump off into the unknown, you will pass through our town. There you can replenish your supplies, shoe your horses and mules, repair your wagons, and find other important support you may need."

"That is no small factor," Silas Smith called out from behind him.

Collett nodded. "No small factor at all. Third, it is about sixty miles from Escalante to the Colorado River gorge. It is desert country, and while we run cattle all through that area, there is no established wagon road. But it is, for the most part, level country—rough, but passable. The route we would take roughly parallels what we call Fifty Mile Mountain, or the

Straight Cliffs, which is the eastern edge of the vast Kaiparowits Plateau. The desert along those cliffs is therefore lower in elevation and the weather more temperate. Also, our route would follow along the base of the plateau where there are water sources at reasonable intervals."

That brought several heads up, especially those of the brethren. This was a telling point.

"We actually call them Ten Mile Spring, Twenty Mile Spring, and so on to Fifty Mile Spring, which makes for an easy run between springs. I should also mention that the road runs roughly parallel to the Escalante River on the east, which ranges from between five to ten miles away. It's deep and not always easy to get to, but it is a year-round source of water in an emergency."

David found himself nodding. The exploring party's thirty-five-mile run across the desert between Bitter Spring and Willow Spring would live long in his memory. Anything they could do to avoid stretches like that was highly significant.

"However—" He stopped and let that word hang for a moment. "However, the Colorado River gorge lies squarely across the route we have explored. Glen Canyon, as it is now called, is surely one of the great wonders of the world. Bishop Schow and I have ridden up and down the western side of that gorge for probably a hundred miles. It is spectacular and awe-inspiring. There are places where the deep red-rock cliffs plunge straight down for two thousand feet. Yes, two thousand! Nearly half a mile deep and straight down. It is truly unbelievable."

There was a fleeting, somewhat sad smile. "It is also impossible to cross." He let that sink in before going on. "Bishop Schow and I had a small, flat-bottomed boat made for us by Brother Charles Hall. This we carried on a two-wheeled cart made from the running gear of a wagon. For a time we despaired of finding anyplace where we could get down to the river. Then we found a great cleft in the cliff face." He paused, letting his eyes sweep across his audience. "We call it the Hole in the Rock."

He glanced back at his partner. "There is some debate about whether we first gave it that name or Brother Hall, who has also explored the area, but that matters not. It is a chasm or very narrow, near vertical cleft that descends from the top all the way down to the river in a series of giant steps."[5]

"An' how do we tek wagons doon that?" someone asked.

David turned. It was Ben Perkins, the Welsh coal miner from Cedar City, who had spoken. His question wasn't meant as a challenge. It had come as a reaction to what he had heard. Collett nodded, having heard the comment. "It is steep, perhaps as much as forty-five degrees. But with some blasting powder and a lot of work, we think it would be possible to make a wagon trail through it."

"Tell dem about da other side," Bishop Schow called out.

He waved in acknowledgment and went on. "Bishop Schow and I found a place a couple of miles upstream from the Hole where we were able to lower the boat over the cliffs down to the river. We paddled across to the eastern bank. There we explored for some time as well. Directly across the river from the Hole is a canyon that we called Cottonwood Canyon. It is a lovely place with plenty of water and grass and provides a natural access to the bluffs beyond. We followed that canyon for some distance to see if it would be possible to take wagons up that way. We found one place where it will take some pretty serious road building, but we believe it's doable. No worse than going down the Hole.

"Once we were up and out of Cottonwood Canyon, we found more smooth going. There were a couple of other challenging spots. I remember one especially. It's like this huge chute, or log flume, carved out of the rock between two sandstone hills. It's pretty steep, but the rock is smooth and we think we can double- and triple-team the wagons up it without a lot of challenge. Beyond that there is a long, gently inclining mesa that is quite flat and stretches eastward as far as we could see. It would be easily passable by wagons. We followed that for a short distance to where we could see down to the San Juan River."

He stopped, letting his eyes search those of the congregation. When he continued, he spoke slowly and deliberately, emphasizing each word. "At that point, we determined that it is possible to build a wagon road through, to create a shortcut to the San Juan, to go in through the back door, as it were. We returned home just in time to receive Elder Snow's letter asking us to come here and share what we found with you."[6]

He turned. "That is our report, Elder Snow. I turn the time back to you."

As he returned to his seat, Elder Snow and Silas Smith put their heads together for a moment. Silas nodded, then nodded again at something the Apostle said. Finally, Elder Snow got to his feet. "Brethren and sisters, we do not wish to curtail your questions, but the afternoon is wearing on and we have other meetings to attend to. I would recommend that we now take about a five-minute stand-up break. Use that time to discuss what you have heard, and consolidate your questions if you can. After the break, we shall take about fifteen minutes for discussion, then call for a recommendation and a vote."

As the family huddled together, Patrick, Carl, and David in the center, the women and Billy Joe around them, Patrick was the first to speak. He looked at David. "What do you think?"

"I'd rather the others speak first, if that's all right."

He nodded and turned to his wife and daughters. "Sarah? Abby and Molly?"

They were hesitant, but finally Sister McKenna spoke. "I think Brother Smith makes a pretty strong case for not going south or north. That seems to leave only one choice."

Abby was thoughtful. "It's hard to say, because we know so little. But it's no wonder Elder Snow has such confidence in those two. And Silas Smith as well. I was very impressed."

"I wanna go," Billy Joe exclaimed. "I think that a hole in a rock sounds neat. And can I paddle when we cross the river?"

They all smiled at his enthusiasm. Then Carl spoke. "There's still a lot of that eastern side that didn't get explored. Sounds like they went only a few miles before they turned around."

"I had the same thought," Patrick said. "But they could hardly go the whole way. They had to get back and report."

As they fell quiet, David was watching Molly. She was listening intently, her face expressionless. But in her eyes, he saw worry. "What do you think, Molly?" he asked.

She turned in surprise. "I . . . I don't know. I guess we have to trust those who do. Maybe we are better off to wait until spring and then take the northern way."

"There's only one real problem with that," David said. "We left two families with nine children over there who are anxiously awaiting our arrival."

"Oh," she said meekly. "I forgot about them."

"So," Patrick said again, "what do you think, David?"

He sighed, not completely comfortable himself. "I wish we knew a lot more than we do about this route, but, like Sarah said, our options are pretty limited. I see no other choice."

"Me too," Molly inserted quickly.

"It's not just the Harrimans and the Davises," Abby said. "I am so ready to leave. We've already waited six months now. To wait another six will be pure torture."

"If that's the case," David said, "and I totally agree with Abby, then it seems pretty straightforward. We take this route and trust that it will work out. After our experience in Arizona, I really like the idea of a shortcut."

"Especially where there are no Indians," Molly murmured.

"Then we're agreed?" Patrick asked, looking to each of them in turn.

One by one they nodded. After a moment, one by one they sat down again, each wondering just what that simple decision would mean for them.

"Brethren and sisters." Elder Snow's face was solemn and concerned. "You have heard the report. You have heard the options. You have had a chance to ask questions. Now it is time to make a decision." After a long, thoughtful pause, he went on. "I was given the assignment by the First Presidency to organize a mission and send them to the San Juan. Brother Silas Smith here was called and appointed to lead that mission. We have conferred together, and it is our recommendation that we here and now choose to go forward, not delaying further. All things considered, we feel that a more central route is our best option. I propose that option to you formally now. All in favor, please manifest it by raising your right hand."

David turned his head quickly, as did almost everyone else. He couldn't tell for sure if every hand was up, but if not, there were very few exceptions.

"Thank you. Are there any opposed to this proposition?"

Again everyone turned. The hall was dead quiet, but not a single hand was up.

There was a deep sigh from the crowd as Elder Snow visibly relaxed. "Thank you, my dear brothers and sisters. I commend you for your faith. The voting has been unanimous in the affirmative. We therefore declare that the mission will depart as soon as possible. We shall gather from our various locations to Escalante in preparation for crossing the Colorado River and taking the shortcut to the San Juan."

Notes

1. It is a common assumption that the first settlers of Escalante named the town for Father Escalante, one of the Catholic fathers who had explored the country much earlier. But Jerry Roundy, in his history of Escalante, notes that the town got its name when some of Major John Wesley Powell's surveying party met some of the Mormons who had come to explore the possibility of a settlement there. Under date of August 5, 1875, a journal entry reads: "Saw four Mormons from Panguitch who are talking of making a settlement here. Advised them to call the place Escalante" (Roundy, *Escalante,* 72–73). The settlers also called the area Potato Valley because they found some wild potatoes growing there (*ibid.,* 18).

2. The information on Bishop Andrew P. Schow comes from Andrew Jenson (*Encyclopedia,* 1:543–44).

3. These details on Reuben Collett come from the Collett family history (as cited by Miller, *Hole,* 39, 42). We do not have a physical description of Collett, nor could I find a photograph of him, so my physical description of him is conjecture, except for the missing arm.

4. We know that Silas Smith was asked to speak to the brethren during the time of the stake conference held in Parowan September 27 and 28, 1879 (see *ibid.,* 40). There are not a lot of details of what he said, but several sources report that he enthusiastically supported a central route scouted out by Andrew Schow, Reuben Collett, and Charles Hall

(see *ibid.*, 34–42; Reay, *Incredible Passage*, 24–25). We also know that Schow and Collett came "to Parowan and other Iron County settlements" to give their report, and "met the San Juan missionaries preparing for the trek" (Miller, *Hole,* 40). Having them do so in a special meeting held in conjunction with stake conference seemed like a logical possibility for that to happen.

5. There is some debate about who first named the Hole in the Rock. Miller concludes that perhaps all three men—Hall, Schow, and Collett—were responsible for its name (see *ibid.*, 36–37).

6. I have chosen to take a different interpretation of the explorations of Schow and Collett than have most historians. Since this is a fairly dramatic departure from the traditional interpretation, I should like to present the case for doing so.

This is more than a mere debate over some trivial historical fact. A few miles either way might normally make little difference, but in this case, there is a greater issue at stake. Many historians and members of the Church have been critical of the decision to take the central route when so little was known about it. Much of this comes from the assumption that Schow and Collett's exploration went only a "short distance" inland.

Members of The Church of Jesus Christ of Latter-day Saints believe the Church is led by prophets, seers, and revelators. They also believe that when an individual person is called and set apart to a specific office, that person is entitled to personal inspiration and revelation. So what is really being questioned here is: How did the system of revelation and inspiration fail so badly in this particular instance?

That is a troubling question. Men and women who are otherwise praised for their wisdom, integrity, and good judgment are suddenly put on trial and condemned by those who are far removed from the realities of their circumstances, and who have only limited information about the situation. I note again the observation by David McCullough, world-renowned historian, included in the preface, where he reminds us that "the character, habits, and manners of those who took part" in historical events must also be considered.

I am not a trained historian. I am only an enthralled amateur, and I am reluctant to disagree with the conclusions of such professional and highly qualified historians as David E. Miller. His work on the Hole in the Rock expedition is remarkable and has been of inestimable value in preparing this book. But in this specific case, the more I thought about the nature and character of such men as Erastus Snow and Silas Smith, ascribing to them a serious error in judgment and inspiration was not in harmony with what we know. Was their decision truly a momentary slip of inspiration—a rush to judgment, as it were, because of the urgency of the situation? Or could there be another explanation?

The key issue is this: How extensively did Schow and Collett scout out the east side of the river? In an "official" account based on interviews with original Hole in the Rock participants such as Kumen Jones and George Hobbs, the San Juan Stake History states that "They [Schow and Collett] had succeeded in crossing the river in their [wagon] box and from the other side, by climbing a short distance, they could see the San Juan River. The two brethren then recrossed the river, and the report of their exploration and the crossing of the Colorado was to the effect that a good road could be made by way of the Escalante desert to the Colorado river, and thence through the country beyond to the San Juan River" (San Juan Stake History as cited by Miller, *Hole*, 39).

Another source, the history of Reuben Collett's family, uses similar language but adds some significant details (cited in *ibid.*, 38, 42).

Those two phrases—"a short distance" and "a good road"—have greatly influenced the conclusions of the historians. Miller's outstanding and definitive work on the Hole in the Rock influenced many other historians when he concluded: "These meager descriptions leave one wondering just how far eastward the two men explored. In order to have reached a point from which the actual waters of the San Juan could have been seen they would have had to hike much farther than 'a short distance.'. . . They did probably reach Cottonwood Creek and no doubt ascended that stream two or three miles. However, they evidently did not go beyond the bald sandstone cliffs at the head of that canyon—else their report must surely have been a negative one" (*ibid.*, 40).

Here are my reasons for disagreeing with that conclusion:

(a) As we have seen, Andrew Schow and Reuben Collett were experienced, seasoned frontiersmen, "veteran scouts" (see *ibid.*, 38). They knew the area well, and fully understood the importance of what they had been asked to do. The Collett family history reports that they "explored for a great length of time, from early spring and on through the summer" (cited in *ibid.*, 38). Are we to believe that when they finally crossed the river to the east side to determine the most critical question of all, they settled for a hasty and cursory exploration, going inland only "two or three miles"? Miller, always the careful historian, adds this, after drawing his conclusions about their limited search: "Of course, this is all speculation; it is not even known how long these men spent in the region" (*ibid.*, 42).

If they went only a short distance, that implies they spent no more than a day exploring there. If they "explored for a great length of time," then it would be strange indeed if they went only two to three miles inland.

(b) We who live in modern times must take care that we do not interpret historical facts through our own "cultural eyeglasses." In our society, people drive two or three blocks to a grocery store, or take their cars to church when it is just around the corner. For most of us, walking "two or three miles" would probably be the upper limit of a definition of a "short distance." But that was not the case in earlier days. First-person accounts from those times frequently speak of walking fifteen or twenty miles in a day as though it were a commonplace thing. Journeys of hundreds of miles on foot are mentioned often. So to assume these two explorers went only two to three miles because the record says they hiked a "short distance" could be the result of cultural myopia.

(c) Miller states that "they evidently did not go beyond the bald sandstone cliffs at the head of that canyon—else their report must surely have been a negative one." That raises another question. What kind of scouts would, when they reached the first real obstacle to wagon travel, decide they had gone far enough, turn around, and then report that a "good road" could be built through the area? Wouldn't those sandstone cliffs have had just the opposite effect on them? Wouldn't they have pushed beyond that difficult stretch to see if this was going to prove an impassable barrier? Were they that tired? That rushed? That negligent? Or have we simply misinterpreted the little data that we have?

(d) The San Juan Stake history states that "by climbing a short distance, they could see in the distance the San Juan River" (ibid., 39). The Collett family history records: "After climbing the mountains a short distance on the east side of the Colorado, the San Juan River could be seen (ibid., 42). Both original sources specifically state that they saw the river. Yet that would have been impossible if they had gone only two or three miles up Cottonwood Canyon. Miller resolves this by concluding that they may have seen the San Juan River gorge but not the river itself. However, if they went all the way to Grey Mesa (a distance of only about seven or eight miles from the top of Cottonwood Canyon), there is a place where one can look almost straight down to the river.

(e) Here's another problem with the "two to three mile theory." In the Collett family record it says this of their exploration of the east side: "The country, being rugged on the San Juan side, made it necessary to blaze a trail by marking anything that would retain a mark. By using this precaution, they easily found their way back to the Colorado and safely to camp" (cited in ibid., 42). "Anything that would retain a mark" sounds like something quite different from making a notch in a tree along a stream bed. Surely, they would not have been concerned about getting lost if all they did was traverse a narrow and well-defined canyon. Yet up on top, away from the river, there are places where, even today, experts on the trail have to paint white arrows on the bare sandstone or mark the trail with small rock cairns because it is so easy to lose one's way.

(f) Grey Mesa is about eight or nine miles long. It is a relatively flat, sagebrush-covered plateau that looks like it continues on for many miles. If these two men did go that far, it would be a natural thing for them to conclude that a "good road" could be made across that country.

(g) But, some might say, there are two very difficult stretches between the river and Grey Mesa. They are Cottonwood Hill, at the top of Cottonwood Canyon, and what is now called The Chute. If the two scouts went all the way to Grey Mesa, they would have to have seen those two stretches. How then could they then return and report that a "good road" could be made through that country?

There is no disputing the difficulty of both of those stretches of the trail. When the main company eventually reached Cottonwood Hill, they stopped for over a week to build a dugway up the steep hillside, and it proved to be almost as challenging as building the road down through the Hole. But they did it. As for The Chute, having personally traversed it both in a Jeep and on an ATV, I fully concur that it is a daunting stretch of trail. One can scarcely believe that wagons and teams could make their way up it. Yet in the company journal, the entry for the day when they went through the area where The Chute is located states only this: "We have been building road over and through solid rock, which we have now completed" (in ibid., 166). No mention of great challenge or hardship is made.

We must remember that Schow and Collett did not say that a road could *easily* be built through that area, only that it could be done. If they did not see the Hole in the Rock as an impossible task, why should we assume they would automatically reject Cottonwood Hill or The Chute as being impassable?

For all of these reasons, I have chosen to assume that Schow and Collett went beyond Cottonwood Canyon, probably as far as the San Juan overlook on Grey Mesa. If that assumption is true, then we can also assume their report to Elder Snow and Silas Smith would have been more detailed—and encouraging!—than most historians have thought. Therefore the decision to take that route was neither irresponsible nor uninspired.

Later experience showed the route to be tremendously challenging, taking them much longer than first predicted, but, when all is said and done, they did do it. Therefore it was not an "impossible journey," as some have suggested.

CHAPTER 47

Sunday, September 28, 1879

At Patrick's request, after having supper in the hotel dining room, the McKenna family, along with David and Carl, gathered in a back corner of the lobby. As they came together, Patrick began pulling the chairs into a semicircle so they would face each other.

It was a sober and mostly subdued group that sat down together. Billy Joe was his usual enthusiastic self, but even he seemed to sense the mood and sat quietly beside his mother. Molly was especially gloomy. She had maintained a forced cheerfulness through the meal, holding an animated debate with Carl on the importance of her knowing how to shoot a rifle. But since the meeting, a pall had settled upon her that hadn't lifted as of yet. Abby had been likewise quiet, but that seemed to be more because she was preoccupied with her own thoughts.

Patrick cleared his throat. "Since we will be leaving early in the morning, and since, once we return home, our lives are going to get very hectic, I thought it might be well to take some time this evening to discuss what has happened and what it means for us." He looked around the group. "We have waited for this day for almost a year now, but at last we know *where* we are going, *how* we are going to get there, and *when* we are leaving. In a way, that is a tremendous relief. But in another way, the realities of it all are now more evident. In approximately two more weeks our lives are going to be changed forever."

He paused, but no one spoke, so he went on. "Therefore, I would like to see how you are feeling about things, and if there are concerns we need to address as we now prepare to leave."

He sat back and folded his hands together in his lap.

David leaned forward quickly. "I hate to start with something so mundane," he said, "but there's something you need to think about as we return home, Patrick."

"What's that?"

"As you know, after the meeting yesterday afternoon, Silas called several of us together who went with him on the first trip. He's asked us, including me, to serve as scouts for the company, especially once we leave Escalante. That means we're going to have to find another driver for the wagons." He turned to Abby. "Assuming we can still count on you to drive one of them."

"And me," Molly snapped. "In spite of what you all may think, I'm not a pansy."

Carl gave her a questioning look. "You told me you didn't want to drive," he said.

Her look was a withering stare. "David didn't ask who *wanted* to drive. Just who could."

"We've assumed," her father came in smoothly, "that you girls will be driving your own sleeping wagon. It will carry the lightest load, and I think we can pull it with just the two mules. But that still leaves us a driver short when David isn't with us." He looked thoughtful. "I totally agree with Silas in this recommendation, so let me think on that some." Then he faced the others. "All right, let's hear what's on your minds and in your hearts."

For almost a full minute, no one spoke. Finally, Billy Joe began to squirm a little in his chair. "Yes, young Patrick," his father said. "Would you like to begin?"

He nodded, swallowed, then began. "My tummy feels like a puppy is crawling around inside of me. I wanna go, but . . . I guess I'm a little scared, too."

His mother put an arm around him and pulled him close. "I think we've all got something inside our tummies, Son. I know I certainly do." She turned to her husband. "I've never doubted that we were going, but now? Suddenly, it's all very real and I have to say that I'm frightened."

"It's a lot more than that for me," Molly said quietly. "Can I speak honestly, Daddy?"

"Of course. That's why we're here."

"Maybe it is just because it's suddenly real and we are frightened, but I don't feel good about it inside. It's like a cloud of darkness has come over me since we voted to go yesterday." Her eyes dropped, and David saw that her hands were clenched tightly together. "I don't know anymore whether we are doing the right thing or not."

Her father nodded slowly. "Is it the decision to take this new route?"

"I . . . I'm not sure what it is. I just feel like something dreadful is going to happen, and it really concerns me."

"Oh, Molly," Sarah said. "I think it *is* just the reality of it hitting us all right now."

David raised his hand, and Patrick motioned for him to speak. When he did, he spoke directly to Molly. "I don't know if this will help, but my family had talked about going to America so long, I was like Billy Joe. I was excited, filled with anticipation. Even when my father and I actually booked passage on the steamship, I was so thrilled I barely slept that night. But then came the time for departure. Suddenly it hit me that I was leaving England forever. I would never see my friends again. I was going to a completely strange land to be with this weird group of people called the Mormons." He smiled briefly. "I never even told my father this, but I spent the night before we embarked bent over the toilet throwing up."

"Really?" Billy Joe exclaimed. "Did it make the puppies in your stomach go away?"

He laughed. "It did." Then he turned back to Molly. "Looking back now, I see that coming was the best thing that ever happened to me. But that night, I felt like the world had collapsed."

"Do *you* feel this is the right thing to do?" she asked, her head coming up.

"I do. I have great confidence in those two men and their recommendation and—"

She waved that aside. "I'm not talking about which route we take. Do you think this is the right thing to do for our family?"

He sat back, struck by the importance of her question. "I . . . I guess I can't speak for your family, so . . ." His voice trailed off. Every eye was on him. Then suddenly he nodded, surprising even himself. "Yes, Molly. I guess I do."

It was Abby who reacted first. "Really!" It was said in surprise, not as a question.

"Yes."

"As do I," Patrick murmured. "Thank you for your honesty, David." Then he turned to Molly. "We still have two more weeks, my dearest Molly. If you still feel that way by that time, then perhaps you should stay behind."

Sarah gasped and Abby visibly started, but Molly just stared at her father. "Do you mean that, Daddy?"

"I do, but I can't speak for your mother."

Sarah's eyes filled with tears as she looked at her youngest daughter. "It would break my heart to leave you, Molly, but if that is how you really feel, yes, I agree with your father."

"Thank you," Molly whispered.

"Abby?" her father said. "Anything you would like to say?"

She started to shake her head, then changed her mind. She looked at Billy Joe. "I guess I have a puppy and a couple of kittens fighting inside my stomach, Billy Joe, but I have felt from the beginning that this is what the Lord wants us to do. I think there will come a time when we understand why we were asked to do this and thank Him for helping us do it."

"Carl?"

Carl Bradford turned to his employer, thought for a moment, then shook his head. "It's not the same question for me, since I will be returning to Cedar City once you're settled. As for the decision made yesterday, I feel that was a good one, and I, like you, am glad things are finally settled. We've waited long enough."

"Thank you." Finally, Patrick turned to his wife. "Anything you wish to say, dear?"

She took a deep breath, then exhaled slowly. Tears still glistened in her eyes, but she managed a tiny smile. "I think you all know that I am the woman who would rather stay in St. George and go shopping with my sister than camp out in Zion Canyon." As they laughed at that, she went on. "I've always wondered how in the world I ever came to be a pioneer woman. Give me the streets of Boston and a concert with a symphony orchestra and I'll be happy. But, the Lord doesn't always see things as we see them. And He certainly doesn't always put us where we feel most comfortable."

She glanced at Molly, then away. "Like Molly, I have grave misgivings. I cannot fathom how we shall make our way across the wilderness, how we shall ever bear to part with our dear friends, or how we shall regain the comforts with which we have been so richly blessed."

Her eyes moved from face to face. "However, there is only one thing of which I am sure, and that makes all the difference. I know this is what the Lord has called us to do, and I know, as it says in the scriptures, that all things work together for good to them that love God. So I shall shut the door on our beautiful home. I shall walk away from our coal stove with its four hot plates and an oven large enough to bake six loaves of bread at the same time. I shall leave behind our pianoforte and my china dishes and our lovely porcelain tub where I can soak in a hot bath as long as I wish. I shall do so because I love your father more than all of these. I shall do so because I love the Lord even more than that."

Both Abby and Molly were sniffing back tears now, and Patrick's eyes were soft and shining. Sarah wiped quickly at the wet streaks on her cheeks and managed a shaky laugh. "The only thing that gives me hope is that there is so much to do in the next two weeks, I won't have time to sit around and bawl. Maybe that opportunity will come, but I don't have time for it now."

Laughing and crying, Molly stood and went to her mother and threw her arms around her. Abby was right behind her. In a moment, Billy and his father had joined them and they all stood together, hugging each other and crying.

David got to his feet, as did Carl. This was a time for the family, not outsiders. As they started to edge away, Patrick saw them and turned. "Sorry," he said in a choked laugh. "We get like this every now and again."

David nodded. "We'll see you at six tomorrow morning,"

"Wait just one moment," Patrick said, stepping back from his family. "I have one more thing I would like to say." The girls and Billy Joe returned to their seats, but Patrick remained standing with the two men. He laid a hand on David's shoulder. "When you were speaking about leaving England, a scripture came to my mind. It was given to Joseph Smith when he first arrived in Jackson County, Missouri. Some of the Saints had come with him and were going to stay and establish settlements there. They were thrilled to think they would be among the first to live in the land of Zion, but they too were nervous. They asked the Prophet to inquire of the Lord what His will for them was at that time. I find the Lord's opening words of His answer very instructive and directly applicable to our own situation."

He paused, his eyes half closing. "I can't quote it exactly, but it goes something like this. 'You cannot behold with your natural eyes at the present time, the design of your God concerning those things which shall come hereafter, and the glory which follows *after much tribulation.* For after much tribulation come the blessings.'"

His eyes opened and he looked around. "I quote that for me, as much as for any of you." Then he turned to David and Carl. "We'll see you first thing tomorrow."

Abby looked up as a soft knock sounded on her door. She looked at the small clock she had brought with her and saw that it was after nine. She then turned and looked at Molly, but she was sound asleep and breathing deeply. She got up and tiptoed to the door and opened it a crack.

"I'm so sorry to bother you," David said, "but I saw your light was on, and—"

"That's all right," she whispered. "I was still reading."

"I . . . I was wondering if you knew where that scripture your father quoted comes from."

She opened the door wider. "It's in the Doctrine and Covenants. Section fifty-eight."

"Oh." He hesitated, clearly embarrassed.

"I have a copy of the Doctrine and Covenants with me. Would you like to borrow it?"

"I don't want to be a—"

"Wait here," she said. A moment later she was back and handed the book to him. "I put a marker in the page where it is."

"Thank you." He took the book and turned away without another word.

She stood there at the door for a long moment, staring after him. Then, as she closed it, she said to herself, "What is happening to you, David Draper?"

Tuesday, October 7, 1879

Billy Joe came busting through the doors of the dry-goods store and slid to a halt. "There you are!" he exclaimed.

"You looking for me?" David said. He was at the counter going through the long list of supplies Sarah had given him earlier that morning.

"Come quick. Daddy says he's found another driver. He wants you in his office right now."

"Who is it?"

His shoulders lifted and fell. "Dunno. He just said to come real quick."

Smiling at the boy's breathlessness, David turned to the clerk and handed him the list. "I'll be back." Then he laid a hand on Billy Joe's shoulder. "Okay, let's go."

When they entered the hotel lobby, David was surprised to see both Abby and Molly standing just outside the office door. They were talking animatedly, but the moment they saw David, their mouths clamped shut. Abby gave a soft knock on the door and stepped back.

"What is it?" he asked. "What's wrong?"

They both just looked at him, faces grave. Before he could ask them anything further, the door opened and Patrick slipped out. He shut the door behind him.

"What is it, Patrick? Billy Joe says you've found us a driver?"

He laughed easily. "I did. But I wanted you to meet him first and see if you approve."

Behind them David heard Molly giggle. "Who is it?" he asked, surprised that Patrick had felt such an urgency about this.

"Come in and see who came in on the morning stage," he said. He opened the door and gestured for David to go inside. As he started to move, David saw that Abby and Molly were now grinning almost as broadly as their father.

Then as he stepped inside the office, he froze. His jaw dropped.

"'owdy, Davee boy," John Draper drawled. "It be a reet keen pleasure ta lay eye on ya agin, laddee. A reet keen pleasure."

"All right," David said, sitting down across the desk from his father, "I'm still in shock here. Start over again and tell me what you are doing here. I haven't heard from you in a couple of weeks now and I was starting to get worried."

After the initial shock had worn off, Patrick and the girls had backed away, leaving David and his father alone in Patrick's office.

"Well, it be marvelous simple," his father began, "an' a bit of a miracle, if Ah do say so meself. As Ah tole ya in one of me letters, after workin' in Liverpool fur a time, Ah was sent ta labor in the Black Country, down in the West Midlands. Guess they thought this ole coal miner might know 'ow ta talk ta them workin' class blokes over thare."

"Yes, I got that letter."

"Sum say they call it Black Country cuz thare be so much coal near the ground that the dirt is aboot 'alf coal dust. But they also call it that cuz thare be so much smoke an' grit in the air from all the steel mills and coke ovens."

"Like Sheffield," David observed.

"Yah, exactly, only mooch worse. Well, that an' the cold wet air doon thare finally got ta me. Ah started coughin' aboot a month after gittin' thare. At first Ah thought it be joost a cold, but it wudn't go away, even when the air turned warmer."

David felt his heart drop. "Not the black lung, Dad. Don't tell me it's that."

There was a slow nod. "Ah be sorry ta say it, but ya be exactly reet."

"But the doctors in Coalville said you didn't have it."

"Naw. They only said Ah didn't 'ave any of the symptoms. Part of that was b'cuz even though the air in Coalville cud get very cold, it was also very dry, very low humidity. So Ah never 'ad problems wit it thare. Ah guess all the pollution in the air 'round Wolverhampton kinda irritated me lungs. That's what cums frum workin' thirty years in the mines."

David put his head in his hands. "I knew I shouldn't have let you go."

That miffed John. "Ah dunna r'member me askin'. Ah joost went."

"How bad is it?" David asked.

To his surprise, his father grinned at him. Then his hand shot out and gripped David's arm. "Naw bad e'nuff to be slowin' me doon mooch, but bad e'nuff that the doc said Ah 'ad ta be in a hot, dry climate. Like in a desert country. Lots of sunshine. That be the best thing fur me."

David gaped at him.

Now the grin spread. "Me mission president in Liverpool, 'e knew awl aboot me call ta the San Juan. So 'e gave me a letter recommendin' that me mission assignment be changed. An' when Ah stopped in Salt Lake, they confirmed that."

David shot to his feet. "You're going with us?"

His grin was so big it filled half his face. "Yah, if'n that be awl reet wit ya." His eyes got a mischievous twinkle. "Ah'll naw be 'avin' ya fightin' me on this one, Son, cuz Ah be determined ta accept that call an' finish oot me mission, no matter what ya 'ave ta say aboot it."

CHAPTER 48

Tuesday, October 21, 1879

"David?"

David turned. Abby was at the door to her father's office, a stack of papers in her arms.

"Hi," he said, veering over to join her. "What are you doing here so late?" The hotel lobby was deserted. Even the night clerk behind the front desk was dozing in his chair.

"I might ask the same question of you."

"I wrote a letter to Jim and Mary Davis and left it in the post office. We'll probably get there before it does—mail down to Montezuma Creek is a bit of a miracle if it happens at all—but I thought I'd let them know we're on our way."

Her face softened. "She is a woman I much admire and respect. And love."

"She's one of my heroes," he said with equal softness.

"I think the proper word is *heroine*."

He shook his head. "If you had seen her stand up to Po-ee-kon, you'd call her a hero too."

"Speaking of letters—" she shifted the stack of papers to one arm, took an envelope from off the top, and handed it to him—"I was going to drop this off to you on my way home."

David looked at the handwriting and recognized it instantly as Molly's. "How is she doing?"

"About like the rest of us," she said. "Knowing this is our final night at home is pretty rough. We've all been bawling our eyes out." That was said with a sardonic smile.

"Abby McKenna bawling?" he said. "I have a hard time picturing that."

Her chin lifted slightly and there was challenge in her eyes. "I try to do it when no one is looking, but I am capable of tears, in spite of my inscrutable manner. And don't worry about Molly. She's tougher than you think."

That surprised him. "I know that—she's going, isn't she?"

"No, David," she said again, "she's tougher than you think. I'm having a rough time of it, and Mom too, but we're committed to going. Molly's not, and yet she's going." She pulled a quick face. "If that makes any sense. Molly dreads it with every fiber of her being, but she's still going. She is one of *my* heroes."

"And you one of hers. In a way, for you this is Angel's Landing all over again, isn't it?"

Her eyes lifted to meet his and he saw the surprise in them.

"I've watched you, Abby," he teased, "so don't play innocent with me. Knowing you're going to be driving a wagon for two hundred miles or more, some of it over some pretty rough terrain, leaves you highly uncomfortable. Understanding your fear of heights, I saw your face when Brother Collett was talking about the Hole in the Rock. You can shoot a rifle well, but you don't enjoy it. You don't hate camping out as much as Molly does, but you would prefer a comfortable bed and hot food each morning. You might as well come clean. For all your pretensions otherwise, you are going to miss Cedar City and your lovely home and your good life as much as your mother and Molly will." He gave a short laugh. "Well, maybe not quite as much as Molly."

"So?" she said, somewhat irked, "that's probably true of every woman going. What has that got to do with Angel's Landing?"

"Because, as much as you dread it, there's something down deep inside of you that says, 'I've got to do this.' Not just because you think the call is from the Lord. Not just because you wouldn't abandon your family. You have to prove something to yourself. It's that rock spine all over again. The eight-hundred-foot drop on both sides scared the spit right out of you and yet—"

She hooted. "It surely did that. My mouth was so dry I thought I would faint."

"But you did it. And you're going to do this, too. And Molly knows that about you. She wants to be more like you. You are one of her heroes, too."

She cocked her head to one side. "Well, aren't you the little analyst."

"Am I wrong?" he shot back.

After a moment, she shook her head. "No."

David decided to change the subject. He reached out and took the stack of papers from her arm. "Where would you like these?"

"I'm taking them home to be put in our cellar. These are the last of Dad's papers. And speaking of having a hard time, I think he asked me to do this because he can't bear the thought of not coming back to his office ever again."

"I'll walk you home, then."

As they walked toward the door, the night clerk awoke with a start, looked around wildly, then gave them a sheepish look. Abby waved one hand. "Good night, Albert. Or, I guess we should say good-bye."

"Good luck to you," he called as they went out.

The streets of Cedar City were mostly deserted. It was past nine o'clock at night, but as they walked slowly along, savoring the crispness in the air and the smell of wood smoke, David noticed that there were very few homes without lamplight in the window. Jens Nielson, captain of the Cedar City contingent, had called for a five A.M. departure, but few of those going tomorrow were sleeping yet. Like David and Abby, they were finishing up last-minute tasks, or doing the last of their packing, or tidying up the house before they left it for good.

"And what about you, David?" Abby said as they approached the McKenna home, where all the windows were still ablaze with light. "Are you dreading it?"

He turned in surprise. "The trip? No. Actually, I'm looking forward to it. I'm glad to be under way finally. And . . ." He debated about sharing this, then saw no reason not to. "I know everyone says that country is wild and desolate, with hardly any inhabitants. But that actually appeals to me.

It's a place to start anew. Hopefully Dad and I can start our own ranch at long last. No, I quite like the idea."

"Only because you are so antisocial," she said.

He chuckled. "Well, yeah. That, too."

"It is wonderful to have your father back with us." She shot him a sideways glance. "So are you going to break this microscope, too?"

He winced. "Meaning?"

"Are you going to tell me what a remarkable coincidence it is that he was sent home just in time to join us for the trip?" She smiled sweetly at him. "It really is a truly remarkable and marvelous coincidence."

"I got it," he growled, remembering his conversation with Mary about those very words. Then he expelled his breath. "Dad called it a miracle the other day."

"And?"

"I didn't disagree with him."

She stopped, her eyes narrowing, searching his. "You really didn't? Not even to yourself?"

He shrugged. "Maybe there's hope for me after all."

"So, have you thanked the Lord for bringing him home?" she asked, eyeing him steadily.

He stopped. "In my own way," he finally said.

She hooted softly. "What's that supposed to mean? Did you thank Him or not?"

"Do I thank Him for the black lung disease, too?" Then, as her face fell a little at the bluntness of his words, he rushed on. "I'm not trying to be difficult, Abby. But that's a question I wrestle with. I am grateful that Dad's back. Incredibly grateful, actually. I do recognize the Lord might have had a hand in it."

"*Might* have?" she chortled. "My goodness, that's big of you."

"All right, *did* have."

"Eh?" she said, putting a hand to her ear. "Say that again." Then she immediately laughed. "Remember, it was you who appointed me to be your humility monitor."

"Do you have to be so darned good at it?" he grumbled. Then he was serious again. "Answer my question. Would the Lord give my father black lung disease so that He could bring him home again?"

"Bring him home just in time to join us," she emphasized. But then she shook her head. "No, I don't believe that. Your father has the black lung disease because he worked all of those years in the coal mine. But did the Lord inspire his mission president to send him to Black Country so it would affect him in such a way that he would have to be sent home? I think there is a very good chance of that. And, again I note, it happened just in time for him to join us on this trip."

"Yes," he said slowly.

She laughed softly. "This must be very hard on you."

"What?"

"Mary Davis gets this remarkable blessing from her bishop, and David Draper, skeptic and doubter, just happens to be with her to see that blessing fulfilled in a most remarkable way. His father, serving a mission seven thousand miles away, suddenly develops a cough and is sent home just in the nick of time to rejoin his son." She cocked her head and gave him a mischievous grin. "You've gotta be thinking you're under siege here, fella."

Now he was the one who hooted. "Ah, Abby. You do have a gift. The title of humility monitor doesn't do you justice."

They had reached the front gate of her house. As David reached out and opened the gate, Abby took the papers from him. "You don't need to walk me to the door, David. Daddy said you and Carl have to have the teams hitched up for us in time to be there at five."

He shrugged. "I don't think many of us are going to be sleeping really well tonight anyway. Good night, Abby. See you in the morning."

"Good night, David." But she didn't move. Her eyes, now black pools in the near darkness, searched his face. "You said the other day that you prayed on the trip. Is it too personal to ask you what your prayer was about?" Then, as she saw his mouth pull down, she retracted her question. "I'm sorry. I have no right to ask that."

"I told God thank you for saving us that day."

"With the old Navajo?"

He nodded. "I know that it wasn't for me. It was for Mary and Emily and the family." He sighed. "And Jim Decker and the others, too. They're good men. So I thanked Him for that."

For a long time she continued to search his face. Then, very softly, she said, "I appreciate you telling me that. Thank you." She stood there for a moment, looking as if she wanted to say something more, but then just shook her head, turned, and started up the walk.

When she was about halfway to the house, David called out one more thing. "I also thanked Him for bringing Dad back home. Even before you told me I should do it."

When she turned, her face was in shadow, but he heard the laughter in her voice. "I know."

David stopped in the main room of the boardinghouse, which was as deserted as the hotel had been. He moved to a chair beside a lamp, took out his pocketknife and slit the envelope open, then sat down. He caught the faint smell of perfume as he withdrew the letter.

My Dearest David,

Knowing that we are going to be together every moment of every day for the next six weeks, it seems odd that I feel compelled to write you the night before our departure. But there is something I needed to say, and I don't think I will have the opportunity to do so once we leave, nor the courage to do so face to face, even if an opportunity arises.

That day out by Coal Creek, we decided to step back, put things on the shelf, as you said it. And then you said something that really hit me hard. You said that if our relationship was meant to be, that the Lord would work it out for us. How ironic! You suggesting that I have more faith. I don't know what possessed you to say what you did that day, but you were like a rock in the middle of my turbulent river—steady, quiet, assured. I stayed awake for a long time that night thinking about it. And though I didn't tell Daddy I was for sure going until just a few days ago, I knew that I had no choice. Not just for us. For me! I had to do it. I had to show you that I do truly believe what I say I do.

And then your father came home. I'm not sure if you see his return as one more evidence that God has not forgotten you, but I surely do!!! I believe that He has heard the "prayers of your heart," as you call them. And that was as much an answer for me as for you. What a powerful reaffirmation to me that God is our Heavenly Father, that He knows us intimately, and loves us infinitely. If He knows how much you needed your father to come home to you, then He knows how much I hate the thoughts of this journey. He knows how weak my faith is.

That doesn't mean that my heart is no longer heavy. I am still filled with dread. I still get sick thinking about leaving Cedar City. But I know that He has not and will not abandon me. Somehow, I will get through it. The only thing that makes that thought bearable is knowing that I will be with my family and that you will be with us too. And by that I mean more than just having you close because of my great love for you. Here again, you are our rock in this river of challenge and change. I thank the Lord every day that Daddy had the wisdom and foresight to ask you to accompany us. Please forgive me if I lean on you too heavily in the next few weeks.

I love you, David Draper. More now than ever before. Don't worry. I will contain those feelings and act in perfect decorum whenever I am around you. But that doesn't change how I feel. Whether it will work out for us, I am no longer sure. But this much I do know. The Lord has not forgotten you, and from that, I also know that He has not forgotten me. And that alone makes what lies ahead something that I can endure.

All my love,
Molly

For a very long time, David sat there in the quiet solitude, reading and rereading her words, thinking about Molly and what it all meant. Finally, the weariness of mind and body began to sink in. He folded the letter, returned it to its envelope, then stood and went up the stairs.

As he reached the door of his room, he paused, thinking of what Abby had said earlier. "You're right," he said to himself. "You're absolutely right, Abby. She is much tougher than I thought."

CHAPTER 49

Wednesday, October 22, 1879

Bishop Jens Nielson had set the gathering place as the tithing office at five A.M. But as David and Carl Bradford turned the first two wagons onto Main Street, it was obvious that they weren't going to be leaving on time. It was already five-thirty, and first light was showing over the mountains to the east, but there were no more than a dozen wagons lined up. Even though the four men—Carl, Patrick, John, and David—had arrived at the barn at four A.M., hitching up sixteen grumpy and balky mules to the four wagons had taken them longer than they had planned. But David suspected that their captain had expected no more and had set the time early so they would still get away at a decent hour.

As if on cue, at that moment David saw the tall, solid figure of their Danish leader on horseback near the lead wagon. He was shouting directions and waving his arms. Closer to them, David saw Joe Nielson, his son, and Kumen Jones, his son-in-law, helping him organize the train. When Joe saw the two approaching wagons, he rode over to them. Joe was as tall and solidly built as his father, and had the same jovial and cheerful nature. When he saw that it was David driving the first wagon, that ready grin of his broke out and he waved. "Mornin', David. Mornin', Carl. I understand you've got two more wagons coming?"

"Yep. Dad and Brother McKenna are only a minute or so behind us."

"Well," Joe said, "I assume you want to keep all four of you together. We've got about twenty-five wagons, so let's start another line on the opposite side of the street. You may as well be the first in that one." He was pointing as he spoke.

Just then Kumen, Joe's brother-in-law, came up to join them. He too had been with David on the exploring party and had become a good friend. Kumen was closer to David's age, whereas Joe was just nineteen. Strikingly handsome with his thick black hair, full beard, and serious dark eyes, Kumen had broken many a heart when he had married Joe's oldest sister just a few days before Christmas of last year. "Mornin', David, Carl."

Nodding, David looked around, thinking of that morning six months earlier in Paragonah. "This has a familiar feel to it, doesn't it?"

"It does," Kumen agreed. "Only this time we're a lot bigger." Then he grinned. "And this time I get to take my wife with me."

"Get to?" Joe guffawed. "You can't be taking any credit for that, Kumen. After leaving your new bride for six months, you think she'd let you go off again without her?"

Kumen looked at David. "Did you hear that Silas Smith won't be joining us for a while?"

"No. Why not?"

"Guess what with all his reporting to the brethren since he returned, he hasn't had time to get ready. He'll join us in Escalante or points south. Says he'll be a couple of weeks behind us."

Then Kumen turned to his brother-in-law. "Aunt Kirsten wants to see you, Joe."

Joe nodded and rode away. Kumen waved and moved down the line to guide the next wagons in As he watched them go, David thought about the use of the title of *aunt*. In plural-marriage families, it was common for the children to refer to the wives other than their own mothers as "Aunt This" or "Aunt That." Like many others of the more established Church leaders in Utah, Jens Nielson had more than one wife. One night on the exploring party, Joe and Kumen had tried to explain to David the complexities of the Nielson family tree.

Jens had married "Aunt Elsie," as everyone called her, before they joined the Church in Denmark. It was tiny little Elsie who had come across the plains with him, pulling him in the handcart when his feet were so badly frozen he could go no farther. They had lost their only son somewhere in Wyoming about that same time. After arriving in Utah, Elsie had been unable to have any more children. When Jens was asked by the Church leaders to live in plural marriage, he promised Elsie that if she would allow him to take another wife, she would be able to have additional children. She had done so and gone on to have two more girls. Her oldest daughter, Mary, was Kumen's wife.

Jens's second wife was "Aunt Kirsten," and her firstborn child was Joe. Joe and his father were very close, and, in fact, it was mostly because of Joe and Mary that Brother Nielson had asked to be called to accompany them.

The third wife, the youngest of the three, was Aunt Katrine. Brother Nielson had married her just a few years before. Thus Joe had a mother, two "aunts," two brothers, three sisters, two half-brothers, three-half sisters, and a brother-in-law. To an only child like David, that seemed like a bewildering tangle of family, but Joe and Kumen were quite comfortable with it all. And, as near as David could tell, in their minds there was no distinction between siblings and half-siblings.[1]

The whole idea of plural marriage had set David's teeth on edge in his first few years in Utah, but since then he had learned firsthand that, with few exceptions, plural marriage was not entered into for salacious reasons, as all the outside world seemed to think. The families were close, often living in a single large house built by the father, as the Nielsons did. The wives viewed each other more like sisters than competitors. In a land and era where men were often gone from their families for months at a time, such an extended family structure provided much support to the women and their children.

Not that he ever intended to take up the practice himself. To his way of thinking, keeping one woman happy would be challenge enough for a lifetime.

"Hello. Are you there?"

David jerked up. Carl was looking at him quizzically, and David realized he had gotten lost in his thoughts. Just then he saw two more wagons and a single rider come around the corner behind them. "Ah, there they are." David jumped down and motioned for Patrick and John to pull the other wagons in behind them. "Billy Joe," he called. "Tie Paint up behind that last wagon for now."

They did so, and got down. As the four men came together, David looked around. "Where are the girls?"

Patrick shook his head with infinite patience. "They'll be along soon. When I left them, they were sweeping the house one last time."

David's eyebrows raised. "But they cleaned the house yesterday."

Patrick turned to David's father. "Your son doesn't know much about women, does he?"

John laughed and shook his head. "Naw in the least." He looked at David. "It be thare way of sayin' g'bye. As fur Sister McKenna, Ah be guessin' she be 'orrified ta think that anuther lady might see 'er 'ouse even the tiniest bit dirty."

"That's exactly right," Patrick said. "I'm guessing they're also having one last good cry."

David blew out his breath. "You're right. I don't understand women. Never will, either."

"Me neither," Billy Joe said in disgust. "Last night both Abby and Molly just kept hugging me and hugging me, and crying and crying."

As they all laughed at the disgust on his face, a movement caught David's eye. Behind them, two more wagons were coming up the street. Kumen was motioning for them to get into line about three wagons back from the McKennas. Although the sun was still half an hour or so from rising, it was light enough now that he could see things distinctly, and David immediately recognized the man driving the first wagon. "Hey, Dad," he said, taking his father's elbow. "Come with me. There's someone I want you to meet."

By the time they walked back, the two drivers were down and checking the barrels, buckets, cages, and other things tied alongside their wagon. "Ben Perkins?" David called.

The man turned. He was surprising small—no more than five feet five inches tall—with a lean, wiry figure, dark hair, dark eyes, and a dark beard worn in the goatee style. He couldn't have weighed much more than ten stone—around 150 pounds, David guessed—and was in his early thirties.[2]

"'Owdy, David." There was a twinkle in his eye. "Whate'er possesses ye ta be out of bed at sooch a dreadful 'our as this?" His accent was pure

Welsh—or Wenglish, as he liked to call it—and had a bit of singsong lilt to it.[3]

"Come on," David laughed, "I hear you're up at four o'clock every morning of the year."

"Nawt true," he said soberly. "In the winter, Ah allow meself an extra hour, Ah do."

"That much, eh?" David turned. "Ben, I would like you to meet my father, John Draper. You probably heard, he just returned from a mission in England about a week ago."

"Ah did 'ear that," he said, "and wur ye so fortunate as ta be assigned ta labor in the green hill country of South Wales?"

"Ah, no," David's father said, feigning great sadness, "Ah were naw so blessed. Most of the time Ah was in the Black Country around Wolverhampton."

Just then, Ben's brother, Hyrum Perkins, came up from the second wagon. David introduced him as well. "Ben and Hy were also coal miners. I thought you ought to know each other."

Ben was shaking his head sadly. "Ah 'urd ye 'ave the black lung, eh?"

"Ah do," John said, shrugging it off, "but it be joost b'ginning. Naw mooch of a problem as yet. And this dry, warm air already be mekin' it better."

Just then a shout turned David around. Joe Nielson was coming toward them astride his horse. "David. Dad would like to see all the scouts up front."

He waved. "Be right there." He turned back. "All right, you three. I know for myself how coal miners love to tell stories, so keep them at least halfway honest." Then to his father, he added, "I'll see you at the wagons."

As he walked away, he heard his father say, "He's got a lot o' cheek, don't 'e?" There was an answering laugh, and David had to smile as he walked on. This was good. He guessed these three were going to become good friends.

***

By the time David came back to their wagons, the McKenna women were there too. He looked around, counting quickly. There were twenty-two wagons in the two lines now, so they were getting close to being ready for departure. All around them was a swirl of activity. People were everywhere, many of them obviously not going on the trip. It was something to behold when a train this size came together and began to form up. It was like a giant carnival. Those who had turned out to see them off and bid them farewell outnumbered the missionaries by two or three to one.

Men, women, and children walked up and down the double line of wagons, stopping to talk, but mostly just gawking at everything around them. The men moved along, checking out the wagons and teams with admiring eyes. Once the company jumped off at Escalante into the desert, there would be no trading of jaded teams for new ones, no running to the nearest tack shop for more harnessing, no crossing the street to restock supplies at the dry-goods store, no pulling a wagon into a blacksmith shop for repairs. Whatever they needed, they were taking with them. So, like the McKennas', most of the equipment here today was new or had been completely refurbished. And though there were a few wagons being pulled by spans of oxen, most of the teams were either horses or mules. With very few exceptions, these were the finest animals to be had—young, strong, well-matched, and a beauty to behold. All up and down the line, men were nodding their approval as they took their measure.

The requirement set by Church leadership—and carefully checked off by local leaders—had been to have food and supplies sufficient for a six-week journey. Most families had packed double that, for they knew that even after they arrived at San Juan, they would be on their own for a significant time. Every wagon was stuffed beyond its capacity with food, tools, bedding, and the other things needed for such an extended journey as this.

The easiest way to ensure that there would be at least some fresh milk, eggs, butter, cheese, and meat along the way was to take it on the hoof. So, in addition to the hundreds of head of beef cattle and the dozens of milk cows, virtually every wagon was laden with cages tied along the sides of the wagon boxes. Mostly chickens, but a few ducks and even some rabbits huddled in their cages, cowed by the chaos around them.

As David rejoined the family, he overheard his father telling Patrick and Sarah about his conversation with the Welshmen. David looked around. "I think we'd better mount up. Brother Nielson is ready to have the prayer, and then we'll be under way."

They nodded and moved to their respective wagons. Patrick and Sarah would drive the lead wagon. Abby went to the second one. Carl took the third, and Molly climbed up with David's father on the last one. David and Billy Joe untied their mounts from behind the last wagon and mounted up. David moved Tillie forward until he was beside Abby's wagon. She already had the reins in her hand. "I can drive if this worries you," he said with a straight face.

"If you see me driving off a cliff, feel free to come help. Otherwise, I'll be fine."

"Fair enough." He grinned and rode to the last wagon. "You okay?" he asked Molly softly.

"Are you kidding?" she cried, straightening. "With this big strong man beside me? Of course I'm all right."

John Draper guffawed. "Ah cahrn't say that Ah be that big—" he was only four or five inches taller than Molly herself—"but Ah be strong, an' Ah surely be handsome."

As David rolled his eyes, Molly punched his father on the shoulder. "You are such a flirt."

David leaned down so his mouth was close to Molly's ear. "I'm proud of you," he murmured.

Her eyes widened a little. "Why?"

"Because you're here." Then, more loudly, "And because you're willing to ride with this old curmudgeon who murders the Queen's English and barely knows how to handle a span of mules."

His father cupped a hand to one ear. "Did ya 'ear sumthin'?" he queried.

Trying to suppress a laugh, Molly shook her head. "I didn't. Did you?"

"Naw. Fur a moment, Ah thought Ah 'eard sumbody flappin' thare gums in the wind, boot Ah reckon it joost be in me imagination."

Laughing merrily, Molly slipped her arm through his again and laid her head against his shoulder. "Brother Draper, I want to ride with you every day. You are exactly what I need." [4]

Notes

1. The details of Jens Nielson's family come from the "Bishop Jens Nielson History and Genealogy" (manuscript copy in LDS Church archives) and Carpenter, *Jens Nielson*, 21–32.

2. This description of Ben Perkins, along with other details shared here, comes from a family history (O'Brien, *Story of Sarah Williams Perkins*).

3. The Perkins family came from South Wales at a time when Welsh was spoken as the national language instead of English, as it is today. One need only look at a map of Wales and see the tongue-twisting spellings of the towns and cities there to realize that Welsh, which is one of the family of Celtic languages, is vastly different from English. Trying to accurately capture the nuances of a Welsh accent on paper were beyond me, so I have taken the easy way out and tried to make it sound somewhat like Scottish or Irish, since both of those are also Celtic languages.

4. The Cedar City contingent, led by Brother Jens Nielson, was the first major party to actually depart for the San Juan Mission. They left on the morning of October 22nd, six months and eight days following the departure of the exploring party. Some of the details and descriptions used here come from the historical sources (see Miller, *Hole*, 43–45; and Reay, *Incredible Passage*, 27–28). Although no exact count was given of the number in the party, it is reported that there were about twenty-five wagons. From the list compiled by Miller of those who are known to have gone on the trek (which he admits is not complete), there were thirty-six individuals listed as coming from Cedar City (see Miller, *Hole*, 143–46). I have supposed that most of them were in the Nielson group.

CHAPTER 50

Sunday, November 9, 1879

They went twelve miles the first day, covering more than half the distance to Parowan. On the second day, they passed through Parowan, moving very slowly because the whole town had turned out to welcome them. Six miles later, they had a similar experience in Paragonah. All of southern Utah was aflame with excitement. Smaller groups of fellow missionaries either did join them or would eventually join them until they all met up around Escalante. These were mostly smaller family groups from as far north as Santaquin and as far south as Kanab. But the largest single contingent was under way. The mission was finally started. A long-term solution to the threat of war with the Navajos was being launched.[1]

The Parowan and Paragonah contingents nearly doubled their numbers. Bishop Nielson held a brief meeting with Captain Silas Smith and learned that Silas would catch up to them somewhere south of Escalante. Until then, Bishop Nielson would be their company's leader.

And so they pressed on. They pushed up Little Creek Canyon, wound through Bear Valley, and dropped down into Panguitch, following the same route as the exploring party. At Panguitch, they were welcomed with another joyous celebration, and more families joined the company.

With nearly sixty wagons now, the train was a sight to behold as it rolled along. It looked like a gigantic, two-mile-long railway train, its white-topped "cars" coupled together by the teams pulling them. The slow-moving mass of horses, mules, cows, and oxen bringing up the rear was like a great, fat caboose.[2]

With their numbers approaching two hundred now, the travelers needed a more formal camp organization. In addition to the normal work assignments—drovers, scouts, blacksmith, commissary, chaplain, firewood gatherers—the old Dane organized them into groups of ten with a sub-captain over each group. Ten was more of an approximate number than a hard and fast one. Mostly the dividing was done along family group lines, with the father or grandfather being the captain of his ten. Because families dominated the makeup of the company, this type of division was natural.

There were eight in the McKenna party, counting David, his father, and Carl, so they became one group, with Patrick as captain. The Deckers were the largest, with twenty people. Ben and Hy Perkins had ten in their party; the Nielsons also were ten. Two families were large enough to form groups of their own without any other extended family: Samuel Rowley and his wife, who were from Parowan, had nine children. The Barneys, from Panguitch, had eight, including a baby in arms. Three women in the company were pregnant.[3]

Most astonishing to David was the number of children. Somewhere around forty percent of the pioneers were minor children, and one in five—fully twenty percent of the total company!—were six years of age or younger. Such a young company brought some unique challenges, but it also dramatically changed the nature of the group. David found it delightful.

The first two weeks things went smoothly. The weather was mostly dry and pleasant. The roads were good. The company made good time and spirits were high.

Their first real challenge was crossing Escalante Mountain, north of Bryce Canyon. The pass there was over nine thousand feet and was blanketed in nearly two feet of snow by the time they reached it. There were several close calls as teams stumbled on the snowpack and wagons started sliding sideways toward the steep drop-offs, but they made it through without undue problems. As they started down the east side, the snow quickly disappeared again. On Saturday, the eighth of November, eighteen days after leaving Cedar City, the long train of wagons made camp just to the west of the settlement of Escalante. That night, they went into town to join the locals for yet another celebration. On Sunday, they returned to join them for worship services.

Monday, November 10, 1879

On Monday, the Cedar City/Parowan/Paragonah/Panguitch contingent left their camp in place just west of town. That morning, Bishop Nielson sent about two dozen of the men, mostly the single young ones like David and Carl Bradford, south with a few wagons and tools. Their specific assignment was to turn the cattle trail and burro track between Escalante and Forty Mile Spring into a road capable of handling wagons.

For the rest of the company, it was a much-needed rest. The teams were exhausted and the rocky road had left many with tender feet. Wagons and harnessing were repaired, tools sharpened, horses and mules re-shod. The greatest excitement, however, was when the women and children, accompanied by their husbands and fathers, went into town to shop.

Restocking their supplies was critical. Escalante would be the last settlement they would see until they reached the San Juan River, where the Harrimans, the Davises, and one or two other earlier settlers awaited their return. Food was the first priority—wheat, milled flour, potatoes, onions, slabs of smoked pork, and barrels of sweet sorghum syrup, which the pioneers called molasses. But they also bought every keg of black powder the dry-goods store carried, along with many other items such as tools, clothing, bedding, and harnessing.

That night, Bishop Jens Nielson called in the captains of ten and told them that anyone who was ready should move out in the morning. They wouldn't move as a full company now, for some still needed to let their teams recuperate. They would make their way in small groups southward to Forty Mile Spring. Based on what Bishop Schow and Reuben Collett and the other settlers told them, it was the best source of water, and the best place for a semi-permanent camp. There they would wait for the other contingents to join them, including one from Oak City, up near Delta. This was led by Platte D. Lyman, the other counselor in the mission presidency, whom most had not yet met. From there they would build a road to the great Colorado River gorge and start the assault on the Hole in the Rock. Here they would also wait for Silas S. Smith to catch up with them. When that happened, they would finally have a full presidency in camp, and their leaders could then decide what happened next.

Saturday, November 15, 1879

Molly McKenna sat beside the small creek that was fed by Forty Mile Spring, resting in the shade of the willows before she returned with the water she had been sent to fetch. She was looking at her surroundings. Though the area would hardly fit the description of being a lush desert oasis, it was pleasant, and had a certain stark beauty to it. The spring itself was set in a wide, shallow canyon or wash. The water sustained a thick growth of willows along the creek and provided enough moisture for grass, shrubs, and brush to keep the whole area green. This was in stark contrast to the desert that surrounded them for miles on every side, or the massive cliffs to the west, which were part of the Straight Cliffs of Fifty Mile Mountain.

Part of what gave the place its beauty were several unusual rock formations that literally sprang up out of the valley floor or formed the sides of the wash. Masses of soft sandstone, colored a brilliant coral-pink, had been sculpted by wind and rain into fantastic shapes. Some were barely bumps or low ridges in the ground. Others were like huge, round loaves of bread, burnt pink in nature's oven.

And most wonderful, at least in Molly's mind, was Dance Hall Rock. This was the most prominent and fantastic formation of them all. Not quite a mile to the northwest of their camp was a single, isolated outcropping of sandstone. What made it so remarkable, in addition to its size and isolation, was its unusual shape. From north to south, it was two or three hundred yards wide and more than a hundred feet high. It sprang from the flat desert so abruptly as to actually startle the mind. Made of smooth, pink Navajo sandstone, it formed the western edge of a long, low, undulating ridge of slick rock, covered with striated erosion marks and dozens of small water pockets that looked almost like swallows' nests. Most astounding, however, was its west-facing front. The whole face of the rock was gently curved, somewhat like the shape of a French croissant, but over the centuries—or millennia—the wind and rain had carved into the sheer western face of the cliff an enormous hollow. Concave in shape, it was big enough and high enough to accommodate a full-masted schooner.

In the shadow of that great hollow was the best part, as far as Molly was concerned. Though it too was pockmarked with small water holes or bumpy patches of stone, the floor beneath the cliff was remarkably level. It was large enough for people to dance on—a lot of people. And thus its name: Dance Hall Rock.[4]

Molly wasn't sure who had first given it such an appropriate name, but she was completely in love with it. In the four days since their arrival, the company had gone there three times already. It was quickly becoming the gathering place after supper when the work was through. Once it was dark—earlier and earlier now—they would build a small fire made from sagebrush and shadscale* to provide light, and settle in for an evening of amusement and entertainment. They might have a speaker or just sit around and tell jokes or share riddles. Sometimes they would lift their voices in hymns or sing some of the more popular folk songs. When they moved up beneath the overhanging lip of the cliff, they were rewarded with a wonderfully rich sound.

The adults sat around and talked while the younger children would play games—hide-and-seek in the darkness, Run-Sheepie-Run, Red Rover, or, a favorite with the girls, cat's cradle. The stone floor also provided a good place for spinning tops. The boys would scratch a circle on the stone with a stick, put a few marbles on the ground inside the circle, then try to throw the tops down in such a way that as they spun they would knock the marbles outside of the circle.

Molly had decided on that first night of their arrival that if they had to be out here in the desert, it was nice to have Dance Hall Rock so near.

---

* A desert bush common to the southwestern United States.

As she returned a few minutes later with two full buckets of water, she saw Billy Joe playing with some of the boys behind the wagons, but she was surprised to see that her father, Carl, David, and David's father were no longer at their campfire. She increased her step, quickly emptied the buckets into the water barrel, dried her hands on her apron, and moved over to join Abby and her mother. "Where's Dad?"

Her mother pointed toward the large tent off to their right. It was the tent of Bishop Nielson. "The bishop has called a meeting for all the men."

"Oh? What's that about?"

Abby didn't turn. She was still looking at the tent, wishing she could hear what was going on inside. "Supposedly, Silas Smith and Platte Lyman are expected to arrive here at any time, but the bishop has decided that simply waiting for them serves no one best."

"And what can he do?" Molly asked.

Abby just shrugged. "We'll know when they come back."

It was another hour before the men returned. They were talking animatedly as they approached the campfire and the McKenna camp.

"Well?" Sarah asked, before Patrick had even reached them.

"It's very simple, actually," Patrick said. "Bishop Nielson is worried that while we wait for everyone to join us, including the rest of the presidency, time is slipping away."

"Hear, hear," Abby said. Of all the family, the waiting was hardest on her.

"Though he expects Silas Smith and Platte Lyman to arrive any day now—and he's left word in Escalante for them to come here to Forty Mile as quickly as possible—in the meantime, he thinks it is time to take action. He is proposing three things. Since they each involve one of us, I'd like the others to tell you what assignments affect them particularly. Carl, why don't you begin."

Carl nodded. "Out here in the desert, not only do we have to take care of the needs of our people, which we think will eventually be about two hundred and fifty individuals, but we also have a huge herd of animals to feed and water. Basically, it's going to take every inch of grazing land and every well, spring, rock tank, and pothole of water we can find. The bishop asked the drovers to start distributing the herd up and down the stretch between here and Escalante, anywhere there is grass and water. We'll keep a few head nearby—the milk cows, a few beef, some saddle horses, and enough teams to pull any wagons we may need to move—but the rest we'll start moving out in the morning. I've been asked to help."

"Thank you, Carl. John?"

David's father stepped forward. "Naw surprise frum me," he said. "Bishop Nielson wants the road crews ta begin work immediately on a road b'tween 'ere an' the 'Ole in the Rock. Ben an' Hy Perkins an' meself 'ave been appointed foremen over three separate crews who will cut, grade, or blast a road passable for wagons. We also start tamorrow."

"And David."

"Well," David began, "mine is pretty simple as well. It's one thing to get us to the Hole in the Rock, but quite another to decide where we go once we get there. The bishop has asked Kumen Jones to lead a group of scouts to explore the east side of the river."

"And you're one of them," Molly murmured.

"Yes. Me, Kumen, George Hobbs—all three of us were together with the exploring party—and Ben Lewis of Kanab and Bill Hutchings of Beaver."

"For how long?"

"No longer than eight to ten days."

She looked stricken. "After you were gone for six months?"

He shrugged. "So were Kumen and George." Then, seeing her dejection, he tried to be a little more helpful. "In a way, it's a good time. The camp's not going anywhere. You can pretty well take care of yourselves here."

"If it's any consolation," her father said ruefully, "they're not sending me out anywhere. I'll be here to keep you company."

"And you leave in the morning too?" Abby asked David.

"Yes. At first light."[5]

Notes

1. George Decker, one of the lead drovers for the company, in an oral history given late in his life, said that the Paragonah portion of the company had already left by the time the Cedar City contingent reached the town and were camped a mile or two up the canyon. He says they did not meet up until the Cedar group reached the head of Little Creek Canyon (see George W. Decker account in Miller, *Hole*, 50–51). To simplify the narrative, I have them leave together.

2. This vivid description of a wagon train comes from "Trail of the San Juan Mission" (as cited in *ibid.*, 45).

3. This information on the camp organization and the various families comes from several sources (*ibid.*, 46–48, 143–46; Carpenter, *Jens Nielson*, 41–43; and Jenson, *Encyclopedia*, 1:801–2; 3:153–54). George Decker also noted: "At this place [Holyoaks Springs], Jens Nielson, Danishman, recognized as leading Elder, proceeded to organize his flock and lay down some simple regulations for the conduct of his charges, the people of the San Juan mission" (as cited in Miller, *Hole*, 50–51).

4. "Dance Hall Rock" was evidently named by the San Juan pioneers because it became a natural gathering place for their recreational activities, including frequent dances. It is less than a mile from Forty Mile Spring. Currently there are interpretive markers at Dance Hall Rock and signs marking the short road that turns into Forty Mile Spring.

5. When the main company reached Forty Mile Spring, which would become the main camp for several weeks, Jens Nielson organized a scouting party consisting of the four men named above (Miller, *Hole*, 57; Reay, *Incredible Passage*, 32–33). Though more specifics are not given, we know that the camp was organized and specific assignments were given, including having Willard Butt serve as foreman of a herd of stock which is variously estimated to have been from 1200 to 1800 head (Reay, *Incredible Passage*, 31). We also know that work on the road south from Forty Mile to the river began immediately (see Miller, *Hole*, 58). Since the Perkins brothers took a major role in building the road down through the Hole, and since the road south from Fifty Mile Spring to the Hole ran through very rough and rocky escarpments, I have given them the lead in the road-building crew.

CHAPTER 51

Saturday, November 22, 1879

Tedium.

To Molly McKenna that was the worst thing of all. It was worse than the desert, worse than the sand, worse than the deerflies that came out in swarms to bite at your legs and arms and face. Day after day, in spite of the work assignments, in spite of the cooking, in spite of having to range ever wider to find fuel for the cooking fires, she found the waiting, the sitting around endlessly talking about what was going to happen next, nearly maddening.

David and the other scouts had been gone now for nine days and she was starting to worry. David's father—her other main source of diversion—was gone about half the time now. The road to the Hole in the Rock had progressed far enough south that the construction crews were taking bedrolls, returning to camp only every third or fourth night. Carl Bradford had been back one night from his drover duties, then had immediately taken another herd north. This time Molly's father had gone with them.

And so she was bored. She was in the doldrums. She was weary, in a malaise, listless, apathetic, sluggish. How many words could she think of to describe how utterly tedious life seemed at the moment? Abby had brought a few books, and spent her free time reading. She had offered them to her, but Molly didn't have the patience for it.

She abruptly stood up. "Mother?"

Sarah looked up. She was darning one of Billy Joe's socks, which seemed to be sprouting holes faster than she could keep up with them. "Yes, dear?"

"Let's invite some company over."

There were four other families parked close enough to the McKennas that they formed a little camp group of their own. They all welcomed the invitation from the McKennas, for ennui was almost epidemic in the camp now. Most of those who came were women and children. Like the rest of the camp, their men were off on one assignment or another.

They made a party of it, bringing their food and cooking supper together. Once that was done, they sent the older children off with the younger ones to play while they sat around the campfire and talked quietly. As they talked, Sarah McKenna watched them, surprised once again at the bonds of friendship that had developed among them.

Samuel and Ann Rowley were from Parowan. They were the family that had nine children with them. Watching Ann manage her family in these limited and trying circumstances had won Sarah's open admiration. Samuel was on the road crew with David's father and hadn't returned yet, even though tomorrow was the Sabbath. There were also two young couples, both childless, traveling together—George and Alice Urie and David and Sarah Jane Hunter. Sarah Jane and George Urie were sister and brother. George was also on John Draper's crew and was expected to return tonight. David Hunter was on Hyrum's crew and had arrived just in time for dinner.

Finally, there were the two Butt brothers. Parley and Willard Butt were also from Parowan and were among the many single brethren who were traveling in the group. They had returned the night before from taking a herd of horses down to the Escalante River.

Sarah had to smile as she watched them. Willard was in his midtwenties, sober of nature, and yet amiable and wonderful with the children. He was one of the lead drovers and so had been gone for over a week seeing to the stock. Parley was younger, closer to Molly's age. He and David Draper had traveled together with the exploring party and were good friends. However, when Molly had suggested it was because of that friendship with David that the two brothers had decided to camp close by, David just hooted. "It ain't me and Carl they're hoping to get close to," he said.

As Sarah watched Parley, she saw that his eyes rarely left one or the other of her two daughters. While both enjoyed his company, neither gave him much encouragement.

Abby looked up as a burst of laughter sounded above their heads. It was almost full dark, but the western sky was still light enough to show several silhouettes on the spine of the round, red-rock formation that guarded Forty Mile Spring. "Halloo the camp!" The sound floated down to them, almost ghostly.

Sarah shot to her feet. "Patrick Joseph McKenna! You get down from there right this minute!" There was another burst of giggles and the figures disappeared.

"It's all right, Mama," Abby observed. "I walked over there with Billy Joe earlier. The backside isn't that steep."

"Makes those boys feel like men," Parley observed. "They're just having fun."

"Maybe it's time we bring them in," Sarah said, looking up anxiously.

"If it worries you," Willard said, "I'll go bring them down."

She blew out her breath, then shook her head. "No, I suppose they're all right for now."

Ann Rowley looked worried too. "Would there be any danger from rattlesnakes there?"

Molly stiffened. "Are there rattlesnakes here?"

"Hey, this is the desert," David Hunter said, grinning.

His wife slapped him. "Don't you say that unless you mean it."

"This cold, most of the rattlers will be holing up now," Parley said. "Besides, the way those boys yell and holler, any intelligent snake will be headed for Fifty Mile Mountain by now."

Ann Rowley suppressed a shudder. "I have nightmares about putting the baby down and—"

"Don't!" Molly said sharply. Then, a moment later, "I hate this place."

They all turned in surprise. What had triggered that outburst? Even more surprising, Ann Rowley jumped in too. "I hate the thought of scorpions. They give me the creeps."

Sarah was giving Molly a chiding look, which she ignored. "Snakes, scorpions, lizards, beetles, horseflies," Molly said. "How long are we going to just sit out here?"

"Molly McKenna," Sarah exclaimed. "What has gotten into you?"

"She's right about one thing, Mama," Abby said. "We've been gone for over a month, and we're not even halfway. And that's the easiest half of the trip."

Sarah Jane Hunter leaned forward. "I have a question." She glanced quickly at her husband for his support. "While we're letting off some steam here, how do you feel about the prices our dear friends in Escalante charged us for supplies?"

At that, Parley's countenance darkened. "Charged? I think the better word is *gouged*. Willard and I were told that since we were missionaries answering a call from the Church, we would be able to buy provisions in Escalante at far below the going prices. Instead, they were double or more what they are in Parowan, or even Panguitch. I know that we got only about a fourth as much as we expected."

"*If* we were lucky and bargained hard," Abby added. She was still fuming from her experience in the town. Her father was better off financially than most of the others, but it had strained even his cash supply.

Sister Rowley spoke again. Normally she was quiet and reserved, and always of good cheer, but her eyes were flashing now. "Someone told us that the people of Escalante, on hearing we were coming, held a convention and unitedly agreed to double the prices."

There were soft cries of indignation and outrage.

Sarah's lips pressed together. This was enough. The mood had been so pleasant just moments before. "I don't believe that," she said quietly.

"Don't be too sure," David Hunter said in support of his wife.

Starting to feel a little beleaguered, Sarah turned to Sister Hunter. "I had some of those feelings too," she admitted, "but when I complained about it to Patrick, he pointed out several things. Sure, the prices were high, but other than what they grow here in the valley, the settlers in Escalante have to bring in everything from the outside for themselves. Virtually everything in those stores came in by wagon. That's not cheap. Also, just the sheer supply and demand would run prices up. Suddenly, two hundred additional people show up, wanting to buy up everything in sight. The amazing thing is that they weren't higher than they were."

Abby felt a stab of shame. She had gotten angry, but her father had not, even though it was his money. Nor had David. She had complained to him, and he had brushed it off.

"These are our brothers and sisters in the gospel," Sarah said, almost pleading now. "I refuse to believe they are taking unfair advantage of us."

The group was silent in response to that, and Abby decided she wasn't the only one feeling a little ashamed.[1] But Molly wasn't ready to give in. "Maybe so, but they sure gave us bad information about this route. We come all this way, and now we're not even sure we can build a road through this country. And what about these so-called springs every ten miles? I think a better title for them would be Ten Mile Ooze, or Twenty Mile Mudpot."

Even Sarah smiled at that. The watering places out here were all in the bottoms of dry washes. Usually, the travelers found water only after digging holes and letting it gradually seep in.

"And when we do finally get enough to drink or to cook with," Sister Urie said, "we have to strain the mud out. I can barely gag it down."

David Hunter threw up his hands. "It's not just the water. Don't you get sick of having sand in everything?"

"Especially in the food," Molly said, jumping on that. "We have sand in our pancakes, sand in our scrambled eggs, sand in our stew, and sand on the bacon. I am sick of feeling my teeth grind or crunch every time I take a bite."

Sarah's head came up slowly. "It does give a whole new meaning to hominy *grits*," she observed, her face completely solemn.

For one second they stared at her—then the laughter exploded, and the tension that had been building between them was gone. Even Molly couldn't sustain her anger and began to giggle. "It does help clean your teeth."

"I never thought of it that way," Ann Rowley managed between bursts of laughter. "But we are living on the world's largest scouring pad."

Willard Butt was trying to hold it in. "If you ever need sandpaper, all you have to do is spit."

Abby bent over, holding her sides. "Please stop!" she begged. "I can't *sand* it anymore."

That did it. They all collapsed as peals of laughter rang out in the evening air. As the laughter gradually died away, they heard footsteps. In the near darkness, three figures were approaching. Then John Draper's voice was heard. "George, Sam. Ah be thinkin' thare be sumthin' strange goin' on at our camp."

Samuel Rowley lowered the pick from off his shoulder and dropped it beside his wagon. Then he came over to his wife and gave her a quick kiss. George Urie came and sat beside Alice. "Want to share what was so funny?" he asked.

There were several suppressed giggles, but Abby was the quickest. "We can't." Her head dropped in shame. "I'm afraid we were telling *dirty* jokes."

That brought new roars of delight as the three men gave each other strange looks. This, of course, only made the others laugh all the harder.

Molly wiped tears from the corner of her eyes, fighting for control. When she had it, she looked up at David's father. "I guess we could share one joke that's not so bad. I got it from Billy Joe, actually, so consider the source, okay? Did you hear what happened to the cat who crossed the desert on Christmas Day?"

John tipped his head to one side, not sure if she was serious. "Naw, Ah cahrn't say that Ah know the answer ta that one."

She held her breath for a moment, fighting for control. Then it burst out of her. "He got sandy claws."

They howled in delight, slapping their legs and punching one another on the shoulder while the three new arrivals just stared at them. "Ah think they may 'ave eaten sum loco weed," David's father said to George. "It looks ta me lek they awl be daft in the 'ead."

Monday, November 24, 1879

Gratefully, there was Dance Hall Rock. Molly smiled at that thought. How many times had she made that statement in the last ten days?

"Miss Molly?" a voice called. Surprised, she looked up. Standing directly in front of her was Sammy Cox. Known to all as "the fiddler in the buckskin pants," Sammy was one of those rare individuals who had a gift for making people smile. Short, lean as a buggy whip, and spry as a monkey, he was irrepressible in both spirit and body. Nothing seemed capable of getting him down. He had endless energy, was quick of wit, and could turn any complaint into a "chuckler," as he liked to call them. He could make a joke about any and every challenge or hardship they faced. He was a tonic to the spirit, a salve to the soul.

And now, with his fiddle tucked under his arm and the bow in one hand, he was grinning impishly down at her. "By golly, Miss Molly," he cried, "by the looks of that lower lip of yours, the end of the world is going to happen before nine o'clock tonight."

"Or sooner," she said, trying not to smile.

"From the look of you, Sister McKenna, I don't think we dare wait any longer." He lifted the fiddle, stuck it between his chin and his shoulder, and ripped off two or three measures of "Turkey in the Straw," saying, "Looks to me like you could use some cheering up."

She couldn't help it. Laughing lightly, she said, "I was just thinking about how much I love it here at Dance Hall Rock."

He feigned sheer horror. "If that's how love affects you, please don't fall in love with me."

This time her laugh was genuine. People had turned to look, and like her were responding to Sammy's boundless enthusiasm. He stretched out his hand, took her hand, and pulled her up. "Come on, people," he shouted. "This girl needs an injection of laughter into her soul."

He spun around, looking. "Abigail McKenna," Sammy called out.

Abby was seated with her parents a few yards away. She raised her hand. "Here."

"Get yourself on up here and help me cheer up your sister. Sister

McKenna, I think we're going to need you too. Abby don't look much happier than Molly."

As Sarah got to her feet, Patrick stirred beside her. Sammy's hand shot out. "Sorry, Brother McKenna. We're only looking for purty ones tonight."

Now the laughter from the group echoed softly against the great stone face behind them. Several stood and started to move in around them to enjoy the fun. Sammy lined the three McKenna women up together, then looked around. Now his face took on a look of exaggerated perplexity. "Hmm," he mused loudly. "I have three lovely young ladies here, hoping for a chance to dance. What we need is a man with the energy and nerve to dance with all three of them at once."

"Joost the job fur a wee Welshman," a deep voice cried. Ben Perkins stood up and bowed to the burst of applause that rolled through the group.

Molly turned to him and gave him an exaggerated wink. "Brother Perkins," she called, "what will your wife think if you dance with all three of us at the same time?"

"Ah'll be forever grateful," sang out a woman's voice. "Me feet are tired."

That brought a burst of applause from all around. As Ben came forward, his short, stout body moving with an easy grace, Sammy Cox again put his fiddle up to his shoulder and stroked the bow across the strings a couple of times. "Brother Perkins, I know you and your brother have been working very hard on the road to the Hole, and I'm guessing you're a bit tired. What would you like me to play for you tonight?"

"Ah do feel a wee bit tuckered," he said gravely. "So let's start wit a couple of Welsh jigs, then maybe we could move ta the Virginia Reel ta give these sisters a bit of a rest. Once they've caught their breath, we could try two or three Scotch reels, a polka or two, maybe some schottisches. And for all of those with tired feet—" he turned and gave his wife a pitying look—"we can stop at some point an' let the old folks do a couple of sedate minuets."

Molly turned to Abby and, over the laughter of the crowd, said loudly, "My dear mother and sister, what say ye? Shall we not dance this proud and vain Welshman under the rug tonight until he begs for mercy?"

"Indeed we shall," Sarah said. She stepped forward and slipped an arm through Brother Perkins's arm. Abby and Molly slipped off their shoes and came forward to join them. "Feel free to holler for mercy when you've had enough," Abby said.

Ben shook his head with great sadness. "My dear sister, r'member what the Proverbs say. 'Pride goeth before destruction, and a haughty spirit before the fall.'"

"Brodder Ben," Bishop Jens Nielson called over another a wave of laughter, "were you speaking of dese tree lovely sisters here, or did ya have reference to yurself?"

Now it was a roar of delight that bounced off the rocks and back in on itself. Without missing a beat, the Welshman sniffed the air in disdain. Then he lifted both of his hands, motioning everyone to stand back. "Good bishop, Ah leeve that judgment in yur capable 'ands. As fur the rest of ya, if ya wud joost move back and leave us enuff room so that when these poor befuddled sisters collapse, no one will be steppin' on their weary an' exhausted bodies."[2]

In the end, the McKennas were saved from being "befuddled" by a startling development. Somewhere about the time they had started on a Scottish dance, something for which the entire group had been anxiously awaiting suddenly occurred. Sammy Cox cut off his fiddling in midstroke and turned to stare. Every head swung around. On the western rim of the dance area, a group of fifteen or sixteen people had appeared. They stood there for a moment, then one of the men near the front stepped forward. "Bishop Nielson? Bishop Jens Nielson?"

A cry of joy exploded from the Paragonah members, who recognized the voice. So did Bishop Nielson. He got to his feet and started shuffling across the stone floor toward the man who had spoken. "Brodder Smith!" he cried. "Brodder Silas Smith. Cud that be truly you?"

After a period of handshaking and backslapping, with hugging among the women, the company separated into groups. The women and younger children moved in to welcome the extended Smith family while the men gathered around Silas and Bishop Nielson.

Captain Smith insisted on hearing the bishop's report first. Much of it he already knew because the bishop was sending reports back to Escalante regularly. But he was pleased to see for himself how smoothly things were going here at Forty Mile Camp. He was especially pleased when Bishop Nielson told him, somewhat apologetically, that rather than wait for his arrival, he had sent five men south to explore possible routes across the river.

"Wonderful! Wonderful!" Silas kept saying. "I'm so glad that you didn't hold back. We need to know what to expect over there, and we need to know quickly."

Then he gave a quick summary of his own journey, and especially what he had learned in Escalante. "You'll be pleased to know that Brother Platte D. Lyman, our first counselor for the mission, is just a few miles behind us. The main part of his group is a little farther back, but he was going to camp at Cottonwood Wash and join us tomorrow."

"Dat is very goot news," Bishop Nielson said. "At last our presidency will be together."

"And, you'll be happy to know, he has three men with him," Silas added. "Bishop Schow, Reuben Collett, and Charles Hall."

He nodded as a murmur of approval swept through the brethren. "That's right. The three men who know the most about this country are here to help us find a way through."

Just then, a noise behind them brought their heads around. There at the edge of the firelight, in the same place where Silas and his family had appeared earlier, five men were coming forward in long strides. As they moved into the flickering firelight, suddenly from the group of women there was a cry of joy. Molly McKenna was staring, one hand to her mouth. It was followed instantly by the heavily accented voice of Bishop Jens Nielson. "Kumen. Is dat you?"[3]

Notes

1. Miller records that about this time the frustrations of the group seemed to increase, and there was some disgruntlement both with the indecision and uncertainty about the

route and with the prices they paid in Escalante for supplies. The criticisms expressed here by Samuel Rowley and Parley Butt come from their family histories (see Miller, *Hole*, 47–48). In his history of Escalante, Roundy makes this observation, which was used in this chapter to counter the criticism:

"It must be remembered that Escalante was only three years old and people had not had time to lay in large supplies. There had been little chance to purchase outside goods and, with this being October and November when the colonists were moving through Escalante, they knew that snow would soon close the road to outside purchases. They, too, had to make it through the winter months, and depleting their supplies could place a hardship on their families before spring came" (Roundy, *Escalante*, 109).

2. These details of the evening times of recreation and relaxation, including Sammy Cox's cheerful nature and musical ability and Ben Perkins's willingness to "challenge three or four women to keep up with him in doing a jig" are drawn from several sources (Redd, "Short Cut," 13–14; Miller, *Hole*, 53–54; Reay, *Incredible Passage*, 49–51; and "Life Sketch of Mary Jane Wilson," 8).

3. While exact dates for this four-man exploring party are not given, Miller estimates that they left around November fifteenth, a few days after the Nielson group arrived at Forty Mile Spring (see Miller, *Hole*, 57). Since they took six days exploring the east side of the river, and it took roughly two days coming and going between Forty Mile Spring and the Hole, ten days would put them back at camp on the twenty-fourth, the very day Smith arrived. In his journal, Silas wrote this brief entry: "Drove five miles to camp. Very unfavorable report from exploring party" (as cited in *ibid.*, 67). So either they were there when he arrived or they came a short time later.

CHAPTER 52

Tuesday, November 25, 1879

After allowing some time for a warm and prolonged welcome for the Smith family and the returning explorers, Silas Smith and Bishop Nielson sent the company back to camp to prepare for bed. Though both leaders were anxious to hear a report on the exploration, due to the lateness of the hour and the fact that the men were completely exhausted, they asked for just a quick summary, which was given by Kumen Jones. Since Platte Lyman planned to arrive in camp sometime the next morning, the five men would give their full report at that time. In the meantime, those in the exploring party were asked to resist answering any questions from the group to prevent the circulation of rumors and half-truths.

Knowing how difficult that was going to be for the McKennas and everyone else, David went straight to bed, saying that he was so tired he could barely make a coherent sentence—which was not much of an exaggeration. The next morning he was out of his bedroll before anyone else and slipped down to the creek unseen. Then he went back to bed and stayed there, sometimes sleeping, sometimes pretending sleep, until after seven o'clock. When he finally did get up, it was clear that Patrick and Sarah had already given the family stern instructions to leave him alone, for breakfast was little more than an awkward commentary on the weather and what the day held. Gratefully, Platte D. Lyman and the two scouts from Escalante walked into camp around eight o'clock, and Silas called for the scouts to come to his tent immediately.

As the five walked out, blinking in the brightness of the sunlight, Kumen Jones held up a hand. "No questions," he called. "President Smith will be making an announcement in about a quarter of an hour."

They ignored the groans and calls of disappointment as they headed back to their individual campsites. Knowing what was waiting for him at the McKennas', David called out to Sister McKenna even before he reached the campfire to forestall any interrogation. "Sarah, is there any chance I could get you and the girls to pack me enough food for two days?"

"What?" Molly cried. "Where are you going?"

Even Patrick was surprised by that. "You're off again?" he asked.

"Brother Lyman wants to hike to the top of Fifty Mile Mountain. He's hoping to use the field glasses to identify a possible route on the east side. We're leaving immediately."

"But you'll only be gone two days?" Sarah asked, deflecting any more questions for him.

"Yes. Silas wants to meet with all the scouts Thursday evening and decide what to do."

"Thursday is Thanksgiving Day,"[1] Molly said.

Sarah nodded. "I'm not sure we'll be able to find a turkey and all the trimmings out here, but we'll do our best. I hope you'll be back by then."

"Me too. Even a jackrabbit with one or two trimmings sounds good to me."

Carl had been silent through all of this. Now he spoke up. "Did you know the road-building crews have completely stopped work on the road now?"

David straightened slowly. "No, I didn't know that. So that's why we didn't see anyone out there when we came back yesterday afternoon." He looked to his father. "Why?"

John Draper frowned. "The men cahrn't see much sense in bustin' their picks if we be turnin' back. So they joost stayed in camp yest'day."

"The camp is pretty discouraged," Patrick said. "Quite a bit of grumbling and complaining."

Molly and Abby exchanged glances, wondering if he had learned about their gripe session the other night, but he didn't look at either of them. "I guess that's why Silas is so anxious to make a decision. Hopefully, this reconnaissance will help."

"But we heard that Schow and Collett brought a boat with them," Carl persisted. "Bigger than the one they used last summer. Doesn't that mean someone's going to cross the river? That there will be further exploration before a decision is made?"

David studied him for a moment. One thing about Carl Bradford: He may not have been the most enthusiastic or experienced pioneer, but he was shrewd. "I'm sure it does," he admitted.

Molly's head came up as the implications of that hit her, but Abby asked it first. "Will you be asked to go on that one, too?"

"Of course you will," Molly said, with a touch of bitterness. "You don't have a family."

"And," her father said pointedly, losing patience, "David has already been over there once."

Molly just tossed her head and turned away. "And how long will that one be?" she muttered.

No one answered, and the silence became awkward as Molly stalked off around to the back of the wagons. Sarah quickly gathered some food, put it in a sack, and handed it to David.

As he took it, Carl spoke. "Take my field glasses. Two pairs of eyes are better than one."

David was surprised and touched. The binoculars were expensive, and Carl was very protective of them. "Thanks, Carl."

As Carl went to get them, David turned to Billy Joe, who had been uncharacteristically quiet through all of this. He pointed at the ragged wall of Fifty Mile Mountain, four or five miles to the west of them. "See that highest peak there?" he asked, pointing. When Billy Joe nodded, he went on, "Now go to the left where the mountain seems to come to an end." He glanced up and saw that Molly had stepped out enough to watch. "That's what they call Navajo Point. Supposedly it looks almost straight down into the gorge. So watch there tomorrow about noon. I'll take my little shaving mirror with me. If you see a flash, you'll know it's me saying hello. All right?"

"Yeah!" Billy Joe said.

He looked up and saw Molly nod gratefully. He lifted a hand to all of them. "See you tomorrow night."

As he started away, Abby looked around. What a dejected and gloomy bunch they were. She walked to Billy Joe and touched his shoulder. "I have an assignment for you. Thursday is Thanksgiving," she said. "Why don't you start a pile of thankful pebbles?"

He gave her a funny look. "Thankful pebbles?"

"Yes," she said, still formulating what she wanted to say. "Every time you can get someone in this gloomy-gus family to laugh, you put a pebble on the pile."

David had heard that and turned back to listen.

"And every time one of us tells you something we're thankful for, you put another pebble on the pile. Can you do that? We'll see how big a pile we can make before David gets back."

"Yes!" Billy Joe said, throwing back his shoulders proudly.

"Let me be the first," Sarah said. She bent down, picked up a small rock, and handed it to her son. "I am thankful the Lord brought David Draper to Cedar City to be a mail rider."

"Amen," Patrick said. He bent down and got a pebble and handed it to Billy Joe.

"Yes," Molly breathed, and did the same.

Abby said nothing, but she bent down, picked up two rocks, and tossed one to Billy Joe. "Is this for David too?" he asked.

Her eyes met and held David's briefly; then her lips curled in a mischievous smile. "No. Actually, this is for Tillie. I am thankful that she never complains, in spite of the company she keeps."

"Ow!" David cried, which brought a hearty laugh all around the circle. Then his head came up. "Did you hear that, Billy Joe. I think I just counted seven people who laughed."

Billy Joe looked confused for a moment, but soon his face was wreathed in smiles. "That's right," he exclaimed, and began scooping up more pebbles.

When he straightened again, Abby's smile faded. She walked over and handed him the other pebble. "And second, I'm thankful for Tillie because she always brings David back safely to us."

Thursday, November 27, 1879

Thanksgiving Day at Forty Mile Creek dawned to reveal a brilliant white landscape as far as the eye could see. Sometime during the night it had started to snow, and now there were two to three inches on the ground. As Abby pulled back the wagon cover and looked out, she drew in her breath quickly. "Oh, Molly," she exclaimed. "Come and see."

Molly moaned, but after a moment she came up on one elbow, clutching the quilt around her. "What is it?" She looked, then dropped back. "Thank you for waking me up for *that*."

Abby stuck her head out and peered around. A few people were stirring and one or two campfires had been started, but for the most part the camp was still just waking up. She tied the flap back so they could see out, then crawled back under the quilt and snuggled in beside her sister. "Not only is it lovely, but when it melts, there'll be water in all the water pockets and rock tanks. Which means we won't have to carry as much from the spring. Surely that's worth another pebble or two for Billy Joe's pile."

Molly sniggered. "When David sees how big the pile is, he's going to be surprised."

"By the way, David is back," Abby said.

Molly jerked to a sitting position. "How do you know that?"

"I just saw Tillie down near the creek. She's unsaddled and grazing, so I guess he must have gotten in late last night."

"Wonderful."

Abby said nothing.

"What?" Molly said. "What was that look for?"

"You may as well know. He'll probably be leaving again in the morning."

"In the morning? No, Abby!"

"Joe Nielson told me last night that Brother Lyman plans to cross the river tomorrow with about a dozen men and see if they can find a route up and out of the gorge."

"And David will be asked to go?" She dropped back again, knowing the answer to that. "It's not fair. He's done his part."

"Oh?" Abby said, with a touch of impatience. "And just exactly what is his part?"

Molly gave her a look. "He was gone six months with the first group," she snapped. "Now that we're on the road again, they're sending him out all the time. Ten days with Kumen. Two days with Lyman. Now another who-knows-how-long trip."

"Somehow I thought that was what scouts did."

"He's not the only scout. It's not right, Abby. Let someone else do it."

Abby's lips pressed together into a tight line. "Go back to sleep. I'm sorry I woke you up."

Molly's hand shot out and grabbed her. "No, Abby. You tell me. Is it asking too much to let him spend some time with us? After all, isn't Daddy paying him to help our family?"

"Then why doesn't Daddy complain to Silas about it?"

"Ohhh! Sometimes you make me so angry, Abby. Always the one to know everything. Always the one to do things just right. You should have married Carl—then you could have spent your time making *him* perfect, instead of me."

Abby stiffened.

Molly's face instantly crumpled. "Sorry, Abby. I didn't mean that. I'm just so frustrated."

There was a soft, sorrowful sound. "No, down deep, Molly, I think you really did mean it. And you're right. It's not my place to tell you how to live your life. I'm sorry."

She sighed, closed the flap, and began to dress. As she finished slipping into her dress and began pulling on her shoes, she finally spoke again. "Today is Thanksgiving. And if David does leave again tomorrow, it's the only day we'll have all together for a while. Just don't make him feel guilty for doing what he's supposed to be doing."

"And you think that's what I was going to do?"

"Not intentionally, no. But if you turn those big, sad eyes on him and look as if your heart is going to break, he will feel guilty."

"You make me sound awful."

Abby started to turn away, then swung back, thoroughly exasperated. "You don't even see it, do you? There are bigger issues here. This isn't just about Molly or Abby or David. Maybe it's about finding a way to San Juan."

"If that's true, then why doesn't God show us the way to go, so we can accomplish His purpose and get on with our life?"

"Maybe," Abby said slowly, "because for now, this *is* our life."

Friday, November 28, 1879

The McKennas stood around, stamping their feet and hugging themselves against the cold, as they watched David tie his bedroll onto the saddle, then shove his rifle into its scabbard. David's father handed him a sack of food, which he stuffed into one side of his saddlebags.

Finally, David turned. "Well, I guess that's it."

His father came forward and shook hands. "Ah'll be oot thare watchin' fur ya," he said. "We 'ope to 'ave the road finished all the way ta Fifty Mile Spring by the time yur back."

David nodded and hugged him. "Do you know," he whispered, "how glad I am that we're here together, Dad? I'm glad the Lord decided England could do without you."

His father's head reared back slightly. "What?" he whispered into David's ear. "Did Ah joost 'ear me own son give credit ta the Lord fur sumthin'?"

David grinned. "Sorry. A slip of the tongue."

"Or of the 'eart," his father responded, letting him go and stepping back.

Patrick came forward. "Godspeed, David." They shook hands, then also embraced. In turn, David hugged Billy Joe, shook hands with Abby and Molly, then went to shake hands with Sarah. She slapped his hand away and threw her arms around him, hugging him fiercely. "Go safely, David. We'll be praying for you. For all of you."

"Thank you. And thank you for yesterday. It was wonderful to just relax and forget about all of this for a day."

Finally, he shook hands with Carl, who again offered David his field glasses. When David thanked him, he said, "They're yours, David. You have more use for them than I do."

Then, as if by unspoken assent, the others moved away, leaving only Molly standing beside him. David searched her face, then grinned ruefully. "Seems like the Lord heard about this deal you and I made before we left, and is doing His part to make it easier on us."

Her head snapped up. "Did Abby talk to you?"

He was genuinely surprised. "About what?"

She shook her head, then gave him a bright smile. "Nothing." She looked up at him, her eyes wide and luminous. "Maybe when you get back we can have some time to talk?" It was said wistfully, and more as a question than a statement.

"I would like that. Maybe even laugh a little again."

She forced a wide smile. "I would like that a lot." She touched his arm briefly, then stepped back. "Godspeed, David."

He swung up in the saddle. Then he remembered something. Removing a glove and fishing in his shirt pocket, he drew out a piece of folded paper and handed it down to her.

"What's this?" she said as she opened it. Then her eyes widened. What was written there was very short. Two words and a number. *Mizpah. Genesis 31:49.* She looked up, puzzled now. "What does it say?"

He lifted a hand. "Gotta go. Good-bye, Molly." And he rode off.

She went straight to the wagon, found her bag, and dug out her Bible. Glancing at the paper again, she turned to Genesis. As she read the verse in the dim light, she began to cry, but she was smiling through her tears. She wiped at her eyes and read it again. *And Mizpah, for he said, The Lord watch between me and thee, when we are absent one from another.*

Wednesday, December 3, 1879

Molly McKenna listened to the soft drumming of the rain on the roof of the tent of Ben and Hyrum Perkins, tuning out the chatter of the women around her. Her thoughts were on David. Where was he in weather like this? She knew they had not taken tents with them, so when the weather turned gray and cold, as it was today, did the group try to find shelter until the rain passed, or did they simply go on exploring? She was pretty sure she knew the answer to that.

She suppressed a yawn that quickly turned into a sigh. This was the sixth day since they had left. When David had gone with the previous group, they had taken ten days. *Four more days. At least!* She sighed again and looked around.

They were having a "hens' day out," as Mary Ann Perkins called it. Ben and Hy Perkins were gone building roads, so she and Hyrum's wife, Rachel, had dug out some of the famous Perkins' Pottawattamie plum preserves[2] and invited some of the other "widows" over for nibbles.

John Draper and Patrick McKenna were also on the construction gang and wouldn't return until Friday or Saturday, so Abby, Molly, and their mother were invited. Anna Maria Decker's husband, Jim, was gone for the day rounding up loose stock. Though he had previous experience as a scout, his wife was now eight and a half months along in her pregnancy, and Silas had told him to stay nearby. But she was alone for the day, and the Perkins women had decided she also needed some cheer on this otherwise lonely and dreary day. Ben and Mary Ann's nine-year-old daughter was also there.

The preserves were gone. Only a few crumbs remained of the loaf of bread, and the butter tin was nearly empty. Little Mary Jane was licking the last of the butter and sticky preserves from her fingers. The mood was bright and they had laughed a lot. Molly had been part of that, but in the last few minutes, concern for David had snuck up on her and darkened her mood.

Then she saw Abby give her a quizzical look. "Are you all right?" the look was saying. Molly forced a quick smile and nodded. She was. If she had to be out in the middle of this vast emptiness; if she had to be sitting in a tent on a cold, rainy day, not knowing what life had in store for them; if she had to do all of that, then being with these sisters was the best way to do it.

Abby was clearly not satisfied. She shot Molly another look, then turned to Mary Ann Perkins. "Mary Ann, I have a question."

"All right."

"Somewhere along the way, and I can't remember who it was now, someone told us that you and that delightful husband of yours had an unusual courtship. Is that true?"

"Aye," she said in her rich Welsh accent. "But unusual be mooch too soft a word."

"Tell us about it," Anna Decker said.

"Oh, yes," her daughter cried, "tell them, Mama. I love this story."

The others joined in chorus, urging her to do the same. Molly glanced sharply at her sister, knowing Abby had asked the question for her benefit. But she always loved to hear about the courting experiences of others, and so she smiled her encouragement too.

The older woman smoothed her skirts for a moment, then finally bobbed her head. "All right. But let me give you some brief background on Ben and Hyrum's family. That will give more significance to my story."

They all settled back to listen.

"Ben's parents were baptized inta the Church in Wales in the early eighteen forties. Ta say that Ben cumes frum a large fam'ly would be a wee bit of an understatement. Ben's mother eventually gave birth to twenty-one children, none of them twins."

"Whoa!" Anna Decker exclaimed. "This is only my fourth. Please don't tell me I have to do this seventeen more times." The look of mock horror sent the others into soft giggles.

"Ben's father was a coal miner, but when the bosses learned 'e was a Mormon, they fired 'im. The fam'ly was immediately ploonged inta poverty an' ended up in the poor hoose fur over a year. But eventually, they were released. Ben and Hyrum both started in the mines as young boys."

Molly felt a pang of guilt. Ben Perkins was one of the most delightful men she knew—jovial, witty, entertaining, always smiling, forever teasing or cracking jokes. Who would have guessed his early childhood had been that hard?

"Ben stayed in the mines fur anuther twenty years, eventually becomin' a blaster."

"Is that when they came to America?" Sarah asked.

"Yes. Eighteen sixty-seven. Ben and five other siblings decided they wuld come ta America ta earn enuff money ta send back for the rest of the fam'ly." She stopped, a slow, secretive smile softening the corners of her mouth.

"What?" Abby teased. "What were you thinking right then?"

Mary Ann laughed, sounding like a young girl. "Ah was thinkin' aboot the day they left fur America. Some of their fam'ly an' close friends came ta bid them farewell. Ah was thare too." Her eyes were soft with the memories now.

"Anyway, thare we were, sayin' gud-bye ta 'em, wund'rin' if we'd ever see them again, me bawlin' me eyes oot because Ah were so sad ta see 'em leavin'. Suddenly, Ah saw Ben standin' there in front of me, joost lookin' at me all funny-like."

"Guess what Daddy said?" Mary Jane blurted, unable to stand it any longer.

"Let me tell it," her mother chided. And Molly saw that Mary Ann had a little bit of the entertainer in her, just like her husband. "Finally, joost about as 'e was ta bust 'is buttons wit embarrassment, 'e looked me reet in the eye an' said, 'Mary Jane Williams, when Ah 'ave made enuff ta send fur the rest of me fam'ly, if Ah send money ta ya, wud ya come wit them?'"

"Just like that?" Molly cried.

"Joost like that." She laughed merrily now. "Ah looked up, wiped me eyes, an' said Ah wud. And that was the full extent of our courtship. Two years later 'e sent the money an' Ah came ta America wit the rest of their fam'ly. Shortly after Ah arrived in Salt Lake, Ben an' me wur married in the Endowment House fur time an' fur all eternity."[3]

"What a wonderful story," Anna Decker said.

"Just like in the fairy tales," Abby observed. "And it all ended happily ever after."

Molly reached out and touched her hand. "It is a wonderful story. Thank you for sharing it."

As the women gathered in around Mary Ann, plying her with questions and sharing some of their own courtship stories, Abby scooted closer to Molly. "What did you think of that?"

"You asked her that for my benefit, didn't you?"

She gave her a mocking look. "I didn't know what she was going to say."

"But you hoped for something to cheer me up, didn't you."

"I was looking for something to cheer us all up," Abby shot right back. Then she smiled. "So did it work?"

Begrudgingly Molly nodded. "It did. It is an amazing story."

"And even though they didn't get to spend any time together before they were married, look how happy they are now."

Molly just shook her head. "You never give up, do you?"

"Not when it's my sister," Abby said. Then she became very serious. "So the way I figure it, you and David still have another eighteen months of separation before—*ow!*"

Molly had grabbed her arm and pinched it hard.

The others turned, giving them both questioning looks. Molly was pure innocence. "She slipped," she explained.

Then, as Abby started to protest, they all turned. Outside, a man was yelling. They heard pounding footsteps. When he shouted again, all but Anna Decker leaped to their feet. Mary Ann threw back the flap of the tent as a man ran by. "What is it?" she called.

He turned. "They're back. Platte Lyman and the men are back."

Notes

1. According to tradition, the first Thanksgiving was held by the early settlers in America to give thanks for their safe arrival and a bounteous crop. President Abraham Lincoln asked Congress to set aside the last Thursday of November as the official day to celebrate Thanksgiving, which custom has been observed since that time.

2. Pottawattamie plum preserves were made by cooking the plums until they formed a syrup. This was run through a colander to remove the stones and skins; then the syrup was poured onto plates and put in the sun to harden and dry. The pancake-like substance could then be stacked up in piles and wrapped in paper or cloth. When wanted for use, the cakes were broken into small pieces, water and sugar were added, and, with a little further cooking, a delicious jam was obtained (see "Life Sketch of Mary Jane Wilson," 8).

3. This account of Ben Perkins's early life and his marriage to Mary Ann Williams also comes from their daughter's life history (ibid., 1–2, 4).

CHAPTER 53

Wednesday, December 3, 1879

"Brethren!"

Instantly the group crowded into Silas Smith's tent stopped talking, and all turned to look at their leader. This was a larger tent, shared by Silas and his extended family, but now the tent was crowded with men. Silas was seated on a small stool behind a collapsible table near the tent's door. He was flanked on both sides by Platte Lyman and Jens Nielson, both of whom were standing. The thirteen men who had just returned sat on boxes and trunks that lined the outer walls of the tent. David was one of those, sitting off in one corner with Joe Nielson, Kumen Jones, and George Hobbs.

"Brethren," Silas said again, his face grave and lined with concern, "we are most grateful for your speedy return. We are badly in need of a decision. As you probably have sensed since returning this afternoon, the company's morale is very low. I fear that a spirit of pessimism now permeates the camp. That is understandable. These people have left their homes, sold their businesses, and bid farewell to family and friends, fully expecting that by now we would be—or at least, soon would be—at our destination. Instead, we languish here in the desert, not going backward, but neither moving forward."

His head came up, and his voice filled with sudden determination. "We cannot live with that indecision any longer. We must decide what we are going to do, and we must decide it *now*."

No one spoke, but heads were bobbing up and down solemnly all around.

"Let us begin with a report from Brother Lyman concerning the explorations just completed." He half turned, motioning to his counselor. "Platte, the time is yours."

Platte took one step forward, nodded briefly at Silas, then turned to face the group. David noticed once again what a striking man he was. He was about the same height as David, just under six feet tall, and solidly built. But there was no fat on him, and David had seen for himself the strength in his arms and hands. After being with him full time now for over a week, David had nothing but the highest respect for the man and his capabilities.

"Thank you, President Smith," he began. "I know there is much to discuss, so I shall be brief. I invite my brethren who were with me to add comments as they see fit." He took a quick breath and continued. "As you know, we left here last Friday morning. We drove ten miles, over some of the roughest country I have ever seen, and camped that night at Fifty Mile Spring. The next day we continued, driving through a lot of sand and over sandstone hills to the Hole in the Rock. After a brief stop to look that over, we continued—"

"Pardon me, Brother Platte," Silas broke in, "but I should like to ask your opinion. Now that you have seen the Hole, do you agree that it is possible to build a wagon road down through it?"

Platte thought on that for a moment, then nodded. "It will take a lot of work. Quite a bit of blasting, but yes, I think it is possible."

"Thank you. Go on."

"We continued on about two miles upstream, where we lowered our boat down to the river. By the way, there is a large, flat area about halfway down there that we called Jackass Flat. It is about a hundred acres and has some excellent grazing. The path is quite steep and precipitous, but we took our animals down it, and with some work believe it could be improved enough to take others."

"Goot," Bishop Nielson said. "Vee need to keep some teams closer to de Hole."

"Once we had the boat down," Platte went on, "after supper and a little rest, we loaded our luggage into the boat and rowed it downstream about a mile to where we tied up. We camped directly across the river from the Hole. By the way, the river at that point is about three hundred fifty feet across. The current is sluggish, the water somewhat milky in color, but pleasant tasting. Building a ferry there should allow easy crossing, especially now at low water."

"The next morning, some of us went downriver, hoping to reach the San Juan River, then row upstream to find a way out in that direction. But before we even reached the San Juan, we could hear a roar of water. There were bad rapids, and we didn't dare risk going farther."

He sighed. David could see in his face the same weariness and discouragement they were all feeling right now.

"So we returned to our camp. We left two men there with the boat, and the rest of us loaded up blankets and food on our backs and started looking for a way up to the eastern bluffs. We found a smooth, open canyon with plenty of water, wood, and grass."

"Brother Collett and I called that Cottonwood Canyon when we were there before," Bishop Schow said. "It would make an excellent campsite."

"Yes, definitely," Platte agreed. "Anyway, we followed that up through the bluffs until we came to some very steep, sandstone hills. These continued all the way to the summit, which is about six miles from the river. Up on top we found plenty of water in potholes and rock tanks."

He hesitated, one hand pulling at his beard. David knew what was coming. They had talked of little else on their return trip to camp.

"Next morning—that would be Monday, day before yesterday—we continued east, looking for a possible route. Very quickly we found the country so rough and broken up, and so badly cut in two by deep gorges of solid rock, that we gave up all hope of a road being made through there."

Silas Smith was staring at his counselor in great dismay. "Say that again, please," he said.

Platte exhaled slowly. "We found the country so badly broken up and cut through with impassable gorges, that we gave up all hope of making a road through there."

"But . . ." Jens Nielson blurted. Then he caught himself, and clamped his mouth shut. He would not speak before his leader had spoken.

"We made one other excursion down a side canyon, but found nothing that way either. So we returned to the river, crossed over, and hauled the boat back up to Jackass Flat. We then returned here as quickly as we could."

He started to step back, then stopped. "In summary, I must say that the country on that side of the river is nothing but hills and mountains made up almost entirely of solid rock, cut through by gulches that are altogether precipitous and impassable. It is certainly the worst country I ever saw."

He looked down at his captain. "I must also say, however, that a few of our party are of a different mind, and I would suggest we hear their opinions, too. But the majority of us are perfectly satisfied that there is no way for this company to get through that country."[1]

Silas let the burst of noise that followed that announcement play itself out as he conferred quickly with his two counselors. Finally he turned and held up his hand. "Brother Lyman suggests that we hear now from our two brethren from Escalante. "Bishop Schow, Brother Collett, you have the floor."

The two scouts were off to one side from the presidency. They conferred briefly, and then Reuben Collett stepped forward. "Bishop Schow asks me to speak for both of us."

When they had spoken at the stake meeting in Parowan, David had been impressed with both Andrew Schow and Reuben Collett. After spending almost a week with them, he found that impression had only deepened. Collett especially, with his one arm, was remarkable.

Now he began, getting right to it. "I would in no way disparage or downplay the concerns that have been so plainly expressed by our leader, Brother Lyman. As he has already noted, his feelings are shared by the majority of our group. However, he has asked that we share our feelings so that when a decision is made, our leaders will have as much information as possible on which to base it. Therefore, I shall speak frankly."

"I cannot disagree with Brother Lyman's assessment—" he hesitated for a fraction of a second as the shock of that hit the group, then went on smoothly—"*based* on the experience we have just completed. However, because of the urgency of our situation, these explorations of the east side of

the Colorado were necessarily limited both in scope and time. This is important to remember. We had only two days of actual exploration on the
east side. And we penetrated inland no more than a few miles at most.
What we saw in that limited time was enough to discourage anyone. It is a
daunting thing to build a road and take a company as large as yours
through such country."

"*But*—" he stabbed the air with his finger—"may I remind you that earlier this summer and fall, Bishop Schow and I also took a boat across the river,
and we spent a considerable time scouting the area over there. We went
much farther inland. We explored several possible routes. And we marked a
track that we were not able to see this time because we had to turn back."

He waited as a soft buzz of whispering moved from man to man.
"There are some tremendous challenges. Everyone agrees on that. The two
biggest challenges that our party saw in the last few days are the steep
bluffs and side hills at the top of Cottonwood Canyon. Unquestionably, we
shall have to cut a road into the mountainside there. But—" again he
jabbed the air emphatically—"it will not be as difficult as cutting the road
down through the Hole. If that is possible, so will the other be.

"The other place is what Bishop Schow and I call 'The Chute.' This is
a few miles farther in. It too is steep and narrow. It is like the bottom half of
a huge pipe, made of solid rock. We shall undoubtedly have to double-
team the wagons, but the footing is good, and with a little work at the top,
we are confident we can make our way through it."

He stopped. No one spoke. Every eye was on him. "In our previous explorations, Bishop Schow and I went beyond The Chute. What we found
there was great, mostly level, mesa. It is tableland thickly covered with
sagebrush and grass and would provide much-needed forage for our stock.
It is easily traversed by wagons."

He went to say more, then changed his mind. There was no sound in
the tent now. The earlier rain had become a light drizzle that was barely a
whisper on the canvas. As Collett moved back, Bishop Schow stood.

"I shall say just dis much. Vee—Brodder Collett an' me—vill not be
goink wit you. So vee cannot be da vuns to say vaht you do. Dat be up to
da presidency. But I say, as does Brodder Collett, vee strongly belief it is

possible to go troo. Vee strongly believe it be the only goot option you haf. But vee vill soostain vahtever President Smit decide to do."

Silas Smith sat there for a moment, deep in thought. Then he looked up. "Brother Lyman tells me that Brother George Hobbs is another who has feelings contrary to the majority. George, we should like to hear from you. After that, I would invite Brother David Draper to speak as well."

David's head jerked up, and he stared at Silas.

Silas smiled. "Brother Lyman tells me that you and he had several long discussions on the way home. So we wish to hear your feelings."

George Hobbs and David had now shared three separate exploring/scouting experiences together—the six-month Arizona expedition, the ten-day trip across the river a couple of weeks previous, and now this experience with Platte Lyman. David liked George. They were about the same age, and both were single. George was sometimes a little more brash than David would have liked, and he sometimes was influenced by the opinions of others, especially others whom he respected, but he was solid in his judgment, quick to throw his full weight into whatever needed doing, and a good man to have along on any expedition.

George stood and went to the front and, like Collett, started without preamble. "Brethren, I too am very reluctant to place myself in arbitrary opposition to my brethren, especially to our leaders, but since I have been invited to do so, I feel obligated to be honest. I must admit that at first, I was of the same opinion as my fellow scouts. I saw no way that we could go through. But as I listened to Brother Collett and Bishop Schow, both on the trip and here again tonight, I became persuaded to take an opposite position. I have seen the country for myself. It is no more difficult than some of the stretches we crossed this summer. Therefore, I firmly believe that under the conditions we now face, our company should endeavor to make a way through to Montezuma Creek on to the San Juan."

Suddenly his voice trembled with emotion. "We must not forget that we have people over there who are anxiously awaiting our arrival. One of them is my sister, Elizabeth Harriman. They have four young children with them. Jim Davis and his wife have five, including a new baby. What happens to them if we do not go through? What shall they do if we turn back now and do not start again until spring?" He searched their faces. "As we decide what we should do now, let us not forget them. Please!"

As he returned to his seat, Bishop Schow stood and put an arm around his shoulder. "Brodders," he said softly, "I fully endorse vaht Brodder Hobbs just say. If your company haf de same backbone as George Hobbs, vee belief dat you vill get troo dis safely."

"Thank you, Bishop," Silas said. "And thank you for your candor, Brother Hobbs." Then he looked at David and motioned him forward.

David's mind had been racing from the moment he had been startled out of his own thoughts by Silas's invitation. He stood and moved forth slowly. As he stopped and looked around at the faces, a rush of great admiration and respect washed over him. There was deep disagreement here, but no animosity. As near as he could tell, there was no selfish purpose being put forward. There were over two hundred men, women, and children waiting outside right now, anxious to find out what they were to do, and these brethren had only one concern, and that was to do what was right for them. That gave him the courage to speak his heart.

"My brethren and friends," he began. "Like George, I too am reluctant to put myself forward, pitting my opinions and judgment against the men I so admire. But as I have been invited by them to do so, I shall." He drew in a deep breath, let it out slowly, and launched in. "I don't know what we should do. I am deeply torn within myself. After seeing that country across the river twice now, I get a sick feeling in my stomach. Will we go on only to reach a point, in another month or two, when we truly can go no farther? How then shall we answer the pain in the eyes of our wives and children? How then shall we fill their bellies when there is no more food and we are even farther from help than we are now?"

Another breath. Another sigh. "The consequences of us turning around are of equal gravity. We may return to Escalante, but we will go no farther. The snows lie deep on Escalante Mountain. And what shall Escalante do with us? Shall we look to them for our salvation and only end up putting them in jeopardy as well? I wish I knew. Oh, how I wish that I had answers." He glanced back at the presidency. "I know our leaders feel that burden even more heavily than we do."

He paused, trying to decide how to express what he was feeling. "Though I am not sure what to do, I have come to two conclusions. First, I think we must decide what to do based on what is right, not what is easy or safe. Second, I am glad that those who will make this decision for us are men like Bishop Jens Nielson, Brother Platte Lyman, and Brother Silas Smith. I have come to know these men under the most challenging and trying of conditions, and I stand ready to accept whatever they decide is the right thing to do."

"Hear, hear," someone murmured. "Amen," a couple of other voices said.

He turned to Silas, nodded briefly, and started back to his seat. Then he stopped. "If I may, I should like to say one other thing."

"Of course," Silas said.

"As some of you know, I have not been what you would call a strong Latter-day Saint. I've been in the Church for some years, but it has been kind of an uneasy partnership between me and the kingdom, between me and the Lord." He glanced at Bishop Nielson, then away quickly. "When I learned that Bishop Nielson had been called to go with us on this mission, and especially that he was to be one of our leaders—" He turned and looked at the old Dane squarely. "I am ashamed to say that I vigorously questioned the wisdom of that decision. 'He is too old,' I said. 'He has a handicap,' I cried." He shook his head. "Now, here we are, two months later, and I have come to know something else of this man. He is large in stature, large in personality, large in enthusiasm, and enormous in his faith. One of his close friends calls him the 'old comic boy'[2] because of his delightful and wry sense of humor. He has also been called a man of indomitable courage and as stubborn as an oak stump."

"Dat vas probably said by my Elsie," Jens called out. "Or perhaps by my boys."

David laughed, as did everyone else, then quickly sobered again. "Since leaving Cedar City, I have come to know that Jens Nielson was exactly what this company needed. How foolish I was to think only of his age or of his crippled feet." He turned and looked directly at the bishop. "I was a fool, Bishop, and I publicly apologize to you now."

"Vee all be fools at sum time or another," came the quiet reply.

"Last December," David went on, his voice soft now, "Elder Snow issued a call to us. At that time he used three words or phrases to describe
what was needed in San Juan. He said this new settlement would be a
buffer between good and evil. He said it would be like the shock absorbers
on a wagon, cushioning the jolts so that others may have a smooth ride.
He said that it would be like a lightning rod to draw down the shafts upon
ourselves. Well, brethren, not one of those phrases describes a people who
simply cave in just because the way ahead is difficult."

To his surprise, he had to stop because his throat had suddenly constricted. He cleared it, then finished with soft conviction. "And not one of
those phrases describes the people in this company that I have come to
know. Brethren, if we turn back now, who will step up to take our place?
Where will the Church find others so eminently qualified for the task that
has been placed upon our shoulders? Let us think of that as we decide."

He dropped his head and returned to sit down between Joe Nielson
and Kumen Jones. To his utter astonishment, Joe's eyes were glistening.
"Thank you, David," he said. "Thank you for coming to know my father."

Silas Smith got slowly to his feet. "Brethren," he said, "I think a recess
would be in order. Rather than have you inundated with questions, I would
recommend you stay here, and my counselors and I shall slip out and find
a quiet place to confer." He looked around at the nodding heads. "Let us
reconvene in half an hour."

⁂

The rain had completely stopped, and there were a few patches of
clear sky and stars as the three leaders filed back into the tent half an hour
later. Immediately the others took their seats.

"Brethren," Silas began, "I wish I could tell you that we have arrived at
a decision, but we have not. I personally am still much perplexed. I have
asked my two counselors to express their feelings as a beginning to this
meeting, Brother Lyman first, and Brother Nielson second."

Platte Lyman stepped forward. He looked even more tired than he had
in the first meeting. His voice was low, and David had to lean forward a little
to hear better. "My dear brethren," he said, "you have heard my concerns

and my feelings about going forward. I do not feel to reiterate them further. I would like to say two things, however. First, I am keenly aware of the challenges that face us if we determine to turn back. I did not address those earlier because I was asked to speak to the question of whether taking a road across the Colorado to San Juan was feasible. Those concerns, so eloquently expressed by both Brother Hobbs and Brother Draper, weigh heavily on my mind too, and must, of necessity, weigh heavily in our deliberations.

"Second, I have full confidence in our president. He has been called by our Church leaders and set apart under the hands of the priesthood. Whatever he determines to be our best course will have my full, unreserved, and indeed enthusiastic support. Thank you."

He stepped back. After a moment, Bishop Nielson stood and came forward. "My goot brodders, it is wit a troubled heart I stand before you. Vee have not come to a decision, even though our president has asked for one. Vee are, like it says in de scriptures about de children of Israel, like a bird hoppink back and forth betveen two branches on a tree. Vee do so because, as our good Brother Draper has pointed out so vell, da choice vee must make has da most grave consequences eeder vay vee go."

He reached up and scratched at his beard, a habit exhibited, David had learned, when he was deep in thought. "But I vud say dis. Vee *must* go troo, even if vee cannot."

The startling contradiction of that sentence brought a few smiles, but David sensed it had not been a slip of the tongue. Bishop Nielson had meant it exactly as he had stated it.

He confirmed that when he smiled. "Vaht vee need now is vaht I call stickity tootie."

David heard Joe Nielson, who was right beside him, chuckle. "Dad," he called, "it's called stick-to-a-tive-ness." He pronounced each syllable clearly and distinctively.

"Yah," came the reply. There was a twinkle in the old man's eyes. "Is not dat vaht I say? Stickity tootie?"

Joe just shook his head as the men chuckled. This was Bishop Nielson all the way. His melodious accent was delightful, and sometimes David suspected he used it to his full advantage.

Bishop Nielson paused, and his eyes grew thoughtful. "I also feel to say, that I do belief dat if vee decide to move forvard across de river, we shall be able to succeed in makink road dere. I say dat again. If vee decide to go forward, vee shall succeed. Brodder Draper said I be stubborn like old mule. And he be right. But I tink dat be exactly vaht the Lord vants right now. I tink vee must go troo vether vee can or not."

Now he turned and looked at Silas Smith. "I vood derefore make a proposink. I proposink that vee all agree to give our full support to President Smit in vahtever he decides vee shud do. As Brodder Lyman has said so vell, he is our called and appointed leader, and he is entitled to revelation on dis qvestion. And dat be all I haf to say on dis matter."

And with that, he was done. He stepped back beside the other two.

Silas Smith stood there for a moment, deep in thought. Finally, his head lifted. "Brethren, I find myself leaning more and more toward a decision to move forward. As you know, when we returned from our exploration through northern Arizona, I had strong feelings that we should seek a central route that passed through Escalante. I was the one who asked two old and trusted friends to do some exploring to see if such a route was possible." He looked to Schow and Collett. "And I do most profoundly thank them for their diligent efforts to do so.

"In addition, since I consider it all but impossible to withdraw through the heavy snows that now lie behind us, I am inclined to declare that we move forward, even if it takes us another three months to build a road through."

That started a low buzz, and he quickly held up his hand for silence. "However, I am not completely settled in that. I deeply appreciate the sustaining voice of my counselors and the expressions of support you have made. So I would like to ask that we retire to our tents now. I have fasted all this day and spent much time on my knees seeking the Lord's will in the matter. I should now like to put our recommendation to Him to see if it is acceptable. I would appreciate your united prayers in my behalf, and I would encourage you to ask your families and all of the company to join us so that I may clearly come to see the Lord's will. We shall then call the company together first thing in the morning and give them our decision."

David was surprised to find himself nodding along with all the others—surprised, not just because he completely agreed with the request, but surprised to find himself planning to fully comply with it. This night, he too would ask the Lord to bless Silas Smith.

Thursday, December 4, 1879

To no one's surprise, the camp was up early. The day was dawning bright and clear, though the temperature was still barely forty degrees. Breakfast was kept simple and quickly put away. Children were not sent out for their usual chores but kept close by their parents. Families congregated together rather than in larger groups and spoke quietly. There was an air of subdued but hopeful expectation.

When David went down to the creek for water, he saw Bishop Nielson and Platte Lyman slip into the tent of Silas Smith. By the time he came back, the word was already passing from mouth to mouth. The meeting would be at eight o'clock.

Half an hour later, they began to gather near the spring itself. To allow easier access to the water, none of the wagons were parked right in its vicinity, so it provided a natural assembly area. Next to the spring, two large boxes had been stacked one on the other. Silas was standing on them, waiting for his congregation to assemble.

David had deliberately not come with the family, but with his father. As they watched for the McKennas, David was surprised to see Bishop Nielson about fifty feet away. He had pulled Abby aside and was talking to her earnestly.

A moment later, the rest of the McKennas showed up and came over to join them. When Abby finally joined them, Molly gave her a strange look. "What was that all about?"

Abby shrugged. "Bishop Nielson just had something he wanted to share with me."

"Oh?" Sarah said.

Abby glanced quickly at David, then away. "It was something he thought I should know."

"But not us?" Molly persisted, a little petulant at the perceived slight.

She smiled sweetly. "No. You know Bishop Nielson. He has his own mind sometimes." And then she turned away to forestall further questions.

A moment later the Perkins family joined them and Abby's strange conversation was forgotten. As more and more of the company arrived, the McKennas and their little group moved off to one side, but still near the front, where they could hear clearly. As they did so, David hung back a little so the McKennas would be in front. To his surprise, so did Abby. She stayed beside him, not looking up at him.

In a moment, when the family began talking quietly with those around them, Abby stepped closer. "It was about you," she said in a low voice.

He looked at her more closely. "What was about me?"

"My little talk with Bishop Nielson."

That totally took him aback.

She glanced forward to make sure they weren't being watched, then lowered her voice even more. "It was the strangest thing. He came over and motioned for me to follow him. And then he told me, in some detail, about the meeting last night. Especially about what you said."

He just stared at her.

Her eyes were suddenly soft and filled with emotion. "He actually began to cry when he told me what you said about him."

"I . . ."

"He also said that you had a profound impact on the group."

"Why? Why would he call you over and tell you that?"

She shook her head. "I don't know. It was so strange."

"Did he ask you not to share it with others?"

"Not exactly, but I . . . I just would rather not. Others will probably be talking about it too, but unless you want me to, I won't say anything."

"I don't. It was just one of those things when . . ." He shrugged.

"I know. I'm glad he told me." She started to say something else, but just then, Molly came back to join them.

"David?"

"Yes, Molly?"

"Do you think we're going to go back to Escalante?"

That startled him. It was said with such wistful hope and longing that he was touched. But he finally shook his head. "I don't think so, Molly. In a way it would be so much easier, but if we do, it creates a whole new set of problems."

"I know," she said, her countenance falling. Then she forced a wan smile. "Whoever thought I would long for a place like Escalante?"

Just then Silas Smith raised his hands and called the group to order. Instantly the crowd went quiet. "Thank you for coming together this morning." His voice caught momentarily, and then he smiled out on them with great love. "Thank you for your faith and your prayers in our behalf. We, the presidency, have been greatly comforted knowing that you fully put your trust in us."

He paused for a moment, his face deep in reflection. "You know the issue before us. You know that we discussed it at some length last evening. I have spent most of the night on my knees, asking the Lord for wisdom and confirmation. And this morning I am at peace. I have made a proposal to my counselors, and they fully sustain it. We now present it to you for your consideration and sustaining vote."

The quiet deepened into a total hush. Every head was turned in his direction, every eye fixed on him. And, as David looked at him, in that instant he knew that the company would be at peace with whatever was about to be said.

Silas took a deep breath and looked down at his two counselors, who smiled and nodded for him to proceed. "After the most careful—and prayerful—consideration of all the issues, it is our decision to press forward across the Colorado River and on to the San Juan."

A collective "ah" exploded from the group, and instantly the air was filled with a babble of noise. Silas stood there, smiling to himself, waiting for it to die away. When it finally did, he continued. "Even if it takes us two or three months to build a road through, we consider this the best option. With the help of the Lord, we also feel that in this way we can fulfill the call we have been given."

He quickly held up his hands as the sound began to rise again. "Bishop Schow and Brother Collett, our two faithful brothers from Escalante who have done us such great service, will leave this morning. They will let all of those who are camped behind us, or who are still coming forward, know of our decision, and urge them to come on with all haste. They have also graciously offered to encourage their fellow Saints in Escalante to send us additional wagonloads of potatoes, pork, sorghum, or whatever else those good people can spare."

Someone cheered and a smattering of applause was heard. Collett and Schow raised their arms and waved back.

"We should like all captains of tens to stay for a meeting when I am finished. There is much we now need to do to move forward, and we need to do it immediately. Our first and most important task will be to push the road forward to the river. We shall move some of the company forward to Fifty Mile Spring, particularly those assigned on the road-building crews. There, we shall be able to better assess the task before us.

"What we ask of you, and of ourselves, is not easy. We know it will require great sacrifice and much hardship. But we have great confidence in you and in your stickity tootie, as Bishop Nielson likes to say."

That brought some laughter and a considerable number of strange looks.

"My brothers and sisters. I am deeply humbled and honored to be at your head. The implications of this decision weigh heavily upon me, but I am at peace. I feel very strongly this is the course the Lord wishes us to pursue. Therefore, I should like to call for a sustaining vote. All of you who feel to sustain the proposal your presidency now puts before you, please show it by raising your hand."

David felt a sudden lump in his throat as he put up his hand and looked around at the group. A sea of hands were up, and each of them was held high. As he turned back, he saw that Molly's was raised as high as anyone's. She turned, as if to make sure he saw her, then she gave him a radiant smile.

"If there are those who feel otherwise," Silas Smith was saying, "please indicate that, too."

The group was large and David couldn't see them all, but from where he was, not a single hand came up.

"Then it is unanimous. We have our decision, my good brothers and sisters. Thank you."

As he jumped down from his "pulpit," suddenly a booming male voice rang out from somewhere behind David. "Ho! Ho to the San Juan!"

A little chill shot up David's back. He turned to see who it was, but there was no way to determine it, for instantly, shouts rang out from every side. "Ho to the San Juan! Ho to the San Juan!"

David raised his own hand, tipped his head back, and shouted it out joyfully. "Ho to the San Juan!"[3]

Notes

1. Platte D. Lyman kept a detailed and almost daily journal of his experience on the Hole in the Rock expedition. It is, without question, the single most valuable and trustworthy source for what happened. Most other accounts were given much later in family histories or oral interviews. While a few things have been brought in from other sources to give a fuller picture of the issues, most of what Platte says in this chapter comes directly from his journal entries (as cited in Miller, Hole, 162–63).

2. The description of Jens Nielson's character and personality come from his biography (see Carpenter, Jens Nielson, 9).

3. The meeting with the thirteen returned explorers and others was held the evening after their return. Those present gave their full support to Silas Smith and left the decision in his hands. The following morning the full company gathered together and were officially told of the decision to go forward, though it was probably pretty well known to all by then (see Miller, Hole, 62–67, 162–63, 181–82; Redd, "Short Cut," 9–10; Reay, Incredible Passage, 33–35; Carpenter, Jens Nielson, 45). That meeting was then turned into a testimony meeting where members could express their feelings, which I chose not to depict here.

Miller says of the effects of that decision: "Gloom and despondency, which had pervaded the camp, were now replaced with optimism and good will. Road work that had come to a standstill with the return of the scouts was recommenced. The company pitched in with a united will and for the first time began to feel and realize the full power it possessed. There would be no more talk of turning back; nothing could stop the expedition now!" (Miller, Hole, 70).

Redd describes it this way: "It may seem strange [after all the unrest and discouragement in the camp] but the decision seemed to be welcomed by all. Immediately someone shouted, 'Ho! for the San Juan,' a cry that re-echoed throughout the camp. At last inertia had come to an end; at last, after weeks of tension and waiting, they were to be on the move" (Redd, "Short Cut," 9–10).

BOOK VII

FULFILLMENT

1879–1880

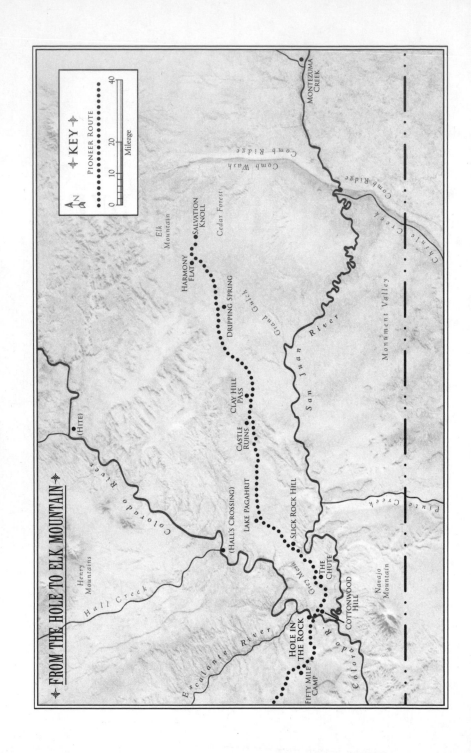

CHAPTER 54

Friday, December 5, 1879

Energized by the decision to move forward, Silas gave the camp an hour or two to celebrate while he and his counselors put their heads together and decided what the decision now meant in terms of practical assignments. When they called the adults back together after the midday meal, they made several announcements:

Forty Mile Camp was basically going to be abandoned. All present there now were to move south and form two new camps. The larger one, made up mostly of the Parowan and Paragonah groups, would be set up at Fifty Mile Spring. Here there was more water and some grass for the stock. The Cedar City group, led by Bishop Nielson, would continue on and set up another camp near to the Hole in the Rock. Since there were no springs there, they would be dependent on winter rain, snowmelt, and water carried in from Fifty Mile Spring. This group was assigned the southernmost location primarily because the Perkins brothers and John Draper, the only experienced blasters in the company, were in it. Other smaller family and community groups were assigned to one of these two camps depending on their work assignments.

The road crews were to return immediately to work, with four primary divisions of labor. First priority was to finish the road to Fifty Mile Spring in the next day or two. A second group was to go straight to Fifty Mile Spring and begin the more challenging task of building a passable wagon road between Fifty Mile Spring and the Hole in the Rock. This last six-mile stretch of trail would be the most difficult they had yet built. Here the flatter desert country gave way to large areas of hard rock pans. The rain and wind had left these rough enough to break a wagon wheel and pockmarked with holes deep enough to break a horse's leg. In other places, low, undulating sandstone ridges, some a hundred feet or more in height, blocked the route. Some had pitches steep enough to require double-teaming the wagons. A third crew would camp at Fifty Mile Spring but leave each Monday morning, walk the seven miles to Jackass Flat, and make their way down to the river. There they would ferry across in the small, flat-bottomed boat owned by Schow and Collett and begin work on a road up out of the gorge to the eastern mesa, returning to camp on Saturday night. Finally, a group led by the three coal miners would tackle the greatest challenge of all—blasting a road down through a cleft in the cliff face that was almost twice as steep as the roof of a two-story barn.

These crews all left for their various sites first thing the next morning. Those men not assigned to the road crews, along with all the families, would round up their stock, pack up their wagons, and follow them as soon as feasible. Hopefully, within two or three days, Forty Mile Spring and Dance Hall Rock would be left behind for the desert to reclaim once again.

Just as the first rays of dawn were starting to lighten the eastern sky, Sarah McKenna approached the front of the wagon. She handed a small flour sack filled with bread and what was left of their brick of cheese to John Draper. "Here's a little something for the road so you don't have to keep digging into the wagon for food."

"Tank ya, luv," John said.

As he took it, she went up on her toes and kissed him on the cheek. "Take care," she said.

Molly came up and also gave him a peck. "Oh, John, now who's going to make me laugh?"

"Ya naw be needin' me, lass," he said with a crooked grin. "Ya 'ave so mooch natural cheer inside ya, girl, that Ah naw be worryin' aboot ya."

David finished tying Tillie to the back of the wagon, then came around to join the others. Patrick stepped forward and gripped his hand. "After all the talk about how rough the road is beyond Fifty Mile Camp, do you really think Carl, Abby, and I can drive the wagons through?"

"I do," David said firmly. "It's very rough, and you'll have to go slow, but it's not that challenging for the teams. There are one or two places where the grade is real bad, but they're not dangerous. You'll be fine."

"Even Abby?" Abby asked.

He smiled. "Especially Abby," he said. "There's something about the softness of your voice that the mules really like. You'll just charm them up and over those rough spots."

She turned and looked at Molly. "I think David's been kissing the Blarney stone again."

Molly hooted softly. "Kissing it? He uses it for a pillow."

Looking wounded, David turned back to Patrick. "If there's any place that especially worries you, or if it gets really muddy, ask Kumen or Joe to help you. They're as good as they get."

He turned. "Well, it looks like Ben and Hy are ready to go. We'll see you in a few days."

Thursday, December 11, 1879

David strode easily up the white sandstone ridge that led to the mouth of the Hole in the Rock. He slowed his step as he moved to its edge. It was like a great block plugging the Hole, and near where David now stood, it sheered off and dropped straight down for fifty or sixty feet. David edged closer to the cliff, then peered down into the notch below it. He immediately saw three figures farther down the notch, totally dwarfed by the immensity of the dark red cliffs on either side. Where they were standing, the cleft in the rock was so narrow that a large man couldn't have slipped through it. He cupped his hands. "Hey! We've got company."

His father, Ben, and Hyrum turned as one and looked up. "Who is it?"

"Silas and Platte. You're gonna want to be here to meet them." He moved back, making sure the rope they used to ascend back to the top was firmly secured to a large boulder behind him.

The four of them had pushed hard that first day and made it past Fifty Mile Spring. But the next day, the road became so rough and slow that it took them until midafternoon to reach the lip of the Colorado River gorge. There the miners got their first look at the Hole in the Rock. They had made camp, seen to the stock, then spent the rest of Saturday and some of Sunday afternoon exploring the notch and assessing the task that lay before them.

The first of their Cedar City group began arriving on Tuesday. Since then, about half the wagons had come in. However, there was no sign of the McKennas as of yet.

David heard a noise and turned to see Hy Perkins pull himself up and onto the top of the sandstone block. A moment later, Ben followed, and David's father a minute after that. The three squinted to the northwest at two riders coming toward them. David handed his father the field glasses. He put them to his eyes, then grunted. "Sure 'nuff. It be Brother Silas and Brother Platte. Gud. It's time they saw this fur themselves."

✳

"So this is the famous Hole in the Rock we've heard so much about," Silas said. His eyes lifted and he looked at the two massive walls of rock that formed the "gateway" to the Hole. The six of them were standing on the lip of the cliff, looking almost straight down for half a mile to the tiny brown line that marked the Colorado River far below.

"This is it," Ben said. He pointed to the rope. "Want to see it for yourselves?"

After an hour of working their way up and down the slot, they returned to the base of the great sandstone plug at the top of the hole. Platte tipped his head back and looked up the face of the cliff. "And you really plan to blast this out?" he said to his three guides.

"Naw the 'ole thing," David's father said. "Joost e'nuff ta mek a road doon ta this point. We'll start back near whare we left yur horses, cut it back until a wagon can mek it doon."

"Gud thing is," Hy came in, "we can use what we blast oot as fill doon below, cover up sum of those pits and holes ya saw."

Ben spoke up. "We be reet short on powder, Cap'n. An' we naw be mekin' a road through 'ere with joost picks and shovels. We be goin' ta need a lot more black powder."

Silas was nodding. "We've been talking about that, and we think we may have a solution." He turned once more and looked at the cliff face above them. "How steep a pitch do you think a wagon can handle once you blast this out?"

Platte Lyman had been thinking the same thing. He closed one eye. "About eight feet per rod* is the maximum, I think."

"Whoo-ee," David said. "I choose not to be the first one to take a wagon down that."

Ben laughed. "It be gittin' yur blood pumpin' a little, that be fur sure."

Silas turned and looked back up at the sheer wall blocking the top of the crevasse. "So just how much more powder are you going to need?" he asked Ben.

The Welshman closed one eye, then grinned wickedly. "We can make do with one trainload. Two would be better."

The two leaders laughed aloud. "I'm glad you dream big, Ben," Platte said. "Let's go back up on top and have some lunch while we talk about what needs to happen next."

"Here's the plan as we see it," Silas began after taking a swig from his canteen to wash down the last of his bread and cheese. "Platte and I will ride on back to Fifty Mile today. Both of our outfits are making their way forward now, but we need to get them settled. I want the Lymans to come up here to the Hole as soon as possible so Platte can take charge. My family will camp back at Fifty Mile for now."

"Your family?" David said. "What about you?"

In answer, he turned to Ben. "Once they're settled, I'll come back up here for one last look. Ben, if you and Hy and John could give me your best estimate of how much powder it's going to take, then—"

Ben looked wounded. "Ya mean yur naw gonna git us a trainload?"

---

* A rod was a measurement used in surveying and was 16½ feet. Thus eight feet per rod would make just under a 50 percent grade. Modern truckers are warned to use low gear on grades of 6 or 7 percent.

"I'll be delighted with a *wagon* full. Once I get your estimate, I am going to return to Parowan and begin—"

"Parowan!" David exclaimed. "How are you going to get over Escalante Mountain? There must be four or five feet of snow up top by now."

"I'm taking my boys with me. We'll go on horseback. We're going to have to beat down a path up over the pass."

When the others just nodded, sobered by exactly what that would mean, he went on. "I'm going to seek contributions from the settlements. After all, they're going to benefit greatly from our mission. But I'm guessing that won't be nearly enough, so I'm also going to ask for an appropriation from the Legislature."

"Gud on ya, mate," Hyrum said.

John spoke up now. "We also be needin' more tools—drills, hammers, bits, chisels."

"And that's all going to take money." Silas gave them a sly grin. "So I am also going to write President Taylor and see if the Church might not contribute some funds as well." Then, sobering, he got to his feet. "We'll be back in a few days, brethren. Get me a list of what you need, and I'll see what I can do."

"One other thing," David said. "As you can see, there is hardly any feed for the teams up here. But we need to keep them fairly close in case we need to move the wagons. There is a place called Jackass Flat. Platte knows it well because we went down that way when we crossed over to explore the east side. We think we can take a bunch of stock down there if we can take a few men off the road project for a couple of days and fix the path somewhat."

Ben nodded. "And we be needin' a path frum the Flat doon ta the river as well. We found a place we can make work, but it be going ta take some fixin' too. We can't be lowerin' and raisin' those boys working on the east side road by ropes every time they come and go."

Silas was nodding. "Take what manpower you need. That's pretty critical too."

"Anything else?" Platte asked.

When they shook their heads, Silas nodded and said, "Then we'd better be getting back."

They shook hands and started for their horses. As they did so, other members of the camp, who had been politely hanging back while their leaders conversed, moved in to shake their hands and ask for news from the camp behind them. At that, Silas suddenly snapped his fingers. "Oh, David, by the way." He fished in his jacket pocket and took out an envelope. "The McKennas and the Nielsons reached Fifty Mile Camp day before yesterday. They had a wheel problem that needed fixing. They'll come on as soon as it's done."

"Are they doing okay?"

"Good, near as we could tell," Platte answered, as Silas nodded. "The Nielsons will wait for them before coming on."

"That be good," David's father said.

"Anyway," Silas said, handing him the envelope. "Sister Molly asked me to give you this."

As Silas and Platte rode off, David eagerly tore into the letter and began reading.

> *My Dearest David,*
>
> *We arrived in camp last night. This morning we learned Brother Smith and Brother Lyman are riding to your camp today. Brother Smith agreed to take this note to you.*
>
> *If all goes well, our family and Bishop Nielson's family should be to you by tomorrow night. We are all anxious to see you and John again, and hope that this letter finds you both well.*
>
> *We did well coming from Forty Mile to Fifty Mile camp, though it took longer than we expected. Going through one of the many washes, a mule pulling Carl's wagon shied at something (perhaps a rattlesnake— shudder!). That jerked the wagon to one side, and the back wheel hit a large rock. This cracked the tire. (Isn't that what they call the iron band around the outside of the wheel?) We were able to limp into camp, but have had to wait for Wilson Daily, our resident blacksmith, to get it*

fixed again. The extra rest has been good for us, and especially for the teams.

By the way, you were right about Abby, Father, and Carl. They have become competent and confident teamsters. I am learning how to drive too (don't look so surprised!) but so far just when the road is level and smooth. Daddy also lets Billy Joe drive from time to time.

Even with an occasional wagon coming down from Escalante with supplies, our food is becoming much more limited in variety. Much of the flour and molasses is gone and we eat mostly ground wheat and corn. The only way to grind the grain is in a coffee mill someone in the company brought with them. This is not only tedious, but very tiring. Though this limited diet is quite boring, it seems to keep us healthy. As George Hobbs observed the other day, "Chopped wheat would shame a dose of Epsom salts in terms of its purging propensities."[1] Modesty forbids me to comment on that further. (I blush even as I write it.)

Well, I must close. The brethren are preparing to leave. You and your father are always in our prayers. We rejoice knowing that we shall soon be reunited.

> *All my love,*
> *Molly*

As David finished and folded the letter, he saw that his father was watching him. "'Ow be things wit the fam'ly?"

"Good," David said, holding out the letter to him. "Here."

He put up his hands. "Ah was naw askin' ta read it. Ah was joost wond'rin'."

"No reason you can't read it," he said, thrusting it at him. His father took it, opened it, and read it slowly. He chuckled once, then laughed aloud. David assumed that was in response to George Hobbs's comment. Finally, smiling, he folded it up again. "She be a gud girl, David."

"I know." He reached for the letter, but his father was looking away now and didn't see his hand. After a moment, David looked at him more closely. "What are you thinking, Dad?"

He turned slowly. "Ah be thinkin' it be a gud thing what ya did back in Cedar City."

One eyebrow raised. "How's that?"

He gave him a long look. "If'n this dunna work oot, it'll be a lot easier naw ta 'ave too much commitment b'tween ya."

David was taken aback. Where had that come from? And then he remembered Mary Davis's final words. *Don't be bringing her back with a ring, David. Not even the promise of a ring.* "Whatever in the world prompted that comment, Dad?"

His father quoted softly. "'My *dearest* David.' An' '*Awl* my love.'"

"Aw," David said, blushing slightly, "that's just Molly."

"Ah know that, which only makes me point."

"Which is?"

He shook his head and started to turn away.

"Come on, Dad," David said, half teasing, half peeved. "You've got something on your mind. Just say it."

He shook his head. "Ah joost be glad yur bein' wise in this."

"Why?" he persisted.

"It dunna matter. Naw question but what Molly be a real charmer. And she be a gud girl. But oot here, things be diff'rent, Son. Maybe doon the road ya be seein' things a little diff'rently." Before an astonished David could say anything more, John stood up and turned his back. "That be awl Ah be 'avin' ta say on the matter."

Note

1. The comment about cracked wheat being a purgative is an actual quote of George Hobbs (see Carpenter, *Jens Nielson*, 46).

CHAPTER 55

Sunday, December 14, 1879

Three days later, both Silas Smith and Platte Lyman returned to the camp at the Hole in the Rock. Platte Lyman had his extended family with him; Silas Smith was alone. By that time, Ben Perkins's construction team had made a trail down to Jackass Flat, though they were still working on the lower trail, and Platte and his sons drove numerous horses down to the bench and turned them loose to graze.[1]

When Platte returned that afternoon, Silas called a meeting and organized the Hole in the Rock camp. He would remain as captain of the entire company, even though he would be gone for a time. Platte Lyman, as assistant captain, would take charge, with Jens Nielson serving with him. Generally, they kept the same captains of tens as before, but added three more—Bishop George Sevy, of Escalante, who had just arrived with several wagons from that settlement, and Henry Holyoak and Samuel Bryson, two more recent arrivals. Ben Perkins was also made foreman for the construction of a road down through the Hole. Some of the Lyman boys were put in charge of the stock, and most of the other men were assigned to road construction.

After the meeting, Silas and Platte sequestered themselves with the Perkins brothers and John Draper and received a list of tools and equipment they would need. First on the list was the request for at least one ton of blasting powder. Promising to do what he could—though not bursting with optimism—Silas Smith shook hands all around and bid them farewell. His plan was to return to Fifty Mile Camp that night, then leave with some of his sons the following morning. With luck, they would be able to cross

Escalante Mountain and return to Parowan, where he would begin his efforts to raise money and purchase equipment.

As he climbed into the saddle, he looked down at Platte Lyman and gave him a somber look. "May the Lord be with you, my friend," he said somberly. "There is much to do, and all rests on your success. I shall try to be back here in about three weeks."[2]

"And the Lord be with you," Platte answered with equal solemnity.

Tuesday, December 16, 1879

Billy Joe McKenna, while playing with some other boys at Fifty Mile Springs, got caught out in a wet, cold sleet storm, and had come down with a bad fever. So the McKennas decided to stay at Fifty Mile Camp, even though Jens Nielson and his family came on. It was Tuesday before the McKennas finally arrived at the Hole. Though David had planned to help his father with their continuing survey of the Hole, he stayed in camp to help the McKennas get settled instead. All expectations now were that they would be here at least a month while road construction on the Hole and on the east side continued.

Platte Lyman spent most of that day climbing up and down the great gash in the cliff face of the Colorado River Gorge with Ben and Hyrum Perkins and John Draper. After numerous calculations and much discussion—often stopping to do additional measurements—they returned to camp and called for a meeting of the camp leaders.

As David and Patrick McKenna left for the meeting, David couldn't help but notice Molly's face. Her eyes were averted, but her hand was resting on Abby's arm, and as he passed, David saw that her fingers were digging into the flesh. And he was pretty sure he knew why. Their "short" separation had turned into twelve days, and once again circumstances conspired to keep them apart. Now, there was a rumor going around the camp that yet another scouting party would be sent out. Unlike other rumors, David fully expected this one was true.

As he passed her, she looked up and gave him a warm smile, though it was somewhat forced. "Don't be late for supper," she murmured. "We're having filet of cracked wheat."

Chuckling, David said, "In the mother tongue, we don't say 'fil-AY,' we say 'FILL-it.' Wouldn't miss it."

There were about ten men in Platte Lyman's tent when they arrived. Platte and Bishop Nielson were talking with David's father as they entered. The two leaders greeted them, then David's father joined David and Patrick and they found a place to sit. The mood inside the tent was somber, but more from curiosity than discouragement. Something was up.

When the Perkins brothers slipped in a minute or so later, Platte immediately stepped forward, signaling for silence. "Brethren, thank you for coming. We shall take only a few minutes of your time, but what we have to discuss is of great importance."

He fell silent, his chin dropping a little. Finally, he gave a quick shake of his head, as if he were tired of searching for the right thing to say. "As you all know so well, we have now been on the road for over two months. That is two weeks longer than we expected to spend on the entire trip and we are still not to our final destination."

There was a deep, weary sigh. "Our hope was to arrive in San Juan early enough to plant crops before the summer heat sets in. And that we must do." He looked from face to face. "If we do not, we shall not survive as a colony."

"An' if vee stay here too lonk," Bishop Nielson broke in quietly, "vee shall haf eaten all our seed corn and veet and vee shall have none to plant."

"Yes," Platte said gravely, "that is part of our reality too. We have known for some time that this obstacle we call the Hole in the Rock would be a great challenge, but not until today, when we have spent hours climbing up and down it, have I finally come to appreciate the magnitude of our task. These brethren, whose judgment I implicitly trust, say that it is going to take us at least one month to complete a road down to the river."

There wasn't a lot of shock at that. That figure had been tossed around earlier.

"Knowing the harsh realities we are facing, we cannot delay further. I have this day sent word to Fifty Mile Camp and asked them to send us additional workers to work on the Hole, even as they continue construction of a road on the other side. As many of you know, Brother Charles Hall is bringing lumber down for the construction of a ferry. This is good. When the first wagons do finally reach the bottom, they can cross the river without delay."

His dark eyes were piercing in their intensity now. "Which brings me to our purpose today. Once our wagons reach the tops of the bluffs on the east side of the river, we must know where we are going. As you know, we have had two additional groups recently arrive at our camp here. Bishop George Sevy, originally from Panguitch but more recently from Escalante, has brought several wagons from his settlement. And we have the Redd family from New Harmony. Both of these brethren have come to me and asked if they can leave their families here and push forward on horseback to see if they can find a way through to Montezuma Creek. Though they do not know the way, they have agreed that if George Hobbs, who went there with the first exploring party, will lead them, they will undertake the journey.

"Bishop Nielson and I believe that their desire and our need coincide and can work to the advantage of all. Therefore, we are asking Brother Sevy to lead another exploring expedition across the river." He raised his voice to override the noise that now filled the tent. "We are also asking Brothers George Hobbs, Lemuel Redd, Sr., and George Morrell to accompany him." There was a fleeting smile. "If three Georges can't accomplish it, I don't know who can. Sorry, Lemuel, but you'll just have to be the odd man out."

There was a soft chuckle, but that quickly died away as he continued. "Now, I want to make one thing perfectly clear. We are not asking these brethren to help us decide whether to go forward or not. That decision was made back at Forty Mile Camp and we are committed to it. No, brethren, their assignment will be to find the way through to the San Juan. No more, no less. I think you all remember how Bishop Nielson put it in our meeting the other day. How did you say it, Brother Jens?"

"Vee must go troo, even if vee cannot," the bishop said softly.

Platte's voice dropped to almost a hush. "That must be our determination. These four brethren must find a way across the vast wastelands that lie between us and Montezuma Creek. This they must do, not only for our benefit, but for the benefit of those two families who are waiting there, desperately hoping that we have not forgotten them."[3]

George Hobbs leaned forward. "Thank you, Brother Lyman. As you know, brethren, I am most anxious to see if my sister is all right, so I accept this call with full purpose of heart."

"President Platte?"

The leader turned. David had his hand up. "Yes, Brother Draper?"

"I would like to request permission to accompany these brethren. As you know, I too, like George Hobbs, have been to the San Juan country and know that area. And although they are not my family, when I left Jim and Mary Davis and their children, I made a solemn promise that I would return as quickly as possible. I should like to keep that promise."

He considered that for a moment, then turned. "Brother McKenna?"

Patrick's response was immediate. "We'll be fine without him. We're not going anywhere."

He turned to Ben Perkins. "You need every man possible to work on the Hole. What do you say to losing one of them?"

A slow grin stole across the Welshman's face. "Davy boy 'ere, 'e be a cowboy, naw a coal miner," he drawled. "Prob'ly be a blessin' ta git 'im outta the way."

David smiled his thanks as the men around him chuckled.

"Brother Draper?" Platte asked, looking at David's father.

His father looked at David for a moment, then turned to Lyman. "Ah be reet prood if David were allowed ta go. Ah think ya awreddy know, 'e be a gud man fur the job."

There was a curt nod, then a smile. "All right. Five men it is."

The meeting ended a minute later. But as the men started to file out, George Sevy spoke up. "Perhaps we could have a brief meeting with the five of us who are going, before we return to our wagons and start to pack."

"Good idea," Platte said. "Use my tent. We will go out and inform the others."

They gathered in a circle, not bothering to sit. When the last man was out of the tent, Sevy began. Of the five of them, he was the oldest, though he was not yet fifty. Everyone called him Bishop Sevy, David had learned, because he had been the bishop in Panguitch for several years. He was wise and steady, a good choice to lead the group, as far as David could determine.

"Brethren," he said, "Brother Silas has given me a rough map of the area that we have to cross. It's hand drawn, and clearly there isn't a lot of detail on it. Our job will be to fill it in. But in scale I think it's pretty accurate. I calculate Montezuma Creek is about seventy miles in a straight line from where we are. I told Captain Lyman that we should allow about fifteen days for coming and going. If we average twenty miles per day, that would still leave us five or six days with the families at Montezuma Creek. He agrees and says he will post some men on the other side of the river to watch for us, starting twelve days from tomorrow."

"Are you figuring twenty miles a day being on foot or on horseback?" David asked.

"Good question, and one we need to decide," was the reply. "I figure we can travel pretty light. Take our bedrolls, some warm clothes, maybe eight days' worth of food." He looked first at Hobbs, then at David. "I say only eight days because I understand that you two helped those two families put in crops last summer."

"That's right," both David and Hobbs said at the same time.

"That's good. We can replenish our food supply there for the return trip. I'm not sure horses can get through that country. In some places, horses might even slow us down."

George Morrell spoke up for the first time. He was from Junction, a town about fifteen or twenty miles north of Panguitch. He too was older than David or George Hobbs. He had left his family back in Junction until he could return for them. He was a solidly built man, quiet in demeanor, but pleasant and amiable. "I was thinking that maybe we might take one small burro to carry our food and bedrolls."

Sevy nodded. "I think a burro is a good idea."

Lemuel Redd spoke now. "Food for five men for eight days and five bedrolls is a lot for one burro. I've got a small mule that can pretty well get through anywhere a small burro can go."

Lemuel Redd, or Lem, as most called him, was in his mid-forties, the second oldest of the five of them. He was a well-known stockman from New Harmony, which was about halfway between St. George and Cedar City, and he had run both sheep and cattle out in the desert. Jens Nielson knew him well and spoke most highly of him, saying there wasn't a better man to have with them on the trail.[4]

Sevy was nodding. "My horse isn't much bigger than Lem's mule. I'll bring him."

David was smiling. It was suddenly as if there was a contest going on. "Well, I've got about as good a horse as you could ask for, but she's a quarter horse and pretty muscular. I'm not sure that's what we're looking for."

"Same with my horse," Hobbs replied, "but Joe Lilywhite has a horse no bigger than Brother Sevy's. He says I can take that if I'd like."

Sevy was satisfied with that. "Then that's it. We'll take two pack animals and two horses. We can take turns riding, maybe switch off every hour or so."

There were nods all around, and that was settled.

"No sense leaving too early tomorrow," Redd said. "We're not going to want to go down that trail to Jackass Flat in the dark."

"Agreed," Sevy said, "so let's meet here at seven o'clock. The captain can give us any last-minute instructions and then we'll be off."

"And maybe a blessing," Morrell murmured. "Sounds like we're gonna need one."

Wednesday, December 17, 1879

Once David had all of his things packed, he sought Molly out. To no one's surprise, she was not waiting with the rest of the family around the fire, but was in her wagon. David went around to the back of it and tapped softly on the canvas. "Molly? Are you in there?"

He heard the wagon squeak with her movements; then she was at the flap and crawling out. He held out his hand and helped her down.

"Thank you," she murmured.

He peered at her more closely to see if she had been crying, but she quickly averted her head.

"I haven't," she said shortly.

"You haven't what?"

"Been crying."

That flustered him. "Oh, I didn't mean to—"

"Yes you did. That's just like you, David Draper. Thinking a girl's going to be crying over you every time you ride off on your horse again. Which happens to be about every week."

"Well, thank you," he said.

"For what?"

"For not crying."

She slapped him again. "But I was crying."

He shook his head, bewildered as always when he was around her. "I'll see you in a couple of weeks," he said finally.

"Will you be careful?"

"Of course I'll be careful."

"No, David. Don't be flippant. Will you *really* be careful?"

"I will."

She hesitated, then gave him a winsome smile. "If you get in trouble, will you ask God for help?" Her smile broadened. "You don't have to answer that."

"Already plan on it."

Her head had dropped, but it came back up sharply. "Really? You'll really pray for help?"

"Yes."

For a long moment she stared up at him, then finally nodded in wonder and satisfaction. "Then let's go before all of my family are convinced that you're kissing me back here."

He laughed aloud. "Ah, Molly girl, you are a tonic for the soul."

"I know," she said cheerfully, giving him a nudge. "So go."

Notes

1. In Lyman's journal under the date of December 14th, he states that he took some horses "down to a bench next to the river" (cited in Miller, *Hole,* 164). In a history dictated some time later by George Hobbs, mention is also made of this trail to Jackass Flat, but with this rather grim addition: "[The trail] was still so dangerous that nine head of the horses

that were taken down to the bench below slid off to the river bottom, about 1,800 feet, and were killed, where they had fallen. This trail was subsequently useful in getting pack animals of the next expedition down to the river" (*ibid.*, 85). Lyman's journal also notes that Silas Smith came to the Hole in the Rock camp and held a meeting with the members there (*ibid.*, 164).

2. As it turned out, Silas Smith did not rejoin his company for another five months. While on his mission to raise funds and secure needed supplies, he became very ill. It was mid-May when he finally caught up with them, and by then they had been in Bluff City for over a month (see *ibid.*, 83). Thus, Platte Lyman became the de facto captain and Bishop Jens Nielson the second in command.

3. Platte Lyman recorded the following under date of December 17th: "Realizing the necessity of having the country more thoroughly explored ahead of us, I have talked the matter over with bro Sevy, and he has consented to undertake a trip through to the San Juan . . . and today he made a start with Lemuel Redd, Geo. Hobbs and Geo Merrell and 4 animals, expecting to be gone about 15 days" (as cited in *ibid.*, 164).

4. The information on George W. Sevy and Lemuel H. Redd, Sr., comes from Jenson's biographical work (see Jenson, *Encyclopedia,* 1:800; 2:116–19).

CHAPTER 56

Thursday, December 18, 1879

The first day passed without incident, though leading their four animals down the trail from the top of the mesa to the river left them all a little shaken. At one point, they were looking nearly straight down over a thousand feet, and far below they could see the carcasses of the nine horses that had slipped off the trail earlier and fallen to their death. Fortunately for David, he was leading Sevy's horse, and he had to concentrate so intently on keeping her from stumbling that he didn't have to think about how much he hated heights like this. But they reached the river safely and camped for the night.

This morning, they had swum the animals across and started up the eastern side. Both David and George Hobbs had been this way with the exploring group, so they led the way. Previously, Collett and Schow had taken them up Cottonwood Canyon all the way to where the canyon gave way to steep red bluffs. Back then, they had been on foot and had been able to scramble and claw their way to the top. Now the men had to spend some time with picks and shovels to make a way for the animals. Even then, the "trail" was so narrow and steep that they had to virtually drag the mule every step of the way up.

Near the top they found a narrow channel through the rock cliffs, which they immediately dubbed "The Little Hole in the Rock,"[1] and they followed it until they came out on top. As they turned back and looked to the northwest, they fell silent. It was a spectacular view. The broad opening of Cottonwood Canyon lay below them, framed on both sides by a fantastic tangle of massive, rounded hills, deep side canyons, and sheer cliffs, all in the soft coral pink sandstone rock so common to this area. Beyond that, the light haze in the air softened the harshness of the tremendous gorge where the river had cut its way through solid rock. On the far side, now three or four miles away, they could clearly see the dark gash that was the Hole in the Rock. Even as they watched, there was a sudden puff of smoke and dust. A couple of seconds later, a faint boom echoed off the cliffs.

Lem Redd poked David. "Looks like your dad and the Perkins boys have started blasting."

David laughed softly. "*Playing* is a better description. They were as excited as a bunch of kids with firecrackers."

They let the animals rest for about half an hour while they refilled their canteens from a nearby rock tank and talked quietly about what lay ahead. When they pushed on, they made their way for the first couple of miles through sagebrush-covered flats with low sandstone hills on both sides. This was country with which David was still familiar, having come this far with Schow and Collett. But as they crested one of those sandstone ridges, they got a glimpse of what was before them. The outcroppings of rock and sagebrush flats through which they were passing were quickly giving way to a scene of nothing but round humps of rock, a hundred to two hundred feet high, which quickly became so numerous that they folded together to form a wall of convoluted rock that blocked the way in both directions.

They were following the rock markers Schow and Collett had put in place the previous summer. The small cairns marked a trail that wound its way between the rock escarpments. This would be no challenge for wagons. But all of that changed when they climbed a low ridge of grey rock. When they topped out on the ridge, the ground dropped away from them in a steep decline. The slope, about a hundred yards long, bottomed out in a narrow wash. Going down this would be challenging enough, for the rock was rough and broken up. One crack was deep enough to swallow half a wagon wheel. But it was what they saw across from them that made them draw in their breath.

Rising even more steeply was yet another wall of solid red rock. Most of it was too steep for even a man to scramble up. Sharp clefts were everywhere to be seen, some with sheer fifty- to hundred-foot cliffs. Directly across from them, however, two rock formations came together, leaving a wide gap between them. Centuries of rain and wind had poured through this gap and eventually shaped the bottom of the narrow defile into a huge natural flume.

David knew what it was instantly. Here was Collett's "half pipe." It was as if someone had sawed off the top of some gigantic drainpipe and wedged it between the two sidewalls of rock. It was about a quarter of a mile long and narrow enough that in some places the wagon wheels would be on the sidewalls rather than on the bottom. At the bottom of the flume, the grade looked like it was maybe ten or fifteen percent, but about a third of the way up, it suddenly angled upward at close to a thirty-degree pitch.

Bishop Sevy gave a low whistle. Lem Redd audibly drew in a quick breath. And George Morrell just gaped.

"We didn't come this far with Captain Lyman," David said. "But I'm sure this is what Schow and Collett call The Chute."

Lem Redd leaned forward, squinting against the brightness of the sun. "It won't be easy, but it looks to me like the rock has a lot of striations, making the footing good for teams. And except right there at the top, it shouldn't require any work to get a wagon through."

Ten minutes later, they stood at the top of The Chute looking back across where they had just come from. Sevy looked at his brethren. "We'll have to double up the teams to get the wagons up this, but other than that I don't see it as a serious hindrance. Not after what we're doing at the Hole in the Rock. You all agree?"

As they nodded, he withdrew the map and made some marks on it. "All right," he said. "Let's go see this Grey Mesa they talked about, see if it's as good as they say it is."

"Oh, my!" George Hobbs exclaimed.

"Would you look at that?" breathed Lemuel Redd.

"Breathtaking," Bishop Sevy agreed.

"Amazing!" said George Morrell.

David was the last to speak, and all he could say was, "Blimey!"

Once they had reached Grey Mesa, they had continued on another two or three miles, moving northeastward and making excellent time. The mesa was a vast, flat plain, two or three miles wide, stretching out ahead of them as far as they could see. They chose to skirt along the southern edge of it. From there they could see out across a vast expanse of badlands to the south of them. This marked the route of the San Juan River, but the water was hidden from their view. And then, almost in an instant, the ground fell away dramatically, and they were looking down almost two thousand vertical feet. And there, amidst the endless emptiness of the desert, the river was visible. It made a great, lazy bend—like a giant gooseneck—to get around a massive fortress of solid rock that blocked its way. It passed almost directly below where they stood before turning south again to make its way on down to the Colorado River.

"So that's what they meant?" David said in wonder.

Sevy turned to him. "Who?"

"Schow and Collett," David said. He looked at Hobbs. "Remember? They said that after The Chute they came up on the mesa and continued on until they could see the river."

"That's right," Hobbs said with excitement. He turned and looked around. Then he pointed. "Look," he said. "There's another rock cairn." He was pointing to a small triangular pile of rocks about twenty yards away, right near the edge. "You're right. They were here."

"Unfortunately," David said, "this is as far as they went. We're on our own now."

Because of its gentle rise, even on horseback Grey Mesa looked as though it continued on for a great distance ahead of them. Then the five scouts began to notice that, in the far distance, the maze of canyons that had been on their south around the San Juan River seemed to be swinging around to the north, filling the full horizon directly in front of them. No one said much, but they all watched it with growing feelings of uneasiness.

Then something else caught their attention. George Morrell saw them first. "Look at that."

All heads turned to see where he was pointing. No more than fifty yards to their left, a herd of some kind of small animal was moving along parallel with their path. Their heads kept turning to look at the men. Several had impressive sets of curved horns.

"Well, I'll be," Hobbs exclaimed. "They're llamas."

"Llamas?" Lem Redd said. "No, llamas come from South America." He lifted a hand to shade his eyes from the sun, which was nearing its zenith. "No, I think they're mountain sheep."

"That's exactly what they are," Bishop Sevy said, "only down this far south we call them desert mountain sheep. We've got a good-sized herd up around Escalante."

"That can't be," David said, peering more closely at them. "We had them up in Wyoming, and these aren't big enough. And not only that, mountain sheep are about as shy as any animal you can name. We'd be lucky to see them at all up there. They could spot us as much as half a mile away and they'd be off like a shot. But look at these. It's like they're actually following us."

"They're just curious," Morrell said. "I'll bet they've never seen humans out here before."

Sevy went to his horse and retrieved a pair of binoculars. While the others moved closer, he focused them on the herd. After a moment, he said, "They're mountain sheep all right." He began to count under his breath. "I count fourteen of them." He let out a soft exclamation. "They're beautiful." He handed the glasses to Redd. "Take a look."

One by one they took turns examining the herd. Only when it was his turn was David convinced. "They're quite a bit smaller than the ones we used to see in the Laramie Mountains," he noted. "But they sure are beautiful."

For the next half an hour, the sheep matched their pace, sometimes moving farther away from the men, sometimes moving to within twenty-five or thirty yards of them. And then, as if they had been given a signal, they broke into a graceful trot, kicking up little puffs of dust. In moments, they were out about two hundred yards and growing smaller every moment.

And then they simply disappeared!

"Whoa!" Sevy cried, coming to a halt. He grabbed the field glasses again and scanned the place where they had last seen the sheep. "Where did they go?"

It took them only about five minutes to answer that question, and with the answer, their optimism and hopes for continuing rapid progress were dashed. In a change so abrupt as to be visually startling, Grey Mesa came to an end. In a matter of just a few yards, the sagebrush-covered ground dropped sharply away and the men looked down three or four hundred feet upon a labyrinth of barren, slick-rock cliffs, gulches, gulleys, and washes. And that sight stretched out ahead of them for as far as they could see to the right and to the left.

They ate a quick, cold lunch, turned the pack animals free to graze, then split up. Sevy took one horse, David the other. They divided the task up. With the horses, David and Bishop Sevy would ride out to the farthest points, then move back toward the center while the others began searching on foot along the rim of the mesa. If anyone found a way down, they were to fire off one shot, and the rest would come back in.

For the next five hours, they moved slowly back and forth along the rim of the mesa. They would find a promising swale or narrow opening into the rocks below, only to have it close off into a blind wall or drop off so steeply one couldn't even get close enough to see how high the cliff was.

As the last rays of the sun disappeared, David met George Hobbs coming along the rim toward him. David had ridden all the way back to the river overlook, a distance of three or four miles, then come back following the rim all the way. "Any luck?" Hobbs called as David got close enough to hear.

"None," David said. When he reached the campfire, he swung down and began unsaddling the horse. "You heard from the others?"

George shook his head. "I thought I'd start supper. It'll be dark in less than half an hour."

"I'd better get some more brush," David said, slapping the horse on the rump to send her away. "They may need a signal fire to find their way back."

But the three other men appeared a few minutes later, walking together with their heads down. Hobbs had some beans and bacon simmering in a pan by then. As they reached the fire, they all looked tired, but Bishop Sevy seemed especially discouraged. "Nothing, I assume?"

Both David and Hobbs shook their heads. "Not even a place where we could lower someone down with a rope," Hobbs replied.

No one said much while they ate their supper. Only when they were finished did they begin to discuss their options. "Let's get up at first light," Sevy finally suggested. "We'll spread out again, only this time we'll all go on foot. Explore every possibility." He shook his head very slowly. "We'll take about three hours. If we haven't found something by then, there's nothing to find."

His voice trailed off. "Brethren, I would suggest we petition the Lord for His help, then retire. Brother David, will you be voice?"

Hobbs gave David a sharp look. On the exploring party, everyone had known that you didn't call on David for prayer. But these men were new.

David just smiled at Hobbs, then nodded. "I'd be happy to."

Friday, December 19, 1879

They barely spoke as they awakened in the morning chill. A deep melancholy lay on each of them. As they went about getting a fire started, their breath made silvery puffs in the growing light. Bishop Sevy seemed especially weighed down. He looked to the east for a long, silent moment. It was going to be another good day. There were puffy high clouds across the northeastern sky, and they were a soft pink with the coming sunrise. The morning light had softened the harshness of the landscape that now lay at their feet. Under other circumstances it would have been a beautiful sight. Now it only deepened their sense of despair.

"All right," Sevy finally said. "I'd recommend we not stop for breakfast. We'll search until ten, each taking a different sector from what we searched yesterday. If by then we've not found anything, we'll come back here, have breakfast, and—" he sighed heavily—"and start back."

No one disagreed. They rolled up their beds and loaded everything but some food and their cooking utensils into the packs so that once they returned, they could strap the packs on the mule and the burro and leave immediately. Finally, it was light enough for them to see clearly, and Sevy signaled for them to gather around him.

"Brother Morrell and I will go south this time," he said. "David, you go north. You'll come to a really deep, narrow canyon. There's no sense going any farther than that. It's all sheer cliffs from there. Lem, you and Hobbs take this central section." He took a quick breath. "Take your time. Follow every possible opening." He gave them all piercing looks. "But be careful! That rock is as smooth as the top of a buttered loaf of bread in some places. One slip and it's over."

As they nodded gravely, he removed his hat. "Brethren, let's once again ask the Lord to accompany us and bless our endeavors."

<hr />

David hadn't brought his watch with him, so he had to guess when it was about ten o'clock. As he trudged back toward their camp, downcast and discouraged, he saw that he was the first to return. The four animals grazed contentedly a short distance away from the campfire, which was now sending up a column of grey smoke in the morning sunshine. But there were no figures in sight.

He stopped, staring east across the unbroken scene of undulating stone, deep canyons, and sheer cliffs. A great sense of despair swept over him. What were those good people so anxiously waiting back there for them going to say when they came back and reported that there was no way through, that their mission was over, at least for this season?

David harbored no illusions that they could return to the river and find another way east. Schow and Collett had spent a lot more time than they had and had finally concluded that this was the only way. He thought about the hope and optimism that had filled the camp after Silas Smith announced that the Lord had confirmed the decision to move forward. Were those hopes now to be dashed?

And what of that supposed inspiration? David wondered. He had felt the rightness of it as strongly as anyone else. When Silas had called for the vote, David's hand was in the air as high as the others. When the decision was confirmed, he too had joyously shouted, "Ho! Ho to the San Juan!" And now the way before them lay blocked by an impassable wilderness.

As he stood there, staring blankly out at nothing, faces began coming into his mind. Emmy Davis. Mary Davis and baby Ethel. Jens Nielson. Molly. The McKennas. His own father. Abby. What would they say? How would they respond when the men rode back into camp to announce that there was no going forward, that it had all been for naught?

He pushed the thought away, the pain too intense. He bowed his head, but suddenly that seemed so inadequate, so insufficient. He looked around once more and, seeing that he was still alone, he dropped his head and closed his eyes. "O God!" he cried from the depths of his soul. Immediately, he heard Mary's voice in his mind and corrected himself. "Our Father in Heaven."

He paused, not sure if after all the years, a desperate cry in a desperate hour qualified as a prayer at all. Angry, he pushed that aside as well. "Dear God. I know I have no right to call on you after so many years of doubt." The words sounded awkward, fumbling. He pressed on. "I do not ask for me, but for them. Those good people back in camp. For the McKennas and so many families like them. For Jim and Mary Davis, the Harrimans, and their families waiting for rescue. O God, don't let us fail. Please! Hear our cries. Heed our prayers. Show us a way through. I have nothing to offer Thee in return except for the submission of my own will to yours. Which I offer now."

He stopped again, searching for words to express his yearnings, for communication deep enough to reach to heaven. Finding nothing, he simply said, "Amen." He got slowly to his feet. Not moving, he let the feelings gradually subside again. Then he pulled his shoulders back and decided it was time to get breakfast started.

Only as he reached the campfire did something finally register in David's mind. They had left almost three hours before. The fire should be nothing but hot coals by now, yet it was burning its way through a thick clump of sagebrush. Then he saw something else. The frying pan, full of half-cooked bacon, was set off to one side. The grease was barely starting to congeal. One or more of his brethren had been here before him and started breakfast as they had agreed to do. He turned slowly. But who? And why had they suddenly left again?

Since he couldn't answer that, he squatted down, picked up the frying pan, and put it back on the fire. Then he started stirring up some flour and water to make flapjacks.

Five minutes later Lemuel Redd returned. In response to David's querying look he simply shook his head. Ten minutes after that, with the tantalizing smell of bacon and fried bread filling the air, Bishop Sevy and George Morrell appeared and trudged slowly into camp. From the slump of their shoulders and the dejection on their faces, it was obvious that they had failed too.

As they joined them, Sevy looked around. "Where's Hobbs?"

"Not back yet," David said. And then he had a thought. "Did any of you start breakfast?"

When they all shook their heads, he said, "It must have been Hobbs then," and he explained what he had found when he returned.

Not sure what to make of it, they sat down around the fire and had breakfast. As they were finishing, a shout pulled them all around. Just to the east, where the mesa abruptly dropped off into the maze of rock below, they saw a head and an arm waving. A moment later George Hobbs appeared. He stopped and bent over nearly double, drawing in huge gulps of air.

Alarmed, the four started toward him. "George!" David called. "Are you all right?"

Still bent over, he waved, and they heard a choked laugh between his gasps. "I found it!" he cried. "I found the way down."

While Hobbs caught his breath, David forked out a flapjack and three slices of bacon onto a tin plate and handed it to him. He nodded gratefully, finally getting some control over his breathing. "I found it, brethren," he said again, grinning like a young boy.

Sevy leaned forward. "You really did, George? Where?"

He pointed in the direction where he had first appeared. "Right over there."

"But," Lem said, looking dubious, "I searched all over there yesterday afternoon."

Hobbs laughed aloud. He was clearly delighted with himself, and so excited that he had already forgotten that he had food in his hand. "So did I this morning." He set the plate aside and stood up so he could use his hands freely. "Finally, greatly discouraged, I gave up and returned and started breakfast."

"So it was you," David said.

"That's right. But I was just getting started when a movement caught my eye. I looked up, thinking it was one of you coming back, but to my astonishment, it was one of those mountain sheep."

"What?" Morrell exclaimed. "Again?"

"Yeah!" Hobbs said as he pointed. "He was standing right over there, not fifteen feet away. He was just standing there, looking at me, like they did yesterday. My first thought was to grab my gun and get us some meat, but as I watched him, he was too pretty to kill. So then I had another idea. I decided to lasso him and show you guys that he was really here."

He paused for a quick breath, then rushed on. "I stood up slowly, not wanting to scare him, and moved over to where we left the pack ropes. I got one and tied a noose in it, all the time watching the sheep. He barely moved. He just kept looking at me with those big brown eyes. So I started edging my way toward him, lasso in hand."

"That is amazing," David breathed.

"That's why I thought you would never believe me." His eyes were dancing as he remembered. "I got within about ten feet of him, but before I could even lift the rope to throw it, he suddenly darted away. But he only went another ten or fifteen feet, then stopped again. So, more slowly now, I moved toward him again. Same thing. I would get just close enough to throw the rope and he'd jump away again."

He stopped, savoring the moment, loving the rapt attention he was getting from his listeners. "After four or five times like that, I thought I'd lost him. Suddenly he disappeared, just like yesterday. I ran forward to the edge of the rim, cursing myself for having let him get away. But there he was, just a few feet below me, staring up as if to say, 'Are you giving up that easily?'"

"Unbelievable," Redd murmured.

"So," Hobbs went on, "I slipped over the edge too, and once again started slowly toward him. Guess what? I'd get about eight or ten feet away, and wham! in three hops, he'd be out of reach again. It was like he was playing a game with me. I could scarcely believe it. Over and over that happened."

He stopped, and now he went very sober. "I followed him for near half a mile before suddenly he gave a toss of his head and leaped away. Only this time he didn't stop. I saw a flash of his tail and he was gone. I never saw him again."

Sevy started. "You went half a mile down the cliff face?" he asked slowly.

"Yes!" He almost shouted it. "When he was gone, I looked around to see where I was. I had been concentrating so hard on catching him that I hadn't paid attention to where I was going. But as I looked around, I realized *I was at the bottom!*"

The others were so absolutely dumbfounded they could only stare.

"Without me even knowing it, that ole rascal showed me a way down."

"Can you take a horse down the way you went?" Redd asked, half in awe.

"Actually, two horses and two mules," he laughed. "They might balk at the sight of the drop-offs, but if we blindfold them, it will be no problem. I marked the way with rocks, coming back up. That's why I was puffing so hard when you first saw me."

Sevy was scratching his beard, his expression unreadable. "What about wagons?" he asked.

That stopped them all. *That* was the real question. But it didn't stop George Hobbs. "It'll be another one of those stretches to turn your hair grey, but give Ben Perkins and his crew some blasting powder and a day or two, and yes, we can make a road wide enough for wagons."[2]

Notes

1. Miller indicates that he is the one who called the narrow notch near the top of Cottonwood Canyon the "Little Hole in the Rock" (see *Hole*, 125), but I have let the explorers name it to make it easier for the reader to identify.

2. George Hobbs is the only one of the four scouts to have left a history of this critical four-man exploration. Even though he is often quoted—or "retold" with some embellishment—he is the only original source for this story about the mountain sheep. As noted in the previous chapter, his was a narrative history given some forty years after the expedition. As is common with such later reminiscences, some details may not be completely correct. For example, Hobbs did call the animals llamas and said there were fourteen of them. Whether he called them llamas at the time when they first saw them cannot be determined. He does say that they "followed us for some distance" and "were quite curious to know what kind of animals we were!"

While some minor details have been added for the flow of the novel, the basic elements come from Hobbs's account. Today the road the pioneers later made down the path where the sheep led Hobbs is still called Slickrock Hill. To see the actual road they cut into the side of the rock hillsides to bring the wagons down is astounding. In several places, notches carved in the rock by the pioneers to give their teams better footing can still be seen.

CHAPTER 57

Wednesday, December 24, 1879

David moaned softly, half asleep and half awake. There was a hard spot—probably a rock he had missed—beneath his left shoulder blade that was hurting enough to have awakened him. He shifted his body, trying unsuccessfully to find a little softer spot in the dirt beneath him.

Irritated that he had been awakened before he was ready, he cracked one eye open to see what was wrong. To his surprise, he saw nothing but blackness. It was the deep, heavy darkness of the coal mine, and for a moment he felt a rush of panic. Then he relaxed as he remembered that he had put his poncho over his head last night in case it snowed. Surprised at how heavy it seemed, he reached up and pushed it away.

That woke him up in an instant. Snow cascaded onto his face and neck. He jerked up, throwing the poncho off to one side. Willing himself to come fully awake, he realized that his whole body seemed weighted down, as if he had on four or five extra blankets. Which meant it had snowed during the night. A lot.

Brushing the snow from his face, he leaned on one elbow. In the first light of dawn, he could see that he was covered with about eight inches of snow. Turning his head to the side, he made out four other mounds in the snow, and a black circle marking where the fire had been.

Careful not to pull any more snow in on himself, he moved his legs and body so that the snow shucked off to one side. Then, with a groan of pure misery, he lay back down and pulled the top blanket up around his neck. Another mistake. It was wet and frozen and it scraped against his neck.

He sighed. Here was yet another setback, another delay, another frustration. After miraculously finding a way down Slickrock Hill, as they called it, the group of scouts were elated. They didn't have to turn back. They had found a way through. His brethren used the word *miraculous,* and, to David's surprise, he found himself comfortable with that term. It had truly been an astounding experience.

That was followed closely by another astonishing development. As they made their way along the highest point between the drainages of the Colorado and San Juan Rivers, off in the distance they saw a long, narrow lake shimmering in the sunlight. At first they thought it was a mirage, but through the field glasses they saw that a pile of rocks and debris—probably from a massive cave-in during a flash flood—had blocked one of the dry washes, forming a natural dam. Behind it, a lake had now formed. From what they could see of the canyon below the dam, there were large trees and considerable forage. This oasis in the desert would make a perfect campsite for a large company and their herds.[1] Amazing!

As they continued eastward, however, wending their way through the tangled network of canyons and gulches, the challenges became more and more daunting. Since the only reasonable route of travel was in the dry washes, they could get no broad perspective of the landscape. When they came to places where a wash was fed by several canyons, they had to stop and make individual forays up each canyon before proceeding.

That became the pattern for the next several days. They inched forward slowly, splitting up again and again to see which canyons boxed up into dead ends, which led off in the wrong direction, and which would take them onward. It was the only way to accomplish their purpose—that was what scouts did—but their progress was maddeningly slow.

They had moments of euphoria, such as when they discovered some magnificent stone ruins below one of the great overhanging cliffs, and then found an ancient cliff dwellers' trail leading from there eastward. They followed it for miles, saving themselves the need to explore alternate routes. But then would come a major setback that dashed their hopes again. For example, four days beyond Slickrock Hill they ran straight into Grand Gulch. This massive canyon, running north and south for miles in both directions, was the deepest they had seen since leaving the Colorado River.

A brief exploration in both directions convinced them that the only way around would be to go straight north until it petered out into the flanks of Elk Ridge. This not only cost them two extra days, it took them straight into the mouth of a major winter storm.

David rubbed at his neck, feeling the cold seeping through his blankets, but feeling a sense of hopelessness pressing down on him even more heavily than the snow. They were eight days out on what was supposed to be a fifteen-day round trip. They had no more than a few ounces of flour for the five of them. Their pack animals were exhausted, their riding horses spent. They were completely lost in a wilderness of baffling complexity, and now the storm blanked out any chance of them finding the landmarks they so desperately needed to find their way. Their situation had gone from challenging to critical, from critical to crisis.

Another thought came, only deepening the gloom. Oh yeah! Today was Christmas Eve.

He should have known better than to start thinking they had hit rock bottom. Any time you did that, fate seemed to delight in proving you wrong. And that was exactly what happened a short time later. As the five men dragged themselves out of their bedrolls and shook off the snow, they didn't say much. They all knew the seriousness of their situation, and moaning about it didn't help anything. They were camped in a thick stand of junipers on the southern slopes of Elk Ridge and the snow continued to fall heavily. From the looks of the sky, it would continue to do so for most of the day. Fortunately, the night before, they had gathered a pile of dead juniper branches. The snow was a light powder, and when they dug the wood out, it was still dry. David and George Hobbs set to work building a fire while the other three went to find the animals. David stirred the last of their flour into a pan of melted snow, then looked at George. "We've got enough mix here to make one large flapjack or five small ones. Any suggestions?"

"Make one, and we'll cut it five ways," he grunted.

"I get to cut it," David quipped.

George actually laughed. "When I was a kid, my mom came up with the perfect solution to situations like this. She didn't care who got to cut the cake, or whatever it happened to be, but the person cutting always got the last choice."[2]

For a moment, David was puzzled, and then he saw it. "Ah," he chuckled. "A wise mother."

"I'll say. I can remember agonizing to make sure every piece was exactly the same size so no one got a bigger piece than me."

David's smile faded. One-fifth of one flapjack. That would have to sustain them now until they reached their destination. Or starved.

Just then a noise off to their left turned their heads. "Uh-oh," David murmured. Their three companions were plowing their way through the snow toward them, but they had no animals in tow. Things had just gotten considerably worse.

<hr/>

Because the snow had covered any tracks, it took them until eleven o'clock that morning to finally find the animals. That was half a day wasted that they could ill afford. The poor creatures were huddled together in a thick stand of junipers, and it was only when one of the horses whinnied that they found them. The snow was too deep for them to forage, and they got no more food than their human masters.

Hungry, cold, wet, and miserable, the little party trudged on, leading the animals now rather than risk having them slip and break a leg. That afternoon, the snow finally stopped, but it turned bitterly cold. Behind them, the sky was clearing, but ahead there was nothing but a solid wall of grey.

Since David and George Hobbs were the only ones in the party who had been to the San Juan River country, the group was counting on them to locate prominent landmarks as they drew closer to their destination. The most important of those were the Blue Mountains,[3] which were about forty miles north of Montezuma Creek. With peaks topping 12,000 feet, they would be hard to miss. However, on a day like today, the Blue

Mountains could have been half a mile away and the men couldn't have seen them. So on they trudged, their despair deepening.

As they rolled out their bedrolls beneath the shelter of juniper trees, their discouragement was almost palpable. Not only had they not arrived at their destination by the time they had planned, but they were wandering blindly through a vast wilderness, and the specter of starvation now stalked them.

As they lay quietly in the bedrolls, each lost in his own thoughts, Bishop Sevy called out softly, "Tomorrow's Christmas, brethren. Let's hope and pray it is a merry one."

"Yeah," George Hobbs muttered. "I'd hang a stocking up for Santa Claus, but it's so cold, I can't bear to even take my boot off, let alone a stocking."

"Knowing what your socks smell like," Lem Redd drawled, "it's just as well. You'd probably knock those poor reindeer right out of the sky."

When Sarah McKenna backed out of the wagon, her husband was waiting for her with a blanket. Though she was bundled up in her winter coat, leggings, mittens, and earmuffs, she still snuggled gratefully into the extra wrap, then moved in close to press up against him. Above them the skies were clear and the stars seemed more brilliant than ever before. Two or three inches of snow still lay on the ground—at least where it hadn't been trampled—and a light breeze out of the northwest made it terribly cold.

As Patrick held her, Molly and Abby moved up beside them. "Is he asleep?" Abby asked.

"Finally," Sarah sighed. "He is so excited, I thought he would never give up." She looked up at her husband. "Know why he insisted that we hang his stocking on the back wheel of the farthest wagon from the fire?"

"No, why?"

"Because the snow isn't all trampled there. He wants to see if Santa Claus leaves footprints, or if there will be reindeer tracks. He's still worried that Santa can't find us out here."

As Patrick shook his head in wonder at how his son's mind worked, Molly fetched a poker from near the fire. She wiped the blackened end in the snow several times, then turned it around and held it by that end. "Billy Joe told me that, too," she said. "So guess what?" She moved to where the wagon tongue protected the snow beneath it, bent over, and pushed the handle of the poker into the snow. Then she did it again, right next to the first. She stepped back, half bowed, and gestured triumphantly with her free hand. "Voilà!" she cried. "I give you: reindeer tracks." They moved in for a closer look. The marks were a little strange, but they looked quite similar to the tracks of a deer.

"Wonderful!" Sarah cried. "He'll be so delighted."

"So who is Santa Claus?" Abby asked. "If Billy's checking for footprints, it had better be Dad."

"Actually," Carl Bradford spoke up, "I have the biggest feet. Why don't I do it?"

"Good." Sarah turned to the others. "Abby, you check the Dutch ovens, see if the cookies are done yet. Molly, get that sack of molasses candy I hid in your wagon."[4]

Molly immediately started for the wagon where she and Abby slept.

Sarah went to the box where they kept their food and brought out a small cloth bag. She came back and handed it to Carl. "I know parched corn isn't much to put into a little boy's Christmas stocking," she said, "but it will make him feel that he at least got something. We'll grind it into cornmeal tomorrow and bake him some corn bread. He loves that."

Carl nodded absently. He was looking at the last wagon where Billy Joe had so carefully hung his Christmas stocking earlier. He turned to Abby. "If I were to climb up the wagon tongue very carefully, then go through the wagon and climb down again while I fill the stocking, I'll leave footprints by the stocking, but none coming or going. What do you think?"

She clapped her hands in delight. "Perfect. Take the poker and make a few reindeer tracks, too. That's brilliant."

He smiled. "You sound like David."

"What about the sleigh?" Sarah asked. "It ought to leave tracks too."

"I'll use the poker to make some long marks."

Patrick stood back, watching this interchange with deep satisfaction. How good it was to have a child as part of Christmas. It infused everyone with the Christmas spirit. When Sarah came back over to join him, and they watched Carl leave proof of Santa's visit, Patrick put his arm around her and pulled her close. "This just might turn out to be the best Christmas ever."

She stretched up and kissed him warmly. "Who would have thought it?"

Thursday, December 25, 1879

Christmas Day dawned perfectly clear, but the wind had picked up during the night and the air had a vicious bite to it. With fuel being as scarce as it was, roaring campfires were not to be found, but all around the Hole in the Rock camp the fires were larger than usual. The people had spent much of yesterday bringing in extra sagebrush and shadscale, and under the supervision of Bishop Jens Nielson, two wagons had been sent to the Straight Cliffs to load up with dead juniper logs and branches. Most of that would be saved for the festivities later in the day, but each family camp had been given an extra measure of fuel for their Christmas morning breakfast.

Because of the snowy, wet weather, work on widening the notch down the Hole and the road on the other side of the river had come to a virtual standstill for the last couple of days. That freed up the men to be in camp for the holiday.

The four adult McKennas stood together around the fire, hands outstretched, trying to keep warm, watching the line of children that snaked out from their last wagon and passed just to the right of them. Even as they watched, three more came running, chattering like squirrels.

"What is taking so long?" Molly asked. "Those poor children are freezing."

Sarah just smiled. "Billy Joe won't let more than two or three come back at a time, lest they tramp out the footprints and ruin the magic."

When Billy Joe had awakened—earlier than anyone else in the

family, of course—his mother had made him wait while the adults all dressed and stepped outside. Then they stood back and watched as he raced to the last wagon. He pulled up short when he saw the bulging stocking, then squealed in delight. He was staring at the ground around his stocking. "He came," he whooped. "He came!"

Pausing only long enough to consume a sugar cookie, he was off on a dead run to find his buddies. Word of the magic spread like a desert wind through the camp, and soon virtually every child—and even a few adults—lined up to see Santa's footprints, the reindeer tracks, and where the sleigh had rested.

Patrick watched his son affectionately for a time. Then, seeing that they wouldn't be eating breakfast for another half hour at best, he wandered over to the Nielson camp to get an idea of the plans for the day. Cries of "Merry Christmas" or "Happy Christmas"—the second greeting coming from pioneers from the British Isles—echoed all around, and there was a general air of merriment and excitement.

When he returned, the others drew in. "When do the festivities begin?" Abby asked.

"Well," Patrick said with a chuckle, "you know Bishop Nielson's sense of humor. The first thing he asked me was if Billy Joe was charging admission to see Santa's footprints."

Sarah started, and turned to look at her son. "He's not, is he?"

Patrick laughed. "No, but Bishop Nielson said—and I shall try to quote him, 'Yah, and if dat boy be charging dem kids to see dem magic tracks, den be shure to tell Billy Joe to pay his tithing. Then vee haf enuff money to buy anudder tousand pounds of black powder.'"

"Did you hear about the shooting match?" Carl asked, coming over to join them. He had been over with Billy Joe, watching with satisfaction the fruits of his efforts of the night before.

"A shooting match?" Abby said in surprise.

"Dat's right," Patrick said. He caught himself, grinned sheepishly, then started again. "That's right. One of the brethren has put up a nice two-year-old steer to be butchered later today. He's selling chances to purchase the best cuts of the meat for one dollar per person."

Molly was perplexed. "How do you sell a chance to buy meat?"

"Simple," Patrick said. "There's going to be a shooting contest. For a dollar, a person buys a chance to shoot three shots at a target. The best shooter gets first choice of the meat, and so on until the last. They're going to limit it to twenty men, though."

Molly clapped her hands. "Oh, that should be fun. Who's going to be shooting?"

"I know one for sure," her father said with a grin.

Sarah slapped him playfully on the arm. "You?"

"Me and Billy Joe," he said. "Actually, I'll let Billy Joe shoot twice. With all the shooting he's done with David, he's pretty darn good now."

"What else is happening?" Abby asked.

"Well, the shooting match will take place just before lunch. Most of those at Fifty Mile Camp will be coming up to join us. After a break for the midday meal, we'll all move up to the dance floor[5] for an afternoon of games, riddles, and jokes. There will be wrestling, sack races, the singing of Christmas carols, and . . ." He left it hanging.

"And a dance?" Molly said eagerly.

"Yep. As soon as it's dark. They say they've got enough wood and brush up there to light up half the desert, and we're gonna dance until our shoes fall off."[6]

Notes

1. To find a lake in that desert country was really quite remarkable. The scouts did not take time to go over to it on the way out, but did stop there on the return trip. The main company arrived at Lake Canyon on February 29, 1880. Platte Lyman recorded the following in his journal entry for that day: "Drove 7 miles over a rough rocky and sandy road to the lake, a beautiful clear sheet of spring water 1/2 a mile long and nearly as wide, and apparently very deep. Cottonwood, willow, canes, flags, bulrushes and several kinds of grass grow luxuriantly, and it would make an excellent stock ranch" (in Miller, *Hole*, 167). The company spent two days there, resting and rejoicing in this restful, cool place.

The lake is no longer there. The dam washed out in November 1915 when a particularly wet year filled Lake Canyon to overflowing (see *ibid.*, 97, 88–89; in the center photo section there is a picture of the lake as it was before 1915). Sadly, another flash flood in the fall of 2008 washed out the narrow road that leads into the canyon, so the canyon can no longer be accessed by vehicles.

2. In the Hobbs narrative, we find this sobering but amusing entry: "That morning [December 24th] we had cooked the last food we had, consisting of a slap jack about one inch thick [also called flapjacks, or what today are frequently called scones]. The man who cut the cake had to take the last choice. This was about our eighth day out" (cited in *ibid.*, 88).

3. The Blue Mountains are a small range of mountains just west of Monticello, Utah. On many modern maps they are marked as the Abajo Mountains.

4. According to Mary Jane Perkins Wilson, daughter of Ben and Mary Ann Perkins, molasses candy was made by boiling sorghum cane stocks in a big, flat vat. "When this boils, skum rises to the top, which must be repeatedly taken off. A barrel was reserved for these skimmings, used by the children to make candy" ("Life Sketch of Mary Jane Wilson," 14–15).

5. The dance held on Christmas Day was not at Dance Hall Rock, which was about fifteen miles to the north of the Hole in the Rock. Fortunately, at the nearer campsite nature had left a large expanse of flat, smooth sandstone, about sixty feet by eighty feet. It lacked the overhanging rock and natural amphitheater shape of Dance Hall Rock, but it provided many a night of entertainment and enjoyment for the Saints (see Miller, *Hole,* 81, 184).

6. Several histories and journals speak of Christmas Day celebrations at the Hole in the Rock camp (see *ibid.*, 78–81; Reay, *Incredible Passage,* 36; "Life Sketch of Mary Jane Wilson," 11; Carpenter, *Jens Nielson,* 46). We're not told the name of the pioneer who came up with this raffle shoot, but it seems to have been a big hit with the Saints. Joseph Stanford Smith claimed to be the winner in an interview given to his biographer some time later (see Miller, *Hole,* 79). Finding Santa's footprints was the creation of the author, based on the fact that parents did put out stockings from Santa.

CHAPTER 58

Thursday, December 25, 1879

The little camp on the flanks of Elk Ridge was not in much of a celebrating mood on this Christmas Day. It was piercing cold. The snow was close to a foot deep. There was no food for them and no forage for their rapidly weakening animals. And they were helplessly lost.

The storm of the day before had swept on eastward into Colorado, and the sky was now clear. The sun sparkled off the snow, bright enough to blind you if you looked directly into it. But they were in a forest of cedar or juniper trees that stretched for miles in either direction. If they looked to the north, they could see Elk Ridge rising above them. If they looked south and west, where the land dropped away, through the trees they got glimpses of Grand Gulch and the countryside they had traversed over the past eight days.

To the east, the direction they needed to go, they could see nothing but trees.

David's stomach twisted and rumbled ominously, reminding him that it had been twenty-four hours since he had eaten one small slice of flapjack. The five of them had built a good fire this morning. That was the one bright note about this place: There was certainly no shortage of firewood. Now they sat around it, trying to come to a consensus as to their next course of action.

The frustrations they were feeling were fueled by the natural irritation that came with hunger and also the frightening reality that their bones could easily end up bleached and bare in this trackless wilderness. As they debated what to do on this Christmas morning, there were several contrasting opinions. Striking out blindly seemed hardly a wise move when they were getting weaker by the day and had no idea how much farther they had to go. One thing they all agreed on: They couldn't go back. They were at least eight days from camp, with no food and no hope of finding any on the way back. They could last four days, maybe five, living on water alone. But what if Montezuma Creek was farther than that? What if they got lost again? There was no margin of error now, and for the moment, they were almost paralyzed by indecision.

This discussion quickly gave way to recriminations and accusations. They shouldn't have taken so much time exploring side canyons. They should have tried harder to find a way to cross Grand Gulch. They should have hobbled the animals two nights ago so they didn't lose half a day trying to find them again. The estimate of eight days to find their destination was woefully inadequate. Whose idea was that? They should have brought more food. If they had brought a horse for each man, they could have made much better time.

Finally, recognizing what was happening, they fell silent. After a few minutes, the three older men—Sevy, Morrell, and Redd, began talking quietly about the families they had left behind. They were rightly worried. What would happen to them now?

David and George Hobbs were not married and so were left out of that conversation. But married or not, they had their own concerns. George was sick with worry about the sister he had left in Montezuma Creek. David shared the same concern for the Davis family. Those two families had been told to expect the arrival of the company somewhere before the first of the year. Yet the company was still months away. Were the families all right? Or was their situation as desperate as their own?

Suddenly, Hobbs stood up. "This is getting us nowhere," he grumped. "I noticed earlier that the wind is clearing the snow off that ridge about a hundred yards above us. I'm going to climb up there and see if we can get a look above these trees."

Without waiting for an answer, he pulled his coat more tightly around his neck and trudged off. After several moments, David stood as well. "I think I'll go with him."

But he didn't follow George directly. As he had sat there, thinking about their situation, worrying about what the McKennas and his father would do if he never returned, brooding about Molly, he remembered Molly's question to him just before he left. "If you get in trouble, will you ask God for help? Promise?"

That morning six days ago, there on the rim of Grey Mesa, he had dropped to his knees for the first time in over ten years and cried out to God. And the answer had come less than an hour later. He laughed softly, mocking himself. How was that for a remarkable coincidence?

He wasn't questioning any longer, not in principle, at least. When Yaheeno, the old Indian, had come and saved their lives, that had been a turning point for David. He could no longer simply explain it away. And a mountain sheep that played "tag" with Hobbs until he led him to the bottom? Absolutely no question there.

But in both of those cases, the answer had come to bless others—Mary Davis, heavy with child; Emmy, the girl with fire in her hair; a missionary who had returned from England so as to accompany his son; the McKennas and two hundred and fifty other good people waiting back in camp. Oh, yes, he knew that if he and his companions didn't get through, all of them would suffer. But what was weighing David down was a terrible fear that *he* wouldn't make it, that *he* might never see his father again. Or Abby. Or Billy Joe. Or . . .

He veered to the left, leaving Hobbs's tracks and striking off on his own. Twenty feet away was a large juniper tree. Beneath its spreading branches, there was no snow. Careful not to knock the snow off the branches above him, David stooped down and found a dry spot. Then he dropped to his knees. And once again he began to talk to his Heavenly Father.

George Hobbs turned around in surprise as he heard the crunch of footsteps in the snow.

"Any luck?" David asked as he came up to join him.

They turned their backs to the wind, which was whipping snow pellets past them, stinging their cheeks. George shook his head in disgust, lifting one arm to point to the east. "It's clear enough, but all you can see in that direction is more trees and more mountain."

David turned. He was right. They were on a series of rolling ridges, one following after the other, that formed the southern flank of Elk Ridge. That and the dense forest blocked any line of sight to the east. He turned. They were high enough now that they could look out across a vast expanse to the south and west. There the green carpet of cedars gradually gave way to the red desert beyond it.

"Good thing we didn't spend any more time trying to cross Grand Gulch," David said, marveling at the enormity of that great rip in the earth. From here they could see that it continued off to the south, widening and deepening until it disappeared in the distant haze.

"Yeah," came the glum response. George lifted a hand and pointed. "Look just to the left of Grand Gulch. See that needle-like mountain way the heck out there?"

Squinting, David immediately saw it. It was almost ethereal, it was so far way. "That's El Capitan," George explained, "or what the Navajos call Mount Aglatha.* We passed just to the south of that last summer with Silas."

David was nodding. "That's got to be sixty or seventy miles from here."

"That's my point," George said. "If we can see that far, then we should be able to see the Blue Mountains, *if* we could just find a place where the view is unobstructed." He was stamping his feet to get them warm. "I know we're close, but we have to know where we are. It's the only chance we have to get out of this alive."

"Agreed," David said. "So how do we do that?"

Instead of answering, George lifted a hand and shaded his eyes, looking down, but more to the southeast now. Then he leaned forward. "Look, David. There's a little knoll down there about half a mile. Do you see it? It looks like a little pyramid sticking up out of the mountain."

"Where are you looking?"

---

* Just north of present day Kayenta, Arizona, on the Navajo Reservation.

"See the smoke from our fire? It's whipping away in the wind, but you can see it." When David grunted, he continued, "Now go a little to the left. There's a lot of snow on it, but it's a cone-shaped knoll. There are several large red boulders near the top."

"I see it," David cried.

"Go get the others. I'm going down there." Not waiting for David's response, he strode down the ridge half a dozen yards, then turned and plowed through the deep snowdrift that had formed below it.

By the time David got the other three, and they reached the base of the knoll, George Hobbs was already at the top. It was a near-perfect cone, and quite steep. David could see where George had slipped several times while clambering up the snow-covered hillside.

"Can you see anything?" Bishop Sevy called, cupping his hands.

"No," came the jubilant reply. "I can see *everything!* Get up here!"

They followed his trail up, grabbing onto the limbs of trees or bracing themselves against rocks to keep their footing. They were all three gasping when they finally reached the top. But all of that was forgotten the moment they straightened and let their eyes turn to where Hobbs was pointing. What lay before them was a grand panorama, stretching out for a hundred miles in every direction except to the north, where Elk Ridge blocked their view. The juniper forest was like a great carpet rolling out from where they stood, a rich green covering that continued for another twenty or thirty miles.

But what Hobbs was pointing at lay to their northeast. As they turned, their eyes widened in awe. Like a massive blot against the horizon, the dark mass of a small mountain range lay about ten or fifteen miles before them. They could see where the deep green of the cedar forest gave way to thick stands of pine, now brilliant white in their snow coverings.

"That's the Blue Mountains!" Hobbs cried.

Instantly David knew he was right. He and several other men had ridden to the base of those mountains last summer. Just to the east of there,

David had found a place where he decided he and his father would start a cattle ranch some day.

"Are you sure?" Sevy blurted.

"He's sure," David answered. "That's them." He half turned. "And look straight out there about twenty miles. Look just beyond where the cedars end. The sun is still a little behind it, so it's hard to see exactly—"

Redd's cry cut him off. "Is that Comb Ridge?"

"Yes!" That came from Morrell, who had never seen it before. But there was no mistaking it. David and Hobbs had told them about it. It was another important landmark to watch for. And now, there it was. It was a long, low ridge that spanned the entire breadth of the landscape below them, maybe fifteen or twenty miles away. But it wasn't a flat ridge or the top of a plateau. Its upper edge was a jagged series of peaks, almost perfectly spaced so they looked exactly like the teeth of some giant comb.

Hobbs was suddenly choked with emotion. "Montezuma Creek is only about twenty miles east of Comb Ridge. Brethren, we've found the way."

Sevy stared out in that direction for a long time before he nodded. "I would suggest that before we descend and return to camp, we kneel in prayer and thank the good Lord for showing us the way. Then we shall get under way as quickly as possible."

"I have one other suggestion," Hobbs said softly. They all turned. "I suggest we call this little mound of dirt and rock 'Salvation Knoll,' for it has certainly proven to be our salvation on this day."[1]

"Amen," Lemuel Redd murmured.

"And a Happy Christmas," David added softly.

Monday, December 29, 1879

"Mama! Mama! Mama!"

Mary Davis gave a low cry, dropped the pan she was scouring out, and darted outside. "Emily! What is it? Where are you?"

Her daughter came flying around the house, hair blowing, legs pumping. She slid to a halt and threw her arms around her mother's skirts. "There's a man hiding in the trees."

"What?" Mary started forward, then stopped. She felt her stomach drop. "Oh, Lord!"

James had taken Eddie and young James with him about a mile upriver to find a place to construct a waterwheel. He wouldn't be back until after noon. She took Emmy's hand and pulled her inside. She grabbed the rifle from above the fireplace, then touched Emmy's cheek. "It will be all right, Emmy. Bar the door behind me." She gave her a gentle shove. "Keep John and baby Ethel quiet if you can."

"Is it Indians, Mama?"

She shook her head, even though that was the first thought that had sprung into her mind. They hadn't seen any Indians thus far, but Peter Shirts,[2] who had come in here two years ago to hunt and trap, traded with both the Utes and the Navajos from time to time. Mary constantly worried about being caught someday when she was alone with the children.

She stepped outside, waited until she heard the bar drop behind her, then gripped the rifle and started around the house. She jumped as a man appeared no more than fifteen feet away from her, walking swiftly toward her. He pulled up short.

"Mary?"

She froze, gaping at him. "David? David, is that you?"

"Good mornin'," he said in a lazy drawl. "You wouldn't happen to have a place where some wand'rin' strangers could sit down and rest their feet awhile, would you?"

After letting Emily nearly smother David with her hugs, and little John climb all over him and tug at his beard, Mary sent Emily off to find her father and her brothers and bring them home as quickly as possible.

As soon as she was gone, Mary plopped the baby on her lap and sat down across the table from him. "Okay," she said, half breathless. "Tell me how far back the rest of the company is."

"You didn't have any food for four days?" Mary was deeply shocked. "No wonder you look so haggard."

"Thanks. We did eat last night with the Harris family."

"Yeah," Lemuel Redd said wryly. "And George Hobbs ate twenty-two of her biscuits."

Mary was aghast. "Twenty-two!"[3]

"Yep," David said. "Said he thought he was going to die, but decided it was well worth it. At least he'd die happy."

"After going without food for four days," Mary replied, "he could have died."

The three men looked at each other. "After four days without food," Bishop Sevy said, "it did seem like we were pretty close to heaven."

There were five of them sitting around the Davis table in front of a crackling fire. The children were all in bed and asleep now. George Hobbs was, of course, staying with his sister, Elizabeth Harriman. The Harrimans had also invited Brother Morrell to stay with them, so it was Brother and Sister Davis, Lemuel Redd, Bishop Sevy, and David. Outside it was raining hard, and it looked like it would continue through most of the next day.

Bishop Sevy spoke up again. "The bigger concern now is getting enough food to get back. It took us twelve days instead of eight to get here. Hopefully we can shorten that on the return, but we can't be sure."

Jim Davis leaned forward. "Wish we could do something for you there. When our crops were washed out last fall, I took a wagon over to Mancos, Colorado. That was a shock. Flour was selling for eighty dollars a hundredweight. I was finally able to buy six bushels of wheat—all they had—and had to pay eleven dollars a bushel at that."

David gave a low whistle. "Now, there's a way to make some quick money."

Jim nodded, quite grim now. "Fortunately, just the other day, Harvey Dunton, who joined us some time back from Colorado, gave Hank Harriman and me some wheat he had. We figure if we are really careful, we may have a sixty-day supply. But from what you say, it's not likely you'll be back by then. So, much as it pains me, I'm afraid we can't spare any-thing."

Redd spoke for all of them. "We wouldn't take it if you offered. We had no idea your crops were lost, or we would never have presumed to replen-ish our supplies here."

"I've already talked to George Hobbs," David said. "Once we get back and get the company on the road, he and I are going to return with some pack mules and bring you wheat and flour."

"You've got your own problems," Jim said. "We'll get by until you re-turn."

David shook his head. "Jim, we'll be lucky to have the road through the Hole done by the end of January. And seeing some of the places we've come through, it could be the first of April before we make it. That's *ninety* days, Jim. If my arithmetic is correct, that leaves you just about a month short." He looked at Mary. "Your children are skinny enough already."

"Thank you," she whispered. And then she brightened. "Can I put in an order?"

"Sure," David said. "What would you like? A piano? A feather mat-tress? Perhaps a new dress with a fancy parasol."

"Salt."

At his surprised look, she explained. "Eating boiled wheat that's been cracked in a coffee grinder gets pretty monotonous, and it has a tendency to give everyone the trots, but a pinch of salt gives it at least some flavor. We ran out of salt several weeks ago."

"Salt we can do," he answered, sobered now. "You have my word on that."

"So what *will* you do for food?" Jim asked.

Sevy and Redd exchanged looks, but Redd answered his question. "I met a trapper with a burro over by the fort this afternoon."

"Peter Shirts?" Mary asked. "With all the beaver skins?"

"That's him. He's headed over into Colorado to trade his pelts, but he was also carrying a sack of flour. Took some hard bargaining and twenty dollars cash, but he finally sold us the sack. It has about forty pounds in it."

"That's not enough," Jim exclaimed.

"It may have to be," Redd broke in. He slapped his stomach, which was already as flat as a griddle. "Besides, we're all getting a little plump of late. Do us good to cut back a little."

Jim Davis got up all of a sudden. "I can't offer you any food, but I can let you take two of my mules. That would give you two more mounts."

"Don't you need them for pulling your wagon or plowing?" David asked.

"We've got two more. That'll be enough." He motioned to them. "Come on, I'll show you. They're a couple of fine animals."[4]

Sevy and Redd stood, but David waved them to go out without him. "I have a question I need to ask Mary," he explained.

He waited until they put on their coats and ponchos and left before he turned to her. "All right, now," he said. "I want an honest answer. How are you doing?"

She sighed. "It's lonesome out here. I guess the biggest disappointment for me is knowing that I have to wait another three months to have some neighbors again. And the food has been a challenge." Then her head came up a little. "But I'm feeling better than I have in probably ten years, David."

"Really?"

"Yes, really." There was a quick, ironic laugh. "Maybe it's all that cracked wheat, but I've got energy—I do all the work and still can play with the children." She touched his arm briefly. "It's wonderful. And what about you, David?" Her eyes were probing his now.

"Well," he said, sobering quickly, "I guess you know you ruined everything for me."

"No," she said in alarm. "How did I do that?"

"That little miracle you put together that day with Yaheeno and Po-ee-kon."

"That I put together? I think it was someone a little higher than me."

"But it was in your behalf. You're the one who got the blessing from Bishop Arthur."

"Yes, I was. So how did all of that ruin you?"

"You left me no choice. I've actually been forced to acknowledge that maybe the Lord does care just a little. First thing you know, I'm gonna have to become a believer." As she laughed delightedly, he grew serious. "We've had some marvelous experiences on this trip, Mary. A couple of real miracles." He told her quickly about the mountain sheep and Salvation Knoll.

"Well, well," she said slowly, her eyes twinkling. "You truly have been corrupted, haven't you." And then suddenly there were tears in her eyes. "That's wonderful, David. Truly wonderful."

"It takes some getting used to," he teased, "but I'm adjusting."

"Does Molly know any of this?" Then she caught herself. "Of course not. That's all happened since you left her." She sat back, watching him thoughtfully, a faraway expression on her face, then finally said, "Something's troubling you."

His surprise showed on his face.

"What is it? Come on, tell Aunt Mary."

He sighed, and this time the weariness showed in his eyes. "I don't know what to think about that whole thing anymore." He quickly told her about the "arrangement" he had made with Molly on his return. "I told Abby about Yaheeno and all of that, but I didn't say anything to Molly. And I'm not sure that I should tell her about these others when I get back. At least not while we're still on the trail. Won't it just create more problems?"

"You mean like making her want to marry you all the more?" she asked dryly.

"Yes. That's it exactly. My father and I were talking about this before I left, and he thinks that out here on the trail isn't the place to work things out between us."

"Your father?" she exclaimed. "I thought he was in England on a mission."

David slapped his forehead. "That's right, you don't know. There's another little miracle for you." And he told her about the black lung and his father's return to Cedar City.

Now the tears spilled over and trickled down her cheeks. "My, my," she breathed. "The Lord has really been knocking you around, hasn't He."

"When your head is harder than a blacksmith's anvil," he said with a sad smile, "I guess it takes more than a nudge to get through to you."

Her eyes were studying him closely now. "So you've told Abby, but not Molly. Interesting." She held up a hand to cut off his response. "And when you got back to Cedar City, you felt compelled to put your relationship on hold. Most men would have tried to push it forward, like President Lunt suggested. Marry them before you go. Does all of this mean you've changed your mind about Molly?"

He was genuinely shocked. "No. I didn't mean it that way."

One eyebrow lifted slowly. "Do you still love her?"

"Of course I do." That came out without the slightest hesitation.

"Wrong question," she said quickly. Her mouth opened as if to ask another, then shut again.

"Go on," he urged. "What's the right question?"

She shook her head, her eyes thoughtful now. Finally she leaned forward, her eyes quite earnest. "I once said that you were devilishly handsome, David, and that if I were ten years younger and didn't love my husband, I would consider marrying you."

"I remember that. Actually," he said, teasing her now, "I didn't care about the ten-year age difference. But the husband was a bit of a problem."

She laughed merrily. "You are such a rogue, David." But then the smile died away. "But as I thought more about what I said later, I decided I was wrong."

"About me being devilishly handsome?"

She ignored that. "You see, David, women like me, we're not looking for handsome and charming and dashing. We're more interested in steady, in strong, in dependable." She smiled softly. "If there's a little charm thrown in there too, all the better. But that's not what makes a strong marriage."

"And maybe the same is true going the other way as well."

"Meaning?"

"Molly is a lovely woman. Really quite beautiful, as you know. But I'm not sure I can make her happy." He grinned. "Not even with all my devilish charm."

"Oh, I have not much question about you being able to make her happy. The bigger question for me is, can you be happy making Molly happy? And, can she be happy making you happy?"

He gave her a quizzical look. "You'd better run that past me one more time."

"Let me ask you some questions first. Do you plan to stay here in San Juan once you get the McKennas settled in safely?"

"I do. My father and I want to start a ranch. Maybe up by the Blue Mountains."

"Does Molly know that?"

"She does. Maybe not the exact location, but, yes, she knows about the ranch."

"And?" she probed softly.

"That's what I mean. I'm not sure she would be happy being a rancher's wife."

"And that's what I meant when I said that I'm not sure she can be happy making you happy. If you decide that the only way she can be truly happy will be in a city or at least a good-sized town, can you be happy giving up your dream of being a rancher?"

He leaned back, considering that. She went on. "Don't get me wrong. I'm not suggesting in any way that this makes Molly flawed somehow. That's just how Molly is. And she's a good girl, David. She'll make a wonderful wife for you. But will she be happy on a ranch? And if she's not, can you be happy keeping her where she is unhappy?"

He looked away, finding the question deeply troubling. "I don't know."

"I think you do, down deep. I think that's why you're so unsettled about this whole thing."

He was nodding. This was exactly why he had been looking forward to talking with Mary again. She understood him in ways that Molly didn't. In fact, in ways that he didn't understand himself. "So do I tell her now, or wait until we get this whole trail thing over with?"

She began to draw little circles on the tabletop with her fingers, deep in thought. Finally, she shook her head. "Not now."

"Why?"

"Well, first of all, I think your father's right. The trail is such an intense experience all by itself, it's not the place to settle things. But more than that, you made a deal with Molly to hold things back until you reached San Juan. And it sounds like she's keeping her part of the bargain. If you suddenly announce in mid-trip that everything's off, it feels like a bit of a betrayal to me."

To his surprise, he felt a great sense of relief. "I agree. It's not fair to her if I change the rules now. It's best to wait."

She stood, looked at him for a moment like she was going to say something more, then moved over to where a blanket hung across a corner of the room, separating the children's sleeping area from the rest of the one-room house. She pulled the blanket back, then stepped inside. All four of the children were asleep on a straw mattress. She bent down and untangled Emily and young Jim from each other, then pulled the blanket up around Emily's neck. Eddie was curled in half a ball, with three-year-old John cuddled within the curl. She brushed a strand of hair back, then touched John's face for a moment. Then she moved to the crib and checked on the baby.

She came back out into the room, stopping to pull the blanket back in place again.

David watched all of this, touched by the love he saw in those simple gestures. "So, one last question?" he said as she sat down across from him again.

"Yes?"

"Where do I find another woman who's looking for steady, strong, and dependable?"

Her look was one of long appraisal before she began to smile. "Oh, David," she laughed. "You still don't know, do you."

Notes

1. The moving account of finding "Salvation Knoll" comes from Hobbs's history (see Miller, *Hole*, 90, 98). In another version, he called it "Xmas Point." Hobbs said that he climbed it alone, then had the others come up and join him. Charles E. Redd, a grandson

of Lemuel Redd, says that all four climbed it together (see Redd, "Short Cut," 16). It was Christmas Day when this occurred.

2. Peter Shirts was a Mormon pioneer from southern Utah who came to the San Juan country in 1877. He was the only known Mormon who was there before the first exploring party arrived. It is said that he had a great love for the history of Mexico, and that he was the one who gave Montezuma Creek its name (see Miller, *Hole*, 25–33).

3. The four scouts arrived at what is now Bluff, Utah, on Sunday, the twenty-eighth of December, after being twelve days on the road, the last four of those without food. A family named Harris had settled in that area since Silas Smith's exploring party had left in August. The four scouts stopped with them overnight before going on to Montezuma Creek where the Harriman and Davis families lived. George Hobbs tells of eating twenty-two of Mrs. Harris's biscuits, much to her astonishment (see *ibid.*, 90).

4. The details of the arrival of the four explorers in Montezuma Creek, the conditions they found there, along with the information on their plans to return back to the Hole in the Rock camp, all come from Hobbs's invaluable account (as cited in *ibid.*, 90–92; and Redd, "Short Cut," 15–18).

CHAPTER 59

Saturday, January 10, 1880

Billy Joe was playing "blaster and blower" with several of his friends. He was John Draper, Yorkshire Tyke. Nate Decker, who was a year older than Billy Joe, was Ben Perkins. They were playing in the rocks above the wagon camp where they had found a narrow crack that somewhat resembled the actual Hole. Both were speaking in a rough imitation of a Yorkshire and Welsh accent.

Nate Decker cupped his hands and bellowed at Billy Joe as if he were a hundred yards away instead of two feet. "Drillers clear?"

"Drillers clear," Billy Joe confirmed.

David Draper stopped behind a small juniper tree, just out of their line of sight. He had come to find Billy Joe, but now he stood transfixed by the little tableau before him.

"Fuse lit?"

Billy Joe dragged a short stick along his pant leg as if it were a match. He carefully held it to something unseen in front of him. "Fuse lit. Fire in the hole!"

"Fire in the hole!" Nate shouted. Both boys dived clear, rolling frantically out of the way.

Just then Hyrum Fielding, another boy about Billy Joe's age, stood up. David hadn't seen him before. He was counting down with his fingers. "Four. Three. Two. One. BOOM!"

He threw a handful of sand against the rock face and a puff of dust billowed outward, looking quite surprisingly like the blast from an explosion.

Then Nate and Billy Joe came bounding back, and they all three did a little dance together.

"Bravo!" David said, stepping out and clapping his hands.

They all jumped, but Billy Joe stiffened in shock. "David?" And then he shot forward like a marble from a slingshot. "Hooray!" he whooped. "The scouts are back. David's back."

———✦———

The family silently watched David as he voraciously emptied a bowl of porridge, using a thick crust of bread as his spoon. He looked up, embarrassed. "Sorry, I was a little hungry."

Sarah McKenna had been studying him as he ate, seeing the hollowness in his cheeks and the gauntness around his eyes. "When was the last time you ate?" she asked.

"About three hours ago, before we crossed the river. The men who were watching for us over there cooked us breakfast. We also ate with them the night before when we found them. I'm afraid we ate everything they had."

"And before that?" Abby asked softly.

He shrugged. "Not sure. Three, maybe four days ago. We were only able to get forty pounds of flour at Montezuma Creek. The two families couldn't help us. Their crops all washed out back last fall."

Molly looked horrified. "No wonder you look like a scarecrow."

David laughed. "Didn't carry a mirror with me, so I hadn't noticed. Probably smell like one, too. I hope there's enough water in that rock tank so that I can take a sponge bath and shave before we report to Brother Lyman and Bishop Nielson."

"Bishop Nielson said the meeting won't be until eleven," Patrick said. "That should give you time." He leaned forward a little. "But you found a way through?" he said. "A way that we can take the wagons?"

"We did," David said with deep satisfaction. "We stumbled around enough trying to do it, but, yes, we did. And we shall so report that. We can move forward with confidence."

"Thanks be to the Lord," Sarah breathed. "We've been so worried about you. We expected you back ten days ago at the latest."

"We imagined every horrible thing," Molly said, her voice low.

"We nearly didn't make it," he said quietly. "If the Lord hadn't intervened, I wouldn't be here talking to you now."

Abby cocked her head and gave him a quizzical look. "So, no more abstract, eh?"

He didn't smile. "Aye."

"Tell us," Molly cried, surprised and delighted.

"You'll hear about it soon enough, I'm sure." Then he looked at Abby. "It wasn't just for me. It was for all of us. And for you back here."

Patrick spoke up. "No more now until Billy Joe comes back with John." He turned to David. "Your father has been sick with worry, as we have."

"I am most anxious to see him again." Then he looked at Sarah. "But while we wait, would you mind if I had another piece of bread?" He picked up a thick slab of cheese. "And where in the world did you get this?"

"From Panguitch and Escalante," Patrick explained. "The Panguitch Ward has been sending stuff from their tithing office—potatoes, salt pork, dried fruit, and an occasional brick of cheese—over the Escalante Mountain on packhorses. Then the Escalante Saints bring it on down to us by wagon, weather permitting."

Sarah broke off another chunk of bread and cut a thick slice of cheese and handed it to him. "Well, bless them all," David said between bites. "This is absolute heaven."

"Carl went with them," Abby said.

David jerked up. "What?"

Patrick was nodding. "The last group brought some mail from Cedar City. We've run into a snag with the sale of the house." He looked at his daughter. "Since Abby has become such an experienced driver now, we decided we could afford to send Carl back with the Panguitch group. He'll go on back to Cedar and see if he can put our affairs in proper order again."

"Well," David said. He was watching Abby out of the corner of his eye. If she was troubled by that turn of events, she was hiding it well. "That's a surprise," he finally said.

"Not really," Molly said, somewhat wistfully. "He was trying hard not to show how relieved he was. He told me that he's really a city boy at heart."

"But," Sarah added, "we kept the number in the camp the same. Anna Decker had her baby."

That brought a broad smile to David's face. "So Jim's a new papa. What was it?"

"A baby girl. Born a week ago today. They're going to call her Lena Deseret."

"And both are fine?" David asked.

They nodded at that. Then Sarah straightened, lifting a hand to point. "Here they come." They turned to see two figures—one small, one large—coming toward them at a dead run.

David set the bread and cheese down on a rock, leaped up, and ran out to meet them. As his father swept him up in a crushing bear hug, swinging him around and around, David finally managed to gasp, "Save me, somebody! I can't breathe."

They sat around him in a half circle, enjoying the warmth of the sun on their backs and the joy of having David back with them. He gave them a pretty thorough account of the scouts' experience, leaving out only the part about his own personal prayers to the Lord.

"You really went four days with no food?" Billy Joe said, when David finished the story of George Hobbs eating twenty-two biscuits. He fell quiet as he remembered the solemnity and the joy that first night they arrived at the Harris place.

But, after a moment, he smiled. "Actually, there were several places I thought about you, Billy Joe. Here's one thing I wish you all could have seen, but Billy especially. I told you a little bit about finding what we called Slickrock Hill going out." As they nodded, he added, "Unfortunately, on the way back, when we reached that same place, we found the road was covered with snow and ice. There was no way we could take the animals up that, so we decided we would try to climb up, maybe chip away the ice enough to make a trail."

Remembering brought a smile to David's lips. "But it was so slippery, we kept falling and sliding back down a few feet. Most of us gave up. We decided we'd wait for the sun to hit it and see if that helped. But George Hobbs is pretty stubborn, so he and Bishop Sevy kept trying. We just lay on the ground at the bottom, laughing and hollering as they tried to claw their way up the rock."

At the shocked look on their faces, he sobered. "Remember, by this time we'd been without food again for a couple of days. We were light-headed and faint, and I think we were a bit delirious with hunger. But at the time, we thought it was a riot."

"An' did they mek it?" his father asked.

"They made their way up about two-thirds of the way to the top, where the sun reached the rock. The snow had started to melt, making the slickrock very treacherous. They were up far enough that they were out of our sight by then, but we heard Bishop Sevy yell, 'Watch out, George. You're gonna fall.'"

Now David laughed aloud. "And he did."

Abby frowned. "And you thought that was funny?"

"He didn't fall off a cliff," David quickly explained. "He just slipped and fell on his backside. But the hillside was so steep and icy, it was like he had fallen into a toboggan. We heard him yelling and looked up. All of a sudden, there he came, shooting around a corner, hands out to steady himself, spraying snow out on both sides of him, yelling like a banshee.

"As I think back on it, he was lucky. He probably slid close to a quarter of a mile.[1] And I mean, he was moving. But at the time it seemed hilarious, and about then, we were looking for anything to cheer us up."

"So he wasn't hurt?" Patrick asked.

"Just his pride," David grinned. "He didn't appreciate us having a laugh at his expense."

"So how did you get up the hill?" his father wondered.

"Well, George is so stubborn, he turned right around and started climbing back up. By that time, the sun had started to soften the snow enough that it could be shaped. So we made a dugway in the snow with our hands. By morning it had frozen solid enough to take the animals up without any serious problems."

Billy Joe drank it all in. "I hope there's snow when we get there. That would be so great."

"Don't even think it," Sarah said, ruffling his hair.

David's voice went soft as he told them about Christmas Day on Elk Ridge and how George had spotted the little knoll, and the view that awaited them when they climbed it.

"What a wonderful Christmas present," Abby murmured when he finished. She was clearly very moved by his account.

"It makes me shudder to think how close you came to dying," Molly said.

But it was Sarah's words that startled David the most. She sniffed back the tears, then came to him and put her arms around him. "If your mother was here right now," she whispered, "she would put her arms around you and weep for joy."

David's head came up with that, as did his father's. It was an astonishing thing for her to say. John turned to his son, nodding. "She be reet, David. She be absolutely reet."[2]

"Dad. Are you still awake?"

"Aye, Son."

David turned on his side to face him. With the weather threatening rain again, and Carl Bradford gone, they were sleeping in one of the wagons now. David had waited until he could hear no further sounds from the rest of the family.

"I . . ." David drew in a quick breath. "I didn't tell the family everything today."

"Ah wundered," came the soft answer. "Ya seemed ta be 'oldin' back a little."

"I prayed out there, Dad."

There was a long silence, then a very soft, "That be gud, Son."

"And in both cases the answer came almost within minutes."

"Aye. That be 'ow the Lord works sumtimes."

"I just wanted you to know that, Dad."

"Tank ya, David." There was another pause. "But ya dunna want the fam'ly ta know?"

"It's not a secret," David said. "It's just that . . ." He sighed. "I'm afraid it will only complicate things with Molly."

"Ah see." That came out very slowly.

So David, speaking in a low voice so as not to awaken the others, told his father about his conversations with Sister Davis. When he finished, his father said nothing, and for a moment David wondered if he had fallen asleep during the narration. "Do you agree with her, Dad?"

"Aboot what? Ya not talkin' ta Molly yet aboot yur little miracles, or that Molly maybe naw be the reet one fur ya?"

"The latter."

"Aye."

David came up on one elbow, peering at him in the dark. "That's all? Just aye?"

"Aye."

"You don't think I should marry Molly?"

"That be naw yur question. Yur question was, do Ah think Molly naw be the one fur ya?"

"What's the difference?"

"Ah think if ya were ta marry Miss Molly, it be a gud marriage. Better than most. But if'n yur askin' if Ah think she be the best one fur ya, the answer is no."

David was dumbfounded. "Why didn't you ever say that before?"

"B'cuz ya never asked befur." There was a soft chuckle. "An' Ah dinna want ya boxin' me lugholes fur buttin' inta yur life."

David lay back, marveling.

"The question be, are ya goin' ta tell her yur thinkin' of changin' yur mind aboot the 'ole thing. And if so, when ya gonna do it?"

The familiar pain returned to David's stomach. "I don't know, Dad. I don't want to hurt her. Heaven knows I've done that enough already. I still love her a great deal, but . . ."

"Ah unnerstand. Be ya askin' fur an opinion?"

"Aye," David said quietly.

"Ah think Sister Mary Davis be a very wise woman, an' Ah wud tek her advice. Ah doon't think it be a gud idee ta 'ave this great talk with Molly until the trek be over. As fur brekin' 'er 'eart, Ah think that be worthy of another prayer to the Lord. She be 'Is daughter, an' maybe 'E can ease the way fur ya sum."

David reached out and laid his hand on his father's arm. "Tank ya, Dahd," he said softly. "Ah luv ya, ya ole Tyke."

Notes

1. The story of George Hobbs's "toboggan ride" down Slickrock Hill comes from his account of the four-man scouting party, as do the other details of this narrative (see Miller, *Hole*, 89–95).

2. Though Kumen Jones was not one of the four scouts, his summary of the significance of their experience for the entire expedition sums it up as well as any source I found:

"The exploring trip of those four men will always be remembered by all those who were acquainted with it, and more especially by those who took part in it, as one of the hardest and most trying in the way of perserverance [sic] and persistent endurance of any undertaking connected with the San Juan Mission. It was one, also, in which the participants must have had the assistance of our Heavenly Father. It has been a source of wonder to all those who since those early days have become acquainted with the country through which these explorers had traveled. How they ever found their way through deep snow and blinding snow storms in such a broken timbered country, all cut to pieces with deep gorges, for such a long distance, without compass, trail, and most of the time no sun, moon, or stars to help them in keeping their course is a mystery. The only answer is that a kind providence came to their assistance in answer to their humble fervent prayers" (as cited in *ibid.*, 183).

CHAPTER 60

Sunday, January 11, 1880

The main camp at the Hole in the Rock had been set up in a large area about a hundred yards from the Hole where the ground was relatively flat and there were no rock escarpments. This helped keep the children away from the construction area, and everyone from the blasting site.

As David and John Draper left camp and started toward the great cleft in the cliff, they passed the place where the two blacksmiths had set up their forges, and then where the tools and other equipment were stored. David's father talked nonstop. David had asked for a tour of the road project, and a tour he was going to get.

"Cap'n Lyman, he be dividin' the work on the 'Ole inta three major projects. The biggest one be cuttin' a road through that ridge ya see joost a'ead of us."

"The one that ends in that sheer drop of about fifty or sixty feet?"

There was a boyish grin. "Naw anymore it doon't. That be what we been tekin' out now fur two weeks or more. Ya be seein' that in a minute. The second task be tekin' the road on doon through the rest of the 'Ole. The third be buildin' a road from the bottom of the 'Ole where it spreads out into foothills on doon ta the riverbank."

"What about the ferry?"

"Ah, that be a sep'rate project. Brother Charles Hall frum Escalante be in charge of that, not us road builders. 'E's supposed ta be arrivin' wit the lumber fur it any time noow."

As they came over a little rise in the ground, David suddenly stopped, staring. What had been a smooth expanse of white sandstone escarpment blocking the whole approach to the Hole now had a deep notch cut into it. "My word," David said. "I had no idea you were going to have to do that."

"Cahrn't do anythin' but," John grunted, pleased that David appreciated what he was seeing. "If'n we joost blast away at that cliff face, still be too steep fur wagons ta negotiate. So, we 'ad ta start the road back 'ere a bit." He squinted in the sunshine. "Still ain't got it doon ta grade yet, but it be comin'. As ya can see, this be still too mooch pitch. Cap'n Lyman, 'e be wantin' ta get the grade through 'ere ta whare it drops no more than eight feet per rod."

David whistled. "That's still pretty steep."

"Yep. Farther doon, it be more like five and a half feet per rod." He grinned. "But hey, that be the 'Ole. She be like a seam of coal. She 'as a mind of 'er own and she be a demandin' mistress. We either mek peace wit 'er, or she be tossin' us off the moontain."

When they reached what had been the first cliff face, David could not believe his eyes. The fifty-foot drop was gone and a road just big enough to accommodate a wagon had replaced it. Like his father said, it was still steep enough to make any teamster draw in a quick breath, but the cliff was gone.

"This is incredible, Dad. You've done a tremendous amount of work."

"Hy Perkins be the foreman on this crew. Ah started as a blaster 'ere, but noow Ah be workin' with Ben on the second part doon below. We cudda done more, if we 'ad more powder. We've used all we brought wit us. A little keeps dribblin' in frum Panguitch and Escalante, but naw nearly e'nuff."

"No word from Silas, then?" David asked.

"Naw anythin' official. Them pack trains comin' over frum Panguitch, they keep tantalizin' us wit news frum the ootside. Thare supposed ta be a keg of twenty-five poonds of powder on its way noow, but cahrn't say we've seen it yet. The latest rumor be that Cap'n Smith got a five thousand dollar appropriation frum the Legislature."

"Wonderful!" David exclaimed.

"Only if it be true," he growled. Then he brightened a little. "But sum men frum Panguitch tole Bishop Schow in Escalante that the Church 'as shipped 'alf a ton of black powder, an' that much again in steel—picks, crowbars, drill bits, and so on. The men said when they got back ta Panguitch, they be puttin' t'gether anuther pack train ta bring it awl over the moontain. If'n that be true, 'twill be a blessin' indeed."

"I would think so," David said. "A thousand pounds."

"If'n that not be so," his father said, turning to look down the steep slope below them, "then we naw be gittin' that notch any wider. Cahrn't do it with picks alone."

David turned to look where he was pointing. What had once been a slot barely wide enough for a man to squeeze through was now three times wider. But it was still not quite enough to let a wagon through.

His father waved a hand and they started down toward the slot. "This be the second major project Ah tole ya aboot," he said. He turned sideways and stepped through the notch. David followed, and once again found himself gaping in amazement at the vista below them. The grade was not as steep as what they had just come down, but it was still breathtaking. They were still at least a thousand feet above the river, but the boulders as big as a wagon or pits deep enough to swallow a team of horses were gone now. The fill from the cuts above now filled the gap and provided a smooth, though steep, roadway.

David turned and looked back at the narrow crack they had just slipped through. "But this is where you're working now?"

His father nodded and tipped his head back. "Thare be me office."

David looked up, not sure what he was looking at, then leaned back even farther. Then he gasped. "That barrel hanging up there?" About a hundred feet above them, what looked like half of a large cider barrel swayed gently back and forth in a light breeze. Four ropes were fastened through eyelets in the rim of the barrel, then came together about ten feet above the barrel to form a single braided line of the four ropes. That was hooked to a block and tackle, which was attached to the end of what looked like the boom of a hay derrick perched at the very top edge of the cliff.

"In a cut like this, ya cahrn't be startin' from the bottom, boy. We be blastin' oot that notch frum the top doon."

"Ya cahrn't—you can't be serious, Dad. You really work from that bucket?"

"Ah do. 'Ow else ya think we be gittin' that cliff face off? They lower me doon an' Ah use a six-poond hammer an' steel drill bits ta punch a 'ole inta the rock. Got me aboot fifty of 'em awreddy done, just waitin' till we git some more black powder."

David stared upward, feeling his stomach twist as he pictured himself hanging there swinging a six-pound hammer.

"Ya think this is bad?" his father snorted. "When we first started, Ah be sittin' on a short length of plank wit a rope tied 'roond me waist an' legs. Noow that be e'nuff ta put 'air on yur chest. But we had ta quit that. Pullin' those ropes up and down over this rough sandstone was like rubbing 'em back and forth across the blade of a knife. Got so nobuddy felt lek trustin' their lives ta a frayed rope. So Platte an' some brethren devised this 'half barrel' approach instead. Works lek a charm."

"Ha!" David said. "I'll gladly go another four days without food before I let you put me in one of those."

His father clapped him on the shoulder. "That be awl reet," he drawled. "This be work fur real men, not boys oot playin' scoutin' games." Then, before David could retort, he turned and started down the steep slope, leaving deep gashes in the sand and dirt with his boots. "Cum on," he called. "Wanna show ya what we be callin' Uncle Ben's Dugway."

Going down that next five hundred feet or so took it out of David. Though he had now had four or five good meals, his body was still feeling the effects of prolonged starvation. And the angle was such that they had to stiff-leg it most of the way down. Farther down, the cleft still needed a lot of fill, and clambering over the large boulders and in and out of the pits didn't help. By the time his father stopped, David was puffing pretty badly, and his legs felt like they were going to melt on him.

His father was standing at the edge of another sheer drop-off. But here, the great gash in the cliff face started to widen out, and the ground directly below the cliff was no longer solid rock but steep hillsides of dirt, rock, and shale that had eroded from the cliffs over the millennia. The drop-offs were very steep right beneath them, but began to smooth out farther down until they leveled out and met the river.

"As ya can see," his father said, moving back to join him. "This 'ere drop be as bad as the one up top. In fact, one of the Decker boys coined a phrase fur it. He calls it 'slantindicular.'[1] Problem is, we dunna 'ave e'nuff powder ta tek this an' the one above both doon. An' we be needin' powder fur the east side, too."

"So?" David said. "How does Ben plan to get around this?"

His father grinned happily. "Thought ya'd never ask. Cum on. This be sumthin' ta see."

Turning hard to the left, his father set out. Now they were going laterally across one of those steep, rock-strewn hillsides that dropped off so sharply. For a moment, David thought his dad was pulling a joke on him because directly ahead of them the hill gave way to a solid expanse of sheer red rock. David could see that it was actually the base of the cliff that went straight up above their heads for nearly a thousand feet. But here, the rock was no longer completely vertical. It was still steep, slanting outward at perhaps a forty-five degree angle, but not completely sheer. The stretch of red rock was somewhere between fifty and seventy-five feet across and the drop-off below it close to fifty feet high.

As David looked at it, he could see no way across it—not for a wagon, not for a man on horseback. Even a man on foot would be at risk if he crossed that without an anchor rope.

He turned to look at his father. "Surely this can't be where you're thinking of taking the road."

Then he saw something that brought him up short. Just ahead, where the rock face actually began, he saw a line of holes drilled vertically into the sandstone. They were maybe three or four inches in diameter, ten to twelve inches deep, and spaced about three feet apart. They formed a line that gradually sloped downward as they followed the drop of the cliff face. "Are those blasting holes, Dad?"

"Naw," came the answer. "They be way too big fur blastin' 'oles."

"Then what are they for?"

John laughed softly. "These provide the base fur Uncle Ben's Dugway."

David moved forward some more, careful where he was placing his feet. He was still puzzled by the line of holes, but his eye had caught sight of something else. Just ahead of where they stood, someone had chiseled a narrow shelf, no more than a foot wide, that paralleled the line of holes, but several inches higher on the rock face.

"Okay, I see where he's started the road." His mind was working hard. "So this so-called dugway of Ben's is going to have to be cut into the side of the cliff?"

His father shook his head slowly, his eyes dancing. "Nope. Cum on, boy, use yur 'ead. That cut ya be lookin' at isn't the beginnin' of a road. In fact, it be awl done noow."

"But . . ." David turned back, studying the cut more carefully. Then his eyes widened. "It's just wide enough to hold the left set of wagon wheels," he murmured, half to himself. He turned and looked at the holes again, squinting a bit as he peered at them. Then suddenly his eyes flew wide open. "Oh my word!" he exclaimed.

"So ya git it noow, do ya?"

David's jaw had gone slack as his eyes darted back and forth between the holes and the narrow shelf. "He's going to tack a road right onto the cliff."

"Aye," John said. "We be drivin' large oak pegs in them 'oles to provide sumthin' ta 'old ev'rythin' in place. Then we be formin' the road base by layin' longer logs at right angles ta the pegs, lettin' the pegs 'old them in place."

"And then you simply fill in the base with brush, then bring in dirt and gravel on top of that until you have a road wide enough and strong enough to carry a loaded wagon."

"And teams," his father added. "That be it, me boy. Brilliant, eh?"

David let his eyes run along the whole length of the cliff, trying to picture how it would work. "Absolutely astonishing. If you can't blast one out, just tack a road onto the mountainside."

His father slapped David on the shoulder. "Ben prefers ta think of it more like nailin' a shelf against a wall, but it be the same principle." He turned abruptly and started back the way they had come. "Cum. Ah'll show you how 'e plans ta do it."[2]

Thursday, January 22, 1880

David paused momentarily as he and his father and several others approached the top of the Hole where the narrow road had now been cut through solid rock. It was late afternoon, and their work was ended for the day. To his surprise, as he looked up toward the top, he saw Molly standing off to one side. Seeing that they had seen her, she waved. David waved back.

"Noow thare be a breath of sunshine on a foggy day," John said, waving too. "An' that smile of 'ers be e'nuff to melt solid rock into mud puddles."

David gave him a sidewards glance. "Are you trying to tell me something?" he asked.

He laughed and shook his head. "Naw. Ah joost be thinkin' she gonna be quite the catch fur the reet man."

"But not me."

John laughed again, then broke into a trot, leaving David behind, taking the grade as easily as if he were passing over an anthill. As he passed by Molly, he sang out, "G'd aft'noon ta ya, Molly gurl. Ya be a reet pleasin' sight fur weary eyes." And leaving her laughing and pleased, he trotted on.

When David reached the top, he moved over to stand beside her. "This is a nice surprise. Is everything all right?"

"Better than all right. Two men arrived from Kanosh today. They brought that keg of black powder Silas Smith promised was coming." Then she withdrew an envelope from her apron pocket and waved it at him. "They also brought some mail."

"Anything interesting?"

She handed him the envelope and let him read the return address. His eyebrows lifted slightly. "So Carl made it back to Cedar City all right. That's good."

"He wrote Daddy to say that he has worked out the situation on the sale of our home."

He examined the envelope again, then gave her a quizzical look. "This is addressed to you."

She snatched it from him and put it back in her pocket. "It's not what you think. He just wrote to tell me how things were back home."

"Did he write to Abby, too?"

"Will you stop it?" she laughed. "You make it sound sinister." Then her smile faded. "The men also brought some bad news about Silas Smith."

"Oh?"

"He's taken seriously ill. He won't be returning anytime soon."

David's shoulders slumped. That *was* bad news. His leadership had been a powerful influence in this undertaking and for David personally as well. "Any idea what it is?"

She shook her head. "They didn't say."

She turned and glanced at the sun, now low in the sky. "Mama will have supper on soon. We'd better start." But when she began walking, it was very slowly. David fell in beside her. Sensing she wanted to talk, he said nothing.

"David?"

"Yes?"

"How long do you think it will take us to get to Montezuma Creek?"

That took him aback a little. "I . . . we told Jim and Mary Davis not to look for us much before the first part of April."

"Two more months!" She looked stricken.

"If not more."

"So instead of six weeks, like they told us, the trip is going to take six months."

"Yes, very likely."

She said nothing. Her step slowed even more.

"Are you thinking of going back to Cedar?" he asked quietly.

She stiffened. "Why do you ask that?"

Knowing he had just stepped out onto thin ice, he chose his words carefully. "I don't know. As you spoke about Carl being home I thought I heard just a touch of envy in your voice."

"Well, I'm not," she snapped. "You think I would just leave my family?"

"I was just asking," he said quickly. "I wasn't assuming anything."

"Yes, you were," she pouted.

"Molly, I was just asking."

She was in a huff now. "You think of me as some little cute powder puff, ready to blow away with the first breeze of adversity."

He laughed easily. "I can honestly say, I have never thought of you as a powder puff. Look, Molly, you're out here, aren't you? You've stuck it out for over three months, making the best of things. That's hardly a powder puff. I can't picture you being blown away by anything."

"You'd better do some fast talking, mister," she growled.

"Molly, you've got more than your fair share of stickity tootie, as Bishop Nielson calls it."

She waved the envelope at him. "Carl asked me if I want to come back. If I say yes, he'll make the arrangements."

David blinked. "Arrangements?"

"Yes. He said he'll give me a room in the hotel for as long as I want it." She smiled briefly. "Says he needs a good postal clerk."

"But . . . ?" Then his eyes narrowed. "Did he ask you to marry him?"

She visibly started. *"No!"*

"Is that what he's got on his mind?"

She started to shake her head, but couldn't. She had asked herself that same question. "He may be hoping that down the road . . ." She shrugged.

"Well, well," he said, not sure exactly how to respond to that. "You can't fault him for his good taste."

"Oh, for heaven's sake, David, I would never marry Carl Bradford. He's more like a big brother than a beau." When he only grunted, she hurried on. "But I don't want to go back. I am not envious, as you suppose. I will see this through. I would never leave my family until I knew they were safely in San Juan."

She stopped, startled by the realization that she had used the word *until*. Why had she said that? And had David picked up on it?

But if he had, he gave no sign. "I know that, Molly. I've never thought otherwise."

"There's another reason I can't leave," she said after a moment.

"What's that?"

"Did you see me talking to the young Decker girls after worship services last Sunday?"

Surprised by that sudden turn, he slowly nodded. "Yes."

"Know what they were asking me? They wanted to know if I was going to marry you."

That wasn't what he expected. "And what did you tell them?"

"I told them that we had no agreement. We would have to wait and see what happened. Know what they said next?"

He shook his head.

"They said that if we didn't marry, would I please ask you to wait long enough for them to grow up so you could marry one of them."

She laughed as he colored deeply. "You never told me that," he said.

"Well, the point is, David Draper, with that kind of competition— young, cute, giggly—I can't just walk away and leave the field. So there."

He laughed a little awkwardly, not quite sure how to respond to that.

She gave him a little shove. "Mama is waiting supper. Why don't you go on and wash up." She turned to the west. "It's going to be a beautiful sunset. I'll be along shortly."

As he walked away, she couldn't bear to watch him. She turned her face to the west, barely seeing the spectacular oranges and reds that had transformed the high, thin clouds over Fifty Mile Mountain. And then the tears came.

Finally, when she was sure that David had reached the camp and could no longer see her, she took a handkerchief from her pocket and wiped her eyes. "You are such a liar, Molly Jean McKenna," she said in a fierce whisper. "Such a shameless liar."

Then her eyes raised upward. *Why?* The cry rose up from somewhere deep inside her. *Why, when we finally resolve our differences, are we farther apart than ever before?*

Then her Irish heritage kicked in, and the grit for which the McKennas were known rose to the surface. She tossed her head angrily, wiped the tears away with two hard swipes of the handkerchief, and shoved it back into her apron pocket. She took out Carl's letter and tore it into tiny shreds, then threw it to the wind. "You have two months, Molly Jean McKenna," she told herself sternly. "Two months to get this longing for home out of your heart. Two months to become the woman that David Draper is looking for." She sniffed back the tears. "So stop your bawling or he *will* end up marrying one of those darling little Decker girls."

Notes

1. In his biography of Jens Nielson, Carpenter gives credit for the word *slantindicular* to Nathaniel Decker, one of the married sons in the extended Decker family (*Jens Nielson*, 47).

2. Any person who has stood either at the base or near the top of the Hole in the Rock and taken in its awesome and rugged majesty finds it almost inconceivable to believe that the pioneers, with nothing but black powder and hand tools, built a wagon road down the entire length of the notch. Words like *heroic, bold, resolute, intrepid, indomitable,* and *undaunted* all come to mind in an attempt to describe the men and women, but all fall short of adequately describing the enormity of their accomplishment.

The details of the construction of a wagon road down through the Hole in the Rock—including the three stages of the work, the number of workers, the tools and equipment used, and the support from outside sources—come from original sources and represent the situation as described therein (see Miller, *Hole*, 100–108, 117; Redd, "Short Cut," 10, 12, 14–15; Reay, *Incredible Passage*, 45–48; "Life Sketch of Mary Jane Wilson," 12).

In what was a series of astonishing and remarkable feats, perhaps the most remarkable and astonishing of all was the building of "Uncle Ben's Dugway." Once again, Miller's description provides one of the best accounts of this incredible feat of amateur engineering.

"At the bottom of the notch, about a third of the total distance to the river, was another sheer drop of approximately fifty feet. This had to be blasted away or otherwise disposed of. Well aware of the shortage of blasting powder and of the difficulty being experienced at the top of the Hole, Benjamin Perkins conceived the idea of avoiding this second sheer drop by tacking a road on to the face of the cliff and thus building a by-pass around that fifty-foot chasm. At this point the notch widens out into a sort of canyon, affording enough room for this type of construction.

"For a distance of some fifty feet along the face of this solid rock wall men were instructed to chisel and pick out a shelf wide enough to accommodate the inside wheels of the wagons. Perkins declared that he would now build the face of the cliff up so that the outside wheels would be level with the inside ones. To accomplish this he instructed the blacksmith to widen the blades of the drills to two-and-a-half inches; then with these tools men were instructed to drill a line of holes, each ten inches deep and about a foot-and-a-half apart, parallel with the shelf that had been chiseled out, and about five feet below it. [Redd says these holes were four feet apart. There are only a few holes still visible today, and these are about three to four feet apart.] Perkins is said to have marked the spot for each hole. At that point the cliff falls off at about a 50 degree angle, so that while they swung the sledges the workmen had to be held in place with ropes secured by their fellows.

"In the meantime men had been sent to scour the river bank and adjacent areas as far back as the Kaiparowits Plateau for oak that could be cut into stakes. When the row of holes was completed, approximately twenty-five feet along the face of the cliff, these stakes, each two feet in length [i.e., two feet above the rock face], were driven firmly into the holes. On top of the stakes poles were secured to the ledge and brush, rock and gravel added until the face of the cliff had actually been lifted and a wagon road literally tacked on. This is one of the most remarkable portions of the whole road. It is rightly named 'Uncle Ben's Dugway' in honor of its engineer. Although the stakes have long since vanished, allowing the poles, brush, and gravel to slip into the canyons below, the drilled holes are still clearly visible and some of the masonry rock work is still in place" (Miller, *Hole*, 105–6).

For modern readers who visit the Hole and try to picture how the road actually looked back then, Miller adds this reminder:

"Most of [the] artificial fill has been eroded away, leaving the bottom of the notch very rough and rugged, much as it must have been before the pioneers began to work on it. Still to be seen, however, are some of the points of jagged rock cliffs picked off to allow the wagon hubs to scrape by, and some of these points are twenty feet above the present floor of the gorge. There are also names of some of the pioneers chiseled in the face of the crevice wall at least twenty feet above the present floor. Nearby are deep scratches, where wagon hubs scarred the wall in 1880 and 1881. . . . One massive block tumbled into the crevice early in 1956, almost completely blocking the upper part of the notch" (*ibid.*, 107).

It should be noted that Miller's book was first published in 1959. In the nearly forty years since that time, further erosion has changed the Hole in the Rock even more, including having an effect on what can be seen on the walls of the crevice.

CHAPTER 61

Monday, January 26, 1880

"All right," Platte Lyman hollered, "I know you're all excited, but let's have your attention for a few moments, then we'll get this show on the road."

He was standing on the back tailgate of his wagon. The entire company of the Hole in the Rock camp stood around him. There was definitely great excitement in the air. Finally, the day had come. The road down to the river was complete. Before this day was out, if all went as planned, the camp would be empty and about three dozen wagons would be on the east side of the Colorado River. They had been waiting for this day now for over a month.

He waited until they were quiet, then, still speaking loudly so all could hear, went on. "As you know, when we first started on this mission, the plan was to take a southern route to bypass the Colorado River gorge. Well, that didn't work. There wasn't enough water, it was too long, and we had some rather hostile natives who didn't want us coming through their land. So we came this way instead. Which was a good idea, except for one thing. We had the Colorado River gorge blocking our way—fifteen hundred feet of sheer cliffs and no way through it."

He grinned broadly. "But now, thanks to Ben Perkins and the other boys, we've busted that gorge open and made a wagon road straight down the face of it. And today, we're ready to start sending wagons down that road and across the river."

He took a breath, then went on quickly. "We plan to take all of the outfits from our camp down today. That's about forty wagons. I'm sure that will take us all day. Tomorrow, the camp at Fifty Mile Springs will move up here. Weather permitting, they'll follow us down as quickly as possible. So, as soon as you reach the bottom of the cleft, just follow the road down to the ferry. Brother Hall and his boys will be waiting to take you across the river. Once on the other side, continue on to what we are calling Cottonwood Camp. You'll find it to be a delightful change from the barrenness of our camp here. But please note, the ferry can take only two wagons at a time, and the round trip over and back takes roughly half an hour, if you count loading and unloading. So it is not likely that we can get all the wagons across today. Some of you later ones may have to camp on this side of the river tonight."

He paused, waiting for questions, but hardly anyone even moved. "Many of you have taken the opportunity to walk down our new road, so you know that the first hundred and fifty or two hundred feet are pretty steep, about a forty-five or fifty percent grade, what Nate Decker calls 'slantindicular.'" A slow smile stole across his face. "For any of you ladies who didn't get a chance to curl your hair this morning, don't worry about it. This will do it for you."

That won him a chuckle of appreciation and not a few rather anxious looks.

"The best part of that is that most of that stretch is narrow enough that you can't overturn your wagons. In some ways, it's going to be like a log going down a three- or four-story log flume. The rest of the crevasse is pretty steep too, but nothing like that initial chute."

"So," Joe Nielson called out, "could you say we're about to 'shoot the chute'?"

"That's a good description, Brother Joe." He paused for effect. "Not very comforting, but a good description." He looked around at what was rapidly becoming a very sober group. "Women and children and those not needed as drivers should walk down to the bottom. Mothers, stay with the smaller children. It's precipitous and rough and we don't want someone tripping and falling off the mountain." The last was said with a sardonic smile.

"I'm not walking," Molly whispered.

Abby turned in surprise. "Why not?"

"Because if I walk, I have to keep my eyes open."

"A word of caution for all drivers," Platte was saying. "If you haven't yet seen what we are calling Uncle Ben's Dugway, you will marvel at that remarkable engineering feat. Thank you, Ben. Only a stubborn old Welshman would simply hang a road on the side of a cliff."

There were cheers and a few whistles and many hats were lifted and waved back and forth as Ben lifted a hand in acknowledgment.

"Drivers, don't be going fast across the dugway. Remember, it is a dirt road hanging in midair. It wasn't designed to take a pounding. Once past that, the rest of the road down is easy."

Jens Nielson stepped forward. "Brodders and sisters, be shure you do not bunch up too close to each odder. Vee cannot be runnink into vun another."

"That's right," Platte said. "The plan is to rough-lock the hind wheels on all wagons and keep them locked all the way down to the dugway. If we only cross-lock the wheels on this grade, they might break loose.* In addition, we'll tie a couple of ropes on the back of each wagon and put about ten men on each rope to help hold the wagon back as you take that first pitch. The biggest challenge will be to not overrun the teams with the wagons."

Their captain stopped and nodded at a man whose hand was up. David saw that it was Stanford Smith from Cedar City, a man the McKennas knew well. "What about using our animals to help hold the

---

* There were two ways to lock the rear wheels of a wagon when going down a steep incline. In cross-locking, the two rear wheels were prevented from turning by placing a sturdy post between the spokes of both wheels, or using a chain to lock each wheel individually to stop them from turning. Rough-locking was developed by freighters and teamsters over the years to handle the worst possible grades with full loads. In this case, short lengths of heavy logging chains were wrapped around the tire and felloe where the wheel made contact with the ground. (The felloe is the inside of the circular rim of the wheel where the spokes are attached.) The chains were then attached to heavy brackets attached to the wagon box. This locked the wheels so that the chains, rather than the tires, made contact with the ground. This provided much better braking than a cross-lock (see Miller, *Hole*, 110).

wagons back?" he asked. "As you know, I've got big Nig. He's old and tired, but he's half as big as a house."

"Twice as big as *our* house," a woman's voice called. That broke the tension, and there were titters and snickers all around. David saw that Arabella Smith, or Belle, as everyone called her, was standing beside her husband. She had a six-month-old baby in her arms and two small children clinging to her skirts. She was a wisp of a woman, but with more spunk than any two women in the company, according to Sarah.

"You can try it," Platte answered with a chuckle. "Every bit will help." He turned back to the crowd. "Don't worry about your loose stock. Once the camp from Fifty Mile is down, the drovers will bring everything down and across the river. Which brings us to our final question. Whose wagon will be the first down? Bishop Nielson and I recommend that Ben Perkins be given that privilege. In a way, this is his road. We feel he ought to lead the way."

There were instantly cries of approval and support. David's father cupped his hands to his mouth. "'E sure e'nuff made the rock an' dirt fly these past weeks."

"All in agreement?" Platte called.

Hands shot up everywhere. This man was not only greatly respected for his work on the road but beloved for his quick sense of humor, his ability to dance the shoes off of anyone in the company, and his never-failing cheerfulness. "Any who disagree?"

As one hand came up, there was another ripple of laughter. The hand belonged to Ben Perkins. "Ah wud lek ta put forth the name of me brother Hyrum ta go first," he said.

"Sorry," Platte said. "Get your outfit up here, Brother Perkins. You will lead the way."

Ben moved up to stand beside the captain. He whispered something to him, and when Platte nodded, Ben turned to the crowd. "Ah be 'onored ta go first. But as ye awl know, Ah be a blower and a blaster, not a teamster. So Ah've asked Brother Kumen Jones ta drive me wagon down this wee 'ill. An' he be usin' 'is team. Mine be a little skittish."[1]

"Now, there's a wise choice," David murmured, as Kumen waved a hand.

As people began to stir, their captain raised his hand once more, and they quickly quieted.

"Brethren and sisters, this is the day we have been waiting for. We are moving on at last. We have asked for the Lord's help in our morning prayer service this morning, but I would suggest another prayer at this point is in order. I've asked Bishop Nielson if he would offer that."

Hats came off, heads bowed, eyes closed. As the sonorous voice with its rich Danish accent echoed softly off the cliffs, every heart added a silent, fervent prayer of its own.

By the time the McKennas pulled their four outfits into line, they were about halfway back. On David's signal, they got down and the whole family came together near the second wagon. Patrick laid a hand on Billy Joe's shoulder, but spoke to all of his family. "David and John and I will be helping with the ropes, holding the first wagons back. The teams will be fine here long enough for you to go up and watch the first wagon go down. After that, you'd better come back here and stay with the teams. All right?"

They each nodded. The earlier excitement had now given way to a deep somberness.

"We're going to be kept pretty busy," he went on, "but you'll know when it's your turn to bring the wagons forward to the chaining area."

David spoke. "With Carl gone, that unfortunately leaves us a driver short for going down the hill. So here's the plan. Dad and I will take the first two down all the way to the ferry and across the river. We'll have to get them out of the way once we're down. But then we'll come back up and help drive down the other two." He looked at Abby. "Unless you've got a hankering to take it down by yourself."

She shook her head, the relief palpable on her face.

"I feel exactly the same," Patrick said.

"I know it looks frightening," David went on, "but in actuality, having the wheels locked and men holding us back, it shouldn't be too bad. Once Ben takes that first wagon down, we'll better know how it's going to work."

He took a breath, glancing at his father, who nodded his encouragement. "However, as Dad and I have talked about it, sometimes you can't always predict how things will go in an operation as complicated as this. Therefore, we would recommend, Patrick, that you and Abby ride down with us in the first two wagons as far as the dugway. If for some reason something happens that we don't make it back up, you're going to have to take them down. It will be helpful to watch how it's done."

"No, David," Molly cried. "They can't."

David didn't look at her. "Do you understand what I'm saying, Abby?"

All color had drained from her face, and she was biting her lower lip, but she nodded. "Yes."

"That first pitch is the worst, and, like Platte said, you can't tip a wagon over in it."

"If I do, do I get extra points?"

He laughed, grateful that she could still joke about it. "But Dad and I will be back." He looked around at them. "Sarah, we'll have you pull the last two wagons out of line until we come back for them. Abby and Patrick will stay with the teams, but we'll let you start walking just before we take the first two down. Okay?"

She too was pale and her eyes were frightened, but there was a quick nod.

"What about you, Molly?" Abby asked. "Were you serious about staying in the wagon?"

"I'm riding," she answered without hesitation. "Either way terrifies me, but if something goes wrong with the wagon, that way I can blame David."

David smiled and nodded. "All right. Let's make one last check of the wagons and teams. Sarah, you and Molly and Billy Joe can go on up to watch. We'll be there in a minute."

A minute or two later, David finished checking the contents of the last wagon to make sure everything was secure. As he jumped down, Abby came around to join him. "Everything set?" he asked.

She nodded.

"Abby," he said, seeing the lines in her face, "try not to worry. We'll be back."

"For Daddy, even more than me," she said quietly. "Mother is really worried, you know."

"I know."

She started away, then stopped. "David, the other day Molly went out to meet you and your father as you finished your work."

"Yes?" he said slowly.

"When she left us, she was all happy and excited. When she came back, after you and John had returned, I could tell she had been crying. Did you say something that really hurt her?"

He was totally taken aback. "When I left her, she was happy. Said she wanted to watch the sunset and would be right along."

Her dark brown eyes bored into him. "Are you sure?"

"Yes, she was fine. She had that letter from Carl. She told me that Carl had asked her if she wanted to come back to Cedar City, and—"

She jerked forward. "He what?"

"Uh-oh," David said. "I thought you knew. Don't tell her I told you. Anyway, she said she wasn't considering that at all and that was that."

Again there was a long, searching look. "What is going on with the two of you now?"

"I . . ." Then he shrugged. "Nothing. That was our agreement."

She blew out her breath. "Don't you hurt her, David. Don't you break her heart."

"The last thing in the world I want to do is to hurt your sister, but—"

She pounced on that. "But what?"

He sighed, wondering how honest to be. Then he decided it needed to be said. "I don't think I'm the only one who's wondering if this is going to work," he said softly.

For a long moment, she just stared at him. Then there was a curt nod, and she turned away.

"Abby? The McKennas are the best thing that ever happened to me. I would never deliberately do anything to hurt anyone in your family."

She came back around. Her chin came up, and he thought he saw a glint in her eyes.

"Including you," he added softly.

———✦———

Crowds of men, women, and children stood on both sides of the crest of the white sandstone ridge. Below them about ten or fifteen feet, a wagon sat right at the crest where the road turned sharply downward. Bishop Jens Nielson, his son Joe, and his son-in-law Kumen Jones were supervising the rough-locking of the hind wheels of Ben Perkins's wagon. About twenty yards back, another group of men were doing the same thing to Hyrum's, though they wouldn't actually lock the wheels until he moved forward and was ready to start down. Just behind both wagons, fifteen or twenty men stood around talking. These would be the ones to hold onto the long ropes attached to the wagon and try to keep the wagon from shooting down the hill and running over the teams. David and John Draper and Patrick McKenna were among them.

As they finished with the chain, Ben looked up, gave his audience a jaunty wave, then climbed up onto the wagon seat. Kumen Jones hopped up beside him and took the reins. Kumen's team was a pair of well-matched blacks. They were powerfully built, and their front shoulders were nearly as high as a man's head.

"All right," Kumen said, "here we go."

He snapped the reins lightly against the horses' backs and started them forward. The chains locking the wheels screeched in protest as they dragged across the bedrock, scoring it deeply. As the horses approached the spot where the road actually dropped away, the crowd above them hushed. This was the critical moment. The horses were already visibly agitated. They didn't like the feeling of being on the edge of a cliff. Their heads were swinging back and forth, and they kept snuffling nervously. Behind the wagon, twenty men had pulled the ropes tight, bracing themselves to take the weight.

"Ho, boys!" Kumen called to them. "Come on. It ain't as bad as it looks." But even as he spoke, the horses began to snort and paw at the ground. Their heads dropped as they tried to see the road in front of them. There was nothing there, and they didn't like that. Their eyes rolled and they began to push back against their tugs.

Kumen slapped the reins sharply across their backs. "Gee-up!" he yelled.

But the two big blacks were having none of it. Neighing loudly, they began backing up, pushing the wagon away from that terrible drop. The men behind the wagon scrambled to get out of the way.

Kumen grabbed the short whip from its holder by the wagon seat and cracked it sharply above their heads. It made no difference. The animals were almost mad with panic now and nothing could make them go forward.

Kumen reined in. "Whoa! Whoa!" They stopped, snorting and trembling, still pawing the ground. He turned to Bishop Nielson. "Dad, see if you can calm them down a little."

Jens Nielson limped forward. He stepped in front of the horses, speaking softly to them in his lilting Danish. At the same time, he began stroking their noses. Then he reached up and took both of their bridles and pulled them forward. Instantly, the horses were fighting back, bowing their necks and swinging their heads back and forth, nearly throwing the Dane aside.

The bishop immediately released the pressure and began stroking their noses again. "Okey dokey, boys. Vee need ta get dis vagon out of da vay, so awl da rest can go down too. Understand?" He pulled on the bridle again, and again they instantly balked.

Stepping back, he looked up at his son-in-law. "Dey no be goink, Kumen. I tink vee better try anudder team."

Joseph Barton, from Paragonah, came trotting up. "Bishop Nielson? I think I have a pair of horses that will go down that chute."

Kumen and the bishop looked at each other and smiled. Both of them knew about Joe Barton's team. "Perfect," Kumen said.

It took seven or eight minutes to make the change. When Joe Barton led his team forward—a beautiful set of bays—murmurs of approval rose up from the crowd. Here was another powerfully built and well-matched team of workhorses, and they came forward with not the slightest sign of nervousness or hesitation. They clopped along behind their owner as placidly as an old hound dog on a leash.

As the pair of blacks was led away, Molly, who was just above Ben's wagon, peered more closely at the bays. Something seemed odd. "Look at their eyes," she whispered to her mother. "Something's wrong."

A man just behind her mother spoke. "They're blind."

Molly, Abby, and Sarah whirled. "What did you say?"

The man laughed. He was one of the Paragonah contingent. "That's why Brother Barton volunteered them. Remember that epidemic of pinkeye we had a couple of years back? Hundreds of horses in southern Utah were blinded, including Barton's team." He chortled aloud, tickled with the very idea of it. "You could drive them off a cliff, and they wouldn't balk."[2]

And he was exactly right. When the team was harnessed up, Kumen and Ben Perkins climbed back into the wagon seat. Kumen picked up the reins and gently snapped them. "Gee-up, boys. Easy now. Nice and steady."

The wagon wheels creaked, and the chains began their horrible grinding as they scraped across the rock. Kumen turned his head and yelled through the wagon to the men behind him, "Hang on, boys. Here we go."

The horses went over the crest first, snorting a little as they felt the ground turning suddenly downward, then planting their big hooves carefully on the rock as they adjusted to the pitch. A moment later, the wagon followed. As soon as the back wheels went over the top, the wagon lurched forward sharply, nearly jerking the men behind it off their feet. The men gripped the ropes and hauled back, digging the heels of their boots against the rock to get a grip. But, to their astonishment, the ropes went slack almost immediately.

David bent down and looked beneath the wagon to see what was happening. In one instant, he understood. When the road builders had blasted out the road through the sandstone cliff, angling it down to the base of what had once been a fifty-foot cliff, they had created a lot of loose dirt and rock. They had used that loose material as fill to provide a more even grade from the top of the pitch to the bottom. Over the last few weeks, the rain and snow and the countless trips of the builders up and down the slot had packed the dirt and gravel down until it made a passable roadway.

But the weight of a man wasn't quite the same as the weight of the wagon. As soon as the front wheels came off the slickrock crest and hit that softer dirt and gravel, they sank to the hubs. Instead of shooting down the hill with twenty men hanging on for dear life, both axles were suddenly pushing dirt and gravel ahead of the wagon. It was like a snowplow, and the wagon slowed to a crawl. The rough-locked wheels in back only added to the drag, and suddenly, instead of holding back the wagon to stop it from overrunning the team, Kumen was snapping the reins to keep the team moving. They were actually going to have to pull the wagon down that impossible descent.

Kumen was standing in the wagon box now. "Hyaw!" he shouted, snapping the reins hard. "Gee-up!" Behind him, David and the others, feeling quite useless now, held onto their ropes, but only to keep them from dragging along the ground. They followed the wagon down until it reached the bottom of that first bad grade.

When they stopped, both Kumen and Ben Perkins climbed down and came around back. They stared in amazement at the new "road" they had just created beneath Ben's wagon. "Well, Ah'll be," Ben breathed. "An' Ah thought Ah might be wettin' me pants aboot now."

But Kumen wasn't quite so delighted. He looked at the men on the ropes. "We'll need you for the rest of the way," he said. Then he turned and looked up. "And this . . ." He shook his head. "This is going to be a problem. Take ten or fifteen more wagons down this grade and all that dirt is gonna be here at the bottom."

David had already come to the same conclusion. "Leaving nothing but naked rock and a steeper grade."

Ben Perkins grunted. "Sumbody better go back up and warn Platte. This be a challenge."

When Patrick, David, and John approached their wagons back up on top about an hour and a half later, covered with dirt and dust and walking very slowly, the waiting McKenna women saw instantly that something was wrong. "What is it?" Sarah cried. "What's the matter?"

"Did someone get hurt?" Molly cried.

"No," Patrick said. "We just have a complication."

John came in. "Ev'rythin' is goin' purty good so far. We crushed a couple of empty water barrels agin the sides of the cliff, an' sumbody lost a cage of chickens." He grinned. "Ya got chickens scattered up an' doon the canyon noow, cacklin' an' flyin' aroond ev'ry time a wagon approaches. But they be easy e'nuff ta catch later. But no, naw even a tip-over so far."

"Ten wagons are down past the notch now," Patrick said. "Things are going pretty smoothly, but . . ."

"Oh," Molly said in a low voice. "Don't say that."

David explained the situation quickly. They had predicted it exactly right. The first hundred and fifty feet of the roadway were no longer covered with fill. That had all been pushed to the bottom, and all that was left was solid rock that looked like it went straight down. There was only one bright spot. The dirt was deep enough at the bottom that it didn't matter how fast the wagon came shooting down. If they could keep it from running up and over the teams, when it hit the bottom, the deep soil provided a natural braking system.

"So," David concluded, "Dad and I will take the first two wagons down as agreed." He looked around and saw that the other two wagons were about fifty yards off to the side, out of the way of the others. "We'll get back up here as quickly as possible to take the others down."

He turned to Sarah. "We think you and Billy Joe ought to start down pretty soon. The canyon's starting to get choked with dust, and with every wagon going down, the footing gets a little rougher."

"Okay."

He turned to Molly. "Are you sure you still want to ride down?"

She suppressed a little shudder. "No. I hate the thought of walking down something that steep, but after watching Ben Perkins go down, I think I'd rather walk."

"Good. I feel better about that." He turned. "All right, Patrick, you and

Abby mount up and we'll take them up to the chaining area." Then to the others, "We'll see you at the bottom."

"When you come back, can you help Belle, too?" Sarah asked. She turned and pointed to where they could barely see the top of a wagon cover behind a large outcropping of rock.

"Stanford's wife?" David asked in surprise. "I thought I saw him go down earlier."

"He did," Abby explained, "but not with his family. He told Belle he had been asked to assist the first wagons going down, then to work at the ferry site with Brother Hall. Someone promised to bring her down if he would do that, but no one's come yet. They asked her to pull out of line and wait over there."

"She's trying to be brave," Molly came in, "but she's quite worried."

"Okay. I'll watch for Stanford and see if I can find out what's going on. If I don't find him, we'll take her down with us when I come back."

"Thank you," Abby said. "I'll run and tell her."

A few minutes later, it was their turn. They pulled both wagons up the road to the brink of the pitch, then dismounted and helped the teams of men rough-lock their wheels and attach the holding rope. Not ropes, David thought with dismay. *Rope.* John had only eight men to help him, David had ten, so one rope each was all they needed. So many of the men had gone down with the other wagons and hadn't had a chance to straggle back up to the top yet.

Satisfied that the chains were in place, David conferred briefly with his father, reminding him to give David a three- or four-minute head start before starting down. Sarah, Molly, and Billy Joe had already begun walking down and were no longer in sight. Patrick wanted Abby to drive with David in the first wagon. He would come with John in the second.

Father and son shook hands quickly, and David climbed up onto the lead wagon seat. Abby sat white-faced, her feet already braced against the front of the wagon box. "You ready?" he asked.

"Never," she said through clenched teeth. Her eyes were wide, the pupils contracted into pinpoints. Her lower lip was trembling, and her fingers, clinging to the iron rail behind the wagon seat, were like claws, the knuckles white.

David suddenly felt sick. The image of a young girl dangling upside down from a tree house, one foot caught in the loop of a rope ladder, had flashed into his mind. "Oh, Abby," he breathed. "I forgot about your fear of heights."

"So get me down from here," she hissed. "And make it fast."

"Got it," he said. He turned. "All right," he called to the men behind. "Here we go."

The mules brayed in protest and began to fight the instant David tried to get them to move, but the company had learned something in the last couple of hours. If the men behind pushed the wagon forward, it impelled the animals over the crest, and they had no choice but to go forward. And that was what happened now. Braying raucously, fighting against the pressure from behind, the mules planted their hooves, only to have them slide forward across the rocks. Then the rear wheels went over the crest, and they were committed.

Abby felt a sickening lurch in her stomach as she was suddenly looking almost straight down over the backs of the mules. She was standing nearly straight up, her feet actually braced against the front of the wagon box rather than the floor, her hands clutching the back of the wagon seat to keep herself from hurtling forward.

The air was filled with terrible noises—the screech of iron across rock; the terrified snorting of the mules; the crash of the wagon wheels. But Abby barely heard them. She was conscious of one thing and one thing only—her fingertips digging into the wood, fighting not to let go and fall.

David was standing now too, leaning back at almost a forty-five degree angle to compensate for the downward pitch. He was yelling and hollering as he whipped the reins to keep the mules from slowing down and being run over by the wagon.

Abby gasped. The narrow cleft at the base of the incline was rushing up at them with incredible speed. If they didn't hit that opening exactly right, they would smash a wheel against the side of the cliff, or maybe even dash one of the mules to death.

Then, just as quickly as it had started, it ended. They hit the soft dirt at the bottom of the ramp and the wagon ground to a halt, dragging the mules to a stop as well.

David sat there for a moment, gasping for breath. The mules were shaking violently. Abby was trembling like she had just awakened from some fiendish nightmare. She didn't look at him. She sank slowly back to her seat, then shoved her hands beneath her hips so that David wouldn't see how badly they were shaking.

One of the men from behind ran around to David. "Everything all right?" he said between great gulps of air. David looked at Abby, who managed a nod.

"Okay," the man said. "You've got to keep moving. Your father's waiting to follow."

David leaned out and looked back up the steep roadway. Two figures were there by the wagon. Seeing David, both Patrick and John waved back.

The rest of the way down was a blur in Abby's mind. They passed through the cut, so narrow that from time to time the hubs of the wheels scored into the stone on either side. Here, as above, each successive wagon had pushed the fill dirt down the canyon or thrown it to off one side, leaving the road very uneven. They bounced and swayed from side to side, still dropping at a stomach-twisting, thirty-five-degree angle. Abby would gasp with each new jarring blow or sudden drop until she started to feel light-headed and realized she was hyperventilating.

About halfway down they stopped and let the men helping them down untie the holding rope and start back up the hill. The rest of the way wasn't quite as bad, but even here, she cursed herself for not riding in the back of the wagon with her eyes tightly closed.

David pulled the wagon to a stop just before they reached Uncle Ben's Dugway. They sat there for a moment, not believing that they had done it.

Up ahead of them, another wagon had just cleared the dugway and was turning onto the track that led down through the foothills to the river-bank. He took a deep breath, looked at her out of the corner of his eye, then stood up. "I've got to take the chains off the wheels before we can cross the dugway."

Not waiting for an answer, he jumped down and went around to the back of the wagon. A few moments later she came around and dropped to her knees beside him, helping him work the chain loose from between the spokes.

They finished without either of them speaking. David gathered the chain into loops and put it into the back of the wagon. Then he turned. "Abby, I think you should go on down with me to the bottom and wait there for your mom and the others."

"What if you don't make it back up?"

"I will. I won't put you through that again."

She gave a quick, almost desperate shake of her head. "It wasn't as bad as I thought."

He shot her an incredulous look.

"It was ten times worse." Then she managed a wan but impish smile. "And now that I've done it once, I can really enjoy it the second time."

He laughed aloud, the sound bouncing off the cliffs behind them. David started to turn away, then swung back around. He stepped to her, took her by the shoulders, and pulled her to him. She stiffened in surprise as he bent down and kissed her very gently on the lips. "Abby, you are something else," he said gruffly.

Almost as stunned as she was, he let her go, face turning scarlet. He almost tripped on the loose rocks in his haste to put some space between them. Then he turned and plunged away. A moment later he was up on the wagon seat again and urging the mules forward, leaving Abby to stare after him, not sure what had just happened.

Notes

1. As Miller notes, several men claimed that they were the ones to take the first wagon down, but most of these claims were made much later, or else were reported by their

families much later. Miller concludes that while Ben Perkins's wagon was the first down, he asked Kumen Jones, son-in-law to Jens Nielson, to drive it for him (see Miller, *Hole*, 109–10).

2. In his description of this day, Kumen Jones states that he did drive the wagon for Ben Perkins but that he took his team, which was "well broken" (*ibid.*, 110, 184). George Decker, who was fifteen at the time, remembers the Perkins teams balking at the sight of that thousand-foot drop, and he is the one who says that Joseph Barton offered his team of blind horses (cited in *ibid.*, 201). He, however, seems to indicate that it was then Barton who drove the first two wagons down. I have combined these two accounts into what I hope is a plausible way of explaining the differences in them.

CHAPTER 62

Monday, January 26, 1880

"There he is." David's father was pointing. "Over there by the ferry."

Then David saw him. "I'll be right back." He broke away and trotted over to where four men were loading a wagon onto the ferry. One of them was Stanford Smith. "Hey, Stanford," David called, waving.

The man straightened, then recognized David and waved. "Hello, David. You're down, eh?"

Stanford Smith was tall and thin, with brown hair and bright blue eyes. Though slender, he was muscular and his belly was hard and flat. He had been the foreman on the road crew that worked on the middle stretch of the Hole. He had a reputation for being able to outwork men younger and more powerfully built than he was. He was nearly thirty, and although David hadn't known him and his wife well in Cedar City, they had met in church several times. But in the last months, they had become good friends.

"Only my dad and I came down," David explained. "We're going back up for Patrick and Abby as soon as we get our wagons across. All the fill dirt has been pushed off that first pitch and it's pretty scary now."

Stanford frowned. "That's what I heard."

"Your wife's not down yet, I understand."

His brow wrinkled as he quickly looked around at the numerous wagons waiting for the ferry. Then he lifted his eyes to the notch that soared majestically upward as far as the eye could follow it. "No, not yet."

"When I left, Sarah told me that Belle had her wagon pulled off to one side waiting for you to come up and get her."

He muttered something under his breath, then snatched his hat off his head and threw it on the ground in disgust. "I knew it. They promised me that if I would help down below, they'd make sure to bring my wife down. I've been getting worried about her."

"That's all I need to know," David said. "Once we get the wagons across, we'll go back up and bring Belle and the kids down too if you'd like."

His relief was evident. "That would be deeply appreciated," he said. "She's got the three little ones up there with her, you know. And right now, they need me badly on the ferry."

"I know," David said. "We'll get them."

Stanford swung around and started waving his hands at the wagon that was approaching the ramp. "Hold it right there," he called. "We have a bit of an emergency." Then he turned to David. "Have your dad bring his wagon on this one. Then you'll be first to load when they return. That lets you get back up the mountain as soon as you can."

Ferry work was maddeningly slow. The one Charles Hall had built here was big enough to carry two wagons and their teams and a few extra people to boot. It had two long oars, one on each side, and crossed the river on its own power rather than being towed through a series of rope pulleys. That meant it had to cross at an angle, landing downstream a couple of hundred yards farther beyond where it started. Then it was towed by a team of horses upstream again until it was well above its initial starting point.

It was almost half an hour before the ferry finally came back and nosed into the riverbank with a solid thud. Charles Hall and one of his sons tossed ropes to those who had waded out to help bring the ferry in. They pulled it up against the bank, the ramp was quickly dropped, and Stanford signaled for David to pull his wagon onboard.

David was already in the wagon seat and clucked to the teams. They had agreed that his father would not come back over on this trip, but would stay on the south side of the river and find someone to watch their teams so they could go back up to the Hole.

The wagon behind him held part of the Barney family, a family with a large number of children who had joined them at Panguitch. Dan Barney's wagon, which was pulled by a yoke of oxen, was boarded without any problems, though the oxen seemed somewhat nervous about being on the water. But to David's surprise, instead of raising the ramp and getting under way, the men then loaded five steers on as well. There wasn't much room behind the wagon, so some of the cattle came up alongside Barney's wagon.

In a few minutes, everything was on board. The ramp was raised and poles were used to push the ferry back out into the current. Using the two long oars, Hall brought the front end around until they were headed downstream.

David made sure his mules were secure. As he finished, Brother Barney came up to join him. "Any problems coming down?" David asked.

Barney chuckled. "You mean, other than turning our hair white?"

"You too, eh?" Then he looked around. "Your son driving the second wagon?"

"Yes. Buren's got Sister Barney and the younger children with him. I've got the—" The bawling of a cow cut him off. There was a crack of horns clashing against horns; then something thudded heavily against the decking.

Both men turned. One of Barney's oxen, more nervous now than before, was swinging its massive head back and forth, and that was crowding one of the steers back against the railing. The steer bellowed and kicked back sharply, catching the cow behind it on the foreleg. It reared, trying to get back.

"Uh-oh," Barney said. The railings on the ferry were two-by-fours nailed to the hull, and were not designed to resist the weight of a steer. Just then, Barney's boy came around from behind the wagon to see what was going on. "Alfred," Barney yelled. "Get them cattle back away from the oxen."

The flat-bottomed boat was now entering the main current and starting to pick up speed, which made the oxen even more nervous. Now both of them were rocking back and forth, lowing mournfully. Alfred, or Al, as everyone called him, was fourteen or fifteen. As he started forward, he saw that he couldn't get through to the lead steer, so he darted back around and came up the other side, then tried to push his way past the oxen. He was a strapping boy and unafraid. He pushed in, grabbing at the horns of the one ox to try to settle it down.

David leaped forward. If Al could contain the oxen, maybe he could push the two steers back out of the way.

Dan Barney had circled around David's wagon and was coming in behind his son. "Be careful, Al. Don't let him catch you with those horns."

David had reached the oxen too, but didn't dare push past them because the nearest ox was rolling back and forth, eyes wild. "Grab this one, Al," he shouted. "Let me get by."

Al did exactly as he was told. He reached in and grabbed the ox nearest to David by the horn and dragged its head toward him. David shot past him and faced the steer. It lowered its head, preparing to charge. "Hey!" David shouted, waving his arms. The steer started backing up, pushing up against the one behind it. It was working. They both started to back up.

Then David heard a shout and jerked around. Al had the ox with both hands, hanging on for dear life. The ox lowered its head, snorting angrily, then hooked up with a powerful thrust of its neck. Al Barney went flying past David. He cleared the rail, then hit the water with a tremendous splash.

"Al!" David spun around. That was a mistake. The front steer charged. One horn snagged David's pant leg. The animal jerked its head upward, and David felt a searing pain across the back of his leg. He crashed backwards, arms flailing. The last thing David saw was Dan Barney, mouth open, arms waving. Then the railing hit David in the small of his back. He did a graceful end-over-end tumble and hit the ice-cold water headfirst.[1]

"Something's happened," Patrick McKenna said. He was standing at the crest of the cut near the top of the Hole in the Rock. He stared morosely down the chasm, which was now totally deserted as far as he could see down it. He glanced up at the sky. The cloud cover had thickened, but he could tell the sun was now two-thirds of the way down toward the western horizon. "We can't wait any longer," he said.

"No, Daddy," Abby cried, greatly dismayed. "He'll come. He promised he would."

He stepped back and walked over to where Abby stood by Belle Smith and her children. Belle had baby George, who was six months old, under one arm. Ada, who had celebrated her sixth birthday just two days before, and Roy, who was not yet four, stood beside her, looking anxious. That only deepened Patrick's sense of foreboding and discouragement. There were three wagons left up here—their two, and Stanford Smith's. Everyone else was either down or on their way down. Those from Fifty Mile Camp wouldn't start arriving until about noon tomorrow, and the thought of spending the night up here alone was not acceptable. The wind was still from the south, promising rain or snow by tomorrow. They simply had to go. And if they waited much longer, it would be dark before they reached the bottom—another unacceptable option.

"We don't have anyone to hold us back," Abby said, feeling a hollowness in her stomach. She clearly remembered how David's wagon had almost shot down that pitch, and that had been with several men hauling on ropes to hold it back.

"We'll just have to make do," her father said. With his mind made up, he sprang into action. "Abby, bring your wagon up to the notch. I'll bring mine up behind it. We'll rough-lock the wheels there. I'm going to drive yours down that first stretch, then I'll come back up for mine."

He turned to Belle. "I'm sorry to leave you, Sister Smith, but I don't see how you can drive a wagon with your children, and I'm not sure we should put them in one of the wagons."

She shuddered. Her head snapped back and forth in quick jerks. "I can barely drive a team on level ground. No, we'll wait here for Stanford. I'm sure he's coming."

"We'll find him the moment we get down," Patrick promised. "And we'll come back too."

"Thank you." She pulled the two little ones closer to her. "Let's go back to the wagon, children. It's starting to get a little cold out here."

Abby rushed to her and gave her a hug. "We'll be back." Then she dropped to one knee. "Ada. Roy. You help your Mama now, okay?"

"Yes, Sister Abby," Ada said. "We will."

Once again Abby stared down at what looked like five miles of sheer drop-off, and she felt a wave of dizziness sweep over her. Her father touched her shoulder. "Ready?"

She nodded grimly. "David said you have to be careful that the wagon doesn't overrun the team and break their legs."

"Thanks," he grunted with heavy irony. "Just what I need." He gripped the reins tightly in one hand and lifted the buggy whip in his other. He gave one last glance, took a deep breath, then yelled at the mules. They balked at the sight of the steep incline, of course, but with no one to push them from behind, Patrick had no choice but to make them go forward. He grabbed the whip, screaming at them as he lashed it across the rump of the nearest one. It lunged forward, dragging its partner with it. It was just enough that they dropped over the crest of the hill, and then they no longer had a choice. Down the hill they went. The wagon careened back and forth, nearly smashing against the side walls. But the logging chains on the back wheels dug into the rock, screeching like a tortured animal in pain, holding the wagon back enough to let the mules stay ahead of it.

To Abby, it felt like they were rocketing downward. Once again she was nearly standing up in the wagon seat, hanging on for dear life. She was nearly thrown free when they reached the pile of soft dirt at the bottom and came to an abrupt halt.

They sat there for a moment, chests heaving, her hands still gripping the wagon seat. Patrick turned to her, face grim. "One down, one to go." He took a breath. "The rest of the way isn't so bad. Are you all right to go on alone?"

"I want to wait here and make sure you make it down safely."

He shook his head. "You can't. This has to be clear before I can start down." He leaned over and kissed her softly on the cheek. "You'll be all right." He handed her the reins and hopped down.

"I'll wait for you at the dugway," she said. "Be careful, Daddy."

✳

Back on top, Patrick checked the chains around his two back wheels one last time before climbing up into the wagon seat. He turned. Belle was on the ridge near her wagon, a solitary, forlorn figure. She waved, and he waved back. "Godspeed," she called.

He waved again, then bowed his head. "O Father," he whispered. "Please watch over this good woman and her children until we can return for her. And help us get down safely."

He picked up the reins and once again took the whip from its holder. "Hee-yah!" he yelled, and cracked the whip twice in rapid succession, nipping both of the animals on their backsides. Startled, they leaped forward, and over the crest they plunged.

About halfway down that hundred-and-fifty-foot stretch of slickrock, Patrick heard a loud snap, then the sound of steel clanging on rock. The wagon lurched forward, nearly throwing him out, and the back end started swinging wildly back and forth, the hubs of the wheels cracking against the sidewall. In that instant, he knew that the wagon was going to overrun the mules, for they were digging in their hooves to stop their precipitous plunge. He laid the whip across their backs, screaming and shouting at them. They leaped forward, and for a moment he thought they were going to make it. The wagon tongue was pushed out ahead of them by three or four feet, dragging them with it. Then suddenly the off mule lost its footing and went down. For a horrifying moment, Patrick thought he was going to go right up and over the both of them, killing him and them both. But the tongue and double trees held. The fallen animal screamed with pain as it was dragged roughly along the sandstone roadway.

Then something jerked the wagon sharply backward, almost as roughly as when it had lurched forward. A screech that nearly split his eardrum exploded from beneath the wagon. The sudden loss of momentum yanked the wagon tongue upward, pulling the downed mule back to its feet again.

Seconds later they reached the bottom and the soft soil and lurched to a stop.

Trembling violently, Patrick climbed down and went to the mule. It stood with its head down, chest heaving, body shaking in great spasms. He patted its neck, talking softly, then bent down. All along its left side, raw patches of flesh were oozing blood.

Patrick watched the mule stomp its feet, trying to shake off the pain, and he momentarily closed his eyes in thanks. No legs were broken. The poor beast was battered and bruised, but still able to stand.

Baffled by what had just happened, he walked slowly around to the back of his wagon, feeling the shakiness in his legs. As he bent down to ex-amine the chain, he saw, as he had expected, that one link had snapped, freeing up one of the wheels. He inhaled sharply. The loose end, which he had heard clanging on the stone, had caught in one of the spokes and wrapped itself twice around the felloe of the wheel, tangling up and lock-ing tight again. He leaned in closer, touching it with his fingers. One loop had crossed over the top of another and the links had bit into the wood. That was what had caused the wagon to slow so abruptly, which had saved the life of his mule.

He pulled on it a couple of times to make sure it was secure, then backed out. He glanced up at heaven. "Thank you," he breathed.

Molly had gone as far as the dugway with her mother and Billy Joe, but then refused to go farther. She was going to wait for Abby and her father, and nothing her mother could say would change her mind. When the next wagon came by and offered Sarah and Billy Joe a ride the rest of the way down, they hugged Molly quickly and left her alone.

Now she had moved back up the trail enough that she could see up into the Hole. She found shelter from the rising wind beneath a large boul-der, pulled her coat tightly around her, and settled down to wait. Time after time, she would leap to her feet as one wagon after another appeared out of the canyon. Time after time she sat back as she saw it was neither Abby nor her father. For the last hour, there had been no one.

She got to her feet, stretched, and moved to the edge of the roadway. From here she had a clear view all the way to the river. She could see the line of white canvas tops waiting their turn for the ferry.

"Where are you, David?" she cried into the wind. "You promised." And then she dropped her head and began to sob.

When she finally raised her head and wiped the tears away with the back of her hand, a movement caught her eye. About halfway up the road, wending its way through the foothills that formed the base of the Hole, a solitary figure was trudging steadily along. For a moment, her heart leaped, but then, as she looked more closely, her hopes were dashed. She could see that the man was wearing a dark coat and a black cowboy hat. David wore a light-colored sheepskin coat and his hat was a light tan. She turned, bitter disappointment swelling up again.

A noise above her pulled her around with a jerk. The crackling sounds of wagon wheels crossing rock came floating down the crevasse. She turned and sprinted up the trail to where the road turned sharply up the canyon. "Please, Lord. Let it be them."

A minute later, a wagon appeared for a moment, then disappeared again behind the cliff. But it was enough. She saw that it was being pulled by two mules and driven by a woman in a dark dress and battered old hat. It was Abby. Molly gave a low cry and sank to the ground, putting her face in her hands.

⁂

A quarter of an hour later, Molly helped Abby and her father remove the heavy logging chain from Abby's wagon wheels. They put it into her wagon, then went back to their father's. "Come here," Patrick said. "I want to show you something."

He led them around to the back of the wagon. There he described his experience, how the wagon had suddenly leaped forward, knocking one of the mules down, then almost instantly was pulled back again. With a voice filled with soft humility, he showed them how the loose chain had wound around the wheel and locked. He straightened. "I couldn't have fastened it in there any better myself."[2]

Abby stared at the battered chain, and then at her father. And she thought *her* ride had been exciting. She turned to Molly. "Still no word from David or John?"

Molly looked away. "Nothing." Then it burst out of her: "What could he be doing that is so important?"

Abby said nothing, just looked away. Was he so embarrassed by what had happened near this very spot that he had decided not to come? She found that hard to believe, but whatever it was, it made her angry. Not only for her and her father—Belle Smith was up on top with three young children, all alone, with dark soon coming on.

Patrick turned, searching the camp below. "Something's happened," he said. "I'm really worried."

"Well," Molly snapped. "He'd better have a broken leg, or I'm going to break it for him."

Just then, the figure that Molly had seen earlier appeared on the far end of the dugway. "Hey!" he called, and broke into a run.

"It's Stanford," Patrick said.

As Stanford reached them, his face twisted angrily when he saw that neither wagon was his, and that his family was not with the McKennas. "Where's David?" he said. "Is he bringing Belle down?"

"We haven't seen David," Abby said. "We were hoping that you had."

He straightened, the shock of that hitting him hard. "But . . ." His face darkened. "I saw him about three hours ago. He and his Dad took their wagons across. He said he was coming right back across, then heading up top to help you. I never saw him again, so I thought that I had just missed him." One hand came up, and he rubbed at his eyes. "He gave me his word that he would bring Belle down too."

"He gave us his word too," Molly murmured.

"Something may have happened," Patrick said. "We're getting worried."

Stanford didn't hear that. He turned and looked up the nearly vertical canyon that rose so majestically above them. "Oh, Belle," he whispered.

The anguish on his face touched Abby, and she pushed her frustrations with David aside. "They were fine when we left them, Stanford," she said. "You have a remarkable wife."

"I know." He removed his hat and slapped it against his leg, sending little puffs of dust shooting outward. "And I'm mad. Everybody promised me they'd bring her down, including your David, and nothing."

As he replaced his hat, still grumping, Patrick spoke. "I'll let Abby and Molly take the one wagon on down. I can leave my wagon here for now and go back up with you."

He shook his head immediately. "Not a good idea to leave animals up here. No, you go on ahead. I'll bring them down."

He turned, looking down at the checkerboard pattern of white-topped wagons scattered along the riverbank. "But when I get back down," he said, his voice tight, "I'm going to give somebody what for. Can you imagine? When I couldn't find her, I asked those who had promised to bring her down why she wasn't there. They got all red-faced and embarrassed and said they were so busy with their own outfits, they just plumb forgot."

Then he softened. "But thank you for staying with her. I'm much obliged."

When Patrick and his two daughters finally reached the bottom of the hill, Sarah and Billy Joe were waiting for them. With a low cry, Sarah came running. Billy outran her, legs and arms pumping, hair flying. The three of them clambered down from the wagons, and for a long, sweet moment, they all just held each other.

Finally, Molly looked at her mother. "Where's David? Have you seen him? I want to give him a piece of my mind."

Her mother looked up in surprise. "What?"

"He never came, Mother," Abby said. "He promised, but he never came."

Billy Joe stepped in front of her and planted his feet, hands on his hips. His lower lip jutted out. "David *couldn't* come."

"What?" Molly cried. "Why not?"

"David was knocked off the ferry into the river by a spooked steer,"

Sarah said quietly. "He has a six-inch gash on his leg and can barely hobble around."

Notes

1. Several report the incident with Al Barney being thrown overboard by an unruly ox, though not all report it quite the same way (see Miller, *Hole*, 120; "Life Sketch of Mary Jane Wilson," 12).

2. Both of the incidents depicted here as happening to Patrick and Abby McKenna actually happened to the pioneers. Here, in their own words, is what happened. The punctuation and spelling—or lack of it—is in the original.

Nathaniel Z. Decker wrote: "My father [Zechariah Bruyn Decker, Jr.] . . . hooked up his two wagons and six horses and mules and when he got to the hole there was none to help hold back with ropes tho some had promised to be there and would have been had they known he was there but no one showed up so he said there isn't any chance for a wagon to tip over and the animals ought to out run the two locked wagons and putting mother and us five children out he seated himself on the front wagon and started. Down they went in a flash and landed in the soft ground at the end of the slick rock slide . . . but one big mule was dragged and seriously hurt" (cited in Miller, *Hole*, 115–16).

Joseph F. Barton, the man who furnished the blind horses for the Perkins wagon, was camped at Fifty Mile Camp. After helping some go down that first day, he hurried back to camp, and brought his outfit forward, hoping to go down with the first group. He writes: "[I] reached the dreaded road just at Sundown and knowing that if he waited for the ten men and rope he would camp on the rim that night after taking a Survey of the cavity & putting on ruff lock and urging his team considerable finally got them to face what seemed almost next to death. However, the next 1/2 minutes landed team wagon and driver at [the] first station about 300 ft. down [others say it was 150 feet] the hole in the rock right Side up, where upon examination he found that the chain to ruff lock had broken but through a providencial act the chain had flipped a lap around the felloe in Such a manner as to Serve for a lock (*ibid.*, 115).

Miller's entire chapter on going through the Hole is excellent (see *ibid.*, pages 101–18; see also various reference in the Appendices, 184, 192–93, 200–201, 208. Others add other small, but important, details of interest. See Reay, *Incredible Passage*, 52–57; Redd, "Short Cut," 18–19; Carpenter, *Jens Nielson*, 46–48).

After reading the various accounts of taking that first, hair-raising drop into the Hole, the following summary by Miller is quite astonishing: "It is a credit to the skill and courage of the expedition that no major tragedy occurred; not a single wagon is reported to have tipped over or have been seriously damaged. Some animals were rather badly mauled, but all came through alive" (*Hole*, 116–17).

CHAPTER 63

Monday, January 26, 1880

Stanford Smith was in excellent shape, but he was puffing heavily as he made his way through the narrow cut near the top of the Hole in the Rock. He had come from bottom to top in just over half an hour—an impressive feat indeed. It was still daylight, but the sun, obscured by clouds all day long, was not long from setting now. Down in the crevasse of the Hole, it was dark and gloomy. If they waited much longer it would make their challenge much more difficult.

As he approached that last final, brutal grade, he stopped. David and his father had mentioned this, but he still could scarcely believe it. All the fill dirt was at the bottom, and there was nothing but very steep solid rock from there to the top. It was scratched and gouged and had many long metallic streaks from where wagon tires had slid across it. He gave a low whistle. Even walking up or down this was going to be treacherous.

Bending over to catch his breath, he felt the anger boil up again. They had left his Belle up here all day with three small children. He snorted in disgust. Too preoccupied with their own troubles? Straightening, he tipped his head back, cupped his hands to his mouth, and shouted, "Belle? Arabelle Smith?"

After a moment the answer floated back, so softly that he almost didn't hear it. "Stanford." There was a sob of joy. "Is that you?" Out of breath or not, he sprinted forward, racing up the steep pitch as quickly as his rubbery legs would carry him.

What he saw there turned anger into rage. Off to one side of the road sat his wife. She had baby George cradled in her arms, heavily swaddled in blankets, and was sitting on a tattered quilt on top of a patch of dirty, crusted snow. "Oh, Stanford," she cried, getting to her feet. "I thought you'd never come."

"I am so sorry, Belle. I thought . . ." He looked around. "But where are the other children and the wagon?"

She half turned, pointing to a spot down off the ridge. At first, he wasn't sure what he was seeing, then he saw the tip of a rusty stovepipe showing above a huge sandstone boulder. "There. In the wagon. Ada is telling young Roy stories."

Stanford's face flushed. He grabbed his hat off his head and hurled it to the ground. Then he began stomping on it, muttering angrily, Belle momentarily forgotten. "With me down there helping them get their wagons loaded onto the raft, I thought sure someone would bring my wagon and family down. Drat 'em all!"

Arabelle Coombs had married Stanford Smith in the Endowment House in Salt Lake City in 1870. She was seventeen; he was twenty. Belle, as everyone called her, was a pretty, dark-haired girl who referred to herself as pleasingly plump. But she had pluck. Everyone knew that. And she was used to her husband's flashes of temper, especially when he saw something that he considered as an injustice. Snatching off his hat and throwing it to the ground was common with him. Stomping it was part of the ritual if he was really exercised. She loved that dirty old crumpled hat because, to her, that was her husband.

Now she watched him for a moment, not reacting. Then she was all business. "Stanford, I have the horses harnessed and everything is packed and ready to go. Standing here stomping on that ole hat isn't going to get us down there any quicker."

He picked up his hat, looking sheepish, dusted it off, and jammed it back on his head. "Ah, Belle, what a jewel you are. How do you put up with this old fool?"

"We need to hurry, Stanford," was all she said.

The Smiths had brought four horses with them. One of them had been crippled and died at Fifty Mile Spring. Two were now hitched to the wagon. The third, a huge old workhorse called Nig that they used to help the team when pulling up the steeper inclines, stood nearby, in harness, head down, waiting patiently. Stanford took him by the bridle, led him to the wagon, and tied him to the back axle with a rope.

Suddenly, the back wagon flap pulled open just above him. "Daddy!" It was a cry of pure joy, and a moment later, Ada and Roy came tumbling out. From the looks of them, they had been asleep. He took them both in his arms, rubbing Roy's hair and tickling Ada's ribs. Then he straightened. "I'm going to drive the wagon over to where we start down the hill, children. Mama and the baby will ride with me, but you can run alongside if you wish."

Delighted with that, they lined up beside the wagon. Reaching under the wagon box, he unlocked the wagon brakes, then held the baby while Belle climbed up. Once she had the baby in his bed inside the wagon, Stanford climbed up beside her. "All right, kids," he called down. "Stay back away from the wagon enough that I can see you."

The wagon had been parked about two hundred yards from the top of the Hole, and the children thought it was grand fun to race their father and the horses to the Hole. He pulled up about ten feet back from the edge, set the brakes, and climbed down. "Belle, I'm going to cross-lock the wheels. Can you toss me the chains?"

He was frowning as he said it, for he didn't have enough chain to rough-lock them, like most of the others had done. He hadn't been too worried about cross-locking before, because he was sure there would be ten to twenty men on the back of the wagon to hold it back. Now, he would just have to pray that the cross-lock held. The children watched with great interest as Belle helped her husband lock the wheels in position. Finished, Stanford took her arm. "You better come look, Belle."

Walking to the edge of the downward cut, they stood there hand in hand. The top ten feet had some loose sand, but after that it was solid rock as steep as a slippery slide for about a hundred and fifty feet. He felt his wife stiffen by his side. "I heard them talking about how the wagons had pushed all the dirt down to the bottom," she said, "but I had no idea."

"I don't know if we can make it," he said, chewing on his lip as he studied the polished, scarred rock just below him.

"We have no choice," Belle answered calmly. "We have to make it."

"If we had even a few men to hold us back," he started, feeling the anger starting to rise again, "then maybe we could make it, but . . ."

Her look cut him off. "I'll do the holding back."

His face blanched. "You?"

"Me and Nig," she corrected. She turned to look at the big horse behind their wagon. "Isn't that why he's back there? I'll hold his lines and pull him back so that he'll hold the wagon back some. It's all we can do."

He was shaking his head even before she finished. "No man with a lick of sense would let a woman do that."

"What else is there to do?" she countered.

"But Belle, what about the children? We don't dare put them in the wagon."

"They'll have to stay up here," she said in that same calm, determined voice.

"And if we don't come back?"

Her eyes momentarily darkened, but then her chin lifted and her mouth set. "We'll come back. We have to."

Without waiting for him to answer, she spun on her heel and walked to the wagon. "Come, children," she called.

She stepped up on the running board beneath the tailgate, and reached inside. She brought out the same tattered quilt she had been sitting on when Stanford first saw her. She handed it to Ada, then crawled inside the wagon. A moment later she reappeared, handed baby George to her husband, then climbed out again. Moving over to one side, back some distance from the edge of the incline, she folded the quilt double, then spread it out on the rocks. "Elroy, you sit here."

As grave as if he were conducting a funeral, the three-year-old came over and sat down in the middle of the quilt. "Make sure you're comfortable, Roy, but spread your legs a little. And button your coat real tight."

He did so. She next took the baby from Stanford. Double-checking that the blankets were tightly wrapped around him, she sat him down between Roy's legs, his back propped against his brother's stomach, his head cradled in one elbow. "All right," she said, smiling brightly at him. "Your job, Roy, is to take care of little George. So you hold on tight to your baby brother until Papa comes back for you, okay?"

He looked up, pleased with such an important responsibility. "Yes, Mama."

Belle took her daughter's arm and guided her onto the quilt. "Ada, I want you to sit right here in front of your brothers. Don't move. Any of you. I don't even want you to stand up."

Ada nodded, her clear blue eyes wide and anxious but trusting.

Belle laid a hand on her shoulder. "I want you to say a little prayer and ask Heavenly Father to bless you children."

"Yes, Mama." Ada looked up at her father. "Will you come back for us, Papa?"

He tried to speak, but suddenly tears had come and his throat was too tight for words to get out. He nodded, then reached out and laid a hand on her head. He nodded again.

At that, she smiled. It was pure and sweet and at peace. "Then I'm not afraid, Papa. We'll stay here with God until you and Mama get the wagon down." And then she bowed her head and spoke slowly but clearly. "Father in Heaven, bless me and Roy and our baby until Father comes back for us."

Unable to bear that look a moment longer, Stanford walked to the back of the wagon. He cleared his throat and wiped surreptitiously at his eyes with the back of his glove. He reached up and untied the reins on Nig's back. Then, to cover his emotions, he handed them to Belle. "You'll have to pull back as hard as you can to hold him in," he said, his voice still husky. He forced a crooked grin. "Little thing like you, though, I'll bet you couldn't pull the legs off a flea."

"Ha!" she said, and took the lines from him. Stanford had given her a pair of his gloves, and she wrapped the reins around them, then pulled back, cinching them tight. "I'm ready."

He stood there for a moment, agonizing over what they were about to do, then gave a quick nod. He went to the front of the wagon, climbed up, untied the lines to the team, and wrapped them around his hands. "Okay, Belle?" he called back.

She turned and smiled at the children, who were watching all of this with wide, anxious eyes.

"We'll be right back," she said, and formed a kiss with her lips. Then she turned forward, bracing herself. "Ready."

She thought she was prepared for the first jolt, but as the back end of the wagon lifted high in the air, it shot forward, nearly pulling her arms out of their sockets and making her gasp. She dug in her heels, leaning back as far as she could as she was dragged over the edge and started shooting downward, feet skidding down the slick rock.

Old Nig hadn't been expecting anything like that either. He neighed wildly as his front hooves shot forward on the slickrock surface. Then his back hooves slipped, and down he went. In a split second he was sitting on his haunches, sliding downward like a kid on a sled. Terrified that she was going to be pulled off her feet and crash into either Nig or the wagon, Belle gave up on holding back and started taking long, stiff-legged hops, frantically trying to keep her balance. Faithful old terrified Nig tried desperately to get to his feet, but in doing so, he threw his head to the right. That change of weight threw him off balance, and he rolled over on his side, still sliding downward.

Belle saw this and, instead of letting go or screaming at him, she had an instant thought: "His dead weight will slow the wagon as much as if he were on his feet." And she was right—the wagon lessened its speed as it careened down the incline.

Just as she was about to congratulate herself, her foot caught between two rocks and she yanked violently forward. She gave a hard kick and her foot came free, but it threw her off balance and she went sprawling, hitting the ground hard just behind Nig's big old behind. Sand flew into her eyes, nose, and mouth. She gagged, spitting and coughing, still clinging to the lines for dear life, bouncing wildly as they shot downward.

The road was rougher now, and there were jagged rocks closer to the side of the cliff where the wagons hadn't knocked them down. She screamed as her hip hit one of them and scraped all the way down her right leg. It was a searing pain, and she nearly let go of the lines, but instinctively her grip only tightened.

"Stanford!" She shouted it out, but there was no way he could hear her over the tremendous racket echoing between the cliffs. There was a loud bang as one of the front wheels hit a rock a glancing blow and veered sharply to the left. That sudden change of direction probably prevented Nig from being dragged headfirst into the rock and saved his life, but there was a shriek of horrible pain as the rock edge scraped along his flanks.

At the same instant, the wagon bounced so hard that Belle was yanked violently upward until she was on her feet again for one instant. But the sharp turn of the wagon snapped the lines and threw her against the side cliff. She bounced off, then went sprawling again, losing her grip on the reins, rolling over and over until she came to a sliding stop.

She lay there for a moment, dazed and battered, and then she realized that she wasn't on hard rock anymore. She was partially buried in soft soil. Amazed, she looked up. Just ahead of her the wagon was stopped, its wheels buried nearly to the hubs in the same soil. A cry of pure joy was torn from her throat. They were down. They had made it.

Dust and sand billowed all around, choking Stanford and making it difficult for him to see. But as soon as he realized they were stopped, he leaped down and ran forward to his team. The wagon had run the animals down, pulling their hind legs clear up beneath the tugs. They were scream-ing in pain. He grabbed frantically at the harnessing, fighting to loosen the tugs before the animals were seriously injured.

That done, he raced around to the back of the wagon to find his wife. He stopped. Old Nig was lying on his side, flesh quivering, eyes closed. Belle was about twenty feet away and just getting to her feet. She was shaking violently. One cheek had a raw, red patch. She was bleeding from a cut on her arm, and she was covered with dust and grime. But he had never seen anything so beautiful, or so magnificent, in his life. "Belle!" he cried.

When she saw him, her chin came up and she planted her feet firmly, daring him to show her one ounce of sympathy. He slowed. "How did you make it, Belle?"

She took a deep breath, brushed at the dirt on her apron and skirt, then lifted her head. "Oh, I just kind of crow-hopped along," she said solemnly.

Once again Stanford felt his eyes burning and he had to turn away. What a woman this was. To his surprise, Nig moaned. He was sure the horse had been killed, but to his amazement, the animal lumbered to his feet. The whole upper side of his body was covered with cuts or large, ugly patches of flesh where the hair had been scraped off. He stood there, head down, chest heaving. But as near as Stanford could determine, he didn't even have a broken leg.

Finally, he turned and looked up the narrow notch through which they had just come. He shook his head in absolute amazement. They had made it. He was just turning away when something caught his eye. About a hundred feet up the hill, he saw a small patch of white atop one of the rocks alongside the roadway. He swung around, staring at his wife.

She had seen what he had seen and was examining her dress. She stretched it out just below the waist to reveal a jagged hole near her hip.

He forced a shaky smile. "I think you lost your handkerchief up there, Belle." Then his throat constricted as he saw the dark stain just below the rip. In three great leaps he was to her. Now he could see a small patch of blood on the rock by her foot.

"You're bleeding." He was frantic. "And we don't have anything here to fix it."

"Old Nig dragged me most of the way down," she admitted. She lifted her skirt to just above the knee, wincing as the fabric brushed across her leg. There was a gash in her leg starting at the hip and going all the way down to her ankle. She gingerly pressed the fabric against the wound. "It's not deep, Stanford. I'll be all right."

"Oh, Belle," he cried, gingerly taking her elbow. "Is your leg broken?"

She didn't feel like being pitied right now. She pulled free and gave him a swift kick in the shins. "Ow!" he yelped. "What was that for?"

"Does that feel like my leg is broken?" she yelled.

And then her chin began to quiver. He put his arms around her. "Belle," he said, smoothing her tangled hair with his fingertips, "I . . . God bless your gallant heart." And then they were both laughing and crying as they stood there trembling and panting for breath.

She pulled away, sniffing and wiping at her tears, then nudged him. "I'm all right. Go up and get the children."

He turned without another word and started up the steep incline. As Stanford approached the top, he heard a small voice calling out to him. "Papa? Papa? Is that you?"

"Papa's coming, Ada. Papa's coming."

He found the three children exactly as they had left them. As he dropped to his knees and took Ada in his arms, she buried her head against his shoulder. "God stayed with us, Papa."

Roy was nodding vigorously, his face wreathed in smiles. "The baby's gone to sleep, Papa, an' my arm's almost broke."

Laughing softly, Stanford gently lifted the baby from between his brother's legs. As he lifted him up, he pulled back the blanket to see if he was all right. Little George opened his eyes at that moment and, at the sight of his father, broke into a large toothless smile.

"Come, children," Stanford said, offering a prayer of gratitude, "Mama's waiting below."[1]

Far below them, among the wagons still left on the west bank of the river, David Draper sat in front of the fire, warming his hands. Anxiously watching him were his father, Sarah McKenna, Molly, and Billy Joe.

"It was just plain stupid," David said, staring morosely into the fire. "I was trying to warn Al Barney about being knocked about and ended up in the water myself."

Molly laid a hand on his shoulder to help steady the shivering that had gripped his body again. She was shocked to feel how damp and cold his coat still was.

He abruptly stood, wincing sharply at the pain. "I'm going up to see if I can help."

"No, David," Sarah cried. She stepped to him and gently pushed him back down again. "Patrick and Abby are already on their way back up."

She looked up, then pointed. "See. There they are, just crossing the dugway."

They all turned and looked up. Sure enough, two tiny figures were visible in the fading light, making their way horizontally across the cliff face.

"But . . ." He started to rise again.

His father pushed him down again more roughly than Sarah had. "David, ya be naw usin' yur 'ead, boy. Yur leg awreddy be swellin' up. They naw be needin' you oop thare. Just give 'em sum ole cripple to worry aboot gittin' off the moontain."

"John!" Molly cried, stunned by the bluntness of his words.

He turned and winked at her. "Sorry, Molly gurl, but ya need ta talk ta this boy in language 'e understands. Otherwise, 'e be 'obbling his way oop thare."

David sank back down. He knew his father was right. Just walking here from the ferry had left his leg throbbing like a bass drum. He looked up again, squinting, watching as the tiny figures of Patrick and Abby finished crossing the dugway. "What do I say to Belle?" he said forlornly. "And how do I face Stanford? I promised."

"I think when they hear what happened," Molly said, squeezing his shoulder, "that you won't have to say anything. Not anything at all."

<hr/>

High above them, Patrick and Abby sat side by side, wheezing heavily as they tried to regain their breath. She stood up and reached out her hand to help him up, but stopped when she saw his face. He seemed far away, lost in his thoughts. "Daddy?"

He looked up, half startled. He took her hand and let her pull him up. But when she went to let go, he held on to it. "Do you regret telling Carl Bradford you didn't want to marry him?"

"*What?*" She gaped at him, stunned by the question.

"Do you?"

She barely hesitated. "Not in any way. Whatever made you ask that right now?"

He shrugged. "Just wondering."

Peering at him more closely, she had a sudden thought. Had he seen what had happened between her and David earlier today? Then she shook her head. There was no way. When she had turned and started back up the canyon, it had been a full ten minutes before she reached him and John. She poked his shoulder. "Come on, Dad, you never 'just wonder' about things. What made you ask that question right now?"

There was an enigmatic shrug. "I don't know. I was just thinking about it for some reason."

She grabbed his arm and held him back. "Oh no you don't, Patrick Joseph McKenna. What's going on in that head of yours?"

He moved closer to her, put his arm around her, and pulled her up against his shoulder. "Sometime we need to talk, my girl, but right now, we need to get up that mountain and see if we can help Stanford and Belle."

Note

1. This story of Stanford and Arabelle Smith is one of the most remarkable accounts to come out of the Hole in the Rock experience. One of Stanford's and Belle's grandsons, after hearing the story many times, wrote it up, and it was published in 1954 (see Raymond Jones, "Last Wagon," 22–25). Miller includes much of this account in his book (see *Hole*, 112–15).

The narrative written by their grandson is so rich in detail and dramatic power that I have added only a very few embellishments for continuity. For the most part, the words attributed to them in this chapter are their own.

BOOK VIII

ATTAINMENT

1880

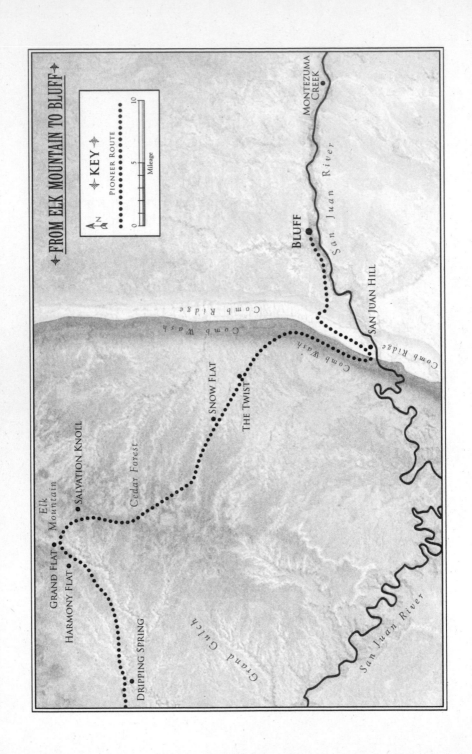

FROM ELK MOUNTAIN TO BLUFF

KEY

N

PIONEER ROUTE ●●●●●●●●

0   5   10
Mileage

MONTEZUMA CREEK

San Juan River

BLUFF

SAN JUAN HILL

Comb Ridge

Comb Wash

Comb Ridge

Comb Wash

SNOW FLAT

THE TWIST

SALVATION KNOLL

Cedar Forest

Elk Mountain

GRAND FLAT

HARMONY FLAT

DRIPPING SPRING

Grand Gulch

San Juan River

CHAPTER 64

Sunday, February 8, 1880

It took five more days to bring the rest of the company across the river. On the day when the McKennas went down the Hole, the company got about forty others down too, and twenty-six of them ferried across to the east side. Tuesday morning the storm that had been threatening finally moved in, blanketing the entire area with snow and turning the air very cold. The second half of the company, those camped at Fifty Mile Spring, came forward to the Hole, but there was no way anyone was going to go down that incline when it was muddy and snow-covered.

The storm lasted for two days, and they had to wait another day to let it dry off enough to begin taking the wagons down. By the time they got them all down and across the river, it was late Saturday afternoon, the last day of January.

Molly shivered a little and pulled her coat more closely around her. It was still bitterly cold—there was ice several feet out on both sides of the river now. But it wasn't the cold that made her shiver. She was remembering Belle Smith. If Stanford hadn't made his way up to her, she would have been caught in that storm up there with those three little children.

She pushed that thought aside. Stanford *had* gone up and he *had* gotten his little family down. The story of Belle's courage and her remarkable "crow-hop" to the bottom of the chute was now the talk of the camp. Molly was as astonished as anyone at what she had done—she and her mother helped bandage Belle's leg when she got down—but it left her with a faint sense of guilt. Molly hadn't even had the courage to ride the wagon down.

She didn't want to start into that chain of thought again, so she deliberately forced herself to look around. That began to cheer her up immediately. This was the closest thing to heaven they'd seen since they left Cedar City. Once they were across the river, the wagons began moving up Cottonwood Creek, where the water was crystal-clear and as sweet as anything they had tasted since Escalante. Once the creek came out of the canyon, it meandered across the valley floor toward the river, dropping here and there into natural rock tanks, some big enough to make good swimming holes if the weather turned warmer.

While the Perkins brothers had been blasting their road down through the Hole in the Rock, another crew had worked on this side of the river and carved out a road up into Cottonwood Canyon. This was a gentle, wide canyon, dramatically different from so many of the rugged, steep, dry-rock canyons in the area. What the builders found about three miles up from the river was a near-perfect campsite. It had shade, plenty of forage for the animals, an abundant supply of clean, fresh water, and plenty of firewood—real firewood, not the sagebrush and shadscale they had been using for almost two months.

Here it was announced, to the great joy of the women, that they would stop while the road builders continued taking the road up to the tops of the bluffs. When the weather turned mild and pleasant a few days later, the women seized the opportunity and began the first major wash and cleanup effort since they had left the settlements. The natural rock tanks provided perfect washtubs for their laundry and bathtubs for their children. Some women wryly commented that it was difficult to determine which of the two was the dirtiest.

The men not assigned to the road crew used the break to prepare for the next leg of their journey. Wilson Daily and George Lewis, the two blacksmiths in camp, set up their forges, using coal they had brought with them in their wagons. They went to work making shoes and nails to reshoe the horses, mules, and oxen. Equipment that had been damaged in the precipitous dash down through the Hole was also in need of repair. There were crushed barrels, smashed cages, cracked tires, split tongues, worn harnessing, all in need of repair.

As Molly looked around at the camp, none of that was going on now, of course. It was the Sabbath. They had enjoyed a worship service earlier that was warmed with a sense of gratitude all were feeling. There would be an evening service later, and Platte Lyman and other brethren would speak to them. But tomorrow, it would all end. The road to the top was now finished, and it was time to move on.[1]

She sighed and continued walking. Move on to what? More sagebrush and shadscale? More tepid, stale water from potholes and rock tanks? More endless, jarring miles? More terrifying grades?

She forced those thoughts aside, too. At least they were moving again. The wait at the Hole, over a month long, had seemed interminable to her. Nice as this camp was, she was ready to move on, to shorten the distance between them and the San Juan.

She stopped at the front of the tent of Jim and Anna Maria Decker. She went to call out to see if anyone was inside, then saw that Jim Decker was at the adjoining tent, talking with his father and brothers. He looked up and saw her. "Go on in," he said. "Anna's there."

From inside the tent came a muffled voice. "Who is it?"

"It's me, Anna. Molly McKenna."

"How nice. Come in, Molly."

Molly cradled the tiny bundle in her arms. "She is so beautiful, Anna."

"And sweet as can be," Anna acknowledged. "Considering where she is and where she was born, she is really a good baby."

"Little Lena Deseret,"[2] Molly crooned, watching her suck on her fist, her eyes squeezed tightly shut, the soft dark lashes lying against her cheeks. "A whole month old now."

Young Anna, the oldest of the three Decker girls, came over. "Can I hold her now, Molly?"

Molly's lips formed into a pout. "That's not fair. You get to hold her all the time." But she handed the baby to her, tucking the blanket in around her feet.

As young Anna sat down on the quilt in the corner, her sister

Genevieve, or Ginny, came over and plopped down beside her. The two sisters began to coo and goo at the sleeping baby, hoping to awaken her. Molly watched the tender scene for a few moments, smiling and feeling a touch of envy. Then she turned to Anna. "So how are you doing by now?"

"I'm doing real good," she said. "The week here in camp has been wonderful for me. I'm finally getting my strength back."

"It's been wonderful for all of us." Molly glanced at the baby. "So, was Jim disappointed not to get a little boy?" she asked, soft enough that the girls wouldn't notice.

"Oh, a little, I suppose. But he adores his girls. Calls them his three little cowgirls."

"I see," Molly said with a smile. "So he plans to go into ranching when we get to San Juan?"

"That would be his dream," she said.

"And what about your dream?"

That brought a look of surprise. "I'm happy with whatever Jim wants to do. He's a hard worker. He'll make a go of it if he sets his mind to it."

Suddenly Molly wished she hadn't asked the question. Anna evidently saw something in her expression. "Doesn't David hope to get a ranch too?"

"Yes. He and his father will work it together."

"You sound like that may not be part of your dream," she observed.

Molly sighed. Was she that obvious? "Maybe it's just because we've been out here so long, but the thoughts of an isolated homestead . . ." She didn't want to finish that, and decided to change the subject. "The good thing about David is, I think he could be successful at about anything he sets his mind to."

She nodded. "Knowing how your father feels about him, I'm sure he'd be happy to have David become part of the family business."

Yes, but would David be happy in the family business? Molly just shrugged in response to the observation. And then a thought struck her with great force. Four months ago, her answer to that question would probably have been, *Yes, but would I want him? Would I want this charming, handsome, cynical, doubting, questioning skeptic as my husband?* That had dominated her thoughts for so long, it seemed strange that it hadn't even surfaced now.

Not liking where that was taking her, she changed the subject. "By the way, Mama and Abby will probably be here in a few minutes. They were writing in their journals when I left, but they really want to see the baby again."

And with that, the conversation turned to other things, and Molly gratefully turned her thoughts away from David, at least for the moment.

※※

Abby moved up to the wagon, listened for a moment, then scratched on the canvas cover. "Anybody in there?"

"Aye, lassie. Stick yur 'ead in an' say 'ello."

She walked around to the back and pulled open the flap. John Draper was propped up against a sack of corn, reading from one of the books Abby had lent him over a week ago. "What are you doing inside there when the weather out here is so pleasant?" she teased.

"Ta be reet 'onest wit ye, Abby gurl, Ah be readin'."

His eyes looked a little droopy. "I'm sorry for disturbing you," she said.

"'Tis awl reet." He looked around. "Whare be David?"

"That was going to be my next question. I need to see him for a moment."

"Sorry, Ah cahrn't 'elp ya thare, Abby." He started to get up. "But Ah can cum 'elp ya look."

She waved him back down. "That's all right," she said, a smile playing at the corners of her mouth. "You stay here and continue your—" one eyebrow arched—"your reading."

He laughed. "Ah, Abby, Ah fear ya been aroond me son too mooch. Ya be pickin' up sum of 'is cheek."

"You have a good read," she said. She pulled back and let the flap fall shut again. Then she tapped on the canvas as she walked past it. "Usually, however, it's easier when you have the book right side up."

※※

After asking several other people, she found David by the creek, downstream from the campsite about a hundred yards. He was beneath some giant old cottonwood trees that shaded one of the rock tanks. To her surprise, he was seated on the ground with his back to her, and in front of him, gathered around the pool, were nearly a dozen children. She stopped and moved behind a tree, curious as to what was going on.

The children included a wide age span, those in their early to mid-teens down to five- and six-year-olds. Billy Joe was visible near the front. One girl about Billy Joe's age was waving her hand back and forth wildly. "I know, I know," she cried, barely able to keep her seat.

David pointed at her. "Yes, Sally?"

"'Bits and bobs' are odds and ends."

"Good." David leaned forward a little. "Are your parents from England?"

"Yep," she said proudly.

"Okay," David said, chiding them a little. "How many of you have parents or grandparents who come from the British Isles?"

To Abby's surprise, nearly half the hands came up.

"I can see I'm going to have to make these a little tougher then," David mused. "Okay, I'll say the word or phrase. If you know what it means, you just sing it out. You don't have to raise your hand. Ready?"

Every child leaned forward, eyes bright with eagerness.

"To 'witter on.'"

A girl about twelve shot up her hand and blurted it out at the same time. "To gab and gab."

"Good, Delia. How about 'dicey'?"

"Questionable or risky," she fired right back.

He laughed. "Okay, I can see you're a real Brit. Come on, you others. How about 'chuffed,' as in 'I'm real chuffed.'"

"Mad?" a younger girl asked tentatively.

"Nope, just the opposite. It means to be delighted." He reached up and pulled on his lip. "All right, let's make this a little more challenging. What's a 'train spotter'?"

"Someone who sees a train," Billy Joe called.

"Spoken like a true Yank," David said. "Sorry. Anyone else?"

Heads were shaking back and forth.

"Ha!" David said. "Got you. A train spotter is a dull person, someone who's really boring."

The children gave him blank looks. Abby stepped forward. "Why's that?" she asked.

David jumped a little as he turned and saw who it was. He looked instantly sheepish. "We're just playing a game," he said. "Seeing if they know the meaning of British expressions."

"I see what you're doing," she said. She walked over and sat down beside Billy Joe. "So why is a dull, boring person called a train spotter?"

He felt even more foolish. "In England there are people who stand by the railroad tracks and write down the serial numbers of all the cars or locomotives as they pass by because they have nothing better to do."

"I see. That does sound pretty boring. Thank you," she said, and sat back.

But she had rattled him, and he looked uncertain about what to do.

"Give us some more," the children called.

"Yes," Abby said. "Give us some more."

He shot her a dirty look. "Okay, a few more, then it's time to get back to your families. How about 'chock-a-block'?"

Frank's hand was up in an instant. "Stuffed full, like the cupboard is chock-a-block."

"Good, Frank. And 'whacked'?"

"Very tired," an eight-year-old said. "Grandpa's always saying that: 'I'm real whacked.'"

"One more," David said. "How about 'dotty'?"

That one had them. They looked back and forth but came up blank. Abby finally raised her hand. "I may know that one."

"Miss Abigail," David said, giving her a low bow.

"To be dotty is to be silly or a little bit crazy."

"Exactly right. Can you use it in a sentence?"

She looked at her brother. "Billy Joe is a bit dotty about guns."

"Am not!" he said hotly as the other children shrieked with laughter.

"I'm afraid you are, Billy Joe," David said, "but would you rather be dotty about guns or nithered?"

His nose wrinkled, as he was not sure he liked either. David looked around. "Anyone?"

No one moved. Even Abby was silent. Pleased that he had them, he stood up. "*Nithered* means to be very cold, nearly frozen. And since we are not nithered at the moment, and this is a lovely day, I would suggest you go back to your families and see how many words they know."

⁂

Abby stood back and watched as the children came up to David to say good-bye or to ask him a question. A five-year-old girl motioned for him to bend down, then kissed him on the cheek. A younger boy gave him a pretty rock he had found in the creek. To her surprise, watching that made Abby want to cry, though she wasn't sure why.

When the last one left, he turned to her, motioning for her to join him as they walked back to the camp. "That was sweet," she said, "and fun."

"They're great kids." They moved slowly, neither speaking. "Where's Dad?" he finally asked.

"In your wagon," she said. She stopped, then moved over to one of the cottonwood trees and leaned back against it. Her eyes never left his. He finally had to look away.

"I have something I want to say, David," she said, speaking very softly now.

"I thought you might."

"I wanted to thank you for the other day. If you hadn't insisted on me and Dad coming down with you that first time, I don't think I could have found the courage to drive down it by myself."

She had surprised him. Trying not to show his relief, he nodded. "When I suggested it, I had no intention that it would ever come to that." He glanced up, his eyes pained. "I am so sorry that I left you up there alone."

She smiled. "It's a good thing you fell into the river," she said, making a face, "or Molly and I would have personally thrown you in. How is your leg, by the way? I see you're not using the cane now."

"It's healing. Fortunately, the hoof didn't cut too deeply."

"Well, anyway. Thank you."

He bent down and picked up a dead twig and began breaking it into small pieces. "Is that what you really came to say?"

She straightened, and he saw that her mouth had pinched tight now. "Would you like to tell me what happened on the mountain the other day?"

Now he began kicking at the dirt with the toe of his boot. "I'm not sure," he finally said.

"And that's it?" she cried.

"I'm sorry, Abby. I . . . I suppose part of it was being so relieved that we made it down safely. I think the adrenaline was still pumping."

"Oh," she snapped, "so it was just adrenaline?"

"Abby, I . . . what I'm trying to say is . . ." He just shook his head. "I am very sorry."

There was a soft sound of disgust. "So is that what you do whenever you're excited and relieved? Grab the nearest girl and give her a kiss?"

"That question is not worthy of you," he said quietly.

Her mouth opened, then shut again. He waited, no longer looking at her. "Do you think Molly would agree with you on that?" she asked with soft bitterness.

When he still neither spoke nor looked up, she threw up her hands. "Don't you even see the irony of it, David? One minute you're saying, 'I would never do anything to hurt your family. *Especially you.*' Then an hour later you grab me and kiss me? What am I supposed to think? You did hurt me, David. And if Molly ever finds out, she'll be absolutely shattered."

"I was wrong, Abby. I shouldn't have done it. Under the circumstances, it was not an honorable thing to do."

"Under the circumstances?" she shot back. "Would those happen to include the fact that you are courting my sister?"

Finally he straightened. "I'm not courting your sister, Abby. Not anymore."

"Well, she thinks you are. Or at least she expects that you will once we reach San Juan."

"I know. And that's why it was not an honorable thing to do. I was just . . ." Then he shook his head. "It doesn't matter. It was wrong, and I planned to apologize to you."

That only frustrated her more. "I'm trying to understand what happened up there, David. Why would you do such a thing?" Her eyes held his, challenging. When it became clear that he wasn't going to answer her, she stepped forward and slugged him hard on the arm. "Oh! You make me *so* furious. How can you do something as wonderful as this—" she waved a hand to take in the pool and the scene she had just witnessed—"and then you do something so . . . so . . ." She couldn't finish it. "If I did have any feelings for you, how am I supposed to feel now?"

That brought his head up with a snap. "Say that again."

She realized what she had just said and her face flamed scarlet. She turned away quickly.

He stepped up behind her, his hands lifting to take her shoulders and turn her around, but, hearing him, she went absolutely rigid. He fell back, moving over to a fallen tree and sitting down heavily. He was remembering that night he had sat across the table from Mary Davis. She had told him that women like her weren't looking for handsome and charming and irresistible, but rather for steady, strong, and dependable. His teasing response had been to ask where one found a woman like that. She had given him a strange look, then had begun to laugh. "Oh, David," she had exclaimed. "You really don't know, do you?"

He had thought much on that. He was pretty sure he understood what Mary had meant, but he had scoffed at it at first. He and Abby? There was no way. They were good friends, but were more prone to battle than to bliss. He was her thorn in the side. She was his humility monitor. She understood his doubts and skepticism and inner struggles with his faith better than Molly did, and saw far more clearly the implications of that for a marriage. From the beginning, she had tried to warn Molly that David was nothing but trouble disguised as charm.

And then had come that wild plunge down the gorge. When they reached the dugway and stopped, he came to the full realization of what she had done. And he knew that she had done it because he had asked her to, in spite of her terrible fear of heights. At that moment, he had realized that she was the most remarkable woman he had ever known. And that included his mother.

That was why he had kissed her. But how could he tell her that? Even now, it was like Molly stood between them. Sweet, wonderful, lovely, courageous, delightful Molly. Molly, who knew full well that David's lack of faith was no longer a barrier between them. Molly, who was patiently waiting for their arrival in San Juan so the courtship could resume and they could marry. Until that was settled, how could he say anything to Abby? If she saw a single kiss as a betrayal, how would she respond if he tried now to express his love for her?

He heard the sound of her footsteps and looked up.

"David." He saw that she had been crying, and that tore at him. There weren't many who were capable of making Abby McKenna cry. But he was one of them. "Don't walk away," she pleaded. "Help me understand."

He stood. "I can't. Not now." He wanted to weep as he saw first hurt, then anger, then coldness sweep across her face. "I am so sorry, Abby." He turned and walked slowly away.

"David!" It came out sharp and hard. He stopped, but didn't turn.

Her voice was like the edge of cold steel. "A woman would be a fool to ever trust you."

Notes

1. The description of Cottonwood Canyon and the campsite the pioneers made there comes from Miller, as does the information on how they used that time to regroup and prepare for the next difficult stretch of their journey (*Hole*, 123–25).

2. Anna Maria Decker, wife of James Bean Decker, while camped at Fifty Mile Spring, gave birth to a baby girl on January 3, 1880. They named her Lena Deseret Decker.

CHAPTER 65

John Draper walked along the line of wagons until he reached the McKennas' lead wagon, which was about a third of the way back from the front. Standing between the first and second wagons, Patrick and Sarah McKenna were conferring with Kumen Jones and Joe Nielson. Molly and Abby were standing off to one side listening.

"Hello, John," Kumen said as he came up. "Do you know where David is?"

"Said 'e was goin' up ta check that sand hill one more time before we 'ave ta cross it."

"Does he plan to come back and drive?"

John nodded. "Fur sure."

Joe Nielson looked at Patrick. "Well, John and David know that road as well as we do, so we'll let them brief you on what to expect. If you need help, let us know."

"Thank you," Patrick said.

"Yes, thank you," Sarah called after them.

"David's not going to leave us alone again, is he?" Abby said to her father.

John pretended not to hear and her father didn't answer. John turned and began searching the road ahead of them, trying to pick out his son from amongst the bustle of activity along the road. And then he spotted him. He and Billy Joe were striding toward them about five or six wagons up the line. John smiled. Billy was only half the size, and he was trotting to keep up with David, but other than that, he looked every bit as much the man as David.

"Thare they be," John said. He hadn't directly looked at Abby, but she seemed to think he had. She came over and touched his arm. "I'm sorry, John. That was uncalled for."

He half closed one eye and squinted at her in the morning sunshine. "Ya awl reet, Abby?"

There was a quick shake of her head. "It's like the Hole all over again. My stomach's twisted so tight that I feel like I can't breathe."

"Ah unnerstand," he said gently. "Thare be a couple of rough places up thare, but they be nothin' like comin' doon the 'Ole." He laughed shortly. "Cahrn't be anythin' in the 'ole world quite like that."

Molly came over. "You're just saying that so we don't turn around and go back home right now."

"Thare be two big differences b'tween Cottonwood Hill an' the 'Ole. First, the grade be only aboot 'alf as steep. Second, we'll be going up the hill, naw doon. That be a big difference."

"Kumen was saying that we'll have to double- or triple-team the wagons to get them up the last pull."

"Aye, maybe even more. Ah predict we'll be puttin' on six or seven span of animals on the 'eavier wagons fur a couple of stretches." He turned. "But 'ere's David."

Billy Joe ran up and put an arm through his mother's. "Hey, Mom, it's really neat up there. You can see all the way back to the Hole in the Rock across the river. And there's a place near the top that they call the 'Little Hole in the Rock.'"

"Oh, great," Abby said, rolling her eyes.

"Only because it's a narrow v-shaped slot between two side cliffs," David said as he joined them. "It's a pull, but not as steep as the Hole, and it's only a hundred or so yards long."

"Ah was joost tellin' 'em a little aboot the road an' what ta expect. Ya be the better teamster, David. Ah'll let you tek it frum 'ere."

David nodded. He was quite sober and businesslike. "The thing about Cottonwood Hill is that it can be quite deceiving. There will be a couple of places where you think you've reached the top, only to crest out and see the next ridge in front of you. "

"Wouldn't you say it's no more than a mile to the top?" Patrick said.

"If you mean clear to the top," David answered, "no, it's about double that. But just beyond the Little Hole that Billy Joe was telling you about, there's some tableland. That's really the end of Cottonwood Hill and the worst of the climb."

"And what lies between here and there?" Sarah asked.

"Well, I won't sugarcoat it for you. This is going to be another challenging day."

Molly looked at him and gave him a bright smile. "It's all right, David. Sugarcoat it for us."

He gave a little grunt and a half smile, then continued in that same matter-of-fact tone of voice. "There are four main features of Cottonwood Hill," he said. "The first, which is just out of sight around the bend there, is a dugway cut into a side hill. That isn't a bad pull, and the first part shouldn't give either the animals or the drivers any serious trouble."

"I think I hear a 'but' coming," Abby said dryly to no one in particular.

"But," David said, ignoring her comment, "the dugway has a very steep pitch that goes through a stretch of fine sand. The sand is deep and constantly drifting across the roadway."

John came in. "We be spendin' a lot of time tryin' ta dig oot a road base thare, but the sand fills it reet in agin."

"If we're going to tip over any wagons, that will be the place."

"Is that on the agenda?" Abby asked innocently.

That finally won her a fleeting smile. "Not on mine, but you never know. Anyway, once we're past that, there is a fairly level stretch of roadway that goes along the top of a ridge. That will give the teams a breather and allow us to stop and regroup a little."

"Do you want us to walk again?" Sarah asked.

"For some parts you'll be fine riding. Others you'll definitely want to walk, so that's up to you—if you don't mind climbing in and out of the wagons on the way up."

"I'm going to walk with Nate," Billy Joe said.

Sarah looked at David to see if he was all right with that. He nodded. "Even walking that strip where the sand is will be tricky, but if you do happen to fall there, it's like falling into a pile of feathers, only grittier."

"So is this where we end up getting sandy claws?" Molly asked, straight-faced.

David actually laughed. "And toes, and hair, and nostrils." He stopped, turned, and lifted his hand to shade his eyes from the sun as he looked up to where they could see the tops of some red rock bluffs. "It's the stretch after the sand hill that will be the most challenging. As you come up along the ridge, the road runs straight into those bluffs you can see up there. That's where that thousand pounds of blasting powder Amasa Lyman brought in from Panguitch came in handy.[1] Ben, Hy, and Dad had to blast a road right out of the side of the hill."

"Hill?" Patrick said. "Not cliff?"

"That's right. It slopes off pretty steeply, but no, it's not a sheer cliff." He paused, and finally looked at each of them. "Once you're past that, it's the Little Hole in the Rock, and then we're on top. Any questions?"

"Are you planning that Daddy and I will drive?" That was Abby. Any lightness was gone from her face now.

"That's up to you. After what you and Patrick did at the Hole, I'd say you're about ready for anything. The challenge will be that Platte's asking every wagon to have seven or eight span. That means we can only take up two of our wagons at a time. We'll unhitch on top and bring them back down to hitch up again. So it's not like we have to have you drive."

"I'm fine with you taking them," Patrick said softly. "Kumen was saying that we're going to put a couple of men on the back with ropes as we cross the sand hill to stop the back ends from sliding off. I can do that."

Abby went to speak, but Molly grabbed her arm. "Walk with Mama and me, Abby. Please? I don't think I can stand another day like that day at the Hole."

"I'm not sure I'm up to another day like that last one either," she said without expression. "I'll walk." She glanced at David to see his reaction to that, but he just nodded.

"Gud," John said. Then to David, "Want me ta go up first?"

"Yeah. Patrick and I will hold the back end for you."

Sarah took in a deep breath, then exhaled slowly. "Well, here we go again." She squinted at David. "About how many more of these do we have between here and the San Juan?"

"Enough to keep us humble," came the soft reply.

As they started to turn away, David cleared his throat. "One more thing." He waited until they were looking at him. "Day after tomorrow, George Hobbs and I and a couple of other men will be leaving."

Molly's head came up sharply. "Not again!"

"Just listen," Patrick said. He seemed not at all surprised by this announcement. Neither was David's father.

"We left Jim and Mary Davis and started back for the Hole on New Year's Eve," David said. "At that time, they had no more than sixty days' worth of wheat left and no way to get any more. It's now been six weeks." He let that sink in for a moment. "We're going to load a few packhorses with what we can spare and strike out ahead while the company builds a road down Slickrock Hill."

His eyes met Abby's for a moment. "It's the only honorable thing to do."

Sarah, Abby, and Molly decided not to go all the way to the top. Once they had crossed the sand hill—slipping and sliding precariously in the shin-deep sand—they found a place at the top of the ridge where they had a clear view of the road below. They sat down to wait for their men to appear. They had plenty of company, as many others had stopped to watch as well.

Platte Lyman, Bishop Jens Nielson, Kumen Jones, and Joe Nielson were nowhere in sight when they arrived, but when Sarah asked, she was told they had been the first to go up. They were expected back to help the others any time. It was a frightening thing to watch the wagons cross that final stretch of deep sand. Not a single wagon had tipped over coming down through the Hole in the Rock, though some barrels had been smashed, and several animals had been dragged and hurt. But by the time the McKennas sat down to watch, the wagons that had gone before had left the roadway completely buried in soft sand again. Each wagon had two ropes tied to the rear axle, and two men walked along behind, pulling back with all their strength to keep the back end of the wagon on the road rather than having it slide off down the hill.

And that was a good thing. There was no way the drivers could be worrying about that. They had their hands full keeping fourteen animals moving up the hill. If the teams ever stopped crossing that stretch, the wagons would be lost. Only the forward momentum of the teams and the men hauling on the back end to keep it on the road prevented a wagon from rolling off.

Men moved up and down along the dugway, checking the harnessing, shouting encouragement, occasionally running up behind to give the wagon a final push up and onto the ridge. John Draper came across without incident. This was where mules proved their value. They were sure-footed and less intimidated by heights. With David and Patrick shouting and yelling, they plowed across the sand. The mules snorted and grunted as the wheels bogged down, but they kept moving, and in a moment John was clear. He waved to the girls as he went by, but kept the mules moving.

"Look," Abby cried a moment later. "Is that Seraphine driving?"

Sarah and Molly stared down in horror. The next wagon up belonged to Zechariah Decker. The Deckers had a large extended family and several wagons. Zechariah's wife, Seraphine Decker, was the mother of five children, including Billy Joe's best friend, Nate Decker. Because of the need for drivers, she had driven one of the wagons most of the way. But to see her now, coming up the dugway, seven sets of reins in her hands, was shocking to all of them. Her husband was behind, holding one of the ropes. Her brother-in-law, Jim Decker, held the other.

As the teams approached the sand hill, her husband shouted up at her, "Don't let them stop, Sera. Keep 'em moving."

Even from this distance, Abby could see that her face was white and her lips were pulled back in a frightful grimace. She whipped the reins and shouted something at the teams. Suddenly, Sarah gasped. "Look. Isn't that the baby right behind the wagon seat?"

"It can't be," Molly cried, one hand flying to her mouth.

But it was. They could see the splash of color tucked in right behind Seraphine. At that moment, the back end of the wagon started to slide sideways in the soft sand. Zechariah and Jim Decker yelled and hauled back on the ropes. It was too late. The wagon dragged them with it, their boots gouging deep furrows in the sand. Other men were shouting now too, and some started running to help. But it was too late. The wagon was now at a sharp angle to the roadway, wheels half buried in the sand. And then, as graceful as a dancer doing a pirouette, the wagon rolled over on its side, dragging the horses to a halt.

A scream pierced the air as Seraphine leaped clear, hit the soft sand, and rolled several times before sliding to a stop. The women on the ridge were up. Everyone was yelling and shouting and crying. Zechariah came running toward the wagon in great leaps. When he reached the wagon, he disappeared for a moment behind the wagon cover, then reappeared again. He shouted as he held a bundle up high in the air with both hands. "I have the baby," he called. "He's all right. He's all right."

Seraphine Decker dropped to her knees, buried her face in her hands, and began to sob.

Over the next hour, the women and children on the ridge above the sand hill grew more and more numbed as they watched the men retrieve the fallen wagon and drag it back up onto the road. It continued as wagon after wagon crossed that treacherous stretch of roadway. Almost every trip across left them gasping, even though most made it safely. David, driving the second wagon, nearly lost it when the back end hit a rough spot beneath the sand and nearly jerked John and Patrick clear off their feet. But David whipped the mules and lunged forward, managing to keep the wagon moving.

Others were not so fortunate. The Barneys, whose son Al had been knocked into the river with David, had a second bout of bad luck. The Barneys had eight children with them, including a baby still in arms. Laura had decided to walk the children up the hill, but Bird Ella, her three-year-old daughter, had fallen asleep in the back of the wagon, and they had left her there rather than wake her. Laura and the other children were now up on the ridge with the McKennas and others, watching nervously as they saw their wagon coming up the dugway.

As Brother Barney reached a narrow part of the road, the outside lead horse began to balk. It didn't like being on the edge of a steep hillside. Again there were shouts of warning, but it was too late. The other horses began turning away from the hill in response to the pressure from the first. That pulled the rear wheel off the road, tipping the wagon at a sharp angle. With a yell, Barney jumped clear, hitting and rolling several feet in the soft sand of the hillside. Laura screamed, thrust the baby at her oldest son, and went racing down the hill, hair flying. There was a tremendous crash as the wagon flipped and hit the ground, then slid down several feet. Shattered pottery, tin pans and kettles, and other debris came flying out. Then a long bundle fell out of the back, and Laura screamed again. "Bird Ella!" To everyone's astonishment, when father and mother reached the little girl, they unwrapped the bedding and found her crying but perfectly unharmed.

Henry Holyoak's wagon was doing fine until a chain broke. His wagon ended upside down with the wagon tongue pointing crazily at the sky and the teams bolting up the hill. The Holyoaks had a hive of bees in the back of their wagon. All operations came to a halt for over an hour while the bees were sacked and returned to their hive, the tongue was taken apart and hauled up the hill, and the wagon was repaired as best as it could be.[2] Little Bird Ella played with her brothers and sisters happily through all of that, completely unconcerned about what had just happened.

Only when David brought the last wagon up and across safely did Sarah and the two girls fall in behind him and make their way up the hill.

Notes

1. Amasa M. Lyman, brother to Platte Lyman, had been sent from Panguitch along with three other men to provide additional manpower for building a road up out of the gorge. When they arrived at Fifty Mile Camp, they found that another man from Panguitch

had left half a ton of black powder there, and the four of them brought it across to the east side of the river (see Platte Lyman's journal for January 31, 1880, in Miller, *Hole,* 166).

2. Cottonwood Hill, and particularly the stretch where the sand was so deep and so fine, saw more accidents than any other part of the road between Escalante and San Juan. The accounts of the accidents given here all involve actual people and accurately represent their account of what happened (see *ibid.,* 126), though they may not have all occurred right at the sand hill.

Much later, Platte Lyman returned to Escalante from San Juan to purchase supplies for the new settlement. His journal entry for May 20, 1880, reads: "Started on this morning, and on the big hill my wagon got loose from my team (which was hitched to the end of the tongue) and ran back and off the dugway and tipped over, breaking the reach [the long beam that connected the two axles and supported the wagon box], box, bows, flour sacks and some other things and scattered my load all over the side of the hill. Spent the balance of the day in mending up and getting things in shape to move on" (*ibid.,* 172).

And yes, for those who are wondering, for about a year, wagons went both directions on the road between San Juan and Escalante, including pulling wagons *up* through the Hole.

CHAPTER 66

Saturday, Feb. 14, 1880: It has been a couple of days since I last wrote here. On Thursday, we packed up the wagons in preparation for leaving our wonderful Cottonwood Camp. We all shall miss its pleasant shade, its clean water, the ample firewood, and the spectacular view across the river to the Hole in the Rock, but it seemed especially hard on Molly.

Yesterday we climbed Cottonwood Hill, spending most of the day getting the wagons up a very precipitous and dangerous road. There were several accidents—tip-overs, mostly—but no one was injured, and wagons can be repaired. I did not drive, which was a tremendous relief. I have said nothing to Father about this, or to David and John, but the experience coming down the Hole has left me deeply shaken, and I do not know how long it will take me to get over it.

We are now camped at what everyone is starting to call Cheese Camp, which is a mile or two above the Little Hole in the Rock. This name requires an explanation. Several days ago, Platte Lyman's brother, Amasa, and some other men came to camp with a wagonload of supplies from the Panguitch Tithing Office. In addition to the black powder which was so important to our road builders, they brought 200 lbs. of pork and a 40 lb. wheel of cheese.

The pork was divided up between the families, but there wasn't enough cheese to share equally with all. So an auction was held. Daddy was able to buy a full pound. It was a treat savored by the family.

Anyway, because the auction created such a stir, we all have taken to calling this place Cheese Camp.

The men from Panguitch also brought mail. To our great surprise, both Molly and I received valentines from Carl. They were simple, but sweet. He writes that he is making much progress on Daddy's business affairs there, which gives Daddy some relief from his concerns. Two of the Decker children also received valentines and are pleased as punch. They have been parading around camp today, showing them to everyone. The other children are much envious.[1]

Strangely, Molly seems in high spirits today. I say strangely because David leaves again tomorrow for the San Juan. He and several others are taking supplies to the Davis and Harriman families there. Normally, his frequent departures and extended absences leave her feeling quite blue. When I said something to her about it, she shrugged it off. "That's how it will always be with David," she said.

David and I have studiously avoided anything but the most polite of interchanges since our conversation last Sunday. Everyone except Molly and Billy Joe seems to have noticed the tension between us. Mother gave me a long, inquiring glance as David's name came up this morning, and I changed the subject. This afternoon, David's father asked me if I knew what was wrong with David. We've all noticed it. He rarely laughs anymore, and only occasionally smiles—and those seem strained. He often doesn't make it back for supper and is gone before breakfast. If I didn't know how concerned he is about Mary Davis and the children, I would almost think he was going there to escape the awkwardness of our situation. I told his father that it was probably just the increased concern for the Davis family causing his change of mood, but I'm sure John doesn't buy that. John likes to call himself a Yorkshire Tyke, but when it comes to shrewdness and tenacity, he's more like a Yorkshire terrier. Why did he ask me what was wrong? How much does he know?

I have relived that conversation numerous times in my head. Though I regret how harshly I spoke—especially my comment about him and women—I still just boil when I think of what happened. Does he really think that he can play with both of our emotions and for—

Abby stopped to dip the pen in the ink bottle. As she prepared to finish the sentence, her eyes lifted and she slowly reread the last three paragraphs. She put the pen down. The paragraph that began with her talking about them avoiding each other took up two lines at the bottom of the previous page, then continued at the top of a new page. She read her words again, thinking about Molly. Though Abby was being circumspect in how she stated it, if Molly were to ever read this, she'd be all over Abby in a minute, demanding to know what she meant.

Abby kept her journal in a small trunk with her other personal possessions. She didn't think that Molly had ever gotten into it and read it, just as she had never read Molly's journal. However . . .

She picked up the pen, dipped it in the ink bottle, and carefully lined out the two bottom lines on the previous page. She did it again so that there was no way anything was legible. Next, she tore out the new page, crumpled it, and put it in her apron pocket. Finally, she dipped the pen once again and began writing at the top of the new page.

I hear someone singing "Come let us anew, our journey pursue," which is usually the signal that evening prayers are about to begin. So I shall close for today.[2]

Sunday, Feb. 15, 1880: *Shortly after breakfast, David left for San Juan in company with George Hobbs. They are on foot, but leading a string of pack mules carrying food and other supplies from Escalante. It was a sad and yet moving sight, two men on foot, rifles in hand, and several mules connected by ropes tied from the tail of one to the head of another.*

Dan Harris, whose family is at the San Juan, and who returned with the Montezuma scouts to get supplies for his family, is going too. But he refuses to go by way of Elk Ridge because of the snow. Hobbs refuses to take a southern route because he says it will take much longer. George and David have asked for other volunteers to accompany them, but

Bishop George Sevy, who was with them last December, said the snow in the cedar forest would be too deep and they would never get through. Neither George nor David were deterred by all of this. As George so eloquently put it, "How could I live with myself knowing that women and children were starving and that I had not done all I could to prevent it?"

There was much gloom at their departure, as many fear they cannot make it alone. Molly's high spirits from yesterday are gone and his departure leaves her in a dark mood. I slipped a short note into David's pack when he wasn't looking, wishing him Godspeed, for I knew I would have no chance to say anything before he left. I fear greatly for his safety, but he is resolute. Strange, that over these past few months—though he rarely ever speaks of it—his faith seems to have become stronger than our own. When Mother questioned the wisdom of his going, he smiled and said simply, "Mary's faith will sustain us."

Monday, Feb. 16, 1880: Left Cheese Camp today and started towards Grey Mesa. Not a pleasant day. Weather cold and threatening. Much rough country. But worst of all, much contention in camp. We have a family by the name of Box with us. They are not members and have expressed no interest in the Church. They joined us because they are taking a large herd of horses to trade with the Indians. Tom Box is a giant of a man from Texas, as are others in his family. He travels with his wife, two sons and their wives, and two daughters and their husbands. They are mild mannered and affable and have been much enjoyed by our company. But there have been some feelings over the grazing. Recently they have been taking their horses ahead of the company so they can feed before it is grazed over. This leaves little for our teams.

This has caused much contention among us, something that is rare for this camp. Today, had it not been for the wise intervention of Platte Lyman and Jens Nielson, it would have come to blows, and maybe even gunplay. Happily, a compromise was made. Box and his family left this morning. They will drive their stock across Grey Mesa and on up the trail as quickly as possible so as to leave sufficient feed for our stock. I was much relieved to see them gone without any violence erupting.[3]

Tuesday, Feb. 17, 1880: Passed through much of the area that Platte Lyman and some of the other scouts said was "impassable." Now I understand why they were reluctant to come forward. This is the roughest country I have ever seen. There is nothing but a world of rocks and holes, hills and hollows, canyons, buttes, cliffs and gorges. The mountains are one solid rock as smooth as an apple. Yet, since leaving the Colorado River, our road crew has built a wagon road through it all.

All of this brought us to a place I have dreaded seeing for some time now. David and the other scouts spoke much of it on their return from San Juan. They called it simply "The Chute," and now I understand why. Our builders took the road down into a steep canyon specifically because it leads to The Chute. The Chute is a U-shaped notch, or better, a water course. This is about a quarter of a mile long with a very steep pitch. In a way it is a gift from heaven, for there is no other access up and out of that canyon without spending another two weeks to cut a road through the rock cliffs. This notch, or flume, as David called it, has been shaped by the wind and water into a nearly perfect half pipe—another term the scouts used.

My fears proved to be unfounded. We had to double-team the wagons, but other than that it was rather uneventful. With David gone, I have little choice but to drive now, and Molly is driving all but the roughest stretches. To my surprise, though they still leave me lightheaded and trembling, I am able to cope with these dangerous stretches more confidently. It helped that the curved bottom of this flume-like notch left nowhere for a wagon to tip over or fall off a cliff. A great relief to those with timid hearts.

I am grateful for my growing confidence because I am embarrassed to call on Kumen Jones or Joe Nielson to come drive for me every time the road looks a little challenging. And Father and John can't keep stopping to come back and bring our wagons forward. I even came back down The Chute today and drove Molly's wagon up for her, because Daddy and John were helping repair one of the wagons.[4]

Friday, Feb. 20, 1880: Camped on eastern rim of Grey Mesa. Mesa is flat tableland about 7 or 8 miles long and 2 to 3 wide. Good grass and easy going. However, it abruptly terminates into steep cliffs and deep ravines, all of solid sandstone. This is where the mountain sheep led G. Hobbs to the bottom. Also where he had his "toboggan ride" for half a mile. Mother is having a difficult time keeping Billy Joe off the rocks. Wants to see if he can find where George slid down on his bottom. Company will stop here, probably for at least a week, as road builders construct a road down, a distance of about half a mile. This is a barren campsite, but has plenty of feed for the animals. Beginning to snow as I write this by lamplight. Very cold.

Saturday, Feb. 21, 1880: Woke up to howling blizzard and four inches of snow. Will likely double that before day's over. Some wagons still coming into camp. Using buckets, pans, and kettles to catch snow so as to conserve water in our barrels. If this writing looks shaky, it is because the wind buffets our wagon so badly.

Great joy in camp today in spite of snow. Received word that Olivia Larson (wife of Mons Larson) gave birth to a baby boy today. Named him John Rio Larson—Rio is Spanish for river—because near here is a magnificent view of the San Juan River far below the mesa. This is the third woman to give birth on our journey, and the second child to be added to our company, the first child being stillborn.[5]

Saturday, Feb. 28, 1880: Road down from Grey Mesa complete! Hooray for Ben and Hy Perkins and John Draper and all who helped. It is called Slickrock Hill, a name given by first scouts. (Maybe also by G. Hobbs after his exciting ride on his backside down to the bottom!) Company moved down from the mesa and camped at bottom, about one mile distance from top.

Said that my confidence as a teamster was back. Not so today. Because of short distance (½ mile), John and Daddy took two wagons down, then returned to take mine and Molly's. As we walked down the hill, we were happy with that decision. The road has several of what the builders call "shoot-the-chutes"—steep dugways cut and blasted out of solid rock. These lead to shelves or small open areas which are more easily traversed, but then immediately become another dangerous stretch. Even in

the easier places, the rock is so smooth and slippery that the men cut striations in the rock and filled them with sand to give the teams better grip.

Very, very glad to have all wagons down safely. VERY!![6]

Sunday, Feb. 29, 1880: *Today is Leap Day! Tradition says on
this day a woman can propose to a man, and if he refuses, he has to pay
her a fine. So far, no known proposals in camp. Perhaps because Molly
and I are among the very few single women traveling in the company,
though there are many single young men. (So far, not tempted to take
advantage of Leap Day.)*

*If David were here, I suppose Molly might use this day to commit
him. However, when I started to tease her about it, she became quite
sharp with me. Said that I shouldn't joke about it. Said they have an
agreement, and nothing will happen until our journey is over.*

*Not that David is in camp to receive such a proposal. He and
G. Hobbs have been gone for two weeks now. No word of any kind and
our worries deepen with each additional day.*

*This is a very lovely day. Drove about 7 miles from the bottom of
Slickrock Hill and came to the lake the scouts told us about. They did
not do it justice. Lake Pagahrit (we're told it's Navajo for "standing
water") is truly an oasis in the desert. The lake is formed by a natural
dam across what would otherwise be a dry wash. Ben Perkins estimates
the dam's height at about 60 to 65 feet high, thus making the water
about 50 feet deep. The lake is J-shaped and backs up about half a mile.
It is about a quarter of a mile wide at one point. Below the dam is a
beautiful canyon, shaded by high, deep vermillion cliffs. There is a
spring here and many trees, rushes, willows, etc. Also many birds. It is
wonderful to hear bird songs again.*

*Happiest of all, Capt. Lyman announced we shall stay here several
days while the men extend the road eastward. Once again we shall have
time to wash and bathe and rest the teams.*

*Who would have thought that such a simple thing as a bath could
bring such wondrous pleasure. To find such a beautiful spot with a*

limitless supply of water in the middle of a vast and desolate desert is
yet another reminder of the Lord's tender mercies in our behalf.[7]

Thursday, March 4, 1880

David Draper nearly wept as he watched Emily Davis lick the bacon grease off her fingertips. Her eyes were half closed as she daintily searched for any lingering flavor with her tongue. Beside her, Jimmie and Eddie were each on their third piece of hot corn bread. There was no butter or honey for it, but from the look on their faces, David knew he wouldn't be hearing any complaints about that. Young John was sitting on his mother's lap. He was gnawing happily on a slice of dried apple in one hand while he eyed four more slices in his other fist. He was clearly trying to figure out how he might enjoy the other pieces at the same time he was working his way through this one.

He turned to Mary and was not surprised to see her cheeks stained with tears. "They're so thin," David whispered.

Nodding, Jim leaned forward and lowered his voice. "About two weeks ago, Hank Harriman and I took stock of what wheat we had left. Not knowing when we might see you, we decided we had to cut back to half rations. The last few days, it's been less than that." His voice caught. "We didn't know what we were going to do."

David had to look away. "I'm so sorry."

"Sorry?" Mary cried, startling the children. "We owe our lives to you and George. How can we ever repay you?" She laughed huskily. "And that bag of salt. It's like gold dust."

David laughed too, then looked around and became very sober. "This is payment enough."

"Mama?"

"Yes, Emmy?"

"Can I have some more bacon, please?"

Wiping at the tears, Mary slowly shook her head. "Not yet, sweetheart. Your little tummy will start hurting if you eat too much of this rich food."

Her face fell, but Mary reached out and laid a hand on her cheek. "We have plenty of food now, children. You go out and play for a couple of hours, and then we'll have supper with David."

"Will you tell me a story when I go to bed tonight?" Emmy asked David.

"I would love to."

"Come on, Emmy," Eddie said, getting to his feet. "David will still be here when we get back." His eyes came around to David's. "Won't you?"

"Absolutely, Eddie. I'm going to stay for a couple of days."

As soon as they were gone, Mary moved over beside her husband. "All right, David, tell us everything. Where is the company by now? When can we expect to see you again? How many are there coming? And how is everything with you and Abby?"

"You mean me and Molly," he said automatically.

She gave him one of her looks that said, "Oh, please!"

David began with a brief summary of the return of the five scouts to the main company at Hole in the Rock. He told them about the road through the Hole, the ferry across the river, and the steady movement eastward. Jim frequently interrupted him with questions. They were so eager for news of any kind that David didn't feel to rush it.

"So," he concluded, "I'm hoping by now they're somewhere near Slickrock Hill or the lake. Which means they still have some pretty rough landscape to cross, a lot of road to build."

"So how much longer?" she demanded.

"Hard to say. There are some pretty easy stretches between here and Lake Pagahrit, but once we hit those cedar forests on Elk Ridge, we're going to have to cut our way through." His eyes crinkled a little as he calculated. "I still think the first of April is a pretty good estimate."

She sighed. "Another whole month. Do you know how good it will be for Lizzie Harriman and me to have other women to talk to?"

David gave Jim a hurt look. "What does that say about me and you?"

"Quite a bit," she retorted. "That's exactly the problem. So tell me, how is the family?"

So David gave a quick report on Sarah and Patrick and their children, and on his own father.

There was a faraway look in her eyes when he finished. "We have so many friends coming. I'm so excited to see them again." She planted her elbows on the table. "Okay, so now are you ready to talk about Abby?"

"You may as well surrender," Jim laughed. "She's been stewing about you and Molly and Abby ever since you left."

"I never talked about Abby when I was here."

Again she gave him that look, only this time she said it. "Oh, please, David. If you'll remember, when you left I was surprised you didn't seem to know. Surely you know by now."

"Know what?"

"Just tell me about you and Abby, and don't be so . . . male."

He wanted to pretend he didn't understand, but he knew exactly what she meant. He took a quick breath, then, blushing a little, quietly told them about kissing her there by Uncle Ben's Dugway after they had come down the slot together.

"Well, donuts and pumpkin pie!" she cried. "You mean you finally saw the light?"

"Yeah," he said glumly. "And care to guess where it got me?" And so he told them about Abby's confrontation with him at Cottonwood Creek. "She wasn't just angry, Mary. She was livid. I thought she was going to slap my face there at one point."

"Of course she was angry."

"I said it was a mistake. I told her I was sorry."

She just shook her head. "I'll bet that helped a lot."

David peered at her. "Why do you say of course she was angry?"

"Because you gave her hope, when she knew there was no hope."

David just stared at her, then turned to Jim for help. He chuckled softly. "Hon, I'm afraid you're going to have to translate that for us boys."

"All right, here it is, as straight as I can say it. I think Abby has loved you for a long time, David. Or, perhaps a better way to say it is, she has *wanted* to love you for a long time. But Molly's been there between you. Sweet, lovely Molly, who has every boy within a hundred miles mooning over her, drowning in the depths of those big eyes of hers. Molly, who is delightful and beautiful and a master at flirting with boys and making them look her way instead of Abby's."

He was dumbfounded. "But . . . ?"

"Hear me out," she said quickly. "Then you and Molly start talking about marriage. Molly, of course, shares everything with Abby. They're sisters, and they're very close. And so Abby sees that once again, she's lost out. And she accepts that. She's used to it, after all. And she does love Molly, and wants her to be happy. But any hope she has for you and her now dies."

His head was down, but his face showed that he was understanding now.

"Then, out of the blue, you take her in your arms and kiss her. She's stunned. Where did that come from? And when she tries to get you to help her understand, all you do is say that it was wrong and that you are sorry. You're lucky she didn't take a stick to you." The last was said with a sad smile.

"But how could I, Mary? She was furious that I kissed her because she thinks I'm still interested in Molly. If I had said I had feelings for her now, before it was over with Molly, that would only make it worse."

"Oh, David. What she was hoping for was that you would tell her it wasn't going to work out between you and Molly. That you didn't *want* it to work out between you and Molly. Don't you see, David? That kiss gave her hope, and then you took it away again."

Jim leaned over and laid a hand on his wife's arm. "I think you're being a little hard on him, dear."

But David burst out before she could answer. "I couldn't, Mary. Not until this thing with Molly is solved. Abby's sense of fairness runs too deep. And she knows how deeply Molly will be hurt. I couldn't do it."

Laughing softly, even as she shook her head, she said, "You've got your plow stuck in some thick clay here, boy. So what are you going to do about it now?"

David considered that, then brightened. When he spoke, it was to Jim. "Would you mind if I stayed here with you and the kids, and sent Mary back to work this out for me?"

That delighted her and she chortled aloud.

"Well," he said ruefully, "all I seem to be able to do is make things worse."

"You're going to be fine," she soothed. "In fact, what you have to do is very simple. Not easy, but simple."

"I'm listening."

"You have to go back and tell Molly that you know now that it isn't going to work out between you. And you need to do that as soon as possible after your return."

"What about our agreement to wait until we're off the trail?"

"Forget the agreement. You can't be making things any easier on Molly by making her wait. The sooner you tell her, the easier it's going to be."

"It will hurt her terribly."

"Probably. But it will hurt her far more if she ever finds out that you loved her sister and never told her that."

"So I just waltz in and say, 'Hi, Molly. Just wanted you to know that it's over between us. And oh, by the way, I'm in love with Abby.'"

Jim chuckled. "I'd try something a little softer than that."

"That will only infuriate Abby all the more," David went on. "She's warned me again and again not to hurt Molly, not to break her heart."

"Of course she has. Abby loves Molly and is her protective big sister. But down deep, Abby is also saying, 'Don't you hurt me either.'"

That struck him like a blow. "Which I did."

"Yes, you did," she said. Then her eyes began to twinkle. "You have a real gift when it comes to women, you know."

David just groaned and put his head in his hands.

Mary laughed again. "Oh, cheer up, David. Jim's right. You have to wait for the right moment to tell Molly, but don't delay too long. And once you do, give it some time before you say anything to Abby. She'll start figuring things out." Then she had a thought. "Since tearing into you there at the creek, has Abby even talked to you?"

He lifted his head. "Oh, yeah. We have all these warm conversations like 'Good morning,' or 'Thank you,' or 'Pass the salt, please.'"

"And that's all?"

He reached in his shirt pocket and withdrew a folded piece of paper.

"Except for this. She put this in my pack the morning I left. I didn't find it until that night." He handed it to her.

She moved closer so Jim could read it too, then read softly: "'David. I am sorry for the breach that now lies between us. You have been a good friend and helped me in many ways. I and my family owe you so much. I hope we can be friends again. As you leave to take food and hope to Jim and Mary Davis, know that my prayers for your safety and theirs will be continual. I was disappointed when others did not see the urgency of your mission. I am not surprised at all that you did. May God speed you on your journey and hold you in the hollow of His hand until you return again to our family. Abby.'"

She read it again silently, then folded it and handed it back. She sat back, deep in thought.

"Well?" David finally said.

"It's going to be all right."

"How can you be sure of that?" Jim asked.

She answered him by answering David. "I was wrong. In spite of her hurt, in spite of her anger, she hasn't lost hope. So you go back there and get this fixed, David." She poked him. "Don't you be messing it up again."

"You sure you won't go for me?" he asked in a small voice.

She laughed. "They say if a skunk's ever going to make any friends, he's got to get rid of his own stink. Only you can fix this one, my friend."

"Thank you so much," he muttered.

She reached out and put both hands over his. "Cheer up, David. If things go really bad, you can always come back here and wait for Emily to grow up. That would make her ecstatically happy." She squeezed his hands gently. "And Jim and me too."[8]

Notes

1. In a letter written from Grey Mesa on February 22, Elizabeth (Lizzie) Decker, wife of Cornelius J. Decker, wrote a letter back to her parents in Parowan. She mentions the fact that two of the children had received valentines two days early and were very proud of them (in Miller, *Hole*, 197). The cheese auction is mentioned by several sources (see *ibid.*, 126; Reay, *Incredible Passage*, 61; Redd, "Short Cut," 19).

2. In that same letter, Lizzie Decker mentioned the singing of the popular hymn "Come Let Us Anew" (now #217 in the LDS hymnal), and said it was used to signal the time for evening prayers. In light of the challenges these pioneers faced, the third verse of that hymn must have taken on special significance for them and may explain its popularity:

> Oh, that each in the day of His coming may say,
> "I have fought my way thru;
> I have finished the work thou didst give me to do."
> Oh, that each from his Lord may receive the glad word:
> "Well and faithfully done;
> Enter into my joy and sit down on my throne."

3. The information on Tom Box and the conflict over grazing priorities comes from accounts by George W. Decker and George Hobbs (see Miller, *Hole*, 201–2, 210). Decker says that he was driving a herd of 800 cows, but Redd, whose father was on the trek, says it was 75 horses that caused the trouble (Redd, "Short Cut," 19, 21). The latter figure seems more realistic.

4. This description of the "impassable" terrain between Cheese Camp and Grey Mesa includes wonderful details furnished by Lizzie Decker and David Miller's gifted writing (see Miller, *Hole*, 128–29, 197; Reay, *Incredible Passage*, 63–64). Having personally driven up and down The Chute four times now, I am truly astonished to realize that those pioneers covered that unique rock formation with wagons and teams. Even more amazing is that after the Hole in the Rock and Cottonwood Canyon, building a road through here and the actual ascent of The Chute is barely mentioned in the journals (see Miller, *Hole*, 166; see also Reay, *Incredible Passage*, 63–64; Redd, "Short Cut," 21–22).

5. Mons Larson was in the process of moving his family to Snowflake, Arizona, when he learned from his good friend Silas S. Smith that a company was taking a shortcut to the San Juan. He decided to accompany them to Montezuma Creek, then continue south on his own from there. The long delay of the company meant Sister Larson had to deliver her baby in the wilderness. A daughter of the Larsons later wrote an account of the birth, portions of which are included here:

"It was February 21, 1880, when the Larsons reached the top of the plateau. A blizzard was raging and it was in this terrible snowstorm, exposed to the desert winds, that Olivia gave birth to a boy. The boy was born while the mother was lying on a spring seat and her husband was trying to pitch a tent so the mother could be made more comfortable. With the help of Seraphine Smith Decker and brother Jim Decker, she was placed in the tent and made as comfortable as circumstances would permit. . . . Because of Olivia's unusual vitality, she was able to be up on the fourth day, packed her belongings and climbed into the wagon, travelling all day over rocky roads. She said the baby never had colic. If it wasn't snowing she could bathe him, otherwise, this wise young mother of twenty-three, who now had three babies, rubbed him well with flannel instead of bathing him" (as cited in Miller, *Hole*, 131–32; see also Reay, *Incredible Passage*, 65).

6. A road down Slickrock Hill was completed in about a week's time, another amazing feat by these pioneer builders. Though the site is very difficult to get into, the dugways cut into the hills and the chiseled striations in the stone are still clearly visible (see Miller, *Hole*, 132; and Reay, *Incredible Passage*, 66). Redd's description is particularly good (see Redd, "Short Cut," 21).

7. Lake Pagahrit (also known as Hermit Lake) was a remarkable find for the pioneers. It no longer exists, as a very wet year in 1915 sent water over the top of the dam and it quickly washed away, sending the entire reservoir roaring down Lake Canyon (see Miller, *Hole*, 133). In the fall of 2008, another series of storms sent a flash flood down Lake Canyon, washing out the very narrow road that provided its only access.

8. These conversations between the fictional David Draper and the real Mary Davis are clearly the creation of the author. Mary Davis is yet another example to me of the remarkable heroism of so many of those pioneer women. She has been an inspiration to me, and I tried to use her in the novel in a way that is in harmony with the incredible woman that she must have been.

CHAPTER 67

Friday, March 12, 1880

Sarah McKenna was bent over a cutting board set up on the back of one of their wagons. She was sawing away at a small piece of beef, cutting it into small squares.

"How is it?"

Sarah turned to Abby, brushing back a strand of hair from her face. "Lean. Tough as leather. But I'm not complaining. It's meat."

"Yes. And it sounds wonderful."

"The stew's ready whenever you are," Molly called. She was standing over the campfire, stirring the last of their potatoes and carrots in a mixture of flour and water.

"Coming," Sarah said. Then to Abby, "I know that poor old beef cow of Brother Lyman's was on its last leg, but it will give at least some flavor to the stew."

"It was nice of Brother Lyman to share it with all the camp." Abby turned and glanced up at the sky. "About another hour before the work crews stop. That should be about right."

"Yes," her mother agreed. "Will you get some cracked corn started boiling, Abby?"

It was about five minutes later that a shout brought the heads of all three women up. They turned and looked to the east. Just over a low ridge was where the road down Clay Hill Pass began. Here was yet another very treacherous piece of road being tamed by the intrepid road builders of the company. The women searched the ridge top, but saw no one. Then the shout came again. "It's John," Abby cried.

And that moment, David's father appeared on the ridge. He was waving his arms wildly. "Bring the binoculars!"

They looked at each other. "Maybe Platte is back." Platte Lyman, his brother, and another man had been exploring the countryside to the south while waiting for the road to be finished.

"They be in that bag in me wagon," John shouted as he ran toward them.

Abby darted over to the wagon David and John used, rummaged quickly, and found them. All three of them broke into a trot toward John. As they reached him, he bent down, breathing hard. "I think it be David."

Molly's hand flew to her mouth. "Where?"

"It's a lone figure on foot, cumin' across the flats aboot a mile oot."

"What about George Hobbs?" Sarah asked, as they turned around and started back.

"Dunno," came the reply. "But Ah'm purty sure it be David."

⁂

John and David Draper lay side by side in the wagon box that served as their bedroom. They could still hear the murmurs of people talking, but for the most part the camp was in bed and quiet. "Ah, Son," John said with a deep, satisfied sigh. "It be so gud ta 'ave ya back agin. We awl be gittin' worried aboot ya. Especially Molly and Abby."

David came up on one elbow. "Abby? Are you sure?"

There was a soft grunt, then a long silence. Finally, John spoke. "Ya wanna be tellin' me what's goin' on b'tween ya an' 'er?" he drawled. "Befur ya left, you two were like a cat an' a dog lookin' at the same bowl of milk."

David chuckled at that image. "Never could put much past you, could I, Dad?"

"Ah be not as dotty as ya think, boy. So, are ya gonna tell me or naw?"

David did. He talked slowly, starting with the plunge down the mountain and the kiss. He went through the conversation at the creek in almost perfect detail—it was still burned keenly into his mind—and finally, he shared Mary Davis's feelings about the whole matter.

"Aye," his father murmured when he was done. "Ah be pretty sure sumthin' was up."

"So?" David said. "I want to know what you think about the whole thing."

"That'll take sum time."

David snickered. "I'm not going anywhere."

Again there was a long silence, and David could almost hear the wheels turning in his father's head. "Awl reet, 'ere be some random thoughts."

"Reet," David snorted, lying back down again. "I've never known you to have a random thought in your whole life."

He ignored that. "First, Ah told ya befur, Molly be a good woman, but Ah dunna believe she be the best person fur ya. An' in me own mind, thare be no question aboot Abby. But yur not outta the woods on this one yet, Davee boy, so go easy. Ya 'ave 'urt Abby real deep, Son. Part of that is 'er own 'urt, but part of it is fur Molly. If ya be destroyin' Molly, Ah naw be sure she be furgivin' ya fur that. Your friend Mary be reet. Go careful. Dunna be riding inta that situation with your spurs clangin' an' yur guns blazin'."

David laughed in spite of himself. "Oh, Dad, we're gonna make a Yank out of you yet." Then he sobered. "Mary thinks I should tell Molly as soon as possible. Do you agree?"

"Naw as soon as possible. That wud be tanight. But as soon as it be wise."

"Well, yes, Mary said that, too. So when do you think is a good time?"

"Naw sure," John said again. "Naw t'morrow, that be certain. We start movin' the cump'ny down the hill in the mornin'. An' this be anuther bad one, Son. Real bad. We're callin' it Clay Hill Pass."

"I saw the grade. About killed me coming up it."

"It be more than joost the grade. Frum the top of the pass ta the base is aboot a thousand feet of vertical drop, but the road is almost three miles long b'cuz it winds back and forth to handle the grade. But the worst part is the clay. The tiniest bit of water, an' it becums slick as an otter's back.

An' we been 'avin' rain and snow now fur a couple of days. Them wagons be slidin' reet over the side if'n we dunna hold 'em back."

"I'm glad I'm back to help drive."

"Ah'm sure Abby be glad fur that too. She's real good noow, but these steep places still frighten 'er sumthin' bad. Anyhoow, yur gonna 'ave ta wait fur a better time ta be talkin' romance and love and marriage."

"I'm not going to say anything to Abby. Not for a long time after I break it off with Molly. Right now, Molly's the problem. Finding a time and a place where we can be alone is . . ." He finally shrugged. "It doesn't come easy in a wagon train."

"Don't rush it, Son. Wait 'til it feels reet. Ya will know it when it cums."

"Thank you, Dahd."

They lay there for several minutes, each far away in his own thoughts. Finally, his father turned so he was facing him. "Yur muther wud be reet prood of ya, Son. Reet prood. What ya did fur the Davises. What yur doin' fur the McKennas."

David swallowed hard. Ironically, he had just been thinking about his mother. "I still miss her. Sometimes real fierce like."

"Aye," came the soft answer. Then, to his surprise, his father rolled over and sat up. He started fumbling in the bag beside his bed.

"What do you need, Dad?"

"Joost a minute." There was a scratching sound, then a match flared. They kept a candle stuck on a tin saucer for use when they were inside the wagon at night. He touched the flame to the wick, then blew out the match.

"Ah been meanin' ta do sumthin' fur a long time, David. Ah think noow be a gud time."

"What is it?"

He didn't answer. Instead he went up on his knees and reached into the sack. He leaned forward, sticking his arm all the way in. David could see his hand searching for something. Finally he straightened, withdrawing his hand. In it he held a small blue-velvet box. He held it out to David.

David stared at it as he slowly took it from his father's hand. His eyes were wide with astonishment. "Is this what I think it is?"

"Open it."

David did. His breath drew in sharply. "Mum's necklace?"

"Aye."

David was incredulous. "You still have it? I thought we lost it somewhere along the way coming to America. You never said anything about it."

John just shook his head. David could see that his eyes were glistening in the candlelight. David took the necklace out and spread it across one hand. The chain was made of tiny filigree links of sterling silver. From the center of the chain hung a small heart-shaped locket. David took it between his fingers and pried it open. There was no picture inside, but David could see an inscription. It was unreadable in the dim light, but he didn't need to read it to know what it said. It read simply, *To my Anne.*

"I remember the day you gave it to her," David said quietly. "She got all mad at you because she knew you spent a lot of money on it."

"Aye, a full week's sal'ry. She never furgave me fur that."

"Oh, yes, she did," David said fiercely. "She once told me that, next to me and you, this was the thing she treasured most in life. I am so glad you still have it, Dad."

"Ah been waitin' fur the reet time ta give it away."

"Give it away?"

"Yah," he said, his voice so low David could barely hear him. "Ah want ya ta 'ave it, Son. It be yurs noow."

"But, Dad—"

"Ah naw be tellin' ya what ta do wit it, but it wud please me if sumday, me first granddaughter were to end up wit it."

David was staring at him.

"Ya 'eard me, ya lunk head," he growled, trying to hide the emotion in his voice. "If'n ya cahrn't do that, then I'll tek it back an' do it meself."

David carefully folded the chain and returned it and the locket to the box. He shut it again. "What made you decide to do this now?" he asked gruffly.

There was a slow smile. "It joost seemed lek the reet time."

Saturday, March 13, 1880

When David came around the back of his wagon, he stopped. Abby was standing beside the mules who would be taking her wagon down, absentmindedly stroking their necks as she stared down at the valley floor far below them.

"I can drive it for you," he said, coming up behind her.

She didn't turn. Nor did she speak.

"But I don't think I need to."

She finally turned. "Are you just saying that to try to make peace between us?"

"Knowing your fear of heights, if I were trying to make peace, wouldn't I be safer not letting you drive?"

She looked down at the ground. It was already churned up into gobs of thick, gooey mud that stuck to their boots and coated the wagon wheels. Using the toe of her boot, she smoothed a little spot, which immediately became wet and shiny and smooth as a tabletop. The snowstorm had left only a skiff on the ground, but the soil was wet. Finally she looked up. "Bishop Nielson says he wants as many men as possible to hold the wagons from sliding off."

He acknowledged that with a nod. The clay was so slick that even a gentle push against a wagon could move it sideways. "That's going to be the challenge. Not the road, and not even the grade."

"Then maybe I'd better drive."

Just then Molly came around the lead wagon with their mother and father. She stopped when she saw them. "Have you decided?" she asked.

There was a moment's hesitation, then Abby gave her an affirmative nod. "Yes, I'm driving."

"Oh, Abby, are you sure?" She turned to David. "And you agree?"

"I do. If Dad and I help with the ropes, she and your father can take the first two down, then Dad and I will bring down the other two when we're through helping on the ropes."

"And who will hold you back?" Sarah said.

He turned, looking at the wagon tracks in the gooey mud. "I hope by then the ruts will be deep enough to hold us in line. If not, we'll have you two come back up again."

David reached inside the wagon and retrieved a coiled rope. "All right, we'll see you down at that first turn." As he pushed past the two girls, Sarah stopped him. She looked at him for several seconds, then leaned up and kissed him on the cheek. "You take care, David. We just got you back. I would rather drive a wagon down there than have you risk getting hurt."

Touched, he managed a smile. "You know, for a woman who prefers to shop in St. George, you're getting to be pretty tough."

She blushed, deeply pleased. Then she smiled and touched his arm, lowering her voice into a conspiratorial whisper. "Don't tell my sister. It would completely shatter her faith in me."

John raised his hand. "Before we start, thare be sumthin' Ah'd lek ta show ya." He turned and started away. "Cum. They naw be startin' fur another few minutes."

The others looked at David, but he shrugged. He had no idea what this was about.

Down about fifty yards from where their wagons were parked, John stopped in front of a large pink boulder. It was rounded but oblong and looked like a loaf of bread with one end buried in the dirt. "Ah discovered this the other night as Ah was cumin' off me shift." He stepped back so they could see the front of the rock. To their amazement, something had been carved into the face of it. They moved in.

It was Molly who read it out for them all. "'Make peace with God.'"

"Who did it?" Patrick finally asked in a soft voice.

John shrugged. "Dunno. Ev'rybody Ah asked says they dunna know either."

"Someone afraid they might not make it safely to the bottom?" Abby asked, very subdued.

"Perhaps," John nodded. "But it occurred ta me, it be gud counsel fur all of us, naw matter whare we are, or what we be doin'."[1]

"Amen," Sarah whispered.

John turned to his son as if to say something, but he had to quickly look away. Seeing that, David also turned his head. When John Draper finally came back around, he was looking directly at his son. "An' Ah joost wanted ta publicly thank the gud Lord fur lettin' me be 'ere ta witness fur meself that David has made his peace wit God. Tank ya, Son. Ah be so prood of ya reet noow, Ah think Ah be aboot to bust me garter belt."

Laughing, and trying to hold in his emotions, David threw his arms around his father, hugging him tightly, while the others looked on and tried not to cry.

Six hours and several close calls later, they were down. In the end, Patrick was needed on the ropes and Abby had to drive the stretch twice. Her mother walked alongside the second time, calling out encouragement both to Abby and to the men on the ropes. When David's father brought the last wagon down with Patrick and David holding him back, the family fell into each other's arms, exhausted, relieved, and exhilarated.

As David and his father clomped over to join the family, their feet so covered with clay and mud that it was like they wore great clodhoppers, John motioned for the family to gather round. When they did so, he reached in his shirt pocket and pulled out an invisible piece of paper and pencil. With an exaggerated flourish, he made a large check mark in the air. "That be one more," he said, then mimed putting the paper away again.

"One more what?" Sarah asked.

"One more impossible obstacle joost made possible." He pulled the "paper" out again and went on. "So far, Ah've got a tick mark by the Hole in the Rock, the Colorado River, Cottonwood Hill, The Chute, Slickrock Hill, an' noow, Clay Hill Pass. Purty impressive, Ah'd say."

"And how many more do you have on that list?" Sarah asked.

David answered for him. "Only two. The cedar forest and Comb Ridge."

Note

1. Clay Hill Pass is located about twenty-five miles east of Hall's Crossing on Lake Powell on Utah Highway 276. Remnants of the pioneer road can still be seen from the

highway, which now bisects the Clay Hills. There are a few trail markers on both sides of the road, though a set of binoculars makes these much easier to locate. On the north side of the highway, near the top of the old pioneer road, there is a large, round boulder with the inscription "MAKE PEACE WITH GOD." Though it is badly eroded now, the inscription is still readable. We have no information about who made this inscription or when it was done, but it is similar in style to other pioneer inscriptions. It has been variously attributed to the pioneers, to a local resident of much later date, and to wanderers sometime in between. That it was done by someone in the pioneer company while they were building a road down those hills is my own supposition.

CHAPTER 68

Monday, March 29, 1880

Step by step, day by day, mile by mile, the company moved slowly eastward, greeting each new challenge with resigned but dogged determination. What should have been a growing sense of excitement as they drew nearer to their destination was lost in a spreading haze of exhaustion. They had left Cedar City on October twenty-second, five months and ten days before. On that day their spirits had been high, their hearts filled with optimism, their teams fresh, their equipment new. Now as they slogged along through the deep sand of Comb Wash, their spirits were flagging, their hearts were weary, their teams were jaded, and their equipment was dilapidated and worn.

They had passed through (or over) some of the roughest, most desolate, least charted country in the United States and its territories. Their inner steel, tempered by the fires of adversity, was now showing metal fatigue and was near the shattering point. The only thing that kept them going was sheer, stubborn endurance, as one challenge after another confronted them.

As if the descent down Clay Hill Pass had not been daunting enough, a day later a raging blizzard swept in. Wagon covers were shredded, tents ripped from their moorings, stock scattered for miles. Many were left exposed to the elements to cope as best they could with their whimpering, shivering children and soggy bedding. When the storm finally blew on to the east, Platte Lyman, a man who had spent much of his life out of doors, claimed that what followed was the coldest night he had *ever* experienced.[1]

When they entered the great cedar forests on the southern slopes of

Elk Ridge, the road builders faced a new and different challenge. They changed from black powder, pick, and shovel to ax and saw. They literally hacked their way through what seemed like an endless expanse of juniper trees. They cut them off as close to the ground as possible so the stumps would not trip the teams or rip out the bottom of the wagons. But that was not all Elk Ridge held in store. Even though it was late in March, the elevation was high enough that when they weren't plowing through the remnants of two-foot-deep snowdrifts, they were buried up to the axles in mud. Horses and mules would finally just stop, quivering and shaking violently, and refuse to budge no matter how much they were urged forward.

As they moved slowly onward, David, who often went ahead to scout the road, began noticing something. Where before there had been an abundance of strong, well-matched teams of horses, mules, and oxen, what he saw now often could not be called "teams" at all. One wagon had an ox and a mule in tandem. Several had milk cows or young heifers in harness. The most unusual pairing was a set of mules harnessed together with a single ox hooked to the front of the wagon tongue. A young girl sat astride the ox's back, guiding him down the road with her feet or an occasional punch on his neck.

Gradually, the tight organization and order that had been a hallmark of the company collapsed as people made their way forward as best they could. Those with the strongest teams—or those who had extra animals— forged ahead, while others lagged farther and farther behind. Some wagons were abandoned, left on the roadside fully loaded to await a time when their owners could return later in the season. By the time they reached the eastern edge of the cedars, some families were as much as thirty miles behind the leaders. The company was like a giant accordion, expanding and contracting as they moved slowly forward.[2]

As if making a road through that country wasn't enough of a challenge, an unusual confluence of events occurred that sent a cold chill of fear through the camp. Shortly after they headed Grand Gulch and started down through the cedar forests toward Comb Ridge, the company spotted a small Ute Indian camp up ahead of them. The company passed by and camped a mile or two farther on. That night, the Indians sent one of their women to the Mormon camp to feel things out. She was treated kindly and given some food from the meager stores. She returned with the others, who were extremely shy, and food was given to them as well. The company's spirits were lifted by being able to render service.

But the very next day, George Hobbs met the wagons. After spending almost three weeks with his sister and her family in Montezuma Creek, he was heading back to Cheese Camp to get the wagon he had left there back in February. David didn't appreciate what happened next.

Hobbs reported that while he was at Montezuma Creek, a cowboy had come in with news of an Indian massacre in Colorado. Some renegade Utes had ambushed a column of U.S. Cavalry and killed ten men, including all of their officers. They had then gone to an Indian agency run by a man named Meeker, where they massacred eight men, including Meeker. Most terrifying to the sisters in the camp was the report that several women had been carried off as hostages.

This was something every woman on the frontier dreaded hearing, for it was part of their own worst imaginings. When someone pointed out that Meeker, Colorado, was nearly three hundred miles away from where they were, and that this had happened several months before, Hobbs told them the renegade band had been seen heading in this direction.

Their encounter the night before now took on a sinister significance, especially in the minds of the women. Was the little band they had seen connected with the renegade group? Had they been sent to spy out the defenses of the Mormons? Though Platte Lyman and Jens Nielson openly scoffed at either idea, it didn't do much to calm the camp. Extra guards were posted for several nights, and many of the women, including Molly and Abby, took rifles to bed with them.

The next morning, Sarah quietly told David that during the night, Molly had had a bad dream. Then she told him something that Molly had never shared with him. When David had returned from the exploring expedition and told the family the story of Po-ee-kon and Mary Davis, Molly had experienced terrible nightmares for weeks after. The very thought of an Indian attack filled her with such enormous dread, it made her physically sick. David wasn't sure whether to kick himself for sharing so much detail about their experience with Po-ee-kon, or to kick George for telling the company that the Utes might even now be coming toward them.

They had one additional Indian experience, but this one turned out to be good for a laugh. As the caravan was making its way slowly through the great forest of cedar trees, an old Ute Indian on horseback happened upon them. He was so utterly stunned by the sight of a wagon train that he sat speechless, watching them roll slowly by. "Where you come from?" he asked the nearest driver in broken English.

"From across the Colorado River," came the answer. "We are Mormons."

"Where you cross big canyon?" the old man demanded.

"At a place called Hole in the Rock. It is like a great crack in the cliff."

The Indian snorted in disgust and rode on, muttering about it not being possible to make a wagon road through this country and insisting that they were lying to him.

That night, at evening prayers, the story brought a great deal of merriment. That turned into a roar of delight when wry old Bishop Nielson raised his hand. "Ven he say it not possible to build a road troo dis country, vee shood haf said, 'Yah, vee know dat now.'"[3]

Wednesday, March 31, 1880

One unmistakable landmark for the pioneers was Comb Ridge, a massive upthrust from the valley floor that ran for over a hundred miles north and south. Its jagged peaks formed a serrated edge that looked very much like the teeth of a comb, and thus its name.

When the company finally dropped out of the upland around Elk Ridge into the great dry wash that ran at the base of Comb Ridge, there was a surge of jubilation. Montezuma Creek lay just twenty-five or thirty miles to the east of the ridge. Their journey was finally nearly over.

But as they made their way slowly down Comb Wash, jubilation died and despair flooded in. Comb Ridge was a thousand-foot-high barrier with no gaps, no canyons capable of taking wagons up and over. And although the wash provided a ready-made and virtually level road to the south, like all of the desert washes, it was an endless sand pit, sometimes deep enough to sink a wheel up to the axles. It quickly proved to be almost more demanding on the teams than the steep dugways, the clay hills, and the thick stands of cedar they had already crossed.

On the morning of the last day of March, Platte Lyman called for three of his scouts—George Hobbs, Kumen Jones, and David Draper. His instructions were terse but clear. The San Juan River was to the south of them. From their previous expedition with Silas Smith, they knew that the river went through Comb Ridge, but by that time, they were too exhausted to see if wagons could be taken through the gap. Their assignment now was to ride south as quickly as possible, find the river, and see if they could make a road through. If for some reason they couldn't follow the river, then the scouts were to find some way to get up and over this last, heartbreaking obstacle. "If the river hasn't made us a road," Platte said, "then you find us a place, and we will have to make our own."

They found the river just ten miles south of where the company was camped in the wash. Normally only forty or fifty yards across, the San Juan River was in the midst of spring runoff, and was near flood stage. The current was swift and filled with debris. They found a large, almost perfectly flat area on the north bank that would provide a good camp for the company. The grass was sparse, but they could see that across the river there was ample forage.

They decided to split up. George and Kumen rode downstream to look for a possible fording place. David turned upstream to find the answer to the more important question: Could they get wagons through the great gap in Comb Ridge carved out by the river?

As he and Tillie made their way up through the willows and cottonwood trees, David also watched for possible fording places. But he quickly lost hope. The channel was narrow here, still squeezed in somewhat by the high ridges on both sides. As he turned and examined the great rise of rock that marked the southern end of this part of Comb Ridge, something caught his eye. He turned the reins and headed in that direction.

The mountain sheared off sharply directly above him, rising a good five or six hundred feet. But sometime in the far-distant past—probably during a flood when the water undercut the cliff face—a huge mass of sandstone had broken free at its base, forming a massive overhang that extended out from the cliff at least thirty or forty feet and ran horizontally for three or four hundred feet. And there, in the deep shade beneath the roof, was what had caught his eye. Blending almost perfectly into the rock were the ruins of an ancient cliff dwelling.

He and the other scouts had seen one of these farther west on their earlier exploration. In fact, when they had climbed up to visit it, they had stumbled on an old trail made by these ancient pueblo dwellers and had then followed it for many miles. This ruin wasn't as large as that one, but it seemed more elegant. There was one large building, at least two stories high, with square, empty windows. A tower of stone masonry—perhaps all that was left of another such building—stood like a solitary sentinel watching out over the river and the flood plain below. David could make out smaller structures, almost hidden in the shadows back farther under the cliff.

Strongly tempted to dismount and explore the ruins on foot, David finally shook his head and turned Tillie away. The group would surely camp not far from here, and when there was time, he promised himself he would come back and make an exploration. Then, as he turned east again, urging Tillie into a trot, he had an intriguing thought. Things had been so demanding since his return from Montezuma Creek these past two weeks, he had never found an appropriate time for his talk with Molly. Each night found all of them so physically exhausted and spiritually spent that they just ate supper and went to bed. He half turned in the saddle and looked back. That might just be the perfect place for their talk—quiet, isolated, serene.

Ten minutes later, he reined Tillie in again. And in that moment, he knew there was no hope for a wagon road through the gap. Here Comb Ridge closed in on both sides of the river, coming right down to the water's edge in nearly vertical cliffs. Perhaps later in the summer, the water level might drop enough to allow passage, but now it was swift, cold water from cliff to cliff.

"Ah, Tillie," he murmured. "We didn't need this."

Thursday, April 1, 1880

Molly watched the people coming from their wagons toward the center of camp, heads down and faces grim. Then she glanced over at Jens Nielson's tent. David, his father, and her father were there, talking quietly with several other men—Bishop Nielson, Kumen Jones, Joe Nielson, and the Perkins brothers. As she watched them, she couldn't help but note the toll this last month had taken on these men she loved. Weariness lined their faces, and discouragement haunted their eyes.

How did Jens Nielson carry on through all of this? she wondered. He looked so utterly spent that she wanted to go over and take him by the elbow and make him sit down. He was over sixty now, and walked with crippled, frostbitten feet. And yet he did carry on. Platte Lyman was absent today. Night before last some of his horses had wandered away, and he had stayed behind to look for them. So even the burden of leadership was solely the bishop's today.

She didn't have to wonder what they were talking about. She didn't have to wonder what was going to be said in the meeting. The news of David's discovery had spread through the camp with the speed of a cholera epidemic, and with pretty much the same results. Ironic that it should be him to discover that there was to be yet another delay, yet another crushing setback.

Her family were also at the end of their tether. Abby stood with her hand resting lightly on Billy Joe's shoulder, he stared at the ground, making patterns with the toe of his boot. That, more than any other thing, pierced Molly's heart. Billy Joe was no longer Billy Joe. His excitement, his exuberance, his endless energy were finally spent. He dragged through the days like the rest of them did, head down, teeth gritted, shoulders hunched.

She turned and looked at her mother, and that too made her want to weep. To Molly, her mother had always been the epitome of graciousness and beauty and class. She stood there now, listless and vacant, her shoulders slumped, her beautiful hair with a patina of red dust, her apron worn in several places, her elegant boots scuffed and battered. The lines of exhaustion at the corners of her mother's eyes looked like they had been penciled in. In a way, they had. The dust of Comb Wash had left its legacy on her face.

Molly laughed softly to herself. Speaking of hair! Hers was so gritty and greasy that she could barely pull a brush through it now. And what about her own face? In the past few days, summer in this south country had begun. The temperature was in the nineties nearly every afternoon now that they were down off of Elk Ridge. The sun not only beat down from above but it bounced upward off the sand and the rocks, radiating heat like the open door of an oven. Her face and arms, already deeply tanned, were now sunburned as well. The skin along the cheekbones beneath her eyes was bright red. Her nose was peeling, and where it had peeled it had sunburned again. Her lips looked like cracked leather. Good thing they had nothing to smile about, for when she did, her lips cracked and bled.

She closed her eyes.

When all but a few stragglers were clustered around the Nielsons' tent, Bishop Nielson moved forward and raised his hands. "Brodders and sisters," he said in a booming voice. "May vee haf yur attention, please."

He paused to let them quiet, then went on, his volume only slightly lower. "As most of you know, Captain Lyman is still behind us. Vee expect he be here later today. But vee cannot vait. Vee must begin immediately. Vee know now dat vee cannot get troo to da Montezuma settlement by way of da river. Derfore, vee must build more road up and over dis." He raised an arm and pointed to the north.

Every head turned to look where he was pointing, even though they had been staring balefully at it all morning. What they were seeing was not red rock cliffs, like so much of what they had passed through before, but it was daunting enough. Here, two ridges came together, forming a slight V. A gentle swale between them reached all the way to the top. To the right of the swale, there was a long, sloping spine of pink sandstone running nearly from bottom to top. To the left was a hillside strewn with a jumble of broken rocks, loose shale, and great slabs of stone. The crest was about a mile from where they stood, though half of that was level ground. The mountain itself was not much more than a quarter of a mile from bottom to top and no more than four or five hundred feet high. Compared to the Hole or Cottonwood Hill or Slickrock Hill or Clay Hill Pass, this was nothing. The lower slopes were somewhat gentle and would be no real challenge. The last hundred yards were noticeably steeper, but again, it was nothing compared to The Chute.

Bishop Nielson waited until they turned back to face him. "Vee are calling dis San Juan Hill. And vee haf no choice but to take our vagons up and over vaht you see der. Da goot news, especially for da vomen and children, is dat vee shall camp here by da river vile a road is built up and over da top. Vee tink dat vill take four to five days. Dis vill gif you goot chance to vash and bathe. Also to let our veary and jaded animals rest. Dis be goot. Dere is plenty of firewood and vater. You like dat, no?"

"Amen," Molly murmured. Many other women actually smiled.

"A few of da men haf been asked to take da stock across da river for better grazing. Vee are asking all odders—except for our blacksmiths—to verk on da road. Da building of dis road is different matter from odder times. Vee haf no more blasting powder. Derfore, Brodder Perkins say vee must build dis road by hand, using pick and shovel, and making stone walls to hold in da dirt."

He stopped and looked around. No one objected. No one said anything. There were a few nods, but that was it. He turned and looked at the Perkins brothers. "Anytink more I should be sayink?" They shook their heads. He turned back to the people. "Den let's go to verk."

David picked up the bag with his tools, water, and food and hefted it on his shoulder. "You ready, Dad?"

"Aye."

But as he turned, David saw Molly walking by herself down toward the river. "You go ahead, Dad," he said. "I'll catch up with you."

His father looked around, then grunted. "Aye, Son. It be time."

"I know. I'm not going to talk to her now. I'll just set a time. So she knows it's coming."

"Naw t'night, if'n ya be askin' me," he said. "Wait 'til t'morrow. Ev'rybody be more rested then. It be mooch better."

David gave him an appraising look, then nodded. "Good idea."

Jens Nielson had been right. From an engineering standpoint, this road was going to be much easier to build. Where there was soft soil, it was cut away with pick and shovel to make a road into the hillside. Where the hill sloped too sharply to allow a wagon to cross without tipping over, a track for the wagon wheels was cut—or chiseled out, if it was rock—then a masonry wall was built on the low side. This was made high enough to allow rocks, gravel, and dirt to be brought in until it made a level road. In other places the rock pan sloped in the same direction as wagons would be moving, but was steep and treacherous. Here striations were chiseled into the rock. Sand would be spread here to give the animals better traction.

It was backbreaking work. And the heat only made it worse. Fortunately, nature had made their task easier. Over the centuries, the sandstone that had fallen from the cliffs above or sloughed off the rock base underneath had broken off in angular chunks. These were not the smooth, round rocks of a creek bottom. The tops and bottoms of these slabs were almost perfectly flat. The men had no mortar, and neither the energy nor the time to cut the stone. This was what in England they had called dry masonry, stonework without mortar. And the sides of San Juan Hill provided the perfect natural quarry.

"Easy, easy," Ben Perkins hissed. "Don't break it."

Four of them—Ben, Hyrum Perkins, David, and David's father—were carrying a slab of rock that was two feet wide, four feet long, and eight inches thick and weighed at least two hundred pounds. The ground was rough, and they grunted as they walked the rock up the hill to where they were building another wall. Gasping with every step, their backs feeling like they were going to break, they inched their way to the end of the wall.

"Okay," Hy said. "Reet thare, just to me right. Ready. One. Two. Three. Swing!"

They swung it up and out away from their bodies, then lowered it into position with a solid thunk. Ben and Hy stood back, panting hard. John sat down on the wall they had already constructed. David bent over, putting his hands on his knees, and drew in great, hungry breaths.

This particular low spot they were filling in was twenty or thirty feet long, and here at its lowest point, the wall would have to be nearly five feet high. All of this was done with muscle and sweat. And it was a wonder. No two rocks were of the same size or shape. Some were nearly square, others only two or three inches thick but two and a half or three feet long. Some were rectangular; one looked like a giant wedge. But Ben and Hy and John had placed them one on top of the other, fitting them together like a jigsaw puzzle, filling in where needed with smaller stones. When it was done, the road would be nearly as solid as virgin rock itself and would carry the weight of eighty or more loaded wagons without a problem.[4]

"Ah be needin' sum water," Ben said. "Let's tek a rest."

David sank down on the rock wall beside his father as Ben and his brother moved over to where they had a porcelain jug of water.

"Ya ready fur a drink?" his father asked.

"In a minute. Let me get my breath first."

They leaned back on their elbows, gradually letting their breathing return to normal. Both looked out on the panorama far below. The green line of cottonwoods and willows meandered lazily through the valley below, marking the course of the San Juan. On the far side, David saw a small cloud of dust, then made out tiny dark specks moving through it. At least some of the herd was across the river.

Closer, lining the banks of the river, were the dozens of small white squares that marked the wagon camp. As he squinted, he could see tiny figures moving in and around them. There were about sixty-five of the eighty-two wagons in camp now. He suspected it could be days before the last of the stragglers came in.

"So," his father grunted, interrupting his thoughts. "Did ya spek ta Molly, then?"

"I did. We're going to go for a walk after supper tomorrow night."

"Gud. Does she know what it's aboot?"

"I said it was time for us to talk. She seemed eager to finally have it come."

"Aye, Ah wud think so."

"Any advice, Dad?"

He pulled at his beard thoughtfully for a moment. Then he shook his head. "Naw, Son. Ya be knowin' what needs to be said, better than me."

"I hope you're right, Dad. I really hope you're right."

Notes

1. The quote from Platte Lyman about the coldest night of his life was recorded in his journal under entry of March 15, 1880 (see Miller, *Hole*, 168).

2. Descriptions of how the wagon train fared after Clay Hill Pass are found in several sources (see Miller, *Hole*, 136; Reay, *Incredible Passage*, 71–72; Redd, "Short Cut," 21–22). The "giant accordion" analogy comes from Redd. The vivid descriptions of the "teams" used to pull the wagons come from George Hobbs's narrative (in Miller, *Hole*, 212).

3. Only Redd talks about meeting the small band of Utes and giving them food. He also says that it was the very next day that George Hobbs rode into camp and reported the Meeker Massacre, and Redd describes how that news affected the camp (Redd, "Short Cut," 23). Several mention the story of the old Ute and his incredulity at seeing a wagon train in that country (see Redd, "Short Cut," 22–23; Reay, *Incredible Passage*, 71–72; Miller, *Hole*, 136). Bishop Nielson's comment on the incident with the old Ute is the author's creation.

4. While nearly a hundred and thirty years of erosion have washed away much of the road up San Juan Hill, from the bottom, the track up the mountainside is clearly discernible. Along the way, one can see—and stand on—the masonry walls put in by those pioneer builders, which are still as strong and solid as they were more than a century ago (see Miller, *Hole*, 138; Redd, "Short Cut," 23; Reay, *Incredible Passage*, 74–75).

CHAPTER 69

Thursday, April 1, 1880

The next evening, as John, David, and Patrick returned from the hill, Molly quietly slipped a note into David's hand. It was three lines, unsigned.

> *Don't want anyone to know of our talk. At least not yet.*
> *Rather not leave together. After supper meet me at the river*
> *where the women do the laundry.*

David crumpled it and tossed it in the fire. When their eyes met next, he nodded briefly.

⁂

As he waited beneath the trees just a few yards from where many items of clothing were still spread across rocks and bushes to dry, David was both elated and filled with dread. The cliff dwelling was just half a mile upriver from the laundry site. It would be the perfect place to talk, and he was happy she had suggested a place that made it easily accessible. They would still be visible from below if anyone happened by, therefore maintaining propriety, but they would be alone, where they could talk things out without interruption.

On the other hand, his stomach was fluttering worse than on that first day he had ridden down the mine shaft with his father. He was already stumbling over how to try to say what had to be said without crushing her. He didn't want to hurt her any more—he had surely done enough of that. This was a woman he had come to admire, respect, cherish, and love. He had watched her change over these last eighteen months from a flirtatious and mischievous girl with an impish smile into a remarkable woman of grace, charm, and faith.

He heard the snap of a twig and lifted his head. She was coming swiftly along the path, searching the trees for him. "I'm over here," he called, stepping into view.

She increased her pace and rushed to him. "Oh, David," she whispered, "Hold me."

He did, taking her gently in his arms, letting her head rest against his chest. They stood there for almost a minute, neither moving nor speaking. Finally she looked up at him, her grey eyes wide and glistening with tears. "It seems like so long since you've done that."

"I know." And he was surprised at how good it felt.

Her head tipped back and her lips parted slightly. For a moment, he thought she was inviting him to kiss her—the one thing he had vowed he must not do—and he felt a little spurt of panic. But she quickly stepped back, and the lips softened into a smile. "Where shall we go? I'm afraid some of the sisters may be coming back here for their clothes."

"I know just the place."

She nodded and fell in beside him. They strolled slowly along, enjoying the first of the evening breezes that were starting to push back the heat of the day. After a time, he spoke. "You look especially lovely tonight, Molly."

She tipped back her head and laughed. "It's an absolute wonder what bathing and washing one's hair does for a girl. It feels so good to be clean again."

"Your mother and Abby looked like new women too."

"The whole camp is different; can't you feel it? We're worn out and ready to stop, but if we have to go on, let us wash our hair and do the laundry first."

David nodded and offered a silent thank you to his father for suggesting that he wait until tonight to do this.

Her step slowed as they approached the cliff face that loomed over them and she saw the ruins. "Oh, David. You didn't tell me these were here."

"Come on. It's a bit of a climb, but they're even more lovely up close."

To his surprise, she shook her head. "No. Let's just talk here." She looked around, found a fallen cottonwood log, and went over and sat down. As he went to sit beside her, she shook her head. "You sit there." She pointed to a flat rock about ten feet away. "I want to be able to see you, and you me, as we talk."

A little taken aback by this sudden decisiveness, he followed her instructions and sat down across from her. He waited a moment, then decided it wasn't going to get any easier. "Molly, I have some things I need to say to you."

"I know," she said softly, "but do you mind if I go first?"

"I . . . well sure, if that's what you want."

"It is." She drew in a breath, and he could see that she was ready to cry again, and he wasn't sure why. Did she sense somehow what was coming? Was she going to try to deflect him before he could say it was over? Was she—

"David, the last thing in the world that I want to do is hurt you."

That cut off his thoughts in a hurry. "And I feel the same—"

"Please. This is going to be hard enough. Let me just talk, and then you can ask questions in a moment if you wish."

"All right."

"First of all, let me say something about you." Her eyes softened and were filled with love. "What you have done over this past year has been truly remarkable. I feel ashamed that I once said that you would never change. Now look at you. No more doubts. No more questions."

"That's a little optimistic," he objected. "I've still got a hundred questions."

"Protest all you wish, David, but I know better. And so does everyone else." She drew in her breath. "You have become all that I hoped and prayed you would become. I need to say that so you'll know that what I am about to say has nothing to do with that. Your faith is no longer an issue between us in my mind."

David was baffled by that. This was not at all what he had expected.

"But I've made a decision, David, and I wanted you to be the first to know about it. Even Mama and Daddy don't know this yet."

Even more surprised, he leaned forward. "What decision?"

She inhaled deeply, as if she was searching for inner strength. "As you know, some of the people in our company are here not because they were called to this mission, but only to help family members get settled. Jim Decker's brother, George; Bishop Sevy's son; Amasa Lyman, Platte's brother; and Ben Perkins's brother-in-law, Thomas Williams, just to name a few."

"Yes, I am aware of that."

"They plan to return to their homes as soon as their families are settled."

"Yes, I knew that, too."

Her head came up now, and her eyes held his. "I plan to go with them."

David's jaw fell open. "*What?*"

There was a fleeting smile. "I plan to go with them, David. Back to Cedar City. As soon as they are ready to leave."

"But . . ." His mouth worked, but nothing came out. He was absolutely flabbergasted.

Now the smile broadened, though it was filled with sadness. "That makes me feel better, that I was able to hide it from you all this time."

"But why, Molly? What about your family? What about . . . what about us?"

"I will miss my family terribly, and I plan to return to visit them once good roads are established. As for us, let me ask you just one question, David. Would you ever consider going back with me? Could you be happy living in Cedar City and becoming a banker or a hotel owner or some kind of clerk somewhere?"

He just stared at her.

"Thank you. That's what I thought."

"Wait a minute, Molly. I'm still catching my breath from that first rock you dropped on my head. Don't throw another one at me."

"No, David, the correct thing to do now is ask me a question. The question is, 'Molly, if we were to be married, could you be happy living in San Juan as a rancher's wife? Could you be happy knowing that I would have to leave you alone many times, sometimes for weeks? Could you live with the knowledge that someday Indians on the warpath might come to our little homestead while I am gone?"

She looked away. "Remember, David. You asked me those very questions some time ago. Back then I thought the answer was yes. Back then I really believed that my love for you was strong enough to make it all work. But now . . ."

Her voice was suddenly filled with a great sorrow. "Do you know when it was that I really knew this for sure?"

He thought for a moment. "When George Hobbs talked about the Meeker Massacre? I was watching your face that night."

She shook her head. "That was just one more clincher, but no. It was the day that you left Cheese Camp and returned to San Juan to help Jim and Mary Davis."

"But I had to do that, Molly. I had to."

"I knew you had to. I wanted you to. I couldn't bear to think of their children without food. But that's exactly my point. As you rode away, I knew I was seeing my future. I knew that there would always be things that you had to do—and that I would want you to do. But I also knew that my heart would break every time you did." She looked away. "Just as it did then."

The tears finally spilled over, but she seemed unaware of them. "I'm sorry I'm so weak, David. But I came to face what I am, and who I am. And once I did that, I finally realized that love wouldn't be enough."

"Molly," he said, getting slowly to his feet. "The last word in the world I would use to describe you is *weak*."

"Thank you, David." She stood too, looking lost and forlorn. "Will you give me a few moments alone? Before I have to go back and face the family."

"Of course. When will you tell them?"

"Tonight."

"I don't know what to say."

"Just tell me one thing, David. Did you really, truly love me?"

"I did. More than I had ever loved a woman before. You are an easy woman to love, Molly Jean McKenna."

"Thank you. And one last question? Will you kiss me good-bye?"

He hesitated not even one second. "Of course," he said softly.

That night in the wagon, Abby held Molly for a long time as she sobbed and sobbed. She had gotten through telling the family with only a few tears. Billy Joe was the hardest. He just looked at her like he had been whipped; then great tears welled up and streaked down his cheeks. That did it, and he and Molly cried together for several minutes. Patrick was stunned, but though Sarah also had a good cry with her daughter, she didn't seem all that surprised.

It was only when she was alone with Abby that the whole story came out and she completely fell apart. "He was going to ask me to marry him, Abby," she cried. "The thing I've hoped for, and worked for, and prayed for, and longed for. And when he's finally ready, I'm the one who says no. I think I broke his heart. He just stood there looking dazed, and hurt, and confused."

"You don't have to say no," Abby said, stroking her hair over and over.

Her head jerked around, and she swiped angrily at the tears. "I do, Abby. You know I do. You know I'm right."

Abby said nothing.

"Say it!" she demanded. "From the beginning you've said we were too different. So don't waffle on me, Abby. Not when I need you to be strong. It was the right thing to do, wasn't it?"

Abby slowly nodded. "Probably."

"That's all, just probably?"

Careful not to answer that too quickly, Abby took a moment, choosing her words carefully. "You could change, Molly. Look how much you've changed already. You drive a team, you sleep on a straw mattress. You go days without washing your hair and hardly get crabby at all."

Abby dodged the blow aimed at her shoulder, then went on. "We all have changed. Look at how David has changed. And Mother. And me and Daddy and John. This experience has changed all of us in some pretty profound ways."

"I know," came the quiet but resolute reply. "I know I can learn to accept being a rancher's wife, being a hundred miles from the nearest drygoods store, being alone for much of the time. But I don't know if I want to. I'm not sure I would ever truly be able to say I was happy here."

Abby pulled her close as a fresh burst of tears began. "Then you *have* done the right thing, Molly," she whispered. "Painful as it is, you have done the right thing."

Friday, April 2, 1880

With supper over and the dishes washed and put away, Molly excused herself and retired to her wagon. Billy Joe was seated on the wagon tongue of David's and John's wagon, and David was teaching him how to braid rawhide thongs into a bridle strap. Abby had a book, but her eyes kept lifting as she stared up at the mountain where now a road was clearly visible two-thirds of the way to the summit. Sarah and Patrick were seated beside the campfire talking quietly.

John looked around at each of them in turn, then said, loudly enough for all to hear. "David. Ah got a hank'rin' ta see them Indian ruins ya was tellin' us aboot. How aboot you, Billy Joe? Wanna go see whare them ancients lived?"

He was up in an instant. "Yeah. I've been asking David to take me there."

"Anyone else interested?" David said, laying the rawhide aside.

Both Patrick and Sarah stood. "I'd love to see them," Sarah said. "I find them just fascinating, how they built them up under the cliffs like they did."

Abby shook her head. "I'll just read for a time."

John went to her, took the book out of her hand, and shut it. "Ya be no more readin' that book than Ah am, Abby gurl. So set it aside. Yur cumin' wit us."

Patrick touched his wife's arm. "Why don't you ask Molly if she would like to go."

Sarah nodded and walked around to the back of the wagon where Molly and Abby slept. A moment later she came back, shaking her head. "She says to go ahead. She's not feeling well."

⁂

David reached down and offered his hand, then pulled Sarah up the last steep incline. She stopped, looking up. "Oh, David! This is incredible."

"I think so too." He bent over again and offered his hand to Abby, but she was already clambering up and didn't see it. But she too stopped, then drew in her breath sharply.

They waited until Patrick and John were up, and then David pointed. "Come. There are stairs over here."

"Oh, my," Abby breathed. "What a place to build a staircase."

They were standing at the base of two gigantic boulders that had fallen from beneath the overhanging cliff, probably centuries or even millennia ago. Both of the great stones were twice the size of a wagon box. Between these there was a narrow gap, barely wide enough to accommodate a single person. In that gap, a set of stone stairs had been built, curving gently upwards, following the contours of the boulders. Abby was right. It looked like a staircase in a grand manor house.

"It be a purfect place ta defend agin attackers," John observed, as Abby and her mother ascended to the top. "Joost put one man up there wit a couple of fist-sized rocks, an' cahrn't no one be comin' up ta bother ya."

David turned and looked both ways. "I hadn't thought about that, Dad, but you're right. Look all along here. The only way anyone could get up is by the stairs or with ladders, which are easily repelled."

"This really is something," Patrick said. "Look at their mortar work. These people were excellent masons."

"Come over here," Abby called. She was standing in the square doorway of the largest structure. It was the building David had seen earlier. It had three walls—the back wall being the cliff face—with several square windows at different levels. The roof—if there had ever been one—was gone, long ago collapsed. But what she was pointing at was the door. "Look how small it is," she said. She stepped beside it, providing a measure.

Abby was no more than five feet two or three inches tall, but the door came only to her neck. "They must have been tiny people." She stooped and went inside.[1]

❈

They explored the ruins for nearly a quarter of an hour, calling out to one another to see this feature or that. Once again it was Abby's sharp eye that spotted something the others hadn't seen. Her head was tipped way back and she was looking almost straight up. "Look up there."

There above them, painted in simple white lines onto the pink stone, were some drawings. David instantly recognized three animals from their stick-figure legs and curled horns. "Mountain sheep," he said. Then he laughed. "Maybe they helped the Anasazi find their way through these mountains, just like they did us."

"Anasazi?" Abby asked, turning to look at him.

"That's what the Navajo call them. I'm told it means 'ancient enemies.' Most people just call them the cliff dwellers or the Pueblos."

"That's got to be the San Juan River," Patrick said, pointing. He was right. A long squiggly line, twice the thickness of the other paintings and about three feet long, ran above the other figures. It was clearly meant to represent a river.

"What strange little men," Sarah said. There were two figures in the rock painting. One was behind the sheep, as if it were driving them. The other was in front. They had round heads, stick arms and legs, but fat little torsos that had been painted in with solid white.

"The one on the left has some kind of horns," Patrick observed.

"Probably a shaman," David replied. "Maybe they're bringing the sheep to him for sacrifice." Both of the men figures had their arms raised in the air, as if supplicating heaven.

"There's more," Abby said, moving away. She was pointing to the rock face, walking slowly as she studied them.

As David started to follow, his father touched his arm. "Ah be reddy ta go back noow," he said softly.

To David's surprise, Sarah nodded. "Yes, I think we are too." Before David could speak, she added, "But there's no need for you two to head down yet." She looked to where Abby was just disappearing around the face of the cliff, still searching the overhang above them. "We'll see you back in camp."

Taking the hands of Patrick and Billy Joe—who looked quite as surprised as David—she turned them around and started back for the stairs. Two minutes later they were down and gone. Sarah looked up and waved just before they disappeared into the cottonwood trees below.

⁂

"Where did everybody go?" Abby stopped dead when she came around the cliff face and saw only David standing there alone.

"Your mother said she wanted to get back."

Her eyes narrowed, and David threw up both hands in his defense. "It wasn't my idea."

She moved slowly toward him, still suspicious. But then the paintings drew her eye again. "These are just wonderful, David. Think how many hundreds of years ago they were painted, and yet they are as fresh as if they were done yesterday."

"It really is amazing."

She moved past him, clambering over one of the low masonry walls. "Well, perhaps we should go too. It will be dark soon."

He didn't move. "Abby?"

She turned back. "Yes?"

"I would like to talk to you for a minute, if we can."

Now she was openly suspicious. "Are you sure you didn't ask them to leave?"

"I am, but I'm not sure but what there may be a little conspiracy going on between your mother and my father."

"About what?"

He hesitated. "About us." She visibly stiffened, and he rushed on.

"Please, Abby. Will you sit down? Just give me five minutes, then I'll not say anything more."

For a moment, he thought she was going to bolt. Her eyes were wide, and she was staring at him with a strange expression. But after a moment, she came back and sat on a low wall.

"Okay, I'm listening." But his heart fell as he saw the set of her jaw and the coldness in her eyes.

He dusted off a flat area of rock and sat down facing her, his mind in a tumble as he realized the moment had come and he had not had any time to prepare himself. "Abby, I . . . look, there's something I would like to explain."

Her eyes flashed. "If this is about the day you grabbed me and kissed me, then—"

"I didn't *grab* you, Abby." He looked down at his hands. "Nor did you fight me."

When he looked up, she was nodding. "All right, I'm sorry that I used that term. But I didn't fight you because I was shocked." Her voice softened, and she was almost speaking to herself. "It happened so fast. That was the last thing I was expecting."

"That day in Cottonwood Canyon, when you and I were talking and you were so angry with me, you said that if you had ever had feelings for me, that ruined it." He took a quick breath. "Have you had feelings for me? Ever, Abby?"

That startled her, and for a moment she was completely flustered. Then her face hardened. "You have no right to ask me that question."

"Probably not, but I'm asking anyway."

She turned her body so she faced away from him.

After almost a full minute, when it was clear she wasn't going to answer, he began talking. "Do you remember the story I told you about Bertie Beames?"

"Yes, what of it?"

"I never even told my mother about that," he said in a near whisper. "Dad was there after it happened, but to this day he doesn't know that I was responsible, that we were playing games."

She half turned. "Why are you telling me this now?"

"You are the only person I have ever told."

She searched his face for several moments, then gave a little toss of her head. "I appreciate your confidence in me, but I don't see what that has to do with anything."

"Now who's breaking the microscope?" he shot back. "You know exactly what it means. Though I was too dense, too big of a fool to see it then, I know now that I've had feelings for you for a long time, Abby."

She leaped to her feet. "Stop it, David!" she cried. "Stop it right now."

He rocked back, stunned by the fury in her. "Abby, I—"

"Are you so colossally stupid that you thought Molly wouldn't tell me everything about last night? I held her in my arms for over an hour last night as she sobbed and sobbed. Do you think I don't know that you brought Molly here last night to propose to her?"

"Propose? What are you—" He stopped as the enormity of what she had just said hit him. Molly had been so anxious to tell David of her decision that he had never had a chance to tell her about his. In actuality, he had been so relieved that he wouldn't now have to hurt her, he had gone back to camp rejoicing.

He dropped his head in his hands and moaned softly. "Oh, Abby. Is that what you think?"

If she had heard him, she gave no sign. She was somewhere between rage and tears. "How dare you?" she whispered. "Molly turns your proposal down, and one night later you bring the old maid sister to the same romantic spot to see if the same line will work with her?" She started to whirl away, but swung back on him. "You know what hurts the most, David? That you think I am so gaga over you that I would throw myself into your arms."

He got slowly to his feet, numbed now as the full realization of what was happening swept over him. "No, Abby. You're right. How presumptuous of me. I'm sorry."

She was trembling, her lips white. "Maybe it's best if you return to Cedar City with her. Maybe eventually your first choice will work out, and you won't have to take second best."

He stepped forward, anger exploding inside of him. He took her by the shoulders, wanting to shake her. "You have never been second best in my mind. That's what I finally realized. I came back from Montezuma Creek this last time knowing that I had to break it off with Molly. Knowing that it was you I loved. *That* was what I planned to tell Molly last night."

Her eyes widened for just a moment, then instantly went hard again. "If that's true, let me ask you one question, and a simple yes or no will do. Did you kiss her good-bye?"

At that moment, he knew he had lost. "Yes," he said softly. "I did."

She jerked free from his grasp and spun away. Then she whirled back and slapped his face hard. "Don't you dare cheapen what you had with Molly, David." She shook her finger in his face. "Don't you dare."

Stumbling, sobbing now, she ran to the stairway and went down it in three leaps. He watched her dart away, disappearing beneath the trees below him. He sat down again and closed his eyes.

"David?"

He leaped up again, hope flooding in. She was standing about thirty feet below him, looking up. "I have no right to ask this, David, but I will anyway. I would ask that you speak to no one about what happened here tonight. No one."

"You didn't have to ask," he said quietly.

"Especially Molly. This will crush her, David. Promise me."

"You didn't have to ask," he said again.

"Whare you been?" John asked as David pulled the wagon flap back and looked inside. "Abby's been back fur over an 'our."

"I went for a walk."

John's dark eyebrows raised. "Ah see," he said slowly.

"Dad, did you leave your tool bag up on top?"

He sat up, really surprised by that. "Yes. Always do. Naw sense packin' it up an' doon the hill ev'ry day." Then he leaned forward, peering more closely at David. "Is that yur bedroll?"

"I noticed one place in that last rocky stretch near the top. I think the groove for the wagon wheels isn't deep enough. I'll sleep up there tonight, then finish it at first light. I'll be back down to help you hitch up the teams."

"Son, are ya awl reet?"

David dropped the flap and walked away before his father could say anything more.

Note

1. Though no mention is made of this in any of the historical sources, there is a wonderfully preserved Anasazi ruin on the north side of the river. It is about a mile east of the site where the company camped while they built the road up and over San Juan Hill. Whoever went east to confirm that no road could be built along the river would likely have seen the ruins. Perhaps, by that point, the company was so exhausted that another set of ruins was not that significant.

CHAPTER 70

Saturday, April 3, 1880

It was somewhere around four-thirty in the morning, David guessed. Off in the far distance, the first tendrils of light were silhouetting a ridge of mountains far to the east. Below him, the desert was still a sea of blackness. He sat on a large boulder at the crest of the ridge, coat pulled tightly around him. Up here, there was none of the lingering heat of the day. His blankets and pack were a few yards down the hill. He had slept fitfully for a time, but finally around two gave it up, dressed again, and came up here to think.

It seemed strange to think that Mary and Jim Davis and the children were out there less than twenty miles away now. Would they be up this early? Not likely. And then he wondered if Abby was awake too, brooding and angry. That was much more likely.

He had tried hard to sustain his bitterness over what had happened at the ruins. One part of him even wanted to blame God for it. In a way, it was Cedar City all over again. Just when he decided to do something right, the roof collapsed on him. Back then, he had agreed to pray with Molly— an enormous concession for him—and within twenty-four hours his father had announced he was going to England and Molly had told him it was over.

But he couldn't sustain his anger at Providence. As he sat on the ridge, watching the half moon pass slowly across the sky, he thought of his prayers that somehow he could tell Molly without it hurting her too terribly. He laughed softly in the darkness. What delicious irony. He hadn't even gotten the chance to tell her it was over before she had told *him* it was over. How was that for an answer? Once again, David Draper had been handed another one of those "remarkable coincidences." There could be no blaming God for that. He closed his eyes and laid his head on his arms, which were folded across his knees. "O beloved Father, I thank thee for what thou hast wrought in my behalf. I thank thee that thou knew of thy sweet daughter's tender heart and purity of spirit. Take her home safely and let her find a man who can truly bring her joy and lasting happiness."

He paused, his thoughts turning to Abby. He closed his eyes again. "And wilt thou help heal the hurt in Abby's heart. I would ask of thee . . ." He stopped, then shook his head. "No. I trust in thee and in thy great wisdom, Father. I have seen that merciful hand in my life again and again. Let thy will be done. And help me to become a worthy and faithful servant in thy work. I pray in the name of Jesus. Amen."

As he got slowly to his feet, a thought popped into David's mind. Speaking of that day in Cedar City, had the roof really caved in? If his father had not received a mission call, David wouldn't have gotten angry and lashed out at God. If he hadn't done that, Molly wouldn't have broken it off with him. And if those two things hadn't come within hours of each other, he would never have joined Silas Smith on that exploring expedition.

He sat down slowly again, his mind in a whirl. And what would have happened then? The answer hit him with tremendous force. *Molly and I would now be man and wife.*

With that stunning thought came another. His father had told him one night that if he didn't change, the Lord was going to knock David about until he learned something. Was that what had happened last night at the Indian ruins? And was his response to skulk about up here, feeling sorry for himself and blaming God?

He laid his head back down on his arms, closed his eyes, and began another silent prayer.

When he awakened, the day had come. The sun was still half an hour from rising, but it was light enough that he could see one or two figures walking about down in camp. He could also see the vast emptiness that lay to the east, and he knew that somewhere down there lay his destiny.

With that, David went back to his little campsite and rolled up his bed. Then he gathered up his father's tool sack and walked down to the place where the rock pan needed a little more work—his excuse for coming up here last night. He fished out his father's hammer and chisel and went to work, finding joy in the simple task of making a better place for a wagon wheel.

Finished, he slipped his bedroll over his shoulder and picked up his father's tool sack. He looked down on the camp once more, watching as more tiny figures moved about far below him. It was time to go. San Juan lay just over the hill.

He had gone down only about forty yards when something caught his eye. At this point, the road ran alongside the long, rounded spine of sandstone that went from the top of the ridge to the bottom of the hill. Where David was passing, it was a twenty-five- or thirty-foot-high wall of solid rock. He pulled up, staring at the face of it for several seconds. Then he removed his bedroll. Once again he fumbled inside the tool sack for the hammer and chisel. Then, at peace at last, he walked over to the wall, moving along it slowly, looking for just the right place.

"Good morning, David."

"Mornin', Abby." While it could hardly be called warm and amiable, there was nothing in Abby's voice or her expression to indicate anything was wrong. He gave her a genuine smile. "Are you ready for today?"

She nodded. "I am *so* ready."

"My goodness, you must have gotten up early," Molly said, coming around to join them. "Did you get your road fixed?"

"Enough," he said. "It wasn't a big thing, but it's right at one of the steepest places, so I thought a little extra measure of safety wouldn't hurt."

"Did you get any sleep at all?" Sarah asked from beside the campfire.

David started a little. Had Abby said something to her after all? But no. Sarah and Patrick and his father knew something had happened— Abby had come back alone and David had spent the night on the mountain—but nothing more. He gave her a rueful smile. "Those flat rocks make a pretty good mattress, believe it or not."

"I don't believe it," she laughed. But she didn't pursue it further.

David turned to his father and Patrick. "We need to decide on drivers."

"Platte and Bishop Nielson were by earlier," Patrick said. "They want us lined up by eight o'clock. We're going to have to hook multiple teams to the wagons again. Normally we could double or triple them for a hill like this, but they are exhausted. Platte says the heavier wagons will need six or seven span."

David turned around and let his eye pick out the route that led to the top. Then he looked at Billy Joe. "I think you and I need to hitch up Paint and Tillie to help the mules. You all right with that?"

After a moment Billy Joe nodded, his eyes grave. "Can I walk alongside her to help her?"

David's eyes softened. "As long as you don't get too close. I think Tillie would appreciate that."

He turned to Abby. "We're going to be shuttling the extra teams down the hill, so we can only take two wagons up at a time. We don't need you to drive, but if you feel up—"

"I'll drive," she said shortly.

"Okay." David looked at his father. "Why don't you and Patrick go first. Billy Joe and I will walk alongside, help keep the teams moving." Then he spoke to Sarah. "I'm going down to the river to wash up. I'll be back in a few minutes."

As he went past Molly, she caught his arm. "Just one more," she murmured. That startled him. Was she asking for just one more talk? But he saw that she too was staring up at the hill, and then he understood.

"That's right. Just one more pull."

Since the McKennas were back some distance in the line, John and David decided to go up and help Bishop Nielson and Joe take their two wagons up the hill. Kumen Jones, the bishop's son-in-law, had his wagon in front, but he had one of the strongest teams in the company and would be fine on his own.

Just then, someone up above them shouted, waving the next outfit forward. Kumen yelled and slapped the reins, and his wagon started up the hill.

Bishop Jens Nielson had started out from Cedar City with a yoke of oxen to pull one wagon, a pair of mules to pull the second, and four steers to pull the third. In the grueling two months since leaving the Colorado River, one of his oxen and two of the steers had died. He had made his way along by hitching up a mule and an ox to pull one wagon, a single mule to pull another, and two steers to pull the third.

"Need some help, Bishop?" David asked as they came up. He couldn't help but shake his head. The bishop had every draft animal he owned hitched to his wagon. The front team was made up of a huge old ox named Buck and one of the Nielson's mules. The two steers were next, looking small compared to Buck. Finally, the bishop had borrowed one of Joe's horses and had it harnessed with his second mule. It was a ragtag collection and it looked pitifully inadequate, but David tried not to show that as he looked up at the old Dane.

"Yah, and vee be very grateful for it, Brodder David and Brodder John."

Joe's head appeared on the other side of his horse. He had been checking the tugs. "We sure do," Joe said. Joe had an ox goad in one hand and tossed it to David. "David, why don't you walk alongside Old Buck, and maybe John and I can worry about the steers and the mules."

"Be kind to Buck," Bishop Nielson said. "He be very much like dis ole, tired Dane. Vee don't haf many more miles left in us."

David turned and looked at the beast. He was massive, probably weighing close to a ton before he had started on the trip. Now he looked exactly as the bishop had said. His head was down. Ribs were visible on his side. His eyes were half closed. His tail barely twitched. Unlike horses and mules, you didn't drive oxen with reins. Someone had to walk alongside and urge them along. Usually, verbal commands were sufficient, but on a pull like this, an occasional jab with the ox goad might prove necessary.

"Sure," David said, moving up to stand beside the ox.

Joe reached up in the seat beside his father and retrieved a short whip. "Sure you don't want me to drive, Dad?"

"Yah," the old Dane said. "Vaht vood the neighbors tink if I let a boy do a man's verk?"

"Yah," David chortled. "Vee can't have dat, Joe."

Joe, pretending to be hurt, ignored them both. He turned and looked up the hill. Kumen was now a good two hundred yards above them and the men up there were waving them on. It was time. Bishop Nielson raised the whip and gave it a sharp crack over the heads of the hodgepodge of animals. "Ha!" he shouted. "Gee up!"

They had to stop and rest the teams three times. Now, at the bottom of the last and steepest pitch, they stopped again. The wagons were bunching up here, and Kumen had just started his ascent. They watched as the twelve horses lunged upward, jerking the wagon forward. What made this final stretch of road so challenging was not just the pitch but also the footing. Much of it crossed rough rock pans with several patches of smooth, slippery rock.

Kumen's team was magnificent, and he was rightly proud of them. They hit the first rock surface, snorting and blowing as their feet fought for some kind of grip. Then, even as those below watched in horror, both horses in the fourth span slipped and crashed to their knees. Kumen was up in an instant, lashing the whip, screaming like a madman. Two men standing nearby leaped in and grabbed the bridles of the lead team, pulling them forward. For a moment, the two downed horses were dragged along on their knees, shrieking in pain, but the forward movement of the lead teams finally pulled them up again. A moment later the wagon went over the top and disappeared.

"All right, Joe," Bishop Nielson said softly. "I tink it be our turn." His face was pale as he reached down and took out a bullwhip from its holder.

David moved over and laid a hand on Buck's massive flanks. "Okay, old boy. Here we go. One last time, then it's downhill from there."

They didn't have the teams to power the wagon up that slope like Kumen had done, but to David's amazement, the animals threw their weight against the harnessing and started up the hill. As they moved steadily upward, all four men were cracking the whips and shouting their encouragement. Buck began to falter about a third of the way up, and David jabbed him hard in the rump with the ox goad. He bellowed in pain but leaned forward, grunting as he tried to keep up with the mule beside him.

They were no more than fifty feet from the top when Buck suddenly went down. The mule brayed loudly as it was nearly pulled off its feet by the weight of the ox. David leaped in, jabbing the goad again and again, drawing blood now. He saw a flash as Joe came up and grabbed the mule's bridle. The whip flashed, and there was a sharp crack. With a squeal, the mule lunged forward. It was to no avail. Buck's dead weight brought the wagon to a halt. Then, to David's horror, he saw it begin to inch back down the hill.

The steers were bawling, the mules and horse squealing or braying, the men screaming at the top of their lungs. Somewhere in the back of his mind, David realized that the bishop was shouting in Danish now. The animals who were still on their feet were pawing at the rock, trying to stop the backward slide, their necks white with lather, nostrils flaring, drool falling from their mouths.

David kicked the ox as hard as he could. "Get up, Buck!" He hammered on his back with the ox goad. "Ha, Buck! Ha!" he shouted with every blow. Great shudders ran through the ox's body, and one knee came up, but the animal couldn't do it. Buck raised his head and gave a great roar of pain. The sound echoed off the cliffs above them and sent chills up and down David's back.

"We're rolling back!" Joe screamed. "Get him up! Get him up!"

David didn't have to be told. Buck was now being dragged slowly backwards, and the momentum of that slide was increasing. David knew that if they didn't stop that backward slide, not only would all the animals be dragged to their death, but Jens Nielson, with his twisted and crippled legs, would not likely survive a jump.

David forgot about Buck. He leaped back to the team of mules, grabbed the nearest one by the ear, and dragged him forward, yelling at him at the top of his lungs. Across from him, his father was doing the same. That did it. The other animals, desperate to get away from the torrent of blows, lunged forward, and that was enough to drag old Buck to his feet.

David heard himself shouting. "Go! Go! Go!" They were moving.

And finally, they crested the ridge. Buck and the mule beside him went first, followed by the steers, then the mules and the horse, and, at last, the wagon. David dropped to his hands and knees, gasping for air. Across from him, his father and Joe collapsed, lying on their backs, heaving in air in hungry gulps. David turned as Jens clambered awkwardly down from his wagon. As he hobbled forward, David saw that tears were streaming down his cheeks.

David got slowly to his feet as the grizzled old Dane hobbled forward past the exhausted animals. Their heads were down, noses almost touching the ground. Lather dripped from their necks. Their legs were trembling so violently that David thought they were going to spasm or even collapse where they stood.

"Help me git him loose," the bishop said as he reached Buck.

"I'm sorry. I'm sorry," David said over and over, between sobs, as they unhooked the chains and led Buck off to one side. The bishop motioned for Joe and John to take the wagon forward out of the way, then turned back and began to stroke Buck's nose. "You gave your all, ole boy," he whispered. "Vee tank you for your courage."

David came over to see if there was anything he could do, but just as he reached the ox, Buck gave a low moan and dropped to his knees. As both men watched helplessly, his hind legs folded as well. Buck grunted as that big body of his finally rested on the ground. There was one last groan, and then the animal rolled over on his side, gave one last weary sigh, and died.[1]

As David reached the line of wagons back down at the bottom, Patrick and a couple of other men were just finishing hitching the extra teams to the McKennas' second two wagons. "Ah, there you are," Patrick said as David came up. "How is it going up there? From here it looks like the teams are struggling, especially over that last hump."

"They're too spent," David said. "Two months of too little grass and hard pulls have taken their toll. It's not very pretty," he added soberly.

"Where's John?"

"He's helping up top. He'll come down when it's our turn."

At that moment, Abby came around the wagon. She pulled up. "Oh. I didn't realize you were here. I thought you were going to help up above."

"I was, but . . ." He glanced quickly at Patrick, then back to her. "I don't think you should drive this one, Abby."

Her head came up sharply. "Why not?"

"I just think it's better if you don't."

"I've driven worse than this," she said. "Sometimes, even without your careful help."

"Abby," her father started, but she whirled and stomped back to her wagon.

The two men looked at each other. As David started to say something, Patrick cut him off. "Look, David, I don't know what's going on between you two, but you're in charge here. You do what you think is best."

"Thank you." He turned and walked back. Abby was at the back of her wagon, reaching inside for something. When he came around, she swung on him. "Why, David? Why now? Earlier, you said you wanted me to drive."

"Because it's not earlier, Abby. Things have changed."

"I know what's changed," she said tightly, "but I didn't think you'd be so petty as to punish me for what happened last night."

He was too weary, too sick at heart to fight with her. "I passed your Mom and Molly going up. I sent Billy Joe with them. They said they'll wait for you on top."

Suddenly she was pleading. "I want to drive it, David. You know I can do it."

"Yes, I do. But the answer is no."

He turned and went forward to begin checking the harnessing on the teams. When he reached the lead team—Tillie and Paint—he came around in front of them and stroked their noses, talking softly to them. He didn't look up as she stalked past him, nor when she muttered something to her father and started up the hill.

"Abby, gurl," John called as he saw her coming up the road toward him, "Ah was joost cumin' doon ta see if yur Pa an' David needed sum help doon thare."

She nearly swept past him without speaking, but then she changed her mind and stopped, planting her feet. "*Ohhh!* That son of yours is impossible."

He grinned. "Ahre ya joost learnin' that, me gurl? Ah cud 'ave tole ya that when he be six years old."

"It's not funny, John. Not funny at all."

He sobered. "Sorry. What be the trouble?"

"Ask *him*. He's the one who won't let me drive." With a jerk, she flounced up the road.

For several seconds, John watched her go, pulling at his beard thoughtfully. Then his jaw set, and he broke into a trot after her. She turned when she heard him and stopped, preparing for battle. But all he said was, "Cum wit me, gurl." He took her by the elbow, not with a lot of gentleness, and guided her up the hill.

When they reached the bottom of the last pitch, he stopped. A wagon was fighting its way to the top, its fourteen horses and mules just starting to clear the ridge. He waited until it disappeared, then turned and looked back the other way. The next wagon was still about fifty yards behind them, making its way slowly upward.

He took her arm again. "Cum. An' keep yur eyes open. Maybe ya can learn sumthin'."

Surprised by his anger, and puzzled by the odd command, she fell in beside him, not speaking. Just what was she supposed to look for? But before they had gone twenty steps, she had her answer. Her stomach lurched and she felt a sudden urge to gag. On the rock pan directly in front of her

was a six-inch streak of fresh blood, like some wounded thing had been
downed here, then dragged along the stone. To the left, there was a splat-
tering of bright red drops. Above that another smear, this one twice as
long.

Her hand flew to her mouth and she had to stop. She felt a nudge and
turned. John was pointing to a rock just off the road. Here the blood was
almost dried, making the patch of matted black hair look all the more
grotesque. "That be from the knee of one of our own mules."

Abby wanted to run, but John wouldn't let her. He held her arm. If she
missed something, he pointed it out. If she tried to hurry past, he made her
slow her step. Finally, he began to speak in a low voice. "The animals be
at their end, Abby. Joost as we are. But thare be no choice. If we cahrn't
git these wagons up an' over 'ere t'day, we awl be done fur. The 'ole purpose of our mission be fur naught."

"I understand," she murmured, feeling sick to her stomach.

"Do ya, gurl? Do ya unnerstand 'ow a good man feels aboot his animals, especially his teams? They be lek 'is own fam'ly. I've seen grown men
weep 'ere t'day, Abby, b'cuz they 'ad naw choice but ta lash and whip these
poor starving beasts up the 'ill. Ah've watched 'orses and mules go into violent spasms—near convulsions—befur they reached the top. Ah've seen
six an' seven span of 'orses go ten feet, then 'ave ta stop befur they can go
the next ten feet."

"I had no idea," she whispered. "I'm sorry."

"It naw be me that needs an apology, Abby. Just know this. Bishop
Nielson's ox almost dinna mek it ta the top. When 'e collapsed in the
shafts, we thought we'd lost 'im and the other animals. If that wagon 'ad
been allowed to roll back, Ah naw be sure the bishop wud 'ave survived.
Ah watched David fall on that ox, beatin' on 'im lek a man possessed, tryin' ta get the poor thing back on its feet."

She looked away, blinded by the sudden tears.

"An' that ole noble animal finally got back up an' went awl the way ta
the top. Then, 'e joost rolled over an' died. And we watched Bishop
Nielson bawl lek a baby over 'is body."

His head came up, and she saw his eyes were glistening too. "Ah 'ave naw idee what be goin' on b'tween ya an' David, Abby. But Ah know this. 'E went back doon b'cuz 'e dinna want ya 'avin' ta be part of this." He looked away, and she saw his Adam's apple bob. "'E went back doon b'cuz 'e cud naw bear the thought of anyone layin' a whip across the back of Paint, or 'is own Lady Tilburn, unless it were 'im."

She felt a shudder as she tried to suppress the sob rising up from within her.

"Ya go on up top noow," he said, his voice filled with gentleness. "Yur mum and Molly and Billy Joe be waitin' fur ya."

As she nodded, he looked her squarely in the eye. "Ah think it wud be better if yur fam'ly were naw waitin' at the top, watchin' Patrick an' David bring those last two wagons up."[2]

When Abby left her family and came back to the top of the ridge, David and his father had their wagon pulled to one side. Tillie and Paint were out of the harness, standing to one side. David was bent over, applying some kind of ointment to Tillie's knees. Abby had to look away. Both legs were raw and bleeding.

When John saw her coming, he took both horses by the bridles. "Ah'll tek 'em forward an' git 'em saddled," he said to David, and without waiting for an answer, he led them away. David had his back to Abby and hadn't seen her. He moved to the mules, who were still wheezing, their entire bodies shaking, their necks and flanks white with lather. He moved to the closest one and began stroking its nose, talking quietly to it.

"David?"

She saw his body tense, but he didn't turn around.

Coming up right behind him, she stopped. She swallowed once, then again, trying to gain control of her voice. "I am so sorry, David."

He turned slowly. The haunted look on his face made her gasp, and that brought the tears, in spite of her determination to hold them back. "Thank you for sparing me this," she said in a strangled whisper. "I was such a fool. I'm sorry."

"This trip has made fools of all of us, Abby," he finally said. "But it's almost over." He turned back and began checking the harnessing.

She stood there for another minute, watching him, making no effort to wipe the tears away. Then she turned and started slowly away.

"Abby?"

She turned back. "Yes?"

He stood there, shoulders slumped, face lined, eyes filled with pain. "I've seen you cry more in the last two days than in the previous eighteen months. I'm sorry. But it's almost over."

Notes

1. The description of Jens Nielson's "team" as he made that last pull up and over San Juan Hill comes from the family's history, though no name is given for the ox. But when it reached the top, it sank to the ground and died (see Carpenter, *Jens Nielson*, 43, 49).

2. It is Charles M. Redd, whose father went on the Hole in the Rock expedition, who gives us the details of that last terrible climb over San Juan Hill:

"Here again seven span of horses were used, so that when some of the horses were on their knees, fighting to get up to find a foothold, the still-erect horses could plunge upward against the sharp grade. On the worst slopes the men were forced to beat their jaded animals into giving all they had. After several pulls, rests, and pulls, many of the horses took to spasms and near-convulsions, so exhausted were they. By the time most of the outfits were across, the worst stretches could easily be identified by the dried blood and matted hair from the forelegs of the struggling teams. My father was a strong man, and reluctant to display emotion; but, whenever in later years the full pathos of San Juan Hill was recalled either by himself or by someone else, the memory of such bitter struggles was too much for him and he wept" (Redd, "Short Cut," 23–24).

CHAPTER 71

In the end, they were simply too exhausted to go any farther.

After the brutal climb up San Juan Hill, the wagons went north along the top of Comb Ridge for a couple of miles before they found a wash that would allow them to descend to the flat land below. They camped at the bottom, too utterly spent to go further.

The next morning they were up and moving again by nine o'clock, but the scouts had already gone ahead and found what the first exploring party had called Butler Wash, one last deep gully that blocked their way. One last numbed effort took a road down and back up again as the camp waited on the western side. On Monday, they started forward again, descending down into the wash, then struggling to make it up the other side. About noon, they reached the river. They were now only twelve miles from Montezuma Creek and their destination.

There should have been an air of excitement, but excitement didn't come cheaply anymore. They had been gone too long and come too far and endured too many things to really care that much. As the wagons began to congregate beneath the shade of the cottonwood trees along the river—some of the families too weary to even climb down—word came back that they would noon here. Up front, Platte Lyman and Jens Nielson walked off to one side and conferred quietly. Ten minutes later, they called for a meeting of all the men present.

Platte waited until the last man joined them, then began without preamble. "Brethren, we don't need to tell you that our little company has reached the end of its tether. It is now the fifth day of April. We had hoped to have our crops in weeks ago. We had hoped to be building houses, barns, and corrals by now. And here we are, still another day from our destination. Maybe two, at the rate we are now going."

Bishop Nielson spoke. "Wit our animals, it may as well be a hundred."

"What are you saying, Dad?" Joe Nielson asked.

"We are saying," Platte came in smoothly, "that perhaps we have come far enough."

Heads jerked up and there were soft exclamations of surprise.

Platte looked around. "This is not a big valley, but it is a pleasant one. There is an abundance of water. The land is flat and easily plowed. We can quarry stone from the hills."

"Are you saying," George Hobbs broke in, "that we're not going on to Montezuma Creek? If so, I object. We have people waiting for us there."

"Thank you, George," Platte said. "We know that, and we know that one of them is your sister. Those families will undoubtedly be disappointed, but they will know we are here. And from the beginning, we've known that not everyone could settle right there around them. There have to be other settlements. Especially as others follow in our path."

"Sounds to me like you've already made the decision," George grumbled.

Platte nodded thoughtfully. "It is settled in our minds. Now we put it to you."

"Well," Ben Perkins said in a loud, booming voice, "Ah be tellin' ya what me wife said as we pulled up a little while ago. She said, 'Ben, ya can go as fur as ya lek, but me? Ah naw be gittin' up in that wagon agin.'"

"Hear, hear," someone in the back called.

"Brodders," Bishop Nielson said. "Dat is our recommendation to you. Cud vee see by show of hands, how many vill support the idee to make dis our home?"

David's hand came up, as did Patrick's and his father's. As he looked around, virtually every other hand was up except for George's. Platte nodded in satisfaction. "We'll not be asking for a negative vote, because no one is required to stay. Those who want to continue to Montezuma are welcome to do so." He took in a deep breath. "Well, that's it, then. Welcome home."

⁂

The word spread like wildfire through the camp and was met with a few expressions of shock and dismay, but mostly it was joy and enormous relief that swept through the company. David told his father and Patrick that he needed to speak briefly with Platte, but would join them at the wagons.

As he walked slowly back about five minutes later, he couldn't help but overhear the reaction going on all around him. Margaret Nielson, teenage daughter of Bishop Nielson, was still sitting up in her wagon. "Does that mean we're staying here, Papa?" A broad smile wreathed the bishop's face. "Why yes, my dear Maggie, where did you want to go?"

Arabelle Smith, wife of Stanford Smith, the woman who had "crow-hopped" down the Hole in the Rock, was best friends with Mary Jones, wife of Kumen Jones. As David passed, the two women were talking excitedly to each other. "Oh, Mary," Belle cried, "Now we can build our houses side by side and be neighbors, like we were back in Cedar City. Let's build us houses of these pretty pink stones."

Farther down, a husband and wife were arguing. She too was up in the wagon seat. He was by the team, looking up at her. "This is the end of the trail," he said, clearly losing his patience. "This *is* the San Juan. We are here."

"But it can't be," his wife protested. "The whole valley is no bigger than our backyard. Where is the fort? Where are the Indians? Where are our own people?"

He sighed. "We are not at Montezuma Creek, but it has been decided that we will stay here."

She harrumphed and folded her arms. "I am not getting down here," she declared.

David wasn't able to hear what the answer to that was, but when he turned back a minute later, her husband was helping her down from the wagon.[1]

In the McKenna camp it was a similar thing. To David's surprise, it was Molly who protested. "But I thought we would be going to live by Jim and Mary."

"We?" Abby asked pointedly.

That flustered her. "Well, I meant our family." Then she pouted a little. "I guess it doesn't matter. Live wherever you like."

"You mean we're staying right here?" Billy Joe crowed. "Great! Can we build our house right by the river? Nate and me saw some great big fish there a few minutes ago."

Sarah put an arm around him and hugged him. "Oh, to have your love of life, Billy Joe."

"How do you feel about it?" Patrick asked her.

She paused and looked around. Then she nodded, somewhat tentatively. That was followed by a second nod, much more emphatic. "I like it. I am so ready to be done with this trip."

"Abby?"

"I'm home," she said simply.

Patrick turned to the Drapers. "And what of you two?" he asked.

David deferred to his father with a nod. "What do you say, Dad?"

"That be simple. Ah came 'ere ta be wit David. Whare 'e goes, Ah go. If'n he'll have me."

"Being together is what all of this is about, Dad," came the quiet reply. Then he looked back at Patrick. "We hope to start a ranch someday, maybe up by the Blue Mountains. But for now, we'll be here to help the company get established." He hesitated, then went on. "However, I'll be riding on now."

"What?" Molly and Sarah cried together.

"I talked to Platte for a minute after the meeting. I'm going on with George to Montezuma. Check on the Davises. Let them know we're here."

"No, David," Abby exclaimed. "Can't that wait at least until tomorrow?"

He shook his head. "No." He looked to Patrick again. "I may spend a day or two with them. Then I think I'll ride north."

"North?" Molly cried. "Where are you going?"

"This valley isn't big enough for cattle. I want to check things out up around the Blue Mountains, take a look at the rangeland, before everyone else starts making claims."

"Without your father?" Molly was clearly close to bawling.

"Ah think it be wise fur David ta go noow," John said quietly. "And alone."

"Platte's also concerned about our lack of cash money right now," David went on softly. "Some of the single men are talking about heading over into Colorado and seeing if they can find work in the mines."

"Ya be goin' back ta minin'?" his father blurted.

"No, no. I was just saying that as an example. Actually, while we were in Escalante, I heard that they're looking for mail riders for a circuit between Green River and Ouray, Colorado."

Now his father was even more dismayed. "An' they also said it be one of the most dangerous routes to ride. The Utes are on the warpath, and there are rustlers and 'ighwaymen everywhere."

"Oh, David, no," Sarah cried.

He smiled briefly. "That's why the pay is half again what it is for other routes."

"But Daddy's paying you," Molly said. "Why do you need to go off somewhere?"

"I haven't been paying David for some time now," Patrick murmured. "Nor his father. They both decided they wanted to do this on their own, just like the rest of us."

That stunned even Sarah. David walked over to her. "I'm not saying I'm going to do that. Only that it's an option. I'm coming back."

She threw her arms around him. "Thank you, David," she whispered. "Thank you for bringing us here safely."

"It has been the best thing that ever happened to me, Sarah. Thank you for letting me be a part of your family."

"You can't go," Molly wailed. "Not now. When will you be back?"

Sarah stepped back, still looking at him. "Your father's right. It's best if you go."

A quarter of an hour later, the family stood together, waving as David rode away. He turned in the saddle and waved once, then disappeared into the trees.

Molly was sobbing. "I'll probably be gone before he gets back. He didn't even say good-bye."

"Oh yes he did," Abby said quietly. "Yes he did."

Patrick turned and watched his two daughters for a moment—Molly weeping openly, Abby weeping inwardly. "Know what tomorrow is?" he finally asked.

It was such a strange question in the context of the conversation that everyone turned to him in surprise. "It's April sixth."

"The anniversary of the organization of the Church," Sarah said, her eyes widening.

"The *fiftieth* anniversary of the organization of the Church," Patrick emphasized. "And why is that important?"

Sarah was nodding. "Because every fifty years is what was known in Israel as a jubilee year."

"A jubidee what?" Billy Joe asked.

"A jubilee year," his father explained. "It comes from the Old Testament. Do you know what happened in a jubilee year?"

Again it was his wife who answered. "Land that had been taken away from or sold by a family, reverted back to the family. Isn't that interesting? Tomorrow, on the start of a jubilee year, we will begin the process of giving this land to the people."

"Slaves were also freed," Abby said with a touch of wonder. She understood exactly what her father was doing. "Bondservants were loosed. Debts were forgiven."

"Ah, yes," her father said with a soft smile. "Debts were forgiven."

John Draper turned slowly. "Thank ya fur remindin' us of that, Patrick. What a wonderful way ta begin a new life."

Friday, April 9, 1880

"Patrick?"

The wagon creaked as someone moved inside it. A moment later, the flap opened and Patrick McKenna stuck his head out. "Good morning, John."

"Mornin'." He chewed on his lower lip for a moment. "Ah 'ave a big favor ta ask of ya."

"Anything, John. You know that."

"Ah'd like to borrow Paint and maybe yur ridin' 'orse fur the day. An' your oldest daughter as well. Ah know thare be a lot goin' on t'day, but . . ." His shoulders lifted and fell. "We probably won't be back 'til after dark."

Suddenly Sarah appeared beside her husband. She was buttoning the sleeves on her dress. "The answer is yes, John. How soon do you want to go?"

"Aboot 'alf an 'our ago."

There was a brisk nod. "Patrick, you go find her. I know she's up because I heard her earlier. I'll get them some food."

When they crossed Butler Wash, Abby spoke for the first time in over an hour. "You're taking me back to the river camp?"

John shook his head. "Close, but naw close e'nuff."

Her eyes widened. "You're not taking me back to those Indian ruins, are you? Because if you are, I'm turning around right now."

"Ah naw be tekin' ya anywhare agin yur will, Abby gurl. Ah promise ya that."

"I don't want to talk about David, either. I mean it, John."

"Ah naw be talkin' aboot anythin' ya dunna want ta talk aboot."

"And that's all you're going to say?"

"That be e'nuff fur now."

⁂

When David's father stopped his horse at the top of San Juan Hill and swung stiffly down, Abby gave him a questioning look. "This is it?"

"Yah."

"I've not forgotten what you taught me here, if that's it," she said quietly.

There was a short laugh. "Ya be bustin' yur bootons tryin' ta guess what we be doin', but it be gettin' ya nowhare. Do ya want ta eat first, or do ya want me ta git it over wit?"

She finally smiled, and her smile was warm and open. How could you stay angry at this man? "Show me what you want me to see."

"'Ow ya know Ah got sumthin' ta show ya?"

She gave him a chiding look. "It's a long way to come for just a talk." He chuckled, but said nothing. Abby dismounted and came over and put her arm through his. "Awl reet, ya old Tyke, lead on. I'm ready."

To her surprise, he led her to a large, flat rock that jutted out of the ground just a short distance from the horses. She sat down, and he squatted down in front of her. His brown eyes were dark and thoughtful as he studied her face. Then he began.

"Ah dunna know what 'appened b'tween ya an' David that night at the ruins, Abby, an'—" He waved a hand, cutting off her protest. "An' Ah dunna wanna know. Let me joost say a few things that need sayin'."

"All right," she said meekly, relieved that he wasn't going to question her on that.

"When Davee cum back frum Montezuma Creek this last time, 'e tole me that 'e an' Sister Davis 'ad a long talk aboot you."

"About me?"

He nodded. "David came back reddy ta tell Molly that 'e cud naw marry 'er noow."

She straightened. "John, there are some things that you don't—"

"Ya be bustin' yur bootons agin, gurl," he growled.

She sat back. "Sorry. But I get to talk when you're finished."

"Agreed. But Ah naw be finished quite yet. So David came back determined ta talk ta Molly an' tell 'er that 'e cud naw be marryin' 'er b'cuz 'e 'ad feelin's fur 'er older sister."

She started to retort, but at his look, bit it back. "Go on."

"But Molly beat 'im ta it. She blurted oot that she was naw goin' ta stay, an' that it be over fur the two of them. Well, Davee was so chuffed— delighted—that this meant 'e naw be havin' ta break 'er 'eart, that 'e joost stood thare an' said nothin'."

"And kissed her good-bye," she said dryly. "That does sound pretty chuffed to me."

If he heard, John gave no sign. "So anyway, Molly comes back an' tells 'er big sister awl aboot what 'appened, but she still be thinkin' that David 'ad cum oot ta propose marriage ta 'er." He stood up, looking down on her, his eyes piercing now in their intensity. "But it naw be true, Abby. It naw be true."

He went on quickly. "Noow, Ah naw be askin' fur ya ta respond ta that, gurl. Ah naw be tellin' ya what ta think or 'ow to feel. Cum. It's time ya see what we cum up 'ere fur."

He started down the road they had traversed just a few days before. As she followed, she averted her eyes from the dark stains on the rocks beneath their feet. He stopped a short distance below the crest. Seeing nothing unusual, she gave him a questioning look.

"When David came up 'ere on the moontain that night after 'e spoke wit ya, Ah be quite worried. Ah cud naw 'elp but wonder if'n 'e might naw turn awl bitter aboot God awl over agin, what wit 'im tryin' ta do what's reet, an' it blowin' up in 'is face like a black-powder rifle." He looked away. "Ah be real worried aboot that, Abby."

"I didn't do it to hurt him, John."

One eyebrow lifted, but he said nothing. He took her elbow and turned her so she was facing east toward the rock face of the sandstone escarpment that ran from here to the bottom. "Walk over thare, Abby, an' tell me what ya see."

Completely baffled now, she pointed. "Over there?" He nodded. As she picked her way across the rocky ground, her eyes began searching the flat wall of pink rock. And then she stopped. Moving slowly now, she veered right and stopped in front of an inscription that had been carved into the stone.

As she read it, John came over to join her. Her fingers were gently tracing the outline of the block letters cut neatly into the sandstone. *WE THANK THEE OH GOD.*[2] Finally, she turned. "And David carved this?" she whispered.

He shrugged. "Ah canna say fur sure. 'E never said anythin' aboot it. But before 'e left, 'e asked me if me tool bag be up 'ere. Ah thought 'e joost wanted it fur workin' on the road. But that next day, joost befur we started doon the t'other side, Ah went lookin' aroond. An' Ah found this." He looked away. "An' when Ah did, Ah knew me son was gonna be awl reet."

Without another word, he climbed back to the top of the ridge and sat down to wait for her.

❦

When Abby rejoined him five minutes later, he had their lunch spread out on the rock. "So let's be eatin'," he said gruffly. "An' then we best be startin' back. It be a long ride."

"And that's all you're going to say." Her voice was soft, and her eyes were still red.

"Ah tole ya, Aw naw be tellin' ya what ta do. An' Ah be in naw mood ta be talkin' aboot this anymore. Naw on the way back, ya 'ear? Ah don't want ya all blubbery an' stuff."

She took a deep breath. "Awl reet," she said, in a near perfect imitation of his accent. "But only if you promise me one thing, John Draper."

"An' what might that be?"

"I would like you to tell me about your wife, John. Tell me about your Annie, and what it was like for the two of you in Yorkshire. Will ya do that for me?"

"Then ya be gettin' *me* awl blubbery."

She laughed aloud, slipped her arm through his, and laid her head against his shoulder. "I doubt that. I doubt that very much."

Notes

1. Margaret Nielson's question about whether this would be their home comes from the Nielson family records (see Carpenter, *Jens Nielson*, 50). Arabelle Smith's desire to build beside Mary Jones comes from the history written by her grandson (see Raymond Jones, "Last Wagon," 25). The account of the woman who thought the valley at Bluff was no bigger than her backyard also comes from that same source.

2. Just a short distance below the top of the ridge, where San Juan Hill comes out on the top of Comb Ridge, there is a faint inscription carved into the face of the cliff. It is barely discernible now, after years of weathering. There is no record as to who may have carved those words (see note on page 734). Because the inscription so perfectly epitomizes the spirit of that gallant and undaunted band of pioneers, I chose to make it an integral part of their story.

CHAPTER 72

Wednesday, April 21, 1880

As David rode slowly along, his head kept swinging back and forth in amazement. Could this really be the same place from which he had left just two weeks before? Stakes with strips of cloth were stuck in the ground everywhere, marking out both sides of what was to be the main street. Virtually every lot now had something on it. About half of the lots had wagons parked on them, but it was the other half that surprised him. He counted about a dozen "wickiups," or dome-shaped huts made of woven willows plastered with mud.

But most astonishing was how many houses were already under construction. As he rode slowly along he counted nearly two dozen foundations, with stone fireplaces already jutting their fingers up like spears stuck in the ground.

As his eyes took in everything, he made a mental note to talk to Patrick about a business idea that was forming in his mind. There were no trees in the valley other than cottonwood trees along the river. Cottonwood lumber was twisted and gnarled, and that showed in the homes now being built. The logs had been squared as much as possible, but because they were so crooked, there were cracks between them, some three and four inches wide. That would take a lot of chinking and plaster.

David had just come from the Blue Mountains, where pine forests stretched as far as the eye could see. That was only forty miles to the north. If someone were to build a sawmill on one of those creeks up there, it could provide lumber to the whole territory. Sooner or later, someone was going to think of that, so why not let it be Patrick? David had found a good ranch site, and had carefully written out a description of the surroundings so as to make his claim. He would ride up there again with his father, perhaps as early as next week, and see if he agreed.

But that was going to take time, and in the last couple of days he had come to another conclusion. Right now, he was needed here. There was so much to do—getting houses built, crops planted, an irrigation ditch dug, corrals and barns put in place. The ranch could wait. In the meantime, a sawmill would be not only an important contribution to the settlement but a source of income until he could get the ranch started.

Seeing Sarah and Patrick standing beside a wagon just ahead, he urged Tillie forward to join them. They called a greeting as he rode up, and when he pulled to a stop, Sarah reached up and patted his arm. "It is so good to have you back. Did you have any luck finding a ranch?"

"I did. There are some very promising places." He looked at Patrick. "And remind me to talk to you about a possible business opportunity. But right now, I'd like to find Dad and let him know I'm back."

"And Abby?" Sarah asked innocently. She didn't wait for an answer. "Your father and Abby and Billy Joe are up working on the ditch."

"I saw some of the crops under irrigation, but I was a little surprised there weren't more."

Patrick grunted in disgust. "It's not for lack of water. It's just that this soil is so sandy, the dams keep collapsing and the ditches fill up with silt."

He acknowledged that with a murmur. "So," he said, looking around. "Molly got off, then?"

"Yes, just four days ago." Sarah pointed to her eyes. "Can't you tell? I haven't stopped crying yet. She went with the Hunters and the Uries. You remember them, don't you? Both young couples from Cedar City."

"Sure. So they were going back? Are they coming back?"

There was a quick shake of her head. "I don't think so."

David fell silent, thinking about how much Molly loved her family. But even that wasn't enough to hold her here. "And what are your plans? Jim and Mary Davis told me you're going to move up to Montezuma Creek and live by them."

"That's right," Patrick said. "You probably haven't heard any of this,

but we had a real brouhaha over the distribution of land. There just isn't
enough here for all of us. Platte finally worked it out to where all were satisfied, but I'm no farmer, David. You know that. I can do business in
Montezuma Creek as well as in Bluff City."

"Bluff City? Is that what we're calling it?"

"Yeah. Bill Hutchings suggested it. Everyone seems to like it because
of the bluffs on both sides of town. Anyway, Abby and Sarah would really
enjoy living by Jim and Mary, so I think we'll move up there in a couple of
days."

"And by the way," Sarah said, "we have another baby in the company.
Alvin and Emma Decker had a little boy."

"Good for them. There's something about this trek that sure makes for
healthy babies."

And then, as an awkward silence settled in, Sarah leaned forward and
poked him. "Oh, for heaven's sake. Go. Go see your—" a slow smile stole
across her face—"father."

"If Abby's up there, do I need to take a sidearm?" he asked ruefully.

Patrick laughed. "We've taken the buggy whip away from her. I think
you'll be all right."

<hr/>

To David's great surprise, when he reached the place where Patrick
had told him to go, the only one working there was Abby. She had a shovel
in her hand and was cleaning out the ditch. When she looked up, she
didn't seem at all surprised to see him. "Hello," she said softly.

"Uh . . . hi," he stammered. "I was looking for Dad. Your parents told
me you were all up here together."

"We were," she said. "But they've gone back to the wagons."

"Oh." He looked back the way he had just come. "I didn't see them."

"They didn't want you to. We heard that you had just passed through
town and thought you might be coming out here."

He turned slowly. There was the hint of a smile in her eyes as they
watched him steadily.

"Is there something I should know?" he asked.

"I can think of several things."

He nearly asked what, but realized she was baiting him and enjoying it very much. He lifted a hand. "Well, I'll go find them. Uh . . . sometime, we need to talk."

"No," she said. "I don't think we do."

"Oh?" He frowned. "Still playing freeze-outs, are we?" He couldn't quite keep the disappointment out of his voice.

Her amusement only deepened. "No, not that, either."

She lifted the shovel and stuck it in the pile of wet sand. Then, to his surprise, she started coming slowly toward him. "I'm glad you're back, David." She took his arm, tugging on it. "Come. There's a nice cool place over there by the river where we can talk."

"But . . . ." He was bewildered now. "You said we didn't need to talk."

"That's right. *We* don't need to talk. But *I* have some things I need to say."

⁂

They sat together, leaning against a fallen cottonwood tree, their shoulders barely touching. He reached over and traced the lines of her mouth with his fingertip, still dazed with wonder. "If I had known all this, I would have come home two weeks ago."

Her head moved back and forth. "No. Even if I had known how to contact you, it was better this way. For all it was Molly's decision to leave you, this would have devastated her. After she's been back in Cedar City for a time, she'll be all right. Now that I know you've forgiven me, I'll write her a long letter."

"Forgiven *you?*" he cried. "What about you forgiving me?"

"Oh yes, that." An impish gleam was in her eye. "Actually, Mary took care of that for you."

"She did?"

"Yes. My goodness, you really have a defender there. Mary tore into me real good. Told me that if I didn't stop being such a brat about you kissing Molly, she was going to marry you off to Emily. And after listening to Emily talk about you, I knew that was not an idle threat."

The wonder only deepened for him. "I came back hoping, Abby. But I thought it might take months before we could work things out."

"Oh, it will," she said sweetly. "Maybe even years. We have a courtship to go through. There's still a lot of rough edges that I'm going to have to iron out."

"I've got more than a lot of those," he said ruefully.

She smiled. "I wasn't talking about you." She reached up and laid her hand against his cheek. "Mary also told me that it was time that I faced the fact that I had loved you for a very long time."

He pressed her hand more firmly against his face. He could feel the roughness of the calluses on her fingertips and along the heel of her hand. Strangely, that touched him deeply. For all of her beauty, for all of her grace and intelligence and wit, somehow the calluses were Abby too. They endeared her to him all the more.

"What about me?" he asked. "I should have known it that day up on Angel's Landing. You were so frightened, but when I came back down, there you were, come across on your own. I was stunned. And then when you told me about your fear of heights, I thought you were the most remarkable woman I had ever met."

She poked him. "Well, it sure took you long enough to say it."

He sobered. "I just needed to grow up enough to where I could see past Molly. I'm sorry I was so dense."

Her smile died away now as well. "When you came back from the scouting trip and told us about the miracles you had experienced, the sheep and Salvation Knoll and so on, did you know I cried myself to sleep that night?"

He was astonished by that. "Why?"

"Because when I saw how you had changed, I knew there was nothing to prevent you and Molly from getting married anymore, and that broke my heart."

He turned his head and softly kissed her hair. "Ah, but there was. There was you, Abby. Dad saw it before I did. So did Mary. I kept telling Molly that we couldn't deal with courtship or romance while we were on the trail, but I see now that that wasn't the real reason I kept stalling. I just feel bad that I made it so hard on her."

"Why do you think I told Carl no, when he asked me if he could come courting?"

"Oh, Abby, Abby, Abby. I can't believe all of this is really happening."

"Nor I."

He sat up. "Well, the first thing to do is go ask your father if I can come courting."

"No," she said. "That's the second thing. First, I want to know something. And I'm deadly serious about this, David."

"All right."

"I need to know if you have any plans of taking me away from San Juan."

That surprised him. "Well, as you know, I'm thinking of becoming a rancher eventually. Probably up around the Blue Mountains. I'm going to take Dad up to look at it sometime. I'd hoped that someday I might take you up as well, and see if you approve. But that's only about forty miles from here and—"

She cut him off. "The Blue Mountains are fine, but no farther." Then she became wistful. "It's really strange, David. But I love this country. We fought too hard to get here to simply turn around and leave again. It feels like home to me already. I know it's going to be hard for a while. Maybe a long while. But I want to raise our children here, and our grandchildren. So don't you be thinking you're going to be taking me away from here."

"You have my word on that," he said gruffly.

He stood and pulled her up. "Now, I have a question for you."

She turned her face up to him. "What?"

"If I were to kiss you right now, would I get myself in trouble all over again?"

She leaned back, considering that carefully. Then the corners of her mouth turned up and her eyes began to twinkle. "Do you remember that buggy whip of mine?"

His eyes widened. "I do."

"Well, if you *don't* kiss me right now, I'm going to go get it."

Patrick McKenna took his daughter in his arms and pulled her close. "Is this what you want, my dearest Abby?"

"Oh, Daddy. More than anything else in the world."

He kissed her cheek, held her a moment longer, then turned to David. "I think the answer is yes, David," he said. "You have our permission to court our daughter."

Abby threw herself into her mother's arms as Billy Joe started jumping up and down. "Yay! Yay!" he cried.

Then Sarah came to David and pressed her head against his chest. "Thank you, David. I knew it would work out."

"How long have you known?" he said.

She laughed. "Since you came back from that first trip with Silas. When you were telling us about your experience with Mary and Po-ee-kon and Yaheeno, I just suddenly knew that it was going to be you and Abby rather than you and Molly."

"Why didn't you tell me?" Abby cried.

"Because," she said archly. Then she slapped David playfully on the arm. "And for a while there, I wasn't sure this lug was going to get it worked out himself."

"Fur a while," David's father drawled, "Ah thought Ah might 'ave ta tek a six-poond 'ammer ta this boy an' knock sum sense inta 'im."

Abby came to John, laughing and crying at the same moment. "And I decided that if David wouldn't marry me, I would marry you instead."

They all had a good laugh at that. As they quieted again, David reached out and took Abby's hand. "I would like you to stand between your parents for a moment, if you would."

She gave him a questioning look, but after a moment she complied. David reached in his pocket and brought out a small blue box. He opened it, extracted a silver necklace, and handed the box to his father. Very somber now, he walked to Abby, holding it out. "My dearest Abby," he said softly, "as a token of my love for you and as a witness of my determination to court and marry you, I now place this around your neck."

She turned her back to him, reaching back to lift her hair out of the way as he fastened it. When she turned back, tears had begun. She brushed at them quickly. "There you go again, David. Making me cry some more."

"Do you know what this is?" he asked, touching the necklace.

"I do," she murmured. "Your father told me all about it that day we rode back from San Juan Hill." Then she turned to him. "You knew, didn't you? Even back then, you knew."

"Ah did," he said happily. "Ah joost dinna know how long it was gonna tek fur you two ta figure it all oot." He raised a finger. "But, what David 'as naw tole you is the necklace cums wit conditions."

"Conditions?"

"Aye. It gets passed on to me first granddaughter."

Abby's mouth softened. "Whose name shall be Anne." She looked at David. "If you agree."

David took her in his arms and kissed her as his answer. When he pulled back, he looked deeply into her eyes. "Abigail Louise McKenna. Will you marry me?"

"I will." She kissed him quickly. "When?"

David turned to her father. "Patrick, if you don't think it is too soon, I would like to marry Abby on June the fifth. That's six weeks from now."

"Ah," his father said in a choked voice, "that be the same day that Ah married me sweet Annie twenty-nine years ago."

"Then I think June the fifth sounds like a wonderful day," Patrick said.

Saturday, June 5, 1880

"I hope you all know," Bishop Jens Nielson said, trying very hard to sound grumpy, "dat dis be not where I usually perform da marriage. Ven dere is no temple, den people do dis in dere living rooms, or at the church house."

Mary Davis just laughed, knowing he was teasing them. "Sorry, Bishop, but our living room is also our bedroom and our kitchen and our study and our . . . well, you get the idea. We're lucky to get the seven of us in our house, let alone several dozen more."

Mary Nielson Jones stood just behind her father. She gave him a poke. "And since there is no church house yet, and since the St. George Temple is about a three-week journey from here, you're just going to have to make do with the riverbank, Papa. So stop giving this poor couple such a bad time. David and Abby have already waited six weeks for this to happen."

"Six weeks!" Abby protested. "I've been working on this man for over a year."

Everyone laughed as David blushed, then grinned. "She's right, Bishop. Why do you think so many people came to watch? They can still hardly believe it."

"Amen," George Hobbs called out.

"Still can't," Kumen Jones chortled.

It was a good crowd that stood under the cottonwood trees at the con-fluence of Montezuma Creek and the San Juan River. Platte Lyman, who had returned to Escalante for a wagonload of flour, had just returned a few days before. Silas Smith, who had finally caught up with the company in San Juan after his long illness, stood beside his two counselors. Many of those who were homesteading Bluff City had come up too. A wedding was something to celebrate. The Davis and Harriman families, now "long-term" residents of the area, having been here for a year, were there, along with others from Montezuma Creek.

Little Emmy Davis was their flower girl. She was barefoot, but wear-ing her best dress and clutching a handful of sunflowers. Billy Joe was the best "man" and was nearly bursting, he was so proud. With the entire mis-sion presidency finally together, David and Abby had debated about who should perform the marriage, but in the end they both agreed that it should be their beloved Bishop Nielson from Cedar City.

"Come on, Dad," Joe Nielson called out. "If you don't hurry up, ole David here is going to lose his nerve and bolt for freedom."

The bishop shot him a dirty look. "Now you see vaht I haf to put up wit from my children." He turned and looked at his son, Joe. "And don't you be gettink any crazy ideas that you and that Lyman girl be gettink married qvick like dese two."

Now it was Joe who blushed right down to the roots of his hair. Standing beside him, Ida Lyman looked like she was going to die. Besides Abby and Molly, there had been only three other single girls of marriageable age in the company. It hadn't been long into the trip before everyone noticed that Joe and Ida Lyman were showing a growing interest in each other.

Then the old Dane grew more serious. "I suppose if vee do not haf a temple, that here beside this beautiful river in our new home be second best." He turned to David and Abby. "If you two vood take your places. Facing me, please. You be looking at each other for many years to come, so it's best if you look at me now."

Now it was his wife who nudged him. "It's time, Jens."

"Brodder David, you may please take Abigail's hand." He waited until he did so. "I know dat dis be a varm day, so I haf only two things to say to dis vonderful couple. I once hear a very vise ole man give two pieces of advice. It vas given to a company of people travelink in de vilds of da desert, but it be goot advice for two people starting on da journey of life as well."

He stopped, letting the anticipation build for a moment. "Advice piece number vun. When difficult times come in your marriage, remember dis. Even ven der is no way to go troo, you must go troo."

That brought smiles and sober nods from everyone as they remembered the night he had spoken those exact words back in Forty Mile Camp. That had been a critical turning point for the company, and his words had made the difference.

"And do you know vaht be the second good advice piece?" His eyes were twinkling as he looked directly at David.

"I think I do," David said. "I think the second important thing for a marriage is that both husband and wife have what that same wise old man called 'stickity tootie.'"

The grizzled old head bobbed with great satisfaction. "Abigail, my dear, your husband to be is very vise too. You make goot choice." He looked around at the others, who were all smiling again. "Yah, dis stickity tootie be a very goot quality for all of us, I tink."

Then the smile died and he grew quite serious. "So, Brodder David and Sister Abby, vood you now turn and face each odder, still holding hands, please?"

They did so.

"Brodder David Dickinson Draper, do you take Sister Abigail Louise McKenna to be your lawful vedded vife, to take her as your own, as bone of your bone and flesh of your flesh, to love with all your heart, and to cherish her above all others, and all things, and troo all time?"

David looked deep into her eyes. "Yes."

"Sister Abigail Louise McKenna, do you take dis man, Brodder David Dickinson Draper, to be your husband, lawfully vedded to him? And do you promise to love and cherish him above all others, and all things, and for all time?"

She smiled through her tears. "Yes."

"Den, as a member of the San Juan Mission presidency and an elder in Da Church of Jesus Christ of Latter-day Saints, I pronounce you, David Draper, and you, Abigail McKenna, to be husband and vife. May your love forever remain as bright and true and pure as it is today." He smiled down on both of them. "You may now kiss each odder as man and wife."

A great cheer went up as David took her in his arms and drew her to him.

When they stepped back from each other, David raised a hand, and the applause and the calls of congratulations died away. "My wife—" he grinned like a little boy—"that sure sounds wonderful—has something she would like to say."

"Say on," the bishop said.

Abby took David's hand again and pulled him up beside her. As she looked around at these friends and family whom she loved so dearly, her face was radiant. "I wanted to have this marriage performed on San Juan Hill, beside an inscription carved in the stone near the top. But it was too far, and there is too much to do here."

She had to stop for a moment to get control of her voice. "All of you know now what that inscription says. It is five simple words. 'We thank thee, O God.'" She drew in a quick breath. "Those words so perfectly signify everything that has brought us here today—as a family, as friends, as a company of missionaries, and, most of all, as husband and wife. Therefore what I have to say is only this."

She grasped David's hand in both of hers. "We thank thee, O God," she said softly. "Oh, how we thank thee, our God."

EPILOGUE

It is hard to say exactly how many participated in the two Hole in the Rock expeditions. David Miller lists forty who went with the exploring party, two hundred thirty-seven who were known to have been with the main company, and at least fifteen more who likely went with them. There were almost certainly others whose names are simply not known.[1]

A few others, both members and nonmembers of the Church, settled in the area independently about that same time. George Harris, his wife, and their two sons emigrated from Colorado and settled near Bluff after the exploring party had departed again, but before the main company returned. But it is not likely that even three hundred people came into the San Juan River Valley that first year.

After an incredibly challenging journey through virtually impossible terrain, the pioneers arrived, not at some lush valley surrounded by verdant mountains, as so many other Mormon settlements had done. They stopped their wagons in the narrow plain of a swift-moving river subject to spring flooding. In spite of enormous effort, the river proved almost impossible to tame for irrigation. Good farmland was limited. They had to hold two different lotteries to assign out city and garden lots. Many families had no choice but to turn to ranching—spreading their herds across vast areas of rich to sparse grazing land—or move on to other settlements.

Another issue was the cultural climate. As Elder Erastus Snow had warned, the area provided an unusual kind of a challenge to those first settlers. Wedged in between the great Navajo nation on the south and the Utes and Paiutes to the north and east, the community was particularly susceptible to petty thievery and livestock rustling. The Mormons got along better with the Indians than most other whites, but there were still some tensions and, occasionally, violent outbreaks. Another problem was that for a time, the presence of the little colony didn't do much to push out the lawless element—the cattle rustlers, horse thieves, bank robbers, highwaymen, moral trash, and renegade Indians still found refuge in the desolate, sparsely populated country. The small fort the settlers built at Bluff was aptly named "Fort on the Firing Line."[2]

But eventually the mission fulfilled its purpose. The members of the Church from across southern Utah called to colonize the San Juan/Four Corners area were sent to establish peace with the Indians and to plant a stabilizing influence there. In that they were successful, becoming a buffer between warring and lawless elements in the area. While there were occasional problems with a few of the natives, there never again was widespread war. As settlements were established, peace and order became the norm.

Ironically, the road that had been carved through the wilderness at such a terrible cost was used only for a short time. For about a year, it was the only road between the southern settlements and the Four Corners area, and people traveled in both directions on it. Then, in 1882, Charles Hall, who had ferried the wagons across the river at the Hole in the Rock, discovered an easier crossing about thirty miles upstream and built a ferry there. Today, a modern ferry service carries vehicles across Lake Powell from Bullfrog to Halls Crossing.

In his impressive work on Bishop Jens Nielson, David S. Carpenter studied what happened to those initial settlers in the years following their arrival. The figures are revealing and give some clue as to the difficulty of life there.

Among those who left within a short time after their arrival were those who either had never planned to stay, and went on to other locations, and those who had come only to help family members get settled. Mons Larson, for example, whose wife gave birth to a baby boy on Grey Mesa in a blizzard, went on to Snowflake, Arizona. This had been their intent from the beginning. Wilson Daily, the company blacksmith, a non-Mormon, went on to Colorado, as did the Box family, who had brought a large herd of horses to sell.

In June 1880, U.S. census takers made their way to the new little outpost and recorded the names of all present. This gives us a good picture of who was there just two months after their arrival. That initial census showed 193 settlers along the San Juan—107 at Bluff and 86 at Montezuma Creek. Ten years later, Bluff's population had grown to 193 on its own.[3] That figure has not changed much in over a hundred years. The population in 2007 was listed as 377.

A glimpse of what happened to the pioneers who played a part in the novel is indicative of the overall picture of what followed the company after their arrival in San Juan.

- Lemuel Redd, Sr., who was one of the four scouts who went to Montezuma Creek, returned home to New Harmony after getting his son settled.
- The Daniel Barney family (whose son Al was knocked into the Colorado River) were gone by June of 1880, possibly to Arizona.
- David and Sarah Jane Hunter and George and Alice Urie, two young couples without children, returned to Cedar City, leaving before June 1880. However, the Hunters were back in Bluff in 1884. (In the novel, Molly returns to Cedar City with them.)
- Bishop George Sevy, another of the four scouts, and his family returned to Panguitch before June 1880.
- Silas S. Smith, captain of the company, had moved to Manassa, Colorado (south of Alamosa), by the end of 1881.
- George Hobbs was gone by 1883 and eventually ended up in Nephi.
- Joseph Stanford Smith and his wife, Belle (who crow-hopped down the Hole) moved on to Mancos, in southwest Colorado, sometime before 1884.
- James and Mary Davis and family, who came with the exploring party in 1879, moved to Bear Lake, Utah, in 1884.

- Henry and Elizabeth Harriman, who also came with the exploring party in 1879, moved to Huntington, Utah, in 1884.
- Platte Lyman, captain of the company, left in 1884 for a time, but eventually returned. He was called as president of the first stake there. He and some family members are buried in the Bluff cemetery.
- Benjamin and Mary Ann Perkins and family, the Welsh coal miner, left in 1884, returned to Cedar City for a time, but eventually came back to San Juan and lived in Monticello. Both Ben and his wife are buried in the Bluff cemetery.
- Hyrum Perkins and his wife are buried in the Bluff Cemetery.
- Jens Nielson returned to Cedar City to get his other two wives and the rest of his family, then returned to Bluff. Jens died in 1906 and is buried in the Bluff Cemetery.
- Kumen and Mary Nielson Jones remained in Bluff with the Nielsons.
- Joe Nielson married Ida Lyman, sister of Platte D. Lyman, and remained in the San Juan area.[4]

Bishop Jens Nielson lived for twenty-six years in Bluff, serving as bishop for the second time for most of those years. Carpenter says of him and of his relationship with his San Juan home:

"Bluff was never far from failure during Jens Nielson's life. . . . By most rational measures, Bluff should have been abandoned, and a farmer as hardheaded as Jens Nielson should have led the exodus. But Bishop Nielson . . . bound himself to stay in Bluff, no matter how impractical. This was not a question of orthodoxy versus apostasy. Those who left Bluff generally did not leave Mormonism. . . . Regardless of others' arguments, until the church's leaders released him from Bluff, Jens Nielson would not go."[5]

Albert R. Lyman shares a wonderful example of Bishop Nielson's courage and his "stickity tootie." About five years after their arrival, Amasa Barton was killed by two Navajos at his trading post down near San Juan Hill. Lyman writes that a short time afterwards, "a hundred Navajos rode into Bluff with faces painted black, carrying guns across their saddles in front of them and demanded to have somebody talk with them—quarrel with them—preliminary to the big row for which their hands were itching. The town had but three men in its borders, the rest being away on the range, on the road or somewhere else, and a helpless community of women and children took terrified account of the fierce looking army, peering out through curtained windows or through holes in the wall.

"Someone went in great haste for the bishop and he came limping readily forward to meet the painted danger. . . . Brother Kumen Jones was there ready to act as an interpreter, and through him the bishop began calmly to tell the Indians that it was not our business to fight, but to make and preserve peace. He stood unmoved there before them, his age, his white hair, his crippled feet indicating nothing of fear. It disturbed them, it contradicted their brave notion that they looked terrible, and that people should flee from their presence. Here was courage, dignity—and it disarmed them.

"Through his faithful interpreter, he told them if they wanted to talk things over to get down from their horses, stand their guns against the wall of the store, and come sit in a friendly circle on the ground. . . . He won them. They all dismounted. They all became friendly.

"Then to complete this movement for peace which he had been inspired to begin, he invited the Navajos to stay overnight. He had some of the people bring and butcher a fat steer, and they got bacon, coffee, flour, and other things from the store that these strangers might be well fed and return to be friends instead of enemies. They ate and remembered "Kagoochee" (crooked feet), and from that time forth, they were friends to him and his people."[6]

This book is titled *The Undaunted*. The definite article is included in the title because the book is not as much about the quality of being undaunted as it is about a remarkable group of men, women, and children who exemplified that quality. Carpenter captures the essence of that astounding courage in a summary statement about the town of Bluff:

"Bluff is an unusually stubborn study in persistence. It reinforces the idea that even into the twentieth century, some Mormon pioneers were committed to religious ideals enough to deny themselves the American dream. But it was always a struggle. The town was settled in that spot almost by accident but became doggedly defended. The colonists who feuded with each other during the first land lottery in April 1880 had no idea that would be the last time people would clamor for land at Bluff. . . . But the pioneers were pragmatic enough to sense not only the faith but the folly of what they were doing. As Parley Butt put it, only half-jokingly, 'I am pretty familiar with the San Juan River, which I wish I hadn't been.' What was said of the Sanpete settlements would easily be echoed further south: 'Every man ought to marry a wife from San Juan because, no matter what happens, she's seen worse.'"[7]

That was David Draper's conclusion as well.

Notes

1. See Miller's list of participants in Appendix I (*Hole*, 142–47).

2. See Albert R. Lyman, "Fort on the Firing Line" series; also his "Indians and Outlaws."

3. Carpenter, *Jens Nielson*, 237–445.

4. Appendix B in *ibid.*, 447–50.

5. *Ibid.*, 6–7.

6. Lyman, "Bishop Jens Nielson," 8–9. Kumen Jones also tells this story about his father-in-law (see Kumen Jones, "Navajo Peace," 248–49).

7. Carpenter, *Jens Nielson*, 416.

BIBLIOGRAPHY

Allen, James B., Ronald K. Esplin, and David J. Whittaker. *Men with a Mission 1837–1841:The Quorum of the Twelve Apostles in the British Isles*. Salt Lake City: Deseret Book Company, 1992.

Bartoletti, Susan Campbell. *Growing Up in Coal Country*. Boston: Houghton Mifflin Company, 1996.

Benson, Ezra Taft. *Come unto Christ*. Salt Lake City: Deseret Book Company, 1983.

Black, William LeGrand. *The Rebirth of the Historic Old Hole-in-the-Rock Trail as a Recreational Trail*. Master's thesis, Brigham Young University, August 1995.

Blankenagel, Norma Palmer. *Portrait of Our Past: A History of Monticello Utah Stake of The Church of Jesus Christ of Latter-day Saints*, no publisher, 1988.

Bloxham, V. Ben, James R. Moss, and Larry C. Porter, eds. *Truth Will Prevail: The Rise of The Church of Jesus Christ of Latter-day Saints in the British Isles 1837–1987*. Germany: The Church of Jesus Christ of Latter-day Saints, 1987.

Brooks, Juanita. "Jacob Hamblin, 'Apostle to the Indians.'" *Improvement Era*, April 1944, 210–11, 249–55.

Carpenter, David S. *Jens Nielson, Bishop of Bluff*. Master's thesis, Brigham Young University, 2003.

Corbett, Pearson S. *Jacob Hamblin: The Peacemaker*. Salt Lake City: Deseret Book Company, 1952.

Dewey, Richard Lloyd, ed. *Jacob Hamblin: His Life in His Own Words*. New York: Paramount Books, 1995.

Garrett, H. Dean, and Clark V. Johnson. *Regional Studies in Latter-day Saint History: Arizona* (Provo, UT: Brigham Young University Department of Church History and Doctrine, 1989), 141–45.

Gibbons, Boyd. "The Itch to Move West: Life and Death on the Oregon Trail." *National Geographic*, August 1986, 146–77.

Hafen, LeRoy R., and Ann W. Hafen. *Handcarts to Zion: The Story of a Unique Western Migration, 1856–1860*. Lincoln, Nebraska: University of Nebraska Press (in association with Spokane, Washington: The Arthur H. Clark Company), 1960.

Hamblin, Jacob. *Journals and Letters of Jacob Hamblin*. Manuscript copies prepared by
    Brigham Young University Library, 1969.
Hayes, Geoffrey. *Coal Mining*. Princes Risborough, England: Shire Publications, 2004.
Hinckley, Gordon B. "The Faith of the Pioneers." *Ensign*, July 1984, 3–6.
"History of the San Juan Stake." Manuscript copy, LDS Church History Library.
Jenson, Andrew. *Latter-day Saint Biographical Encyclopedia: A Compilation of Biographical
    Sketches of Prominent Men and Women in The Church of Jesus Christ of Latter-day Saints*.
    4 volumes. Salt Lake City: Publishers Press, originally published by the Andrew Jenson
    History Company, 1901.
———. "Pioneers and Pioneering in Southern Utah." *Improvement Era*, June 1915, 710–11.
Jones, Kumen. "Navajo Peace." *Improvement Era*, April 1941, 214–15, 247–49.
———. "Notes on the San Juan Mission." Manuscript copy, LDS Church History Library.
———. "Writings of Kumen Jones." Manuscript copy, LDS Church History Library.
Jones, Raymond Smith. "Last Wagon Through the Hole-in-the-Rock." *Desert Magazine*,
    June 1954, 22–25.
Lake, Fiona, and Rosemary Preece. *Voices from the Dark: Women and Children in Yorkshire
    Coal Mines*. Overton, England: Yorkshire Mining Museum Publications, 1992.
"Life Sketch of Mary Jane Wilson." Manuscript copy, LDS Church History Library.
Ludlow, Daniel H., ed. *Encyclopedia of Mormonism*. 4 volumes. New York: Macmillan, 1992.
Lyman, Albert R. "Bishop Jens Nielson: A Brief Biography." Manuscript copy, LDS Church
    History Library (copy in author's possession).
———. *Indians and Outlaws: Settling of the San Juan Frontier*. Salt Lake City: Deseret Book
    Company, 1962.
———. "Fort on the Firing Line, Parts I-XVIII." *Improvement Era*, October 1948–March
    1950.
McKay, David O. "Pioneer Women." *Relief Society Magazine*, January 1948, 4–9.
McPherson, Robert S. *A History of San Juan County: In the Palm of Time*. Utah Historical
    Society, San Juan County Commission, 1995.
Miller, David E. *Hole-in-the-Rock: An Epic in Colonization of the Great American West*, Salt
    Lake City: The University of Utah Press, 1959.
O'Brien, Alberta Lyman. *The Story of Sarah Williams Perkins*. Revised by Elaine Perkins
    Walton, 1993. Manuscript copy, LDS Church History Library.
Reay, Lee. *Incredible Passage: Through the Hole-in-the-Rock*. Provo, UT: Meadow Lane
    Publications, 1980.
Redd, Charles E. "Short Cut to the San Juan." In *The Westerners: A Baker's Dozen of Essays
    on the West: Its History, Places, and People*. Don Bloch, ed. Denver: Brand Book, 1950.
Roundy, Jerry C. *"Advised Them to Call the Place Escalante."* Springville, UT: Art City
    Publishing, 2000.

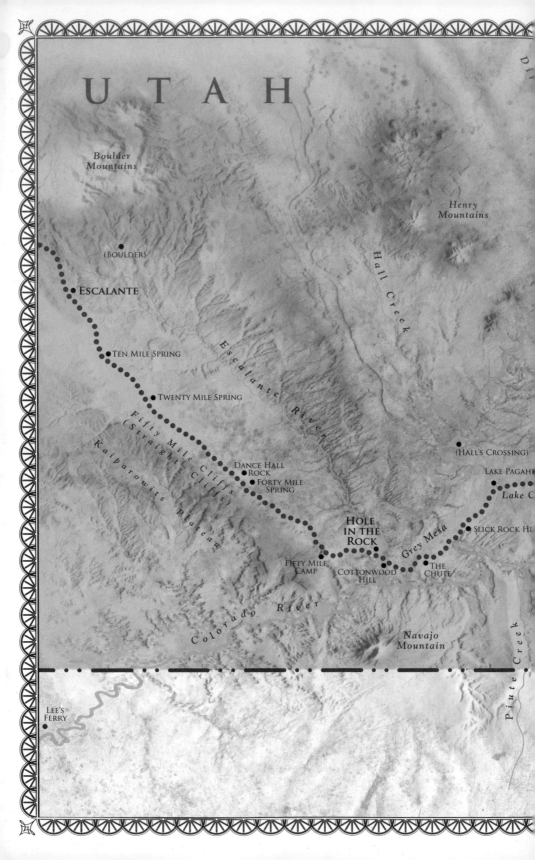